STAR WARS®

THE HAN SOLO ADVENTURES

Han Solo drove his swoop into the weather station's giant emission cylinder. The pursuing craft hung back a moment, then followed.

"Stay gripped!" he called to the woman behind him, jockeying the swoop to face his enemies. They scattered, then dropped onto his tail again, ready to trap him at the cylinder's far end.

Han speeded up once more. The end of the emission cylinder was swinging, first revealing and then concealing meter-and-a-half-wide openings in the gridwork. The opening Han had selected expanded before him as he drove toward it. There was a terrible moment of doubt . . . then the gridwork passed him like a shadow, and they were in the open.

He took a quick look behind. Pieces of wreckage were raining slowly toward the ground; one of his pursuers had tried to emulate him and failed . . .

Star Wars® Titles
Published by Ballantine Books:

STAR WARS: A NEW HOPE
THE EMPIRE STRIKES BACK
RETURN OF THE JEDI

THE STAR WARS TRILOGY

SPLINTER OF THE MIND'S EYE

STAR WARS: THE HAN SOLO ADVENTURES
STAR WARS: THE LANDO CALRISSIAN ADVENTURES

A GUIDE TO THE STAR WARS UNIVERSE,
SECOND EDITION

STAR WARS:
THE NATIONAL PUBLIC RADIO DRAMATIZATION
THE EMPIRE STRIKES BACK:
THE NATIONAL PUBLIC RADIO DRAMATIZATION
RETURN OF THE JEDI:
THE NATIONAL PUBLIC RADIO DRAMATIZATION

STAR WARS: THE ESSENTIAL GUIDE TO CHARACTERS
STAR WARS: THE ESSENTIAL GUIDE TO VEHICLES AND VESSELS
STAR WARS: THE ESSENTIAL GUIDE TO WEAPONS AND TECHNOLOGY
STAR WARS: THE ESSENTIAL GUIDE TO DROIDS

THE STAR WARS TECHNICAL JOURNAL

THE QUOTABLE STAR WARS:
"I'D JUST AS SOON KISS A WOOKIEE!"

STAR WARS ENCYCLOPEDIA

THE HAN SOLO ADVENTURES

HAN SOLO AT STARS' END

HAN SOLO'S REVENGE

HAN SOLO AND THE LOST LEGACY

From the Adventures of Luke Skywalker

By Brian Daley

Based on the characters and situations
created by George Lucas

A Del Rey Book
BALLANTINE BOOKS • NEW YORK

A Del Rey® Book
Published by The Ballantine Publishing Group

www.randomhouse.com/delrey/

ISBN 0-345-37980-2

Manufactured in the United States of America

First Ballantine Books Edition: June 1992

28 27 26 25 24 23 22

CONTENTS

HAN SOLO
AT
STARS' END

To Poul Anderson and Gordon R. Dickson,
for their kind words to a new guy

and

Owen Lock: learned editor and friend,
who'll race to Antares for pinks, any time

The author wishes to thank Eleanor and
Diana Berry for timely assistance

I

"IT'S a warship all right. Damn!"

Instrument panels in the *Millennium Falcon*'s cockpit were alive with trouble lights, warning flashers, and the beeps and hoots of the sensor package. Readout screens were feeding combat-information displays at high speed.

Han Solo, crouched forward in the pilot's seat, coolly flicking his eyes from instrument to screen, hastily assessed his situation. His lean, youthful face creased in a frown of concern. Beyond the cockpit canopy, the surface of the planet Duroon drew steadily nearer. Somewhere below and astern, a heavily armed vessel had detected the *Falcon*'s presence and was now homing in to challenge her. That the warship had, in fact, picked up the *Millennium Falcon* first was a matter of no small worry to Han; the ability to come and go without attracting notice, especially official notice, was vital to a smuggler.

He began relaying fire-control data to the ship's weapons systems. "Charge main batteries, Chewie," he said, not taking his eyes from his part of the console, "and shields-all. We're in prohibited space; can't let 'em take us or identify the ship." Particularly, he added to himself, with the cargo we're hauling.

To his right, Chewbacca the Wookiee made a sound halfway between a grunt and a bark, his furry fingers darting to his controls with sure dexterity, his large, hairy form hunched in the oversized copilot's seat. Wookiee-style, he showed his fierce fighting teeth as he rapidly surrounded the starship with layers of defensive energy. At the same time, he brought the *Falcon*'s offensive weaponry up to its maximum charge.

Bracing his ship for battle, Han berated himself for ever having taken on this job. He'd known full well it could take him into conflict with the Corporate Sector Authority, in the middle of a steer-clear area.

The Authority ship's approach left Han and Chewbacca just seconds for a clutch decision: abort the mission and head for parts unknown, or try to pull off their delivery anyway. Han surveyed his console, hoping for a clue, or a hit off the Cosmic Deck.

The other ship wasn't gaining. In fact, the *Falcon* was pulling away. Sensors gauged the mass, armaments, and thrust of their pursuer, and Han made his best guess. "Chewie, I don't think that's a ship of the line; looks more like a bulk job, with augmentative weapons. She must've just lifted off when she got wind of us. Hell, don't those guys have anything better to do?" But it figured; the one major Authority installation on Duroon, the only one with a full-dress port layout, was on the far side of the globe, where the dawn line would just be lightening gray sky. Han had planned his landing for a spot as far away from the port as possible, in the middle of the night-side.

"We take her down," he decided. If the *Falcon* could shake her follower, Han and Chewbacca could make their drop and, with the luck of the draw, escape.

The Wookiee gave a grumpy growl, black nostrils flaring, tongue curling. Han glared at him. "You got a better idea? It's a little late to part company, isn't it?" He took the converted freighter into a steep dive, throwing away altitude in return for increased velocity, heading deeper into Duroon's umbra.

The Authority vessel, conversely, slowed even more, climbing through the planet's atmosphere, trading speed for altitude in an attempt to keep the *Millennium Falcon* under sensor surveillance. Han ignored the Authority's broadcast order to halt; telesponders that should have automatically given his starship's identity in response to official inquiry had been disconnected long ago.

"Hold deflector shields at full capacity," he ordered. "I'm taking her down to the deck; we don't want our skins cooked off." The Wookiee complied, to shed thermal energy generated by the *Falcon*'s rapid passage through the atmosphere. The starship's controls trembled as she began to buck the denser air. Han worked to put the planet between himself and the Authority vessel.

This he soon accomplished, as indicators registered increased heat from the friction of the freighter's dive. Between watching sensors and looking through the canopy, Han quickly found his first landmark, a volcanically active crevasse that ran on an east-west axis, like a stupendous, burning scar on the flesh of Duroon. He brought the *Falcon* out of her swoop, her control systems rebelling against the immense strain. He leveled off only meters above the planet's surface.

"Let's see them track us now," he said, self-satisfied. Chewbacca snorted. The meaning of the snort was clear—this was temporary cover only. There was little danger of being detected either optically or by instrument over this seam in Duroon's surface, for the *Falcon* would be lost against a background of ferrous slag, infernal heat, and radioactive discord. But neither could she remain there for long.

In the vivid orange light of the fissure that illuminated the cockpit, Han conceded that fact. At best, he'd broken trail so the Authority ship would be unable to spot the *Falcon* should the pursuer gain enough altitude to bring her back into sensor range. He poured on as much airspeed as he dared in an effort to keep Duroon's mass between himself and the vessel hunting him while he sought his landing site. He cursed the fact that there were no proper navigational beacons; this was seat-of-the-pants flying, and no chance of leaning out the cockpit and stopping a passerby for directions.

In minutes the ship had neared the western end of the

fissure. Han was compelled to dump some velocity; it was time to look for road signs. He reviewed the instructions given him, instructions he'd committed to memory alone. Off to the south a gigantic mountain range loomed. He banked the *Falcon* sharply to port, slapped a pair of switches, and bore straight for the mountains.

The ship's special Terrain Following Sensors came on. Han kept the freighter's bow close above a surface of cooled lava and occasional active rifts, minor offspring of the great fissure. For whatever small edge it might give against detection, he trimmed the *Falcon* off at virtual landing altitude, screaming over eddied volcanic flatlands. ''Anybody down there better duck,'' he advised, keeping one eye pinned to the Terrain Following Sensors. They bleeped, having located the mountain pass for which he'd been searching. He adjusted course.

Funny. His information said the break in the mountains was plenty wide for the *Falcon*, but it looked mighty narrow on the TFS. For a second he debated going for altitude fast, hurdling the high peaks, but that just might put him back onto the Authority's scopes. He was too close to his delivery point, and a payday, to risk having to cut and run. The moment of option passed. He shed more airspeed, committed now to taking the pass at low level.

Sweat collected on his forehead and dampened his shirt and vest. Chewbacca uttered his low rumble of utmost concentration as both partners synched to the running of the *Millennium Falcon*. The image of the pass on the TFS grew no more encouraging.

Han tightened his grip on the controls, feeling the press of his flying gloves against them. ''Pass, nothing—that thing's a *slot*! Hold your breath, Chewie; we'll have to skin through.''

He threw himself into a grim battle with his ship. Chewbacca caterwauled his dislike for all unconventional maneuvers as he cut in braking thrusters, but even those would not be enough to avert disaster. The slot began to take on shape, a slightly lighter area of sky lit by bright stars and one of Duroon's three moons, set off by the silhouette of the mountains. It was, just barely, too narrow.

The starship took some altitude, and her speed slackened. Those extra seconds gave Han time to pilot for his life, calling on razor-edge reflexes and instinctive skills that had seen him through scrapes all across the galaxy. He killed all shields, since they'd have struck rock and overloaded, and wrenched his controls, standing the *Millennium Falcon* on her port-side. Sheer crags closed in on either side, so that the roar of the freighter's engines rebounded from the cliffs. He made minute corrections, staring at rock walls that seemed to be coming at him through the canopy, and rattled off a string of expletives having nothing whatsoever to do with piloting.

There was a slight jar, and the shriek of metal torn away as easily as paper. The long-range sensors winked out; the dish had been ripped off the upper hull by a protrusion of rock. Then the needle's eye was threaded sideways, and the *Falcon* was through the mountains.

Perspiration beading his face, dampening his light brown hair, Han pounded Chewbacca. "What'd I tell you? Inspiration's my specialty!"

The starship soared over the thick jungle that began beyond the mountains. Han leveled off, wiping a gloved hand across his brow. Chewbacca emitted a sustained growl. "I agree," Han replied soberly in the wake of his elation. "That *was* a stupid place to put a mountain." He took up scanning for the next landmark and spied it almost at once: a winding river. The *Falcon* skimmed in low over the watery coils as the Wookiee lowered the ship's landing gear.

In seconds they'd reached the landing area near a spectacular waterfall that dropped two hundred meters to the river in a flume like a blue-white, ghostly scrim under stars and moonlight. Han, reading the TFS, found a clearing in the heavy cover of vegetation and settled the ship slowly. The broad disks of the landing gear sank a bit in soft humus; then the hydrolics sighed briefly as the *Millennium Falcon* made herself comfortable.

Han and Chewbacca sat at their controls for a moment, too drained to do more. Outside the cockpit canopy, the jungle was an irregular darkness, tangles of indefatigable growth topped by a roof of fernlike plants that stretched up twenty meters and more. Gauzy ground fog rolled through the undergrowth and clearing.

The Wookiee gave a long, gusty, bass-register exhalation. "I couldn't have said it better," Han concurred. "Let's get at it." Both removed headsets and left their seats. Chewbacca picked up his crossbow weapon and a bandolier of metal ammo containers, which also supported a floppy carryall pouch at his hip. Han already wore his side arm, a custom-model blaster with rear-fitted macroscope, its front sight blade filed off to facilitate the speed draw. His holster was worn low, tied down at the thigh, cut so that it exposed the weapon's trigger and trigger guard.

According to directories, Duroon's atmosphere would support humanoid life without respirators. The two smugglers moved directly to the ship's ramp. The hatch rolled up and the ramp lowered silently, letting in smells of plant growth, of rotting vegetation, of hot, humid night and animal danger. The jungle was filled with sounds, calls, clacks, and cries of prey and predator, and, over all, with the monumental spillage of the waterfall.

"Now it's up to them to find us," Han said. Checking the jungle, he saw no sign of life. Not surprising. The freighter's landing had probably frightened most wildlife out of the area. He turned to his shaggy first mate/copilot/partner. "I'll wait for them. Turn off sensors, shut down the engines, the works; kill all systems so the Authority can't spot us. Then see how much structural damage she suffered topside when she got her back scratched."

Chewbacca barked acknowledgement and shambled off. Han stripped off his flying gloves, tucked them in his belt, and stepped down the ramp, which stretched down and out from the ship's starboard side, astern the cockpit. He thumbed his gun's sights to set it for night shooting, then glanced around. A lean young man dressed in spaceman's high boots, dark uniform trousers with red piping, and civilian shirt and vest, Han had cast aside his uniform tunic, stripped of its rank and insignia, years ago.

He ran a quick check of the *Falcon*'s underside, assuring himself that she had taken no damage there and that the landing gear had come to rest properly. He also made certain that the interrupter-templates had automatically slid into place along the servo-guides for the belly turret, so that the quad-mounted guns wouldn't accidentally blow away the landing gear or ramp if he had to fire them while the ship was grounded.

Satisfied, he went back to the foot of the ramp. He gazed up at the empty sky and the stars beyond, thinking: *Let the Authority look for me; this whole part of Duroon's spotted with hot springs, thermal vents, heavy-metal magma seepages, and radiation anomalies. It'd take them a month to find me, and in an hour or three, I'll be gone like a cool breeze.*

He sat at the end of the ramp, wishing for a moment that he'd brought along something to drink; there was a flask of ancient, vacuum-distilled jet juice under the cockpit console. But he didn't feel like going for it. Besides, he still had business to conduct.

Duroon's nocturnal life forms began reappearing in the mossy clearing. Lacy white things swam through the air with ripples of their thin bodies, resembling flying doilies, while nearby fern-trees held creatures that looked like bundles of straw, making their slow way along the wide fronds. Han kept an eye on them but doubted they'd approach the alien mass of his starship.

As he watched, a smallish green sphere sailed out of the undergrowth in a high arc, landing with a *boink*. It appeared perfectly smooth at first, but then extruded an eyelike bump that studied the *Falcon* with jerky motions. But when it noticed the pilot, it flinched. The eye-bump disappeared, and the sphere-thing's underside compressed. With another *boink* the thing bounced away into the jungle.

Han returned to his musing as he listened to Chewbacca tramping around on the ship's upper hull. The unfamiliar constellations here were how many light-years from the planet of Han's birth? He couldn't even make a close guess.

Being a smuggler and a flyer-for-hire had its dangers, and those he accepted with a philosophical shrug. But a run into a prohibited sector with a cargo that would earn him a summary execution if caught, those were different table stakes altogether.

The Corporate Sector was one wisp off one branch at the end of one arm of the galaxy, but that wisp contained tens of thousands of star systems, and not one native, intelligent species was to be found anywhere. No one was sure why. Han had heard that neutrino research showed abnormalities in the solar convective layers of every sun hereabout, something that might have spread like a virus among the stars in this isolated sector.

In any case, the Corporate Sector Authority had been chartered to exploit—some called it plunder—the uncountable riches here. The Authority was owner, employer, landlord, government, and military. Its wealth and influence eclipsed that of all but the richest Imperial Regions, and the Authority spent much of its time and energy insulating itself from outside interference. Competition, it had none; but that didn't make the Corporate Sector Authority any less jealous or vindictive. Any outside ship found off established trade corridors was fair game for the Authority's warships, which were manned by its feared Security Police.

But what do you do, Han asked himself, when your back's to the wall? How could he have said no to a nice, lucrative run when usurious Ploovo Two-For-One described the riches that were to be had.

I could always hit the beach, he thought. Find a nice planet somewhere, go native. It's a big galaxy.

But he shook his head. No use fooling himself. If he were grounded, he might as well be dead. What could one planet, any planet, offer someone who had knocked around among the stars? The need for the boundless provinces of space was now a part of him.

And so when, broke and in debt, he and Chewbacca had been approached for a run deep into Authority steer-clear territory, they'd jumped at the job. In spite of all the perils and uncertainties, the run still let them raise ship again and experience the freedom of star-travel. Risk of death or capture had been, in their eyes, the lesser of two evils.

But that brought up another point. The Authority ship had somehow picked up the *Millennium Falcon* before her own sensors had detected the other. No doubt the Security Police had something new in the way of detection equipment, thereby making Han's and Chewbacca's lives more complicated by an order of ten. This situation would require immediate future attention.

Han kept a close watch on the jungle around him, wishing he could have left the ship's floodlights on. So, when a voice at his side announced, "We are here," he twisted around with a yelp, his blaster appearing in his fist as if conjured there.

A creature, barely out of arm's reach, was calmly standing next to the ramp. It was almost Han's height, a biped, with a downy, globular torso and short arms and legs boasting more joints than a human's. Its head was small, but equipped with large, unblinking eyes. Its mouth and throat were a loose, pouchy affair; its scent was the scent of the jungle.

"That," Han grumbled, recovering his composure and putting his blaster away, "is a good way to get yourself roasted."

The creature ignored the sarcasm. "You have brought what we need?"

"I've got cargo for you. Beyond that, I know zero, which is the way I want it. If you came alone, you've got your work cut out for you."

The creature turned and made an eerie, piping noise. Figures seemed to grow up out of the ground, dozens of them, motionless, regarding the pilot and his ship with silent gazes. They held short objects of some sort, which he assumed to be weapons.

Then he heard a growl from above. Stepping forward, Han looked up and saw Chewbacca standing out on one of the ship's bow mandibles, covering the newcomers with his bowcaster. Han gave a signal. His hairy first mate put up the bowcaster and headed back inboard.

''Time's wasting,'' Han told the creature. It moved toward the *Falcon*, taking its companions with it. Han stopped them with upheld hands. ''Not the whole choir, friend. Just you, for starters.'' The first one burbled to its fellows and came on alone.

Inside the ship, Chewbacca had turned up the blackout lights to a minimal glow in strategic parts of the interior. The towering Wookiee was already drawing cover plates off the hidden compartments, concealed and shielded to be undetectable, under the deck near the ramp. Into this space, where he and Han usually hid whatever contraband they were carrying, Chewbacca lowered himself to stand with his waist at deck level. Releasing clamps and strapping, the Wookiee began lifting out heavy oblong cases, the huge muscles beneath his fur bulging with effort.

Han pulled the end of a case around and broke its seals. Within the crate weapons lay stacked. They had been so treated that no part of them reflected any of the scant light. Han took one up, checked its charge, made sure the safety was on, then handed it to the creature.

The firearm was a carbine—short, lightweight, uncomplicated. Like all the others in the shipment, this one was fitted with a simple optical scope, shoulder sling, bipod, and folding bayonet. Though the creature obviously wasn't used to handling an energy weapon, its ready acceptance, grip, and posture showed that it had seen them often enough. It shifted the carbine in its hands, peered down the barrel, and examined the trigger carefully.

"Ten cases, two hundred rifles," Han told it, taking up another carbine. He flipped up its butt plate, pointing out the adapters through which the weapon's power pack could be recharged. These were obsolete weapons by current standards, but they had no internal moving parts and were extremely durable, so much so that they could safely be shipped or stored without Gel-Coat or other preservative. Any one of these carbines, left leaning against a fern in the jungle, would be fully operable ten years from now. Those advantages would be important on this world, where the carbines' new owners would be able to provide little maintenance.

The creature nodded, understanding how the recharging worked. "We have already stolen small generators," it told Han, "from the Authority compounds. We came here because they promised us jobs, and a good life, and we celebrated our good fortune, for our world is poor. But they worked us like slaves and would not let us leave. Many of us escaped to live in the wilds; this world is not unlike our own. Now, with these weapons, we will be able to fight back—"

"Stop!" Han snarled with a slashing gesture of his hand, and a violence that made the creature recoil. Reining in his temper, he went on, "I don't want to hear it, get me? I don't know you, you don't know me. It's none of my business, so *don't tell me*!"

The large eyes were fixed on him. He looked away. "I got half my pay on account when I lifted off. The other half comes when I get out of here, so why don't you just take your stuff and scratch gravel? And don't forget: no firing those things until I've left. An Authority ship just might register the noise."

He recalled that advance, paid in glow-pearls, fire nodes, diamonds, nova-crystals, and other precious gems smuggled off this mining planet at terrible risk by whatever sympathizers the contract-slaves had found. Rather than buy their own freedom in a quick dash aboard the *Falcon*, these fugitives were about to throw themselves into a doomed rebellion against the power of the Corporate Sector Authority. Morons.

He stepped out of the creature's way. It watched him for a moment, then went and piped at the open hatch. Others of its kind came scampering up, crowding around the hatch. Their weapons could be seen now, primitive spear-throwers and blowguns. Some carried daggers of volcanic glass. They had clever hands, all three fingers of which were mutually opposable. They filed inboard, surrounding the rifle cases and straining to lift them in teams of sixes and sevens. Chewbacca looked at them in amusement. The cases, being borne away down the ramp and into the jungle, reminded Han of some bizarre funeral procession.

Remembering something, he took the solemn leader aside, "Does the Authority have a warship stationed here? Big-big ship, with lots of guns?"

The creature thought for a moment. "One big ship, which carries cargo, carries passengers. It has big guns on it, and meets other ships up in the sky, to load and unload them, sometimes."

Just as Han had thought. He hadn't encountered a true combat vessel, but rather a heavily armed lighter. Bad, but not as bad as he'd thought. But the creature wasn't finished. "We will need more," it said; "more weapons, more help."

"Consult your clergyman," Han suggested dryly, helping Chewie replace the deckplates. "Or fix up a deal through your own channels, like this run. I'm out; you won't see me again. I'm just doing business."

The creature cocked its head at him, as if trying to understand. Han thrust aside the thought of what life must be like in a forced-labor camp, a driven, joyless existence if ever there was one. That was a common pattern in the Corporate Sector, naive outworlders lured by false promises, signing on only to become prisoners once they reached the compounds. And what could these few fugitives hope to accomplish?

The luck of the draw, he reminded himself. Hits off the Cosmic Deck didn't always make things Right, but Right wouldn't fill an egg timer on Tatooine. You played the cards you got, and Han Solo liked to be on that end of things with the largest profit margin.

But Chewie was staring down at him. Han sighed; the big lug was a good first mate, but a soft touch. Well, the tip about the Authority ship was worth something—a hint, maybe, a useful lesson. Han snatched the carbine from the leader irritably.

"Just remember this, you're prey. Got me? You've got to think like prey, and use your brains."

The creature understood and moved closer, standing on tiptoe to see what Han was doing with the carbine.

"It's got three settings, see? Safety, single shot, and constant fire. Now, the Security Police here use those riot guns, right? Sawed-off, two-handers? They're real fond of using constant fire, because they can afford to waste power, just hosing it around. You can't. What you do is, lock all your carbines on single shot. And if you get into a firefight at night or in the deep jungle where visibility's poor, shoot at the constant-fire sources. You'll know it's none of your people, so it must be Security Police. You've got to start using your brain."

The creature looked from the man to the carbine and back again. "Yes," it assured him, retrieving the weapon, "we will remember. Thank you."

Han sniffed, knowing how much they still had to learn. And they'd have to learn it on their own, or the Authority would grind them under its vast heel. And on how many worlds, he asked himself, was the Authority doing just that?

His thoughts were interrupted by distant sounds of blaster fire off in the jungle. The creature had moved to the hatch, with its carbine leveled at them. "I am sorry," it told them, "but we had to test some of the weapons here, now, to make certain they work."

It lowered the carbine and fled down the ramp, heading

for the jungle. So much for world-saving. "I take it all back," Han said to Chewie as they leaned on the open hatch. "They might do all right at that."

Their long-range sensors had been knocked out by the destruction of the *Falcon*'s dish antenna on the approach run. The ship would have to make a blind lift-off, taking her chances on running into trouble.

Han and Chewbacca stood atop the *Falcon* for nearly an hour, straining to patch the damaged antenna mount. Han didn't begrudge the time; it had been a worthwhile effort and, if nothing else, had given the fugitives time to leave the rendezvous area. Because, sure as stink in a spacesuit, the *Falcon*'s lift-off would be plotted and its point of origin thoroughly searched.

They could wait no longer. The first lightening of the sky would bring every flitter, skimmer, and armed gig the local Authority officials could lay hands on, in a tight visual search grid. Chewbacca, sensing Han's mood, made a snarling comment in his own language.

Han lowered his macrobinoculars. "Correct. Let's raise ship."

They adjourned below, buckled in, and ran through a preflight—warming up engines, guns, shields. Han declared, "I'm betting that lighter will be holding low, where his sensors will do him the most good. If we come up any distance away from him, we can outrun him and dive for hyperspace."

Chewbacca yelped. Han poked him in the ribs. "What's eating you? We just have to play this hand out." He realized he was talking to hear himself. He shut up. The *Millennium Falcon* lifted, hovering for just a moment as her landing gear retracted. Then Han tenderly guided her up through the opening in the jungle's leafy ceiling.

"Sorry," he apologized to his ship, knowing what abuse she was about to take. He fired her up, stood her on her tail, and opened main thrusters wide. The starship screeched away into the sky, leaving the river steaming and the jungle smoldering. Duroon fell away quickly, and Han began to think they had the problem licked.

Then the tractor beam hit.

The freighter shook as the powerful, pulling beam fixed on her. High above, the Authority captain had played it smart, knowing he was looking for a faster, more maneuverable foe. Having outwitted the smuggler, he now brought his ship plummeting down the planet's gravity well, picking up enough speed to compensate for any dodge the *Falcon* might try in her steep climb. The tractor pulled the two ships inexorably into alignment.

"Shields-forward, all. Angle 'em, and get set to fire!" Han and Chewbacca were throwing switches, fighting their controls, struggling desperately to free their ship. In moments it became clear their actions were futile.

"Ready to shift all deflectors astern," Han ordered, bringing his helm over. "It'll have to be a staring match, Chewie."

The Wookiee's defiant roars shook the cockpit as his partner swung the freighter onto a new course, straight at the enemy vessel. All the *Falcon*'s defensive power was channeled to redouble her forward shields. The Authority ship was coming at them at a frightening rate; the distance between ships evaporated in seconds. The Authority lighter, making hits at extreme range, jounced the two around their cockpit but did no major damage.

"Hold fire, hold fire," Han chanted under his breath. "We'll train all batteries aft and kick him going away." The controls vibrated and fought in their hands as the *Falcon*'s engines gave every erg of effort. Deflector shields struggled under a salvo of long-range blaster-cannon fire, lances of yellow-green annihilation. The *Falcon* ascended on a column of blue energy as if she lusted for a fiery double death in collision with her antagonist. Rather than fight the tractor beam, she threw herself toward its source. The Authority ship came into visual range and, a moment later, filled the *Falcon*'s canopy.

At the last instant, the warship's captain's nerve gave. The tractor faded as the lighter began a desperate evasion maneuver. With reflexes that were more like precognition, Han threw everything he had into an equally frantic bank. The two ships' shields couldn't have left more than a meter or two between them in that blindingly fast near miss.

Chewbacca was already shifting all shields aft. The *Falcon*'s main batteries, trained astern, hammered at the Authority vessel at close range. Han scored two hits on the lighter, perhaps no more than superficial damage, but a moral victory after a long, bad night. The Authority ship rocked. Chewbacca howled, and Han exulted, "Last licks!"

The lighter plunged downward, unable to halt her steep dive quickly. The freighter bolted out of Duroon's atmospheric envelope, out into the void where she belonged. Far below her, the Authority vessel was just beginning to pull out of her dive, all chance of pursuit lost.

Han fed jump data into the navicomputer as Chewbacca ran damage checks. Nothing irreparable, the Wookiee decided, but everything would have to have a thorough going-over. But Han Solo and Chewbacca the Wookiee had their money, their freedom, and, for a wonder, their lives. And that, Han thought, should be enough for anyone, shouldn't it?

The starship's raving engines carved a line of blue fire across infinity. Han engaged the hyperdrive. Stars seemed to fall away in all directions as the ship outraced sluggard Light. The *Millennium Falcon*'s main drive boomed, and she disappeared as if she'd never been there.

THEY knew they'd be watched, of course, from the moment they docked their battered freighter.

Etti IV was a planet open to general trade, a world where dry winds swept amber, moss-covered plains and shallow, saline seas beneath vermilion skies. It had no remarkable resources in and of itself, but was hospitable to humans and humanoids and occupied a strategic spot on star-routes.

On Etti IV, great wealth had been gathered by lords of the Corporate Sector, and with this wealth had come its universal corollary, a thriving criminal element. Now, Han and Chewbacca made their way down a street of fusion-formed soil, between low buildings of press-bonded minerals and tall ones of permacite and shaped formex. They wove through the spaceport toward the Authority Currency Exchange, with the Wookiee guiding a rented repulsor-lift handtruck. On the handtruck were cases resembling strongboxes, and it was for that reason that the two assumed they'd be watched. The boxes were just the sort of thing to pique the curiosities of assorted criminal types.

But the duo also knew that any watchers would weigh risk against revenue. In the risk column would be Han's gunman's rig and his loose, confident gait, plus Chewbacca's looming presence and ready bowcaster, not to mention the strength and ferocity to twist any attacker's body into new and different shapes.

So they went their way in confidence, knowing that, as

targets, they would appeal to neither the good business sense nor the survival instincts of any would-be stickup artist.

The Authority Currency Exchange had no idea it was abetting a transaction involving gunrunning and insurrection. Han and Chewbacca had already managed to unload the gems with which they'd been paid, exchanging them for precious metals and rare crystalline vertexes. In a Corporate Sector encompassing tens of thousands of star systems, the kind of record-keeping that could keep track of every debt and payment was beyond even the most sophisticated data system. So, without a hitch, Han Solo, tramp freighter captain, smuggler, and freelance law-bender, had converted most of his payment into a nice neat Authority Cash Voucher. If he'd had a hat, he'd have tipped it to the chirping disbursements auto-clerk that spat the voucher at him. He tucked the little plastic chit into a vest pocket.

When they'd left the Exchange, the Wookiee let out one of his long, hooting barks. Han answered, "Yeah, yeah, we'll pay Ploovo Two-For-One, but first we've got one stop to make."

His sidekick growled loudly, startling bystanders with his displeasure and inviting a dangerous sort of attention. A detachment of Security Police appeared out of the swirl of humans, 'droids, and nonhumans moving along the street.

"Hey, lighten up, pal!" Han murmured out of the side of his mouth. The brown-uniformed Security Police, their suspicious eyes darting beneath battle helmets, sauntered along four abreast, their weapons held ready, as pedestrians moved quickly out of their way. Han saw two of the black battle helmets bob, and knew they'd heard the Wookiee's outburst. But the disturbance apparently didn't merit their attention, and the detachment went its way.

Han stared after them, shaking his head. There were all kinds of cops in the galaxy, some of them good, some not. But the Authority's private Security Police—"Espos," in slangtalk—were among the worst. Their enforcements had nothing to do with law or justice, but only with the edicts of the Corporate Sector Authority. Han had never been able to figure out what turned a man into an unquestioning Espo bully-boy; he merely tried to ensure that he didn't cross trails with any of them.

Remembering Chewbacca, he resumed their conversation. "Like I said, we'll pay Ploovo. This stop-off won't take a minute. We'll meet him right after, like we planned, square things, and go our way free and clear."

The placated Wookiee carped noncommittally but fell in beside his partner again.

Because Etti IV's monied classes required conspicuous means of demonstrating their wealth, the spaceport harbored several exotic pet stores, featuring rare or unique stock from the immeasurable expanses of the Empire. *Sabodor*'s was, by general consensus, the best of them. It was there that Han went.

The store's muting system, expensive as it was, couldn't mask all the scents and sounds of the curious life forms somewhat loosely collected there under the dubious classification: *Pets*. Among the species on display were such premium specimens as the spidery night-gliders of Altarrn, the iridescent-feathered song serpents from the deserts of Proxima Dibal's single planet, and the tiny, tubby, clownish marsupials from Kimanan that were commonly called furballs. Cages and cases, tanks and environmental bubbles, teemed with glowing eyes, restless tentacles, clicking chelae, and wobbling pseudopodia.

The proprietor instantly appeared, Sabodor himself, a denizen of Rakrir. His short, segmented, tubular body scuttled along on five pairs of versatile limbs, his two long eyestalks moving and rotating constantly. Seeing the pair, Sabodor rose up on his last two sets of limbs, his uplifted eyestalks reaching nearly to the level of Han's chest, inspecting him from all angles.

"Ever so sorry," Sabodor's voice twittered from the cantilevered vocal organ located at the center of his midsection.

"I don't deal in Wookiees. They're a sentient species; can't use them as pets. Illegal. I've got no use for a Wookiee."

Chewbacca cut loose with a furious roar, showing his fearsome teeth, stamping a hairy foot the size of a platter. Display racks shook and cases vibrated. Emitting a squeal, the terrified Sabodor scooted past Han, his foremost limbs clapped over his hearing orifices. The pilot tried to calm his big friend, while dozens of pets began chorusing their answering chitters, hums, screams, and tweets, bouncing around their respective confinements in fear and agitation.

"Chewy, easy! He didn't mean it," Han soothed, blocking the Wookiee from a violent laying of hands upon the quivering shopkeeper.

Sabodor's trembling eyestalks appeared, one to either side of Han's knees. "Tell the Wookiee no offense. An honest mistake, was it not? No insult intended."

Chewbacca quieted somewhat. Han, remembering all the Security Police in port, was grateful. "We came in to buy something," he told Sabodor as the proprietor rippled away from him in reverse gear. "Hear me? Buy."

"Buy? Buy! Oh, come, sir, and see-see-see! Any pet worth having is to be had at *Sabodor*'s, best in the Sector. We have—"

Han had waved him to silence. He laid a friendly hand on the spot where the overwrought little shopkeeper's shoulder would have been, if he'd had one. "Sabodor, I'm going to make this transaction easy. What I want is a Dinko. You have one?"

"Dinko?" Sabodor's tiny mouth and olfactory cluster somehow cooperated with his recoiling eyestalks to convey disgust. "What for? A Dinko? Revolting, ugh!"

Han's mouth tugged in a wry smile. He produced a handful of cash, riffling it invitingly. "Got one for me?"

"Can do! Wait right here!" Sabodor, undulating excitedly, flowed away into a back room. Han and Chewbacca barely had time to gaze around before the proprietor was back. In his upper two pairs of appendages he held a clear case. Inside was the Dinko.

Few creatures enjoyed the dubious notoriety accorded to Dinkoes, whose temperament came quite close to pure psychopathy. One of the mysteries of the zoological world was how the little terrors tolerated one another long enough to reproduce. Small enough to fit in a man's palm—if that man were indiscreet enough to pick it up—the Dinko glowered out at them. Its powerful rear legs moved constantly, and the twin pairs of grasping extremities on its chest pinched the air, longing for something upon which to fasten. Its long tongue flickered in and out between wicked, glittery fangs.

"Is it de-scented?" Han asked.

"Oh, no! And it's been in rut ever since it was transshipped. But it's been de-venomed."

Chewbacca grinned, his black nose wrinkling.

Han asked, "How much?"

Sabodor named an exorbitant sum. Han counted through his sheaf of cash. "I'll give you exactly one half that, agreed?"

The eyestalks, flopping about in distress, seemed close to tears. The Wookiee, snorting, leaned down at Sabodor, who shrank again behind the dubious safety of Han's knees. "Admit it, Sabodor," Han invited cheerfully, "it's a good deal."

"You win," wailed the proprietor. He proffered the case. The Dinko threw itself from side to side of its container, foaming at the chops.

"One more thing," Han added blithely. "I want you to give it a light sedation dosage so I can handle it for a moment. Then you can give it to me in a different box, something opaque."

That was really *two* things, but Sabodor agreed dejectedly, eager to have the Wookiee, the human, and the Dinko all out of his establishment as soon as possible.

Ploovo Two-For-One, loan shark and former robber, smash-and-grab man, and bunko-steerer out of the Cron

Drift, looked forward with pleasure to collecting the outstanding debt from Han Solo.

He was elated, not only because the original loan would reap a splendid profit for himself and his backers, but also because he thoroughly hated Solo, and an interesting form of revenge had materialized.

The message from Solo, promising repayment, had stipulated a meeting here on Etti IV, in the spaceport's most elegant bistro. That had been all right with Ploovo Two-For-One; his creed was that toil and enjoyment should be combined whenever feasible. *The Free-Flight Dance Dome* was more than satisfactory; it was opulent. Ploovo himself was far from charming, a bad-tempered hulk of a man whose face was subject to a nervous tic; but his income gave him a certain conspicuous social viability.

He sprawled onto a conform-lounger at a corner table, joined by the three retainers he'd brought along. Two of these were humans, hard-bitten men with a number of weapons concealed on and about their persons. The third was a long-snouted, scaly-skinned biped, native of Davnar II, who possessed a true flair for execution.

Ploovo, flashing more than enough currency to create an inspired sense of hospitality in the waitress, primped at his black, oily topknot. While he waited, he gloated over his anticipated revenge on Han Solo. Not that the pilot wouldn't repay. The loan shark was certain of getting his money. But Solo had long been an irritant, always ready with some dazzling evasion of payment, jeering Ploovo and bewildering him at the same time. On a number of occasions Ploovo had lost face with his backers because of run-ins with Solo, and his backers weren't the sort to be amused by that. The code of ethics necessary to the conduct of illegal enterprises kept Ploovo from turning in the captain-owner of the *Millennium Falcon* to the law; nevertheless, a convenient local circumstance would serve the loan shark's purpose just as well.

* * *

Entering with Chewbacca beside him, a metal case in hand, Han Solo appraised *The Free-Flight Dance Dome* with a great deal of approval.

As on almost any civilized planet, many species mixed and mingled here in a taxonomic hodgepodge, their appearance familiar or alien by turns. Having seen about as much of the galaxy as a man might reasonably expect to, Han still found he couldn't identify half the nonhuman types he saw here. That wasn't unusual. The stars were so many that no one could catalog all the sentient races they'd spawned. Han had lost count of the times he'd entered a room like this one, filled with a kaleidoscope of strange shapes, sounds, and odors. Without straining, he could spot a dozen types of respirators and life-support apparatus being used by entities whose biology wasn't compatible with standard human atmosphere.

Han particularly appreciated those human and near-human females dressed in shimmersilks, chromasheaths, and illuminescences. One swept up to him, fresh from the bank of coin-games that offered such diversions as Mind-Jam, Senso-Switch, Reflex Races, and Starfight. She was a tall, lithe girl with a wine-dark cast to her skin and hair like plaited silver, wearing a gown that seemed to have been knit from white mist. "Welcome down, spaceman," she laughed, throwing an arm around him. "How about a turn through the dance dome?"

Han shifted his burden to his other arm as Chewbacca looked on disapprovingly; several of their less auspicious adventures had begun just this way. "Sure!" Han responded enthusiastically. "Let's dance, let's snuggle up, let's get *grafted together*!" He gently pushed her away. "A little later."

She showed him a truly stunning smile—to let him know it was nothing personal—and moved on to greet another customer before he'd moved out of earshot.

The Free-Flight Dance Dome was a first-class trough. It was equipped with a top-of-the-line gravity field, its console visible among the bottles, spigots and taps, and other paraphernalia encircled by the bar. The field permitted the management to alter gravity anywhere on the premises, and so the dance floor and the dome over it had become a low-gee acrobatic playground in which singles, couples, and groups looped, floated, and spun with effortless grace. Han also spotted individual booths and tables where species from low-gravity worlds were taking their ease in comfort, the specific gravity of their area having been lowered for them.

Han and Chewbacca moved farther into the twilight of the place, hearing the clink of drinking vessels of many kinds and the interweaving of any number of languages over the blast from the sound system. They breathed in the aromas of diverse inhalants and aerosols; a profusion of smoke and vapors of various hues, defying the ventilation unit, had drifted by thermoclines into multicolored strata.

He had no problem spotting Ploovo Two-For-One; the big glom had found a large table in the corner, the better to watch for his debtor. Han and Chewbacca sauntered over. Ploovo applied a labored, unconvincing smile to his well-upholstered face. "Solo, old colleague. Come, sit."

"Spare us the guano, Two-For-One." Han sat down next to Ploovo. Chewbacca slung his bowcaster over his shoulder and took a place across the table so that he and Han could watch each other's backs. Han set down the box he carried. Ploovo's greedy eyes caressed it. "Feel free to drool," Han bade him.

"Now, Solo," Ploovo chided, volubly ready to ignore any insult in the heady presence of money, "that's no way to talk to your old benefactor." Ploovo had already been informed by contacts here that these two freighter bums had exchanged a large quantity of negotiables for cash. His hand went for the box. Han's got there first.

The pilot challenged the loan shark with a raised eyebrow. "Your payment's in there. With interest. We're quits after this, Ploovo."

Strangely unperturbed, Ploovo nodded, his topknot jiggling along with his jowls. Han was about to question this when Chewbacca's warning snarl interrupted. A detail of Security Police had entered *The Free-Flight*. Some stationed themselves at the doors while the others made their way around the room.

Han snapped the retaining strap off his holstered blaster. The sound made Ploovo turn. "Now, um, Solo, I swear I had nothing to do with this. We are, as you so recently pointed out, quits. Even *I* wouldn't presume to turn informer and risk my livelihood." He put a fat, covetous hand on the box. "I believe those gentlemen in institutional brown are seeking a man who answers your description. While I no longer have any interest in your well-being, I suggest that you and your fuzzy comrade absent yourselves from here at once."

Han didn't waste time wondering how the Authority had gotten on his tail after he'd obtained new registration for the *Falcon* and identification certificates for himself and Chewbacca. He leaned close to Ploovo, right hand still close to his blaster.

"Why don't we just sit here awhile, *colleague*? And as long as we're at it," he addressed Ploovo's flunkies, "you all have my permission to put your hands right up on the table here, where Chewie and I can see them. *Now!*"

Ploovo's upper lip beaded with sweat. If anyone made a play now, he would certainly become corpse number one. He stuttered an order; his men complied with Han's proposal.

"Compose yourself, Solo," Ploovo implored, though Han was quite serene; it was Ploovo's face that had become pasty white. "Don't let that, er, renowned temper get the better of you. You and the Wookiee can be so irrational at times. Take the occasion when Big Bunji was careless enough to forget to pay you, and you two strafed his pressure dome. He and his staff barely had time to get into their survival suits. Things like that give a man a bad reputation, Solo!" Ploovo was shaking now, having very nearly forgotten his money.

The Security Police had been circulating. They stopped

by the table, two rankers and a sergeant. Their timing couldn't have pleased Ploovo less.

"Everyone at this table, produce identification."

Chewbacca had assumed his most innocent expression, his big, soft blue eyes upturned to the soldiers. He and Han offered their falsified IDs. The pilot's hand hovered near his weapon's grip, even though a shootout now, in this position and at these odds, with the door firmly held by reinforcements held little promise of survival.

The Espo sergeant ignored the credentials of Ploovo and his gang. Skimming Han's he asked, "These are correct? You're the master-owner of that freighter that made planetfall today?"

Han saw no margin for deception there. And if the Authority had already connected his new persona with events surrounding the illegal landing on Duroon, he was as good as dead. Still, he managed to look faintly amused and somewhat bewildered by all this interrogation.

"The *Sunfighter Franchise*? Why, yes, Officer. Is anything wrong?" Guileless as a newborn, he gazed up at them.

"We got your description from the docking bays supervisor," the Security Police sergeant answered. "Your ship's been impounded." He threw the IDs back on the table. "Failure to conform to Authority safety standards."

Han's mental processes switched tracks. "She's got all her approvals," he objected, thinking he ought to know, having forged them himself.

The Espo waved that way. "Those're outdated. Your ship fails to meet new standards. The Authority redefined ships' performance profiles, and from what I heard, buddy, your freighter violates hers about ten different ways and doesn't appear on the Waivers List. Just on external inspection, they found her lift/mass ratio and armaments rating way out of line for nonmilitary craft. It looks like a lot of radiation shielding got removed when the thruster ducting was chopped and rechanneled. Also, she's got all that irregular docking tackle, augmented defensive shields, heavy-duty acceleration compensators, and a mess of long-range detection gear. That's some firecracker you've got there.''

Han spread his hands modestly; this was one time when he didn't feel like boasting about his pride and joy.

The Espo sergeant went on. ''See, when you run a hot rig like that, small payload, overmuscled, the Corporate Sector Authority starts thinking you might take a notion to do something illegal with it. She'll have to be refitted to original specs; you'll have to appear and make arrangements.''

Han laughed airily. ''I'm positive there's some error.'' He knew he'd been lucky they hadn't forced the locks for an inboard search. If they'd seen the anti-sensor equipment, jamming and countermeasures apparatus, and broad-band monitoring outfit, this would have been an arrest party. And what if they had found the contraband compartments?

''I'll drop by the portmaster's office as soon as my business is done,'' Han promised. He now realized that this was why Ploovo Two-For-One had been so content. The loan shark hadn't even had to violate criminal protocol or risk his own rank hide going against Han and Chewbacca; Ploovo had known the *Millennium Falcon,* under any name, would run afoul of these Authority regulations.

''No good,'' the Espo sergeant was saying. ''My orders are to escort you down as soon as you're found. The portmaster wants this matter cleared up right away.'' The Espos were suddenly more alert.

Han's smiled became pained and sympathetic. Platitudes of understanding rolled from him. Meanwhile, he considered his dilemma dispassionately. The Authority would want a full accounting of ship's papers, log, master's credentials. When those showed discrepancies, there'd be a full ID scan: pore patterns, retinal and cortical indexes—the whole routine. Eventually, they'd find out who Han and his first mate were, and then the trouble would really start.

It was axiomatic to Han Solo's philosophy that you never go one step closer to jail than necessary. But seated here, he could offer no decent resistance. He shot a glance at Chewbacca, who was amusing himself by showing his teeth to the wary Security Police in a frightening smile. The Wookiee caught Han's look, though, and inclined his head slightly.

Whereupon the pilot rose. "Shall we get this unpleasantness taken care of, then, Sergeant, so we can all go our way?" Chewie shuffled away from the table, his attention on Han, one paw on the sling of his bowcaster. Han leaned down for a last word with Ploovo.

"Thanks for the good time, old colleague. We'll get back to you as soon as we can, I promise. And before I forget, there's your payment." He flipped down the box's front end and stepped back.

Ploovo dug into the box, expecting to fill his itchy palm with wonderful, sensuous money. Instead, sharp little fangs clamped down on the fleshy part of his thumb. Ploovo screamed as the enraged Dinko swarmed out and sank its needlelike claws into his pudding of a stomach. Fastened to the Dinko's dorsal vane was the Authority Cash Voucher, Han's thoughtful way of repaying debts both financial and personal—with interest.

The Espos' attention switched to the table as the criminal boss howled. One of Ploovo's henchmen tried to tear the Dinko off his employer while the others gaped. The Dinko wasn't having any; it slashed the fumbling hands with the serrated spurs on its rear legs, then sprayed everyone at the table with vile squirts from its scent sac. Few things in nature are more repugnant than a Dinko's defensive secretion. Men and humanoid fell back, coughing and gagging, forgetting their boss.

The Security Police were trying to understand what was happening as beings stumbled from the table, lurching past them, leaving Ploovo to the mercies of the rabid little beast. The Dinko was now trying energetically—if overoptimistically—to devour him, starting with his nose, which rather reminded it of one of its many natural enemies.

"Yahhh!" Ploovo complained, wrenching at the determined Dinko. "Ged it off of me!"

"Chewie!" was all Han had time to yell. He punched the nearest Espo, not wanting to shoot at close quarters. The Espo, caught off guard, fell backward, thrashing. Chewie did better, picking up the other two by their harnesses and bashing them together helmet to helmet, eliciting a gonging sound from the ultrahard surfaces. Then the Wookiee ducked into the crowd with notable agility, following his friend.

The Espos at the doors were unlimbering wide-bore, shoulder-fired blasters, but the confused crowd was milling around and no one had a clear idea yet of just what was going on. The antigrav dancers began alighting as beings raised their attention from assorted intoxicants, stimulants, depressants, psychotropics, and placebos. The room buzzed with a sort of befuddled, translingual *"Huh?"*

Ploovo Two-For-One, having finally dissuaded the Dinko from his abused nose by main force, flung it across the room. The Dinko landed upon the dinner of a wealthy dowager, destroying the appetite of everyone at that table.

Ploovo, still caressing his wounded snout, turned just in time to see Han Solo vault the bar. "There he is!" the underworld boss exclaimed. The two bartenders rushed to stop Han, swinging the stun-staves they kept behind their bar for the preservation of order. He met the first with crossed wrists intersecting the bartender's, stopping the descending stun-stave, brought his knee up, and elbowed the first mixologist into the second. Chewbacca, following his partner over the bar with a joyous bellow that made the lighting fixtures tinkle, fell on top of the bartenders.

A blaster bolt, fired by one of the Espos at the doors, shattered a crystalline globe of four-hundred-year-old Novanian grog. The crowd bleated, most of them diving for the floor. Two more shots blew fragments out of the bar and half slagged the cash repository.

Han had struggled past the vigorous tangle of Chewie and the bartenders. He grabbed for his blaster and threw down on the Espos, peppering their general location with short bursts. One dropped, his shoulder smoking, and the others scattered for cover. Off to one side, Han could hear Ploovo and his men clubbing their way through yelling, charging customers. He headed for the bar.

Han turned to his objective, the gravity controls. With no leisure to analyze them, he frantically began moving indicators toward maximum. Luckily for everyone not within the insulated area of the bar, he noticed when he'd happened on the general field override, and there were no longer any free-flight dancers in the air. Thus, no one was crushed, or dashed to smithereens.

As it was, Han ran the place's gee-load up to three-point-five Standard. Entities of all descriptions sank to the carpets, borne down by the staggering weight of their own bodies, proving there were no heavy-gee natives here today. The Espos flopped with the rest. Ploovo Two-For-One, Han noted in passing, strongly resembled a beached bloatfish.

There was silence except for the grunts of determined breathing and the smothered groans from those who'd suffered some minor mishap in hitting the deck. No one seemed badly hurt, though. Han put his smoking blaster away, studying the gravity-field's controls, telling himself, Yo, now; what we need is a tight corridor out of here. But he was biting his lip, and his fingers poised indecisively over the adjustments.

With an impatient hoot, Chewbacca, who'd put away both bartenders, picked Han up by the shoulders and set him aside. The Wookiee stood over the console, his long fingers moving with nimble precision, peering frequently from his work to the door. In moments the bodies of the two or three patrons lying along his corridor of lighter gravity stirred weakly. Everyone else, the Espos and Ploovo's underworld contingent included, remained pasted to the floor.

Chewbacca eased himself carefully back over the bar and into the normal-gee passageway. He clamored smugly to Han.

"Well, *I* was the one who thought of it, wasn't I?" the pilot groused, trailing after his friend. Outside the Free-Flight, he discreetly closed the doors behind him and straightened his clothes, while Chewie gave himself a fastidious brushing.

''Hey, Chewie, you were slow with your left just now, weren't you?'' Han queried. ''Is your speed going, old-timer?'' Chewbacca belched savagely; age was a standing joke between them.

Han stopped a group of laughing revelers who'd been about to enter the *Free-Flight*. ''This establishment is officially closed,'' he proclaimed with weighty importance. ''It's quarantined. Fronk's Fever.''

The merrymakers, intimidated by the sinister sound of that imaginary malady, didn't even think to question. They left at once. The two weary partners grabbed the first robo-hack they saw, and sped off toward their ship.

''Things are getting tough for the independent businessman,'' Han Solo lamented.

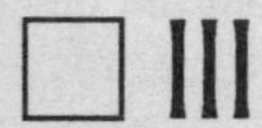

SEVERAL minutes later, the robo-hack deposited Han and Chewbacca around the corner from their docking bay, Number 45. They'd decided it would be wise to scout the landscape to determine whether the forces of law, order, and corporate dividends had gotten there first. Peering cautiously around the corner, they saw a lone portmaster's deputy dutifully locking an impoundment-fastener on their bay's blast doors. Han pulled his first mate back into concealment for a conference. "No time to wait until the coast is clear, Chewie; they'll be sorting things out back at the *Free-Flight* any time now. Besides, that geek is about to lock up the bay, and Espo patrols would get kind of curious if they saw us burning our way through the blast doors."

He peeked out again. The deputy had nearly finished making connections between alarms and the blast-door solenoids. No doubt the bay's other door was fastened as well. Han looked around and noticed an Authority liquor and drugs outlet to his rear. He took his partner's elbow.

"Here's the plan . . ."

A minute later, the portmaster's deputy had wrestled the massive lock halves into place and finished securing the impoundment-fastener. The blast doors slid shut with a shrinking of diamond-shaped opening that disappeared with a clang. The deputy pulled a molecularly coded key from its slot in the fastener, and the device was activated. Now if it were disturbed or damaged, it would instantly inform Espo monitors.

The deputy tucked the key into his belt pouch and prepared to report his errand completed. Just then a Wookiee, a big, leering brute, came wandering past in a drunken stagger, with a sloshing ten-liter crock of some vile-smelling brew cradled in his thick, hairy arm. Just as the Wookiee drew even with the deputy, a man coming from the other direction failed to avoid the shambling creature's dipsomaniacal lurches. There was a rapid, complicated three-way collision, resulting in the Wookiee's stumbling into, and spilling his liquor all over, the luckless deputy.

The instant pandemonium included accusation and counteraccusation, all in raised voices. The Wookiee gobbled horribly at both men, shaking knotted fists and gesturing to the spilled crock. The portmaster's deputy was brushing uselessly at his soaked tunic. The other participant in the accident did his best to be of help. "Oh, say, that's really a shame," Han *tsk*ed with a sad, solicitous tone. "Hey, that stuff's really in there, huh," he said as he tried to wring some of the brew out of the tunic fabric. The deputy and the Wookiee were swapping inprecations and contradictory claims about whose fault the accident had been. The occasional passerby kept right on moving, not wishing to become involved.

"Fella, you better get that tunic washed right away," Han advised, "or that smell'll never come out."

The deputy, with a last threat of legal action against the Wookiee, stalked off. His pace quickened as he realized with apprehension that a supervisor might happen by at any time and catch sight—or even worse, a whiff—of him. He hurried on, leaving the other two to argue liabilities and culpabilities.

The argument stopped as soon as the deputy was gone. Han held up the key he'd lifted from the deputy's belt pouch during the confusion. He handed it to Chewbacca. "Go warm up the ship, but don't call for clearance. The portmaster's most likely got us posted for grounding. If there's a patrol ship, it'd be on our necks in no time." He estimated that eight minutes had passed since they'd fled the *Free-Flight;* their luck couldn't hold much longer.

Chewbacca ran a hasty preflight while Han dashed off along the row of docking bays. He passed three before he came to the one he wanted. In it was a stock freighter, not unlike what the *Millennium Falcon* had once been, but this one was clean, freshly painted, and shipshape. Her name and ID symbols were proudly displayed on her bow, and labor 'droids were busily loading general cargo under the supervision of her crew, who looked nauseatingly honest. Han leaned through the open blast doors, waving a friendly hand. "Hi there. You guys still raising ship tomorrow?"

One of them waved back, but looked confused. "Not tomorrow, bud; tonight, twenty-one hundred planetary time."

Han feigned surprise. "Oh? Well, clear skies." The crewman returned the traditional spacer's farewell as Han strolled away casually. As soon as he was out of their sight, he took off at a run.

When he got back to Bay 45, he found Chewbacca finishing locking the impoundment-fastener on the inner sides of the blast doors, reconnecting them. Han nodded approvingly. "Bright lad. Are we revved up?"

The Wookiee yipped an affirmative and slid the blast doors shut. Locking them again, this time from the inside, he threw the molecularly coded key away.

Han had already reached his seat in the cockpit. Taking his headset, he called port control. Using the name and ID code of the freighter down in Docking Bay 41, he requested that liftoff time be moved up from twenty-one hundred planetary time to immediately, not an unusual request for a tramp freighter, whose schedule might change abruptly. Since there wasn't much traffic and clearance for that ship had already been granted, immediate liftoff was approved at once.

Chewbacca was still buckling in when Han raised ship. Her thrusters flared, and the *Falcon* made, for her, a moderate and restrained departure from Etti IV. When the Espos showed up at Docking Bay 45 and cut their way in, Han reflected, they'd have one interesting time trying to figure out how somebody had sneaked a starship out from under the portmaster's nose.

The starship parted company with Etti IV's gravitational field. Chewbacca, elated over what had been a fairly nifty escape, was in high spirits. The Wookiee's leathery muzzle was peeled back in a nice-hideous smirk, and he was singing—or what passed among his people as singing—at the top of his capacious lungs. The volume of it, in the confines of the cockpit, was incredible.

"C'mon, Chewie," Han implored, rapping a gauge with his knuckle, "you're making all the instruments jump." With a behemothish sort of yodel, the Wookiee ceased. "Besides," Han continued, "we're not out of the heavy weather yet."

Chewbacca lost his placid look and lowed an interrogative. Han shook his head. "Naw, Ploovo's got his money; no matter how torqued off he is, his backers'll never unpocket for a contract on us now. No, what I meant was, the long-range dish we patched together won't last forever. We need another, a top-of-the-line model. Besides, the Espos and, I guess, most other folks who like to arrest people have some kind of new sensor that evades detection on old equipment. We need one of those, too, to get back over with the smart money. One more thing—we need one of those Waivers if we're going to operate around here; we have to wrangle ourselves onto that list somehow. Dammit, the Corporate Sector Authority's wrung out thousands of solar systems; I can almost smell that money! We ain't passing up on fat pickin's just because somebody around here doesn't like our lift/mass ratio."

He finished plotting his hyperdrive jump and turned to his partner with a sly grin. "Now, since the Authority doesn't owe you and me any personal favors, what's that leave?"

The long-pelted first mate growled once. Han spread a hand on his chest and pretended to be shocked. "Outside the law, did you say? *Us?*" He chuckled. "Right you are, pal.

We'll take so much money off the Authority we'll need a knuckle-boom to haul it all away."

The hyperdrive began to cut in. "But first, it's time to meet and greet old friends. After that, everybody'd best hang on to their cash with both hands!" Han finished.

They had to do it in steps, of course. A hyperspace jump took them to an all-but-deserted, played-out mining world where the Authority didn't even bother to maintain offices. A lead there, from an old man who had once seen better days, put them in touch with the captain of a long-orbit ore barge. After some finagling, during which their *bona fides* were checked, with their lives forfeited if that check had turned up the wrong answers, they were given a redezvous.

At that rendezvous they were met, in a deep space, by a small ship's gig. When an inboard search by armed, wary men revealed that the *Falcon* carried no one but her pilot and copilot, the two were led to the second planet of a nearby star system. The gig parted company with them, and they came in for a landing, tracked by the upraised snouts of turbo-laser cannons. The site was a huddle of quickly assembled hanger domes and habitation bubbles. Parked here and there was a wide assortment of ships and other equipment, much of it gutted and decaying, cannibalized for spare parts.

When Han stepped down the starship's ramp, his face lit with that intense smile that had been known to make men check up and see what their wives were doing. "Hello, Jessa. It's been too long, doll."

The woman waiting at the foot of the ramp looked back at him scornfully. She was tall, her hair a mass of heavy blond ringlets, and her shape did extremely pleasant things to the tech's coveralls she wore. Her upturned nose held a collection of freckles acquired under a variety of suns; Jessa had been on almost as many planets as Han. Just now, her large brown eyes showed him nothing but derision.

"Too long, Solo? No doubt you've been busy with religious retreats? Mercantile conferences? Milk deliveries for the Interstellar Childrens' Aid Fund? Well, it's no wonder I haven't heard from you. After all, what's a Standard Year, more or less, hey?"

"A lifetime, kid," he answered smoothly. "I missed you." Coming down to her, he reached for her hand.

Jessa eluded him, and men with drawn guns came into view. They wore coveralls, fusion-welders' masks, tool belts, and greasy headbands, but they were plainly comfortable with their weapons.

Han shook his head mournfully. "Jess, you've really got me wrong, you'll see." But he knew he had just received an explicit warning, and decided he'd better turn the conversation to the matter at hand. "Where's Doc?"

The scorn left Jessa's features, but she ignored his question. "Come with me, Solo."

Leaving Chewbacca to watch the *Falcon*, Han accompanied her across the temporary base. The landing field was a flat expanse of fusion-formed soil (almost any sort of solid material would do for fusion-forming, Han knew; minerals, vegetable matter, or any old enemies for whom you had no further use). Male, female, human, and nonhuman techs scrambled over vehicles and machinery of every category, aided by a wild assortment of 'droids and other automata, engaged in repair, salvage, and modification.

Han admired the operation as he walked. A tech who'd do illegal work could be found almost anywhere, but Doc, Jessa's father, had an operation that was famous among lawbreakers everywhere. If you wanted your ship repaired without questions as to why you'd been through a firefight, if you needed a vessel's ID profile and appearance changed for reasons best left unmentioned, or if you had a hot piece of major hardware to buy or sell—the person to contact, if you met his rigorous background check, was Doc. If something could be done with machinery, he and his outlaw-techs could do it.

Several of the modifications done on the *Millennium Falcon* had been performed through the outlaw-tech's good offices; he and Han had dealt with each other on a number of occasions. Han admired the shifty old man because he'd been sought by Authority and other official forces for years but never apprehended. Doc had kept himself well buffered, and piped into as many crooked bureaucrats and scuttlebutt sources as anyone Han knew. More than one strike unit had moved against the outlaw-techs only to capture a target area empty of everything but abandoned buildings and useless junk. Doc had joked that he was the only felon in the galaxy who'd have to set up an employee pension plan.

Threading among disassembled hulks and humming repair docks, Jessa led Han through the largest hangar on the base. At one end, slabs of Permex had been joined into a stark cube of an office. But when its door slid up at her command, Han could see that Doc's taste hadn't coarsened. The office featured carpets of Wrodian weave, glittering in rich colors, each one representing generations' work. There were shelves of rare books, lavish hangings, and paintings and sculpture, some by history's greatest artists and others by unknowns who'd simply struck Doc's fancy. There was a monolithic, hand-carved scentwood desk with only one item on it, a holocube of Jessa. In it she was wearing a stylish evening gown, smiling, much more like a pretty girl at her first formal reception than a top-flight outlaw-tech genius.

"Where's the old man?" Han asked, seeing the room was empty. Jessa slid into the conform-lounger behind the desk. She clenched her hands on the lounger's thick, luxurious arms until her fingers made deep indentations.

"He's not here, Solo. Doc's gone."

"How informative; I'd never have guessed it just from seeing the room's empty. Look, Jess, I have no time for games, no matter how much you'd like to play. I want—"

"I know what you want!" Her face was bitter; it took him by surprise. "No one comes to us unless we know what they want from us. But my father's not here. He's disappeared, and nothing I've tried has turned up a hint. Believe me, Solo, I've tried it all."

Han eased down into a seat across the desk from her. Jessa explained, "Doc went off on one of his buying trips—you know, shopping for stuff that would fit the market, or for some customer's special order. He made three stops and never arrived at the fourth. Just like that. He, three crewmen, and a star yacht just dropped out of sight."

Han thought for a moment about the old man with work-hardened hands, a quick, crusty grin, and a halo of frizzy white hair. Han had liked him, but if Doc was gone, that was that. Few people who vanished under circumstances like that ever showed up again. Luck of the draw. Han had always traveled light, with emotional baggage the first thing he jettisoned, and grief was far too heavy to lug around among the stars.

So that only left thinking, *Goodbye, Doc,* and dealing with Jessa, the old man's only surviving kin. But when his brief distraction broke, he saw that she'd studied the entire play of his thoughts on his face. "You got through that eulogy pretty fast, didn't you, Solo?" she asked softly. "Nobody gets too far under that precious skin of yours, isn't that so?"

That pricked him. "If it was me who'd checked out, would Doc have gone on a crying jag, Jess? Would you? I'm sorry, but life goes on, and if you lose sight of that, sweetheart, you're asking to be dealt out."

Her mouth opened to reply, but she thought better of it and changed tack. Her voice became as sharp as a vibroblade. "Very well. Let's do business. I know what you're looking for, the sensor suite, the dish, the Waiver. I can take care of all of it. We got our hands on a sensor suite, powerful, compact, a military package built for long-range scoutships. It found its way to us from a supply depot; got misrouted by a happy coincidence I arranged. I can handle the Waiver, too. That only leaves"—she gazed at him coldly—"the question of price."

Han wasn't crazy about the way she'd said it. "The money's got to be right, Jess. I've only got—"

She cut him off again. "Who said money? I know *just*

how much you have, high roller, and where you got it, and how much you gave Ploovo. Don't you think we hear everything sooner or late? Would I assume an imbecile who's been gunrunning would be flush?'' She leaned back, interlacing her fingers.

He was confused. He'd planned to arrange long terms with Doc, but doubted if he could with Jessa. If she knew he couldn't meet a decent price, why was she talking to him? ''Are you going to explain, Jess, or am I supposed to do my famous mind-reading act?''

''Give your jaws a rest, Solo, and pay attention. I'm offering you a deal, a handwash.''

He was suspicious, knowing there'd be no generosity from her. But what were his alternatives? He needed his ship repaired, and the rest of it, or he might as well go somewhere out on the galactic rim and bid on a contract to haul garbage. With exaggerated sweetness, he answered, ''I'm hanging on your every word. By what, I won't mention.''

''It's a pickup, Solo, an extraction. There are details, but that's basically it; you make contact with some people and take them where they want to go, within reason. They won't be expecting you to drop them anywhere risky. Even your stunted attention span ought to suffice for that.''

''Where's the pickup?''

''Orron III. That's mostly an agricultural world, except that the Authority has a data center there. That's where your passengers are.''

''An Authority Data Center?'' Han exploded. ''And how do I get into a place like that? It'll look like the Espos' Annual Picnic and Grand Reunion. Listen, toots, I want that stuff from you, but I want to live to a ripe old age, too; I plan to sit in a rocker at the Old Spacemen's Home, and what you're suggesting will definitely exclude that option.''

''It's not so terrible,'' she replied levelly. ''Internal security's not especially bad, because only two types of vessels are cleared to land on Orron III—drone barges for the crops and Authority fleet ships.''

"Yeah, but in case you haven't noticed, the *Falcon*'s neither."

"Not yet, Solo, but I'll change that. We have a barge shell, hijacked it in transit. That wasn't much of a trick; they're robot hulks, and they're pretty dumb. I'll fit the *Millennium Falcon* with external control couplings and set her in where the command/control module usually goes, and partition into the hold space. My people can mock up the hull structure so it'll con the Espos, port officials, or anybody else. You land, contact the parties in question, and off you go. Average ground time for a barge is about thirty hours, so you'll have plenty of leeway to get things done. Once you're in transit, you ditch the barge shell and you're home free."

He thought hard about that one. He didn't like anyone messing with his ship. "Why pick me for this thrilling honor? And why the *Falcon*?"

"Because you need something from me, for one thing, so you'll do it. Because, for another, even though you're an amoral mercenary, you're the hottest pilot I know; you've flown everything from a jetpack to a capital ship. As for the *Falcon*, she's just the right size, and has computer capacity to spare, to run the barge. It's a fair deal."

One thing had him puzzled. "Who's the pickup? It sounds like you're going to an awful lot of trouble for them."

"No one you'd know. They're strictly amateurs, and they pay well. What they're doing's no concern of yours, but if they feel like telling you, that's their decision."

He gazed up at the ceiling, which was patterned with glow-pearls. Jessa was offering everything he needed to make the Authority ripe for the plucking. He could give up gunrunning, petty-cash trips to backwater worlds, all that low-ante stuff.

"Well," coaxed Jessa, "do I tell my techs to get busy, or do you and the Wookiee plan to teach the galaxy the folly of crime by starving in poverty?"

He brought his chair upright. "You better let me break the

news to Chewie first, or your wrench jockies will be nothing but a mound of spare parts for the organ banks.''

Doc's organization—now Jessa's—was nothing if not thorough. They had the factory specs for the *Millennium Falcon*, plus complete design holos on every piece of augmentative gear in her. With Chewbacca's help and a small horde of outlaw-techs, Han had the *Falcon*'s engine shielding removed and her control systems exposed in a matter of hours.

Service 'droids trundled back and forth while energy cutters flared, and techs of many races crawled over, under, and into the freighter. It made Han jittery to see so many tools, hands, tentacles, servogrips, and lift-locks near his beloved ship, but he gritted his teeth and simply did his best to be everywhere at once—and came close to succeeding. Chewbacca covered the things his partner missed, startling any erring tech or 'droid with a high-decibel snarl. No one doubted for a moment what the Wookiee would do to the being or mechanical who damaged the starship.

Han was interrupted by Jessa, who had come up to inspect his progress. With her was an odd-looking 'droid, built along human lines. The machine was rather stocky, shorter than the woman, covered with dents, scrapes, smudges, and spot-welds. Its chest region was unusually broad, and its arms, hanging nearly to its knees, gave it a somewhat simian aspect. Its finish was a flat brown primer job peeling in places, and it had a stiff, snapping way of moving. The 'droid's red, unblinking photoreceptors trained on Han.

''Meet your passenger,'' Jessa invited.

Han's features clouded. ''You never said anything about taking a 'droid.'' He looked at the aged mechanical. ''What's he run on, peat?''

''No. And I warned you there'd be details. Bollux here is one of them.'' She turned to the 'droid. ''Okay, Bollux, open up the fruit stand.''

''Yes, ma'am,'' Bollux replied in a leisurely drawl. There was a servomotor hum, and the 'droid's chest plastron split down the center, the halves swinging away to either side. Nestled in among the goodies that were the 'droid's innards was a special emplacement; secured in the emplacement was another unit, a separate machine entity of some kind that was approximately cubical, with several protrusions and folded appendages. Atop it was a phtoreceptor mount, monocular lensed. The unit was painted in deep, protective, multilayered blue. The monocular came on, lighting red.

"Say hello to Captain Solo, Max," Jessa instructed it.

The machine-within-a-machine studied Han up and down, photoreceptor angling and swiveling. "Why?" it demanded. The pitch of its vocal mechanism was like that of a child.

Jessa countered frankly, "Because if you don't, Max, the nice man is liable to chuck your teensy iron behind out into deep space—that's why."

"Hello!" chirped Max, with what Han suspected to be forced cheer. "A great pleasure to make your acquaintance, Captain!"

"The parties you're picking up need to collect and withdraw data from the computer system on Orron III," Jessa explained. "Of course, they couldn't just ask the Authority there for probe equipment without raising suspicions, and your walking in with Max under your arm might cause a few problems, too. But nobody's going to bother much about an old labor 'droid. We named him Bollux because we had so many headaches restructuring his gut. We never did get his vocal pattern up to speed.

"Anyway, that cutie in Bollux's chest cavity is Blue Max; Max because we crammed as much computer capacity into him as we could, and blue for reasons that even you, Solo, can see, I'm sure. Blue Max was a piece of work, even for us. He's puny, but he cost plenty, even though he's immobile and we had to leave out a lot of the usual accessories. But he's all they'll need to tap that data system."

Han was studying the two machines, hoping Jessa would admit she'd been joking. He'd seen weirder gizmos in his time, but never on a passenger roster. He didn't like 'droids very much, but decided he could live with these.

He bent down for a better squint at Blue Max. "You stay in there all the time?"

"I can function autonomously or in linkage," Max squeaked.

"Fabulous," Han said dryly. He tapped Bollux's head. "Button up." As the brown segments of plastron swung shut on Max, Han called up to Chewbacca, "Yo, partner, find a place and stow this mollusk, will you? He's with us." He turned back to Jessa. "Anything else? A marching band, maybe?"

She never did get to answer. Just then klaxons went off, sirens began to warble at deafening levels, and the public-address horns started paging her to the base's command post. Everywhere in the hangar, outlaw-techs dropped their tools in a ringing barrage and dashed off frantically for emergency stations. Jessa sprinted away instantly. Han took off after her, yelling back for Chewbacca to stay with their ship.

The two crossed the complex. Humans, nonhumans, and machines charged in every direction, necessitating a good deal of dodging and swerving. The command post was a simple bunker, but at the bottom of the steps leading to it, Jessa and Han entered a well-equipped, fully manned operations room. A giant holo-tank dominated the room with its phantom light, an analogue of the solar system around them. Sun, planets, and other major astronomical bodies were picked out in keyed colors.

"Sensors have painted an unidentified blip, Jessa," said one of the duty officers, pointing out a yellow speck at the edge of the system. "We're awaiting positive ID."

She bit her lip, eyes fastened to the tank along with those of all the others in the bunker. Han moved up next to her. The speck was moving toward the center of the holotank, which would be, Han knew, the planet on which he was standing, represented by a bead of white light. The bogie's speed decreased, and sensors painted a cluster of smaller blips breaking away from it. Then the original object accelerated, kept on accelerating, and faded from the tank a moment later.

"It was an Authority fleet ship, a corvette," the officer said. "It launched a flight of fighters, four of them, then ducked back into hyperspace. It must've detected us and gone for help, leaving the fighters to harass and keep us busy until it can return. I don't see how they happened to be searching this system."

Han realized the officer was looking directly at him. In fact, everybody in the command post was, and hands had gone to side arms. "Whoa, Jess," he protested, meeting her eyes, "when did I ever stooge for the Espos?"

For a moment an expression of uncertainty crossed her face, but only for a moment. "I guess if you'd tipped them you wouldn't have stuck around while they dropped in," she admitted. "Besides, they would have shown up in full strength if they'd known we were here. You've got to concede, though, Solo, it's some coincidence."

He changed the subject. "Why didn't the corvette just put through a hyperspace transmission? They must be close enough to a base to call for support."

"This area's full of stellar anomalies," she said absently, focusing back on those ominous blips. "It fouls up hyperspace commo; that's why we picked it, partly. What's the fighters' estimated time of arrival?" she asked the officer.

"ETA less than twenty minutes," was the reply.

She blew her breath out. "And we haven't got anything combatworthy except fighters ourselves. No use ducking it; get ready to scramble. Order evacuation to start in the meantime."

She looked to Han. "Those are probably IRDs'; they'll eat up anything I can send up right now except for some old snubs I have here. I need to buy time, and I have almost nobody who's done any combat flying. Will you help?"

He saw all the grave faces still staring at him. He led Jessa to one side, caressed her cheek, but spoke in a low tone.

"My darling Jess, this definitely was *not* in our deal. I'm for the Old Spacemen's Home, remember? I have no intention of ever plunking my rear into one of those suicide sleds again."

Her voice was eloquent. "There are lives at stake! We can't evacuate in time, even if we leave everything behind. I'll send up inexperienced pilots if it comes to that, but they'll be cold meat for those Espo flyers. You've got more experience than all the rest of us put together!"

"All of which cries out to me that there's no percentage fighting the good fight," he parried, but he burned from the look she gave him. He nearly spoke again but held his tongue, unable to untangle his own nagging ambiguities.

"Then go hide," she said so low he could barely hear, "but you can forget your precious *Millennium Falcon*, Solo, because there's no power in the universe that can make her spaceworthy before those raiders hit us and pin us down. And once their reinforcements arrive, they'll carve this base and everything in it to atoms!"

His ship, of course; that's what must have been biting at the back of my mind, Han told himself. Must have been. The turbo-laser cannon would never stop fast, evasive fighters, and the raiders would indeed take the base apart. He and Chewbacca might possibly escape with their lives, but without their ship they'd be just two nameless, homeless pieces of interstellar flotsam.

In the confusion of the command post, with the giving and receiving of frantic messages, she still heard his voice among all the others.

"Jess?" She stared, confused, at his lopsided smirk. "Got a flight helmet for me?" He pretended not to see the sudden softening of her expression. "Something sporty, in my size, Jess, with a hole in it to match the one in my head."

HAN tagged after Jessa in another quick run across the base. They entered one of the lesser hangar domes where the air was filled with the whine of high-performance engines. Six fighters were parked there, their ground crews attending them, checking out power levels, armaments, deflectors, and control systems.

The fighters were primarily for interceptor service—or rather, Han corrected himself, had been a generation ago. They were early production snubships; Z-95 Headhunters; compact, twin-engined swing-wing craft. Their fuselages, wings and forked tails were daubed with the drab spots, smears, and spray-splotches of general camouflage coats. Their external hardpoints, where rockets and bomb pylons had once been mounted, were now bare.

Indicating the snubs, Han asked Jessa, "What'd you do, knock over a museum?"

"Picked them up from a planetary constabulary; they were using them for antismuggling operations, matter of fact. We worked them over for resale, but hung on to them because they're the only combat craft we've got right now. And don't be so condescending, Solo; you've spent your share of time in snubs."

That he had. Han dashed over to one of the Headhunters as a ground crewman finished fueling it. He took a high leap and chinned himself on the lip of the cockpit to eyeball it. Most of its console panels had been removed in the course of years of repair, leaving linkages and wiring exposed. The cockpit was just as cramped as he remembered.

But with that, the Z-95 Headhunter was still a good little ship, legendary for the amount of punishment it could soak up. Its pilot's seat—the "easy chair," in parlance—was set back at a thirty-degree angle to help offset gee-forces, the control stick built into its armrest. He let himself back down.

Several pilots had already gathered there, and another, a humanoid, showed up just then. There was little enough worry on their faces that Han concluded they hadn't flown combat before. Jessa came up beside him and pressed an old, lusterless bowl of a flight helmet into his hands.

"Who's flown one of these beasts before?" he asked as he tried the helmet on. It was a bad fit, too tight. He began pulling at the webbing adjustment tabs in its sweat-stained interior.

"We've all been up," one pilot answered, "to practice basic tactics."

"Oh, fine," he muttered, trying the helmet on again. "We'll rip 'em apart up there." The headgear was still too tight. With an impatient click of her tongue, Jessa took it from him and began working on it herself.

He addressed his temporary command. "The Authority's got newer ships; they can afford to buy whatever they want. That fighter spread coming in at us is probably made up of IRD ships straight off the government inventory, maybe prototypes, maybe production models. And the guys flying those IRDs learned how at an academy. I suppose it'd be too much to hope that anybody here has ever been to one?"

It was. Han went on, raising his voice over the increasing engine noise. "IRD fighters have an edge in speed, but these old Headhunters can make a tighter turn and take a real beating, which is why they're still around. IRDs aren't very aerodynamic, that's their nature. Their pilots hate to come down and lock horns in a planetary atmosphere; they call it *goo*. These boys'll have to, though, to hit the base, but we can't wait until they get down here to hit them, or some might get through.

"We've got six ships. That's three two-ship elements. If you've got anything worth protecting with those flight helmets, you'll remember this: stay with your wing man. Without him, you're dead. Two ships together are five times as effective as they would be alone, and they're ten times safer."

The Z-95s were ready now, and the IRDs' arrival not far off. Han had a thousand things to tell these green flyers, but how could he give them a training course in minutes? He knew he couldn't.

"I'll make this simple. Keep your eyes open and make sure it's your guns, not your tail, that's pointed at the enemy. since we're protecting a ground installation, we'll have to ride our kills. That means if you're not sure whether the opposition is hit or faking, you sit on his tail and make sure he goes down and stays down. Don't think just because he's nosediving and leaving a vapor trail that he's out of it. That's an old trick. If you get an explosion from him, fine. If you get a flamer, let him go; he's finished. But otherwise you ride your kill all the way down to the cellar. We've got too much to lose here."

He made that last remark thinking of the *Falcon*, shutting out human factors, telling himself his ship was the reason he was about to hang his hide out in the air. Strictly business.

Jessa had thrust his helmet into his hands. He tried it on again; it was a perfect fit. He turned to say thanks and noticed for the first time that she was carrying a flight helmet, too.

"Jess, no. Absolutely not."

She sniffed. "They're my ships, in the first place. Doc taught me everything; I've been flying since I was five. And who d'you think taught these others the basics? Besides, there's no one else even nearly qualified."

"Training exercises are different!" Of all things, he didn't want to have to worry about her up there. "I'll get Chewie; he's done some—"

"Oh, brilliant, Solo! We can just build a dormer onto the

canopy bubble and that hyperthyroid dust-mop of yours can fly the ship with his kneecaps!''

Han resigned himself to the fact that she was the logical one to fly. She turned to her other pilots. ''Solo's right; this one'll be a toughie. We don't want to engage them out in space, because all the advantages out there are theirs, but we don't want to let them get too close to the surface, either. Our ground defenses couldn't cope with a fighter spread. So somewhere in the middle we'll have to draw the line, depending on how they play it when they come at us. If we can buy time, the ground personnel will have a chance to complete evacuation.''

She turned to Han. ''Including the *Falcon*. I gave orders to finish her and close her up as soon as possible. I had to divert men to do it, but a deal's a deal. And I sent word to Chewie what's happened.''

She pulled her helmet on. ''Han's flight leader. I'll assign wing men. Let's move.''

With high screeches the six Z-95 Headhunters, like so many mottled arrowheads, sped off into the sky. Han pulled down and adjusted his tinted visor. He checked his weapons again, three blaster cannons in each wing. Satisfied, he maneuvered so that his wing man was above and behind him, relative to the plane of ascent. Seated in his sloped-back easy chair, situated high in the canopy bubble, he had something near 360-degrees' visibility, one of the things he liked most about these old Z-95s.

His wing man was a lanky, soft-spoken young man. Han hoped the guy wouldn't forget to stick close when The Show started.

He thought, *The Show—fighter-pilot jargon.* He'd never thought he'd be using it again, with his blood up and a million things to keep track of, including allies, enemies, and his own ship. And anything that went wrong could blow him out of The Show for good.

Besides, The Show was the province of youth. A fighter

could hold only so much gee-compensation equipment, enough to lessen simple linear stress and get to a target or scrap in a hurry, but not enough to offset the punishment of tight maneuvering and sudden acceleration. Dogfighting remained the testing ground of young reflexes, resilience, and coordination.

Once, Han had lived, eaten, and slept high-speed flying. He'd trained under men who thought of little else. Even off-duty life had revolved around hand-eye skills, control, balance. Drunk, he'd stood on his head and played ring-toss, and been flung aloft from a blanket with a handful of darts to twist in midair and throw bull's-eyes time and again. He'd flown ships like this one, and ships a good deal faster, through every conceivable maneuver.

Once. Han was by no means old, but he hadn't been in this particular type of contest for a long time. The flight of Headhunters was pulling itself into two-ship elements, and he found his hands had steadied.

They drew their ships' wings back to minimize drag, wing camber adjusting automatically, and rose at high boost. They would meet their opposition at the edge of space.

"Headhunter leader," he announced over the commo net, "to Headhunter flight. Commo check."

"Headhunter two to leader, in." That was Han's wing man.

"Headhunter three, check," sang Jessa's clear alto.

"Headhunter four, all correct." That had been Jessa's wing man, the gray-skinned humanoid from Lafra who, Han had noticed, had vestiges of soaring membranes, suggesting that he had superior flying instincts and a fine grasp of spacial relationships. The Lafrarian, it had turned out, had over four minutes' actual combat time, which was a good sign. A good many fighter pilots were weedcd out in the first minute or so of combat.

Headhunters five and six chimed in, two of Jessa's grease slingers who were brothers to boot. It had been inevitable that they'd be wing men; they'd tend to stick together, and if paired with anyone else, would have been distracted anyway.

Ground control came up. "Headhunter flight, you should have a visual on your opposition within two minutes."

Han had his flight tighten up their ragged formation. "Stay in pairs. If the bandits offer a head-on pass, take them up on it; you can pitch just as hard as they can." He thought it better not to mention that the other side had a longer reach, however.

He had Five and Six, the brothers, drop far back to field any enemies that might break through. The two remaining elements spread out as much as they could without risking separation. Their sensors and those of the approaching ships identified one another, and complex countermeasures and distortion systems switched on. Han knew this engagement would be conducted on visual ranging; all the complicated sensor-warfare apparatus tended to cancel out, no longer to be trusted.

Short-range screens painted four blips. "Go to Heads-Up Displays," Han ordered, and they all cut in their holographics. Transparent projections of their instrumentation hung before them in the canopy bubbles, freeing them of the need to divert their eyes and attention from the task of flying in order to take a reading.

"Here they come!" someone shouted. "At one-zero-slash-two-five!"

The enemy ships were IRD models all right, with bulbous fuselages and the distinctive engine package that characterized that latest military design. They were IRD prototypes. As Han watched, the raiders broke formation into two elements of two ships each in perfect precision.

"Elements break!" he called. "Take 'em!" He led his wing man off to starboard to face that brace of IRDs as Jessa and her humanoid wing man banked to port.

The net came alive with cries of warning. The Espo flyers had disdained evasionary tactics, coming head-on, meaning they were out to put some blood on the walls. Their orders,

Han thought, must've been to hit the outlaw-techs as hard as they could.

The IRDs began firing from extreme range with yellow-green flashes of the energy cannon in their chin pods. Deflector shields were up. Han ground his teeth, his hand tight on the stick, disciplining himself not to fire until it could do some good. He fought the urge to rubberneck and see how his other element was doing; each two-ship pair was on its own for the moment. He could only hope everybody would hold together, because the pilot who became a straggler in a row like this seldom came out of it.

Han and the opposing wing leader squared off and bore in on each other. Their wing men, keeping out of the way, were too busy holding position and adapting to their leaders' actions to do any shooting.

The IRD's beams began to make hits, rocking the smaller Headhunter. Han came within range and still held his fire; he had a feeling about this one. The IRD pilot might not even be sure about the old Z-95's reach, but Han suspected he knew what the man would do as soon as he returned fire. Riding the jolting Headhunter through the hail of incoming shots, he bided his time and hoped his shields would hold.

He played it for as long as he dared, only a matter of an extra moment or two, but precious time and vital distance. He let one quick burst go. As he'd suspected, the enemy never intended to face off to the very end. The IRD rolled onto its back, still firing, and Han had the snap shot he'd hoped for. But the IRD fighter was into his gunsight ring and out again like a wraith, so although he scored, Han knew he hadn't done it any damage. The Authority ships were even faster than he'd thought.

Then all bets were off because, despite everything taught in classrooms, the IRDs split up, the wing man peeling away in an abrupt bank. Han's wing man went after him, exclaiming excitedly, "I'm on him!" Han hollered for him to come back and not throw away the security of a two-ship element.

The IRD leader swept by underneath Han. He knew what that meant, too; the enemy was almost certain to split-S, loop under, and try for a tail position—the kill position. What Han should have done with the slower Headhunter was to firewall the throttle and go for clear space until he knew what was what. But the interchange of chatter between Jessa and her wing mate told him that the other pair of IRDs had split up as well, drawing her and her companion out of their pairing.

Han sent his Headhunter into a maximum-performance climbing turn, trying to look everywhere at once, still yelling to his wing man, "Stick with me! They're baiting you!" But he was ignored.

The IRD leader he'd shot at hadn't split-S. The raiders' whole strategy of drawing the defenders out of formation was clear now, too late. The IRD leader had half rolled again, half looped, and come around onto the tail of Han's wing man. The other IRD, the bait, was already racing on toward the backup element, Headhunters five and six. One of the IRDs Jessa had faced joined that one in a new two-ship element.

The Espos had counted on the inexperienced outlaw-techs' breaking formation, Han thought. If we'd stayed together we'd have mopped the floor with them. "Jess, dammit, we've been robbed," he called as he came around, but Jessa had her own troubles. Because she and her wing mate had become separated, an IRD had found the opportunity to fasten itself on her tail.

Han saw that his own wing man was in trouble, but just didn't have the speed to intervene. The IRD leader had attached himself to the Headhunter in the kill position, and the lanky young outlaw-tech was pleading, "Help me, somebody! Get him off me!"

Still way out of range, Han fired anyway, hoping to shake up the IRD leader's concentration. But the enemy was steady and undistracted. He waited until he had the Headhunter perfectly set up and hit the firing button on his control grips in a brief burst. The Z-95 was caught by a yellow-green blast and vanished in a nimbus of white-hot gas and debris.

What Han should have done was draw his remaining ships together in a weaving, mutually protective string or circle. But even as he breathed profanities to himself, he cut a course for the victorious IRD, his blood up, caution forgotten, thinking, *Nobody gets into me for a wing man, pal. Nobody.*

It came to him that he didn't even know that lanky boy's name.

Jessa's wing man, the Lafrarian, shouted, "Scissor right, Headhunter three! Scissor!"

Jessa broke right in a flurry of evasive maneuvers while lines of destruction probed for her. She poured on all speed as her wing man came in at a sharp angle, decreasing his own velocity so that Jessa and her pursuer came across his vector. The Lafrarian settled calmly into the kill position, quickened up, and opened fire.

Lines of red blaster-cannon fire broke from the trailing Headhunter's wings. The raider ship shuddered as pieces of its fuselage were sheared off. There was an explosion, and the crippled IRD went into a helpless flutter, as if it were dragging a broken wing. It began its long fall toward the planet, sentenced to death by simple gravity.

Far below, Headhunters five and six, the two brothers, had engaged the IRDs that had broken through. Off in the distance Han Solo and the IRD leader swept and wove through the permutations of close combat, making their statements in beams of devastation in red, in green.

But Jessa knew where priorities lay, and Five and Six were her weakest flyers. Even now they were calling for help. She and her humanoid wing man closed and sped off to rejoin the fray.

A raider was glued to Headhunter five's tail, chopping at it and holding position through all the insane turns and evasions, refusing to be unseated. The outlaw-tech shoved his stick up into the corner for a pushover but was too slow. The IRD's beams sliced through his ship, depressurizing it and severing him at the waist. The IRD turned toward the other brother, Headhunter six, as its companion raced on toward the planet and its outlaw base.

Just then Jessa and her wing man arrived, calling for Headhunter six to come under their cover.

"I can't; I'm latched!" the man answered. The IRD that had remained behind had come out of a smooth barrel roll and attached itself to him. Jessa's wing man threw himself in to help and she came right behind. The sliding, jockeying string of four ships plunged toward the planet's surface.

The IRD made its kill a moment later. Headhunter six split apart in a blossom of fire and wreckage just as its killer came under Jessa's wing man's guns.

The Espo flyer applied more of his ship's amazing speed to improve his lead and came up as if he were going into a loop, making the Lafrarian misjudge. The IRD flashed out of the maneuver instead, in a lightning-fast turn, banked, and managed to make a high deflection shot.

The IRD's cannon scored, and her wing man's Headhunter shook as Jessa raised her voice in alarm, sheering off as quickly as she could. She banked and sensed a shadow near. The IRD swooped past. She swerved and shot at it instinctively. The burst scored, penetrating the IRD's shields. As the IRD dropped away in an emergency power dive, its pilot struggling to adjust his craft's thrust bias and avert disaster, Jessa ignored Han's dictum that she ride her kill. She returned to see what she could do for her wing mate.

Exactly nothing. The Lafrarian's ship was damaged but not in danger of crashing. He'd put it into a shallow glide, extending his wings to their fullest.

"Can you make it?"

"Yes, Jessa. But at least one of the IRD has gotten through. The other may manage to rejoin him."

"Nurse your ship back. I've got to get down there."

"Good hunting, Jessa!"

She opened her ship's engines in a power dive.

* * *

Han found out right away that the IRD leader was a good pilot. He discovered it by nearly getting his easy chair shot out from underneath him.

The Espo flyer was hot, accurate with his weaponry, deft with his maneuvers. He and Han quickly joined in circling, pouncing, cloverleaf battle, the upper hand alternating between them. Rolling, looping, doing their best to turn inside each other's turns, sliding into and out of each other's gunsights over and over, they never let their sticks sit still for an instant.

For the third time Han shook the IRD off, playing on his Headhunter's greater maneuverability against the IRD's superior speed. He watched the Espo flyer try to pick him up again. "I guess you must be the local champ, huh?" The IRD came at him once more. "Have it your way, bozo, Let's see what you've really got."

He split-S down deeper into the planet's atmosphere as the IRD sprang at his tail, gaining in the descent but unable to hold the Headhunter in his sights. Han pulled up sharply, twisted his ship into a half loop, flipped over, and went into a diving aileron roll with another loop thrown in, coming out of the combo in the opposite direction.

Cannon blasts streaked by over the canopy bubble, barely missing. Man, this Espo can really *latch*, Han told himself. But he has a few things left to learn. School ain't over yet.

He rammed the stick into the corner for a pushover and began a power dive. The IRD hung in but couldn't quite draw a bead on him. Han pushed the Headhunter to its limits, ducking and slipping as the Espo pilot raked at him. The snub's engines moaned, and every particle of her vibrated as if desiring to fly apart. Han jostled, watching his Heads-Up Display for the reading he wanted. The IRD's shots ranged closer.

Then he had it. He began pulling out of his dive, nosing up slowly and dreading the shot from behind that would end all his problems and hopes.

But the IRD pilot held off, not wanting to waste the opportunity, waiting for the Headhunter to present a spread-eagled silhouette in his gunsight. Han thought, *Sure, he wants this one to be the perfect kill.*

He yanked into a turn as the IRD aligned itself trailing him into it and edging for a lead. Han cheated the turn tighter, and tighter yet. But the IRD pilot clung doggedly, to end the frustrating chase and prove who was the hotter pilot.

And then Han had the turn tighter than ninety degrees, the thing he'd been working toward all along. The Espo hadn't paid enough attention to his altimeter, and now the thicker air was working against the IRD, cutting down on its performance. It couldn't hold a turn this tight.

And just as the IRD broke off its run, Han, with the instincts that had given him a reputation for telepathy, threw his Headhunter into a vertical reversement. The IRD was close enough now. Han fired a sustained burst and the IRD became a cloud of light, throwing out glowing motes and bits of wreckage in every direction.

And as the Headhunter zipped past the showering remains of its opponent, Han crowed, ''Happy graduation day, *sucker*!''

The fourth IRD had already made three strafing runs on the outlaw-tech base. The base's defensive guns couldn't keep up with it; they'd been set up for actions against large ships and mass assault, not agile, low-angle fighter attacks.

The raider had concentrated on flak suppression for his first runs. Now most of the gun emplacements were silent. Outlaws dead and dying lay in a base where several buildings were already holed or ablaze.

Then Jessa showed up. Maintaining the velocity she'd picked up in her dive, ignoring the fact that the wings might be ripped off her stubborn little Headhunter at any moment, she threw herself after the IRD just as it came out of its pass. Those people down there were hers, were suffering and perishing because they worked for her. She was absolutely adamant that no more runs would be made at them.

But as she was lining up on the IRD a volley of cannon

fire sizzled down from above, nipping at the leading edge of her starboard wing. Another IRD flashed by with speed it had picked up in its own dive, the ship she had thought to be disabled. Its shots had penetrated her shields and come close to cleaving her wing.

But she held position, determined to get at least one of the raiders before they got her.

Then the second IRD itself became a target. Han had it in his sights for an instant in a side-on, high deflection shot. He jinxed the nose of his ship, laying out sleeper rounds ahead of the Espo, investing in the future. It paid off; the IRD vanished in an outlashing of force and shrapnel.

"You're on the last one, Jess!" he informed her in a crackle of static. "Swat him!"

She was lined on the IRD again. She fired, but only her portside cannon worked; the damage to her starboard wing had knocked out its guns. Her target being slightly off to starboard, she missed.

The IRD began surging ahead, capitalizing on its raw ion power, slipping away to starboard. In another split second it would get away. Jessa snap-rolled, sliding to starboard belly-up, and fired again. Her remaining guns reached out with red fingers of destruction and hit. The IRD flared and flamed, breaking apart.

"Nice shooting, doll," Han called over the net. Jessa's Headhunter continued along, canopy lowermost, not far from the ground. He cut in full power and went after her, saying, "Jess, in aerospace circles, what we call what you are is upside down."

"I can't get back over!" There was desperation in her tone. "That damage I took must've started a burn-out creep-age. My controls are dead!"

He was about to instruct her to punch out but stopped himself. She was too close to the surface; her ejection seat would never have time to right itself. Her ship was losing altitude rapidly. Only seconds were left.

He swept in and matched speeds with her. "Jess, get ready to go when I give you the word."

She was mystified. What could he mean? She was dead, crashing or ejecting. But she prepared to do as he said. Han eased the wing of his Headhunter under her overturned one. She saw his plan and her breath caught in her throat.

"On three," he told her. *"One!"* On that count he brought his wing tip up under hers. *"Two!"* They both felt the jar of hazardous contact, knowing the most minuscule mistake would strew them both all over the flat landscape.

Han rolled left, and the ground that had been streaking by beneath Jessa's dangling head seemed to rotate away as Han's Headhunter imparted spin to hers. He finished his roll with additional force.

"*Three!* Punch out, Jess!" He himself was fighting to keep his jostled ship from going out of control.

But before he'd even said half of it, she'd gone, her canopy bubble propelled up and back by separator charges, her ejection seat—the easy chair—flung high and clear of her descending ship. The Headhunter plowed into the planet's surface, making a long strip of fiery ruin along the ground, becoming the day's final casualty.

Jessa watched from her ejection seat while its replusor units steadied and eased her down toward the ground on gusts of power. Off in the distance, she could see her Lafrarian wing man nursing his damaged craft in for a landing.

Han maneuvered his Headhunter through a long turn, coaxing with his retrothrusters until he was at a near stall. He brought his ship down nearby just as Jessa touched down.

The bubble popped up. He removed his helmet and jumped out of the aged fighter just as she slid free of her harness and threw her own helmet aside, feeling around and finding herself generally whole.

Han sauntered over, stripping off his flying gloves. "There's room for two in my ship if we squeeze," he leered.

"As I live and breathe," she scoffed. "Have we finally seen Han Solo do something unselfish? Are you going soft?

Who knows, you may even pick up a little morality one day, if you ever wake up and get wise to yourself."

He stopped, his leer gone. He glared at her for a moment, then said, "I already know all about morality, Jess. A friend of mine made a decision once, thought he was doing the moral thing. Hell, he *was*. But he'd been conned. He lost his career, his girl, everything. This friend of mine, he ended up standing there while they ripped the rank and insignia off his tunic. The people who didn't want him put up against a wall and shot were laughing at him. A whole planet. He shipped out of there and never went back."

She watched his face become ugly. "Wouldn't anyone testify for—your friend?" she asked softly.

He sniggered. "His commanding officer committed perjury against him. There was only one witness in his defense, and who's going to believe a Wookiee?"

He fended off her next remark by glancing at the base. "Looks like they never touched the main hangar. You can have the *Falcon* finished in no time and still evacuate before the Espos show up. Then I'll be on my way. We've both got things to do."

She closed one eye, looking at him sidelong. "It's lucky I know you're a mercenary, Solo. It's lucky I know you only flew that Headhunter to protect the *Falcon*, not to protect lives. And that you saved me so I could hold up my end of our bargain. It's lucky you'll probably never do a single selfless, decent thing in your life, and that everything that happened today fits in, in some crazy way, with that greedy, retarded behavioral pattern of yours."

He stared at her quizzically. "Lucky?"

She started for his fighter, walking tiredly. "Lucky for me," Jessa said over her shoulder.

"WHAT'D you say, Bollux? Quit whispering!"

Han, seated across the gameboard from Chewbacca, glared at a crate on the other side of the *Millennium Falcon*'s forward compartment, where the old 'droid sat. The compartment's other clutter included shipping containers, pressure kegs, insulated canisters, and spare parts.

The Wookiee, seated on the acceleration couch, chin resting on one enormous paw, studied the holographic game pieces. His eyes were narrowed in concentration and his black snout twitched from time to time. He'd spotted Han two pieces, and was now on the verge of wiping out that advantage. The pilot had been playing poorly, his concentration wandering, fretting and preoccupied with the complications of the voyage. The new sensor package and dish were working perfectly, and the starship's systems had been fine-tuned by the outlaw-techs. Nevertheless, Han's mind couldn't rest easy as long as his cherished *Falcon* was hooked up to the huge barge like a bug on a bladderbird. Furthermore, the trip was taking far longer than the *Falcon* alone would have required; the barge wasn't built for speed.

Han could hear the barge's engines now, their muffled blast vibrating through the freighter's deck and his boots, into the soles of his feet. He hated that barge, wished he could just dump it and zoom off; but a bargain was, after all, a bargain. And, as Jessa had explained, the Waiver for the *Falcon* was being arranged by the people he was to pick up on Orron III, so it behooved him to hold up his end of the agreement.

"I didn't say anything, sir," Bollux replied politely. "That was Max."

"Then what did *he* say?" Han snapped. The two-in-one machines sometimes communicated between themselves by high-speed informational pulses, but seemed to prefer vocal-mode conversations. It always made Han nervous when Bollux's chest was closed up, with the diminutive computer's voice rising spectrally from an unseen source.

"He informed me, Captain," Bollux replied in his slow fashion, "that he would like me to open my plastron. May I?"

Han, who'd turned back to the gameboard, saw that Chewbacca had sprung a clever trap. While his finger hovered indecisively over the programming keys controlling his pieces, Han muttered, "Sure, sure, go on, you can fan the air for all I care, Bollux." He scowled at the Wookiee, seeing there was no way out of the trap. Chewbacca threw his head back with a toss of red-brown hair and woofed with laughter, showing jutting fangs.

With a soft hiss of escaping air—his plastron was airtight, insulated, and shockproof—Bollux's chest swung open as the labor 'droid moved his long arms back out of the way. Blue Max's monocular came alive and tracked over to the gameboard just as Han punched up his next move. His gamepiece, a miniature, three-dimensional monster, jumped into battle with one of Chewie's. But Han had misjudged the two pieces' subtle win-lose parameters. The Wookiee's simulacrum-beastie won the brief fight. Han's gamepiece evaporated back into the nothingness of computer modeling from which it had come.

"You should have used the Second Ilthmar Defense," Blue Max volunteered brightly. Han swung around with murder in his eye; even the precocious Max recognized the look, hastily adding, "Only trying to be of assistance, sir."

"Blue Max is quite new, quite young, Captain," Bollux supplied, by way of mollifying Han. "I've taught him a bit about the board game, but he doesn't know much yet about human sensitivities."

"Is that so?" Han asked, as if fascinated. "So who's teaching him, Mr. Pick and Shovel, you?"

"Sure," Max bubbled. "Bollux's been *everywhere*. We sit and talk all the time, and he tells me about the places he's seen."

Han swiped at the gameboard's master key, clearing it of his defeated holo-beasties and Chewbacca's victorious ones. "Do tell? Well, now, that must be some kind of education: *Slit Trenches I Have Dug—a Trans-Galactic Diary.*"

"The great starship yards of Fondor was where I was activated," Bollux responded, in his slow way. "Then, for a time, I worked for a planetary survey Alpha-Team, and after that, for a construction gang on weather-control systems. I had a job as general roustabout for Gan Jan Rue's Traveling Menagerie, and as maintenance helper in the Trigdale Foundaries. And more. But one by one, the jobs have been taken over by newer models. I volunteered for all the modifications and reprogramming I could, but eventually I simply couldn't compete with the newer, more capable 'droids."

Interested now despite himself, Han asked, "How'd Jessa pick you for this ride?"

"She didn't sir; I requested it. There was word that a 'droid would be selected from the general labor pool for some unstated modification. I was there, having been purchased at open auction. I went to her and asked if I might be of use."

Han chortled. "And for that they yanked out part of you, rearranged the rest, and stuck that coin bank inside you. You call that a deal?"

"It has its disadvantages, sir. But it's kept me functioning at a relatively high level of activity. There would probably have been some lesser vacancy for me elsewhere, Captain, even if it were only shoveling biological byproducts on a nontechnological world, but at least I have avoided obsolescence for the time being."

Han gaped at the 'droid, wondering if he were circuit-crazy. "So what, Bollux? What's the point? You're not your own master. You don't even have a say in your own name; you have to reprogram to whatever your new owner decides to call you, and 'Bollux' is a joke. Eventually you'll be of no further use, and then it's Scrap City."

Chewbacca was listening intently now. He was far older than any human, and his perspectives were different from a man's . . . or a 'droid's. Bollux's leisurely speech made him sound serene as he replied, "Obsolescence for a 'droid, sirs, is much like death for a human, or a Wookiee. It is the end of function, which means the end of significance. So it is to be avoided at all costs, in my opinion, Captain. After all, what value is there to existence without purpose?"

Han jumped to his feet, mad without knowing exactly why, except that he felt dumb for arguing with a junk-heap 'droid. He decided to tell Bollux just what a deluded, misfit chump the old labor 'droid really was.

"Bollux, do you know what you are?"

"Yessir, a smuggler, sir," Bollux responded promptly.

Han, confused, looked at the 'droid for a moment, his mouth hanging open, taken off balance by the reply. Even a labor 'droid ought to recognize a rhetorical question, he thought. "*What* did you say?"

"I said, 'Yessir, a smuggler, sir,' " Bollux drawled, "like yourself. One who engages in the illegal import or export of"—his metal forefinger pointed down at Blue Max, nestled in his thorax—"concealed goods."

Chewbacca, paws clasped to his stomach, was rolling around on the acceleration couch, laughing in hysterical grunts, kicking his feet in the air.

Han's temper blew. "Shut up!" he shouted at the 'droid. Bollux, again with that strange literalness, obediently swung his chest panels closed. Chewbacca's laughter had him close to suffocation, as tears appeared around his tight-shut eyes. Han began looking around for a wrench or a hammer, or another instrument of technological mayhem, not intending to have any 'droid one-up him and survive to tell the tale. But at that moment the navicomputer bleeped an alert. Han and Chewbacca instantly charged for the cockpit, the Wookiee still clasping his midsection, to prepare for reversion to normal space.

The tedious trip to Orron III had gnawed at their nerves; both pilot and copilot were grateful for the reappearance of stars that marked emergence from hyperspace, though it was accompanied by a wallowing of the gigantic barge shell. The barge's ovoid hull bulged beneath them, a metal can of a ship with a minimum of engine power. Jessa's techs had executed their hull mock-up so that the *Falcon*'s cockpit retained most of its field of vision.

Han and Chewbacca kept their hands off the ship's controls, letting the computer do the work, maintaining the role of an automated barge. The automatics accepted their landing instructions, and the composite ship began its ungainly descent through the atmosphere.

Orron III was a planet generous to man, its axial tilt negligible, its seasons stable and, throughout most of its latitudes, conducive to good crop production, and its soil rich and fertile. The Authority had recognized the planet's potential as a bread basket and wasted no time in taking advantage of its year-round growing season. Since the planet had more than adequate resources, room, and a strategic location, they had opted to build a data center there as well, thus simplifying logistics and security for both operations.

Orron III was undeniably beautiful, wreathed with strings and strands of white cloud systems, and showing the soft greens and blues of abundant plant life and broad oceans. As they made their approach, Han and Chewbacca ran sensor readings, taking the layout of the Authority installations.

"What was that?" Han asked, leaning forward for a closer look at his instruments. The Wookiee woofed uncertainly. "I thought I caught something for a second, big blip in a slow transpolar orbit, but either it went around the planet's horizon or we've dropped too low to pick it up. Or both." He worried about it for a moment, then firmly instructed himself not to borrow trouble; whether or not there was a picket ship should make no difference.

Ground features began to resolve into gently rolling country divided precisely into the huge parcels of individual fields. The various shades of those fields reflected a wide range of crops at various states of maturity. Planting, growing, and harvesting must be done on a rolling basis on a large agriworld, for optimal utilization of equipment and manpower.

Eventually they could discern the spaceport, a kilometers-wide stretch of landing area built to the immense proportions of the great robo-barges. The main part of the port, which supported the Authority fleet ships, occupied only a small corner of the installation, even taking into consideration its communications and housing complexes. The majority of the place was simply mooring space for the barges, abysslike berths where maintenance gantries could reach them for repair work and the lumbering mobile silos, aided by gravity, could load them. A constant flow of bulk transports, ground-effect surface freighters, came by special access routes to the port, unloaded their cargoes of foodstuff into the silos, and turned back again, bound for whatever harvest was presently going on.

The bogus barge carrying the *Falcon* settled to its appointed berth among hundreds of others on the field. They touched down, and the computers stopped their chatter. Han Solo and Chewbacca locked down the console and left the cockpit. As they entered the forward compartment, Bollux looked up. "Do we disembark now, sirs?"

"Nope," Han answered. "Jessa said these people we're going to pick up will find us."

The Wookiee went to the main lock and activated it. The hatch rolled up, and the ramp eased down, but didn't admit light or air from Orron III's atmosphere; the camouflaging hull design covered most of the *Falcon*'s superstructure, and a makeshift outer hatch had been installed just beyond the ramp's end.

The ramp had barely lowered when there was a clanging

on the outer skin there. The Wookiee snorted warily, and Han's hand dipped and came up with his blaster. Chewbacca, seeing his partner was ready, hit the switch to open the outer hatch.

Standing just beyond was a man of incongruities. He wore the drab green coveralls of a port worker and had a tool belt slung at his waist. Yet he radiated a different aura, nothing like that of a contract tech. He was native to a sun-plentiful world, that much was apparent, for his skin was so dark that its black approached indigo. He was half a head taller than Han, with broad shoulders that strained the seams of his issue coveralls, and a body that spoke of waiting, abundant power. His tightly curled black hair and sweeping beard were shot through with streaks of gray and white. For all the size and weight of dignity of him, he had a lively glint of humor in his black eyes.

"I'm Rekkon," he declared at once. He had a direct gaze, and although his tone was moderate, it resonated in the air, its quality deep and full. He replaced at his belt the heavy spanner he'd used to rap on the hatch. "Is Captain Solo here?"

Chewbacca gestured to his partner, who had just come further down the ramp. The Wookiee hooted in his own language. Rekkon laughed and—to their astonishment—roared back a polite response in Wookiee. Few enough humans even understood the giant humanoids' tongue; fewer still had the range and force of voice of speak it. Chewbacca boomed his delight in an earsplitting yowl and patted Rekkon's shoulder, beaming down at him.

"Now that you're all through with the community sing," Han interrupted, stripping off his flying gloves, "I'm Han Solo. When's liftoff?"

Rekkon appraised him frankly, but there was still that jovial light to his face. "I'd like it to be as soon as possible, as I'm sure you would, Captain Solo. But we must make one brief trip to the Center, to cull the data I need and pick up the other members of my group."

Han looked back to the head of the ramp, where Bollux waited, and gestured to him. "Let's go, Rusty. You're back in business."

Bollux, his chest plates closed once again, clanked down the ramp, his stride as stiff as ever. He'd explained during the trip that his odd manner of walking came from the fact that he'd been fitted with a heavy-duty suspension system at one point in his long career.

Rekkon was holding out two cards for Han and Chewbacca, bright red squares with white identification codes stamped on them. "Temporary IDs," he explained. "If anyone asks, you're on short-term labor contracts as tech assistants fifth class."

"Us?" Han sputtered. "We're not going anywhere, pal. You take the 'droid, get your gang and whatever else, and you come back. We'll keep the home fires burning."

Rekkon's grin was dazzling. "But what will you two do when the decontamination crew arrives? They'll be irradiating the entire barge, and your ship with it, to make sure no parasites feed on the shipment. Of course, you could switch on your deflector shields, but that would surely be noticed by port sensors." The two partners glanced at each other dubiously. It was true that a decontam-treatment would be normal procedure, and that a man and a Wookiee hanging around the landing area while the team did its work would make somebody curious.

"And there is another matter," Rekkon continued. "The Waiver status for your ship, and its doctored identification codes; I shall be taking care of those, too. Since you and your first mate have a vested interest in that, I had thought you might wish to accompany me."

Han's mouth began watering at the thought of the Waiver, but he always got the sweats in the halls of power, and that Authority Data Center was precisely that. His inbuilt caution came forward. "Why do you want us on this side trip? What is it you're not telling?"

"You're right, there are other reasons," Rekkon answered, "but I do think it best, for you as well as for me, if you come. I would be much in your debt."

Han stared at the tall black man, thinking about the Waiver and the inevitable decontam-team. "Chewie, get me a tool bag." He unfastened his blaster belt, knowing he couldn't be seen armed in an area of tight security. Chewbacca returned with the bag and his bowcaster. Both dropped their weapons into the tool bag, and the Wookiee slung it over his shoulder.

With Bollux trailing after, they walked through the outer hatch, locked it closed, and followed Rekkon across the maintenance gantry. The barge's hull stretched far below and to either side. A utility skimmer with a work platform and enclosed cab was hovering on the other side of the gantry. The living beings climbed into the cab, Rekkon getting behind the controls and Han crowding next to him, while Chewbacca filled the rear seat. Bollux settled himself on the work platform, securing himself with his servo-grip. The skimmer swung away from the barge.

"How'd you find us so fast?" Han wanted to know.

"I received word of what markings your craft would have, and its estimated time of arrival. I came as soon as the data systems registered your approach. I've been waiting here for some time, with forged field-access authorization. I presume this 'droid is my computer-probe?"

"Sort of," Han answered as Rekkon upped the skimmer's speed to the legal limit, guiding it between rows of berthed barges. "There's another unit built into his chest; that's your baby."

The port was surrounded on every side by ripening grain, showing the ripples of the gentle winds of Orron III. While he glanced about, Han asked, "What're you looking for in Authority computers, Rekkon?"

The man studied him for a moment, then turned back to the controls as he pulled onto a service road. Except for the immediate area of the barges, Han knew the skimmer would have to adhere to authorized routes, and would be intercepted if it flew too high, too fast, or cross-country. Off in the distance, gargantuan robot agricultural machines moved through the crops, capable of planting, cultivating, or harvesting vast tracts of land in a single day.

Rekkon adjusted the polarization of the skimmer's windshield and windows. He didn't make it reflective, or opaque to outside observation, which might have been conspicuous, but darkened it against the sun. The cab's interior dimmed, and Han felt as if he were in one of Sabodor's pet environment globes. As they sped along the service road, cutting between seas of bending grain, Rekkon asked, "Do you know what my mission here has been?"

"Jessa said it was up to you whether or not to tell us. I nearly passed up the bargain because of that, but I figured there must be a fair piece of cash involved for this kind of risk."

Rekkon shook his head. "Wrong, Captain Solo. It's a search for missing persons. The group I organized is made up of individuals who've lost friends or relatives under unexplained circumstances. Same thing's begun to happen with suspicious regularity within the Corporate Sector. I found that a number of others were abroad, as I was, seeking their lost ones. I'd detected a pattern, and so I gathered about me a small group of companions. We infiltrated the Data Center in order to carry out our search, with Jessa's help."

Han tapped his finger on the window, thinking. This explained Jessa's commitment to Rekkon and his group, her determination to see that he got all the required assistance. Doc's daughter obviously hoped that Rekkon and his bunch, in locating their own lost ones, would turn up her father.

"We've been here for nearly one Standard month," Rekkon continued, "and it's taken me most of that time to find windows of access into their systems, even though I'm rated as a contract computer tech supervisor first class. Their security is diligent, but not terribly imaginative."

Han shifted around on his seat to look at the other. "So what's the secret?"

"I won't say just yet; I'd rather be sure and have absolute proof. There is a final correlation of data for which I need a probe; the terminals to which I have access at the Center have governors and security limiters built into them. I lack the resources and parts and time to construct my own device. But I knew Jessa's excellent techs could provide what I needed and thereby decrease the risk of detection."

"Which reminds me, Rekkon. You haven't told us that other very good reason why we should come with you to the Center."

Rekkon looked pained. "You're persistent, Captain. I selected my companions carefully; each of them was close to a lost one, yet—"

Han sat up. "But you've got a traitor in there somewhere." Rekkon stared hard at the pilot. "It wasn't just a guess. Jessa's operation got hit while I was there; an Authority corvette dropped a spread of fighters on us. The chances of them just stumbling onto us, out of all the star systems in the Corporate Sector, are so small they're not even worth talking about. That left a spy, but not one who was there at the time, or the Espos wouldn't have been scouting, they'd have come in force. They must've been checking out a number of solar systems." He leaned back, self-satisfied. He was proud of his chain of logic.

Rekkon's face was a mask cut from jet. "Jessa gave us a contingency list of places where we might be able to contact her if our lines of communication were broken. Plainly, that solar system was one of them."

That surprised Han. Jessa would never ordinarily have trusted anyone with that sort of information. She must be investing all hope of finding her father with Rekkon. "Okay, so you've got somebody who's on two payrolls. Any idea who?"

"None, except that it cannot be either of the two members of my group who have already perished. I believe they discovered who the traitor was. There were indications in the final com-link conversation I had with one of them before she died. And so, of course, I've told no one of your arrival, and came to meet you myself. I wanted your help, to make sure none of them can give the alarm before we depart. I have called each of them to my office, without telling them the others would be there."

Han disliked the idea of going to the Center even more now, but saw it was vital that Rekkon have help, vital to the survival of Han Solo. If the traitor managed to turn in an alarm, chances were that the *Falcon* would never raise ship again. He made a mental note to bill Jessa and whoever else he could for additional services rendered. He angled around in his seat again. "Who're the other people you recruited for Amateur Night?"

Driving with only part of his attention, Rekkon responded, "My second-in-command is Torm, whose cover role is contract laborer. His family controlled large ranges on Kail, independent landowners under the Authority. There was some sort of dispute over land-use rights and stock prices. Several family members vanished when they wouldn't yield to pressure."

"Who else?"

"Atuarre. She is a female of the Trianii, a feline race. The Trianii had settled a planet on the fringes of Authority space generations before the Corporate Sector was chartered. When the Authority finally annexed the Trianii colony world recently, they met with resistance. Atuarre's mate disappeared and her cub was taken from her and placed in Authority custody. They must have used some sort of interrogation procedure on the cub, Pakka, for when Atuarre finally managed to rescue him, he could no longer speak. The Authority is no respecter of ages or conventions, you see. Atuarre and Pakka eventually made contact with me; her cover here on Orron III is that of apprentice agronomist."

The service road, winding through the fields, had met a main artery leading toward the Center. The place was a small city unto itself, handling record keeping, computations, and data flow and retrieval for much of the Corporate Sector. It radiated from an operations complex that rose like a glittering confection from the rolling farmland.

Rekkon, lips pursed in thought, wasn't finished. "The last member of our group is Engret, who is scarcely more than a boy, but has a good heart and a kindly temperament. His sister was an outspoken legal scholar, and she too dropped from sight." He was silent for a moment. "There are others abroad searching for their lost ones, and many more, I'm certain, who've been frightened into silence. But perhaps we shall be able to help them, too."

Han half snickered. "No way, Rekkon. I'm just here as part of a trade-off. Save the old school fight songs until I'm clear, got it?"

Rekkon's face was sculpted in amusement. "You only do this sort of thing so that you can become a wealthy man?" He eyed Han up and down and went back to his driving, but added, "A callous exterior isn't an uncommon way of protecting ideals, Captain; it hides the idealists from the derision of fools and cowards. But it also immobilizes them, so that, in trying to preserve their ideals, they risk losing them."

What this big, bluff, amiable man had just said carried so much of hit and of miss, insult and compliment, that Han didn't take time to unravel it. "I'm a guy with a hot ship and places to go, Rekkon, so don't let yourself get carried away with the philosophy."

They entered the Center, maneuvering along wide streets between rearing buildings housing the various offices and storage banks, personnel dormitories and recreational areas, shops and commissaries. The traffic was thick—robo-hacks, ground-effect cargo lifters, skimmers, Espo cruisers, and innumerable mechanicals.

Making a final turn, Rekkon entered a subterranean garage and descended more than ten levels. Nosing the skimmer into a vacant spot, he cut the engine and stepped out. Han and Chewbacca followed as Bollux clambered down. The Wookiee and his partner affixed their badges to their chests and vests, respectively. Rekkon slipped out of his coveralls and tool belt and stuffed both into an equipment locker on the skimmer's side. That left him attired in long, flowing robes of bright, geometric patterns. His supervisor's badge was prominent on his broad chest. His feet were shod in comfortable-looking sandals. Han asked him how he'd gotten the skimmer and other equipment.

"Not difficult, once I'd made a partial penetration of the computer systems. A false job-request form, an altered vehicle-allocation slip—those things were elementary."

Chewbacca took up the tool bag again. Bollux, who hadn't had the chance before, now drew himself up before Rekkon. "Jessa has instructed me to place myself and my autonomous computer module completely at your service."

"Thank you—Bollux, isn't it? Your aid will be critical to us." At this, the old 'droid seemed to straighten with pride. Han saw that Rekkon had found the way to Bollux's heart, or rather, to his behavioral circuitry matrix.

The Authority had spared no expense on this Center, and so, rather than to an elevator or shuttle car, it was to a lift chute that Rekkon led them. They stepped into its confluence and, seemingly standing on air, were wafted upward by the chute's field. Two techs drifted into the lift chute on the next level, and conversation among Han's group stopped. The Wookiee, the two men, and the 'droid continued to ascend, with others entering or leaving the field, for another minute and more, rising past garage and service levels, the lower bureaucratic offices, and at last through the levels where data processing and retrieval operations of one kind and another took place. Most passengers in the chute wore computer techs' tunics. Occasionally, one would exchange a greeting with Rekkon. Han gathered, from the lack of curiosity he and his companions drew, that it wasn't unusual for a supervisor to have tech assistants and 'droids in tow.

Rekkon eventually tilted himself, to drift into the disembarkation-flow. Han, Chewbacca, and Bollux followed. They found themselves standing in a large gallery. Here, two floors had been combined, the upper one opening onto a balcony that ran around the gallery's midsection, looking down on the banks of lift and drop chutes.

Rekkon led on, down a hallway of darkly reflective walls, floor, and ceiling. Han caught sight of himself in the tinted mirror of the walls and wondered how he had ever wound up a reckless-eyed predator, contaminating these antiseptic inner domains of the juggernaut Authority. What he did know was that he would much rather have been hotting the *Falcon* along between the stars, unencumbered.

Rekkon stopped at a door and covered its lock face with his palm, then stepped through as the door swished open. The others followed him into a spacious, high-ceilinged chamber, three walls of which were lined with a complex array of computer terminals, systems monitors, access gear, and related equipment. The fourth wall, opposite the door, a single sheet of transparisteel, gave a commanding view of the bountiful fields of Orron III from one hundred meters up. Han went over and took a bearing on the spaceport across the gentle rise and fall of the land. Chewbacca, seating himself by the door on a bench that ran the length of the wall there, laid the tool bag down between his long, hairy feet. He watched the chatter and wink of sophisticated technology with only mild curiosity showing on his face.

Rekkon turned to Bollux. "Now, may I see what it is that you've brought me?"

Han clucked to himself softly, amazed that anyone should be so palsy-walsy with a mere 'droid.

Bollux's plastron opened as the stubby 'droid pulled his long arms back out of the way. The computer-probe's photoreceptor came on. "Hi!" he perked. "I'm Blue Max."

"You certainly are," Rekkon answered in his full, amused bass. "If your friend here will release you, we'll have a look at you, Max."

Bollux said an unhurried, "Of course, sir." There were minute clicks from his chest, the withdrawal of connector jacks and retaining pins. Rekkon drew the computer forth without trouble. Max was smaller than a voice-writer; he looked unimposing in Rekkon's big hands.

Rekkon's laughter rang. "If you were much smaller, Blue Max, I'd have to throw you back!"

"What's that mean?" Max asked dubiously.

Rekkon crossed to one of several worktables. "Nothing. A joke, Max." The table, a thick slab resting on a single service pillar, was studded with outlets, connectors, and complex instrumentation. Along its front edge ran an extremely versatile keyboard.

"How would you like to do this, Max?" Rekkon asked. "I have background and programming data to feed you, information on systems-intrusion. Then I'll patch you into the main network."

"Can you feed it in Forb Basic?" Max piped in his high, childish voice, like an eager kid with a new challenge.

"That presents no difficulty; I see you have a five-tine input." Rekkon drew a five-tine plug and line from his table and connected it to Max's side. Then he took a data plaque from his robes and inserted it into an aperture in the table, punching up the proper sequence on the keyboard. Max's photoreceptor darkened as the little computer gave his complete attention to the input. Several screens in the room came to life, giving high-speed displays of the information Max was ingesting.

Rekkon joined Han Solo at the window-wall and handed him another plaque, one he'd taken from his worktable. "Here is the new ship's ID for your Waiver. Alter your other documentation accordingly, and you should have no further problem with mandatory-performance profiles within the Corporate Sector."

Han bounced the plaque once or twice on his palm, visualizing enough money to wade through with his pants rolled up, then tucked it away.

"The rest of this shouldn't take terribly long," Rekkon explained. "The others in my group are due to show up in short order, and I don't expect someone with Max's brainpower to find this task too difficult. But I'm afraid there's nothing in the way of refreshment around here—an oversight of mine."

Han shrugged. "Rekkon, I didn't stop off to eat, drink, or observe quaint local ceremonies. If you really want to make me dizzy with delight, just wrap it up here as fast as you can." He glanced around the room, with its perplexing lights and racing equations. "Are you honestly a computer expert, or did you get the job on sheer charm?"

Rekkon, hands on lapels, gazed out the window. "I'm a scholar by trade and inclination, Captain. I've studied a good many schools of the mind and disciplines of the body, as well as an array of technologies. I've lost track of my degrees and credentials, but I'm more than qualified to run this entire Center, if that's of any importance. At one point I specialized in organic-inorganic thought interfaces. That notwithstanding, I came here with forged records, playing the part of a supervisor, because I wished to remain inconspicuous. My only desire is to locate my nephew, and the others."

"What makes you think they're here?"

"They're not. But I believe their whereabouts can be discovered here. And when Max over there has helped me do that, by sifting through the general information here, I shall know where I must go."

"You never did get around to mentioning your own lost one," Han reminded him, thinking that he was beginning to sound like Rekkon. The man was infectious.

Rekkon paced to the opposite wall, stopping near Chewbacca. Han came after him, watching the man lost in thought. Rekkon took a seat, and Han did the same. "I raised the boy as if he were my son; he was quite young when his parents died. Not long ago, I was hired as instructor at an Authority university on Kalla. It is a place for higher education, mostly for Authority scions, a school rooted in technical education, commerce, and administration, with minimal stress on the humanities. But there were still some vacancies for a few old crackpots like me, and the pay was more than adequate. As nephew of a university don, the boy was eligible for higher study, and that's where the trouble began. He saw just how oppressive the Authority is, stifling anything that even remotely endangers profit.

"My nephew began to speak out and to encourage others to do the same." Rekkon stroked his dense beard as he thought back on it. "I advised him against doing so, although I knew he was right, but he had the convictions of youth, and I had acquired the timidity of age. Many of the students who listened to the boy had parents highly placed in the Authority; his words could not go unnoticed. It was a painful time, for although I couldn't ask the boy to ignore his conscience, I feared for him. As an ignoble compromise, I decided to resign my post. But before I could do so, my nephew simply disappeared.

"I went to the Security Police, of course. They made an appearance of concern, but it was clear that they had no intention of exerting themselves. I began making inquiries of my own and heard accounts of other disappearances among those who'd inconvenienced the Authority. I'm accustomed to looking for patterns; one wasn't long in emerging.

"Picking carefully—very carefully, I assure you, Captain!—I gathered a close group of those who'd lost someone, and we began a careful penetration of this Center. Word had come to me of the disappearance of Jessa's father, Doc, as he's called. I approached her, and she agreed to help us."

"All of which leaves us sitting here," Han interrupted, "but why here?"

Rekkon had noticed that the race of characters and ciphers across lighted screens had stopped. Rising to return to Max, he answered. "The disappearances are related. The Authority is attempting to remove those individuals who are most conspicuously against it; it has decided to interpret any natural, sentient individualism as an organized threat. I think the Authority has collected its opponents at some central location that—"

"Let me get this straight," Han broke in. "You think the

Authority's gone into the wholesale kidnapping business? Rekkon, you've been staring at the lights and dials too long."

The man didn't look offended. "I doubt that the fact is generally known, even among Authority officials. Who can say how it happened? Some obscure official draws up a contingency proposal; an idle superior takes it seriously. A motivational study crosses the right desk perhaps, or a cost-benefit analysis becomes the pet project of a highly placed exec. But the germ of it was in the Authority all along—power and paranoia. Where no real opposition existed, suspicion supplied one."

As he spoke, he paced back to the worktable, unplugging Max. "That stuff was really interesting," the little computer bubbled.

"Please show a little less enthusiasm," Rekkon entreated, taking Max up from the table. "You give me the feeling I'm contributing to the delinquency of a minor." The computer's photoreceptor zeroed in on him as he continued. "Do you understand everything I've shown you?"

"You bet! Just give me a chance, and I'll prove it."

"I shall. The main event's coming up." Rekkon took Max over to one of the terminals and set him down by it. "You have a standard access adapter?" In reply, a small lid in the computer's side flipped down, and Max extended a short metal appendage. "Good, very good." Rekkon moved Max closer to the terminal. Max inserted his adapter into the disk-like receptor there. The receptor and the calibrated dial around it circled around and back as Max accustomed himself to the fine points of the linkup.

"Please begin as soon as you're ready," Rekkon bade Max, and took a seat again between Han and Chewbacca. "He'll have to sift through an enormous amount of data," he told the two partners, "even though he can use the system itself to help him at his work. There are numerous security blocks; it will take even Blue Max awhile to find the right windows."

The Wookiee growled. Both humans understood the expression of Chewbacca's doubt that the information Rekkon wanted would actually be found in the network.

"The location as such won't be there, Chewbacca," Rekkon responded. "What Max will have to do is find it indirectly, just as you must sometimes turn your eyes away to locate a dim star, finding it out of the corner of your eye. Max will analyze logistical records, supply and patrol ship routings, communications flow patterns and navigational logs, plus a number of other things. We'll know where Authority ships have been stopping, and where coded traffic has been heaviest, and how many employees are on payrolls at various installations, and what their job categories are. In time, we'll find out where the Authority is keeping the members of what it has come to believe is a far-flung plot against it."

Rekkon got up again to pace the room briskly, clapping his hands with sounds like solid-projectile rifle shots. "These fools, these execs and their underlings, with their enemies' lists and Espo informers, they're creating just the sort of climate to make their worst fears come real. The prophecy fulfills itself; if we weren't talking about life and death here, it would make a grand joke!"

Han was reclining against the wall, watching Rekkon with a cynical smile. Had the scholar actually thought that people were any different from the Authority execs? Well, anybody who let his guard drop or wasted his time on ideals was in for just the same sort of rude shock Rekkon had gotten, Han thought. And that was why Han Solo had gone and would always go free among the stars.

He yawned elaborately. "Sure, Rekkon, the Authority better watch out. After all, what's it got going for it except a whole Sector's worth of ships, money, manpower, weapons, and equipment? What chance does it have against righteous thoughts and clean hands?"

Rekkon turned his hearty smile on Han. "But look at yourself, Captain. Jessa's communication mentioned a little about you. Just by living your life the way you chose, you've already committed deadly offenses against the Corporate Sector Authority. Oh, I don't look for you to wave a banner of freedom or to mouth platitudes. But if you think the Authority's the winning side, why aren't you playing its game? The Authority won't meet with disaster because it abuses naive schoolboys and idealistic old scholars. But as it increasingly hampers intractable, hardheaded individualists such as yourself, it will find its real opposition."

Han sighed. "Rekkon, you'd better take it easy; you've got me and Chewie confused with somebody else. We're just driving the bus. We're not the Jedi Knights, or Freedom's Sons."

What Rekkon's rejoinder would have been became academic. The door-lock buzzed just then, and a man's voice at the intercom demanded: "Rekkon! Open this door!"

With a cold feeling in his stomach, Han caught the blaster Chewbacca tossed to him as the Wookiee leveled his bowcaster at the door.

VI

REKKON interposed himself between Han and Chewbacca and the door. "Kindly put your weapons up, Captain. That is Torm, one of my group. Even if it weren't, would it not have been wiser to find out what was happening before preparing to shoot?"

Han made a sour face. "I happen to *like* to shoot first, Rekkon. As opposed to shooting second." But he lowered his weapon, and Chewbacca did the same with the bowcaster. Rekkon worked the door controls.

The panel snapped up, revealing a man of about Han's height, but bulkier through the torso, with brawny arms and wide, blunt hands. His face was fine-featured, with high cheekbones and alert, roving eyes of a liquid blue. His hair was a long shock of bright red. His darting eyes found Han and Chewbacca first, as his right hand made a reflexive spasm toward the thigh pouch of his coveralls. But he arrested the motion, turning it into the rubbing of palm against trouser leg on seeing Rekkon. Han didn't blame the man for being skittish at this point, with several of his teammates already dead.

The man's mind worked quickly. "We're leaving?" he was asking, even as he stepped through the door.

"Presently," Rekkon replied, gesturing over to where Blue Max sat linked to the data system. "We'll soon have the data we require. Captain Solo there and his first mate, Chewbacca, will be transporting us offworld when we're ready. Gentlemen, may I present Torm, one of my companions."

Torm, his poise recovered now, inclined his head to the two, then went over to inspect Blue Max. Han followed; someone in this band might be an informer, and he wanted to acquaint himself with each one of them, to do all he could to safeguard himself and his ship.

"Not very impressive, is it?" Torm asked, staring down at Max.

"Not too," Han answered fake-pleasantly.

A nod from Torm. "You think Rekkon'll find what he's looking for?" Han asked. "I mean, this long shot's your only hope of finding your folks, right? Or shouldn't I ask?"

Torm fastened a frank gaze on him. "It *is* a personal matter, Captain. But since your own safety is at stake, I suppose you're within your rights. Yes, if I can't locate my father and brother in this way, I'll have no idea how to proceed. We've fixed all our hopes on Rekkon's theory." For a moment he glanced over to Rekkon, who was showing Chewbacca features of the room's equipment. "I didn't throw in with him lightly, but when I saw that the Authority was dragging its feet in its investigations, and my own inquiries led me to him, I knew I must commit myself to follow Rekkon's belief."

Torm's voice had drifted as his thoughts had. Now he came back to himself. "It's most unselfish, very admirable of you, Captain Solo, to take on this mission. Not many men would willingly risk—"

"Jet back: you got it all wrong," Han interrupted. "I'm here 'cause I struck a deal, Torm. I'm strictly a businessman. I fly for money and I look out for number one, clear?"

Torm reappraised him. "Quite. Thank you for clarifying that, Captain. I stand corrected."

The door was sounding again. This time, Rekkon admitted two of his co-conspirators. There were Trianii, members of a humanoid species of feline. One was an adult female, trim and supple, who stood just about the height of Han's chin. Her eyes were very large, yellow, with vertical slits of green iris. Her pelt, a varied, striped pattern along her back and sides, lightened to a soft, creamy color on face, throat, and torso front. It tufted out to a thick mane around her head, neck, and shoulders. Behind her curled and swayed a meter of restive tail, mixing the colors of her pelt. She wore the only clothing her species required, a belt at her hips to support loops and pouches for her tools, instruments, and other items. Rekkon introduced this being as Atuarre.

With Atuarre was her cub, Pakka. He was a miniature copy of his mother, standing half her height, but his coloring was darker, and he wasn't as slender or as graceful. He still had some of the fuzzier fur and baby fat of cubhood, but his wide eyes seemed to hold an adult's wisdom and sorrow. Though his mother spoke, Pakka said nothing. Then Han recalled Rekkon's saying the cub had been a mute since enduring Authority custody. Like his parent, Pakka wore a belt and pouches.

Atuarre pointed a slim, clawed finger at Han and Chewbacca. "What are they doing here?"

"They're here to aid our escape," Rekkon explained. "They brought the computer element I needed to extract the final data. The only one yet to arrive is Engret; I couldn't contact him, but left a message on his recorder with the code word for him to contact me."

Atuarre seemed agitated. "Engret didn't make his check-call and didn't answer his com, so I stopped by his billet on the way here. I'm sure his quarters are under surveillance; we Trianii do not mistake such things. Rekkon, I believe Engret's been killed, or taken."

The leader of the small band sat down. For a moment Han saw the strength and determination leave Rekkon's features. Then it was back, that special vitality. "I suspected that was the case," he admitted. "Engret would not forgo contact for days, no matter what. I trust your instincts in this completely, Atuarre. We must presume him to have been eliminated."

He had said this with absolute finality. This wasn't the first time he had come up against an unexplained disappearance. Han shook his head; on one side was the near-absolute power of the Authority, and on the other, nothing more substantial than friendship, than family ties. Han Solo, loner and realist, considered it a gross mismatch.

"How do we know he's what he says he is?" Atuarre was demanding, pointing to Han.

Rekkon looked up. "Captain Solo and his first mate, Chewbacca, come to us by way of Jessa. I presume we all trust her aid and counsel? Good. We leave as soon as possible; I'm afraid there'll be no time for luggage or arrangements. Or com-calls, for any of us."

Atuarre took her cub's paw-hand as Pakka studied Han and Chewbacca silently. "When do we go?"

Rekkon went back to Max, to find out just that. Just then the computer module's photoreceptor came back on. "Got it!" he chirped. A translucent data plaque emerged from the slot at the terminal's side.

Rekkon seized it eagerly. "Fine. Now we must match it against the Authority's installations charts—"

"But that's not all," Max blurted.

Rekkon's dense brows knit. "What more, Blue Max?"

"While I was in the system, I monitored it, you know, to get the feel. This intrusion is fun! Anyway, there's a Security alert on in the building. I think it's directed at this level. The Espos are moving into position."

Atuarre hissed and pulled her cub closer. Torm's face seemed impassive at first, but Han noticed a tic of anxiety along his jaw. Rekkon tucked the data plaque into his robes, and from them drew a big disrupter pistol. Han was already buckling on his gunbelt, as Chewbacca settled his ammo bandolier over his shoulder and threw the empty tool bag aside.

"Next time I fall for one of these tempting offers," Han instructed his partner, "sit on me till the urge passes."

Chewbacca growled that he definitely would.

Torm had taken a handgun from his tight pocket, and Atuarre had produced another from one of her belt pouches.

Even the cub, Pakka, was armed; he pulled a toylike pistol from his belt.

"Max," Rekkon said, "are you still in the network?" Max indicated he was. "Good. Now, look at deployment plans for alerts in this Center. At what corridors, junctions, and levels will the Espos be stationed?"

"I can't tell you that," Max answered, "but I could clear a way through them, if that's what you want."

That grabbed Han's attention. "What'd that little fusebox say?"

The computer-probe elaborated. "The Security Policemen are all supposed to respond to alarms, it says here, and redeploy to cover any new trouble spots. I could just make enough alarms in other places and draw them away in different directions."

"That may not get them all out of the way," Han pointed out, "but it could sure thin out the opposition. Do it, Maxie." Another thought struck him. "Wait a second. Can you fake alarms anywhere else?"

Max's voice burst with pride. "Anywhere on Orron III, Captain. This network's got so much capacity that they've hooked just about everything into it. Good cost reduction, but bad security, right, Captain?"

"No foolin'. Yeah, give it everything you've got: fires in the power plants, riots in the barracks, indecent exposure in the cafeteria, whatever appeals to you, all over the planet." He was thinking that if there *were* a picket ship in orbit, she might also be kept busy by a rash of false alarms.

Bollux, who had remained silent during all this commotion, now came to the terminal and prepared to take Max back the moment the computer's work was done. Rekkon stood with him.

"There're two ways out of here that might be open," Max announced, and flashed the positions on the screen. The two paths, picked out on the level's layout, both led back to the gallery where the lift and drop chute banks were located. One route was on their floor, the other on the floor above.

Security alarms began clanging and warbling in the corridors. The room's equipment blazed with ripples of light as every circuit reacted to Max's prompting. Then, suddenly, the room became dim, except for light from the window-wall. The Center's automatics had shut down main power sources in response to the supposed emergency. Alarms continued to sound, running on reserves.

"Illumination in the corridors will be very low, on standby power," Rekkon told the others as they gathered by the door. "We may be able to slip by." He carefully set Blue Max back into his emplacement. As his plastron swung shut, Bollux, followed by Rekkon, joined the rest of them at the door.

"If I may suggest," said the 'droid, "I would, perhaps, attract less suspicion than any other individual here. I could walk well in advance of you others, in case there are Security Policemen present."

"That makes sense," Atuarre said. "Espos won't waste time and power shooting a 'droid. They'll halt him, though, and that will warn us off from any traps."

The door slid up, and Bollux started off down the corridor, preceded by the noise of his stiff suspension. The others followed after—Rekkon and Han in the lead, with Torm behind. Atuarre and Pakka came next, and Chewbacca brought up the rear, his bowcaster cocked and ready. The Wookiee was watching the conspirators as well as rear-guarding. With the possibility of a traitor in the group, he and Han trusted no one, not even Rekkon. The first wrong move on the part of any of them would be the Wookiee's signal to shoot.

They came to a turn. Bollux went around first, but as the others approached it, they heard:

"Halt! You, 'droid, get over here!"

Han, peeking cautiously around the corner, spied a contingent of heavily armed Espos clustered around Bollux. He picked up bits of the conversation, mostly questions about whether the 'droid had seen anyone else. Bollux put up a front of supreme ignorance and lethargic circuitry. Beyond the gathered Espos, the corridor opened onto the chute gallery, but it might just as well have been on the other side of the Corporate Sector.

"It's no good this way," Han said.

"Then it's the more desperate route for us," Rekkon replied. "Follow me." They went back the way they had come, at a trot. As they rounded the next corridor, the footfalls of the Espo detachment drifted to them. They hadn't gone far when they heard another squad approaching from the opposite direction.

"Nearest stairwell," Han instructed Rekkon, who led them a few meters more, then ducked through a door. "Keep it as quiet as you can," Han whispered in the semidarkness of the emergency-lighted stairwell. "Up one floor, and we'll make our way to the balcony overlooking the chutes." Of course, Chewbacca, for all his bulk, moved quietly, as did the sinuous Atuarre and her cub. Rekkon, too, seemed used to running with stealthy efficiency. That left only Han and Torm to guard their steps, both laboring to keep the noise of their movements to a minimum.

When they reached the second floor of that level, they found it empty. Blue Max's flurry of crazy alerts had drawn the security forces away from their contingency posts. The fugitives raced along the corridors as through a hall of mirrors, keeping close to the walls.

They came to the balcony overlooking the gallery. Crouching low, they edged up to its railing. Han risked a quick peek over the top, then drew his head down again. "They're setting up a crew-served blaster down by the chutes," he told them. "There're three Espos working it. Chewie and I will fix that up; the rest of you get set to jump. Chewie?"

The Wookiee rumbled softly, his finger tightening on the bowcaster. He moved off, staying low, along the railing. Han leaned close to Rekkon's ear and whispered, "Do us a favor and watch things here; we can only look one way at a time." He scuttled off in the opposite direction from his partner. With Rekkon armed and watchful, Han doubted that any turncoat would show his hand now.

He paralleled the railing, rounding its corner, down to the far wall. Peering over the rail, he saw the Wookiee's big blue eyes edging up over the opposite railing. Halfway between them and several meters below, the gun crew was making final adjustments on the heavy blaster and its tripod mount. In a moment they would be ready to activate the weapon's deflector shield; going after them would then become an almost hopeless venture, and the drop chutes would be inaccessible. Apprehension would be a matter of time. One of the Espos was bending even now to throw on the shield.

Han stood, drew, fired. The man who had been about to activate the shield slumped, clasping a burned leg. But one of the others, with no regard for niceties like fire-discipline, spun and sprayed a steady stream of destructive energy from a short riot gun. The riot gun's fire blasted material from the walls and railing; the Espo slewed the weapon around carelessly, searching for his target.

Han was forced to duck back out of the way as the rain of energy lashed through the air, striking walls, ceiling, and most things in between. That innocent bystanders might've been hurt didn't seem to have entered into the Espo's calculations.

But the Espo gave a cry and fell, his finger easing off the trigger, accompanied by the metallic twang of Chewbacca's bowcaster. Han looked over the rail again and saw the second man slumped over the first, brought down by one of the short quarrels from the Wookiee's weapon. Now Chewbacca stood, jacking the foregrip of his bowcaster down to recock it and strip another round off its magazine.

The third gun crewman kicked the bodies of his fellows out of the way while firing wildly with his pistol and yelling for help. Han shot him just as the Espo's hands were closing on the heavy blaster's grips. Chewbacca was already over the balcony railing. Han, straddling the railing on his side, called, "Rekkon, get 'em moving!" He pushed himself off.

He missed his footing and fell to all fours, then raced to help his partner throw assorted Espos off the blaster cannon.

Torm leaped down, landing lightly for all his weight, and Atuarre came after him, all grace and form. Her cub launched himself off the rail, gathered his limbs and tail in for a somersault, and landed next to her. Atuarre slapped him on his way, as if to say this was no place to show off, even for an acrobatic Trianii.

Last to come was Rekkon, moving skillfully, as if this were something he did all the time. Han wondered for a half-second about this versatile university don who never seemed to lose track of the problems at hand. In sending all the others ahead, Rekkon made sure no potential spy remained behind, to be tempted by an unguarded back.

Torm stopped short of the drop chutes, luckily for him. "The fields have been shut off!" he shouted. Rekkon and Atuarre were with him in a moment, fumbling at the emergency panel beside the chute opening. Rekkon's sturdy fingers closed around the panel's grille, and he yanked it away without apparent effort.

Calls and a general hubbub could be heard in the upper corridors. Han squirmed himself down behind the blaster cannon, setting his feet on the pegs of its tripod, and switched on the deflector shield. "Heads up!" he warned his companions. "The party's starting!"

A squad of Espos, wearing combat armor and carrying rifles and riot guns, burst out onto the balcony above, fanning out along the rail, and started firing down. Their bolts splashed in polychrome waves from the cannon's shield. Torm, Rekkon, and the others, directly behind Han as they worked on the drop-chute panel, were protected, too, for now. Chewbacca stood behind his partner, firing his bowcaster whenever he had an opening. Soon his weapon was empty, and he pulled another magazine from his bandolier. He chose explosive quarrels and started firing again. The detonations filled the gallery with smoke and thunder.

Han had raised the cannon's snout to extreme elevation, and now he swept it across the railing. Heavy blaster charges flashed and crackled; parts of the railing and the balcony's edge exploded, melted, or burst into flames. Several Espos were hit, falling to the floor below, and the rest backed hastily out of the line of fire, darting out to snap off a volley when they could, in a constant, determined exchange of shots. The firefight and its echoes, heat, and smoke enveloped the gallery.

Han kept the Espos' heads down with long traverses of the cannon, letting go at the floor of the balcony, scoring the walls. The gallery heated up like a furnace from the energies unleashed. Red beams of annihilation bickered back and forth, and Han knew that the cannon's shield wouldn't hold out forever against constant fire from the riot guns and rifles.

A squad of armored figures appeared in the low corridor, the one leading directly onto the gallery. Han depressed the cannon's mouth and filled the lower hallway with raging destruction. These Espos drew back, too, like the others, stayed just out of range to risk firing whenever they could. Atuarre, Pakka, and Torm, drawing their guns, joined Han and Chewbacca in returning fire, while Rekkon kept working at the chute.

"Rekkon, if you can't get that drop field working, that'll be all for us," Han hollered over his shoulder. A Security man leaned out from the balcony above and snapped off a shot. It rebounded from the gun's shield, but Han could tell from the residual heat the deflector let through that it was beginning to fail.

"It's no use," Rekkon decided as his strong, sensitive fingers probed the mechanisms. "We'll have to find another way out."

"This is a one-way street!" Han shouted without looking back. Chewbacca's angry, frustrated roars sounded above the din.

"Then *you* dive headfirst down the shaft!" Torm bellowed back. Han's rejoinder was lost in an electronic whooping that filled all their ears, catching at their hearts. It was a warning signal, standard throughout much of the galaxy.

"Hard radiation leak," Rekkon shouted. "That wasn't one of the alarms Max put in."

Not only that, Han thought, but it had only just begun to sound, and it was sounding right in the corridors off the gallery. A hard radiation exposure would leave little chance for any of them to live; they'd be receiving lethal dosages even as they listened. Han swore at himself for ever having gotten out of a nice, cushy racket like gunrunning sideways through mountains. He scrambled up. "Get ready. We're going to have to shoot our way through them, or else we all get signed off."

Over the alert sirens, Atuarre shrilled, "Wait—look!"

Han's blaster was out again, ready to target on what he presumed to be another Espo. But the figure tottering down the lower hall toward them was moving stiffly, its arms extended horizontally, holding some burden.

"Bollux!" cried Torm, and it was. The 'droid stiff-legged out into the stronger light of the gallery, holding a globular public-address speaker in either hand. Wires from them ran back to his open chest, patched in near Blue Max's emplacement. From the speakers beat the whooping radiation alarm.

They gathered around Bollux, yelling in Standard, Wookiee, Trianii, and one of two other tongues, but nobody could hear anybody else because of the alarms. Han was getting a headache that he was willing to ignore only because he was too overjoyed at being alive.

Then the alarms stopped. Bollux carefully lowered the P.A. speakers and patiently unplugged their cables from himself while the others clamored for an explanation.

"I'm gratified that my plan worked, sirs and ma'am; but I confess it was merely an extension of Max's false alarms," Bollux told them. "He learned about the radiation alarms while he was in the network. Under his guidance, I vandalized these two speakers from the corridor walls and adapted them. The corridors are empty now; the Espo armor is for combat, not radiation protection. They appear to have withdrawn hastily."

Han broke in, "Get Max over there by the drop chutes. If he can't get one running again, we're still gonna be old news." He tugged Bollux over that way.

"All the chutes cut out, right?" Blue Max piped up. "No sweat, Captain!"

"Just turn 'em on, huh?" Han pleaded, adding, "What's a runt like you know about sweat, anyway?"

Bollux's plastron swung wide as the 'droid approached the panel. But the adapter input was too high. So Chewbacca, who was closest, slung his bowcaster, took Max out of his emplacement, and held the computer up to the chute's control panel. Max's adapter extended itself and engaged the receptor. The metal tumblers twirled back, forth, back again. The panel lit up.

"It's working!" Rekkon exulted. "Quickly, follow me, before someone notices and has the thing shut down again." He made a hand motion to Han, so fast that no one else caught it, and the pilot knew he was to go last. Rekkon was still unsure of the loyalty of his people. He hopped into the drop chute and Atuarre followed after him. Then came Pakka, spinning, tumbling, and chasing his own tail playfully in the chute's field. Torm leaped after, gun in hand.

They could hear the tread of cleated boots in the corridor. With Blue Max still tucked under his arm, Chewbacca jumped into the drop chute, too. Han held back long enough to fire at the blaster cannon from its unshielded side. There was a bright eruption as its power pack began to overload. Han spun and dived headlong down the shaft, as Torm had invited him to do. Behind, he heard the explosion of the portable cannon.

They plunged down, in varying postures and attitudes, strung out behind Rekkon in a ragged line. Craning their heads upward, they waited nervously for the first blaster bolt to come raving down the chute, but none did. Han decided that the Espos had been delayed by the exploding cannon. He hoped it would take them awhile to figure out that the drop chute was on, but feared that any moment would bring the stomach-wrenching fall, once the field was shut down again, that would plunge him, Chewie—all of them—to their deaths.

They descended all the way to the garage levels. Rekkon left the chute at last, beckoning them to do the same. They found themselves standing in a large parking area as alarms sounded off in the distance. "I thought there would be a flyer of some sort here," Rekkon said sourly; "worse luck."

"We're not going back into that chute, and that's that," Han stated.

"There's a ground skimmer. Let's take it," Atuarre suggested. They piled in, with Han taking the controls and Rekkon next to him. Chewbacca sat back in the cargo bed with the others, keeping his back to his partner and his eyes on the others as he fit a new magazine into his bowcaster. Before the Wookiee could take time to return Max to Bollux's chest, Han had thrown the skimmer into motion and shot away, barely making the turn onto the up-ramp, scarcely avoiding the wall.

He kept the control stem's steering grips pushed forward, giving the skimmer all the acceleration she could safely stand and a good deal more. The ramp went by in a wild corkscrewing of Formex, the walls whirling past the skimmer's front cowling at hair-raising speed. Rekkon saw at once the wisdom of yielding the controls to the younger man.

Han hoped that nobody had gotten around to sealing off the computer complex yet, and they hadn't. The security network was inundated with everything from reports of insurrection to drunk-and-disorderly calls from the executives' club, spread across the Center and the face of Orron III. The skimmer left the garage like a missile out of a launch tube. In his haste, Han had departed through a door clearly marked ENTRANCE. A traffic-monitoring scanner dutifully logged the skimmer's license number for a citation and mandatory court appearance.

The skimmer tore through the city, guided partly by Rekkon's instructions and partly by Han's instincts. Han left the city's edge behind in a blur, drilling a hole through the air down the fusion-formed road, as other traffic dodged and skidded hysterically away from him. He was glad he'd taken the time to orient himself on the spaceport while in Rekkon's office. Since its cab was open, the wind plucked and tugged hard at everyone on the skimmer, ruffling hair, fur, and clothing alike, making conversation impossible as the passengers braced however and wherever they could.

But rounding a turn in the last stretch approaching the spaceport, Han discovered that somebody somewhere in the bureaucracy had actually done a bit of thinking. The skimmer nearly crashed head-on into a roadblock, an Espo troop-hovervan parked across the roadway, its twin-mounted guns nosing for a target.

Han jerked the controls hard, kicking the foot auxiliaries, and sent his small vehicle sailing off the road's surface. The engine sang with effort; the low-built skimmer slammed down among the rippling grain and raced off through it erratically. The tall grain, an Arcon Multinode hybrid, was so high that it instantly swallowed them up, hiding them from the startled Espos. But Han zigzagged anyway, for luck, and sure enough, the Espos fired even though they had no clear target, most probably from sheer frustration. The troop-hovervan was a ground-effect vehicle, unable to climb above the field, Han knew. That meant that if his pursuers wanted to give chase, they'd have to eat a little cereal themselves.

He had to stand up, poking his head above the windscreen as he drove, in a mostly unsuccessful attempt to see where he was going. The skimmer sliced through thick rows of hybrid grain, sending a spray of mangled plants and chaff back over and around it. Han slitted his eyes and tried to peer through the hurricane of vegetable matter as best he could, which wasn't very well. In moments, all of the skimmer's grillework and trim was decked with stalks of grain that had gotten lodged there, and the craft looked like a strange agricultural float.

Chewbacca, standing and exhorting, reached forward over

his partner's shoulder and pointed. Han, asking no questions, changed course. He had to steer hard to slide past the hazard, a mountain of yellow metal, one of the enormous automated farm machines slowly and patently working this part of Orron III's limitless fields.

Han broke out onto bare ground, reaped clean by the harvester. He conned the skimmer around in a wide arc, got his bearings on the spaceport and the ranked colossi of the berthed barges, and hotted off that way.

At that moment the Espo hovervan broke through, too, but farther down the field, away from the spaceport. Han couldn't take time to watch it; instead he tried to throw enough twists and dodges into his course to keep them out of the Espo gunner's sights. Heavy blaster salvos scored around the skimmer, starting small fires smoldering among the stubble of shorn stalks.

Han took the skimmer through a hairpin turn, trying to jump out of the line of fire, but the hovervan's twin-mounted guns scored closer and closer to starboard, making the shaven field erupt. He jammed the control stem back to port. But the Espo gunner, trying for a bracketing salvo, had outguessed him. The ground blew apart just beyond the skimmer's undercarriage.

The skimmer jarred violently, its nose plowing at the rich soil, crumpling, as the engine cowling was smashed and compressed. Smoke rolled from its engine compartment, and the little craft grounded, carving long scars in the crop-stubble.

Han, fighting to keep control, lost his grip on the control stem at the last moment, clipped his head on the windscreen, and was flung clear of the cab as it stopped short, ending up on his back. He watched the sky of Orron III, which appeared to be spinning, and wondered if his entire skeleton had actually been turned into confetti. That was just how he felt.

"Everybody off," he announced woozily; "baggage claim to your left."

The others tumbled off the wrecked skimmer. Han found himself being lifted as easily as a child; Rekkon's dark fists were hoisting him by his vest. He was pleased to find himself more or less whole. "Run for the spaceport fence!" Rekkon ordered the others. The whine of the Espo hovervan grew in the distance.

Han shook off the fall. The hovervan was closing quickly. Rekkon pulled him down into the shelter of the skimmer's nose and began working at the adjustments of his oversized disrupter pistol. Han drew his blaster. "Chewie, get 'em moving," he called.

The vociferous Wookiee, still lugging Blue Max in one arm, shoved or shouted the others into motion. Atuarre and Pakka sped away, the Trianii female half dragging her cub, half carrying him, with Torm not far behind. Even Bollux moved at top speed in long, jarring bounds made possible by his heavy-duty suspension system, disregarding the damage he might do his gyros and shock absorbers. Chewbacca came last, casting frequent glances over his shoulder. Before them rose another stand of grain, being reaped by another of the giant machines, and past that was the spaceport security fence.

Han felt a warm liquidity on his forehead, swiped at it, and saw blood on his fingers, courtesy of the skimmer's windscreen. Rekkon, having finished adjusting his disrupter, was waiting for the hovervan to come into range, which it was doing with frightening speed.

The hovervan driver, watching the figures running for the fence, failed to notice the two men hiding behind the disabled vehicle. When the Espo was close enough, Rekkon, forearms braced across the skimmer's nose, fired. He'd set his disrupter on overload, and now the powerful handgun emptied itself in a brief flood of ruinous energy. Han had to shield his face from it, thinking what a chance Rekkon was taking; the disrupter could just as easily have blown up in his hands, killing both men.

But the jet of disrupter fire splashed across the hovervan's cowling and windshield. The Espo craft slid side-on, spun once, and planed into the ground, plowing up a mound of soil before it.

Han, lowering his hands, saw that the barrel of Rekkon's pistol was white-hot, and the scholar's face was sweating and seared. Rekkon tossed aside the useless pistol. "You must've taught in some tough damn schools," was Han's only comment as he struggled to his feet, preparing to run again.

Rekkon, watching the overturned hovervan, didn't hear. Body-armored Espos were already stumbling from it, to continue the pursuit on foot. The twin-gun mount, twisted underneath the vehicle, was useless. Rekkon, backing away a step or two, said, "The moment has come for our departure, Captain Solo!"

Han pegged a couple of shots at the Espos. The range was long, but they still hit the dirt. Then he put his head down and pounded off behind Rekkon, wondering if the Espos could get into range before the fugitives made the fence and somehow got over, under, or through it. All things considered, the smart money appeared to be with the Espos, he conceded.

For long moments all he did was race after Rekkon's flying sandals and wait for a blaster bolt to fry his shoulder blades. Then he raised his head, gulping breath. The monstrous harvester was working its way back down the rows of grain, its gaping maw cutting down a swatch twenty meters wide, pouring the grain into a tandem load-carrier. Han and Rekkon cut wide around it, and Han scanned the terrain in front of him. He spotted figures thrashing through the stalks, but could make none of them out.

A shot kicked up dirt and flame off to the left, proof that the Espos were gaining. Han and Rekkon dodged right to put the enormous agrirobot between themselves and their pursuers. Then they were shoving, running, tearing through a world of golden-red stalks, occasionally spying one of their companions in the distance.

Han dug his heels in, sliding to a stop. Rekkon, who'd

come abreast of him, caught the movement and halted, too. Both of them panted hard, as Han demanded, "Where's Chewie?"

"Ahead of us, to the side; who can tell in this field?"

"He's not. He's the only one who'd be easy to spot, even here." Han straightened, his side aching. "That means he's back there!" He shagged back the way he'd come, ignoring Rekkon's cries.

When he broke into the open again, he saw at once what had happened. Chewbacca had realized the Espos stood a good chance of overtaking his companions before they could make it to the spaceport and get past the fence. Some major distraction had been needed to save all their lives, and so the Wookiee had paused to set one up.

As Han cried out for him to come back, Chewbacca, his bowcaster slung over his shoulder and Blue Max under his long arm, pulled himself up the side of the giant harvester as the machine went on its pre-programmed way. The harvester had already borne the Wookiee most of the way back toward the Espos. He finished climbing the last few feet, reaching the top of the agrirobot, where its control center was situated.

Chewbacca began tugging and heaving at the protective cover over the controls. It was a durable industrial design and resisted him. Han and Rekkon watched as Chewbacca seated himself for better leverage, then applied all his strength in a tremendous effort. The cover popped loose, and the Wookiee threw it aside. He began working furiously, uncoupling hookups and moving components around in order to make room for Blue Max. There was no way he could hear Han's hoarse shouts over the noise of the harvester, and the distance, and no way could the Wookiee see, from his position, the three Espos who had managed to catch hold of one of the maintenance ladders and clamber after him.

Han was too far away to shoot. The Espos swarmed quickly upward. The huge harvester gave a lurch, then went through a series of disturbed tremors as Blue Max usurped control of it and tried his touch. Just as the Espos, having worked their way to the top of the ladder, leveled their weapons at Chewbacca's spine, the harvester gave the most violent shudder of all.

One Espo nearly fell, and must have yelled, because the Wookiee's head snapped around just as the three crouched to keep from being dislodged. Chewbacca's bowcaster shot exploded against one man's chest, flinging him backward to roll off the harvester's side. But in turning and firing, Chewbacca had lost his own balance. The harvester went into a sharp turn, and the Wookiee had to make a desperate lunge to catch hold of a stanchion. He managed to do it but lost hold of his bowcaster.

"Chewie!" Han bawled, starting back, but Rekkon's big hand closed around his shoulder, holding him resolutely.

"You can't get to him now," the scholar shouted, and that seemed certain. More Espos were closing in around the slow-moving harvester.

Chewbacca, unarmed, got his feet back under him and threw himself at the two remaining Espos before they could recover. He gathered one in a lethal hug, kicking the second, before either man could raise his weapon. But the second man somehow managed to cling to the Wookiee's leg, and held on for his life.

Blue Max now had the harvester under control, that much was clear. He pivoted the machine, attempting to swallow an entire square of Espos. But, using the harvester's primitive guidance system, Max was unaware of the Wookiee's predicament. The pivot dislodged Chewbacca and the two Espos. They fell, limbs gyrating, and the Wookiee somehow managed to land on top. But it was still a long drop, and before the stunned humanoid could rise, he was buried under a pile of rifle-swinging Espos.

Han, struggling to get loose of Rekkon's grip, felt himself shaken until his teeth rattled. Rekkon implored, "There are dozens of them! You have no hope. Better to live, and stay free, to help the Wookiee later!"

Han spun, pulling his blaster. "Hands off. I mean it."

Rekkon saw by his eyes that he did indeed; Han would kill anyone who stood between himself and Chewbacca. The broad black hands fell away. Gun in hand, Han went off toward the mass of Espos.

He couldn't tell just how Rekkon hit him then. Han's whole spinal column seemed to light up, and a blinding paralysis descended on him. Perhaps it was a nerve-punch, or a blow to a spot selected for its hydrostatic shock value. In any case, Han dropped like a unstrung puppet.

The harvester, moving much more quickly now, circled back at the Espos. They fired on it, but the giant machine, an uncomplicated device, was difficult to stop with small-arms fire. Unimportant pieces of plating and cutter blade were shot away, but the harvester ground on. Several Espos, failing to move quickly enough in the thick grain, vanished into its cavernous mouth.

Max had finally seen Chewbacca's predicament and moved in to give the Wookiee an opportunity to jump back aboard. But Chewbacca, his arms and legs dangling limply, was now being rushed away by a squad of Espos. Max couldn't go after them for fear of injuring Chewbacca with the clumsy harvester. Moreover, the Espos' fire was becoming more concentrated. Blue Max wished desperately that Bollux were there to tell him what to do; the computer didn't feel that he'd been operative long enough to make decisions like this one. But with no other apparent option, Max recognized that he must go join the others. He headed the ponderous harvester around, cut out its speed governor, and gunned it for all it was worth.

Han only dimly felt Rekkon hoist him up on one shoulder; he could hardly focus his eyes. But as Max came past, Rekkon took a pair of wide steps, propelled himself into the air, and caught a foothold at the harvester's side. He pulled himself up a short ladder and deposited Han on a narrow catwalk. Somehow, Han managed to lift his head. He could make out, through the machine's rough ride and the distance, the knot of Espos bearing his friend away, a prisoner.

Han clawed at the metal under him, to throw himself off the machine, to go back. Rekkon was on him instantly, pinning his arms with a strength and an intensity that were frightening. "He's my friend!" Han grimaced, writhing.

Rekkon shook him once more, with more emphasis than violence. "Then *help your friend!*" urged the rich basso voice. "Face hard fact: you must save yourself to save him, and not throw both lives away!"

The giant, imprisoning strength retreated and Han was left enervated, knowing Rekkon was right. Holding the catwalk railing, he stopped staring at the indistinguishable specks of Chewbacca and the Espos.

"Ahh." He lowered his eyes disconsolately. "Chewie . . ."

AS he overtook each of the escapees in turn, Max slowed the harvester just enough for them to board. First was Bollux, who had fallen behind the others despite his best efforts; he made a last bound with a deep *sproing* from his suspension, found a servo-grip hold, and drew himself aboard. Then came Torm, who, pacing the harvester, made an athletically skill-ful mount. Lastly, Atuarre and Pakka came aboard, the cub clinging to his mother's tail. Blue Max accelerated for the spaceport perimeter.

Rekkon still held Han to the catwalk, but now it was to make sure he wouldn't fall. ''Captain, you must accept that there's no more you can do here. Your chances of getting to Chewbacca here on Orron III are vanishing small. And, more to the point, it's doubtful he'll be here for long. Surely he'll be taken for interrogation, just like the others. Our mission is yours now; it's nearly certain the Wookiee will be put in with the rest of the Authority's special enemies.''

Han wiped blood from his forehead, pulled himself up-right, and began climbing a maintenance ladder.

''Where are you going?'' Rekkon demanded.

''Someone has to tell Max where he's going,'' Han an-swered.

The spaceport was guarded by a security fence of fine mesh, ten meters high, carrying a lethal charge maintained by transmitting posts along its length. An unprotected man, or even an armored one, would stand no chance of making it through, but the harvester offered a special form of protection.

"Everybody get to a catwalk," Rekkon called. "Stand on the insulated strips!" His various companions, Han included, rushed for positions, bracing their feet on the thick runners of insulation on the mechanic's catwalks.

The harvester hit the field area as Max threw his cutter blades into motion again. Defensive energy spat and spattered all around the agrirobot, discharging across its bow in skittering strands. Then the fence was torn apart by the harvester's blades, a twenty-meter length of it ripped loose and engulfed. The defensive field faded along that part of the fence, its continuity broken. Whereupon the giant machine churned out onto the flat, press-bonded landing area.

Han hauled himself up and looked down at Max, nestled in the control niche. "Can you program this crate so it'll run without you?"

The computer probe's photoreceptor swiveled around, coming up to bear on him. "That's what it's built to do, but it'll remember only simple things, Captain. For a machine it's pretty dumb."

Han weighed his suspicions, presumptions, and a knowledge of security procedures. "They'll be rushing their men to the passenger-ship end of the port; they won't think the barges are any good to us. But they'll certainly be looking for this tub, Max. Set it up so it'll give us a few seconds to get clear, then head itself down toward the main port area." To the others, he called, "Checkout time! Everybody pound ground!"

From Blue Max came low buzzes, beeps, and wonks of his labors. Then he announced, "Done, Captain, but we better get off right now."

Han reached down as Max disengaged himself from the harvester's controls, pulled free the connector jacks Chewbacca had inserted, and lifted the computer out of the niche. There was a carrying strap in a recessed groove on Max's top. Han pulled it out and slung Max over his shoulder.

When he reached the ground, Rekkon and the others were already there. They all stepped back as the harvester ground into motion again, wheeled promptly, and tore off between rows of barges. From the harvester, Han had already spotted, not far away, the barge shell concealing the *Millennium Falcon.* He handed Blue Max back to Bollux and started for his ship at a dead run, with the rest keeping up as best they could.

The outer hatch, the makeshift one, wasn't dogged, of course. He pushed it aside, palmed the ramp and inner hatch open. Then he dashed to the cockpit and began swiping at controls, bringing his ship back to life, yelling: "Rekkon, say the word the second everybody's onboard, and hang onto your heirlooms!" He pulled on his headset and deserted all caution, thinking, *Hell with preflight.* He brought the barge's engines up to full power all at once, and simply hoped they wouldn't blow or dummy out on liftoff.

His best hope lay in the nature of bureaucracy. Somewhere back in the fields, the Espo detachment commander was trying to explain to his superior what had happened. That man, in turn, would have to contact port security and give them the rundown. Given a creaky enough chain of command, the *Falcon* still stood a chance.

Han pulled on his flight gloves and ran through his preparations with a sharp feeling of incompleteness; he was used to dividing the tasks with Chewbacca, and each detail of the liftoff drove home the fact that his friend wasn't there.

He checked the barge's readouts—and swore several of his choicer curses. Bollux, stumping into the cockpit to relay Rekkon's word that all was secure, added, "What's wrong, Captain?"

"The motherless barge is what's wrong! Some over-eager Authority expediter filled it up already!" The instruments proved it; several hundred thousand metric tons of grain were stowed in the barge's vast shell. There went Han's plan for rapid ascent.

"But, sir," Bollux asked in his unhurried speech pattern, "Can't you release the barge shell?"

"*If* the explosive-releases worked, and *if* I didn't damage the *Falcon*, I'd still have to get above the port's close-proximity defenses, and maybe a picket ship." He turned and yelled back down the passageway, "Rekkon! Get somebody in those gun turrets; we may have to stand tall!" Han could operate the ship's top and belly turrets by means of servos from the cockpit, but remote control was a poor substitute for sentient gunners. "And screw your navels in; we go in twenty seconds!" He fumed over the fact that the barge's engines took so much longer to heat up than the *Falcon*'s.

Port control, having noticed that the barge was preparing to lift, began transmitting to what it still presumed to be a robotized ship orders to abort liftoff. Han hit the overrides and had the barge's computer answer by acknowledging clearance as if it had received permission to go. Port control repeated the command to hold, convinced it was dealing with a computer malfunction along with all its other problems.

Han brought the engines up. The barge wallowed up from its pit, bending aside the boarding gantry, ignoring all directions to do otherwise. As his radius of vision increased with altitude, Han spied the abandoned harvester. It was halfway to the other end of the giant port, surrounded by Espo hovervans, skimmers, and self-propelled artillery. The harvester had been partially disabled, but still obeyed its present programming mindlessly, trying to grind forward.

As Han watched, a cannonade from all sides stopped the huge machine for good, gouging large chunks from it, turning most of the harvester's lower chassis into wreckage. Someone no longer cared whether prisoners were taken or not. The harvester's power plant went up in a fireball, and the harvester split in half with a force that rocked the Espo field pieces back.

As the barge rose higher, responding sluggishly under its burden of cargo, ignoring chatter from the port control, Han saw the place where Chewbacca had been captured. Other

Espo vehicles were gathered near the wreck of the hovervan. Han couldn't tell whether his partner was there or had already been taken away, but the fields were crawling with Security Police, like a pestilence among the golden-red grain, searching for possible stragglers. Rekkon had been right; going back would've spelled certain disaster.

The barge gave a sudden, convulsive shudder, and the *Falcon*'s passengers felt as if someone had caught them by the collar and given a yank. With an ominous feeling, Han punched up the rear screens. Bollux, having nearly fallen, lowered himself into the navigator's chair, inquiring what was wrong. Han ignored him.

It *had* been a picket ship, in transpolar orbit, that he and Chewbacca had picked up just prior to landing. Even Rekkon hadn't realized how security-minded the Authority was about Orron III. Moving up hard astern the barge was a dreadnaught, one of the military's old Invincible Class capital ships—over two kilometers long, bristling with gun turrets, missile tubes, tractor-beam projectors, and deflector shields, armored like a protosteel mountain. The dreadnought hailed them with the demand that the barge halt, and at the same time identified herself: the *Shannador's Revenge*. She'd locked her tractors onto the barge, and compared with her raw power, the lighter's beam back on Duroon had been a mere beckoning finger.

"Church is out," Han observed, bringing his ordnance up to charge and preparing to angle deflector shields, for all the good it would do. The dreadnought had enough weaponry to hold and vaporize a score of ships like the *Falcon*. Han opened the intercom. "That shake-up was a tractor. Everybody stay cool—things could get rough." As if we have a prayer, he finished to himself. But he had no intention of being caught alive. Better to shorten a few Espo careers, and go out in style.

There were sounds of banging, tearing metal from the barge shell, of parting supports and struts. Some of the superstructural features, weakened or loosened by alterations to the hull, had been pulled free by the tractor beam and gone flying back toward the *Shannador's Revenge*.

Han took inspiration from it. He had at his side breadboarded computer overrides for the barge's every function. His fingers stabbed at them as he shouted, "Everybody brace! We're gonna—" and was slammed back in his seat. He'd hit the cargo release, opening the barge's rear dump-doors. Hundreds of thousands of tons of grain were poured into the dreadnaught's tractors, pulled toward the *Shannador's Revenge* by her own brute power, fanning out in a blinding contrail, as the barge surged ahead with a lightening load.

The dreadnought was engulfed, her sensors muffled by the tidal wave of grain. Han, with one eye on his own sensors, saw that the warship was driving straight on through the hail of grain, closing quickly on the barge even though she was blinded. Her tractor beams were still clamped onto the barge's stern, and Han wondered how long it would be before her skipper gave the command to open fire.

There was only one other possibility. He hit the controls, cutting in the barge's retrothrusters, and with virtually the same motion, slapped the emergency releases. His other hand hovered over the main drive control of the *Millennium Falcon.*

The barge shell shook, losing much of its velocity, while the reports of exploding bolts sounded through both the freighter and the larger ship around it. Superstructural elements, added to secure the *Falcon* and disguise her lines, were blown clear. A split second later, the *Falcon*'s engines howled to life, their blue fire tearing the smaller ship free of the breakaway supports holding her and severing her external control hookups.

Han took the *Falcon* on the same course he'd been holding, keeping the barge shell between himself and the Authority warship. The *Shannador's Revenge*, her sensors impaired, had failed to note the barge shell's drastic drop in speed. The dreadnought's captain was calling for a vector change just as the warship rammed the decelerating barge. The *Shanna-*

dor's Revenge's forward screens flared with impact, and her anticoncussion fields cut in instantly on collision, as she cut the floating hulk of the barge shell in half in a terrific impact and suffered structural damage of her own. The warship's forward sensor suite was disabled; she resounded with alarms and damage reports. Airtight doors began booming shut automatically, triggered by decompressive hull ruptures.

The *Millennium Falcon* was clawing for the upper atmosphere. The thought that he'd bloodied the nose of a battlewagon, escaping against all odds, didn't lighten Han's mood, nor did the thought that hyperspace and safety were only moments away. Occupying his mind was one simple, intolerable fact: his friend and partner was now in the merciless hands of the Corporate Sector Authority.

When the stars had parted before him and the ship was safely in hyperspace, Han sat for long minutes thinking that he couldn't remember the last time he'd spaced without the Wookiee beside him. Rekkon had been right in arguing for escape, but that didn't change Han's feeling that he'd let Chewbacca down.

But regrets were a waste of time. Han stripped off his headset and shoved himself out of his seat. Rekkon was his only hope now. He headed for the forward compartment, the ship's combination lounge-mess-rec area, and realized something was wrong while he was still in the passageway. There was the pungent smell of ozone, the smell of blaster fire.

"Rekkon!"

Han ran to where the scholar slumped over the gameboard. He'd been shot from behind, by a blaster set on needlebeam at low power. The sound of it probably hadn't even carried across the compartment. On the gameboard, under Rekkon's body, was a portable readout. Next to it a clear puddle of molten liquid bubbled, the remains of the data plaque. Rekkon was dead, of course; he'd been shot at close range.

Han leaned on a bulkhead pad, rubbing his eyes and wondering what to do next. Rekkon had been his sole hope for rescuing Chewbacca and for getting himself out of this insane jam. With Rekkon dead, the hard-won information gone, and at least one traitor-murderer onboard, Han felt alone for one of the few times in his life. His blaster was in his hand, but there was no one else in the compartment or in the passageway.

A clattering on the rungs of the main ladderwell. Han ran to it just as Torm came climbing up from the *Falcon*'s belly turret. As he came up, Torm found himself staring into the muzzle of Han's gun.

"Just give over your pistol, Torm. Keep your right hand on the rung, and do it with your left, easy. Don't make a mistake; it'd be your one and only."

When he had the other man's weapon, Han let him ascend, then made him shuck his tool belt. Patting him down and finding no other weapons, Han motioned for him to move into the lounge, then called up the ladderwell for Atuarre to come down from the ship's top quad-mount.

He kept one eye on Torm, who was staring in shock at Rekkon's body. "Where's her cub?" he asked the man quietly.

The redhead shrugged. "Rekkon told Pakka to look around for a medi-pack. You weren't the only one who was injured along the way. The cub went off to rummage around. I guess when you yelled for everyone to stay put and hang on, he did." He looked back to Rekkon, as if he couldn't fathom the fact of the man's death. "Who did it, Solo? You?"

"No. And the list of possibilities is awfully short." He heard Atuarre's light tread on the rungs and covered her as she came down the ladderwell.

The Trianni's features became a mask of feline hatred. "You darc point a weapon at me?"

"Gag it. Toss your gun out here, careful, then step out and drop the tool belt. Somebody's killed Rekkon, and it could be you as easy as anyone. So don't push me. I'm not telling you twice."

Her eyes were wide now, the news of Rekkon's death appearing to shock her out of her fury. But how can I tell if it's real or an act? Han asked himself.

When he had them both in the forward compartment, he still found he couldn't pick up anything but shock and dismay. Theirs, at least, served to prod him out of his own.

A clanking on the deckplates marked Bollux's arrival from the cockpit. Han didn't look around until he heard the urgency in the 'droid's voice.

"Captain!"

Han whirled, dropping to one knee, blaster up. Beyond the cockpit offshoot from the passageway crouched the cub, Pakka, his small pistol held in one paw-hand, a medi-pack swinging from the other. He seemed to be wavering indecisively.

"He thinks you're threatening me!" Atuarre rasped, moving toward her cub. Han swung his blaster to cover her and looked back to the cub. "Tell the kid to drop it and come to you, Atuarre. Do it!"

She did, and the cub, shifting his wide eyes between Han and his mother, obeyed.

Torm took the medi-pack from the cub and handed it to Han. Still covering his passengers, Han moved to an acceleration chair and opened the pack with his free hand. He held the nozzle of an irrigation bulb against his forehead injury, then wiped at it with a disinfectant pad.

Putting the medi-pack down, he took up the three confiscated weapons, put them aside, and confronted Torm, Atuarre, and Pakka. His mind ran in circles. How to tell who had done it? They'd each had a weapon, and time. Either Pakka had doubled back from his search, or one of the others had left his turret long enough to murder. Han almost regretted not having exchanged fire with the *Shannador's Revenge;* at least he'd have known if either of the quad-mounts was untended.

Atuarre and Torm were trading suspicious looks now.

"Rekkon told me," Torm was saying, "that he took you and the cub on against his better judgment."

"Me?" she shrilled. "What about you?" She turned to Han. "Or, for that matter, *you*?"

That shook him. "Sister, I'm the one who got you out of there, remember? Besides, how could I lift off and shoot Rekkon at the same time? And anyway, Bollux was with me." Han rummaged again in the medi-pack, dug out a patch of synth-flesh, and pressed it over his injury, his mind in a turmoil.

"That all could've been done by computer, Solo, or you could have killed him just before I came down," Torm said. "And what good's a 'droid for a witness? You're the one pointing the blaster around, hotshot."

Han, pushing the medi-pack aside, replied, "I'll tell you what: you're all, all three of you, going to keep an eye on one another, and I'm going to be the only one with a gun. If anybody has the wrong look on his face, it's going to be all over for him. You're all fair game, understand?"

Atuarre moved to the gameboard. "I'll help you with Rekkon."

"Keep your hands off him," Torm shouted. "It was either you or that cub who killed him, maybe both." The big redhead's fists were balled. Both Atuarre and Pakka were showing their fangs.

Han cut them off with a wave of the blaster. "Everybody relax. *I'll* take care of Rekkon; Bollux can help. The three of you move down to that cargo hold off the main passageway." He stifled their objections with a motion of the gun's muzzle. First Torm, then the two Trianii, began to move.

Han stood to one side as they filed into the empty hold. "If anybody sticks his face out of here without my say-so, I'll figure he's out to get me, and I'll fry him. And if anybody's hurt in here, I'll space whoever is left, no questions asked." He closed the hatch and left them.

In the forward compartment, Bollux waited silently, with Blue Max on a console nearby. Han regarded the corpse.

"Well, Rekkon, you did your best, but it didn't get you far, did it? And you dumped it into my lap. Now my partner's captured and your murderer's onboard with me. You weren't a bad old man, but I somehow wish I'd never heard of you."

Han picked up one heavy arm, dragging at the corpse. "Bollux, you get ready to take the other side; he was no lightweight."

Then he noticed the scrawl. Han pushed Rekkon's body back clumsily and bent to examine a stylus's scribble on the gameboard that the dead man's arm had hidden. The writing was difficult to read, dashed off in a pained, distorted hand, hastily and weakly. Han turned his head this way and that, puzzling the message out aloud: "Stars' End, Mytus VII." He knelt and quickly found Rekkon's bloodstained stylus on the floor by the gameboard base. With his last strength, after he'd been left for dead, Rekkon had managed to leave word of what the computer plaque had told him. Dying, he hadn't abandoned his campaign.

"Foolish," Han told himself. "Who was he trying to tell?"

"You, Captain Solo," Bollux answered automatically. Han turned on him in surprise.

"What?"

"Rekkon left the message for you, sir. The wound indicates that he was shot from behind, and therefore quite probably never saw his assailant. The only living entity he could trust would be you, Captain, and it would be logical to assume you would be present when his body was moved. He made sure in this manner that the information would reach you."

Han stared down at the body for a long moment. "All right, you stubborn old man; you win." He reached over, smearing and eradicating the words with his hand. "Bollux, you never saw this, understand? Play dumb."

"Shall I erase that portion of my memory, sir?"

Han's answer was slow as if he was catching the habit from the 'droid. "No. You may be the one who'll have to pass it along if I don't hack it. Make sure Blue Max keeps zipped, too.''

''Yes, Captain.'' Bollux moved to take Rekkon's other arm as Han prepared to hoist again. His joints creaked, and his servos whined. ''This was a great man, was he not, Captain?''

Han strained under the corpse's weight. ''What d'you mean?''

''Just, sir, that he had a function, a purpose he cared about above and beyond his life. Doesn't that indicate a greatness to the purpose?''

''You'll have to read the obituaries, Bollux; all I can tell you is, he's dead. And we're going to have to eject him through the emergency lock; we might get boarded yet, and we can't have him around.''

Without further conversation, the two dragged at Rekkon, who had reached out from beyond death and given Han the answers he needed.

Han opened the hatch. Atuarre, Pakka, and Torm looked up in unison. They'd taken seats on the bare deck, the man at the opposite side of the empty hold from the two Trianii.

''We had to ditch Rekkon,'' Han told them. ''Atuarre, I want you and Pakka to go square away the forward compartment. You can throw some eats into the warming unit, too. Torm, come with me; I need a hand repairing the damage we did on liftoff.''

Atuarre objected. ''I am a Trianii Ranger, and a rated pilot, not a drudge. Besides, Solo-Captain, that man is a traitor.''

''Save it,'' Han cut her off. ''I've locked up all the other weapons in the ship, including Chewie's other bowcaster. I'm the only one armed, and things stay that way until I figure out what to do with you all.''

She gave him a sullen look, telling him, ''Solo-Captain, you're a fool.'' She left, with Pakka trailing behind.

Torm rose, but Han stopped him with an arm across the hatchway. The redhead retreated back into the hold and waited. "You're the only one I can trust," Han told him. "Bollux isn't really much good, and I just figured out who killed Rekkon."

"Which of them did it?"

"The cub, Pakka. He was in Authority custody, and they messed with him. That's why he doesn't talk. I think they brain-set him, then let Atuarre recover him. Rekkon wouldn't have let any of you others near."

Torm nodded grimly. Han produced the man's pistol from the back of his gunbelt and handed it to him. Its charge indicator read full. "Keep this on you. I'm not sure Atuarre's figured it out yet, but I'm willing to play them along and find out if either of them know anything that'll help."

Torm stashed the gun in his coverall pocket. "What will we do next?"

"Rekkon left a message as he was dying, scrawled it on the gameboard. The Authority's keeping its special prisoners at something called Stars' End, on Mytus VI. After we've checked the ship over, we'll gather in the forward compartment and run down everything we've got in files and computers on it. Maybe Pakka or Atuarre will let something slip then."

When the light damage suffered by the *Millennium Falcon* in her breakout from Orron III had been repaired insofar as was possible, the ship's complement gathered in the forward compartment. Han had brought four portable readouts. He gave one to each of the others and took one himself. Bollux watched, seated to one side, with Max back in his usual place, gazing out from the 'droid's chest.

"I patched these readouts into the ship's computers," Han explained. "Each of them's keyed to one kind of information. I'll pull navigational, Atuarre's got planetological; Pakka can retrieve the Authority's unclassified stuff, and Torm's got operational files from the outlaw-techs. Okay, punch up Stars' End and let's get at it."

Each of the other three complied. Torm's screen, except

for the retrieval request, remained blank. Atuarre's too. She looked up, as they all did, to see Han scan his own readout.

"Your portables aren't hooked up to anything," he told them, "only mine. Atuarre, show Torm your screen."

Dubious, she still did as he asked, turning her readout so that the redhead could see it. On her screen was the simple retrieval request, MYTUS VIII. "Yours too, Pakka," Han bade the cub. That readout showed MYTUS V.

"Catch his face," Han told the others, meaning Torm, who had become pallid. "You know what you've done, don't you, Torm? Show everybody your readout. It says MYTUS VII, but I told you that Stars' End was on MYTUS VI, just as I told the others the wrong planet. But you already knew the right one, because you read it over Rekkon's shoulder before you killed him, right?" His voice lost its false lightness. "I said right, *traitor*?"

Torm jumped to his feet with impressive speed, gun drawn. Atuarre pulled hers out too, and pointed it at him. But neither Torm's shot at Han nor Atuarre's at him worked.

"Two malfunctions?" Han inquired innocently, unlimbering the blaster at his side. "I betcha mine works, Torm."

Torm heaved his pistol wildly. Han reacted with a star pilot's reflexes, slapping the gun out of midair with his left hand. But Torm had already whirled and seized the surprised Atuarre in a savage infighting hold, prepared to break her neck with a slight twist. When she started to resist, he forced her neck to the brink of fracture, making her subside.

"Put down the blaster, Solo," he grated, "and get your hands on the gameboard, or I'll—"

He was interrupted as Pakka, in a spectacular leap, landed on Torm's shoulders, sinking fangs into his neck, clawing at his eyes, wrapping a supple tail around the traitor's throat. Torm was forced to release his hold to keep from being blinded. Atuarre sought to turn and fight, and even Bollux had risen in the moment of crisis, unsure of just what to do.

Torm gave Atuarre a vicious kick. His superior weight and strength sent her sprawling, blocking Han, who had been moving for a clear shot. As Han skirted Atuarre, Torm tore Pakka from his shoulders and threw the cub aside just as Bollux blundered into the pilot's path. Pakka bounced off one of the pads of safety cushioning lining the compartment hatch, as Torm dashed into the passageway.

Dodging, moving as quickly as he could, Torm raced past the cockpit, main ladderwell, and ramp hatch; none of them held any promise of even temporary safety. He heard Han's bootsteps close behind and ducked into the first compartment he came to, damning himself for not having taken time to learn the ship's layout. He hit the hatch-close button as he came through. The compartment was empty, offering no tools, nothing he might use as a weapon. He'd been hoping this was the escape-pod chamber, but fortune had passed him by. At least, he thought, he had a moment's respite. He might be able to buy time, perhaps even wrest Solo's blaster from him. His thoughts were moving so quickly that he didn't realize, for a moment, where he was. But when he did, he threw himself back at the hatch through which he'd come, tearing at the controls, screaming obscenities.

"Don't waste your time," came Han's voice over the intercom. "Nice of you to choose the emergency lock, Torm. It's where you would've ended up anyway."

Han stood looking through the viewport set in the lock's inner hatch. He'd overridden the lock's controls to make sure Torm couldn't get back in. All the *Falcon*'s access systems had inboard overrides, to make life complicated for anyone interested in forced entry, a wise smuggler's option.

Torm tried to wet his lips with a very dry tongue. "Solo, stop and think a minute."

"Save your breath, Torm. You're gonna need it all; you're going swimming." There were, of course, no spacesuits stored in the lock. Torm's eyes opened wide with fear.

"Solo, no! I never had anything against you; I never would have come, except that bastard Rekkon and the Trianii never took their eyes off me. If I'd cut, they would have shot me.

You can understand that, can't you? I had to look out for number one, Solo!"

"So you shot Rekkon," Han told him in a soft voice, no questioning to it.

"I had to! If he'd passed on word about Stars' End, it would've been my neck! You don't know these Authority people, Solo; they don't accept failure. It was Rekkon or me."

Atuarre came up behind Han, and Pakka and Bollux after her. The cub climbed up the 'droid's shoulders for a better view. "But, Torm," Atuarre said, "Rekkon found you, recruited you. Your father and brother really have disappeared."

Without facing away from the viewport, Han added, "I'm sure they did. Your father and older brother, right, Torm? Let's see, now, that wouldn't by any chance make you heir to the Kail Ranges, would it?"

The traitor's face was waxen. "Yes, if I did as the Authority asked. Solo, don't play righteous with me! You said you're a businessman, didn't you? I can get all the money you want! You want your friend back? The Wookiee is on his way to Stars' End by now; the only way you'll ever see him again is by bargaining with me. The Authority's got no grudge against you; you can name your price!"

Torm reasserted control over himself, going on more calmly. "These people keep their word, Solo. They don't even know your names yet, any of you; I was operating under deep cover, saving the information I developed so I could up the price. Strike a deal. The Authority's just good business people, like you and me. You can have the Wookiee back and go free with enough money to buy a new ship."

He got no answer. Han's gaze had gone to his own reflection in the metal of the emergency lock's control panel. Torm pounded his fists on the inner hatch, a dull thudding.

"Solo, tell me what you want; I'll get it for you, I swear! You're a guy who looks out for number one, aren't you? *Isn't that what you are, Solo?*"

Han stared at his own lean reflection. In another man, he'd have said those eyes were too used to concealing everything but cynicism. His thoughts echoed Torm: *Is that what I am?* He looked back to Torm's face, straining against the viewport.

"Ask Rekkon," Han answered, and hit the lock release.

The outer latch snapped open. With an explosion of air into vacuum, Torm was hurled out into the chaotic pseudoreality of hyperspace. Once outside the *Millennium Falcon*'s mantle of energy, the units of matter and patterns of form that had been Torm ceased to have any coherent meaning.

"SOLO-CAPTAIN," Atuarre interrupted his thoughts, leaning into the cockpit, "isn't it time we spoke? We've been here for nearly ten Standard Time-Parts, and our course of action is no clearer than when we arrived. We must reach some decision, don't you agree?"

Han broke off gazing out the canopy at the distant speck, barely visible, of Mytus VII. All around the *Millennium Falcon* rose the peaks and hills of the tiny asteroid on which she was concealed. "Atuarre, I don't know how Trianii feel about waiting, but me, I hate it worse than anything. But there's nothing else we can do; we have to sit tight and play out our hand."

She wouldn't accept that. "There are other courses of action, Captain. We could attempt to contact Jessa again." Her slit-irises dwelled on him.

Han shifted around in the pilot seat to face her directly, so quickly that she drew back reflexively. Seeing this, he reined in his temper, "We could waste all kinds of time looking for Jessa. When her operation ran, after we got hit by the IRDs, she probably dug a hole and pulled it in after her. The *Falcon* can cook along at point-five factors over Big L, but we still might waste a month looking for the outlaw-techs and not find them. Maybe word will find its way to Jessa, or one of the prearranged blind transmissions, but we can't bank on her. I don't count on anybody but me; if I have to bust Chewie out of there alone, I'll do it."

Some of the tension left her. "You aren't alone, Solo-

Captain. My mate is there at Stars' End, too. Your fight is Atuarre's." She extended a slim, sharp-clawed hand. "But come, now, take some food. Staring at Mytus VII cannot help and may be distracting us from solutions."

He pushed himself up out of the seat, taking one more look at the distant planet. Mytus VII was a worthless rock, as worlds went, revolving around a small, unexceptional sun at the end of the wisp of stars that was the Corporate Sector. Stars' End, indeed. There'd be scant danger of anyone's happening on the Authority's secret prison facility here, unless he came looking for it specifically.

Since Mytus VII had been listed in the charts as being at the outermost edge of its solar system, Han had broken into normal space nearly ten Standard Time-Parts before, deep in interstellar space, far out of sensor range. He'd come in from the opposite side of the system, entering a thick asteroid belt halfway between Mytus VII and its sun, and hunted up what he'd wanted, this jagged hunk of stone. Using his starship's engines and tractors, he'd brought the asteroid onto a new course, one that would allow him to take a long-range peek at Stars' End, sure that no one there would notice the slightly unusual behavior of one tiny mote in the uncharted asteroid belt.

He'd spent most of his time monitoring the planet's communications, studying it by sensors, and watching the occasional ship come and go. Monitored commo traffic had told him nothing; most of it had been encrypted in codes that had resisted his computers' analyses. Plaintext messages had been either mundane or meaningless, and Han suspected that at least some of them had been sent strictly for appearances' sake, to make Stars' End look like an ordinary, if remote, Authority installation.

Now he trailed Atuarre into the forward compartment. Bollux was seated near the gameboard, his plastron open. Pakka was stalking a jetting remote back and forth. The remote, a small globe powered by magnetic fields and repulsor power, turned, dove, climbed, and dodged unpredictably.

The cub hunted it with tail twitching and quivering, obviously enjoying the game. The remote eluded him time and again, demonstrating more than its usual maneuverability.

As Han watched, Pakka nearly caught the globe, but it evaded his pounce at the last second. Han looked to the 'droid. "Bollux, are you directing that remote?"

The red photoreceptors trained on him. "No, Captain. Max is sending information pulses to it. He's much better at anticipation and dictating random factors than I, sir. Random factors are extremely difficult concepts."

Han watched the cub make a final, long spring and catch the remote in midair, pulling it to the deck and rolling over and over with it in sheer delight. Then the pilot sat at the gameboard, which often doubled as a table, and accepted a mug of concentrate broth from Atuarre. They had used up fresh supplies several Time-Parts before and were now sustaining themselves on the *Falcon*'s ample, if bland, emergency rations.

"There have been no new developments, Captain?" Bollux asked. Han presumed the 'droid already knew the answer and had asked only out of a sort of programmed conversational courtesy. Bollux had turned out to be an entertaining shipmate who could spin hours of tales and accounts of his long years' work and the many worlds he'd seen. He also had a repertoire of jokes programmed into him by a former owner, and an absolutely deadpan delivery.

"Zero, Bollux. Absolutely zilch."

"May I suggest, sir, that you assemble all available information in sum, recapping it? Among sentient life forms, new ideas sometimes emerge that way, I have noticed."

"I bet. After all, aren't most decrepit labor 'droids armchair philosophers?" Han put his mug down, rubbing his jaw thoughtfully. "Anyway, there isn't much to tote up. We're on our own—"

"Are you sure there's no other resource?" Max chirped.

"Don't start that again, lowpockets," Han warned.

"Where was I? We've found the place we want, Mytus VII, and—"

"How high is the order of probability?" Max wanted to know.

"Up an afterburner with the order of probability," Han snapped. "If Rekkon said it's here, it's here. The installation has a pretty big power plant, almost fortress class. And quit interrupting, or I'll take a drill to you.

"Let's see. We can't hang around forever, either; supplies are running low. What else?" He scratched his forehead where the synth-flesh patch had flaked away, leaving new, unscarred skin.

"This is a strictly off-limits solar system," Atuarre contributed.

"Oh, yeah, and if we get nailed here without a mighty good alibi, they'll stick *us* in jail, or whatever." He smiled at Bollux and Blue Max. "Except you boys. You, they'd probably recycle into lint filters and spittoons."

He dragged the toe of his boot back and forth on the deck. "Not much more to it; only that I'm not leaving this stretch of space without Chewie." Of all the things he'd mentioned, he was surest of that. He'd spent many long watches in the *Falcon*'s cockpit, haunted by what his Wookiee partner might be undergoing. A hundred times since taking up this vigil, he'd almost cut in the ship's engines to shoot his way into Stars' End and get his friend out or get flamed in the attempt. Each time, his hand had been stayed by the memory of Rekkon's words, but it was a constant struggle for Han to restrain his impulses.

Atuarre had plainly been thinking along the same lines. "When the Espos came to evict us from our colony world," she said slowly, "some Trianii tried armed resistance. The Espos were brutal in their interrogation of prisoners, seeking the ringleaders. It was the first time I had seen anyone use The Burning. You know what I refer to, Solo-Captain?"

Han did. The Burning was a torture involving the use of a blaster set at low power, to scorch and sear the flesh off a prisoner, leaving only blood-smeared bone. Usually, a leg would be first, immobilizing the victim; then the rest of the skeleton was exposed, inch by inch. Any other prisoners could be made to watch, to break their will. The Burning seldom failed to obtain answers, if answers were to be had; but in Han's opinion, no being who employed such methods deserved to live.

"I will not leave my mate in the hands of the kind of people who would do that," Atuarre was saying. "We are Trianii; death, if it comes to that, is not something we fear."

"Not a very linear analysis," Blue Max piped up.

"Well, who said *you'd* understand it, birdhouse?" Han scoffed.

"Oh, I comprehend it, Captain," Max said with what Han could've sworn was a note of pride. "I just said it wasn't very—"

He was interrupted by a beep from the commo monitoring suite. Han was out of his chair and halfway to the cockpit by the second beep. Just as he slid into the pilot's seat, a last, sustained beep signaled the end of the transmission.

"The recorder bagged it," Han said, hitting the playback. "I don't think it was encrypted."

It was a cleartext message, sent economically, in burst. He had to slow down the playback by a five-to-one factor before it ungarbled.

"To: Corporate Vice-President Hirken, Authority facility at Stars' End," the audio-reconstruction began. "From: the Imperial Entertainers' Guild. We beg the Viceprex's indulgence and forgiveness, but the troupe scheduled to stop at your location has been forced to cancel its itinerary because of transportational mishap. This office will schedule a replacement immediately, when a troupe with a 'droid of the requisite type becomes available. I am, distinguished Viceprex, your abject servant, Hokkor Long, Secretary in charge of scheduling, Imperial Entertainers' Guild."

Han's fist hit the console on the last syllable. "That's it!"

Atuarre's expression mixed befuddlement with doubt of Han's soundness of mind. "Solo-Captain, that's what?"

"No, no, I mean that's *us*. We're in! We just got dealt a wild card!"

He whooped, slammed his fist in his palm, and nearly ruffled Atuarre's thick mane from glee. She retreated a step. "Solo-Captain, has the oxygen pressure dropped too low for you? That message was about entertainers."

He snorted. "Where've you been all your life? He said *replacement* entertainers. Don't you know what that means? Haven't you ever seen the broken-down acts the Guild'll throw in to fill a playdate, just so they can hang on to their agent's fee? Haven't you ever gone to some bash where they promised a class act, then at the last second they pull a switch and stick in some . . ."

It dawned on him that they were all staring at him now, photoreceptors and Trianii eyes. He half sobered. "What else can we do? The only other thing I've thought of is to fly into Mytus VII backward so they'd think we were leaving. But this is even *wilder*. We can do it. Oh, they'll think we stink like banta droppings maybe, but they'll buy the lie."

He saw Atuarre was far from convinced, and turned to Pakka. "They want entertainers. How'd you like to be an acrobat?"

The cub made a little bounce, a kind of strain to speak, then, frustrated, sprang into a backflip to swing upside down from an overhead control conduit by his knees and tail.

Han nodded approval. "What about it, Atuarre, for your mate's sake? Can you sing? Do magic tricks?"

She was nonplused, resenting his appeal to Pakka and his invocation of her mate. But she saw, too, that he was right. How many chances like this would come their way?

The cub began clapping his paws for Han's attention. When he got it, Pakka shook his head energetically in answer to Han's last question; then, still hanging upside down, he put paws on hips and made wriggling motions.

Han's eyebrows knit. "A . . . dancer? Atuarre, you're a dancer!"

She cuffed her cub's rump sharply. "I am not, er, unskilled in the rites of my people." Han saw she was embarrassed; she riveted him with a defiant stare. "And what of you, Solo-Captain? With what will you astonish your audience?"

He was too exhilarated with the prospect of action to be dampened. "Me? I'll think of something. Inspiration's my specialty!"

"A dangerous specialty, the most dangerous of all, perhaps. What of the 'droid? What 'droid? We don't even know what kind of 'droid they meant."

"Ah, a *replacement* 'droid, remember?" Han talked fast, to sell his point, gesturing at Bollux. The 'droid made strangely human prevocal sounds, a creak of astonishment, and Blue Max got out a "Wow!" as Han rattled on.

"We can say the Guild got it wrong. So Stars' End wanted a juggler or whatever and they get a storyteller. So what? We'll tell them to go sue the Entertainers' Guild!"

"Captain Solo, sir, if you please," Bollux finally interjected. "With your kind permission, sir, I must point out—"

But Han already had his hands on the 'droid's weatherbeaten shoulders, eyeing him artistically. "Hmm, new paint, of course, and there's plenty aboard; it often pays to slap a coat on something before resale, especially if you didn't own it to begin with. Scarlet liqui-gloss, I think; a five-coat job's all we have time for. And maybe some trim. Nothing flashy, no scrollwork or filigree; just some restrained silver pinstriping. Bollux, boy, you can stop worrying about obsolescence after this, 'cause you're gonna lay 'em in the aisles!"

Their approach and planetfall were uneventful. Han had altered the drift of their captive asteroid to take him back out of range of the Authority's sensors and then abandoned it. Once back in deep space, he'd made a nanno-jump, barely brushing hyperspace, to emerge near Mytus VII and its two small moonlets.

The *Falcon* identified herself, using the Waivered registration obtained by Rekkon. To that was added the proud announcement that she was the grand touring vehicle of Madam Atuarre's Roving Performers.

Mytus VII was a place of rocky desolation, airless, its distance from its sun rendering it dim and cheerless. If anybody escaped Stars' End, he'd have no place to go; the rest of the solar system was untenanted, none of its planets being hospitable to humanoid life.

The Authority's installation was marked by groupings of temporary dormitories, hangars and guard barracks, hydroponics layouts, dome-sheds and weapons sites. The ground was gouged and pocked where construction of permanent subsurface facilities was in progress, but there was at least one finished structure already. In the middle of the base reared a tower like a stark, gleaming dagger.

Evidently no tunnel system had been completed yet. The whole complex was interconnected by a maze of tunnel-tubes, like giant, pleated hoses radiating from their boxy junction stations, a common arrangement for construction sites on airless worlds.

There was only one sizable vessel on the ground, an armed Espo assault craft. There were also smaller craft and unarmed cargo lighters, but Han had checked carefully for picket ships this time and was satisfied that there were none.

Han, checking visually for that heavyweight power plant his sensors had spotted, failed to locate it and wondered if it might be in that tower. He shot a second look at the tower, thinking something about it looked strange. It was equipped with two heavy docking locks, one at ground level and the other near its summit, the former hooked up to a tunnel-tube. He would very much have liked to run a close sweep of the place to see if he could pick up a high concentration of life forms that might indicate prisoners, but dared not for fear of counterdetection. Being caught probing the base would spell the end of the masquerade.

He made an undistinguished approach, nothing fancy, revealing none of the *Falcon*'s hidden capabilities. The attentive snouts of turbo-lasers tracked the ship exactingly. Ground control guided the starship down, and one of the tunnel-tubes snaked out, its folded skin extended by its servoframe, its hatch-mounted mouth sealing to the *Millennium Falcon*'s hull, swallowing the ship's lowering ramp.

Han shut down the engines. Atuarre, in the oversized copilot's seat, said, "I tell you one last time, Solo-Captain: I don't wish to be the one to do the speaking."

He brought his chair around. "I'm no actor, Atuarre. It'd be different if we were just going to jump in, spring the prisoners, and kiss off, but I can't cut all that chitchat and play the role."

They left the cockpit. Han was wearing a tight-cut black body suit, converted into a costume by the addition of epaulets, piping, shining braid, and a broad yellow sash, over which he'd buckled his blaster. His boots were newly polished.

Atuarre was bedecked at wrists, forearms, throat, forehead, and knees with bunches of multicolored streamers, Trianii attire for festivals and joyful occasions. She'd applied the exotic perfumes and formal scents of her species, using up the tiny supply she had in her belt pouch.

"I am no actress, either," she reminded him as they met the others at the ramp hatch.

"Did you ever see a celebrity?"

"Authority execs and their wives, when they came to our world as tourists."

Han snapped his fingers. "That's it. Smug, dumb, and happy."

Pakka was costumed as his mother was, wearing the scents appropriate to a pre-adolcscent male. He handed his mother and Han long, billowing metallic capes, hers coppery and his an electric blue. Han's small wardrobe had been ransacked for material for the costumes, and the capes had come from the thin insulating layers of a tent from the ship's survival gear.

The fitting, seaming, and alterations had been a problem. Han was all thumbs when it came to tailoring, and the Trianii, of course, were a species who had never developed the art because they never wore anything but protective clothing. The solution had come in the form of Bollux, who had been programmed for the necessary skills, among others, while serving a regimental commander during the Clone Wars.

The ramp was already down; all that remained was to open the hatch. "Luck to us all," Atuarre bade them softly. They piled hands, including Bollux's cold metal ones, then Han reached for the switch.

As the hatch rolled up, Atuarre was still objecting. "Solo-Captain, I still think you ought to be the one to—" At the foot of the ramp, the tunnel-tube was crammed with body-armored Espos brandishing heavy blasters, riot guns, gas projectors, fusion-cutters, and sapper charges. Whirling, Atuarre gushed, "Oh, my! How thoughtful! My dears, they've sent us a guard of honor!"

She touched up her glossy, fine-brushed mane with one hand, smiling down at the Security Policemen charmingly. Han wondered why he'd ever worried. The Espos, keyed up for a shootout, stared popeyed as she swept down the ramp, the profusion of streamers rippling and snapping behind her, her cape shimmering. Her steps sounded with the anklet-chimes that Han had run off for her from shipboard materials, using his small but complete tool locker.

At the front of the Espo ranks was a battalion commander, a major, his black swagger stick held behind his back, spine stiff, face rigid with officiousness. Atuarre descended the ramp as if she were receiving the keys to the planet, waving as if to acknowledge a standing ovation.

"My dear, *dear* General," she halfsang, intentionally giving the man a promotion, "I'm simply beyond words! Viceprex Hirken is too kind, I'm sure. And to you and your gallant men, thanks from Madam Atuarre and her Roving Performers!'' She swooped right up to him, ignoring the guns and bombs and other items of destruction, one hand playing with the major's ribbons and medals, the other waving her gratitude to the massed, dumbfounded Espos. A dark, high-blood-pressure blush rose out of the major's collar and climbed swiftly for his hairline.

''What is the meaning of this?'' he sputtered. ''Are you saying you're the entertainers Viceprex Hirken is expecting?''

Her face showed cute confusion. ''To be sure. You mean word of our arrival wasn't forwarded here to Stars' End? The Imperial Entertainers' Guild assured me it would communicate with you; I *always* demand adequate advanced billing.''

She swept a grand gesture back up the ramp. ''Gentlemen! Madam Atuarre presents her Roving Performers! First, Master Marksman, wizard of weaponry, whose target-shooting tricks and glittering gunplay have astounded audiences everywhere!''

Han walked down the ramp, trying to look the part, sweating under the tunnel-tube's worklights. Atuarre and the others could use their real names with impunity here, since those names had never appeared in Authority files. But Han's might have, and so he'd been forced into this new persona. He wasn't altogether sure he liked it now. When the Espos saw his blaster, weapons came up to cover him, and he was cautious to keep his hand away from it.

But Atuarre was already chattering. ''And, to amaze and amuse you with feats of gymnastics and spellbinding acrobatics, Atuarre presents her pet prodigy—''

Han held up a hoop he had brought down with him. It was a ring-stabilizer off an old repulsor rig, but he'd plated it and fitted it with an insulated hand-grip and a breadboarded distortion unit. Now he thumbed a switch, and the hoop became a circle of dancing light and waves of color as the distortion unit scrambled the visible spectrum, throwing off sparks and flares.

"—Pakka!" Atuarre introduced. The cub dived through the harmless light-effects, bounced off the ramp, and executed a triple forward somersault, into a double twist, and ended bowing deeply to the surprised major. Han scaled the hoop back into the ship and stepped to one side.

"And lastly," Atuarre went on, "that astonishing automaton, robotic raconteur, and machine of mirth and merriment, *Bollux*!"

And the 'droid clanked stiffly down the ramp, long arms swinging, somehow making it all look like a military march. Han had knocked out most of his dents and dings and applied a radiant paint job, five layers of scarlet liqui-gloss, as promised, with glinting silver pinstriping, painstakingly limned. The 'droid had been converted from an obsolescent into a classic. The mask-and-sunburst emblem of the Imperial Entertainer's Guild embellished one side of his chest, a touch that Han had thought would raise their credibility.

The Espo major was stumped. He knew Viceprex Hirken was expecting a special entertainment group, but was not aware of any clearance for one's arrival. Nevertheless, the Viceprex attached particular importance to his diversions, and wouldn't take kindly to any meddling or delay. No, not kindly at all.

The major put on as cordial an expression as his gruff face could achieve. "I'll notify the Viceprex of your arrival at once, Madam, ah, Atuarre?"

"Yes, splendid!" She gathered her cape for a curtsy and turned to Pakka. "Fetch your props, my sweet." The cub skipped back up the ramp and returned a moment later with several hoops, a balance-ball, and an assortment of lesser props scrounged up aboard ship.

"I'll escort you to Stars' End," said the major. "And I'm afraid my men will have to hold on to your Master Marksman's weapon. You understand, Madam: Standard Operating Procedure."

Han steeled himself and handed his blaster over butt-first to an Espo sergeant as Atuarre nodded to the major. "Of course, of course. We must never ignore the proprieties, must we? Now, my dear, *dear* General, if you'd be so gracious . . ."

He realized with a start that she was waiting for his arm, and extended it stiffly, his face livid. The Espos, knowing their commanding officer's temper, hid their grins carefully. They formed up a hasty honor guard as Han hit the ramp control. The ramp pulled itself up quickly and the hatch rolled closed. They would reopen for no one but himself, Chewbacca, or one of the Trianii.

The major, after sending a runner ahead, led the group off through the tunnel-tube mazework. They were a long walk from the tower, and passed through several of the tread-mounted junction stations, to the surprised gazes of black-coveralled tech controlmen. Their footsteps and Bollux's clanking joints echoed through the tunnel-tubes, and the new arrivals noticed a gravity markedly lighter than the Standard gee maintained onboard the *Millennium Falcon*. Air in the tubes had the tang of hydroponics recycling, a welcome change from shipboard.

They came at last to a large, permanent air lock. Its outer hatch swung open at a verbal order from the major. Han caught a quick glimpse of what he knew must be the tower's side, surrounded by the tunnel-tube's seal, that confirmed something he'd thought he'd seen when landing.

Stars' End, or at least the tower's outer sheath, was molecularly bonded armor, of a single piece. That made it one of the most expensive buildings—no, he corrected himself, *the* most expensive building—Han had ever seen. Enhancing the molecular bonding of dense metals was a costly process, and doing it on this scale was something he'd simply never heard of.

Inside the tower, they passed down a long, broad corridor to the central axis, which was a service core that also housed elevator banks. They were hurried along, with little chance to gawk, but they did see techs, Authority execs, and Espos coming and going. Stars' End itself didn't appear to be particularly well manned, which didn't jell with the theory that it was a prison.

They entered an elevator with the major and a few of his men and were whisked upward in a high-speed ride. When the elevator opened and they trailed the major out, they found themselves standing beneath the stars, which shone so brightly and were packed so tightly overhead that they seemed more like a mist of light.

Then Han realized they were on top of Stars' End, which was covered with a dome of transparisteel. There was an apron of bright flooring by the elevators. Beyond that began a small glen, complete with miniature streamlet, and flowers and vegetation from many worlds, landscaped down to the last bud and leaf. He could hear the sounds of birds and small animals, the hum of pollinating insects, all of which were confined to the roof garden, he assumed, by partition fields. The glen was cleverly lit by miniature sun-globes of various colors.

Footsteps to their right made them turn. A man came around the curve of the tower's service core, a tall, handsome patriarch of a man. He wore superbly cut uppermost-exec's attire—a cutaway coat, formal vest, pleated shirt and meticulously creased trousers, set off by a jaunty red cravat. His smile was hearty and convincing, his hair white and full, his hands clean and soft, his nails manicured and lacquered. Han instantly wanted to bop him in the skull and dump him down the elevator shaft.

The man's voice was sure and melodious. "Welcome to Stars' End, Madam Atuarre. I am Hirken, Vice-President Hirken, of the Corporate Sector Authority. Alas, you come unheralded, or I'd have greeted you with greater pomp."

Atuarre feigned distress. "Oh, honorable sir, what shall I say? We were contacted by the Guild and asked to serve as a replacement act, at the last moment, as it were. But I was told the Secretary in charge of scheduling, Hokkor Long, would make all arrangements."

Viceprex Hirken smiled, a charming drawing back of red lips from chalk-white teeth. Han thought how useful that smile and smooth voice must be in Authority board sessions. "Totally unimportant," the Viceprex announced. "Your appearance is thus an unexpected pleasure."

"Why, how gracious of you! Never fear, my kind Viceprex; we'll distract you from the problems and pressures of your high office!" To herself, though, Atuarre swore Trianii vengeance: *If you've hurt my mate, I vow I'll see your living heart in my hand!*

Han observed that Hirken wore, at his belt, a small, flat instrument, a master-control unit. He assumed that the man liked to keep close watch on everything in Stars' End; the unit gave him total control of his domain.

"I have gathered some of the most prestigious entertainers in this part of our galaxy," Atuarre continued. "Pakka here is a premier acrobat, and I myself, in addition to being mistress of ceremonies, perform the traditional music and ritual dance of my people. And here stands our handsome Master Marksman, peerless expert with firearms, to amaze you, worshipful Viceprex, with his trick shooting."

There was a whistling laugh and a jeering: "Trick shooting of what? Of his mouth, as appears likely?"

The speaker appeared behind Viceprex Hirken. He was a reptilian creature, slender and quick of movement. Viceprex Hirken chided the humanoid gently. "There, there, Uul; these good folks have come a long way to relieve our tedium." He turned to Atuarre. "Uul-Rha-Shan is my personal bodyguard, and something of an adept with weapons himself. Perhaps a contest of some sort could be arranged later. Uul has such a droll sense of humor, don't you agree?"

Han was eyeing the reptile, whose bright green scales were marked with diamond patterns of red and white, and whose big black, emotionless eyes were studying Han. Uul-Rha-Shan's jaw hung open a bit, exposing fangs and a restless pink tongue. Strapped to his right forearm was a pistol, a disrupter, Han thought, in a spring-loaded or power-driven holster of some kind.

Uul-Rha-Shan had taken up a position to Hirken's right. Han recalled having heard the bodyguard's name before. The galaxy was filled with species, all boasting their exceptional killers. Nonetheless, some individuals rose to a kind of prominence. One of those, an assassin and gunman who, it was said, would go anywhere and slay anyone for the right price, was Uul-Rha-Shan.

Hirken's manner had shifted to businesslike demeanor. "Now, that is the 'droid I requested, I take it?" He inspected Bollux unsmilingly, with a look that put cold danger in the air. "I was most specific with the Guild; I told Hokkor Long precisely what sort of 'droid I desired and stressed that they were to send nothing else. Has Long acquainted you with my desires?"

Atuarre swallowed, trying not to let her effusive manner slip. "Of a certainty, Viceprex, he did."

Hirken threw one more skeptical look at Bollux. "Very well. Follow me." He set off, back the way he had come, Uul-Rha-Shan at his heels. The travelers and their escort came behind. They left the garden area, coming to an amphitheater, an open expanse surrounded by banks of comfortable seats, separated by partitions of transparisteel.

"Automated fighting is combat at its purest, don't you agree?" Hirken said chattily. "No living creature, no matter how savage, is free of the taint of self-preservation. But automata, ah! They are without regard for themselves, existing only to follow orders and destroy. My own combat-automaton is a Mark-X Executioner; there aren't many of them around. Has your gladiator 'droid ever fought one?"

Han's nerves were screaming; he was trying to figure out whom to jump for a weapon if, as he feared, Atuarre bobbled her reply. Any show of hesitation or ignorance now would surely tip their hand to Hirken and his men.

But she improvised smoothly. "No, Viceprex, not the Mark X."

Han was struggling with the jarring revelation. Gladiator 'droid? So that was what Hirken assumed Bollux was. Han had known, naturally, that matching 'droids and other automata in combat was a fad among the wealthy and jaded, but it hadn't occurred to him that Hirken would be among those. He put his brain into overdrive, looking for a way out.

As they walked, a woman joined them, coming from what was evidently a private lift tube. She was short, extremely fat, and trying to hide it with expensive, well-tailored robes. Han thought she looked as if somebody had draped a drogue parachute over an escape pod.

She took Hirken's hand. The Viceprex endured the gesture with ill humor. She fluttered a fat, beautifully maintained hand and chortled, "Oh, darling, do we have company?"

Hirken turned upon the woman a stare that, Han calculated, was enough to dissolve covalent bonding. The chubby birdbrain ignored it. The Viceprex gritted his teeth. "No, dearest. These people have brought a new competitor for my Mark X. Madame Atuarre and Company, I present my lovely bride, Neera. By the way, Madam Atuarre, what did you say your 'droid's designation is?"

Han jumped in. "He's one of a kind, um, Viceprex. We designed him ourselves and call him Annihilator." He turned to Bollux.

Bollux looked from Han to Hirken, then bowed. "Annihilator, at your service. To destroy is to serve, exalted sir."

"But our troupe has other acts to offer," Atuarre was quick to tell Hirken's wife. "Tumbling, dancing, trick shooting, and more."

"Ooh, dearest!" the obese woman exclaimed, clapping her hands, sliding up against her husband. "Let's see that first! I grow so tired of watching that old Mark X demolish other machinery. How boring and uncouth and crude, really! And live performers would be such a relief from those dreadful holotapes and recorded music. And we have company here so seldom.'' She made puckering noises which, Han took it, were intended to be kisses to her husband. Han thought they sounded more like the attack of some invertebrate.

He saw a chance to solve two problems at once: how to get Bollux out of the match and how to get a look around Stars' End on his own. ''Uh, honored Viceprex, I'm also gaffer for the troupe. I have to tell you, our gladiator 'droid, Annihilator there, was damaged in his last match. His auxiliary management circuitry needs to be checked. If I could use your shop, it'd only take a few minutes. You and your wife could enjoy the other performances in the meantime.''

Hirken looked up at the stars through the dome and sighed, while his wife giggled and seconded the proposal. ''Very well. But make these repairs quickly, Marksman. I'm not much taken with acrobats or dancing.''

''Sure, right.''

The Viceprex summoned a tech supervisor who had been checking the amphitheater's systems and explained to the man what was needed. Then he offered his arm, unwillingly, to his wife. They went to find seats in the amphitheater, with the Espo major and his men ranging themselves around in a loose guard formation. Uul-Rha-Shan, with a last, menacing look at Han, followed along, again positioning himself near Hirken's right.

Since Pakka's acrobatics and Atuarre's dancing would pose no danger to the audience, Hirken hit a control on his belt unit, and the transparisteel slabs forming the arena's walls slid away into floor slots. The Viceprex and his wife settled into luxurious conform-loungers. Pakka readied his props.

Han turned to the supervisor tech who'd been placed at his disposal. ''Wait for me by the elevator; I'll get the circuit box out, be with you in a second.''

The man left. Han, loosening his cape and sliding it from his shoulders, turned to Bollux. ''Okay, open up just enough for me to get Max.''

The plastron opened partway. Han leaned close, shielded

by the plastron halves. As he freed the computer-probe, he warned, "Not a sound, Max. You're supposed to be a combat-control component, so no funny stuff. You're deaf and dumb as of now." As a signal that he understood, Blue Max's photoreceptor went dim. "Good boy, Maxie."

Han straightened, slinging the computer's shoulder strap over his arm. As Bollux closed his chest up, Han handed his cape and gunbelt over and patted the 'droid's freshly painted head. "Hold these for me and stay loose, Bollux. This shouldn't take long."

As Han joined the tech supervisor at the elevator, Pakka was just beginning a marvelous exhibition of tumbling and gymnastics. The cub was a competition-class acrobat and covered the amphitheater floor in a series of flips, twists, and cartwheels, somersaulting through a hoop he held and, perching on the balance-ball, moving himself around the arena with both hands and feet. Then Atuarre came in to act as thrower as Pakka became a flyer.

Hirken's wife thought it all charming, *ooh*ing at the cub's prowess. Subordinate Authority execs began to show up and take seats, a handful of the privileged who had been invited to see the performance. They muttered approval of Pakka's agility, but stifled it when they saw their boss's deadly look of discontent.

Hirken thumbed his belt unit. A voice answered instantly. "Have the Mark X readied at once." He ignored the crisp acknowledgment from the duty tech, eyed the waiting Bollux, and turned his attention back to the acrobatics. Authority Viceprex Hirken could be very, very patient when he wished, but wasn't in the mood now.

RIDING down in the elevator, Han concentrated furiously on his predicament.

He'd led the others into this jam thinking that, if nothing else, he'd at least get an idea of what he was up against. At worst, he'd thought, they'd be told they weren't welcome. But this was an unanticipated twist.

That Bollux was committed to a match against a killer robot of some sort shouldn't bother him, Han reminded himself. Bollux was, after all, only a 'droid. It wasn't as if a living entity would die. Han had to keep repeating that because he was having a hard time selling it to himself. Anyway, he had no intention of giving Viceprex Hirken the enjoyment of seeing the superannuated 'droid taken apart.

Times like this, he wished he were the slow, careful type. But his style was the product of Han himself, defying consequences, jumping in with both feet, heedless of what he might land in. His plan, as revised in the elevator, was to do all the scouting he could. If nothing more could be accomplished, he and the others would have to wing it, withdraw from the performance and, it was to be hoped, Stars' End, on the plea that Bollux was irreparable.

He watched floor numbers flash and kept himself from asking questions of the tech supervisor beside him. Any outsider, particularly an entertainer, would be scrupulously uncurious about an Authority installation. For Han to be otherwise would be a matter causing instant suspicion.

A few other passengers entered and left the car. Only one

was an exec; all the rest were Espos and techs. Han looked them over for keys, restraint-binders, or anything else that might indicate detention-block guard duties, but saw nothing. Again he noticed that the tower seemed very lightly manned, contrary to what he'd expect if there really was a prison here.

He followed the tech supervisor out of the elevator, alighting at the general maintenance section, nearly back at ground level. Only a few techs were there, moving among gleaming machinery and dangling hoisting gear. Disassembled 'droids, robo-haulers, and other light equipment, as well as commo and computer apparatus, were to be seen everywhere.

He resettled Max's carrying strap at his shoulder. "Do you guys have a circuit scanner?"

The tech led him to a side room with rows of booths, all of them vacant. Han set Max on a podium in one of them and lowered a scanner hood, hoping the tech would go off and take care of his normal duties. But the man remained there, and so Han found himself staring into the computer-probe's labyrinthine interior.

The tech, watching over his shoulder, commented, "Hey, that looks like a lot more than just an auxiliary component."

"It's something I worked up, pretty sophisticated," Han said. "By the way, the Viceprex said when I'm done here I could take it up to your central computer section to recalibrate it. That's one level down, right?"

The supervisor was frowning now, trying for a better look at Blue Max's guts. "No, computers are two levels up. But they won't let you in unless Hirken verifies it. You're not cleared, and you can't go into a restricted area if you're unbadged." He leaned closer to the scanner. "Listen, that really looks like some kind of computer module to me."

Han chuckled casually. "Here, look for yourself."

He stepped aside. The tech supervisor moved closer to the scanner, reaching down to work its focus controls. Then his own focus went completely dark.

Han, rubbing the edge of his hand, stood over the unconscious tech and looked around for a place to stow him. He had noticed a supply closet at the end of the scanner room. Han fastened the man's hands behind him with his own belt, gagged him with a dust cover off a scanner, and lugged the limp form into the closet. He paused to take the man's security badge, then closed the door.

He went back to the little computer-probe. "All right, Max; perk up."

Blue Max's photoreceptor lit up. Han removed his own sash and stripped the gaudy homemade medals and braid off his outfit. He yanked the epaulets and piping away, too, and what remained was a black body suit, a fair approximation of a tech's uniform. He placed the supervisor's security badge prominently on his chest, took Max up again, and set out. Of course, if anyone were to stop him or compare the miniature holoshot on his badge to his real face, he'd be tubed. But he was counting on his own luck, a convincing briskness of stride, and an air of purpose.

He went up two levels without mishap. Three Espos lounging in the guard booth near the elevator bank waved him on, seeing he was badged. He fought the impulse to smile. Stars' End was probably an uneventful tour of duty; no wonder the guards had gotten lax. After all, what could possibly happen here?

At the amphitheater, Pakka's amazing deftness hadn't even drawn an approving look from Viceprex Hirken. The cub had been using a hoop while rolling a balance-ball with his feet, doing flips.

"Enough of this," Hirken proclaimed, his well-tended hand flying up. Pakka stopped, glaring at the Viceprex. "Isn't that incompetent Marksman back yet?" The other execs, conferring among themselves, managed to reach a group decision that Han was still gone. Hirken's breath rasped.

He pointed to Atuarre. "Very well, Madam, you may dance. But be brief, and if your sharpshooting gaffer isn't back soon, I may dispense with him altogether."

Pakka had removed his props from the arena floor. Now Atuarre handed him the small whistle-flute Han had machined up for him. While the cub blew a few practice runs on it, Atuarre slipped on the finger-cymbals Han had fashioned for her and clinked them experimentally. The improvised instruments, even her anklet-chimes, all lacked the musical quality of Trianii authentics, she decided. But they would suffice, and might even convince the onlookers that they were seeing the real thing.

Pakka began playing a traditional air. Atuarre moved out onto the arena floor, following the music with a sinuous ease no human performer could quite match. Her streamers blew behind her, many-colored fans flickering from arms and legs, forehead and throat, as her finger-cymbals sounded and her anklets rang, precisely as they should.

Some of the preoccupation left Hirken's face and the faces of the other onlookers. Trianni ritual dancing had often been touted as a primitive, uninhibited art, but the truth was that it was high artistry. Its forms were ancient, exacting, demanding all a dancer's concentration. It required perfectionism, and a deep love of the dance itself. In spite of themselves, Hirken, his subordinates, and his wife were drawn into Atuarre's spinning, stalking, pouncing dance. And as she performed, she wondered how long she could hold her audience, and what would happen if she couldn't hold them long enough.

Han, having found a computer terminal in an unoccupied room, set Max down next to it. While Max extended his adapter and entered the system, Han took a cautious look in the hall and closed the door.

He drew up a workstool by a readout screen. "You in, kid?"

"Just about, Captain. The techniques Rekkon taught me work here, too. There!" The screen lit up, flooded with symbols, diagrams, computer models, and columns of data.

"Way to go, Max. Now spot up the holding pens, or cells, or detention levels or whatever."

Blue Max flashed layout after layout on the screen, while his search moved many times faster, skimming huge amounts of data; this was the sort of thing he'd been built for. But at last he admitted, "I can't, Captain."

"What d'you mean, can't? They're here, they've gotta be. Look again, you little moron!"

"There're no cells," Max answered indignantly. "If there were, I'd have seen them. The only living arrangements in the whole base are the employees' housing, the Espo barracks, and the exec suites, all on the other side of the complex—and Hirken's apartments here in the tower."

"All right," Han ordered, "put a floor plan of this joint up, level by level, on the screen, starting with Hirken's amusement park."

A floor plan of the dome, complete with the garden and amphitheater, lit the readout. The next two levels below it proved to be filled with the Viceprex's ostentatious personal quarters. The one after that confused Han. "Max, what're those subdivisions? Offices?"

"It doesn't say here," the computer answered. "The property books list medical equipment, holo-recording gear, surgical servos, operating tables, things like that."

A thought struck Han. "Max, what's Hirken's title? His official corporate job-slot, I mean."

"Vice-President in charge of Corporate Security, it says."

Han nodded grimly. "Keep digging; we're in the right place. That's no clinic up there, it's an interrogation center, probably Hirken's idea of a rec room. What's on the next floor down?"

"Nothing for humans. The next level is three floors high, Captain. Just heavy machinery; there's an industrial-capacity power hookup there, and an air lock. See, here's the floor plan and a power-routing schematic."

Max showed it. Han leaned closer to the screen, studying the myriad lines. One, marked in a different color and located near the elevators, attracted his attention. He asked the computer what it was.

"It's a security viewer, Captain. There's a surveillance system in parts of the tower. I'll patch in."

The screen flickered, then resolved into the brightness of a visual image. Han stared. He'd found the lost ones.

The room was filled, stack upon stack, with stasis booths. Inside each, a prisoner was frozen in time, stopped between one instant and the next by the booth's level-entropy field. That explained why there were no prisoner facilities, no arrangements for handling crowds of captive entities, and only a minimal guard complement on duty. Hirken had all his victims suspended in time; they'd require little in the way of formal accommodations. The Security Viceprex need take prisoners out only when he chose to question them, then pop them back into stasis when he was done. So he robbed his prisoners of their very lives, taking away every part of their existence except interrogation.

"There must be thousands of them," Han breathed. "Hirken can move them in and out of that air lock like freight. Power consumption up there must be terrific. Max, where's their plant?"

"We're sitting on it," Max answered, though that anthropomorphism couldn't really apply to him. He filled the screen with a basic diagram of the tower. Han whistled softly. Beneath Stars' End was a power-generating plant large enough to service a battle fortress, or a capital-class warship.

"And here are the primary defense designs," Max added. There were force fields on all sides of the tower, and one overhead, ready to spring into existence instantly. Stars' End itself was, as Han had already noticed, made of enhanced-bonding armor plate. According to specs, it was equipped with an anticoncussion field as well, so that no amount of high explosives could damage its occupants. The Authority had spared no expense to make its security arrangements complete.

But that helped only if the enemy were outside, and Han was as inside as he could get. "Is there a prisoner roster?"

"Got it! They had it filed: *Transient Persons*."

Han swore under his breath at bureaucratic euphemisms. "Okay, is Chewie's name on it?"

There was the briefest of pauses. "No, Captain. But I found Atuarre's mate! And Jessa's father!" He flashed two more images on the screen, arrest mugshots. Atuarre's mate's coloring was redder than hers, it turned out, and Doc's grizzled features hadn't changed. "And here's Rekkon's nephew," Max added. The mug was of a young black face with broad, strong lines that promised a resemblance to the boy's uncle.

"Jackpot!" Max squealed a moment later, a very uncomputerish exclamation. Chewbacca's big hairy face flashed on the readout. He hadn't been in a very good mood for the mugshot; he was disheveled, but his snarl promised death to the photographer. The Wookiee's eyes looked glassy, and Han assumed that the Espos had tranquilized him as soon as they'd taken him.

"Is he okay?" Han demanded. Max put up the arrest record. No, Chewbacca hadn't been badly injured, but three officers had been killed in apprehending him, the forms said. He hadn't given a name, which explained why it had been difficult for Max to locate him. The list of charges nearly ran off the screen, with a final, ominous, handwritten notation at the bottom listing time of scheduled interrogation. Han glanced at a wall clock; it was no more than hours before Chewbacca was due to enter Viceprex Hirken's torture mill.

"Max, we're up against it. We have to do something right now; I'm not going to let them take Chewie's mind apart. Can we deactivate defensive systems?"

The computer replied: "Sorry, Captain. All the primaries are controlled through that belt unit Hirken carries."

"What about secondaries?"

Max sounded dubious. "I can get to the standby, but how will you deactivate the Viceprex's belt unit?"

"I dunno; how's he wired up? There must be ancillary

equipment; the damn box is too small to be self-contained and still control this whole tower."

Max gave the answer. Receptor circuitry ran through Stars' End, built into the walls on each level.

"Show me the top-level circuitry diagrams." Han studied them carefully, memorizing points of reference—doors, elevators, and support girders.

"Okay, Max, now I want you to cut into the secondary control systems and rearrange power-flow priorities. When the secondaries cut in, I want that umbrella shield, the deflector directly overhead, to start load-shedding its power back to the plant, but I want you to prejudice the systems' safeguards, so that they notice the deflector droppage but not the feedback."

"Captain Solo, that'll start an overload spiral. You could blow the whole tower up."

"Only if I get to Hirken's primaries," Han said, half to himself, half to Max. "Get crackin'."

High above, Viceprex Hirken had realized that he was being played for a fool.

As fascinated as he'd been by Atuarre's dance, he'd recognized in a fundamental, ever-suspicious part of his mind that he was being diverted. What he desired was to see mechanized combat. This dance artistry, though pretty enough, was no substitute.

He stood, fingering a button on his belt unit. Lights came up, and Pakka stopped playing. Atuarre looked around her, as if awakening from a dream. "What—"

"Enough of this," Hirken decreed. Uul-Rha-Shan, his reptilian gunman, stood at his side, hoping for the order to slay. But instead, Hirken said, "I've seen enough, Trianii. You're clearly stalling. You think me an imbecile?" Then he motioned to Bollux. "You ridiculous excuses for entertainers brought this obsolete 'droid to me purely as a fraud, never planning to give me value for my money. You'd hoped to plead mechanical failure and get me to reimburse you for your trip, or even reward you for your efforts. Isn't that so?"

Her quiet "No, Viceprex" was ignored.

Hirken was not convinced. "Prepare that 'droid for combat, and bring out my Mark X," he ordered the techs and Espos around him.

Atuarre drew herself up, enraged, and afraid for Bollux. But she could see Hirken was adamant, and she had her cub to think of. Furthermore she could do Han and her mate little good here. "With your permission, Excellency, I will return to my ship." Onboard the *Falcon*, at least, more options would be available.

Hirken waved her away, preoccupied with his Executioner, laughing his humorless laugh. "Go, go. And if you see that worthless liar of a Marksman of yours, you'd be wise to take him with you. And don't think I won't lodge a complaint. I'll have your Guild membership revoked."

She glanced to where Bollux was being ushered down to the arena, helpless to aid him. "Lord Hirken, surely this is illegal. That is our 'droid—"

"Brought here to defraud me," he finished for her, "but I'll have my value from it. Now leave, if you're going to, or watch if you wish." He wagged a finger, and an Espo sergeant barked an order. Tall, stern guards fell in, one to either side of the two Trianii.

Atuarre couldn't restrain her hiss. She grabbed Pakka's paw and stormed toward the elevator, the cub bouncing along behind. Uul-Rha-Shan's dry laugh was like a stab of hatred.

Down in the computer center, the readout screen, which had been showing a small part of the modification Blue Max was making, went blank for a moment.

"Max? You all right?" Han asked worriedly.

"Captain Solo, they're activating that combat machine, the Mark X. They're putting it in with Bollux!" Even as the computer-probe spoke, the rapid-fire images of the Mark-X Executioner's engineering details replaced one another on the screen. Max's voice was filled with alarm. "The Mark X's controls and power are independent of this system; I can't touch it! Captain, we have to get back upstairs right now. Bollux needs me!"

"What about Atuarre?"

"They're summoning an elevator and notifying security that she's leaving. We've got to get up there!"

Han was shaking his head, unmindful that Max's photoreceptor was off. "Sorry, Max, there're too many other things I need to do here. Besides, we couldn't help Bollux now."

The readout went blank and the photoreceptor came on. Blue Max's voice trembled. "Captain Solo, I'm not doing anything else for you until you take me to Bollux. I *can* help him."

Han struck the probe, not gently, with the heel of his hand. "Get back to work, Max. I'm serious." For answer, Max withdrew his adapter from the network. Han, infuriated, snatched the little computer up and held it high overhead.

"Do what I told you, or I'll leave you here in pieces!"

Max's reply was somber. "Go ahead, then, Captain. Bollux would do whatever he had to if I were in trouble."

Han paused in the midst of dashing the computer to the floor. It occurred to him that Max's concern for his friend was no different from Han's own for Chewbacca. He lowered the probe, looking at it as if for the first time. "I'll be damned. You sure you can help Bollux?"

"Just get me there, Captain; you'll see!"

"I hope. Which car was going to the dome?"

Max told him, and he set out for the elevators at once, slinging the probe over his shoulder. When he got there, he removed the security badge and punched for a downward ride. The wrong car stopped; he let it wait and go on, and punched the descent button again.

He lucked out. The car containing Atuarre, Pakka, and their two guards had stopped a number of times on its way down. She saw Han and pulled her cub off the car with her. The Espos had to hurry to avoid being left behind.

Han took the two Trianii aside a pace or two, but the Espos made it plain that they were keeping an eye on all three.

"We were going to the ship," Atuarre told him in low tones. "I didn't know what else to do. Solo-Captain, Hirken is putting Bollux in with that Executioner machine of his!"

"I know. Max has some kind of angle on that." He saw one of the Espos speaking on a com-link. "Listen, the lost ones are here, thousands of 'em. Max rigged the tower; Hirken'll have to let everybody go if he wants to keep breathing. Go get the ship ready. If I can just get my hands on a blaster, the fix is in, sister."

"Captain, I meant to tell you," Max interrupted. "I was rechecking the figures. I think you should know—"

"Not now, Max!" Han pulled Atuarre and Pakka back toward the elevator, hitting both the up and the down buttons. One of the Espos fell in with the Trianii again, but the other stationed himself with Han, explaining, "The Viceprex says it's all right for you to come up. You can take home what's left of your 'droid after the fight."

The techs and Espos hurried Bollux down into the arena as the transparisteel slabs raised from their hidden slots in the floor. Hirken knew now that this was no gladiator 'droid, and so gave the command that Bollux be equipped with a blast shield, to make things more interesting. The shield, an oblong of dura-armor plate fitted with grips, weighed down the old 'droid's long arm as he tried to adjust to what was happening.

Bollux knew he would never escape so many armed men. He had known many humans in his long years of function and could recognize hatred by now. That was what he saw on the Viceprex's face. But Bollux had come through a number of seemingly terminal situations and had no intention of being demolished now if he could avoid it.

A door panel slid up in the far wall forming one arc of the arena. There was a squeal of drive wheels, the rattling of treads. The Mark-X Executioner rolled out into the light.

It was half again as tall as Bollux and far broader, though it moved on two thick caterpillar tracks instead of legs. From the treads and support housing rose a thick trunk, armored in gray alloy plate. The Executioner's many arms were folded close to it now, inactive, each one furnished with a different weapon.

Bollux employed a trick he had learned from one of his first human owners, and simply omitted from computations the logical conclusion that his destruction was now a high order of probability. Among humans, he knew, this tactic was called ignoring certain death. Bollux thought of it as excluding counterproductive data. He'd been doing it for a long time now, which was why he was still functional.

The Executioner's cranial turret swung, its sensors locking in on the 'droid. The Mark X was the latest word in combat automata, an extremely successful, highly specialized killing machine. It could have zeroed in on the unarmed, general-purpose labor 'droid and vaporized him right then and there, but was, naturally, programmed to give its owner a more enjoyable show than that. The Executioner was also a machine with a purpose.

The Mark X began rolling, moving with quick precision, maneuvering toward Bollux. The 'droid backed away clumsily, contending with the unfamiliar task of holding and manipulating his blast shield. The Executioner circled, studying Bollux from all sides, gauging his reactions, while the 'droid watched from behind his shield.

"Commence!" called Viceprex Hirken through the arena's amplifiers. The Mark X, voice-keyed to him, changed to attack mode. It came directly to bear on Bollux, rushing at him at top speed. The 'droid dodged one way, then another, but his efforts were all anticipated by the Executioner. It compensated for his every move, rumbling to crush him under its tread.

"Cancel!" rasped Hirken over the amplifiers. The Mark X stopped just short of Bollux, allowing the old 'droid to totter awkwardly back from it.

"Resume!" ordered the Viceprex. The Executioner cranked

into motion again, selecting another destructive option from its arsenal. Servos hummed and a weapon arm came up, its end supporting a flame projector. Bollux saw it and brought his shield up just in time.

A gush of fire arced from the nozzle of the flame gun, splashing against the walls of the arena, throwing a burning stream across Bollux's shield. The Mark X brought the nozzle of its weapon back for another pass at low angle, to cut the 'droid's legs out from under him. Bollux barely managed to crash clumsily to his knees and ground his shield before flame washed across it, making puddles of fire on the floor around him. The Mark X was rolling again, preparing for a clearer shot, when Hirken canceled that mode, too.

Bollux struggled to his feet, using the shield for leverage. He could feel his internal mechanisms overheating, his bearings especially. His gyro-balance circuitry hadn't been built with this sort of constant punishment in mind.

Then the Mark X was coming in again. Bollux ignored the inevitable, making his sluggish parts respond, moving with some mechanical equivalent of pain, but still functional.

Han came out of the elevator at a run. The Espos there, aware that the Viceprex wished him to see the spectacle, let him pass.

He skidded to a stop at the top row of the little amphitheater. Hirken was seated below with his wife and subordinates, cheering their champion and laughing at the ludicrous Bollux as the Executioner raised another weapon arm. This one was provided with a bracket of flechette-missile pods.

Bollux saw it, too, and used a trick, or, as he thought of it, a last variable. Crouching, still holding his shield, he loosed the heavy-duty suspension in his legs and jumped out of the Mark X's cross hairs like some giant red insect. Miniature missiles exploded against the clear arena walls in a cloud, filling the amphitheater with crashing eruptions in spite of the sound-suppression system out in the seating area.

Hirken and his people roared their frustration. Han flung

himself down the steps to the arena, three at a time. Bollux had landed badly; the strain on his mechanisms was becoming insuperable. The Viceprex changed his combat-automaton's programming once more.

The Executioner retracted its missile-arm. Articulated catch-cables extended from ports in its sides, like metallic tentacles, and two circular saws swung out, their arms locking into position. The sawblades spun, creating a peculiar sound, the molecules of their cutting edges vibrating in a way that would shear through metal as easily as through air. The Mark X moved toward Bollux, its cables weaving, for a terminal embrace.

Hirken spied Han reaching the arena's edge. "Fraud! Now, watch a true combat-automaton at work!" He shook with gruesome laughter, all the affected charms of corporate board rooms stripped from him now. His wife and subordinates followed suit dutifully.

Han ignored them and held up the computer. "Max, tell him!" Blue Max sent burst-signals at top volume, concentrated pulses of information. Bollux turned his red photoreceptors to home in on the probe. He listened for a moment, then returned his attention to the onrushing Mark X. Han, knowing it was crazy, still found himself holding his breath.

As the Executioner bore down on him, Bollux made no move to avoid it or raise his shield. The Executioner recognized that as only logical. The 'droid had no hope. Questing catch-cables spread wide to seize Bollux; circular saws swung close.

Bollux hefted his shield and threw it at the Mark X. Cables and cutters changed course; the shield was easily intercepted, caught, and sliced to pieces. But in the moment's reprieve, Bollux had thrown himself, stiffly—with a huge metallic *bong*—down between the crushing treads of the Executioner.

The combat-automaton ground to a halt, but not in time. Bollux, lying beneath it, fastened one hand to its undercarriage and locked his servo-grip there. The other hand reached in among the components of the Mark X, ripping at its cooling circuitry.

The Executioner emitted an electronic scream. If it had sat there and pondered for an age, the killing machine would still never have considered the possibility that a general-labor 'droid could have learned how to do the irrational.

The Mark X broke into motion, rolling this way and that, randomly. It had no way to get at Bollux, who clung beneath it. No one had ever programmed the Executioner to shoot at itself, or cut at itself, or to crush something it couldn't reach. Bollux was in the single safe place in the entire arena.

The Mark X's internal temperature began rising at once; the killing machine produced enormous amounts of heat.

Hirken was on his feet now, screaming: "*Cancel! Cancel!* Executioner, I order you to *cancel*!" Techs began running around, bumping into one another, but the Mark X was no longer receiving orders. Its complicated voice-keyed command circuitry had been among the first things to go out of whack. Now it charged aimlessly around the arena, discharging blasters, flame guns, and missile pods at random, threatening to overload the noise-suppression system.

The arena's transparisteel walls became a window into an inferno as the Executioner roamed, its trunk rotating, its weapons blazing, its malfunctioning guidance system seeking an enemy that it could confront. It was hit by shrapnel from its own missiles. Smoke and fire could be seen pouring from its ventilators. Bollux hung on to the Mark X's undercarriage with both hands now, being dragged back and forth, wondering calmly if his grip would fail.

The Executioner rebounded from one of the arena's walls. Surviving targeting circuits thought the killing machine had found its enemy at last. It backed up, preparing for another charge, its engine revving.

Bollux decided correctly that it was time to part company. He simply let go. The Executioner howled off again, all its remaining attention focused on the unoffending wall. The 'droid began to drag himself, squeaking laboriously, toward the exit.

The Executioner crashed head-on into the arena wall, bouncing back with a mighty concussion. Frustrated, it fired all weapons at close range and was engulfed in the backwash of blaster beams, flechette fragments, and acid spray. Then, as Hirken cried a last "*No-ooo!*", the Mark X's internal heat reached critical, compounded by external damage.

The Mark-X Executioner, latest word in combat automata, was ruptured open by a spectacular explosion just as Bollux, semiobsolete general-labor 'droid, got his tired chassis out of the arena.

Han knelt by him, pounding the old 'droid on the back while Blue Max somehow produced a cheer from his vocoder. The pilot threw his head back and laughed, forgetting everything else in the absurdity of the moment.

"Give me a minute, please," Bollux begged, his drawl even slower now. "I must try to bring my mechanisms into some sort of order."

"I can help!" Max squeaked. "Link me through to your brain circuits, Bollux, and I'll handle all the bypasses. That'll leave you free to deal with the cybero-stasis problems."

Bollux opened his plastron. "Captain, if you'd be so kind?" Han put the little computer back into place.

"Touching, whoever you are," said a smooth, dry voice behind Han, "but pointless. We'll pick them both apart for the information we want. What happened to all your pretty braid and medals, by the way?"

Han turned and stood fast. Uul-Rha-Shan was waiting there, gun in hand. Han's holstered blaster hung over the reptilian gunman's shoulder.

Hirken came up behind Uul-Rha-Shan, followed by the major and the other Espos, his execs, and his wife, all the trappings of his corporate importance. The air was filled with the smell of charred circuitry and molten metal, all that remained of the precious Mark X. Hirken's face held inexpressible rage.

He pointed a quivering finger at Han. "I should've known you're part of the conspiracy! Trianii, 'droids, the Entertainers' Guild—they're all in on it. No one on the Board will be able to deny it now; this conspiracy against the Authority and against me personally involves *everyone*!''

Han shook his head, amazed. Hirken was sweating, bellowing, with a maniacal look on his face. ''I don't know your real name, Marksman, but you've come to the end of this plot. What I need to know, I'll dig out of your 'droid, and the Trianii. But since you've spoiled my entertainment, you'll make up for it.''

He went with the rest of his entourage and stood just inside the arena, safe behind the transparisteel slabs. Uul-Rha-Shan took Han's gunbelt from his shoulder and held it out to him. ''Come, trick shooter. Let's see if you have any tricks left.''

Han moved warily and collected the belt. He checked his holstered blaster by eye, and saw that it had been drained of all but a microcharge, not enough to damage the primary-control circuitry. His gaze went to Hirken, who stood gloating behind invulnerable transparisteel. The belt control unit was out of the question. Han climbed the amphitheater stairs slowly, buckling the gunbelt around his hips, tying down the holster.

Uul-Rha-Shan came after, returning his disrupter to its forearm holster. The two stepped out onto the open area overlooking the arena; the gathered Authority officials looked up at them.

It had been a good try, Han told himself, just a touch shy of success. But now Hirken meant to see him dead, and Chewbacca and Atuarre and Pakka in his interrogation chambers. The Viceprex held all the cards but one. Han made up his mind on the spot that if he was going to die anyway, he'd take all these warped minds of Corporate Security with him.

He went, carefully, and stood by the wall, unsnapping the retaining strap of his holster. His opponent, squared off a few paces away, wasn't through taunting.

''Uul-Rha-Shan likes to know whom he kills. Who are you, imposter?''

Drawing himself up, Han let his hands dangle loosely at his sides, fingers working. ''Solo. Han Solo.''

The reptile registered surprise. ''I have heard your name, Solo. You are, at least, worthy of the killing.''

Han's mouth tugged, in amusement. ''Think you can bring it off, lizard?''

Uul-Rha-Shan hissed anger. Han cleared his mind of everything but what lay before him.

''Farewell, Solo,'' Uul-Rha-Shan bade him, tensing.

Han moved with a dipping motion of the right shoulder, a half turn, all done with the blinding abruptness of the gunfighter. But his hand never closed on the grip of his blaster.

Instead, feigning his draw, he hurled himself out on the floor. As he fell, he felt Uul-Rha-Shan's disrupter beam lash over him, striking the wall. It set off a belching explosion that caught the reptile full in the face, flinging him backward. His shot had blown apart the ancillary circuitry for Hirken's belt unit, freeing swirls of energy. Secondary explosions told of the destruction of power-management routers.

Han had hit the floor rolling, surviving the blast with little more than singed hair. His blaster was in his hand now, the cautionary pulser in its grip tingling his palm in silent, invisible warning that the gun was nearly empty. As if he needed to be reminded. Uul-Rha-Shan, somewhere in the din and smoke, was shrilling, *''Solo-ooo!''* in furious challenge. Han couldn't pick him out.

A far-off vibration reached him, the overload spiral he'd had Blue Max build into the secondary defense program. Now that the primaries had been damaged and Hirken's belt unit circumvented, the power-rerouting had taken over. Won't be long now, he told himself.

Everyone in Stars' End suddenly felt as if he were being immersed in thick mud, as the weight of a planet seemed to be pressing down. The anticoncussion field—Han had forgotten about it, but it didn't matter.

Then, with an explosion beyond words, the power plant blew.

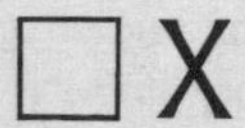

X

ATUARRE restrained herself from running back through the maze of tunnel-tubes, conscious of the Espo guard at her heels. Han's desperate plan left her so much room for doubt. What would happen if the bluff failed? But on that thought she corrected herself at once—Solo-Captain was not bluffing, and was more than capable of taking all his enemies with him in an act of awesome revenge.

But she approved of the gamble. This might be Stars' End's only vulnerable moment. Even so, she took her longest strides now, dragging a stumbling Pakka along breakneck-quick.

They passed into the final junction station, the one nearest the *Falcon*. A tech lounged on duty behind his console. The Espo's com-link signaled for attention, and Atuarre heard the crackled order, relayed from Hirken through the Espo major, as clearly as did her escort himself. The two Trianii were to be brought back to the tower. She wondered if that meant Han had successfully intervened in Bollux's combat.

But Atuarre had no intention of going back now; Solo-Captain specifically wanted her onboard the *Millennium Falcon*. She tried her most reasonable tone. "Officer, I have to pick up a very important item on my ship, then we can return. Please? It's very vital; that's why I was given clearance to go in the first place."

The Espo wasn't paying heed. He drew his side arm. "Orders say *at once*. Move it!"

The attention of the duty tech was aroused now, but the guard was the immediate danger. Atuarre held Pakka's paw high, so that his toes barely touched the floor, showing him to the guard. "You see, I was also told to leave my cub onboard ship. His presence displeased the Viceprex." She felt Pakka's short, elastic muscles tighten.

The Espo opened his mouth to reply, and she whipped the cub up. Pakka took snapping momentum from the launch, and both of the Trianii split the air with predatory howls, astounding the Authority men.

Pakka's dropkick caught the astonished Espo in the face and throat. Atuarre, coming in behind her cub, threw herself on the man's arm, prying his hand loose from his blaster. The Trianii bore their antagonist over backward, the cub with arms and legs and tail wrapped around the Espo's head and neck, Atuarre wrenching the blaster free.

She heard a scuffle of sound behind her. Whirling, she saw the duty tech half standing from his chair behind the console. His left forefinger was stabbing some button on his board, hard. She assumed it to be an alarm, but the tech's right hand was bringing up a blaster, and that was first on the agenda. She fired with the dispatch of a Trianii Ranger. The brief red flash of the blaster knocked the tech off his feet backward, overturning his chair.

The Espo, bleeding from his wounds, threw Pakka off and charged at Atuarre, hands clutching for her. She fired again, the red bolt lighting the junction station. The Espo buckled and lay still. She could hear alarms jangling through the tunnel-tube layout.

Atuarre was about to go to the junction station console, to disconnect the tunnel-tubes and cut off pursuit, when the station jolted on its treads, as if the surface of Mytus VII had surged up under it. She and Pakka were bounced in the air like toys by the tremors of an explosion of incredible force.

Atuarre picked herself up dazedly and staggered to one of the thick exterior observation ports. She couldn't see the tower. Instead, a column of incandescent fire had sprung up where Stars' End had stood. It seemed impossibly thin and high, reaching far up into the vacuous sky of Mytus VII.

Then she realized that the force of the explosion had been contained by deflector-shield generators around the tower. The pillar of destruction began to dissipate, but she could see nothing of Stars' End, not a fragment. She couldn't believe that even an exploding power plant could utterly vaporize the nearly impregnable tower.

Then, on some impulse, she looked up, beyond the tip of the explosion's flare. High above Mytus VII she saw the wink of the small distant sun off enhanced-bonding armor plate.

"Oh, Solo-Captain," she breathed, understanding what had happened, "you *madman*!"

She pushed herself away from the port unsteadily and assessed her situation. She must move without hesitation. She raced to the console, found separator switches, and matching them with indicators over the junction station's tunnel-tubes, worked the three not connected to the *Falcon*. The tubes disengaged, their lengths contracting back toward the junction, pleating in on themselves.

Then she brought the junction station's self-propulsion unit to life, setting its treads in motion, steering it toward the *Millennium Falcon*, gathering in the intervening tube length as she went.

She chilled the discord in her mind with the discipline expected of a Trianii Ranger, and a plan began to form. One minute later, the *Millennium Falcon* raised from Mytus VII.

Atuarre, at the controls with Pakka perched in the copilot's chair, scanned the base. She knew the personnel must be coping desperately with pressure droppages and air leaks through their ruptured systems. But the armed Espo assault ship had already boosted clear of the base; she could see its engine glowing as it climbed rapidly in the distance. That someone had comprehended what had happened and responded so quickly gave her one more worry. No more Authority ships must be allowed to lift off.

She guided the starship in a low pass at the line of smaller Authority vessels. The *Falcon*'s guns spoke again and again in a close strafing run. The parked, pilotless ships burst and flared one after another, yielding secondary explosions. Of the half-dozen craft there, none escaped damage. She swooped past the deep crater where Stars' End had once stood.

She opened the main drive, screaming off after the departed Espo assault craft. She kept all shields angled aft, but there was only sporadic, inaccurate turbo-laser cannon fire. The personnel at the base were too busy trying to keep the breath of life from bleeding off into the vacuum. That was one advantage, a small help to her in what seemed like a hopeless task.

Stars' End's anticoncussion field must very nearly have overloaded, Han thought; for the first seconds after the power plant blew, stupendous forces had been exerted on the tower and everything in it. But the immobilizing effect began to recede as the systems adjusted.

Smoke and heat from both the ruined Executioner and the now-defunct primary-control ancillaries rolled and drifted through the dome, choking and blinding. There was a universal rush of indistinct bodies for the elevators. Han could hear Hirken yelling for order as the Espo major bellowed commands and the Viceprex's wife and others shrilled in panic.

Han skirted the mob headed for the elevators, wading through the anticoncussion field and the drifting smoke. Like all standbys, the anticoncussion field fed off emergency power inside Stars' End. The tower's reserves would be limited. Han grinned in the murk and confusion; the Espos were in for a surprise.

He made his way down the steps of the amphitheater, groping along, coughing and hoping he wasn't being poisoned by burned insulation and molten circuitry. His toe hit something. He recognized Viceprex Hirken's discarded belt unit, kicked it aside, and went on. He located Bollux when he stumbled over the 'droid's foot.

"Captain sir!" Bollux hailed. "We'd thought you'd quite left, sir."

"We're bowing out now; can you make it?"

"I'm stabilized. Max improvised a direct linkup between himself and me."

Blue Max's voice drifted up from Bollux's chest. "Captain, I *tried* to tell you when I rechecked the figures that this might happen."

Han had gotten a hand under the 'droid's arm, helping him to rise to his wobbly legs. "What *did* happen, Max? Not enough power in the plant?" He started moving Bollux off unsteadily through the drifting reek.

"No, there was plenty of power in the plant, but the enhanced-bonding armor plate is a lot stronger than I thought at first. The exterior deflector shields contained the force of the explosion, all except the overhead one, the one that dissolved in the overload. All the force went that way. Us too."

Han stopped. He wished he could see the little computer, not that it would have helped. "Max, are you telling me we blew Stars' End into *orbit*?"

"No, Captain," Max answered darkly. "A high-arc trajectory, maybe, but never an orbit."

Han found himself leaning on Bollux as much as the 'droid was leaning on him. "Oh my! Why didn't you warn me?"

"I *tried*," Max reminded him sulkily.

Han was in mental overdrive. It made sense: Mytus VII's relatively light specific gravity and lack of atmospheric friction must give it an escape velocity that was only middlin'. Still, if the tower's anticoncussion fields hadn't been on when the large charge had gone off, everybody in Stars' End would've been colloidal slime by now.

"Besides," Max added testily, "Isn't this better than being dead? So far?"

Han brightened; there was no arguing with that logic. He shouldered part of Bollux's weight again. "Okay, men; I have a new plan. Forward!" They reeled off again, away from the elevators. "All the elevators will be out; life-support and whatnot will have pre-empted all the reserve power. I saw a utility stairwell in the floor plans, but Hirken and Company will be remembering it pretty soon, too. Shag it."

They rounded the curve of the utility core as Han took his bearings. They were almost to a yellow-painted emergency door when the door snapped open and an Espo jumped out, riot gun in hand. Cupping his hand to his mouth, the man called, "Viceprex Hirken! This way, sir!"

Then he noticed Han and Bollux and swung his weapon to bear. With only a microcharge in the blaster, Han had to make a quick head shot. The Espo dropped.

"Brown nose," Han grunted, still hanging on to the 'droid, stooping to grab the riot gun. He manhandled himself and his burden through the emergency door. A furor of shouting reached him; the others had found the elevators useless, and someone had remembered the stairwell. Han secured the door behind him and fired several sustained bursts at its latching mechanism. The metal began to glow and fuse. It was a durable alloy that would shed its heat again in moments, leaving the latch welded shut. Those remaining on the other side would be able to blast their way through with hand weapons, but it would take precious time.

As he and Han half fell, half ran, down the stairs, Bollux asked, "Where to now, sir?"

"The stasis-booth tiers." They careened around a landing, nearly falling. "Feel that? The artificial gravity's fluctuating. In time the power-management routers will cut off everything but life-support."

"Oh, I see, sir." Bollux said. "The stasis booths you and Max mentioned!"

"Give the 'droid a prize. When those booths start conking out, there're gonna be some pretty cranky prisoners on the loose. The guy who might be able to pull our choobies out of thc conflagration is one of them—Doc, Jessa's father."

They made their way down, past Hirken's living quarters and the interrogation levels, cncountering no one else in the stairwell. The gravity fluctuations lessened, but footing remained unpredictable. They arrived at another emergency door, and Han opened it manually.

Across a corridor was another door, which had been left open. Through it Han saw a long, wide aisle between high tiers of stasis booths like stacked, upright coffins. The lowest rows of booths were already darkened, empty, the highest still in operation. Booths in the middle two rows flickered.

But down in the aisles a line of six guards wavered before a mass of humans and nonhumans. The released prisoners, members of dozens of species, growled and roared their hostility. Fists, tentacles, claws, and paws shook angrily in the air. The Espos, waving their riot guns and advancing, tried to contain the break without firing, afraid they might be overwhelmed if they opened up.

A tall, demonish-looking being broke from the mob and launched himself at the Espos, his face splitting with mad laughter, hands grasping. A burst from a riot gun brought him down in a groaning heap. The prisoners' hesitation disappeared; they advanced on the Espos in unison. What did they have to fear from death, compared with life in the interrogation chambers?

Han pushed Bollux aside, knelt behind the emergency-door frame, and cut loose at the guards. Two of them fell before they realized they were taking fire from their rear. One turned, then another, to exchange shots, while their fellows tried to hold back the seething prisoners.

Red darts of light crisscrossed. Smoke from charred metal rose from the doorframe with the ozone of blaster fire. The smell of burned flesh was in the air. The unnerved guards' bolts zipped through the open emergency door or hit the wall, but failed to find their target. Han, kneeling to make himself as small a mark as possible, winced and flinched from the intense counterfire and cursed his own riot gun's poor sighting characteristics.

He finally nailed one of the two Espos shooting at him. The other dropped to the floor to avoid being hit. Han, seeing that, used an old trick. Reaching through the door frame, he placed his weapon flat on its side on the floor, triggering frantically. The shots, aligned directly along the plane of the floor, found the prone Espo and silenced him in seconds.

The remaining guards broke. One let his piece fall and raised his hands, but it did him no good; the mob poured over and around him like an avalanche, burying him in murderous human and alien forms. The other Espo, trapped between Han's sniping and the prisoners, started scaling one of the ladders connecting the catwalks along the tiers of stasis booths.

Partway up, the guard paused and shot those who had tried to follow him. Han's shots, at the wrong angle, missed. Han gathered up Bollux, headed for the tier room.

The last Espo's gunfire had made the prisoners draw back as he climbed for the third catwalk. From out of the pack of prisoners, three shaggy, simian creatures swarmed up after him, disdaining ladders, swinging up arm over long arm along the tiers' outerworks. They overtook the Espo in moments.

He hung from the rungs long enough to shoot one of the simians. It fell with an eerie caw. The other ape-things drew even with the Espo, one on either side. As he tried to fire again, his weapon was snatched from his hand and dropped to those below. The yowling guard was then caught up by both his arms, swung, and hurled with incredible strength straight upward. He slammed against the ceiling above the highest row of booths and fell to the floor in a windmilling of arms and legs, with an ugly sound of impact.

Han, setting Bollux aside, ran to join the milling prisoners. Overhead, more and more of the stasis booths were being shut down to power the overtaxed life-support systems, yielding inhabitants of many planets. Now that the immediate challenge of the guards had been eliminated, the recent escapees were at a loss. Many of them had been killed or wounded by the guards' fire, and many others were dead or dying, unwounded, because their physiologies weren't compatible with Stars' End's atmosphere and they hadn't entered stasis with their life-support equipment. Voices overbore one another: "Hey, where are—" "The gravity's funny! What's happ—" "What place is this?"

Han, yelling and waving, got their attention. "Grab those guns and take up positions in the stairwell! Espos will be finding their way here in a minute!" He spotted a man in the uniform of a planetary constabulary, probably a bothersome official the Authority had decided to put on ice. Han pointed to him. "Get them organized and set up defenses, or you'll all find yourself back in stasis!"

Han turned, heading for the corridor. As he passed the 'droid, he told him, "Wait here, Bollux; I've got to find Doc and Chewie."

As the prisoners scrambled for the fallen Espos' weapons, Han dashed into the connecting corridor, swung right, and headed for the next tier block. But as he closed on the next door, it snapped open, unlocked from the inside. Three Espos crowded, elbows and hips, each trying to be the first to get out of the tier block, as a pandemonium of fighting and shooting echoed from the room behind them.

The guards made it only halfway through the door. There was a deafening roar, and a familiar pair of long hairy arms reached out to gather all three of them back into the fray.

"Yo, there you are now," Han called happily. "Chewie!"

The Wookiee had finished draping the guards' limp forms over a nearby handrail. He saw his friend and hooted ecstatically. Han, his protestations ignored, was caught up in a comradely embrace that made his ribs creak. Then the artificial gravity waffled for a second and Chewbacca nearly fell. He let Han down.

"If we ever get out of this, partner," Han panted, "let's go settle down on a nice, quiet, stellar delivery route, what d'you say?"

This tier block had been taken with less trouble than the other; apparently fewer guards had been here when its stasis fields began to go. There was the same confusion, though, in a multitude of tongues and sound levels. The Wookiee, jostled into Han, turned with a truly stentorian roar, holding his fists aloft. A space cleared around him instantly. Into the interval of silence Han inserted the order that the prisoners take up what guns they had and join the other defenders.

Then he grabbed Chewbacca's shoulder. "C'mon, Doc's here somewhere, Chewie, and we haven't got long to find him. He's our only chance of coming out of this alive."

The two went on to the next tier block, of which there were five altogether, as Han recalled from the floor plan. They encountered a door already open. Han brought the riot gun up and peered cautiously into the chamber. Its stasis booths were empty, and a disturbing silence hung over all. Han wondered if, perhaps, the Authority hadn't gotten to use this portion of its prison yet. He stepped into the tier block; Chewbacca followed after.

"Stand where you are!" ordered a voice behind them. Men and other creatures jumped up from concealment on the catwalks and outerworks, and along the walls. More appeared from around the bend in the corridor.

But both Han and his first mate had identified the voice that had commanded them. "Doc!" Han cried, though he and the Wookiee prudently held their places. No use being fried.

The old man, his head wreathed by a white, frizzy cloud of hair, blinked at them in utter surprise. "Han Solo! What in the name of the Original Light brings you here, son? But I suppose that's obvious: two more inmates, eh?" He faced the others. "This pair's okay."

He trotted over to them. Han was shaking his head, "No, Doc. Chewie was here. A few of us came to see what we—"

Doc hushed him. "More important things to get to, youngster. All these tiers in the first three rooms went at once; that's how we took the blocks so quickly. The demands on the systems must've been extraordinary; and now I notice the gravity's unstable."

Three tier blocks going all at once figured, Han thought,

what with that first giant demand placed on the anticoncussion fields when the power plant went. "Uh, yeah, Doc. I meant to mention that. You know you're in a tower, right? Well, I, I sort of blew it into space; overloaded the power plant and cut the overhead deflector shield so that—"

Doc clapped a hand over his eyes. "Han, you *imbecile*!"

Han became defensive. "You don't like it? Climb back into your shipping crate!" He saw he'd made his point. "No time to argue; there's no way Stars' End can make it all the way out of Mytus VII's gravity. We're due for a crash, and I'm not sure how soon. The only thing that'll save us is that anticoncussion field, and it's faded. It's up to you to make sure it's juiced up when we hit."

Doc was staring at Han with his mouth open. "Sonny, energizing an anticoncussion field is *not* like hot-wiring somebody's skyhopper and going for a joy-ride!"

Han threw his hands up. "Fine; let's just sit and wait to smash ourselves flat. Jessa can always adopt a new father."

That struck home. Doc sighed. "You're right; if it's our one shot, we shall take it. But I don't think much of your taste in jailbreaks." He turned to the others, who had been kept from intruding in the conversation only because of Chewbacca's looming presence. "Pay attention! No time for chatting! Come with me, and do as I say, and we may make it yet; at least I can promise you an end to interrogation."

He elbowed Han. "Blaze of glory, and all that, eh?" Then he started off at the head of a shuffling, loping, hoof-clacking horde, each individual moving on whatever extremities or in whatever fashion was his.

As they went, Han rapidly told Doc the bare bones of the story. The old man interrupted: "This Trianii is onboard the *Millennium Falcon*?"

"Should be, but it won't do us much good; the *Falcon*'s tractors could never hold back this tower from re-entry."

Doc stopped. "I say, did you hear something, boy?"

They all had, the mew and crackle of blaster fire. They broke into a run. For all his apparent age, Doc kept up with the pilot and the Wookiee. They reached the emergency door just as the limp body of a prisoner was passed into the corridor from the stairwell. It was a gangling, saurian creature with a blaster burn in its midsection. From the stairwell came the irregular sounds of a firefight.

"What's going on?" Han shouted, trying to elbow his way through. Chewbacca got in front, shoving and yelping, and opened a way. The prisoner who Han had arbitrarily put in charge appeared on the stairs. "We're holding an upper landing. There are a number of Authority people up there, trying to fight their way down. I put some lookouts on the lower stairs, but nothing's happened down there yet."

"Hirken and his bunch are trying to make their way down because the air locks are located here and on the lowest level. He's hoping for a rescue," Han told them.

Doc and the others looked at him in surprise. He remembered that Stars' End must be largely unknown territory to them. The constabulary officer asked, "Just what's happened?"

"Our time's running out, is what," Han answered. "We have to hold up here and give Doc there a chance to get down to the engineering levels. Take whoever's armed on point; there'll be some resistance down there, but it ought to be light. The rest can follow at a distance."

The expedition down the stairwell began, with Doc hurrying because none of them knew when the tower would hit its apogee and begin its plummeting descent.

Meanwhile, Han and Chewbacca dashed upstairs. Han felt himself breathing hard and understood that life-support systems were beginning to fail. If the oxygen pressure in the tower fell too low, all their efforts would mean nothing.

They joined the defenders holding the second landing above the tier blocks. Blaster beams from above sizzled and crashed against the opposite wall as the remaining armed prisoners here fired quick, unaimed shots around the corner when they could, with little chance of hitting anyone up on the next landing. Several defenders lay dead or injured. As

Han topped the stairs, one man edged his weapon around the corner, quickly squeezed off a few shots, and drew back hastily. He spied Han. "What's going on down there?"

Han crouched beside him and was about to ease around the corner for a squint upstairs when a volley of red bolts burned and bit at the floor and walls out in the field of fire. He shrank back.

"Get your damn bulb down, man," the defender cautioned. "We ran into their point men right here at the turn. We drove them back, but the rest came down. It's a standoff, but they have more weapons." Then he repeated, "What's going on below?"

"The others are headed for the lower levels, to rig a, a way out of this. We're here to keep the riffraff out." He began to sweat, thinking that the tower must surely be succumbing to the pull of Mytus VII by now.

The steady salvos from the next landing lit the stairwell. Chewbacca, checking it out with narrowed eyes, gobbled something to Han.

"My pal's right," Han told the other defenders. "See all the incoming bolts? They're hitting the far wall and the other side of the floor, and that's all, nothing on this side."

He slid around on the seat of his pants, cradling the riot gun high across his chest. Chewbacca braced Han's knees solidly to the floor. Han squirmed back on his buttocks, centimeter by centimeter, until his back was almost into the line of fire.

He and Chewbacca traded looks. The man's was rueful, the Wookiee's concerned. "Hang it out."

Han let himself fall backward. The riot gun, clamped across his chest, pointed straight upstairs. Still dropping, he saw what he'd expected. A man in Espo brown was stealing down the stairs, hugging the near wall to avoid his covering fire. The scene burned into Han's mind with an abrupt, almost painful clarity as he cut loose with a flurry of shots. Without waiting to see their effect, he leaned up again, long before his back could touch the floor. Chewbacca felt the move, pulled hard. Han came sliding to safety; his pop-up appearance had begun and ended so suddenly that nobody upstairs had managed to redirect his aim.

There was a rapid clattering on the stairs, and an Espo-issue side arm spun to a stop on the landing. A moment later, with a weighty bouncing, the pistol's owner rolled to a halt next to it, more than adequately dead. It was the Espo major.

Han nodded in tribute to the major's devotion to duty.

The barrage from the next landing became more intense. The defenders answered with what weapons they had. Chewbacca picked up a pistol dropped by one of the fallen defenders, a feathered creature lying in a pool of translucent blood. The corpse's beaked face had been partly obliterated by a blaster shot. The Wookiee found that the barrel of the pistol had been hit, and was twisted and useless.

Chewbacca, pointing at Han's empty, holstered blaster, threw him the unusable gun. Han threw back the riot gun in exchange and drew his own side arm, to charge it from the ruined pistol. Chewbacca, whose thick fingers didn't fit the human-sized weapon well, tore off the trigger guard, then began firing around the corner without looking—high, low, and in between, at every angle.

Han mated the adapters in the pistol's grip to those in his own blaster's power pack, just forward of the trigger guard. He wound up with only half-charge capacity, but it would have to do. Finished, he tossed the useless Espo pistol aside and joined the Wookiee. To frustrate counterfire, the two fired unpredictably, and they could be very unpredictable indeed. None of the Authority people seemed to want to emulate the major's heroism.

Suddenly the firing from above stopped. The defenders also stopped, watching for a trick. It occurred to Han that if Hirken had even one shock-grenade—but no; he'd have used it already.

A flat, hissing voice called down, "Solo! Viceprex Hirken would speak with you!"

Han leaned back against the wall nonchalantly. Without

showing himself, he answered, "Send him down, Uul-Rha-Shan. What the hell, come on down yourself, old snake! Happy to oblige."

Then came Hirken's strong-sales-experience voice. "We'll talk from here, thanks. I know now just what it was you did."

Han wished to himself he'd known, too, beforehand. "I want to strike a bargain," Hirken went on. "However you're planning on getting away, I want you to take me with you. And the others with me, of course."

Of course. Han didn't even hesitate. "You got it. Throw your guns down here and come down one at a time, hands on your—"

"Be serious, Solo!" Hirken interrupted, depriving Han of the chance to tell him where to put his hands. "We can keep you occupied here so that you won't be able to get out yourself! And Stars' End is at the top of its arc; we've seen that much through the dome. It'll be too late soon for any of us. What do you say to that?"

"No way, Hirken!" Han wasn't sure whether Hirken was bluffing about the tower's having reached apogee, but there was no way to check it short of leaning out one of the locks—a poor idea in view of the scarcity of spacesuits. "Hirken's dead center about one thing," he whispered. "They *could* pin us here if we let them make the rules."

The others followed him quickly down to the next landing, the last one before the tier-block level. They slipped around the corner and took up positions, waiting. Now it'd be the Viceprex's turn to sweat. From what Han could hear, it sounded like the majority of the prisoners were still in the tier blocks, unsure of what they should do. Han just hoped they wouldn't panic and come his way.

He had his blaster raised, knowing a questing head must come around the corner they'd abandoned, but it was impossible to anticipate exactly when it would come.

A head did flick around the corner, Uul-Rha-Shan's, high up; he'd stood on someone else's back or shoulders. He flashed out, saw the disposition of the defenders, and pulled back with astounding speed. Han's tardy shot merely chipped a little more wall away; the pilot marveled at how quickly the reptilian gunman had moved.

"Is that how it is to be, Solo," came Uul-Rha-Shan's hypnotic voice. "Must I hunt you from level to level? Strike a bargain with us; we only desire to live."

Han laughed. "Sure, it's just everybody *else* that you *don't* want to live."

There was a noise from below, boots on the stairs. Doc reappeared, puffing. He threw himself down next to Han, his face composed in alarm. Han hand-signaled him to speak quietly so that those above wouldn't hear.

"Han, the Espos have come! Their assault craft is at the lower lock, unloading a strike force. They've linked up with the Authority people who were hiding from us down there. They drove us off the engineering levels; many were shot, and we were forced back. More died on the stairs before a rear guard was organized, but the Espos are pushing a heavy blaster up, step by step. We're in it where it's deep, this time!"

A stream of prisoners was already pouring frantically up the stairwell, bound for the only shelter left, the tier blocks. "The Espos down there have spacesuits on," Doc said. "What if they bleed off our air?"

Han abruptly saw that the men around him were looking to him for an answer, and thought, *Who, me?* I'm just the getaway driver, remember?

He shook his head. "I'm tapped out, Doc. Get yourself some machinery; we'll play them one last chorus."

Hirken's voice boomed down triumphantly. "Solo! My men just contacted me by com-link! Surrender now, or I'll leave you here!" As if to emphasize that, they heard the oscillation of a heavy blaster somewhere in Stars' End.

"Well, they'll still have to come through to us," Han muttered. He grabbed Doc's shirt, but recalling Hirken, spoke in a low, hard tone. "Don't sweat the air; the Espos can't bleed it off or they'll kill their Viceprex. That's why they hit the lower lock instead of the one at prisoner level; they knew they'd have a much better chance of getting in without having to burn and rupture the tower. Send up everyone you can, anyone who'll come. We'll rush Hirken, whatever it costs, and use him as a hostage."

Remembering the barrage the Authority people could lay down in the narrow stairwell, he knew that the price would be terrible. Doc did, too, and pushed himself off looking, for the first time, like the very tired old man he finally felt himself to be.

"Don't stop for anything," Han was telling the others. "If somebody falls, somebody else grabs his machinery, but *nobody stops*."

He caught Chewbacca's eye. The Wookiee peeled back his lips from his curved fangs, scrunching his black nose, and sounded a savage, appalling howl, shaking his shaggy head—a Wookiee's way of defying death. Then he grinned and rumbled at Han, who smiled lopsidedly. They were close enough friends not to have to make any more of it than that.

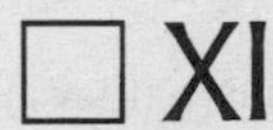

MORE inmates had come up to the landing, but they were unarmed. Han repeated instructions about weapons and not stopping. His heart pounded when he thought how concentrated the energy beams would be in that stairwell. Goodbye, Old Spacemen's Home.

He rose to a half crouch, and the others emulated him. "Chewie and me first, to lay down a cover. On three; one, two"—he edged to the corner—"th—"

A small, furry form, vaulting over those behind Han, landed on his shoulders, tugging at his neck. Its limber tail looped out to encircle the surprised Chewbacca's wrist.

Han staggered, valor forgotten. "What the flying—" He identified his assailant. *"Pakka!"*

The cub swung down from Hans's neck, bouncing up and down urgently, tugging at his leg. For a moment no fact seemed reliable. "Pakka, didn't you, I mean where's Atuarre? Dammit, kid, how'd you get here?" He remembered then that the cub couldn't answer.

Doc was shouting from below. "Solo, get down here!"

"Sit on things here; don't charge and don't fall back unless you have to," Han told Chewbacca. He pressed through his troops and raced down the stairs, trailing the fleet Pakka. Inside the emergency door leading to the tier blocks, he slid to a halt. *"Atuarre!"*

She was surrounded by Doc and the other prisoners. "Solo-Captain!" She seized his hands, her words tumbling out on top of one another. She'd brought in the *Millennium*

Falcon and clamped onto the cargo lock here at the tier-block level, on the opposite side of the tower from the Espo assault ship.

"I don't think they noticed me; energy fluxes in Stars' End are distorting sensors completely. I had to link up purely by visual tracking."

Han drew Doc and Atuarre aside. "We could never, never fit all these people into the *Falcon*, not if we use every cubic centimeter of space. How do we tell them?"

The Trianii broke in. "Solo-Captain, *shut up!* Please. And listen: I have a tunnel-tube junction station secured to the *Falcon*. I drove it right up against the ship and made it fast with a tractor beam."

"We can certainly fit inmates in the tunnel-tubes if we extend them," Doc began.

Hans's excited voice overbore him. "We'll do better than that. Atuarre, you're a genius! But will the tunnel-tube reach?"

"It should."

Doc was looking from one to the other. "What are you two— Oh! I *see*!" He rubbed his hands together, eyes bright. "This will be novel, for a fact."

One of the defenders from the upper landing poked his head through the emergency door. "Solo, the Viceprex is calling for you again."

"If I don't answer, he'll know something's doing. I'll send Chewie down to help you. Work fast!"

"Solo-Captain, we have only minutes remaining!"

He bounded up the stairs, though it left him huffing and heaving, and threatened to black him out. Air's going, he thought. In hushed tones he explained everything quickly and dispatched the Wookiee and most of the others down to join Atuarre and Doc.

Then he answered Hirken. The Viceprex shouted, "Time's short, Solo. Will you yield?"

"Yield?" Han sputtered, unbelieving. "What d'you have in mind, defloration?" He pegged a shot around the corner, beginning a steady harassing fire, and hoped that those below could hold the Espo assault team for the required time.

Ninety seconds later a cycling light came on over one of the unused stern air locks of the Authority assault craft. No one was there to notice, because, except for a skeleton watch, the entire ship's complement had been turned out to rescue the Viceprex, at his order.

The lock opened. Through it stepped a very incensed Wookiee, hefting a captured wide-bore blaster. He was pleased, however, that he hadn't been compelled to waste time and power burning through the lock doors. He'd secured the outer hatch open. Behind him, floating in the weightlessness of the extended tunnel-tube, were more prisoners, waiting with weapons and with claws and stingers and pincers and bare, eager hands. Even farther back, at the junction station, other prisoners were being crowded aboard the *Falcon*, while more waited to leave the tower. Since the freighter could never hold them all, this ship had to be captured.

Chewbacca gave a hand motion and set off. The others drew themselves in after, touching down as they entered the assault craft's artificial gravity.

The lock's opening had been noted on the bridge. An Espo crewman, coming to check out what he thought would be a malfunction in the air-lock apparatus, rounded a corner and almost fetched up against the Wookiee's enormous, furry-haired torso. A stroke of the blaster's butt sent the Espo flying back through the air. He landed in a brown-clad heap, his helmet skittering along the deck.

Another Espo, down a side passageway, heard the noise and came running, tugging at his holstered pistol. Chewbacca stepped out of concealment and swung the blaster's stovepipe barrel, downing him. As prisoners rushed to pick up the felled men's weapons, Chewbacca led the rest on, past engineering and crew's quarters, as small parties split off from the main group to take and hold those areas. More and more prisoners poured from the aft lock, making way quickly for the many who were to follow.

The Wookiee came to the hatch of the ship's bridge. He hit its release and, as the hatch slid up, stepped through. A junior officer did a foolish double take and fumbled for his pistol, saying, "How in—"

Chewbacca struck the officer down with a giant forearm, then threw his head back and roared. Those behind him surged into the bridge. Little of the fighting done in the next twelve seconds was with artificial weapons. None of the bridge watch ever reached an alarm button.

Setting the wide-bore aside, Chewbacca prepared to cast off from Stars' End.

Atuarre watched anxiously as she and a few chosen helpers in the big tier-level cargo lock almost threw milling prisoners into the tunnel-tube, where they thrashed like swimmers, moving and helping one another toward the junction station. Doc had already gone ahead to take the *Falcon*'s controls. As soon as Chewbacca had control of the assault craft, he was to free it gently from the tower so that it couldn't be retaken, and the Espos' withdrawal route would be cut off.

So many! Atuarre thought, hoping there'd be room enough for all of them. Then she saw a familiar face in the crowd and abandoned her place, keening with joy.

Pakka came, too, and clung to his father's back, holding on to both his parents for the first time in months, his wide eyes tearing.

Just then, Stars' End's general power conduits, weakened by erratic flow management, began to explode.

Up on the landing, Han heard it, the beginning of Stars' End's death throes. He was holding with three others, all of them armed. Hirken's people had been quiet for the last few minutes; the Viceprex was probably hoping that relief wasn't far off. And he could be right, since Espo assault troops were working their way up through the tower quickly, mowing down the prisoners' opposition.

But the exploding conduits constituted a new factor. Han ordered everybody back. "We'll hold at the tier-block level; pass the word below to come running." They could pull back to the air lock, which lay beyond the fifth tier block, if they had to.

He fired a few more shots up the stairwell as his runner took off. He tried to figure out how long it had been since the tower had been blown free. Twenty minutes? More? They were asking a great deal of their luck.

As Han and his men fell back, the clatter of the lower-level defenders was heard. Both groups met at the emergency door leading to the tier blocks and crowded through. Han, among the last, turned to give the man behind him a hand, only to see him die with an odd, disappointed look on his face.

Han pulled the falling body out of the way as the final prisoner leaped through. Several others helped him shoulder the ponderous door shut as blaster and disrupter fire lashed against it, and made it fast with scraps of metal jammed in the latch. But it wouldn't hold long, especially if the heavy crew-served blaster were brought up. Han surveyed the prisoners with him. "How many left to load?"

"Almost done, fella," someone called. "Just a few left, not more than a hundred or so."

"Then anybody who's not armed, hat up! The rest spread out and take up a firing position. We're almost home."

They were still moving down the corridor when the emergency door crumpled inward, burned from its frame in a rain of glowing slag. The snout of the crew-served blaster stood in the gap, pointing straight into the abandoned first-tier block. Han didn't bother firing at its shielded barrel.

The heavy blaster erupted into the empty tier block, and an armored Espo came worming around it to enter the corridor. One of the prisoners stopped long enough to shoot him. At the curve in the corridor, the defenders paused to take up firing again. The gunners were having trouble getting their piece through the emergency door without exposing themselves to counterfire.

Han and three others were the only ones left; a few prisoners had gone on to set up a new line of defense. Smoke from ruptured power conduits was getting thicker, the air thinner. Han's senses strayed for a moment. He was opposite the door to the second tier block and crossed to it, bent over double, for a better field of fire.

But he spied something propped up against one of the stasis booths, halfway down the tier's aisle. "Bollux, what the hell are you doing there?" Evidently the 'droid either had been dragged or had managed to drag himself this far toward the air lock, then had been shunted aside, and pausing in the shelter of the tier block for a moment, was unable to rise again. Han realized that no prisoner in fear of his life would have taken time to worry about an antiquated labor 'droid.

He ran to his side and dropped to one knee. "Up and at 'em, Annihilator. We're beatin' feet."

It took all his strength to get the 'droid up. "Thank you, Captain Solo," Bollux drawled. "Even with Max in direct linkage, I couldn't— *Captain!*"

Simultaneously with the 'droid's warning, Han felt Bollux throw all his mechanical weight against him, sending the two of them spinning around. In the same stopped frame, as it seemed, a disrupter beam meant for Han sliced into the 'droid's head.

As they spun, Han's draw was automatic. In that frozen instant, he saw Uul-Rha-Shan standing in the door frame at the head of the aisle, the bodies of the other defenders on the corridor floor behind him.

The reptilian gunman had his weapon held at arm's length, knowing that his first shot had missed. The disrupter pistol was realigning. Han, with no time to aim, fired from the hip. Everything seemed to him to take forever, and yet to happen instantly.

The blaster bolt flowered high against Uul-Rha-Shan's

green-scaled chest, lifting him and hurling him backward, while his own disrupter shot lanced upward and splashed off the ceiling.

Han and Bollux were sprawled together on the floor. There was no light in the 'droid's photoreceptors, no evidence of function. Han rose shakily, locked the fingers of his left hand around Bollux's shoulder pauldron, holding on to his blaster with his right, and began hauling, heaving for breath.

He never saw the Espos who, following in Uul-Rha-Shan's wake, were ready to cut him down. Nor did he see them fall, downed by the fire from the prisoners' counterattack. Han's lightheadedness had narrowed his vision down to a dark tunnel; through the tunnel he would drag Bollux back to the *Falcon*, nothing less.

Suddenly another figure was at his side, a furred and sinuous Trianii Ranger, bearing a smoking blaster. "Solo-Captain?" It was a male's voice. "Come, I will aid you. We have but seconds."

Han let the other do so, both of them tugging the 'droid's hulk along much more quickly. Dull curiosity made Han ask, "Why?"

"Because my mate, Atuarre, said not to bother coming back without you, and because my cub, Pakka, would have come if I had not." The Trianii called out, "Here, I've found him!"

Others arrived, to give supporting fire, throwing the Espos into a brief confusion. The assaulting troops, not having gotten their heavy blaster into the corridor yet, fell back. More willing hands dragged at Bollux.

Then, somehow, they were all standing at the air lock, and the Espos seemed to have broken off their attack. The 'droid was floated into the tunnel-tube, along with the other defenders and Atuarre's mate. Only then did Han enter the air lock, leaving behind a strangely silent chamber. The fresher, thicker air of the tube hit him like a drug. He waved the rest on. The *Millennium Falcon* was still his ship, and he would be the one to cast off.

"Solo, wait!" A man stumbled out of the smoke. Viceprex Hirken, looking a century older. He spoke with hysterical speed.

"Solo, I know they've moved the assault ship away from the lower lock. I told no one, not even my wife. I ordered the Espos back and came in by myself."

He shuffled closer, hands imploring. Han stared at the Vice-President for Corporate Security as if he were a specimen under a scope.

"Please take me, Solo! Do anything-anything-anything to me, but don't leave me here to—"

Hirken's handsome face jumped, as if he'd forgotten what he was about to say, then he fell, squirming and reaching uselessly for the wound in his back. His obese wife came waddling up behind him with Espos at her back and a smoking pistol in her hands.

Han had already hit the inner air-lock hatch closure. He dived through the outer, into the tunnel-tube, hitting that switch, too. As the outer air-lock hatch closed, he irised the tunnel-tube shut, released its seal with an outgushing of air, and unclamped the tube. He floated there, watching through a viewport as Hirken's wife and the Espos beat at the air lock's outer-hatch viewport, unavailingly. Stars' End's descent speed had already drawn it away, and it plunged deeper into the planet's gravity well.

Around him he could see and hear the wobble of the tunnel-tube as packed prisoners were gradually absorbed into the assault craft and the *Millennium Falcon*.

Everyone in the two ships and the tunnel-tubes was so busy crowding elbow to pseudopod, or helping the injured or the dying, that only one survivor thought to watch the tower's fall.

As his mother and Doc labored over the *Falcon*'s controls, conning the freighter under its extreme burden and maintaining tractor-grip on the junction station, Pakka hung from an overhead conduit in the cockpit, the only one with both an unoccupied mind and a vantage point.

The cub stared down at Stars' End's descent, the flawless trajectory of an airless world. And even the sudden, brilliant flash of its impact didn't distract the others, who had lives to worry about. But Pakka, unblinking, unspeaking, saw the symbol of Authority flare and die with the brevity of a meteor.

The wind pulled hard across the landing field on Urdur, a no-nonsense wind, chilling, biting, but fresh and free. The former inmates of Stars' End, those who had lived to reach this latest outlaw-tech base, breathed it without complaint as they were herded off to temporary quarters.

But Han still pulled his borrowed greatcoat tighter around him. "I'm not arguing," he argued. "I just don't understand, is all." He was addressing Doc, but Jessa was listening, as were Pakka, Atuarre, and her mate, Keeheen.

Nearby rested the *Falcon*, the tunnel-tube junction still clamped to her side, and the Espo assault craft. Doc had guided both stuffy, overcrowded ships into quick contact with Jessa, and they'd been directed to this latest hide-out world.

Chewbacca was still onboard the *Falcon*, surveying the damage done to her since the last time he'd seen her. A new *yaup* of inconsolable sadness echoed from the ship each time he found another item of damage.

Doc, rather than reiterate his explanation, said, "Youngster, check the 'droid out for yourself. There." Outlaw-techs were just offloading Bollux's mutilated, beam-scorched form from the ship. An entire segment of his cranium had been shot away by Uul-Rha-Shan. At Doc's order, his men brought over the repulsor-lift handtruck with the 'droid strapped to it. With force bars and pinch-jacks, they prized open the plastron.

And there sat Blue Max, unscathed, running off his own power pack. Han leaned over him. "Uh, Maxie?"

The computer's voice still sounded like a child's. "Captain Solo! Long time no see. In fact, long time no see anything."

"Gotcha. Sorry; things were really jumping this trip. Is Bollux in there with you for a fact?"

In response, he heard the unhurried drawl of the labor 'droid coming from Max's grille, sounding strangely high-pitched through the vocoder. "Right enough, Skipper. Blue Max was in direct link with me when the disrupter hit me. He pulled all my essential information and basic matrices down here, safe and sound with him, in microseconds. Imagine that? Naturally, I've lost a lot of specifics, but I guess I can always relearn camp sanitation procedures if I have to." The voice became dejected. "I suppose my body's unsalvageable, though."

"We'll get you a new one, Bollux," Doc promised. "One for both of you, a custom puff; you have my word. But now you have to go; my boys will make sure all that circuitry in there remains stable."

"Bollux," Han said, and found himself with nothing to say. He hit that problem from time to time. "Take it slow."

"I always do," the vocoder drawled.

"G'bye, Captain Solo!" Blue Max added.

Jessa, shading her eyes, pointed to the assault craft. "There's a problem we won't solve in the shop."

A dark-skinned figure sat by the ship's ramp, head bent to his chest. "He took his uncle's death pretty hard," Jessa continued. "Rekkon was quite a man; losing him would be hard on anybody." She looked to Han. Han was studiously looking elsewhere. He saw the boy's head come up from his private grief; he bore a startling resemblance to Rekkon.

"What do we do with him?" Jessa went on. "Most of the prisoners will find a new life somehow, even Torm's father and brother. The majority of them will leave the Corporate Sector; a few hotheads plan to take it to the courts, as if they had a prayer. But the boy's by far the youngest you rescued, and he's got no one now."

She was watching her father expectantly. Doc's eyebrows shot up. "Don't goggle at me, girlie. I'm a certified businessman and criminal. I don't collect strays."

She giggled. "But you never turn them away, either. And you always say there's always room for one more at the table, we'll just—"

"—scramble the eggs," he anticipated her, "and water the soup. I know. Well, I suppose I could at least talk to the lad. He might have some usable aptitude, hmm, yes. Atuarre, you worked with his uncle quite closely; would you mind coming with me?"

Doc went off with all three Trianii at his side. Pakka turned and flipped Han a parting wave, his other pawhand caught up in his father's.

Jessa looked at Han. "Well, Solo, thanks. See you around." She turned to go.

He couldn't stifle an involuntary *"Hey!"* She turned back with a cant to her head that let him know he'd have to talk fast. Which he did. "I put my life—my one and precious life, mind you—on the line for your father—"

"—and all those other fine people," she cut in, "including your good friend Chewie—"

"—and went through a couple of types of hair-raising situations, and all you have to say is *thanks*?"

She evinced shock. "Why, you only carried out your part of our deal. And I carried out mine. What else did you expect, a parade?"

He glared at her, hoping she'd wither from his gaze. She didn't. He spun on his toe and headed for the *Falcon*'s ramp with long strides. "You win! Women, hah! I've got the whole galaxy, sweetheart, the whole galaxy. Who needs this?"

She caught up, whirled him around. Jessa looked good even in cold-weather gear. "Numbskull! What's wrong with striking another deal?"

His brow furrowed. I am somehow slipping into something tricky here, he thought, but I can't quite see what. "What kind of deal?"

She considered it, looking him over. "What are your plans? Are you going to join this campaign against the Authority? Or clear out of this part of space?"

He looked up, sighing. "You should know better than that. Rob 'em blind, that's my kind of revenge."

Jessa leaned around him and called up into the ship: "Hey, Chewie, how'd you like an all-new guidance system? And a complete overhaul?"

The Wookiee's delighted honks, preceding his appearance at the ramp, sounded like a happy foghorn. Jessa finished cheerily, "And to show you what a sport I am, boys, I'll throw in some body work, repair all minor hull damage. I'll reroute the ducting in the cockpit, too; get all those conduits and other head-knockers out of your way."

Chewbacca was close to tears of joy. He threw his hairy arm around the *Falcon*'s landing gear and gave it a wet Wookiee kiss.

Jessa said, "See, Solo? It's easy when you're the boss's daughter."

He was flummoxed. "Jess, what am I supposed to offer?"

She slipped her arm through his, grinning slyly. "What've you got, Han?" She led him away, ignoring his objections. His outbursts became fewer as the pair walked across the landing field toward the distant buildings. Halfway there, Chewbacca saw, Han held his greatcoat open so that she could slip into it, safe from the bitter winds of Urdur, though her own suit was quite well insulated.

Leaning casually on the *Falcon*, the Wookiee watched them go, and thought about what he and Han Solo could do with a ship milled and tuned fine by the full resources of the outlaw-techs. His muzzle wrinkled back from his fangs. He was glad for the breather they'd have here on Urdur.

But after that, everybody had best hang on to his cash with both hands.

HAN SOLO'S REVENGE

For Cargo-master-apprentice Dane Thorson, Chief Scout Adam Reith, Jason dinAlt, Jame Retief of the *Corps Diplomatique Terrestrienne* and all others of that rare stripe

And who are they anyway, these so-called free traders and independent spacers? Rogues, scoundrels, and worse! The common slangtalk term "freighter bums" is more applicable, surely. Beware to the shipper who would entrust them with cargo; woe to the being who books passage with them!

At best, they are feckless ruffians whose unconscionable social values allow them to undercut the fee rates of established, reliable companies. More often, they're con artists, frauds, tariff-dodgers and, yes, even smugglers!

Is any rascal with a spacecraft to be entrusted with your livelihood? Overhead, administrative apparatus, and managerial proprieties—these are the best guaranties of a dependable business arrangement!

(Excerpted from Public Service Message #122267-50, sponsored by the Corporate Sector Authority)

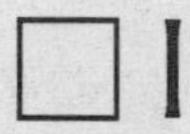

I

"CHEWIE, hey, I've got it!"

Han Solo's happy shout surprised Chewbacca so much that the towering Wookiee straightened involuntarily. Since he'd been hunkered down under the belly of the starship *Millennium Falcon* welding her hull with a plasma torch, he bumped his shaggy head against her with a resounding gong.

Snapping off the torch and letting its superheated field die, the Wookiee tore off his welding mask and threw it at his friend. Han, knowing Chewbacca's temper, skidded to a stop and ducked with the reflexes of a seasoned star pilot as the heavy mask zipped by overhead. He took a step backward as Chewbacca stalked out from under the grounded *Falcon* into the brilliant light of Kamar's white sun. Making temporary repairs on the damaged ship had brought the Wookiee peevishly close to mayhem.

Han pulled off his wraparound sun visor and grinned, raising his free hand to ward off his copilot's pique.

"Hold on, hold it. We've got a new holofeature; Sonniod just brought it." To prove it, Han held up the cube of clear material. Chewbacca forgot his anger for the moment and made a lowing, interrogative sound.

"It's some kind of musical story or something," Han replied. "The customers probably won't understand this one either, but are we going to pack them in now! Music, singing, dancing!"

Han, waving the cube, beamed happily over their good fortune. He still retained a good deal of the ranginess of youth, but combined it with much of the confidence of maturity. He had shucked his vest in the heat of Kamar, and his sweat-stained pullover shirt clung to his chest and back. He wore high spaceman's boots and military-cut trousers with red piping on their seams. At his side was a constant companion, a custom-made blaster that was fitted with a rear-mounted macroscope. Its front sight blade had been filed off with the speeddraw in mind. Han wore it low and tied down at his right thigh in a holster that had been cut away to expose his sidearm's trigger and trigger guard.

"Chewie, we're gonna be pulling in customers from all over the Badlands!"

With a noncommittal grunt Chewbacca went to pick up the fallen plasma torch. Kamar's sun was lowering at the horizon, and he'd done just about all he could to make the ship spaceworthy anyway.

He was large, even for a Wookiee—an immense, shambling man-shaped creature with radiant blue eyes and a luxurious red-gold-brown pelt. He had a bulbous black nose and a quick, fang-filled smile; he was gentle with those whom he liked and utterly ferocious toward anyone who provoked him. There were few of his own species to whom Chewbacca was as close as to Han Solo, and the Wookiee was, in turn, Han's only true friend in a very big galaxy.

Gathering his equipment, Chewbacca trudged back out from under the ship.

"Leave that stuff," Han enjoined him. "Sonniod's coming by to say hello." He indicated Sonniod's ship, a light cargo job, parked on her sandskid-mounted landing gear some distance out on the flats. As he had been close to the blast of his plasma torch, Chewbacca hadn't even heard the landing.

Sonniod, a compact, gray-haired little man with a cocksure walk and a rakish tilt to his shapeless red bag of a hat, was approaching slowly behind Han. He took in the *Falcon*'s temporary resting place with an amused eye, being a former smuggler and bootlegger. One of the fastest smuggling ships in space, she looked out of place here in the middle of the Kamar Badlands, with little to see in any direction but sand, parched hills, miser-plants, barrel-scrub, and sting-brush. The hot white sun of Kamar was lowering and soon, Sonniod knew, night scavengers would be leaving their burrows and dens. The thought of digworms, bloodsniffers, nightswifts, and hunting packs of howlrunners made him shiver a little; Sonniod hated crawly things. He waved and called a greeting to Chewbacca, whom he'd always liked. The Wookiee returned the wave offhandedly, booming a friendly welcome in his own tongue while ascending the ramp to stow his welding equipment and run a test on his repair work.

The *Millennium Falcon* sat on her triangle of landing gear near a natural open-air amphitheater. The encircling slopes showed the prints and tail scuffs left on previous occasions by the Badlanders. Down in the middle of the depression the stubborn plantlife of Kamar had been cleared away. There rested a mass-audience holoprojector, a commercial model that resembled in size and shape a small spacecraft's control console.

"I got word that you wanted a holofeature, any holofeature," Sonniod remarked, following Han down the side of the bowl. "*Love is Waiting* was all I could find on short notice."

"It'll do fine, just fine," Han assured him, fitting the cube into its niche in the projector. "These simpletons'll watch anything. I've been running the only holo I had, a travelogue, for the past eleven nights. They still keep coming back to gawk at it."

The sun was ready to set and dusk would come rapidly; this part of the Badlands was close to Kamar's equator. Removing the sweatband he'd been wearing around his forehead, Han bent over the holoprojector. "Everything checks out; we have ourselves a new feature tonight. Come on back to the *Falcon* and I'll let you help me take admission."

Sonniod scowled at having to turn around and climb the bowl again. "I got word on the rumor vine that you were here, but I couldn't understand how in the name of the Original Light you and the Wookiee ended up showing holo to the Kamar Badlanders. Last I heard, you two took some fire on the Rampa Rapids.''

Han stopped and scowled at Sonniod. ''Who says?''

The little man shrugged elaborately. ''A ship looks like a stock freighter but she's leaking a vapor trail on her approach, and the Rampa Skywatch figures she's a water smuggler. They shoot at her when she won't heave to, but she dumps her load, maybe five thousand liters, and cuts deeper into the traffic pattern. What with the thousands of ships landing and lifting off all the time, they never got a positive I.D. on her. And you were seen on Rampa.''

Han's eyes narrowed. ''Too much chatter can get you into trouble. Didn't your mother ever tell you that, Sonniod?''

Sonniod put on a big grin. ''What she told me was never to talk to strangers. And I haven't, not about this, Solo. But I'd have thought you'd have known better. Didn't you check for leakage?''

Han relaxed and shifted his feet. ''Next time I'll install the damn tanks myself. That was pure R'alla mineral water, sweet and natural and expensive as hell to haul—worth a fortune on Rampa, where all they've got is that recycled chemical soup. Too bad. Anybody who makes it down the Rampa Rapids with a load of fresh water these days is a rich man.''

What Han didn't mention, though he assumed Sonniod had concluded as much, was that he and Chewbacca had lost all the money they had saved during those two-and-a-half minutes of fun and excitement in the Rampa approach corridors.

''As it was, I landed with nothing but the general cargo I was lugging as cover. And somebody messed up on that, too! Instead of twelve of the Lockfiller holo models, I had eleven of them and this old Brosso Mark II. The consignee would only accept the eleven Lockfillers and finally wouldn't pay because he'd been shorted. The shipper liquidated right after I lifted off, and you know how much I hate police and courts, so I was stuck with that holoprojector."

"Well, I see you didn't let it put you out of business, Solo, I'll say that for you," Sonniod granted.

"Inspiration's my specialty," Han agreed. "I knew it was time to get out of the Corporate Sector for a while anyway, and I figured the locals out here in the Badlands would be crazy over holos. I was right; wait till you see. Oh, and thanks for fronting for the holo."

"I didn't," Sonniod answered as they resumed their way. "I know someone who rents them, and *Love Is Waiting* is about the oldest he's got. On my return leg I'll swap him whatever you've got and pick up a bit of cash on the side. My cut, all right?"

The deal sounded good to Han.

They returned to the *Falcon*, where a variety of local trade goods had been heaped at the foot of the starship's main ramp. As Han and Sonniod arrived, a labor 'droid came clumping down the ramp bearing a plastic-extrusion carton containing more Kamarian wares of various sorts.

The 'droid was somewhat shorter than Han, but barrel-chested and long-armed, and moved with the slight stiffness that indicated a heavy-duty suspension system. It had been designed in the image of man, with red photoreceptors for eyes and a small vocoder grille set in his blank metallic face where a mouth would have been. His durable body was finished in a deep, gleaming green.

"How's you afford a brand-new 'droid?" Sonniod asked as the machine in question set down its burden.

"I didn't," Han answered. "He said they wanted to see the galaxy, but sometimes I think they're both circuit-crazy."

Sonniod looked puzzled. "Both?"

"Watch." The 'droid having completed his chore, Han commanded, "Hey, Bollux, open up."

"Of course, Captain Solo," Bollux answered in a casual drawl, and obligingly pulled his long arms back out of the way. His chest plastron parted down the center with a hiss of pressurized air and the halves swung outward. Nestled among the other elements in his chest was a small, vaguely cubical computer module, an independent machine entity painted a deep blue. A single photoreceptor mounted in a turret at the module's top came alight, swiveled, and came to rest on Han.

"Hello, Captain," piped a childlike voice from a diminutive vocoder grille.

"Well, of all the—" Sonniod exclaimed, leaning closer for a better look as the computer's photoreceptor inspected him up and down.

"That's Blue Max," Han told him. "Max because he's packed to his little eyebrows with computer-probe capacity and Blue for obvious reasons. Some outlaw-techs put these two together like that." He thought it best not to go into the wild tangle of crime, conflict, and deception surrounding a previous adventure at the secret Authority installation known as Stars' End.

Bollux's original, ancient body had been all but destroyed there, but the outlaw-techs had provided him with a new one. The 'droid had opted for a body much like his old one, insisting that durability, versatility, and the capacity to do useful work had always been the means to his survival. He had even retained his slow speech pattern, having found that it gave him more time to think and made humans regard him as easygoing.

"When they were manumitted they asked to sign on with me," Han told Sonniod. "They're swapping labor for passage."

"Those are the last of the trade articles we've accumulated, sir," Bollux informed Han.

"Good. Close up and go re-stow all the loose gear we had to move around." The plastron halves swished shut on Blue Max, and Bollux obediently returned up the ramp.

"But, Solo, I thought you always said you disavow all machinery that talks back," Sonniod reminded him.

"A little help comes in handy sometimes," Han answered

defensively. He avoided further comment, remarking "Ah, the rush is about to start."

Out of the gloom, figures were hurrying toward the starship, pausing at a cautious distance. The Kamar Badlanders were smaller and more supple than other Kamarians, and their segmented exoskeletal chitin was thinner and of a lighter color, matching the hues of their home terrain. Most of them rested in the characteristic pose of their kind, on their lowermost set of extremities and their thick, segmented, prehensile tails.

Lisstik, one of the few Badlanders whom Han could tell from the others, approached the *Falcon*'s ramp. Lisstik had been among the very few to watch the holos on the first evening Han had offered them, and he'd shown up every evening thereafter. He seemed to be a leader among his kind. Now Lisstik was sitting on his tail, leaving his upper two sets of brachia free to gesture and interweave as Kamarians loved to do. The Badlander's faceted, insectile eyes showed no emotion Han had ever been able to read.

Lisstik wore an unusual ornament, a burned-out control integrator that Chewbacca had cast aside. The Kamarian had scavenged and now wore it, bound by a woven band to the front of his gleaming, spherical skull. Lisstik spoke a few phrases of Basic, possibly one of the reasons he was a leader. Once more he asked Han the question that had become something of a formula between them. In a voice filled with clicks and glottal stops, he queried, "Will we see *mak-tk-klp*, your holo-sss, tonight? We have our *q'mai*."

"Sure, why not?" Han replied. "Just leave the *q'mai* in the usual place and take a—" he almost said "seat," which would have been a difficult concept for a Kamarian, "—a place below. The show starts when everybody's down there."

Lisstik made the common Kamarian affirmative, a clashing-together of the central joints of his upper extremities, sounding like small cymbals. From his side he uncorded a wound scrap of miser-plant leaf and laid it down on a trading tarp Han had spread out at the base of the ramp. Lisstik then scuttled down into the open-air theater with the swift, fluid gait of his species.

Others began to follow, leaving this leaf-wrapped treasure or that handicraft or artwork. Often one Badlander would offer something that constituted the contributions for himself and several companions. Han raised no objection; business was good and there was no reason to push for all the market would bear. He liked to think he was building good will. The Badlanders, who weren't used to congregating, tended to find their places on the slopes in small clusters, keeping as much distance between groups as possible.

Among the payments were water-extraction tubes, pharynx flutes, minutely carved gaming pieces, odd jewelry intended for the exotic Kamarian anatomy, amulets, a digworm opener chipped from glassy stone and nearly as sharp as machined metal, and a delicate prayer necklace. Earlier on, Han had been forced to dissuade his customers from bringing him nightswift gruel, boiled howlrunner, roast stingworm, and other local delicacies.

Han picked up the twist of leaf Lisstik had left, opened it on his palm and showed it to Sonniod. Two small, crude gemstones and a sliver of some milky crystal lay there.

"You'll never get to be a man of leisure at this rate, Solo," opined Sonniod.

Han shrugged, rewrapping the stones. "All I want is a new stake so I can lay in a cargo and get the *Falcon* repaired."

Sonniod studied the starship that had once been, and still looked very much like, a stock light freighter. That she was heavily armed and amazingly speedy was something Han preferred not to have show externally. Such display of force would have been too likely to arouse the curiosity of those entrusted with enforcement of the law.

"She looks spaceworthy enough to me," Sonniod commented. "Same old *Falcon*—looks like a garbage sledge, performs like an interceptor."

"She'll run, now that Chewie's welded the hull," Han

conceded, "but some of the control circuitry that was shot up over Rampa was about ready to give up when we got here. Before we came out into the Badlands we had to lay in some new components, and about the only thing you can get here on Kamar is fluidic systems."

Sonniod's face turned sour. "Fluidics? Solo, dear fellow, I'd rather steer my ship with a blunt pole. Why couldn't you get some decent circuitry?"

Han was poring over the rest of this take. "This is a nowhere planet, pal. They've still got nationalism and their weapons—in the advanced places, I mean; not out here in the Badlands—are at the missile-delivered, nuclear-explosive stage. So, of course, someone developed a charged-particle beam to mess up missile circuitry, and naturally everyone turned to fluidics, because shielded circuitry was a little beyond them. So now fluidics is the only type of advanced systems they've got here. We had to load up on adaptor fittings and interface routers and use gas and liquid fluidic components. I *hate* them."

Han stood up again. "I can't stand the thought of all those flow-tracks and microvalves in the *Falcon* and I can't wait to rip 'em out and retool her." He held up and studied with pleasure a statuette carved from black stone, exquisitely detailed and no bigger than his thumb. "And the way things are going, that shouldn't take too much longer."

He put the statuette down in the much smaller of two piles of goods that had been stacked around the starship's ramp. The larger one consisted of trade articles of relatively great bulk and little value, including musical instruments, cooking utensils, tunneling tools, chitin paints, and the portable awnings the Badlanders sometimes used. The smaller pile held all the semiprccious stones, much of the artwork, and a number of the finer tools and implements. The amassed goods had been cluttering up the *Falcon*, stored here and there in available corners of the ship over the past eleven local days. While Chewbacca had been completing repairs that afternoon, Bollux and Han had hauled all the stuff out for sorting and to determine just what it was they had accumulated.

"Maybe not," Sonniod agreed. "Badlanders don't usually trade like this; they're very jealous of their territory. I'm amazed that you've got them flocking together here."

"There's nobody who doesn't enjoy a good show," Han told him. "Especially if they're stuck out in a hole like this place. Or else I wouldn't have all this junk." He watched the last of the stream of Kamarians make their way down and take up their three-point resting positions. "Wonderful customers," he sighed fondly.

"But what'll you do with all the bulky stuff?" Sonniod asked, falling in as Han started down for the center of the amphitheater again.

"We're planning a going-out-of-business sale," Han declared. "Very good deals, everything must go. Super discounts for steady customers and compact items offered in trade." He rubbed his jaw. "I may even sell old Lisstik the holoprojector when I go. I'd hate to see the old Solo Holotheater close down."

"Sentimentalist. So I don't suppose you need work right now?"

Han looked quickly at Sonniod. "What kind of work?"

Sonniod shook his head. "I don't know. Word's out back in the Corporate Sector that there're jobs to be had, runs to be made. Nobody seems to know the details and you never hear names, but word is that if you make yourself available, you'll be contacted."

"I've never worked blind," Han said.

"Nor I. That's why I didn't get in on it. I thought you might be sufficiently hard up to be interested. I must say I'm glad you're not, Solo; it all sounds a bit too tricky. I just thought you might like to know."

Assuring himself of the holoprojector's settings, Han nodded. "Thanks, but don't worry about us; life's a banquet. I might even do this some more, hire out a few projectors and hire local crews on these slowpoke worlds to run them for a split. It could be a sweet, legal little racket, and I wouldn't even have to get shot at."

"By the way," Sonniod said, "what's the other feature, the one you've been showing all along?"

"Oh, that. It's a travelogue, *Varn, World of Water*. You know, life among the amphiboid fishers and ocean farmers in the archipelagoes, deep-seat wildlife, ocean-bed fights to the death between some really big lossors and a pack of cheeb, things like that. Want to hear the narrative? I've got it all memorized."

"Thank you, no," Sonniod replied, pulling his lower lip thoughtfully. "I wonder how they'll react to a new feature?"

"They'll love it," Han insisted. "Singing, dancing; they'll be tapping their little pincers off."

"Solo, what was the word Lisstik used for the admission price?"

"Q'mai." Han was finishing fine adjustments. "They didn't have any word for 'admission,' but I finally got the idea across to Lisstik in spotty Basic and he said the word's *q'mai*. Why?"

"I've heard it before, here on Kamar." Sonniod put the thought aside for the moment. The holofeature appeared in mass-audience projection, filling the air over the natural amphitheater. The Badlanders, who had been swaying gently in the hot night breeze and clicking and chittering among themselves, now became utterly silent.

Love is Waiting was standard fare, Han recalled. It opened without credits or title, which would appear shortly, superimposed on the opening number. That was just as well, Han reflected, since abstract symbols would mean about as much to Kamar Badlanders as particle physics meant to a digworm. He wondered what they would think of human choreography and music, of which there had been none in *Varn, World of Water*.

The feature opened with the woebegone hero stepping off a transporter beltway en route, with some misgiving, to a job with a planetary modification firm. A catchy beat, intended to inform the viewer that a production number was coming, began. Something appeared to make the Badlanders uneasy, however. The clicking and chittering grew louder, nor did it abate when the hero collided with the ingenue and their introduction led to his song cue.

Before the hero had even gotten through the first of his lyrics, discord among the Kamarians was drowning out the music. Several times Han caught the name of Lisstik. He raised the volume a little, hoping the crowd would settle down, puzzling over what had them so agitated.

A stone sailed out of the darkness and bounced off the holoprojector with a crash. From the light spilled by the dancing, singing figures overhead there could be seen the angry waving of Kamarian upper extremities. Multifaceted eyes threw the light back out of the dark in a million fragments.

Another rock clanked against the holoprojector, making Sonniod jump, and a flung howlrunner thighbone, remains of someone's dinner, just missed Han.

"Solo—" began Sonniod, but Han wasn't listening.

Having spotted Lisstik, Han shouted up the slopes at him. "Hey, what's going on? Tell 'em to calm down! Give it a chance, will you?"

But it was no use yelling to Lisstik. The Kamarian was surrounded by an irate crowd of his fellows, all waving their upper extremities and thrashing tails, making more noise than Han had ever heard Badlanders make. One of them swiped at the burned-out integrator banded to Lisstik's skull. Elsewhere on the slopes around the holoprojector, shoving, arguments and differences of opinion had erupted into violent disagreement.

"Oh, my," said Sonniod in a very small voice. "Solo, I just remembered what *q'mai* means; I heard it in one of the population centers to the north. It doesn't mean 'admission,' it means 'offering.' Quick, where's the other holo, the travelogue?"

By then a mob of hostile Badlanders was slowly closing

in around the holoprojector. Han's hand descended toward his blaster. "Back onboard the *Falcon*, why? What are you talking about?"

"Don't you stop and analyze things, *ever*? You've been showing them holos of a world with more water than they'd ever dreamed existed, filled with cultures and life forms that they've never even fantasized about. You haven't set up a holotheater, you idiot; you've started a *religion*!"

Han gulped, pulling his blaster indecisively as the Badlanders closed in. "Well, how could *I* know? I'm a pilot, not an alien-contact officer!"

He took a handful of Sonniod's coverall sleeve and, pulling gently, led him back slowly toward the *Falcon*. He heard Chewbacca's alarmed roaring from farther up the slope. Overhead, the hero and the ingenue and everybody else at the transporter beltway were engaged in a meticulously choreographed dance routine built around the ticket kiosks and turnstiles.

The Badlanders at that side of the circle began to give way uncertainly before Han, who tugged the frightened Sonniod along after him. A number of the bolder Kamarians rushed the holoprojector and began beating at it with sticks, stones, and bare pincers. Overhead, the dance number began to dissolve into distortion. Some of the vandals—or outraged zealots, depending on one's orientation—turned from the projector after a moment and advanced in a vengeful throng on Han.

Sensing correctly that by simply refunding the *q'mai* he stood little chance of mollifying his former audience-cum-congregation, Han fired into the ground before them. Sandy soil exploded, throwing up rocky debris and burning cinders. Whatever flammable material there was in the soil caught fire. Han fired twice more to his right and left, gouging holes in the ground in spectacular bursts.

Badlanders fell back for the moment, their enormous eyes catching the crimson of blaster beams, ducking their small heads and shielding themselves with upraised brachia. Han didn't have to fire at the disgruntled Kamarians between himself and his ship; they were giving way. "Stay up there," he hollered up into the darkness at Chewbacca, "and get the engines started!"

The crowd was doing a pretty fair job of disassembling the holoprojector. Its sound synthesizer was making simply random noises now, though at high volume. *Love is Waiting* had devolved to a sluggish flow of multicolored swirls in the air.

As Han watched, walking backward as calmly as he could, Lisstik rushed in from the darkness, wrenched the integrator from his forehead and hurled it to the ground, stamping and grinding it into the dust as he beat at the holoprojector with his pincers.

"It looks like your high priest has split with the church," observed Sonniod. Lisstik succeeded in wrenching loose a piece of the control panel casing and flung it in Han's general direction with a vindictive series of clicks.

Feeling himself more the aggrieved party than the one at fault, Han lost his restraint. "You want a show? *Here*'s a show, you rotten little ingrate!" He fired into the holoprojector. The red whining blaster bolt elicited a brief, bright secondary explosion from somewhere in the projector's internal reaches.

Suddenly the sound synthesizer was producing the most appalling string of loud, piercing, unrecognizable agglutinations of noise Han had ever heard. The projection filled the sky over the amphitheather with nova bursts, solar flares, pinwheels, sky rockets, and strobe flashes. The entire crowd gave a concerted bleat and charged off in all directions up the slopes of the bowl.

Han and Sonniod took considerable advantage of the confusion by sprinting madly toward the *Millennium Falcon*. They could hear harsh chitters and clacks from both sides as Badlanders, having not yet vented their full outrage, began giving chase. Han pegged unaimed shots into the air and the ground behind him. He still hesitated to fire at his former customers unless it meant life or death.

As they neared the *Falcon*'s gaping ramp, Han and Sonniod were gratified to see the starship's belly turret fire a volley. The quad-guns spat lines of red annihilation, and a rocky upcropping already passed by the racing men was transformed into a fountain of sparks, molten rock, and outlashing energy. The heat scorched Han's back and a stone chip whistled past Sonniod's ear, too close for comfort, but it put a halt to the Badlanders' chase for the moment.

When they reached the ramp, Sonniod dashed up at maximum speed while Han slid to a stop on one knee to gather up what he could from the more valuable *q'mai*. A hurled stone bounced off the *Falcon*'s landing gear and another ricocheted from the ramp while Han groped.

"Solo, get up here!" Sonniod screamed. Spinning, Han saw Badlanders closing in around the ship. He fired over their heads and they ducked, but kept coming. Backstepping rapidly up the ramp, Han fired twice more and fell when he dodged a thrown rock. He ended up crawling through the hatch.

As the main hatch rolled down, Chewbacca appeared at the passageway, leaning out of the cockpit with an incensed snarl in this throat.

"How should *I* know what went wrong?" Han bellowed at the Wookiee. "What am I, a telepath? Get us up and head for Sonniod's ship, *now*!" Chewbacca disappeared back into the cockpit.

As Sonniod helped him up off the deck, Han tried to reassure him. "Don't worry, we'll get you back to your ship before the grievance committee arrives. You'll have time to lift off."

Sonniod nodded thankfully. "But what about you and the Wookiee, Solo?" The starship trembled slightly as she hovered on her thrusters and swung away toward Sonniod's parked vessel. "I wouldn't come back for my profits if I were you."

"I suppose I'll have to head back for the Corporate Sector," Han sighed, "and see what kind of jobs there are floating around. At least the heat should be off; I doubt if anyone's looking for me or this freighter anymore.''

Sonniod shook his head. ''Try to find out what the job is before you get into it,'' he encouraged. ''Nobody seems to know what kind of run it is.''

''I don't care; I'm in no position to be picky. I'll have to take it,'' Han said, resigned. They heard Chewbacca's dejected hooting drifting aft from the cockpit. ''He's right,'' he said. ''We just weren't cut out for the honest life.''

THE *Millennium Falcon* seemed a ghost ship, a spectral spacecraft like the long-lost, sometimes-sighted *Permondiri Explorer*, or the fabled *Queen of Ranroon*. Trailing sheets of crackling energy, with dancing lines of brilliant discharge playing back and forth over her, she might have flown directly out of one of those legends.

Around the starship seethed the turbulent atmosphere of Lur, a planet quite close, as interstellar distances go, to the Corporate Sector. Its ionization layer was interacting with the *Falcon*'s screens to create eerie lightninglike displays. The shrieking of the planet's winds could be heard through the vessel's hull, and the fury of the storm had cut visibility virtually to zero. Han and Chewbacca paid scant attention to the uproar pounding at their canopy with rain, sleet, snow, and gale-force winds.

They lavished closest attention on their instrumentation, courting it for all the information it could provide, as if by concentration alone they could coax a clearer picture of their situation from sensors and other indicators. Chewbacca growled irritably, his clear blue eyes skipping all over his side of the console, leathery snout working and twitching.

Han was feeling just as cross. "How am *I* supposed to know how thick the ionization layer is? The instrumentation's jittery from the discharges, it doesn't show anything clearly. What do you want me to do, drop a plumb line?" He went back to closely monitoring his share of the console.

The Wookiee's rejoinder was another growl. Behind him,

in the communications officer's seat that was usually left vacant, Bollux spoke up. "Captain Solo, one of the indicators just lit up. It appears to be a malfunction in some of the new control systems."

Without turning from his work, Han uncorked some of his choicer curses, then calmed down somewhat. "It's the miserable fluidics! What timing, what *perfect* timing! Chewie, I told you there'd be trouble, didn't I? *Didn't I?*"

The Wookiee flailed a huge, hairy paw in the air by way of dismissal, wishing to be left to his tasks, rumbling loudly.

"Where's the problem?" Han snapped back over his right shoulder.

Bollux's photoreceptors scanned the indicators that were located next to the commo board. "Ship's emergency systems, sir. The auto-firefighting apparatus, I believe."

"Go back and see what you can do, will you, Bollux? That's all we need, for the firefighting gear to cut in; we'd be up to our chins in foam and gas before you could ask the way to the exit." As Bollux staggered off, barely staying upright on the bucking deck, Han resolutely thrust the problem out of his mind.

Chewbacca yowlped. He had gotten a positive reading. Han dragged himself halfway out of his chair for a look as another spitting globe of ball-lightning drifted out and spun off the *Falcon*'s bow mandibles. The ionization levels were dropping. Then he threw himself back into his seat and cut the ship's speed back even further. He had terrible visions of the ionization level extending down, somehow, to the surface of Lur, blinding them right up to the time of collision.

Of course, the party who had hired the *Millennium Falcon* for this run hadn't mentioned the ionization layer, hadn't mentioned anything very specific for that matter. Han had put the word abroad that he and his ship were available for hire and disinclined to ask questions, and the job had come, as Sonniod had predicted it would, from unseen sources in the form of a faceless audio tape and a small cash advance.

But with creditors hounding them and their other resources exhausted in the wake of the debacle in the Kamar Badlands, Han and his partner had seen no alternative but to ignore Sonniod's advice and accept the run.

Was I born this stupid, Han asked himself in disgust, *or am I just blossoming late in life?* But at that moment both the storm and the ionization layer parted. The *Falcon* lowered gently through a clear, calm region of Lur's atmosphere. Far below, features of the planet's surface could be seen, mountain peaks protruding through low-hanging, swirling clouds. Another light flashed on; the freighter's long-range sensors had just picked up a landing beacon.

Han switched on the Terrain Following Sensors and poised over the readouts. "They picked us a decent spot to land at least," he admitted. "A big, flat place slung between those two low peaks over there. Probably a glacial field." He flipped the microphone on his headset over to intercom mode. "Bollux, we're going in. Drop what you're doing and hang on."

Correcting his ship's attitude of descent, he brought her in toward the landing point at very moderate speed. The TFS rig showed no obstacles or other dangers, but Han wished to take no chances with instrumentation on this stupid planet.

They settled into the clouds as precipitation was driven at the canopy, only to slide away when it met the *Falcon*'s defensive screens. Sensors had begun functioning normally, giving precise information on altitude. Visibility, even in the storm, was sufficient for a cautious landing. Lur materialized below them as a plain where winds hurried along endlessly, aimlessly.

Han eased the vessel down warily; he had no desire to find himself buried in an ice chasm. But the ship's landing gear found solid support, and instrumentation showed that Han's guess had been correct; they had landed on a glacial ice field. Off to starboard some forty meters or so was the landing beacon.

Han removed his headset, stripped off the flying gloves he

had been wearing, and unbuckled his seatbelt. He turned to his Wookiee copilot. ''You stay here and keep a sharp watch. I'll go let the ramp down and see what the deal is.'' The unoccupied navigator's seat behind him held a bundle that he snagged and carried along as he left the cockpit.

On his way aft to the ship's ramp he found Bollux. The 'droid was stooping down by an open inspection plate set in the bulkhead at deck level. Bollux's chest plastron was open, and Blue Max was assisting him in his examination of the problem at hand.

''What's the routine?'' Han inquired. ''Is it fixed?''

Bollux stood up. ''I'm afraid not, Captain Solo. But Max and I caught it just before the last safety went. We shut down the entire system, but repair is beyond the capability of either of us.''

''You don't need a tech for those fluidics, Captain,'' Max chirped. ''You need a damn *plumber*.'' His voice held a note of moral outrage at the inferior design.

''Tell me about it. And watch your language, Max. Just because I talk that way is no sign you should. All right, boys, just leave things the way they are. This trip should make us enough to have all those waterworks replaced with good old shielded circuitry. Bollux, I want you to close up your fruit stand; we've got cargo to pick up and I don't want you making the clients jumpy. Sorry, Max, but you do that to people sometimes.''

''No problem, Captain,'' Blue Max replied as the halves of Bollux's chest swung shut to the hum of servomotors. Han reflected that, while he still didn't care much for automata, Bollux and Max weren't too bad. He decided, though, that he would never understand how the pseudo-personalities of an ancient labor 'droid and a precocious computer module could hit it off so well.

Han opened the bundle he had brought from the cockpit—a bulky thermosuit—and began pulling it on over his ship's clothes. Before fitting his hands into the thermosuit's attached gloves, he adjusted his gun-belt, rebuckling it over the suit, then removing the weapon's trigger guard so that he'd be able to fire it with his thermoglove on. He wouldn't have dreamed of going out unarmed; he was always wary when the *Millennium Falcon* was grounded in unfamiliar surroundings, but especially so when he was doing business on the shady side of the street.

He donned protective headgear, a transparent facebowl with insulated ear cups. Touching a button on the control unit set in his thermosuit's sleeve, he brought its heating unit to life.

"Stand by," he ordered Bollux, "in case I need a hand with the cargo."

"May I inquire what it is we're to carry, Captain?" Bollux asked as he drew aside the covers of the special compartments hidden under the deckplates.

"You may guess, Bollux; that's about all I can do right now myself." Han prodded at the hatch control with a gloved finger. "Nobody mentioned what it's going to be, and I was in no position to ask. Couldn't be anything too massive, I guess."

The hatch rolled up and a blast of frigid wind invaded the passageway. Han shouted over the wail of the storm. "Doesn't look like it's going to be heat rash salve though, does it?"

He started down the ramp, leaning into the force of the gale. The cold in his lungs was sharp enough to make him think about going back for a respirator, but he judged that he wouldn't be outside long enough to need one. His facebowl polarized somewhat against the ice glare as snow hissed against it. Specific gravity here on Lur was slightly over Standard, but not enough to cause any inconvenience.

At the foot of the ramp he found that the wind was moving a light dusting of snow across the blue-white glacier. Miniature drifts were already accumulating against the *Falcon*'s landing gear. He spied the beacon, a cluster of blinking caution lights atop a globular transponder package, anchored to glacial ice by a tripod. There was no one to be seen, but visibility was so low that Han couldn't have made out much beyond the landing marker.

He walked over to it, inspecting it and finding it to be nothing more than a standard model, designed for use in places lacking sophisticated navigational and tracking equipment.

Suddenly a muffled voice behind him called out. "Solo?" He spun, right hand dropping automatically to the grip of his blaster. A man stepped out of the swirl of the storm. He, too, wore a thermosuit and a facebowl that had muted his voice, but the thermosuit was white and the facebowl reflective, making him nearly invisible there on the glacier.

He moved forward with hands empty and held high. Han, squinting past him, saw the vague outlines of other figures moving just at the edge of his range of vision.

"I'm him," Han responded, his own words muffled somewhat by his facebowl. "You're, uh, Zlarb?"

The other nodded. Zlarb was a tall, broadly built man with extremely fair skin, white-blond beard and clear gray eyes with creases at their corners that gave him an intense, threatening look. But he showed his teeth in a wide smile. "That's right, Captain. And I'm ready to go, too. We can load up right away."

Han tried to peer through the curtain of snow behind Zlarb. "Are there enough of you to bring up the cargo? I brought along a repulsorlift handtruck in case you need it to haul your load. Want me to run it out for you?"

Zlarb gave him a look Han couldn't quite read, then smiled again. "No. I think we can get our shipment onboard without any problems."

Something about the man's behavior, the hint of a private joke or the sardonic tone to his reply, made Han suspicious. He had long since learned to listen to inner alarms. He looked back at the blurry outline of the *Falcon* and hoped Chewbacca was alert and that the Wookiee had the starship's main batteries primed and aimed. The two seldom encountered trouble from their pickup contacts. Usually at the other end, the drop-off and payment end of things, trouble tended to occur. But this just might be the exception.

Han backed away a step, eyes meeting Zlarb's. "All right then, I'll go get ready to raise ship." He had more questions to ask this man, but wanted to move the proceedings to a more auspicious spot, say, next to the freighter's belly turret. "You drag your shipment to the ramp head and we'll take it from there."

Zlarb's grin was wider now. "No, Solo. I think we'll both go onboard your ship. Right now."

Han was about to tell Zlarb that it was against his and Chewbacca's policy to let smuggling contacts onboard when he noticed that the man had turned his hand over. In it he held a tiny weapon, a short-range palmgun that, like a conjuror, he must have held hidden between gloved fingers. Han thought about going for his blaster but realized that at best he could probably manage no more than a tie, in which case both of them would die.

The blinking lights of the landing beacon, gleaming off Zlarb's facebowl, gave the man's smirk an even more sinister look. "Hand the blaster over butt-first, Solo, and keep your back to the ship so your partner can't see. Carefully now; I've been warned about you and that speeddraw, and I'd rather shoot than take a chance."

He tucked Han's sidearm into his belt. "Now let's get aboard. Keep both hands at your sides and don't try to warn the Wookiee."

He turned for a moment and motioned to unseen companions, then indicated the *Falcon* with the palmgun. From a distance, Han thought, it probably looked like a polite you-first gesture.

As they walked Han tried to sort through the situation, his mind roiling. These people knew exactly what they were doing; the whole job had been a setup. Zlarb's frank willingness to use his weapon was proof that he and his accomplices were playing for very high stakes. The question of being cheated of payment or even of having his vessel hijacked suddenly bothered Han less than the thought of not surviving the encounter.

The bulk of the *Millennium Falcon* became more distinct as they approached her. "No bright stunts now, Solo," Zlarb warned. "Don't even twitch your nose at the Wookiee or you'll die for it."

Han had to admit that Zlarb thought in advance, but he hadn't covered everything. Han and Chewbacca had a signal system for pickups and dropoffs, whereby Han didn't need to communicate that something was wrong; all he had to do was approach the ship and fail to give the subtle all's-well.

Over the moan of the gale they heard the whine of servomotors. The quad-guns in the *Falcon*'s belly turret traversed, elevated, and came to bear on them.

But Zlarb had already stepped behind Han, pulling the captured gun from his belt and holding its muzzle up close to Han's temple. They could see Chewbacca now, his hairy face pressed close to the canopy, gazing down apprehensively. The Wookiee's left arm was stretched behind him, down near the console. Han knew his friend's fingers would be only millimeters from the fire controls. He wanted to yell *Get out! Raise ship!* But Zlarb anticipated that. "Not a word to him, Solo! Not a sound, or you're canceled." Han didn't doubt him a bit.

Zlarb had the Wookiee's attention and was motioning him to come down out of the ship, indicating with the blaster's muzzle just what would happen to Han if Chewbacca failed to obey. Han, familiar with his shaggy first mate's expressions, read indecision then resignation, on his face. Then the Wookiee disappeared from the cockpit.

Han muttered something, and Zlarb poked him with the blaster. "Save it; it's lucky for you he paid attention. Just play along and both of you will come through this alive."

Two of Zlarb's underlings had come up and stopped near their boss. One was a human, a squat, tough looking ugly who could have come from any of 100,000 worlds. The other was a humanoid, a giant, burly creature nearly Chewbacca's size, with tiny eyes beneath jutting, boney brows. The humanoid's skin was a glossy brown, like some exotic, polished wood, and vestigial horns curled at his forehead. He seemed to feel the need for neither thermosuit nor facebowl.

But it was what the other man, the squat one, had brought that surprised Han most. He had a control leash fastened to his wrist; at the end of the leash was a nashtah, one of the storied hunting beasts of Dra III. The nashtah's six powerful legs, each armed with long, curving, diamond-hard claws, shifted restlessly on the ice. It strained at its leash, tongue arcing, its steamy breath rasping between triple rows of jagged white teeth, its long barbed tail lashing. Its muscles, tensing and untensing, sent ripples along its green, sleek hide.

What in the name of the profit-motive system can they be doing with a nashtah? Han asked himself. The creatures were bloodthirsty, tireless and impossible to shake once they scented their prey, and were among the most vicious of all attack animals. That seemed to indicate poaching of some kind, but why would a gang of poachers go to all this trouble? Han disliked moving pelts or hides and, given a choice, would not have carried them. But that surely didn't call for this kind of extreme action on Zlarb's part; there were plenty of smugglers who would have taken the job.

Chewbacca appeared at the ramp head. The nashtah, sighting him, gave throat to a piercing scream and lunged, dragging its handler until he dug in his heels and pressed a stud on the control leash handle. The nashtah gave a yeowl of displeasure at the mild shock that stopped its advance for the moment. Chewbacca watched impassively, his bowcaster held ready, eyes sweeping the scene below.

Zlarb started Han off with a shove, staying close behind, and the two climbed the ramp. When they were near the top, Zlarb addressed Chewbacca. "Put down the weapon. Do it now and step back or your friend here gets fried." There was the nudge of the blaster between Han's shoulder blades.

Chewbacca debated the variables involved, then complied,

seeing no other way to save his friend's life. Meanwhile, Han evaluated his chances for a fast move. He knew he might stand a chance of neutralizing Zlarb, but the other two gang members were backing their boss up and each had a handgun out now. And then there was the nashtah. Han elected to postpone his most desperate option for the time being.

When they reached the top of the ramp, Zlarb pushed Han hard, then stooped to take up Chewbacca's bowcaster. The Wookiee caught his friend as Han stumbled from the shove and kept him from falling. Han removed his facebowl and threw it aside. Taking a quick look around, he noticed Bollux still standing where Han had left him. The 'droid seemed to be rooted to the spot, immobile with surprise, his circuitry struggling to absorb the bewildering rush of events.

Zlarb's men had come in behind him along with the nashtah, whose claws scraped the deckplates. Again it had to be curbed from leaping at the Wookiee, and Han wondered for a moment what it was about Chewbacca that antagonized it so. Something about his first mate's scent, or perhaps a resemblance to one of the beast's natural enemies?

Zlarb turned to the hulking humanoid who had been eyeing Chewbacca with nearly as much hostility as the nashtah. "Go tell the others to start moving. We'll get things ready here." Then he turned to Han. "Open up your main hold; we're going to start loading." And finally, to the handler who still restrained the spitting nashtah, Zlarb indicated the Wookiee. "If he moves, burn him down."

They set off aft, Zlarb being careful to stay well back from Han, watchful for any surprise move the pilot might make. Following the curve of the passageway, they came to the hatchway of the *Falcon*'s main cargo hold. Han tapped the release, and the hatch slid back to reveal a compartment of modest size, ribbed by the ship's structural members, featureless except for air ducts, safety equipment, and the heating-refrigeration unit. A stack of panels and disassembled support posts lay there, to be erected as shelving or retaining bins if they were needed. Dunnage and padding were heaped in a pile to one side near coils of strapping and fastening tackle.

Zlarb, looking around, nodded in approval. "This'll do fine, Solo. Leave the hatch open and let's get back to the others."

Another of Zlarb's men had arrived and was standing at the top of the ramp, a disruptor rifle leveled at Chewbacca. The nashtah handler had dragged his beast back farther toward the cockpit. The big humanoid had returned, too, carrying a small shoulder pack. Zlarb pointed to it. "You've got your equipment there, Wadda?"

Wadda inclined his head. Zlarb pointed to Bollux. "First I want you to stick a restraining bolt on the 'droid. We don't want him wandering around; he might give us trouble."

Bollux started to protest but weapons moved to cover him and Wadda closed in on him, looming over him and unlimbering the ominous pack from his shoulder. The labor 'droid's red photoreceptors went to Han in what seemed to be an entreaty. "Captain Solo, what shall I—"

"Keep still," Han instructed, not wanting to see Bollux destroyed and knowing Zlarb's people would do just that if the 'droid resisted them. "It'll only be for a while."

Bollux looked from Han to Chewbacca, then to Wadda and back to Han again. Wadda closed in on him, fitting a restraining bolt into a hand-held applicator. The big humanoid pressed the applicator against Bollux's chest and the 'droid gave a split-second bleep. There was a wisp of smoke as bolt fused to metal skin. Just as Bollux shuffled, resettling his changing feet as if some new posture would be of help to him, his photoreceptors went dark, the restraining bolt deactivating his control matrices.

Satisfied that the *Falcon* was his, Zlarb began issuing commands. "Let's get busy." Han was directed to Chewbacca's side. The nashtah handler and the man with the disruptor rifle continued to watch them while Wadda hurried down the ramp, making it tremble under his great weight.

"Zlarb," Han began, "don't you think its time you told us what's so flaming . . ."

He was distracted by the ramp's vibrations and the sound of many light footfalls. A moment later he understood just what had happened to him and in how dangerous a situation he and Chewbacca had become involved.

A file of small figures trooped aboard, heads hung in fatigue and despair. These were obviously inhabitants of Lur. The tallest of them was scarcely waist-high to Han. They were erect bipeds, covered with fine white fur, their feet protected by thick pads of calluslike tissue. Their eyes were large, and ran toward green and blue; they stared around the *Falcon*'s interior in dull amazement.

Each neck was encircled by a collar of metal, the collars joined together by a thin black cable. It was a slaver's line.

Chewbacca bellowed an enraged roar and ignored the answering scream from the nashtah. Han glared at Zlarb, who was directing the loading of slaves. One of his men held a director unit, its circuitry linked to the collars. The director, a banned device, had an unfinished, homemade look to it. Any defiance from the captives would earn them excruciating pain.

Han fixed Zlarb with his eye. "Not in my ship," he stated, emphasizing each word.

But Zlarb only laughed. "You're not in much of a position to object, are you, Solo?"

"Not in my ship," Han repeated stubbornly. "Not slaves. Never."

Zlarb aligned Han's own blaster at him, sighting down the barrel. "You just think again, pilot. If you give me any trouble, you'll end up locked in a necklace yourself. Now, you and the Wookiee go forward and get ready to lift."

A second line of slaves was being led aboard and ushered aft to the hold. Han scowled at Zlarb for a moment, then turned toward the cockpit. Chewbacca hesitated, bared his fangs at the slavers once more, and followed his friend.

Han lowered himself unwillingly into the pilot's seat, and

Chewbacca took the copilot's. Zlarb stood behind them watching their every move carefully. He mistrusted the two, of course, but knew that they could get more speed and better performance out of the *Falcon* than he or any of his men could. And that might well mean survival in the perilous business of slave-running.

"Solo, I want you and your partner to be smart about this. You take us to our point of delivery and you'll both be taken care of. But if we're halted and boarded, it's the death sentence for all of us, you included."

"Where are we going?" Han asked, tight-lipped.

"I'll tell you that when the time comes. For now, you just prepare to raise ship."

Han brought the *Falcon*'s engines to full power, warming up her shields and preparing to lift. "What are they paying you? Even *I* can't think of enough money to get me mixed up in slaving."

Zlarb chuckled derisively. "They told me you were a hard case, Solo. I see they were wrong. Those little beauties back there are worth four, five, maybe even six thousand apiece on the Invisible Market. They're natural-born experts at genetic manipulation, and in great demand, my friend. Not everyone is happy with the rigid restrictions that were imposed after the Clone Wars. It seems these creatures like their own world too much, though, and wouldn't sign out on contract labor for anything. So my associates and I rounded up a bunch. A few of them are sick or wounded, but we'll deliver at least fifty of them. I'll make enough off this run to keep me happy and lazy for a long time."

Contract labor. That sounded like the Corporate Sector Authority was involved. But though the Authority had been known to use contract hoaxes and deceptive recruitment, Han found it hard to believe that it would be so bold as to practice out-and-out slavery, particularly raiding a planet outside its own boundaries. That was something even the Empire couldn't afford to ignore.

"Your board looks good to me, Solo," Zlarb commented, studying the console. "Raise ship."

As Han, Chewbacca, and the slavers left the passageway, Bollux still stood precisely where he had been deactivated near the ramp's head. The restraining bolt had interdicted all his control centers, immobilizing him.

But hidden within the labor 'droid's thorax, still functioning off his own independent power supply, Blue Max was assessing his situation. Though he realized that the emergency might mean disaster for the *Falcon*'s entire complement, the undersized computer probe could see little he could do to change the situation. He had no motor capability of his own and contained no communications equipment except his vocoder and various computer-tap adaptors. Moreover, Max's own power source was minuscule in comparison to Bollux's, and he couldn't possibly move the labor 'droid's body far enough or fast enough to do any good before exhausting himself.

Blue Max wished he could at least talk to his friend, but the restraining bolt's interdiction extended to all of Bollux's brain functions. The computer, who had seldom been separated from Bollux's host body, felt very much alone.

Then he remembered the short bleep emitted by Bollux just before he'd been immobilized. Max ran the bleep back, slowing it by a high factor and finding, as he had thought, that it was a squirt, a burst transmission. It was garbled; Bollux had been dealing with a number of things at the time. But at length Max made sense of it and saw what the labor 'droid had been trying to do.

Blue Max linked himself in carefully with some of Bollux's motor circuitry, prepared to withdraw and close off instantly if the bolt's influence threatened to impair him.

But it didn't. The restraining bolt worked against Bollux's command and control centers, not his actual circuitry and servomotors. Still, Max knew he had a very difficult task, one that would have been impossible if Bollux hadn't repositioned his feet at the last instant before being paralyzed.

The computer lacked the power to make Bollux's body take more than a few steps but he did have enough to effect a single servo. Though it drained him dangerously, Max fed all the power he could into the knee joint of his companion's left leg. The knee flexed and the labor 'droid's body tilted. Max, trying desperately to gauge the unfamiliar leverages and angles, stopped for a moment and redirected his efforts toward the central torsion hookup in Bollux's midsection, turning him a little to the left. That demanded so much of his scant power that Max had to pause for a moment and let his reserves build a bit.

He shut down all nonvital parts of himself to hoard the energy he needed, then addressed himself to the knee joint once more as the roar of the *Millennium Falcon*'s warming engines made the deckplates chatter and filled the passageway with a hollow rumble.

The 'droid's balance passed the critical point; he tottered, then toppled to the left, landing with a clamorous din. Bollux's body ended up resting on its left arm and side, barely stabilized by its right foot, which also touched the deck.

Max found that, with the body in this position, he couldn't get both chest panels open, but that hardly mattered since he lacked the power to do so anyway. As it was, he had to stop twice in working the right panel outward, wait for his reserves to build up, then channel power into the panel servo. He stopped when the right panel was open sufficiently for him to see his objective.

The last move was the hardest. Max extended an adaptor to the exposed fluidics systems on which he and Bollux had been working prior to planetfall. The fluidics were fitted with standard couplings, but that still left the problem of making a connection with them. Extending his rodlike adaptor arm as far as it would go, Max found his goal just out of reach. The coupling waited beyond and below his adaptor. In desperation Max tried to push his adaptor arm out even farther and nearly damaged himself. It availed nothing.

The computer saw he had only one chance left. That it involved risk of personal damage to him didn't make him hesitate for an instant. He shifted power back to Bollux's midsection, turning the torsion hookup again in an all-out effort that nearly overloaded him. The labor 'droid's body twisted slowly, then rolled over.

But in the last moment, the roll brought Max's adaptor close enough to make contact with the fluidics coupling. He linked up with the systems and had time to send out a single command. Then the torso's descending weight bent his fragile adaptor arm, breaking the connection, and sending feedback washing into Blue Max with a computer analogue of blinding pain.

While Max fought his lonely battle, Han was staring at his controls. He was perspiring and had the front of his thermosuit open, wondering if he should let things go any further or try to jump Zlarb now.

Zlarb was scanning the control console. "I told you to get going, Solo. Raise ship."

He was still waving Han's blaster around to emphasize his command when he took a gush of thick, white foam full in the face.

Nozzles in the cockpit and throughout the *Millennium Falcon* had begun to spew anti-incendiary gas and suppression foam when Max's single command cut in the ship's autofirefighting apparatus. Under the computer probe's override, the system behaved as if the entire ship were aflame.

Han and Chewbacca, unsure of what was happening, didn't stop to think, but seized instead upon whatever freak opportunity this was. The Wookiee struck out with a huge paw, backhanding Zlarb against the navigator's seat, located just behind Han's. Zlarb, blinded, let off a shot at random. The blaster blew a jagged hole in the canopy, its edges dripping with molten transparisteel.

Just then Han flung himself on the slaver, followed closely thereafter by his first mate. Zlarb was punched, shaken, kneed, bitten, and slammed head-first into the navi-computer before he could get off a second shot.

The cockpit was already ankle-deep in foam, and blasts of anti-incendiary gas made it nearly impossible to see. The racket of sirens and warning hooters was deafening. Nevertheless, both partners' spirits had risen appreciably. Picking up his blaster, Han cupped his hand to his mouth and hollered into Chewbacca's ear.

"I don't know what's going on, but we've got to hit them before they can recover. I counted six of them, right?"

The Wookiee confirmed the number. Han led the way from the cockpit as quickly as he could, both of them slipping and sliding in the deepening foam.

Han dashed out into the main passageway. Fortunately he looked to his right first, toward the forward compartment. There one of the slavers stood open-mouthed, staring at the belching auto-firefighting gear. He caught sight of Han and started to bring his disruptor rifle around. But Han's blaster bolt took him high in the chest, knocking him backward through the air, his weapon dropping from his hands.

Han heard a horrible growl and whirled. The handler appeared from the other direction and released the nashtah, which sprang at Han with such speed that it was no more than a blur. Before he could even get off a shot the beast hit him, sending him sprawling against the squares of safety cushioning that rimmed the cockpit hatchway, his shoulder and one forearm slashed with parallel furrows from the creature's claws.

But the nashtah never completed its pounce. Instead it was grabbed and held in midair and sent hurtling against a bulkhead. Chewbacca, having lost his footing in the act of throwing the nashtah aside, scrambled to his feet once more. Han brought his gun up but hesitated to shoot because the fall had shaken him. In that moment the nashtah, with an angry flick of its tail and a hideous cry, sprang at the Wookiee, driving him back into the cockpit passageway.

Chewbacca somehow managed to maintain his footing. Exerting to the fullest his astounding strength, he absorbed the force of the nashtah's attack, locking his hairy hands around its throat, hunching his shoulders and working with legs and forearms to ward off its claws.

The nashtah screamed again, and the Wookiee screamed even louder. Chewbacca held the attack beast clear of the deck and slammed it against the bulkhead to his left, then to his right and to the left again, all in less than a second. The nashtah, its head dangling now at a very odd angle, slumped in his grasp. Chewbacca let it fall to the deck.

The beast's handler gave an outraged shout, seeing his animal's unmoving body. He brought his pistol up, but Han's blaster reacted first. The man staggered, tried to bring his weapon up again, and Han fired a second time. The handler fell prone on the deck not far from the body of his nashtah.

Han grabbed Chewbacca's elbow, pointed and started aft toward the main hold. They found Bollux's inert bulk where Blue Max had caused it to fall, and it was apparent just what the two automata had done. Foam had crept in around the 'droid's body and had begun seeping in through the open chest panel.

Chewbacca gave a grating snarl alluding to the ingenuity of the two. "I'll second that; they're pretty nervy," Han concurred. He'd taken a grip on the 'droid's shoulder. "Help me sit him up so the foam doesn't get at them."

There was no time to do anything else. They propped the 'droid's body against the bulkhead in temporary safety and hurried on. They were going full-tilt when the giant humanoid appeared around the curve of the passageway from the opposite direction, a riot gun in his hand.

Han made an awkward attempt to dodge for cover, bringing his blaster up at the same time. With the deck slippery with foam, he lost his footing and took a spill. Chewbacca, on the other hand, adapted quickly to these unusual conditions. Without decreasing speed he hurled himself into a feet-first slide along the deck-plates, cutting a bow-wave through the drifting foam, his enthusiastic bellow rising above the hiss of gas projectors and the alarms.

The slaver's aim wavered from Han to the Wookiee, but Chewbacca was moving too fast; one shot mewed, a miss that crackled on the deck, raising steam from the foam. The Wookiee rammed the humanoid with his outsized feet, and the humanoid bounced with astonishing abruptness into a mound of foam wherein he was joined directly by Chewbacca. The foam mound quivered and shook, strands and clumps of it flying loose, as there came from it the sounds of snarls and roars, and heavyweight collision.

Han was back on his feet, rushing on, feeling somewhat lightheaded from the anti-incendiary gas. He was still uncertain what to do when he encountered the last two slavers, the ones carrying the collar-boxes. If he hesitated they might just hit the kill switches, slaying every captive on the lines. He steeled himself to fire accurately and without an instant's delay.

But the responsibility wasn't his. The main hold was in pandemonium. Both remaining slavers were staggering under swarming, flailing captives. All the creatures moved with agonized, twitching motions, fighting both their captors and the pulses of excruciating pain being inflicted by their collars. Many were on the deck, unable to overcome the punishment and join the fight.

But those who had mastered their agony were carrying the battle well. As Han watched, they dragged the slavers to the deck, wrestling away weapons and director units and pounding the two into submission. Apparently the creatures knew enough about the director units to deactivate them. All the slaves slumped visibly as their torture ended.

Han stepped cautiously into the hold. He hoped his unwilling passengers understood the situation well enough to know that he wasn't their enemy, but reminded himself he'd better be charming until they were sure.

One of the creatures, its thick white fur ruffled and tufted from its struggle, was studying the collar-box. It made a decisive stab at a switch and all the collars along that particular cable sprang open. The creature tossed the director unit aside contemptuously, and one of its companions passed it a captured disruptor. The sidearm looked big and clumsy in its small, nimble hands.

Han holstered his blaster slowly, holding empty palms up for them all to see. "I didn't want this either," he told them in an even tone, though he doubted that they spoke a shared language. "I had no more to do with it than you."

The disruptor was moving slowly. Han argued with himself the wisdom of reaching for his pistol but doubted his own ability to shoot the creature down. It had no fault in this matter either. He decided to reason on, but the skin on his neck was trying to crawl up into his scalp.

"Listen: you're free to go. I'm not going to stop—"

He sprang sideways as the disruptor swung up at him. It took an iron, conscious effort to keep from drawing. He heard the disruptor's blaring report. And unexpectedly, he heard a small clatter and a gasp from behind him.

Framed in the hatchway, looking down without comprehension at the broad wound in his chest, was Zlarb. At his feet lay the little palmgun. He sank against the hatchway and slid slowly to the deck. The creature had lowered its disruptor once more. Han went and knelt by Zlarb.

The slaver was breathing very unevenly between clenched teeth, his eyes screwed shut. He opened them then, focusing on Han, who had been about to tell him to save his strength, but saw that it made no difference. Perhaps, in a full-facility medicenter, the slaver could have been saved, but with the limited resources of the *Falcon*'s medi-packs Zlarb was as good as gone.

He didn't avoid the slaver's gaze. "They weren't quite as meek as you thought, were they Zlarb?" he asked quietly. "Just real, real patient."

Zlarb's eyes began to flutter shut again. He only managed

"Solo . . ." He put more hatred into the name than Han would have thought possible.

"And how did Zlarb get past you? He almost scored me, you big slug!"

Chewbacca gobbled angrily in response to Han's indignant question and pointed to where the burly humanoid slaver, the one with whom the Wookiee had collided, lay battered and bound by the main ramp.

"So what?' Han demanded with elaborate sarcasm, enjoying himself. He was kneeling by Bollux's side, setting the cap of an extractor over the restraining bolt. "You used to handle three of his kind before breakfast. What I *don't* need is a first mate who's turning into a geriatric case."

Chewbacca barked so loudly that Han ducked involuntarily. A Wookiee's lifespan is longer than a human's—age was a standing joke between the two.

"That's what *you* say." Han thumbed the extractor's switch. There was a pop and a tiny burst of blue discharge around the bolt's base.

Bollux's red photoreceptors came on. "Why, Captain Solo! Thank you, sir. Does this mean the crisis has passed?"

"All but the housework. I got the firefighting outlets shut down, but the ship looks like an explosion in a dessert shop. You can skate from here to the cockpit if you want. That was a good move you and Maxie—"

"Blue Max!" Bollux interrupted, a rarity for him. "Sir, he's not in linkage; I think he's been damaged."

"We know. His adaptor arm was bent and he took some burnout creepage. Chewie says he can fix him up, though, with components we have onboard. Just leave Max be for now. Can you get up?"

The labor 'droid answered by rising and swinging his chest panel shut over the computer module protectively. "Blue Max is remarkably resourceful, wouldn't you say, Captain?"

"Bet your anodes. If he had fingers we'd have to start locking up the tableware. You can tell him that for me later, but for now just take it easy." Han stood and beckoned Chewbacca and the two went aft to the hold again.

The former captives had laid out the bodies of their several dead, those who hadn't survived the terrible ordeal of the slave collars. They were assembling litters from materials in the hold, which Han had offered them, with which to bear their fellows home.

Han stopped by the corpse of Zlarb. In searching the man a few minutes earlier, he had noticed the hard, rectangular lump of a breast-pocket security case under his thermosuit. Han had seen a few such cases before and knew he had to be careful with it.

Settling down with one of the *Falcon*'s medi-packs, he dug out a flexclamp and a vibroscalpel and began cutting away the tough material of the thermosuit. In the meantime, Chewbacca began cleaning his own wounds with an irrigation bulb and a synth-flesh dispenser. More by fortune than design, neither of the two had received deep wounds from the nashtah's claws.

Han quickly had the security case exposed. It was anchored to the pocket by a slim clip to which it was attached by a fine wire. Han carefully felt for and found the safety, a small button concealed at the case's lower edge. Pressing it, he disengaged the security circuit. Then he began working the clip loose from the pocket lining with his other hand. To try to remove the case in any other fashion would invite a neuroparalysis charge from the case. A numb arm would be the best he could hope for, depending on the case's setting. Some security cases were capable of giving lethal shocks.

He reprimed the clip, and the case was rendered harmless. Humming a half-remembered tune, he got busy with some fine-work instruments he had fetched from the ship's small but complete tool locker. The lock itself was a fairly common model; the neuroshock was the case's main line of defense. He had it open in fairly short order.

And spat some sizzling Corellian oaths. There was no money.

All the case contained were a data plaque, a message tape, and a smaller case that turned out to be a Malkite poisoner's kit. That Zlarb was a practitioner of the Malkite poisoner's arts reaffirmed Han's conviction that the universe wouldn't mourn the man's passing, but it did little to alleviate his frustration or his financial situation.

He threw aside the security case and glowered at the two surviving human slavers. They both began to quake visibly. "You have one chance," he said quietly. "Somebody owes me money; I have ten thousand credits coming for this run and I want it. Not telling me where I can get it would be the dumbest thing you'll ever do in your lives, and one of the very last."

"We don't know anything, Solo, we swear," one of them protested. "Zlarb hired us on and he arranged everything; he handled the contacts and all the money himself. We never saw anybody else, that's the truth." His comrade confirmed it energetically.

The ex-slaves had finished their preparations and were ready to depart. Han walked over to where the empty collars and director units lay. "That's really rotten luck for you two," he told the slavers and fastened a collar around the neck of each, ignoring their protests. He handed the collar-box to the leader of the ex-slaves and pointed to the bodies of the dead.

The creature understood, patting the case. The slavers would pay for the deaths with their own servitude. How long a sentence they'd have to serve would be entirely up to their one-time captives. Han couldn't have cared less.

"Take your boss's body with you," he ordered the two. They looked at one another. The creature's finger poised near the controls of their collars. They scrambled to obey, hoisting the late Zlarb between them.

Chewbacca led the way as the ex-slaves, preceded by their new servants, bore their dead from the cargo hold. "Don't forget to get rid of the other casualties," Han called after his friend. "And collar up that other slaver for them. Then bring me a reader!"

Exhausted, he resolutely set to the task of cleaning up his injuries with another irrigation bulb, thinking ominous thoughts about how little money he and Chewbacca had left and wondering if their rotten luck would ever break. Then it occurred to him that Zlarb would undoubtedly have killed him, and Chewbacca as well, if Blue Max and Bollux hadn't given the situation a twist. As it was, he and the Wookiee were alive and free and, with a little cleaning up, would have their starship in something like running order again very shortly. By the time Chewbacca returned, Han was applying synth-flesh to his wounds and whistling to himself.

The Wookiee was carrying a portable readout. Han shoved the medipack aside and fit the data plaque into the reader. His copilot leaned over his shoulder and together they puzzled over what they saw.

"Date-time coordinates, planetary index numbers," Han muttered. "Ships' registry codes and rental agents' IDs. Most of them for a planet called Ammuud." Chewbacca rumbled his own mystification.

Han again cursed Zlarb. Removing the plaque, he inserted the message tape into the readout's other aperture. On the screen appeared the face of a young, black-haired man. The tight closeup told Han nothing about the man's surroundings, whereabouts, or even the clothing he wore.

The face in the portable readout began speaking. "The measures you suggested are being taken against the Mor Glayyd on Ammuud. When delivery of your current consignment is made, payment will take place on Bonadan. Be at table 131, main passenger lounge, Bonadan Spaceport Southeast II at these coordinates." Standard date-time coordinates appeared on the screen for a moment, then it cleared.

Han tossed the reader into the air with a burst of laughter. "If we pour it on, we can still get there in time. Let's get the canopy patched; we can tidy up and see to Bollux and Max while we're in jump."

He kissed the reader and the Wookiee brayed, muzzle wrinkling, tongue curling, fangs showing. It was time to see about payments due.

HAN Solo was obliged to raise his voice to deliver the punch line. A gargantuan ore barge was settling in with such a booming of brute engines that, even though it was grounding halfway across the vast spaceport, it set up tiny wavelets in drinks in the passenger terminal's main lounge.

The main lounge of Bonadan Spaceport Southeast II was colossal and, besides the unceasing rumble of arriving and departing ships, was filled with the conversation of thousands of human and nonhuman customers that overtaxed its sound-muting system. The lounge's transparent dome revealed a sky teeming with ships of every description, their comings and goings orchestrated by the most advanced control system available. Planetary and solar system shuttles, passenger liners, the enormous barges carrying food and raw materials, Authority Security Police fleet ships, and bulk freighters bearing away Bonadan's manufactured goods—all combined to make this one of the busiest ports in the Corporate Sector.

Although it encompassed tens of thousands of star systems, the Corporate Sector Authority was no more than an isolated cluster among the uncountable suns known to humankind. But there wasn't one native, intelligent life form to be found in this entire part of space; a number of theories existed to explain why. The Authority had been chartered to exploit the incalculable wealth here. There were those who used words like ''despoil'' and ''pillage'' for what the Authority did. It maintained absolute control over its provinces and employees, and guarded its prerogatives jealously.

Leaning closer to Chewbacca, Han chuckled. "So the prospector says—get this, Chewie—the prospector says, "Well, how do you think my pack-beast got knock-kneed?"

He had timed the delivery just right. Chewbacca had raised a two-liter mug of Ebla beer to his lips and a spasm of laughter caught him right in the middle of a long draught. He choked, snorted, and woofed mightily into his mug. White beer-spume exploded outward. Though they registered displeasure, patrons at nearby tables, inspecting the Wookiee and noting his size and the fierce, fanged visage, refrained from complaining. Han chortled, as he scratched a shoulder made itchy by the somatigenerative effects of the synth-flesh.

Chewbacca uttered a guttural accusation. The pilot raised his eyebrows. "Of course I timed the punch line that way. Bollux told that joke to me while I was eating and it did the same thing to me." Chewbacca thought about the joke again and laughed abruptly, something halfway between a grunt and a bark.

Throughout his story and most of the long Bonadan morning Han had kept an eye on table 131. It was still vacant and the little red light over its robo-bartender indicated that it was still reserved. The closest overhead chrono showed that the time for Zlarb's rendezvous with his employer was long past.

The lounge was nearly filled, which tended to be true of this place at any hour of the day or night, what with the number of passengers and crew members passing through the port in addition to resident personnel. It was a light, airy, and open place constructed in levels of meandering terraces where plants from hundreds of Authority worlds had been nurtured. Though every table had a clear view of the constant traffic above, foliage tended to screen one terrace from the next. The two partners had selected a table from which they could observe table 131 through a lush curtain of D'ian orchid vine freckled with sweet-smelling moss and still remain inconspicuous.

It had been their uncomplicated plan to observe who came to meet Zlarb at the table, follow them out and accost them, collecting their ten thousand by dint of whatever threats or intimidation seemed appropriate. But something was plainly wrong; no one had come.

Han began feeling uneasy despite his joking; neither he nor Chewbacca was armed. Bonadan was a highly industrialized, densely inhabited planet, one of the Authority's foremost factory worlds. With masses of humanity and other life forms packed together in such number, the Security Police—"Espos," as they were called in slangtalk—were at great pains to keep lethal weapons out of the hands and other manipulatory appendages of the populace. Weapons detectors and search-scan monitors were to be found almost everywhere on the planet, including thoroughfares, places of business, stores, and public transportation. And, most particularly, surveillance was maintained at each of Bonadan's ten sprawling spaceports, the largest of which was Southeast II.

Carrying a firearm—either blaster or Wookiee bowcaster—would be grounds for immediate arrest, something the two could hardly afford. If their true identities and past activities ever came to light, the Corporate Sector Authority's only regret would be that it could only execute them one time apiece. The one positive aspect of this situation, the way Han saw it, was that Zlarb's contact would in all probability be unarmed as well.

Or, would have been. It was beginning to look like their wait had been for nothing.

Chewbacca punched a series of buttons on the robo-bartender and fed it some cash, very nearly their last. A panel slid back and a new round of drinks waited. The Wookiee took up a new mug enthusiastically, and for Han there was another half-bottle of a strong local wine. Chewbacca drank deeply and with obvious bliss, eyes closed, lowering the mug at last to wipe the white ring of suds out of his facial hair with the back of one paw. He closed his eyes again and smacked his lips loudly.

Han approached his bottle with less ardor. Not that he

didn't like the wine; it was the intrusive nature of this over-civilized planet, as reflected in the design of the bottle, that he abhorred. He pressed hard on the cap's seal with his thumb and the cap popped off. Once off, it was almost impossible to re-affix. Then came the part Han really loathed; breach of the cap triggered the release of a small energy charge. Light-emitting diodes, manufactured into the bottle, began a garish show. Figures and lettering marched around the bottle extolling the virtues of its contents. The LEDs scintillated, giving what were intended to be winning statements about the wine's contents, bouquet, and the high standards of personal hygiene embraced by the bottler's employees and automata. Consumer information appeared, too, though in far smaller letters and less blinding hues.

Han, glaring at the bottle, refusing to touch it as long as it persisted in flaunting itself, thought *I should've had some of these back on Kamar. The Badlanders would probably've danced around them holding hands and singing hymns.*

After a minute or so the tiny charge was exhausted and the bottle reverted to an unaggressive container. Han's attention was attracted by a conversation going on by table Number 131, only a few meters away on the next terrace down. An assistant manager, a blue-furred, four-armed native of Pho Ph'eah, was engaged in a difference of opinion with an attractive young female of Han's own species.

The manager was waving all four arms in the air. "But the table is reserved, human! Can you not see the red courtesy light that so designates it?"

The human appeared to be several years younger than Han. She had straight black hair that fell just below the nape of her slender neck. Her skin was a rich brown, her eyes nearly black, indicating that she came from a world that received a good deal of solar radiation. She had a long, mobile face that showed, Han thought, a sense of humor. She wore an everyday working outfit—a blue one-piece bodysuit and low boots. She stood, hands gracefully on hips, and stared at the Pho Ph'eahian, unconvinced.

Then she contorted her face in a very close imitation of the manager's, waving her arms and shrugging her shoulders in precisely the way he had, though she was a couple of arms short. Han found himself laughing aloud. She heard him, caught his eye and gave him a conspiratorial smile. Then she went back to her dispute.

"But it's been reserved ever since I came in, hasn't it? And nobody's claimed it, have they? There're no other small tables and I'm tired of sitting at the bar; I want to wait for my friends right here. Or should we take our business elsewhere? It doesn't look like you're making much money off this table right now, does it?"

She had hit him in a vital spot. Lost revenue was something a good Authority employee simply never permitted. The blue-furred manager looked around worriedly to make sure the party or parties for whom the table was reserved wouldn't materialize out of thin air and object. With an eloquent four-shouldered gesture of resignation, he flicked off the red courtesy light. The young woman took her place with a look of satisfaction.

"That's that," Han sighed to Chewbacca, who had noticed the incident, too. "No collections today; Zlarb's boss is as slippery as he was."

The Wookiee grumbled like a drumroll in a deep cave. He added a surly afterword as he rose to check on the *Millennium Falcon*.

"After you check the ship," Han called after him, "go hunt around the guild hiring halls and the portmaster's headquarters. I'll meet you later at the Landing Zone. See if anybody we know is in port; maybe somebody can tell us something. Chewie, if we don't come into some cash pretty soon, we're not even going to be able to get off Bonadan. I'm going to finish my wine, then make a few more stops to look for familiar faces."

The Wookiee, scratching his shaggy chest, acknowledged with a basso honk. As his copilot ambled off, Han took another sip of his wine and another look around, hoping that a last-minute arrival would give him a chance to pick up the ten thousand somebody owed him. But he saw no one who looked interested in table 131. Penury loomed before him and he felt the near-undeniable craving for money to which he was especially susceptible in times of financial distress.

He whiled away a few more minutes sipping at the wine and admiring the young woman who had preempted table 131. At length she happened to turn and catch his eye again. "Happy landings," she toasted, and he raised his glass in response to the old spacer's greeting. She eyed him speculatively. "Long time out?"

He made an indifferent face, not sure why she was interested. "No home port for me, just a ship. It's simpler."

She had drained her goblet. "How about a refill?"

Her lively, amused face appealed to him, and it didn't make much sense to carry on the conversation through intervening plant life. He took his bottle and goblet and joined her at table 131.

"You and your friend were the only other ones keeping an eye on this table," she ventured as Han was refilling her goblet.

He stopped pouring. She reached out one forefinger and gently tilted the bottom of the bottle up, filling her goblet nearly to the brim.

"It was obvious, you know," she went on. "Every time someone approached this table, you and your sidekick looked as if you were going to jump through the foliage. I know; I'm very good at reading expressions."

Han was looking around for her backup men, support troops, deputies, accomplices, or whatever. Nobody else in the lounge that he could see was paying any particular attention. He had envisioned meeting a slaver's contact, someone hard and mean enough to stomach and prosper in onc of the vilest enterprises there was. This attractive, breezy female had taken him completcly off guard.

She sipped the wine. "Mmm, delicious. How are things on Lur, by the way?" She was now watching him vigilantly.

He kept his face blank. "Chilly. But the air's clearer than it is here." He batted the air with his hand. "Not as much smoke blowing around, know what I mean?" Sounding as casual as he could, he went on. "You have something for me by the way, don't you?"

She pursed her lips as if in deep concentration. "Since you bring it up we do have a little business. But the main lounge is a little public, wouldn't you say?"

"I didn't pick the place. Where would you suggest, sis, a dark alley? Down a mineshaft somewhere, maybe? Why meet here if not to take care of things?"

"Maybe I just wanted to look you over in the light." She glanced at an overhead chrono. "But you can take it for granted that you've been checked out and approved. After I've left, wait ten minutes then follow." She slid him a folded durasheet with stylus markings on it. "Meet me at this private hangar. Bring proof of delivery and you'll get your money." She raised an eyebrow at him. "You *can* read, can't you?"

Han took the durasheet. "I'm better at feeling my way. Why all the sneaking around?"

She gave him a sour look. "You mean why didn't I just come up to you and dump a mound of cash on the table and have you pass your receipt over? Work that out for yourself."

She slid out of her seat and made her way out of the lounge without a backward glance. Han enjoyed the view in a dispassionate manner; she had a very nice way of moving. His first impulse was to go find Chewbacca, and perhaps even take a chance on arming himself. But if he had to hunt the Wookiee among the guild halls and portmaster's offices, it could take the rest of the long Bonadan day. Han possessed what he regarded as a certain flair for innovation, though, as well as a confidence in his own ability to cope. None of what the woman had said rang quite true, and her allowing Chewbacca to leave before speaking to Han definitely indicated that she was angling.

Still, minutes ago he had been worrying about where his

next meal was coming from, and now he had what might be a chance to get the money he felt was due him. That sort of thing always went a long way toward quieting Han Solo's misgivings.

In any case, he had no intention of following her instructions precisely. He would cheat enough to give himself an advantage. After all, it was daylight and the spaceport was buzzing with activity.

As soon as she was out of sight, Han rose to go. On impulse he put a little more money into the robo-bartender and got himself another half-bottle, taking two more throwaway goblets from the dispenser. He told himself *If she's on the level she might still be thirsty. I hope this makes up for grabbing her money.*

Bonadan Spaceport Southeast II took in a larger square area than many cities, though little of it extended very high above or far beneath the planet's surface. There were shipbuilding and refitting yards, dock facilities for the barges and bulk freighters, an Espo command center, an Authority Merchant Marine academy, and the portmaster's headquarters. Added to that were passenger terminals, maintenance depots, ground transportation installations, warehouses, and living and recreational arrangements for the thousands upon thousands of human and nonhuman types who either lived there or passed through Southeast II. Its immense expanse of fusion-formed soil supported fixed structures of permacite and shaped formex and more transient ones of quick-throw and lock-slab.

Because he had shipmaster's credentials, even though they were forged, Han didn't have to wait for the interport shuttleskimmer. Flagging one of the special courtesy cabs, he set off with the conviction that he could get across the huge port before the woman and whatever friends she might have.

He had the cab let him off a short distance from the hangar whose number she had given him. This part of the port was far less active; these hangars were rental structures, cheap, lock-slab constructions intended for private ships that might not be used for extended periods of time.

As he approached his destination, he passed one of the weapons detectors that covered Bonadan. It tracked him for a moment, like some exotic, overgrown flower following sunlight. Detecting no firearms on him it swung away without issuing an alarm. *Busybody*, grumped Han, hastening on his way.

Rather than enter the small rental hangar through the smaller portal set in the main doors, he located a rear door. It was unlocked and he did a prudent amount of listening and peeking-through before entering.

It was a windowless building containing some maintenance equipment and a compact, six-seater Wanderer. A number of tools lay around the Wanderer, suggesting that whoever had been working on her had gone out for some reason and left the rear door open.

Satisfying himself that the hangar was deserted, he found a place behind a pile of shipping crates, from which he could watch the main door without being seen. Hiking himself up onto an insulated shipping canister, he set down the goblets and half-bottle and waited. If the woman showed up with reinforcements, he'd be able to withdraw and follow them; if she came alone, Han figured, he'd soon be counting his money. Nevertheless, he began to wish Chewbacca was with him. He felt naked without his blaster, and the Wookiee's brawn would have been reassuring.

He was still thinking that when the lights went out.

Han jumped to his feet in a flash, pivoting slowly in absolute darkness without daring to breathe. He thought he heard sounds, a light skittering somewhere on or among the crates, but he couldn't get a fix on its direction. He had his hands and feet ready for defense but felt useless and quite vulnerable in the dark. He wished his sense of smell were as keen as Chewbacca's.

A weight hit his back and shoulders, driving him forward to hands and knees with a violence that knocked the breath from him. Then a rough, cold, damp surface was pressed up against his face. It felt like a hand within a heavy glove, but that was unimportant as he realized that the dampness was releasing fumes of some kind. He had caught his breath again when he had fallen and his reflexes kept him from getting more than a whiff, but that alone set his head spinning.

Fearing the anesthetic, Han tried to wrench his head away, but he succeeded only partially and the glove fumbled for him again. With a terrific effort he managed to continue holding his breath as he clamped down on the invisible hand and bit hard. His silent, invisible attacker wrenched madly and pulled the hand loose, breaking away.

Han lurched to his feet, head still swimming. He swung blindly, trying to land a blow or catch hold of his unseen opponent, but without effect. Rotating slowly, listening to his own heart pound, he was taken by surprise again as he was butted from behind.

Flying headlong, he struck the base of the shipping canister where he had been sitting. It was a double-walled container but luckily it was empty and light enough to yield somewhat. Still, he saw points of light circling before his eyes. He concluded woozily that his assailant must have taken the logical precautions of wearing snooper goggles and breathing filters as well, conferring an enormous advantage.

Something fell on Han's back and rolled onto the floor, then the attacker was on him again and it was all he could do to remember to hold his breath again. He struggled unsuccessfully to rise, protecting his head with one arm. As he did, his groping hand encountered something. It suddenly penetrated his dazed brain that what had landed on his back a moment before had been the half-bottle of wine, which he now held, jostled off the canister by the impact of Han's head. Unfortunately he was in no position to swing it, being held down by his assailant's weight on his back.

With desperate pressure of his thumb he broke the bottle's seal. The cap snapped off, and the bottle's combination LED light display and commercial advertisement began throwing out a garish light, dispelling the blackness.

The oppressive weight on his back shifted, then was gone. He could hear a scuffing of footsteps as his attacker retreated, confused or repelled by Han's unexpected trick. Han pushed himself back over, mouthing denunciations in four languages and trying to ignore the pain of his injuries and the effects of whatever it had been that he had inhaled.

He dragged himself up, using the canister for support. His attacker was nowhere in sight. Han held the half-bottle up but its glare didn't reach far into the gloom; the LEDs weren't, after all, meant for illumination.

He knew he had no time to waste looking for either his enemy or the controls to the lights. The minor charge that powered the bottle's LEDs would last only a little longer. He stumbled back to the hangar's rear door, trying to keep watch in every direction, without further incident.

Back in the glare of Bonadan's sun, he leaned against the hangar wall, closed his eyes and panted until his head cleared. The bottle was dimming. He tossed it aside and it bounced, rolling away rather than breaking. It was made of very tough glass.

What bothered him most was the thought that his attacker might have been the girl. He really thought she had been more kindly disposed toward him, but the facts seemed to add up. She would hardly be working alone, though, and that meant that both Han and Chewbacca might have been watched in the passenger lounge.

If Chewbacca had been followed from the lounge, he might really be in trouble.

Han sprinted off, looking desperately for a courtesy cab, hoping he would get to his ship before somebody tore her apart.

IV

THERE were, perversely, no courtesy cabs to be had in the private hangar area of the spaceport. Han used up long minutes at a dead run to locate one. The thought of his friend in desperate trouble, and that of possible damage to his beloved ship, kept him fuming and fidgeting the entire way. He was only marginally relieved when he saw the converted freighter resting, apparently unharmed, where he had left her.

Because they were short of funds, the partners had been compelled to leave their ship parked on an approach apron rather than in a rented docking bay as was their preference. Han took the ramp in two long bounds. Even before reaching the main hatch he had noticed, with a meticulous eye for every detail of his ship, a variety of tool marks and discolorations where power implements had been used. He covered the lock with his palm, ready to charge through the hatch the instant it rolled up, unmindful that he wasn't armed, all self-concern overriden by his anxiety over Chewbacca and fear that strangers were working who-knew-what atrocities on his source of freedom and livelihood, the *Millennium Falcon.*

But when the hatch was up he found himself, ready to spring into mortal combat, face-to-faceplate with Bollux. The 'droid's blank, glittering visage didn't convey much emotion, but Han could have sworn there was a note of relief in the vocoder drawl.

"Captain Solo! Are Max and I glad to see you, sir!"

Han brushed past him. "Where's Chewie? Is he all right? Is the ship all right? What happened? Who was here?"

"Aside from minor damage to the main hatch lock, all is in order. First Mate Chewbacca made a brief visual inspection earlier, and left. Then the surveillance systems alerted Max and me that someone was attempting to make a forced entry. Evidently the equipment they brought wasn't sufficient to compromise the ship's security arrangements."

That made sense to Han. The *Falcon* was no ordinary ship, and she had been modified to resist boarding or break-in efforts. Among other things, the relatively unsophisticated lock and other security gear had been replaced with the best Han could build, buy, or steal. Tools and equipment that could crack a stock freighter in minutes wouldn't even make the *Falcon* nervous.

Bollux continued his narration. "I warned them over the hatch comlink that I would alert port Espos if they didn't cease and desist and depart at once. They did, although in keeping with your standing orders I would have been very reluctant to involve any law-enforcement agency."

Han was back out at the ramp, checking the lock. Its palm plate showed nicks and scratches where a decoder had been fastened to it in a futile attempt to unlock it. The armored cover plate was scorched from a plasma torch or baffled blaster. The cover plate was barely touched and probably could have resisted entry for an additional fifteen to twenty minutes. It would have taken a light cannon to burn through in a hurry. But the damage to his ship left Han beside himself with outrage.

The labor 'droid went on, undaunted. "I went forward to the cockpit to observe them as they left."

"You stupid stack of factory rejects! You should've climbed down into the belly turret and erased 'em!" Han was so angry he could scarcely see straight by now.

The 'droid's slow speech made him seem imperturbable. "That's one thing I could not do. I'm sorry, Captain; you know my built-in constraints against harming or attacking intelligent life forms."

Han, still brooding over the affront to his pride and joy, murmured, "Yeah. One of these days when I've got some time I'll have to see about those."

Alarmed at the thought of fundamental personality alterations as performed by Han Solo, Bollux quickly changed the subject. "Sir, I did get a view of the individuals who attempted to force entry. Both were human and wore blue standard coveralls. One was a man, but he wore a hat and I couldn't discern very much about him from the elevation of the cockpit. The other was a female with short black hair and—"

"I've met her," Han cut in, the color rising in his face. He was trying to calculate times and distances and determine whether it could have been her or her companion who had jumped him in the hangar. If, as he suspected, they had their own private transportation, it could easily have been. "Which way'd they go?"

"As a matter of fact, at Blue Max's suggestion I followed their departure through the macrobinoculars you keep in the cockpit. They parted and the man went off toward the passenger terminal, but the woman boarded a repulsorlift scooter, one of the green rental-agency models. In addition to her safety helmet, I noted, she was carrying a homing unit. Blue Max plugged into the ship's communication countermeasures package and resonated the homer; I've made a notation of the unit's setting. Then she flew away at a course of approximately fifty-three degrees west of planetary north, Captain."

Han was looking at Bollux in amazement. "You know, you two lads constantly wozzle me."

"You're very kind, sir." There was a brief squeal of electronic pulse-communication from deep within the 'droid's chest cavity. "Blue Max thanks you, too."

"A pleasure." Han considered his next move. The woman's course would take her out over some of the only open country in this part of Bonadan. He couldn't go after her in the *Falcon*; strict local airspace regulations prohibited taking spacecraft out of approach-departure corridors. The only remaining alternative was renting a repulsorlift scooter of his own and locating her that way. But that also meant going past who-knew-how-many more of the omnipresent weapons scanners and forgoing his blaster. Taking Chewbacca along would be a logical precaution, but waiting for the Wookiee to return decreased his chances of catching up with the woman. Han was still boiling about having been jumped in the hangar, madder still about the damage to the *Millennium Falcon*, minor though that was. In this sort of mood he had seldom been noted for his cool reasoning.

That left one more problem, communicating with Chewbacca. "Bollux, I want you to leave Max here, linked to the ship's surveillance system. If anybody else tries to tamper with the *Falcon*, he can do just what you did; if worse comes to worst, he can call in the Espos. Then I want you to go track down Chewie. He'll be either making the rounds of the guild hiring halls or portmaster's offices or waiting for me at a joint called the Landing Zone just outside the spaceport. I'll catch up with you both there as soon as I can or, if I'm gone more than a few hours, I'll meet you back here. Tell him everything that's happened."

The repulsorlift scooter was the fastest one the spaceport rental agency had, which was no particular mark of distinction. Han pushed the craft to its limits, its tiny engine sounding as if it had developed a lung condition, scanning ahead with the macrobinoculars he had brought from the ship.

He set a course to match the one Bollux had observed the woman to be taking. He had also brought a homing unit, adjusted to the setting Blue Max had resonated from hers.

The city was a dreary mosaic of factories, refineries, offices, dormitories, worker housing, warehouses, and shipping centers that stretched on and on. He moved, as was required, through the lowest levels of air traffic. Around him skimmers, gravsleds, and other scooters passed and flowed according to the directions of Traffic Control. Below, wheeled and tracked transportation and ground-effect vehicles moved along the city's avenues and byways, and high overhead in the hazy smog cover the lanes were monopolized by long-distance mass transport craft, bulk haulers, and cargo lifters. Espo patrol ships swam among the flow at all levels like predatory fish.

Eventually he left the city behind, whereupon Traffic Control notified him that guidance and navigation of his little vehicle had been returned to him. The repulsorlift scooter was little more than a bucket-chair with attached control board, a cheap, simple, easily mastered vehicle common to any number of worlds. He'd slung the visored safety helmet given him by the rental agency from its storage clip at the board's side; he wanted as wide a field of vision as he could get. The fact that helmets were mandatory didn't matter much to him.

Once out of the metropolitan restrictions, Han poured on more speed than the scooter's engine was supposed to be able to provide. Crouching behind the little windscreen, he ignored the ominous noises coming from the propulsion plant located under his seat.

Beneath him the surface of Bonadan came fully into view for the first time—it was barren, parched, eroded, and leached of its topsoil because plant life had been destroyed by large-scale mining, pollution, and uncaring management. The surface was predominantly yellow, with angry strips of rust-red in its twisted gullies and cracked hillocks. The Corporate Sector Authority cared little about the long-range effects of its activities on the worlds it ruled. When Bonadan was depleted and unlivable, the Authority would simply move its operations to the next convenient world.

The landscape gave way gradually to steeper peaks and crags. These mountains must have had little mineral wealth and no industrial value, for they were relatively intact. The single incursion made here by the grasping technology of the

Authority was an automated weather-control station, a titanic cylinder set lengthwise on its giant aiming apparatus. At present it was directed seaward, no doubt to dissipate a storm center the Corporate Sector Authority found inconvenient. To hell with Bonadan's natural weather patterns; ocean mining and drilling must go on, Bonadan's seas were dying.

The homing unit began registering. Han turned onto the course it indicated, hurdling the peak on which the weather station stood. He passed down over the lower hills beyond, scanning with the macrobinoculars, checking the homing unit from time to time.

A movement below caught his eye. Han brought the scooter to a hover while he focused on it more clearly. Another small air vehicle, something faster than a scooter, was dropping toward a flat table of land. Han could make out, already waiting on the ground, a tiny figure standing next to another scooter, a green rental job.

He cut in full thrust again. In a more leisurely moment he might have held off and surveyed the situation before going in, but he and his copilot had been cheated of ten thousand in cash and almost killed, which had made them vengeful ever since. Then somebody had pummeled Han to the ground and an attempt had been made to cut his ship open. Given conditions on Bonadan, the fact that no one below was likely to be carrying a firearm counted only lightly in his decision.

As he dove toward the ground, his rage built into something that was closer to an adrenaline seizure than to courage. He hit full emergency braking thrusters at the last instant, turning what should have been a prodigious crash into a startlingly abrupt precision touchdown, taking delight in the bone-shaking force of it.

Leaping from the scooter, Han was greeted by a dumbfounded stare from the woman and angry suspicion from the man who had landed just seconds before him. The man was a bit taller than Han, but very lean, with deep-set eyes and gaunt cheeks. He, too, wore standard worker's coveralls. The vehicle he had ridden, though, was far from commonplace.

It was what was usually called a "swoop"—essentially an overpowered repulsor engine pod with handlebars. It was sitting on its landing skids, its engine making it throb gently.

The swoop-rider turned to the woman with an odd smile. "I thought you said Zlarb sent you alone." He then stared at Han. "You have a fatal sense of timing, friend." His hand dipped into the utility pouch on his belt. When it came up again it held something that filled the air with an insistent hum.

Han identified it as some sort of vibroblade, perhaps a butcher's tool or surgeon's instrument that the weapons scanners would register as an industrial implement. It had been home-altered to include a large blade, and its haft was fitted with a bulkier power pack. The blade, half again as long as Han's hand, was difficult to see, vibrating at an incredible rate. It would cut through flesh, bone, and most other materials with little or no resistance.

Han jumped backward as the vibroblade slit the air where he had stood, its droning field sounding aroused now. The woman's voice rang out firmly, "Just stop right there!"

Both men saw that she had produced a small pistol, but when she motioned with it the vibroblader turned on her, blade held ready. His defiance put doubt on her face, but she still pointed the weapon directly at him.

"Quit fanning him with it and shoot!" Han yelled. He saw her finger convulse at the trigger.

Nothing happened. She looked at the pistol in amazement and tried to fire again with no more success. The vibroblader turned to advance at Han again, light-footed, making quick cuts and exploring Han's defenses, which, in brief, were retreat and avoidance. Against a regular blade Han might have tried to block or parry; a simple laceration, even a deep one, could be set right with the contents of any medi-pack and would have been a price he would have accepted to end the match. But a vibroblade would simply lop off anything that got in its way; standard responses would only get him carved to bits slowly.

Whoever he was, the vibroblader was good. Han was suddenly and tardily sorry he had descended. The man advanced on him more confidently now, weaving his blade in the air, driving Han back step for step, ready to leap forward in an instant if the pilot turned to withdraw.

Han caught sight of his scooter out of the corner of his eye. He side-stepped that way hastily, still facing his opponent. The man circled that way just as quickly, slashing where he thought Han would be, assuming he meant to escape.

But Han stopped and bent sideways at the last moment, snatching his safety helmet off its clip. Enraged at having been tricked, the vibroblader hurried a clumsy backhand stroke. Han swung the helmet by its chinstrap with all his might but only caught the man with a badly aimed blow that bounced from his shoulder and glanced off the side of his head. The light material of the helmet wasn't enough to down him.

The vibroblader brought his weapon around and up in a move that would have opened Han vertically, but he had jumped back out of range. They shuffled on again, Han still retreating.

The fight had changed subtly. Han swung away with the helmet, aiming for the hand that held the weapon. Though he was still at a tremendous disadvantage, he just might connect, opening the vibroblader's guard. Then he might close with the man and immobilize his wrist, the only chance he needed.

But his opponent knew that as well as Han. His advance was still strong, but he was careful to avoid the flailing helmet. Then the vibroblader caught the safety helmet with a slash; a broad segment of the tough duraplas went flying free. Seeing that the helmet was too slow and clumsy, Han whirled what was left of it underhand and flung it upward at his opponent's face.

The man avoided it, ducking quickly to one side, but in that split second Han was inside his guard, his left hand around the wrist that held the weapon. Their free hands locked and they strained against one another. The man was far stronger than he looked; he forced his vibroblade nearer.

Han heard the dull burring of the knife's field by his left ear and, distracted by it, fell victim to a deft leg-trip. He fell to his back and the vibroblader fell with him, the two still locked together.

Han managed to roll over, gaining the top position, but his antagonist used the momentum to force another roll, regaining it and bringing Han up sharply against some unseen obstruction. The vibroblader rose a bit, using his weight, straining to bring the blade down. Its drone filled Han's ears as the duel narrowed to a singleminded contest over the few centimeters that separated the blade from Han's neck.

Suddenly the atmosphere of Bonadan seemed to be filled with a tremendous roaring, a flood of sounds. The vibroblader was ripped away so quickly that Han was almost dragged with him. As it was, he was hauled around, nearly wrenching his shoulder before his grip was torn free of the other's hand and wrist.

Han sat up, confused. Looking in one direction he saw the vibroblader lying some meters away, not doing a great deal of breathing. Turning his head slowly, shaking it a little to clear it, Han saw the young woman, off some distance in the other direction. She was clumsily bringing the swoop around in a slow turn.

She guided the vehicle with a jerky lack of skill. Failing to coordinate braking thrust and lift, she stalled it out completely. Giving it up, she dismounted and finished the rest of the way back on foot. By that time Han had risen and brushed much of the dust off himself.

She studied him, left hand on hip.

"That wasn't a bad move, rocketsocks," he admitted.

"Don't you ever pay attention to anybody?" she scolded. "I kept hollering 'look out, look out'; I was going to toss a rock at him but you kept getting in the way. I don't know what I would've done if he hadn't been right behind the engine pod. If he'd been any farther— Hey!"

Han had stepped forward, grabbed both her hands and pulled her palms up roughly, inhaling them deeply. He detected no scent of either the anesthetic that had impregnated the gloves of his assailant at the spaceport or any solvent that might have been used to remove it. But her companion might have executed the ambush in the hangar, or it was possible that the stuff in the gloves might not have contacted her skin. This didn't prove she was innocent; it only failed to prove she was guilty.

He let her go. She was watching him with arch interest. "Should I sniff you back or clap my hands on your nose or what? You're a really strange one, Zlarb."

That explained a few things anyway, if she meant it. "My name's not Zlarb. Zlarb's dead, and whoever he worked for owes me ten thousand."

She stared at him. "That tallies, provided you're telling the truth. But you were where Zlarb was supposed to be, doing more or less what he was supposed to be doing."

Han angled a thumb at the vibroblader's body. "Who was that?"

"Oh, him. That's who Zlarb was supposed to meet at the lounge. I was playing off both sides, Zlarb and his boss. Or, I thought I was."

Han began warming up to an interrogation session when she interrupted. "I'd love to chat this over at length but shouldn't we get out of here before *they* arrive?"

He looked up and saw what she meant. Bearing down on them was a flight of four more swoops. "Scooters are too slow. Come on." He snagged his macrobinoculars from his repulsorlift scooter and ran for the swoop belonging to the late vibroblader. Climbing on, he brought the engine pod back to life. The woman was bent over the vibroblader's body.

Working the handlebar accelerator, he tugged the swoop through a tight turn, helping with his foot. A quick surge of power took him to her side in a moment.

He braked hard. "Are you coming or staying?" he asked

as he fit his knees into the control auxiliaries. She set her boot on a rear footpeg and swung up into the saddle behind him, showing him the vibroblade she had stopped to collect.

"Very good," he conceded. "Now belt in and hold on." He did the same, securing the safety belt tightly at his waist, and each donned a pair of the flying goggles that hung from clips at the swoop's side. He gave the accelerator a hard twist and they tore away into the air, the wind screaming at them over the swoop's low fairing. She clasped her arms around his middle and they both bent low to avoid the fairing's slipstream.

The oncoming swoops were approaching from the direction of the city, so Han turned deeper into open country. At the edge of the table of land he threw his craft into a sudden dive over the brink, straight down into a chasm beyond. The ground rushed at them.

He threw his weight against the handlebars and leaned hard against the steering auxiliaries. The swoop came up so sharply that he was nearly torn from the handlebars by centrifugal force and the woman's grip on him. The rearmost edge of the engine pod brushed the ground, making it skip and fishtail. Han just avoided a crash, slewed in midair and headed off down the sharply zigzagged chasm.

He calculated that, due to the steep, twisty nature of the gulches and canyons in the area, his pursuers couldn't simply stand off at high altitude and search for him, for he might escape through a side canyon or simply hide under an overhanging ledge and out-wait them. If, on the other hand, they came in direct pursuit; they would have to hang on his tail through these obstacle course gullies and draws.

Han hadn't been on a swoop in years but had once been very good on them, a racer and a course rider. He was willing to match himself against the four who rode after him. The one thing that worried him was the chance that they might split their bet, one or two of them going high and the others clinging to his afterblast.

"What're you worried about anyway?" his passenger

yelled over the engine's howl and the quarrelsome wind. "They won't have guns or that first man would've had one, right?"

"That doesn't mean they can't jump us," he called back over his shoulder, trying not to let it distract him from negotiating the crazy turns and switchbacks of the maze. He decided that she must have little experience with swoops. She made some remark he didn't catch, sounding as if she understood, but he was too busy conning the aircraft to answer.

Then he found out what she'd been worried about. Coming out of an especially sharp turn he almost lost control and had to touch his braking thrusters, swearing at the necessity.

It saved both their lives. A sudden blast of force erupted in the air to their right. Even the turbulence at its very edge was nearly enough to send them into the rock wall so close to their left. Under Han's desperate efforts the little swoop wobbled, then righted and flew on.

Overhead and to the right banked one of the other swoops; its pilot had brought it down in a steep dive and snapped past, opening his accelerator at the bottom of the dive in an effort to knock Han's vehicle out of the air or tear its riders from their saddle with the sheer force of an engine blast. Played for near-misses and scares, this sort of thing had been a game Han had known well in his youth; played for real, it was an efficient form of murder.

He knew there would be at least one backup man; they wouldn't leave more than half their number on high cover. He came up on a forking of the way, took a split second's bearing on the angle of the sun and dodged into the canyon he had selected. The woman was pounding him on the back, demanding to know why he'd taken the more confining way.

There was a long overhang running along one side of the canyon, but he clung to the other side, dividing his time between the harrowingly fast decisions of the ride and stolen, microsecond glances at the canyon floor. He fought the urge to pull up and get clear of the insane obstacle course; with its double burden, his swoop would almost certainly be overtaken and hemmed in and someone flying high cover was a good bet to buffet him right out of the sky.

A flash of warning was all he got. The sun's slanting rays showed him another shadow not far behind his own on the canyon's floor. His instantaneous brake-and-accelerate sequence was based more on intuition than on computation of angles and speeds. But it served its purpose; the other swoop overshot, its rider's aim thrown off by Han's maneuver. The other rider pulled out of his dive, but by then Han had pulled into a position to meet him as he brought his swoop into an ascending curve. As he rose, the other rider found himself gazing into the rear end of Han's swoop's engine pod.

He couldn't avoid Han's afterblast. The other swoop careened off the canyon floor, wobbled in the air for a moment, then plowed into the ground. Han didn't stop to see whether the rider survived the spill or not; he poured on all the speed he safely could, and considerably more besides. Climbing, diving, and sideslipping, it was all he could do to keep from having a collision of his own.

It was a shock when, coming out of a frantic bank that had their swoop's underside within centimeters of a vertical canyon wall, Han and his passenger broke into the open, leaving the hills behind. Unexpectedly, the other three pursuers, who had lost track of Han in the maze, came flying at an almost leisurely pace across his course.

He had a moment's view of their astounded faces, a human and two humanoids whose gold-sheened skins gleamed in the hazy sunlight of the long Bonadan afternoon. They swung their swoops around to resume the chase as Han accelerated.

Even as he did, he knew a straight run would be futile. With the woman aboard he was bound to be overtaken before he could reach the safety of the patrolled city traffic patterns. What he needed was something to break off the pursuit.

Something off to his left attracted his attention. The huge cylinder of the automated weather-control station was just beginning a slow swing on its aiming apparatus, realigning for a new assignment. Han yanked at the handlebars and cut a new course for it.

His passenger screamed. "What are you doing? They'll catch us!"

He couldn't take time to tell her they would be overtaken anyway. Closing fast on the station's supporting framework, he had to cut speed. Quick looks told him that his swoop was being bracketed above and to either side by the remaining pursuers. He cut speed even more as the support framework loomed directly before him.

For the moment his pursuers held back, not sure why he was riding straight at this huge obstruction. They had no desire to be lured into a fatal accident.

At the last second he shed almost all his speed and threaded in through the girderwork support. It wasn't a particularly hard maneuver; the thick girders were widely spaced, and his speed was, by then, comparatively low. The pursuers, closely grouped behind him, chose to follow rather than detour around the support tower. They were determined not to lose him as he broke out the other side. That wasn't, however, his plan.

He pulled at the handlebars and went into a vertical climb, straight up the central well of the support tower, hoping that this station followed standard design.

It did; he shot between two catwalks and directly out into the cavernous emission cylinder, a gridwork with open squares some meter and a half or so on a side. The emission cylinder was 150 meters long, less than a third of that in diameter. He swung down toward one end of the slowly rotating cylinder, orienting himself and figuring out just which way the station was pivoting.

He turned back to see the three pursuers soar into the cylinder in determined chase. They were moving a good deal slower than Han; they had never played this game before.

"Stay gripped," he shouted over his shoulder and swung back toward the others. The cylinder was more than spacious enough for them to scatter and avoid him, thinking he was trying to ram. Then they dropped in on his tail again, following him down toward the far end of the cylinder where, they were sure, they could trap and halt him.

Until he speeded up again. The engine pod blared its power. The far end of the emission cylinder was still swinging and Han had to compensate carefully for its movement. He crouched forward, sighting carefully through the fairing, lining up the swoop precisely. The openings in the gridwork were frighteningly small.

The woman saw what he was about to do and burrowed her head into his back. The opening he had selected expanded before him. There was a terrible moment of doubt, far too late to change his mind.

The gridwork passed him like a shadow. And he was in the open, pointed more or less toward the city, the swoop's engine howling. He took a quick look behind. Pieces of wreckage were raining slowly to the ground and some lengths of gridwork stuck out jaggedly; one of his pursuers had tried to emulate him and failed.

The woman's face was pallid.

"Are you all right?" he asked.

"Just fly this thing, you psychopath!" she shouted back.

He faced forward again with an arrogant smirk. "Deft hands and a pure heart triumph again! You were never in any—" He gulped as he saw that the top edge of the fairing had been neatly sheared away. He'd been spared by no more than millimeters.

"—danger," Han Solo finished in a much more subdued voice.

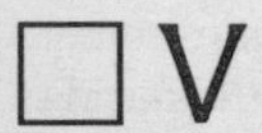

V

CHEWBACCA, still some distance from the *Millennium Falcon*, smelled a strange odor and knew something was wrong. Black nostrils flaring in a futile effort to identify the aroma, he approached the starship as quietly as he could. Despite his great size and weight, the Wookiee, a veteran hunter, moved with total stealth.

After leaving the lounge, Chewbacca had made only a cursory check of the *Falcon*, eyeballing her to make sure no one on any of the grounds crews had attempted to move the freighter or block her in. Then he had begun a round of inquiries at the portmaster's headquarters and guild hiring halls. But the *Falcon*'s first mate had turned up nothing of use.

His errand had caused him to miss both the abortive attempt to break into the ship and Han's subsequent appearance and departure. But now he had discovered still another threat to the starship. Silently easing up to the foot of the ramp, he saw an unfamiliar form hunched over and working busily at the freighter's main hatch lock. Next to the figure was an open tool bag containing a fusioncutter, some probes, a drill, and other instruments of illegal entry. The intruder's ears were covered with some sort of headphones.

Chewbacca ascended the ramp like a wraith, reached out, seized a broad handful of the nape of the intruder's neck, and lifted. The headphones shook loose and from the creature's neck dangled the thing to which they were attached, apparently a listening device for the opening of locks.

"Eee-ee!" The figure writhed and wriggled with such sinuosity that the Wookiee lost his hold. But as the would-be burglar sought to dodge past him, Chewbacca's long arms scooped out to either side, blocking the way. Trapped, the intruder shrank back against the *Falcon*'s main hatch, panting and trembling.

The being was small, perhaps a head shorter than Han Solo when standing erect rather than cowering. He had the sleek, glossy pelt of an aquatic mammal, colored a deep gleaming black. He was a biped with short, strong-looking fingers and toes; between those fingers and toes were webs of pinkish-gray skin. He had a thick, tapering tail and pointed ears that stood close to his skull, moving independently, aiming this way and that, first at the Wookiee, then away. His long, moist snout snuffled and quivered nervously. From this whiskered snout protruded a set of long buckteeth. It was plain from his squinting eyes that his vision wasn't very acute.

The being seemed to gain a good deal of information by his ears; Chewbacca assumed it was only because he had been wearing the headphones that he'd failed to notice the Wookiee's approach.

The intruder collected himself and drew himself up to his full height (which wasn't very imposing against Chewbacca's), nose quivering and tail vibrating in righteous indignation. Unfortunately his voice, when it came, was something of a quavering squeak with a slight lisp, reducing the effect. Still, it held conviction.

"What's the idea of assaulting me, you big overstuffed oaf of a Wookiee? How *dare* you? I'll have you know I'm a licensed collections agent. This vessel appears on the *Red List*!" He snagged a card out of his open bag and presented it with the formal flourish of a webbed hand.

It was a document of identification and authorization for one Spray, of the planet Tynna, to act in the interests and on the behalf of Interstellar Collections Limited, pursuant to the collection of debts, garnishing and repossession proceedings and any and all activities connected thereunto. On it was a flat two-dee depicting the little collections agent.

Chewbacca, satisfied that the document was real, looked up with a snarl of displeasure directed at all skip-tracers in general and at Spray in particular. Like Han, he sincerely detested them.

Jumping out on a debt seldom meant trouble with law enforcement agencies; it was such a common practice among members of the fringe society of independent spacers that every lawman in the galaxy could have spent every waking moment looking for, apprehending, and prosecuting them to the exclusion of all other activity. Thus the Espos, Imperial forces, and other legal authorities tended to ignore the problem, leaving the collection of debts and/or repossession of spacecraft to agency skip-tracers like Spray who roamed the galaxy with the voluminous and infamous *Red List*.

Spray appeared not to notice the Wookiee's snarl. Having identified himself, he reverted to being a company man. The Tynnan dug out, from somewhere, an incredibly thick little notebook, squinting into it, his moist nose nearly touching the page.

He mumbled to himself as he read. "Ah, here, yes," he said finally. "Would you by any chance be Captain, um, Solo?"

Chewbacca barked an irritated negative and jerked a thumb back at the spaceport, indicating Han's present location as well as he could. Then he moved Spray rudely out of his way and bent to see what had been done to the lock. When he noticed the same damage Han had seen earlier he let out a horrible howl and turned back on the skip-tracer with mayhem in mind.

But the Tynnan, back on familiar territory, was indignant rather than intimidated. He snuffled. "I most certainly am *not* responsible for that damage! Do you mistake me for a bungler and a thug? A brainless primitive unconversant with modern technology? I am a trained collections agent, my dear Wookiee, equipped with the latest tools of my profession; I avoid doing any unnecessary damage to repossessed property. I have no idea who was tampering with the hatch lock before me, but you may depend upon it that it wasn't *me*! I simply deactivated the surveillance system and was about to neutralize the lock—*without* damaging it, if I may say so—when you so violently accosted me. Now that you're here, however, the need no longer exists."

Spray was burrowing his bucktoothed proboscis into the notebook again and lisping mumbles to himself, insinuating himself between the Wookiee and the *Falcon*'s main hatch. Chewbacca found himself somewhat off stride; his wrath and threats were sometimes greeted by fear, sometimes by hostility, and occasionally with combat, but never had the towering first mate met anyone quite so preoccupied that he actually paid him no attention.

"Ah, here we are," Spray went on, having riffled back to the correct page. "Your captain has failed to settle on an outstanding debt of some two thousand five hundred Credits Standard owed to Vinda and D'rag, Starshipwrights and Aerospace Engineers Incorporated, of Oslumpex V. Your Captain Solo has ignored seven—no, eight dunning notices."

He glared myopically at the Wookiee. "*Eight*, sir. Vinda and D'rag have therefore presumed default on your captain's part and referred the matter to my employers. Now, if you'll be good enough to open the hatch, I can continue the repossession process. Of course, you're free to remove all personal effects and non—"

Chewbacca had been making deep, reverberating noises in his throat up to now, which someone more familiar with him would have taken as a danger signal. His annoyance burst forth in a roar that drove Spray back a step with its sheer physical impact, ruffling the little skip-tracer's nose fur and bending back his whiskers.

But he stood waiting patiently, eyes squeezed shut against the vocal gale, as Chewbacca railed horrible Wookiee oaths at him. The Tynnan flinched every now and then as the crescendo rose, his ears swinging back protectively, but he held his ground resolutely. The *Falcon*'s first mate periodically punctuated his ranting by slamming his enormous fist against the ship's hull, evoking deep percussives from her armor.

But when he finally ran down, Spray began again in the mildest of tones. "Now then, as I was saying: I have a document here entitling me to take possession of—"

Chewbacca snatched up the papers proffered by Spray. It was a thick legal instrument of several pages; the Wookiee crushed it into a tightly compressed wad in his powerful hands and stuck it into his fanged mouth. Sneering hideously at the skip-tracer, he chomped on the document a few times, shredding it handily, then swallowed it.

But it did little to alleviate his frustration over how to deal with Spray. This was the first time in memory that Chewbacca had ever had such difficulty with a creature whom he outweighed three to one. He was beginning to feel embarrassed; the scene had already attracted the attention of several local idlers and a number of passing automata. The idea of simply demolishing the Tynnan was now out of the question.

"That will do you precisely no good whatsoever, my dear Wookiee," Spray hastened to assure him. "I have many duplicates. Now, unless your captain is prepared to make immediate and total defrayal of the entire sum of his debt, I'm afraid I *must* demand that you open that hatch, or permit me to do so."

Chewbacca surrendered at last, growling and motioning Spray to follow him back down the ramp. He would take the skip-tracer to talk to his partner; he could see no alternative short of losing the ship or committing premeditated murder in a public place.

But Spray was shaking his head briskly, his whiskers quivering. "I'm afraid it just won't do, my good fellow. It's too late to begin negotiating; immediate payment or immediate repossession are your only choices."

In the course of a long life Chewbacca had learned that

there come times when the most bellicose roar is insufficient. He clamped one vast paw on either of Spray's shoulders and effortlessly hoisted the skip-tracer up close, until their gazes were level. Suspended furry muzzle to bucktoothed muzzle with Chewbacca, his webbed feet dangling somewhere above the Wookiee's knees, the Tynnan watched as the *Millennium Falcon*'s first mate wordlessly peeled his lips back from ferocious rows of teeth.

"Then again," the collections agent resumed hastily, "perhaps we *could* work out some sort of agreement and spare my employers the expense and inconvenience of public auction. Point well taken, sir. Where might I find your captain?"

Chewbacca carefully set Spray back down on his feet and, gesturing to the lock surveillance system, growled harshly. Taking his meaning clearly, Spray dug some tools from his bag and quickly reactivated the device.

Blue Max's chirp instantly sounded over the intercom. "Who's there? Why was this instrument deactivated? Reply at once or I'll notify port security!"

Chewbacca barked once at the comlink. "Oh, First Mate Chewbacca, sir," Max replied happily. "I thought the ship was being burglarized again. There was already one attempt earlier. Captain Solo's gone off to investigate. He dispatched Bollux to the Landing Zone with word, and said he'd meet you there. Are you coming aboard, sir?"

The Wookiee barked irritably as he marched Spray down the ramp. The Tynnan had to trot to match Chewbacca's long strides.

Blue Max called after them. "But what are my instructions?"

As the Wookiee dragged him off, the skip-tracer shrilly called back, "In the name of Interstellar Collections Limited, make sure no harm comes to the vessel!"

"What's your name, anyway?" the woman asked as they passed through the entrance to the Landing Zone. It was a well-known spot among spacers, prominent on the avenue of bars, rub-shops, gambling dens, and pawnbrokers' establishments outside the spaceport's main crew gate. "Mine's Fiolla," she encouraged.

Han hadn't had much chance to talk to her on the ride back, at the end of which they had abandoned the swoop and the vibroblade several blocks away, in the middle of the teeming Alien Quarter. It was a good bet that the swoop already had a new coat of paint or was dismantled.

But he saw no reason to cudgel his brain for a cover; the slavers already knew his name, and anyone else who wanted to badly enough could find out.

"Han Solo," he said. She gave no sign of recognizing it.

Bollux, having failed to find Chewbacca in the spaceport's wide confines, had had no more luck at the Landing Zone. But by soliciting the bartender's permission with particular fervor, he had been allowed to wait by the entrance.

Now he approached Han who, sighting the 'droid, sighed. "I don't feel like talking standing up. Come and have a seat, Bollux."

The Landing Zone and all its furnishings were built from pieces and fittings from the spaceport salvage yards. Han led the way to a small table made from an obsolete charts-computer from an old survey ship.

When Bollux and Fiolla had taken seats he turned to her. "Bollux, general labor 'droid, at your service."

Han interrupted Fiolla's courteous reply. "Never mind that," he snapped. "Bollux, where's Chewie?"

"I was unable to locate him, Captain. I came here assuming this to be the place where you'd eventually contact him."

The waiter came by, a many-tentacled Sljee with a broad tray firmly fastened to the top of its low, slab-shaped body. There was a hole in the middle of the tray and through it the Sljee's olfactory antennae waved like some strange centerpiece.

"What're you folks having?" it asked them hurriedly, the second afternoon rush just having begun. Then it noticed

Bollux. "Sorry, but it's against house policy to allow 'droids at the tables. You two gentlemen will have to leave him outside."

"*Who's* a gentleman?" Fiolla demanded sharply.

"Beg pardon," apologized the Sljee. "I've only been working here since this morning. It's my first time away from home and I've never dealt with aliens before. Non-Sljee, I mean. The smells are so confusing. Frightfully sorry."

"The 'droid stays," Han stated flatly. "Now go bring us two Flameouts, or I'll tell the manager you insulted this lady. I'm a very close friend of his."

"At once, sir. Coming right up." The Sljee pirouetted on its many short podia and sailed off in the direction of the service bar.

"So we know I'm not Zlarb," Han resumed to Fiolla. "Who are you not?"

She chuckled. "I'm not a slaver, but you know my real name, or at least part of it. I'm Hart-and-Parn Gorra-Fiolla of Lorrd, Assistant Auditor-General, Corporate Sector Authority."

An Authority exec, Han groaned to himself. *Why don't I just go down to the Espo prison, pick a comfortable cell, and get it over with?* Instead he pursued the conversation. "Slavers must have interesting audits, fascinating expense vouchers."

"Doubtless, but I've never read one. I'm an auditor-at-large, sort of a roving assignment conducting random checks of Authority operations. I was working here with my assistant when I found out that there's a slavery ring operating inside the Authority. Some top execs are implicated, and a number of Espo officials. I think it might go as high as the territorial manager for this entire part of the Authority, Odumin, and that's a shock in itself. Although I've never met him, I've heard that Odumin's always shunned the limelight, but he's always been a decent administrator, a regular humanitarian as managers go. Anyway, I'm conducting my own investigation. When I've developed all the information, I'm going to dump it right in the lap of the Board of Directors."

She smiled brightly. "Then I'm going to nail myself the juiciest promotion and raise you ever saw. You're looking at Fiolla of Lorrd, heroine of the spaceways. Now how about you?"

He spread his hands. "I fly for hire. I rendezvoused with Zlarb without knowing he wanted me to move slaves. We disagreed and he got shot. And I don't care who's doing what to whom; I've got ten thousand in cash coming and I want it. Zlarb had a tape message to meet someone here for payment so I kept his appointment. How did you end up there in the lounge?"

"It was part of the information I came across. Did Zlarb tell you anything else?"

"Zlarb made the Final Jump shortly after being burned with a disruptor, but he had a record of ship registrations and leasing permits. Almost all of them were funneled through an agency on Ammuud."

She was listening distractedly, but he went on. "Do you mind telling me how come I'm in your confidence all of a sudden? Not that it doesn't stir me deeply, of course."

"Simple; this thing's even bigger than I'd thought. I need some additional help and I can't go to the Espos. You seem to know what you're doing in an unsubtle sort of way. And you definitely aren't a member of the slavery ring unless murder is a standard business pay-down."

"You'd be surprised. But don't get any ideas; I'm not the helpful type. How'd you end up out there today, by the way?"

"My assistant, Magg, got his hands on a message that the management was holding for Zlarb back there at the lounge. When I decided you weren't going to tell me much I sent you off to chase yourself and—"

Han leaned forward with a certain look on his face that caused Bollux to fear for Fiolla's safety. "And Magg followed me to put my lights out, right?"

She looked honestly shocked. "Are you saying someone attacked you?"

"Somebody did everything except zeroize my rotors."

She drew a deep breath. "I gave you the number of an Authority pool hangar. The ship there was the one Magg and I arrived in. I knew it was on down time, waiting for parts, and there'd be no one around. But listen—Magg trailed your hairy friend when he left the lounge and that's how we found out which ship was yours. When we couldn't get aboard for a search, I went off to keep Zlarb's appointment myself because the instructions said one person and one scooter. I sent Magg to see what he could find out about you."

Han was so busy trying to unravel what she had said that he forgot to be angry at her mention of the attempted break-in. He was impressed with her resourcefulness, antagonized a bit by her self-assurance, and surprised by her naïveté.

The Sljee waiter had returned. Two tentacles whisked two tall glasses off its back-tray while two more placed absorb-mats before Han and Fiolla. "There we are," the Sljee said cheerfully. "Will that be pay as you go, or shall I put it on a tab?" it asked hopefully. It had already been stiffed twice that day by unscrupulous customers who had taken advantage of its difficulty in differentiating among individual non-Sljee.

"Run the tab," said Han immediately. The Sljee retreated in disappointment, trying its best to memorize Han's odor without much confidence.

The Flameouts were perfect, burning their tongues and freezing their throats, making them gasp a bit. "Don't you think it was stupid to ride out there alone?" Han asked.

"I had a gun," she argued. "A special, one that doesn't register on scanners. Lots of execs carry them. How did I know the worthless thing would let me down?"

"Where's your assistant now?"

"After Magg checks on you he'll go to our hotel and get ready to leave. It occurred to me that we might have to get off-planet in short order."

"Very possible," allowed Han. A sudden thought struck

him and he became hostile again. "I owe Magg for damaging my ship, don't I?"

"I ordered him to try to break in, to see if there was any information onboard; I thought you might just be playing very, very dumb. If you want to get even, you can take me on another swoop ride sometime. By the way, what kind of security system is that you've got? Magg was sure he could open up a freighter without breaking stride, but that lock of yours stopped him cold. He said he'd need a tool shop to get in."

"I like my privacy," Han explained simply, avoiding the mention of smuggling.

"Magg said it was like trying to crack the Imperial Currency Reserve."

"Sounds like an experienced guy."

"Oh, very versatile, yes. I handpicked him because he had, ah, a range of abilities. I think you two will find one another quite—"

At that moment Chewbacca arrived with Spray. The Wookiee forcefully sat the little Tynnan down with the pressure of a giant paw and took a seat himself, filling it to overflowing.

"I met Fiolla here and almost got killed," Han told his friend pleasantly. "How was *your* afternoon?"

Chewbacca studied the woman with his large, lucid blue eyes and she returned the scrutiny. Then the Wookiee motioned to Spray and, in his growling, barking language, explained to Han what had happened as the skip-tracer squinted from one to the other.

"I hate skip-tracers," announced Han Solo at length.

"In that case I think I'll just be toddling along . . ." Spray said, starting to rise. Chewbacca clapped a paw on him and pushed him back down.

Han's head was spinning with this new development, and he wished he could process information as quickly as Blue Max. Theoretically, Spray could enlist the aid of the Espos in taking possession of the *Falcon*. Once again Han wondered when his string of rotten luck would break.

Just then the Sljee waiter showed up again, having noticed Chewbacca's and Spray's presence. It endeavored to speak in its most hospitable tones, still aware of its previous gaff.

"Yes, *sir*," purred the Sljee to the Wookiee, "and what can I bring you and your strapping young hatchling here?"

Chewbacca snarled at the Sljee. Spray, already visibly disturbed, exploded. "We're not even the same species!"

"What've I told you about that?" Han asked the Sljee menacingly.

"A thousand pardons," wailed the Sljee, rotating back and forth through nervous quarter-turns and intertwining its tentacles imploringly.

"What in the world is going on?" Fiolla wanted to know, not having understood anything Chewbacca had said.

Spray held his paws up, webbed fingers spread, until the others were quiet, including the Sljee. "First of all, we have no need of any refreshments, thank you," the Tynnan told the waiter. The Sljee retreated gratefully.

"Now," Spray continued, "the central issue, Captain Solo—please stop *shush*ing me, sir; I will be heard! At issue are two thousand five hundred Credits Standard owed Vinda and D'rag, Starshipwrights. Unless you're prepared to make payment, I am empowered to attach and take possession of your ship, which, by the way, appears to have had her marking altered in illegal fashion."

Han narrowed his eyes and glared at Spray. "I am thinking right now," he said, "of how a certain chisel-beaked runt is going to get his just desserts."

"It's a bit public for threats of aggravated assault, isn't it, Solo?" Fiolla asked.

"You keep out of this! For all I know, you two work together."

"Bullying will do you no good, Captain," Spray plowed on insistently in his squeaky voice. "Either remittance arrangements must be made this very moment or I shall be forced to go to the portmaster and the Security Police."

Han had his mouth open, uncertain whether he would try to lie or simply instruct Chewbacca to render the skip-tracer unconscious. He heard Fiolla say: "*I'll* pay for him."

Han's mouth stayed open as he turned on her. "Better close it," Fiolla cautioned, "before your tongue gets sunburned. Look, this problem of mine is a lot more complicated than I'd thought. It will take more investigation before I'm ready to go to the Board of Directors. I need a way to get around fast, and I'm not particularly anxious to go by public transportation. And the last thing I want is to take an Authority pool ship. Solo, you ought to be eager to leave, too, before the Espos start asking about missing rental scooters and several swoop riders smeared out on the landscape. If you'll chart out to me, I'll cover your debt. Besides, you want your ten thousand, don't you? Your best chance of finding it is to stick with me."

She turned to Spray. "How about it?"

The Tynnan nervously scratched up tufts of fur on his skull, blinking and wriggling his nose back and forth in consternation. "Cash?" he asked at last.

"An Authority Cash Voucher," Fiolla replied. "Half now, half when we're done. They're as good as money in a vault."

"Interstellar Collections Limited does prefer repayment to repo procedures," the skip-tracer admitted. "But I'm afraid I couldn't let you out of my sight until restitution is made."

"Just a second," Han snapped at Fiolla. "I'm not carting that little bloodsucker along anywhere."

Spray remained unexpectedly firm. "Captain Solo, her proposal is absolutely the only alternative to having your ship attached."

"There's always the famous Disappearing Ship-Tracer Trick," suggested Han darkly.

"Be civilized," Fiolla chided. "This won't take long, Solo. And if you don't help me, maybe I'll have to drag your name into my report. But if you take me to check out this shipping agent on Ammuud, the one you mentioned, I'll forget about you completely."

Han hoped it would be mutual. He poured down half of what remained of his Flameout. It felt corrosive but didn't help much otherwise. He looked to his first mate, who was looking back, no help at all, willing to go with whatever decision Han made.

He put his chin on his fist. "Chewie, you take Bollux and paddlefoot, here, back to the ship. I'll go with our new employer and pick up her assistant. Get liftoff clearance and punch up a jump to Ammuud."

Fiolla scribbled quickly on a pad of forms and pressed her thumbprint against the authorization square. She presented the voucher to Spray, whereupon Han realized that she was carrying an open expense account and that her position with the Authority must be an important one indeed.

The Wookiee had risen and moved near Spray as a general precaution, with Bollux close behind. But the Tynnan only made a polite parting bow to Fiolla. "Thank you for remaining reasonable about this entire incident," he said.

He started for the door. Chewbacca growled a farewell to Han, then to Fiolla. She returned it, not getting the vocal sounds right but contorting her face around into a very close approximation of the Wookiee's, even to getting both corners of her upper lip up high and baring her lower teeth along with the uppers in true Wookiee fashion. Chewbacca was startled, but yipped laughter. Then he went quickly, Bollux at his side, to catch up with the departing Spray.

"You're a pretty good mimic," Han commented, remembering her imitation of the four-armed manager in the terminal lounge.

"I told you, I'm from Lorrd," she reminded him, and he understood. The Lorrdians had, for many generations, been a subject race during the Kanz Disorders. Their masters had forbidden them to speak, sing, or otherwise communicate as they worked at their slave labors. The Lorrdians had evolved a complicated language of extremely subtle hand and facial movements and body signals and become masters of kinesic communication. Although it had been generations since their servitude had been ended by the Jedi Knights and the forces of the Old Republic, the Lorrdians remained among the galaxy's very best mimes and mimics.

"So that's how you knew Chewie and I were watching table 131 today?"

"I read you like a pair of message tapes; you tipped it every time someone went near the table."

And, thought Han, Fiolla's Lorrdian background gave her an added interest in ending the slavery ring. Still, it was unusual to find a Lorrdian working this far from home, and especially for the Corporate Sector Authority.

About to down the last of his Flameout, Han pointed to the open voucher pad. "There are plenty of times when you can get more with a blaster than with one of those, but if I had one I'd buy myself a nice little planet and retire."

"Which is why you'll never have one," she assured him, rising and following him from the table. "This slavery business is going to be my big break; nothing's keeping me out of a Board chair."

The Sljee waiter returned, its olfactory stalks tilting and waving when it took cognizance of the empty table. Then it noticed Han and Fiolla and approached them tentatively, the check extended before it on a metal salver.

"Ah, I believe this is your check, humans," ventured the Sljee.

"Us?" Han, who was broke, cried indignantly. "We just arrived, and for your information we've been waiting to be seated for quite a while now. And you're trying to stick us with somebody else's check when we haven't even had a drink yet? Where's the manager?"

The Sljee was spinning around and back, tangling its tentacles in total consternation. Its sensory equipment was really quite excellent at fine distinctions and subtle perceptions concerning other Sljee, but it found humanoid species dreadfully anonymous.

"Are you certain?" the Sljee moaned abjectly. "I'm sorry; I, I suppose I had you confused with two others." It studied the vacant table, wringing its tentacles in distress. "You didn't happen to see them leave, did you? If I'm stiffed again it will cost me my job."

Unable to endure any more, Fiolla drew a generous handful of cash from her thigh pouch and tossed it on the salver. "Solo, you're impossible."

The Sljee withdrew, showering her with its gratitude. Fiolla headed for the door.

"It's every life form for himself," opined Han Solo.

FIOLLA'S hotel was, predictably, the finest lodging place at the spaceport, the Imperial. Han tried his best not to look uncouth and out of place as he followed her through a lobby of soaring gem-set columns, vaulted ceilings, resilient plush carpeting, delicate glow-orb lighting, expensive furnishings, and lush shrubbery.

Fiolla, on the other hand, was a picture of cool, nonchalant poise, aristocratic even in coveralls. She led the way to the lift shaft and punched for the seventieth level.

Her suite was luxurious without being overdone. Han suspected that, though Fiolla could have afforded something far showier, she would have deemed it vulgar.

But the second she palmed her door open, he knew something was wrong. Things were in disorder. Conform-lounge furniture had been pushed and shoved out of place, suspension cushions and floater pads ripped or overturned. Storage panels were hanging open and the data plaques and tapes with which Fiolla worked were strewn all over the floor.

As Han pulled Fiolla out of the doorway, he suddenly remembered that he was unarmed. "Do you have another gun?" he whispered to her. She shook her head, her eyes very wide. "Then give me the special; it's better than nothing."

She passed the inoperative weapon to him. He listened closely but heard no sound to indicate that whoever had ransacked her room was still there. He moved cautiously into the suite, listening at each doorway before he went through.

He found signs of search everywhere on his wary sweep, but satisfied himself that no one remained in the rooms.

He engaged her door's security mode at FULL ISOLATION. "Where's Magg's room?"

She pointed. "There's a connecting door behind that hanging; we usually take adjoining quarters. An audit can demand very long hours."

Sliding Magg's door open slowly, ear cocked for any warning, he heard none. Magg's suite was in the same state at Fiolla's.

"You sent him back here to pack?" Han asked. Fiolla nodded, gazing around the ransacked place in some shock. "Well, somebody forwarded him for you. Grab whatever you can put in your pockets; we're getting out of here right now."

"But what about Magg? We have to report this outrage to the Espos." Her voice trailed away as she returned to her own suite. He began feeding instructions into the programming panel for the servant-drones that took care of domestic chores, then went back to Fiolla's suite.

"We don't go to any Espos," he called to her. "They may be part of it, isn't that what you told me? Then don't go cutting the charter short."

He began inserting orders into the programming panel for her rooms, too. Fiolla returned, her various coverall pockets and pouches bulging and a slim day-tote slung over one shoulder. "I don't like it, but you're correct about the Espos," she admitted. "What are you doing?"

He turned from the panel. "Well, what do you know, a female who can travel light. What I did was issue instructions for your stuff and Magg's to be put into storage. You can come back for it later"—*I hope*, he thought to himself. "Are the rooms already paid for? Good, let's jet."

He peeked into the corridor before easing out into it. Han felt as tense as a wound spring as they rode down the drop shaft, but they encountered no trouble there or in the foyer. A robo-hack dropped them at one of the spaceport's side gates, a freighthauler's entrance near the *Falcon* that Han's shipmaster's credentials allowed him to use.

But when they reached the side of the approach opposite from the apron on which the *Falcon* was parked, Han suddenly yanked Fiolla back behind the shelter of a small orbital skiff and directed her attention to several loiterers in the area. "Recognize any of them?"

She frowned at them in the hazy sun. "Oh, you mean those goldskins? Aren't they the other swoop riders from this afternoon? But what are they doing here?"

He made an elaborate face at her. "They came to ask us to join their aerobatics club, what else?"

"What now?" Fiolla wanted to know.

Han took his macrobinoculars from their case at his side. Through them he could see Chewbacca moving around the cockpit of the *Millennium Falcon*, running a pre-flight check of the ship.

"At least Chewie's onboard," he told her, lowering the macros. "Spray and Bollux, too, I guess. Our friends are probably waiting for you and me to show up before they spring whatever they've got planned." Shooting their way out wouldn't work, he knew. Even if he and Fiolla could reach the *Falcon* under cover of her belly guns, their chances of evading the patrol network and picket ships overhead and making hyperspace would be almost nonexistent.

Fiolla held her lower lip between her teeth, pondering. "There are regular passenger connections between here and Ammuud; we could leave now, while they're watching your ship, and meet Chewbacca there. But how to let him know?"

Han looked up and down the rows of spacecraft on their side of the approach. "There's what we need," he said and, taking her head, led her back through several rows of grounded vessels.

They came to the one Han had spotted, a large cargo lifter connected to a refueler, its outer access panels open. Han crawled up through an access panel and twenty seconds later threw open the small cockpit hatch.

"Nobody home," he told her as he gave her a hand up. Together they squeezed into the cramped cockpit. Han trained the macrobinoculars on his first mate across the way, and when the Wookiee chanced to look in his general direction, flashed the cargo lifter's running lights. Chewbacca took no notice.

It took four more tries to get the Wookiee's attention. Han saw his first mate's long, shaggy arm go to the console and the *Falcon*'s running lights blinked twice in acknowledgment.

Fiolla kept an eye on those individuals watching the *Falcon* to ensure that they hadn't noticed what was going on. In so doing she spotted at least four more idlers mounting an inconspicuous guard on the freighter. Chewbacca pretended to be running a warmup while Han sent him a series of longs and shorts explaining their predicament and what the revised plan was. Throughout the process, Han was very aware of Fiolla pressed up against him in the confining cockpit; her perfume, he found, had a tendency to distract him.

When Han was finished, the *Falcon*'s lights blinked twice again. As he helped Fiolla down from the cargo lifter's cockpit hatch, a tech came up. "What were you people doing up there?"

Fiolla turned a scathing, imperious glare on the tech. "Is it now required that Port Safety overseers answer to ground crew? Well? Who's your supervisor?"

The tech murmured something apologetic, shuffling her feet and saying that she'd only been asking. Fiolla gave her one more haughty glare and departed with Han at her elbow. "And now we book passage out?" she asked once they had passed out of the tech's earshot.

"Yeah, I'll teach you all about getting offworld under a phony name. Chewie's going to stay put till we're clear, then lift off. They won't be expecting him to leave without us, so he shouldn't have any trouble. We will meet him on Ammuud."

* * *

"We're in luck," Fiolla said as she and Han stood studying the soaring holos that listed departures in the main passenger terminal. "There's a ship that goes straight to Ammuud, leaving this evening."

Han shook his head. "No, there's the one we want, departure 714, the shuttle."

Her brow furrowed. "But it's not even leaving this solar system."

"Which is why no one will be covering it," he countered. "They're likely to have watchers on the through-ships. We can change ships and book passage for Ammuud at the first stop, it says in the index. Besides, the shuttle's leaving now, which appeals to me a whole lot more. We'll have to hurry."

They tried not to appear too anxious as they bought tickets and barely made it to the departure gate in time. Since the ship was only an inter-system shuttle, it offered no sleeping accommodations beyond big, comfortable acceleration chairs. Han buckled himself in and let his chair back, sighing and preparing to drop off to sleep.

Fiolla had grabbed the window seat with no objections from Han. "Why did you make me pay for the tickets in cash?"

He opened one eye and studied her. "You want to go around passing out Authority cash vouchers from an open expense account? Good, go ahead; you might as well hang a sign around you neck: AUTHORITY EXEC—WON'T SOMEBODY PLEASE SHOOT ME?"

Her voice suddenly held a tremor. "Do, do you think that's what's happened to Magg?"

He shut his eye again, lips tightening. "Absolutely not; they'll hang on to him as a bargaining piece. All I meant was that we don't want to leave a trail. Don't pay any attention to me; sometimes I talk too much."

He could hear attempted cheer in her tone. "Or you don't talk enough, Solo. I haven't decided which." She settled herself to watch their liftoff. Han, who had seen more of them than he'd ever be able to count, was asleep before they left the troposphere.

At their destination, Roonadan, fifth planet out from the same sun that warmed Bonadan, they discovered they had missed their starship connection. The shuttle had been slightly delayed en route by injector problems, but of course starships on interstellar jump schedules are never held for mere interplanetary traffic. They run on precise timetables for which hyperspace transitions are meticulously calculated in advance by both onboard and ground-based computers. Straying from the strict timing of the jump schedules was something the passenger lines hated to do.

"But they don't mind leaving people stranded on some rock," fumed Han, who had been known to calculate a hyperspace jump with one hand while dodging the law with a hold full of Kessel spice with the other.

"Stop complaining. There's nothing we can do about it," Fiolla reasoned. "There's another ship that can get us to Ammuud, see? Departure 332."

He checked the holo listings. "Are you crazy? That's an M-class ship, probably a tour. Look at that, they're going to stop at two, no, three other planets. And they're not exactly going to be burning up hyperspace either."

"It's the quickest way to Ammuud," Fiolla said sensibly. "Or would you rather go back and try to make peace with the people who were chasing us all over Bonadan? Or wait for them to trace us here?"

Han was painfully aware that Chewbacca and the *Millennium Falcon* would be waiting on Ammuud. "Uh, I don't suppose you have enough cash to charter a ship of our own without using a voucher?"

She smiled at him sweetly. "Why, yes, growing right here off my petty-cash vine; I was saving up the harvest until I had enough to buy my own fleet. Try to be rational, will you, Solo?"

"All right, lay off. At least it won't cost us more than a few Standard timeparts."

On the way to the reservations deck they passed travelers from dozens of worlds. There were wobbly-fleshed Courataines in their exoskeletal travel suits, breathing the thinnest of atmospheres through their respirators; octopedal Wodes, heavy-stepping and unused to less than two Standard gravities; beautifully plumed Jastaals trilling their phrases to one another as they half-glided along, wings partially extended; and human beings in all their variety.

A hand dropped onto Han's shoulder. He started, pivoting with a blurringly fast motion that freed him of the hand, put distance between himself and the other, and brought his right hand down to where his blaster would ordinarily have been.

"Easy, Han; old reflexes die hard, I see," laughed the man who had stopped him. Braced to confront Zlarb's business associates or a flying squad of Espos, Han felt abrupt relief not unmixed with a new worry as he recognized the man.

"Roa! What are you doing here?" Roa had put on weight, too much of it, but it didn't conceal the open, friendly features of one of the best smugglers and blockade-runners Han had ever known.

Roa smiled, looking as pleasantly paternal and trustworthy as ever. "Passing through, just like everyone else, son, and I thought I recognized you." Roa was carrying an expensive command case, a compact, self-contained business office. He wore a conservative beige suit with soft white shoes and rainbow girth-sash. "You remember Lwyll, I'm sure."

The woman introduced by Roa had been standing to one side. Now she came forward. "How's it been with you, Han?" she asked in that rich voice he recalled so well. Lwyll hadn't gone as far to flesh as her husband; she was still a striking woman with masses of wavy white-blond hair and an elegant face. Han thought that she certainly didn't look—how many Standard years older?

Seeing them brought back a surge of memory of the fast, furious time he had spent working for Roa, when he had tired of trying to be just one more honest, unassuming spacer a few credits away from poverty, like uncounted others wandering the stars, having abandoned a planet and a life.

It had been Roa who had taken Han on his first exhilarating, harrowing Kessel Run—very nearly his last. In Roa's organization Han had risen quickly with a reputation for taking mad chances, daring any odds, running fearsome risks in the pursuit of illegal profit.

But they had parted company a long time ago, and honor among thieves was a more romantic myth than a dependable institution. Han's immediate reaction on seeing Roa was pleasure, but close on its heels was suspicion that this wasn't altogether an accident. Could word be out already, carrying a price on Han's head, through the interstellar underworld?

Still, Roa showed no sign of hailing the Espos. Fiolla cleared her throat, and Han made introductions. Roa waved at Han's lack of gunbelt. "So you're out of the game, too, eh? Well, I don't blame you, Han. Bowed out myself, just after we parted company. Lwyll and I had one close call too many. And, after all, doing business isn't too unlike our old line of work. A background in felony can be a real plus. What's your new line of endeavor?"

"A collections agency. Han Solo Associates, Limited."

"Ah? Sounds like your ideal; you always fought for what you had coming. How's your old sidekick, the Wook? Do you ever see any of the others? Tregga maybe, or even Vonzel?"

"Tregga's doing life at hard labor on Akrit'tar; they caught him before he could dump a load of *chak*-root. Sonniod's running a delivery service, living hand to mouth. The Briil twins are dead; they shot it out with a patrol cruiser out in the Tion Hegemony. And Vonzel messed up an emergency landing; most of what's left of him will be in a life-support clinic for good. He started a regular one-man run on the organ banks."

Roa shook his head sadly. "Yes, I'd forgotten how the deck is stacked. Few make it, Han."

He came back to the present. Squaring his shoulders,

he dipped two fingers into his gaudy sash and drew out a business card. ''Fifth largest import-export firm in this part of space,'' he boasted. ''We've got some of the best tax-and-tariff men in the business. Drop around one of these days, and we'll talk over old times.''

Han tucked away the card. Roa had turned to his wife. ''I'll see that our baggage is transferred. You make sure our shuttle reservation's confirmed, my dear.'' He looked wistful for a moment. ''We're lucky to be out of it, aren't we, Han?''

''Yeah, Roa, we sure are.'' The older man clapped him on the shoulder, made a polite leave-taking to Fiolla, and marched away.

Lwyll, waiting until her husband was gone, gave Han a knowing, amused look. ''You're not out of it at all, are you, Han? No, I can tell; not Han Solo. Thanks for not telling him.'' Lwyll touched his cheek once and left.

''You've got interesting friends'' was Fiolla's only comment, but her perspective on him had changed. Youthful looks belied the fact that he was a survivor in a calling with a very high rate of attrition.

Watching Roa's retreating back, Han thought about tax-and-tariff men and fingered the business card. ''Solo, hey, wake up!'' Fiolla assailed him. ''It's our necks we're supposed to be preoccupied with here.''

He sauntered off toward the interstellar reservations desks. *Things could be worse*, Han reflected.

''Bugging your eyes out at them won't help,'' said Fiolla, referring to the gambling tables and other games of chance in the swank wagering compartment just off the passenger liner's main salon.

She was wearing a sheer, clinging gown and soft evening slippers of polychromatic shimmersilk. She had brought the outfit with her, packed away in her upper-right thigh pouch and lower-left calf stuffpocket, on the assumption that her coveralls would do for all but the most formal places. She wore it now for a change of pace and a morale booster. Han still wore his ship clothes, but had closed his collar.

"We could go over what we know so far," she proposed.

"That's all we've been doing since we came onboard," he grimaced.

That wasn't entirely true. They had spoken of any number of things during the trip; he found her a spirited and amusing companion, much more so than any of the other passengers, aside from a frustrating tendency to keep her stateroom door locked during the liner's "night." But they had exchanged stories.

For instance, Fiolla had explained to him how she and her assistant, Magg, had been doing an audit on Bonadan when her portable command-retrieval computer terminal malfunctioned. She had turned to Magg's, which, having a more comprehensive cybernetic background, was a more complicated instrument with a number of keyboard differences. Some miskeying or accident had opened up a restricted informational pocket in Bonadan's system. There she had found records of the slavery ring's activities and the notation of Zlarb's impending payoff.

Han's eyes were still riveted to players trying their luck or skill at Point Five, Bounce, Liar's Cut, Vector, and a half-dozen other games. For two Standard timeparts, ever since coming aboard the passenger liner *Lady of Mindor*, he had been trying to come up with a way to get into a game. Now that he was completely rested, inactivity was nearly intolerable.

Fiolla had absolutely refused to back him, though Han had promised bountiful returns on her investment. He then pointed out that if she hadn't squandered money on separate accommodations, she would have had plenty to loan him.

"I didn't have time to brush up on my hand-to-hand" had been her retort. "And besides, if you're such a good gambler, how come you're flying around in that cookie-box freighter instead of a star yacht?"

He changed the subject. "We've been on this mud cart for two Standard timeparts. To get to Ammuud! No wonder I'm going crazy; the *Falcon* could've gotten us there in the time it took these idiots to clear port.''

He rose from the little table where they had eaten an indifferent meal. ''At least we'll make planetfall soon. Maybe I'll go run my clothes through the robo-valet one more time for fun.''

She caught his wrist. ''Don't be so depressed. And please don't leave me here alone; I'm afraid that priest of Ninn will corner me for another lecture on the virtues of formalistic abstinence. And no comments! Come on, I'll play you a game of Starfight. *That* we can afford.''

Not many passengers remained in the lounge, for the *Lady of Mindor* was due to reenter normal space shortly; most of them were packing or making other last-minute preparations. He gave in and they crossed to the bank of coin games.

She mimicked his rangy walk, swaggering along next to him, arms dangling a bit and shoulders slumped back. There was an exaggerated sway to her hips as she swept the room arrogantly with narrowed eyes and an invisible blaster weighting her side, right in step with him.

When he noticed, he recognized himself at once. He glared around the salon in case anyone was inclined to laugh. ''Will you quit that?'' he said out of the side of his mouth. ''Somebody's liable to call you out.''

She chuckled. ''Then they'll stop a blaster bolt, handsome; I've been studying with the master.'' He found himself laughing, as she'd intended.

The Starfight game consisted of two curved banks of monitors and controls, almost surrounding each of the two playing stations. Between them was a large holotank with detailed star charts. With the stacks and stacks of controls, each player sent his myriad ships out to do battle in computer modeled deepspace.

He stopped her as she was about to drop a coin into the game. ''I've never been too partial to Starfight,'' he explained. ''It's too much like work.''

''What about a last stroll through the promenade?''

* * *

It was as good a diversion as any. They ascended the curved staircase to find they had the promenade to themselves. The novelty of the place must have worn off for the other passengers. A single pane of transparisteel ten meters long and five high curved to follow the ship's hull, showing them the tangled luminosity of hyperspace. They stared with the age-old fascination, their human minds and eyes trying to impose order on the chaos beyond the transparisteel so that, at times, they believed they saw shapes, surfaces, or fluxes.

She noticed he was still distracted. "You're thinking about Chewie, aren't you?"

A shrug. "He'll be all right. I just hope the big lug didn't worry himself sick when we were overdue and start shedding or something."

The ship's public-address system announced final warning of transition, though it was for crew members rather than passengers. Shortly thereafter Fiolla pointed and breathed a soft exclamation as the distortions and discord of hyperspace melted away and they gazed out at a field of stars. Due to the liner's position they could see neither Ammuud nor its primary.

"How long to—" Fiolla was saying, when emergency klaxons began hooting all through the ship. The lighting flickered and died and was replaced by far dimmer emergency illumination. The outcries of frightened passengers could be heard as distant echoes in the passageways.

"What's happening?" Fiolla yelled over the din. "A drill?"

"It's no drill," he said. "They've shut down everything but emergency systems; they must be channeling power into their shields."

He grabbed her hand and started back for the staircase. "Where are we going?" she hollered.

"The nearest escape-pod station or lifeboat bay" was his shouted answer.

The salon was deserted. As they got into the passageway the entire liner rocked under them. Han recovered with the agility of a seasoned spacer, keeping his balance and stopping Fiolla just before she collided with a bulkhead.

"We've been hit!" he called. As if to underscore what he said, they heard massive airtight doors sliding into place automatically throughout the ship. The *Lady of Mindor* had taken hull damage of some sort and been breached.

A steward came running down the passageway with a medipack under one arm. When Han saw he wasn't about to stop, he grabbed a double handful of the man's heavily braided jacket.

"Let go," the steward said, trying to twist free. "You're supposed to proceed to your quarters. All passengers proceed to quarters."

Han shook him. "First tell me what's going on!"

"Pirates! They shot out the main drive as soon as we made transition from hyperspace!" The news shocked Han so much that he released his grip.

As he ran off on his way, the steward shouted back at them. "Return to your quarters, you fools! We're being boarded!"

“THIS vessel is a fraud,” Spray announced, keying his next move into the gameboard in the *Millennium Falcon*’s forward compartment.

Chewbacca took just enough time from what he was doing—analyzing Spray’s unorthodox stratagem—to snarl threateningly.

Spray, who had grown more used to the Wookiee’s outbursts, didn’t flinch much at all. He was dividing his time between the compartment’s technical station and the gameboard, giving the *Falcon*’s first mate a very difficult match while running a combination inventory and inspection of the ship out of a sense of duty to Interstellar Collections Limited. Chewbacca permitted it more to keep the skip-tracer busy than anything else, but this slandering of the *Falcon*, if unchecked, could only lead to retribution.

Come to think of it, the Wookiee reflected, *the Tynnan wasn’t a bad technical pilot*. He had even assisted on the liftoff from Bonadan, once Chewbacca had judged that Han and Fiolla had won enough time to get offworld. Spray had copiloted and aided in hyperspace transition with a fussy proficiency, though he’d been startled to learn that Han and Chewbacca habitually spaced by themselves, Han reaching back to his left to carry out navigator’s chores and the Wookiee leaning to his right to run the commo board when needed.

“The exterior is a deception,” Spray was continuing. “Why, some of the equipment you’ve installed is restricted to military use; are you aware of that? And her armament rating's way too high, as is her lift/mass ratio. How did Captain Solo ever get a Waiver to operate within the Authority?''

The Wookiee, cupping his hirsute chin in both hands, leaned down even closer to the gameboard, ignoring the question. Even if he had been able to communicate eloquently with Spray, he wouldn't have explained about the Waiver, which had involved an amazing variety of lawbreaking and the total destruction of the covert Authority facility known as Stars' End.

Miniature holomonsters waited on the circular gameboard, throwing challenges to one another. Chewbacca's defenses had been penetrated by a lone combatant from Spray's forces. The question of external versus internal threat was a very subtle one, involving closely matched win/lose parameters. The Wookiee's nose scrunched in thought. He reached a hairy finger out very slowly and punched his next move up on the game's keyboard, then reclined on the curving acceleration couch, arm pillowing his head, his long legs crossed. With his free hand he scratched his other arm, which the somatigenerative effect of the flaking synth-flesh had made itchy.

''Uh-oh,'' blurted Blue Max, who was following the contest from his habitual place in Bollux's open thorax. The 'droid sat on a pressure keg among the other clutter to one side of the compartment, amid plastic pallets, hoisting toggles and a rebuilt fuel enricher that Han hadn't gotten around to installing yet. The computer probe's photoreceptor swiveled to track on Spray as the Tynnan returned to the board and made his next move without hesitation.

Spray's lone combatant had been a decoy. Now one of his supporting monsters slithered across the board and, after a brief battle, threw Chewbacca's defenses wide open.

''It's the Eighth Ilthmar gambit; he drew you out with that loner. He's got you,'' Blue Max observed helpfully.

Chewbacca was filling his lungs for a vituperative outpouring and levering himself up to the board again when the navicomputer clamored for attention. The starship's first mate forgot his ire and scrambled up from the acceleration couch, but not before he cleared the board of his humiliating defeat. He hastened off to prepare for the reversion to normal space.

"And just look at this; some of these systems are fluidic!" Spray squeaked after him, whiskers aquiver, waving a tech readout screen. "What is this, a starship or a distillery?"

The Wookiee paid him no heed. "Good game, Spray," attested Max, who was himself a fair player.

"He held me for three extra moves," admitted the skip-tracer. "I wish things were going as well with this technical survey. Everything's so modified that I can't trace the basic specifications."

"Maybe we can help," Max piped brightly.

"Max *is* conversant with ship's systems," Bollux said. "He might be able to dig out the information you require."

"Just what I need! Please, step over to the tech station!" Spray was behind the 'droid, webbed feet scrabbling on the deckplates, pushing him to a seat at the station. As Bollux sat heavily into the acceleration chair, Max extended an adaptor, the one Chewbacca had repaired after the encounter with the slavers.

"I'm in," Max announced as technical readouts began marching across scopes and screens at high speed. "What d'you want to know, Spray?"

"All data on recent jumps; you can patch into the navicomputer. I want to see how the ship's been operating."

"You mean accuracy factors and power levels?" Max asked in his childish voice.

"I mean hyperspace jumps, date-time coordinates, all relevant information. It'll give me the simplest evaluation of how the ship performs and what she's worth."

There was a momentary hesitation. "It's no use," Max told Spray. "Captain Solo's got all that stuff protected. He and Chewbacca are the only ones with access."

Exasperated, Spray pursued. "Can't you find a window to it? I thought you were a computer probe."

Max achieved a wounded tone. "I *am*. But I can't do

something like this without the Captain's permission. Besides, if I make a mistake, the safeguards will wipe everything clean."

As the Tynnan sat and stewed, Bollux drawled, "As I understand it, a general examination would begin with things like power systems, maintenance records, and so forth. Would you like Blue Max to run a thorough check of current status?"

Spray seemed distracted. "Eh? Oh, yes, yes, that would be fine." Then he sat, bucktoothed chin poised on a stubby paw, stroking his whiskers in concentration.

"Whoops," chirped Max, "what d'you suppose *that* is? Whatever it is wasn't there when we did the preflight warm-up."

The skip-tracer suddenly became attentive. "What are you—oh, that power drop? Hm, that's a minor conduit on the outer hull, isn't it? Now what could be draining power there?"

"Nothing in design schematics or mod-specs," Max assured him. "I think we should tell Chewbacca."

Spray, never one to trust the unexplained, was inclined to agree. Yielding to the skip-tracer's nervous exhortations, the Wookiee left the cockpit only under protest, and seated himself at the tech station. But when he saw evidence of the highly improbable power drain, his thick red-gold brows beetled and his leathery nostrils dilated reflexively, trying to catch a whiff of what was wrong.

He turned and brayed an interrogative at Spray, who had been around the Wookiee long enough to understand that much.

"I haven't a clue," the skip-tracer answered stridently. "Nothing in this slapdash ship makes any sense to me. She looks like a used loadlifter, but she's got higher boost than an Imperial cruiser. I don't even care to think about how jury-rigged some of those reroutings must be."

At Chewbacca's order Blue Max showed him, on a computer model, exactly which length of the conduit was experiencing drainage. The Wookiee marched to the tool locker, withdrew a worklight, a scanner and a huge spanner, and continued on aft with Spray and Bollux bringing up the rear.

Near the engine shielding, the *Falcon*'s first mate removed a wide inspection plate and wormed himself down into the crawlspace there. He had even less room than normal—a good deal of the fluidic systems had been installed here.

He barely managed to turn his wide shoulders and squeeze the scanner in by the hull. He played its invisible tracer beam over the metal, watching the monitor carefully. At last he found the spot where, on the other side of the hull, the power conduit was showing droppage. It didn't look like any malfunction he had ever seen; there should be no reason for the conduit simply to lose power. Something must be drawing it from the conduit, but Chewbacca could think of nothing that would do so. Unless, of course, something had been added.

In a moment he was wriggling his way back out of the crawlspace like an enormous red-gold-brown larva, honking his distress. Bollux's vocoder and Max's vied with Spray's high-strung squeak, demanding to know what was wrong. Sweeping them out of his way with one wide swing of his arm, Chewbacca headed for the storage compartment where his oversized spacesuit was stored.

The Wookiee detested the confinement of a suit and loathed even more the idea of clambering along the hull and undertaking delicate and dangerous work while protected from the annihilation of hyperspace only by the thin envelope of the *Falcon*'s drive field. But more than that he dreaded what he believed he would find on the other side of the hull.

The decision was taken out of his hands. There was a loud *ploow!* Out of the still-open inspection port came a burst of flame and explosive force along with gasses and vaporized liquids from the fluidic components. There followed a sustained whistle of air that let them know the vessel had been holed, confirming the Wookiee's worst fears. During the ground-time on Bonadan, someone, most probably the enemies waiting for Han and Fiolla, had taken precautionary measures to ensure that the *Millennium Falcon* wouldn't escape. They had fastened a sleeper-bomb to the starship's hull where it would do the worst damage. It had been applied inert, unpowered, undetectable except by the most minute inspection. Once in flight it had become active, draining power from the ship's systems to build its explosion. Then it had released in a shaped charge and blown out control systems in flight. The device was meant to produce the cleanest possible kind of murder, one that would leave no evidence, blasting the ship and all it contained into meaningless energy anomalies in hyperspace.

Chewbacca and Spray were driven back by the multicolored reek belching from the ruptured fluidics. Unprotected, they could be killed as easily by breathing those concentrated gases as by a miscalculated transition.

But Bollux could get along quite well where they couldn't. They saw the 'droid clank through the billowing smoke, lugging a heavy extinguisher he had pulled from a wall niche. Chewbacca had occasion now to curse the same auto-firefighting gear that had saved them all on Lur; the system's inability to operate now might spell their deaths.

Bollux's chest panels closed protectively over Blue Max even as he set the extinguisher down and lowered himself stiffly into the crawlspace, his gleaming body poorly suited to an area designed for limber living creatures. Once he had entered the space, his lengthy arm reached back out to drag the extinguisher after him. There was still the shriek of escaping air and the *whoop* of warning sirens to tell them the *Falcon* was depressurizing.

Chewbacca had run for the cockpit with Spray crowding behind. At the control console he kicked in filtration systems full-all, to carry away toxic fumes, and checked damage indicators.

The bomb must have been relatively small, placed in a precise location by someone who knew stock freighters like the *Falcon* well. The Wookiee realized it before Spray—whoever had planted the sleeper-bomb hadn't been aware of the starship's tread-boarded fluidics setup. With the control design radically altered, the bomb had failed to do a complete job of rendering the starship derelict.

Transition to normal space was imminent. Without taking time to seat himself, Chewbacca reached over his seat and worked at the console. At least some of the fluidics were functioning; hyperspace parted around the freighter like an infinite curtain.

The *Falcon*'s first mate bellowed an angry imprecation at the Universe's sense of timing, picked Spray up bodily and deposited him in the pilot's seat, bayed a string of uninterpreted instructions while pointing at the planet Ammuud, which had just appeared before them, and tore off in the direction of the explosion.

He paused long enough to pick up a hull-patch kit and a respirator. Hunkering down over the inspection plate, he saw Bollux sitting in the midst of shards and fragments of fluidic tubing and microfilament. The fire had been quelled. The shriek of escaping air had stopped: Bollux had firmly planted his durable back against the breach, an adequate sort of temporary seal.

The labor 'droid looked up and was relieved to see Chewbacca. "The hole is rather large, sir; I'm not sure how long my thorax will withstand the pressure. Also, the armor surrounding the breach is cracked. I suggest using the largest patch you have."

Chewbacca analyzed the thorny problem of getting Bollux out of the crawlspace and simultaneously plugging the hole. He settled on the plan of preparing two patches, one smaller and lighter that could be set in place quickly, and the other a sturdy plate that would hold up even against the massive force exerted by the *Falcon*'s air pressure toward the utter vacuum outside. He handed the smaller patch down to Bollux and yipped instructions, gesturing to make himself understood, frustrated that he'd never mastered Basic.

But the 'droid grasped what he meant and gathered himself for the effort. Using the agility of his special suspension system and his simian arms, Bollux managed to push himself free, swing around, and slap the patch into place in rapid sequence. He swarmed for the inspection opening, having seen that the temporary patch was trembling before the strain placed upon it.

Chewbacca had seen it, too, and worried; the hole was bigger than he had thought. He reached down with both arms and hauled the 'droid up through the inspection opening. Just as he did the patch gave way, sucked into nothingness so quickly that it seemed to vanish. With it went several jagged pieces, enlarging the hole.

It was suddenly as if Chewbacca was standing in the middle of a wild river-rapids, fighting raging currents of air that, in escaping the ship, were dragging him inexorably toward the hole. Scraps and loose debris swirled around and past him and zipped down the inspection opening.

Bracing the muscular columns of his legs on either side of the opening, the Wookiee fought to retain his hug on Bollux and resist that flood. The giant sinew of his back and legs felt as if it were about to come apart. He clutched the 'droid to him with one arm, bracing the other on the deck, sustaining himself on a tripod of arm and legs, head thrown back with effort.

Bollux recovered somewhat, only to find that in the position in which the Wookiee was holding him, he could do little to exert any force of his own. What he could and did do was grasp the corner of the inspection plate and swing it over on its pivot, something Chewbacca hadn't a free limb to accomplish. It almost jammed halfway, but with a final tug the 'droid cleared it. Once it was past that point the airflow caught it and hauled it shut with a ringing alarm. Fortunately none of the Wookiee's fingers or toes were poised on the lip of the opening.

The depressurization was confined to one small compartment for the time being. How serious that was remained to be seen. Chewbacca wanted to lie on the deck and catch his breath for a moment but knew he didn't have the time. He squirted thick, gluey sealant all around the inspection plate, then paused long enough to pat Bollux's cranium with a gruff compliment.

"It was Max who brought the inspection plate to my attention," said the 'droid modestly. Then he hauled himself to his feet and trailed off after Chewbacca, who had already dashed off toward the cockpit.

There, Spray was engaged in an uncertain contest with the controls. "We retain considerable guidance function," he reported, "and I've put us on an approach path to the planet's only spaceport. I was about to alert them for an emergency landing under crash conditions."

The Wookiee loudly countermanded that plan, dropping into his outsized copilot seat. He, like Han, shunned involvement, and the consequent fuss or furor, that could possibly be avoided. He found that the controls responded adequately and thought he stood a good chance of landing the freighter without sirens, crash wagons, stop-netting, firefighting robos, and ten thousand official questions.

Already in Ammuud's upper atmosphere, he brought the ship onto a steady approach path. Her hyperspace drive seemed to have suffered damage, but the rest of her guidance system responded within tolerance.

Bollux, who had just caught up, came up next to Chewbacca, his panels open. "I think there's something you should know, sir. Blue Max just ran a quick check at the tech station. The damage has stabilized, but some of the filament tubing for the guidance systems has been exposed; its housing was cracked."

"Will it blow?" Spray asked. Below them, they could make out features of the terrain quite clearly. Ammuud was a world of immense forests and oceans with rather large polar ice caps.

Max answered. "It's not a question of blowing *out*, Spray; they're secure, but they're delicate low-pressure filaments. Going too deep into the planet's atmosphere will implode them."

"You mean we can't land?" Spray blinked.

"No," Bollux replied calmly. "He merely means that we can't land too deep in Ammuud's—"

The starship gave a convulsive shudder.

"Be careful!" squawked the skip-tracer to Chewbacca. "This vessel is still in lien to Interstellar Collections Limited!"

Chewbacca gave out a vociferous growl. One of the control filaments had imploded, the planet's atmosphere having overcome the lesser pressure within it. The Wookiee snarled. Working to bypass the line, he had one bit of luck in that he could cut the ship's speed back to a very gentle descent.

"—atmosphere," Bollux finished.

"How deep is that?" Spray asked urgently. The Terrain Following Sensors had already shown them the planet's spaceport at the foot of a high mountain range.

"Not very much lower at all, sir," commented Bollux in neutral tones.

The Wookiee pulled the *Falcon*'s bow higher and reset the Terrain Following Sensors to display the features of the mountain range beyond Ammuud's spaceport. His plan was clear; since he couldn't set down in the lower atmosphere, he would find as suitable a site as he could in the higher mountains and hope that the lower air pressure there wouldn't collapse the rest of the guidance system before he could set the ship down. He waved a shaggy paw at Bollux and Spray, indicating the passageway.

"I believe he wants us to stow all loose gear and prepare for a rough landing," Bollux told Spray. The two turned and began working their way along the passageway together, frantically cramming loose items into storage lockers and securing their lids.

They had reached the escape pods when Spray thought of something important. "What about Captain Solo? How will he know what's happened?"

"I'm afraid I can't say, sir," Bollux confessed. "I see no

way in which we can safely leave word for him without compromising ourselves to port officials.''

The skip-tracer accepted that. ''By the way, I think there's some welding equipment in that second pod there; you'd better bring it out so that we can secure it.''

Bollux obligingly leaned into the open pod. ''I don't see any—'' He felt an abrupt push from behind. Spray had worked up just enough momentum, with a running start, so that shoving with all his might he toppled Bollux into the pod.

''Find Solo!'' Spray yelled, and hit the release. Inner and outer hatches rolled down before the confused 'droid could get out another word. The pod was blown free by its separator charges.

And as the *Falcon* nosed up, driving for the high mountains of Ammuud, the dumpy escape pod began its fall toward the spaceport.

☐ VIII

GENERAL Quarters or any call to stations can be disorderly in even a well-run military spacecraft. On a passenger liner like the *Lady of Mindor*, where runthroughs and practices were all but ignored, it was total confusion. Therefore, Han Solo paid scant attention to the garbled and frequently contradictory instructions blared by the public-address annunciators. With Fiolla in tow he plunged down the passageway as panicky passengers, frightened crew members, and indecisive officers immobilized one another with conflicting aims and actions.

"What are you going to do?" Fiolla asked as they sidestepped a mob of passengers hammering at the purser's door.

"Get the rest of your cash from your stateroom, then find the nearest lifeboat bay." He heard airtight doors booming shut and tried to remember the layout of these old M-class ships. It would be disastrous to be trapped by the automatic seal-up.

"Solo, *tractor in*!" Fiolla bawled, dragged her slippered feet, and finally halted him. Catching her breath, she continued. "I have my money with me. Unless you want to tip the robo-valet, we can get going."

He was once again impressed. "Very good. We keep going aft; there should be a boat just forward of the power section." He recalled that his macrobinoculars were back in his cabin, then wrote them off. Ahead of them an airtight door had just begun grinding shut. They made it in a sprint, though the hem of Fiolla's shimmersilk caught in the hatchway and she had to tear a ragged edge off it to free herself.

"A month's pay, this thing cost me," she complained ruefully. "What's it going to be now, fight or run?"

"A little of both. The fool captain of this can must've tripped every door in the ship. How does he think his crew'll get to battle stations?" He started on.

"Maybe he doesn't intend to fight," she puffed, staying right at his heels. "I hardly think a liner's crew could make a fight of it against a pirate, do you?"

"They'd better; pirates aren't famous for their restraint with captives." They came to a long, cylindrical lifeboat tucked into its bay. Han broke the seal on the release lever and threw it back, but the lifeboat's hatch failed to roll open. He threw the lever forward and back again, condemning the liner's maintenance officer for not looking after his safety equipment.

"Listen," Fiolla stopped him.

The ship's captain seemed to have reasserted a certain amount of self-control. "For the safety of all passengers," his voice came from the PA, "and crew members alike, I've decided to accept terms of surrender offered by the vessel that disabled us. I have been assured that no one will be harmed so long as we put up no resistance and no attempt is made to launch lifeboats. With this in mind I have overridden boat and pod releases to keep them onboard. Though the ship is damaged, we are in no immediate danger. I hereby order all passengers and crew members to cooperate with the boarding parties when the pirate craft docks with ours."

"What makes him think they'll keep their word?" Han muttered. "He's been larding it on passenger runs too long." A small part of him chased after that thought. When *was* the last time a pirate raid had been made near the well-patrolled inner environs of the Authority? An attack of this sort was nearly unheard of in this part of space.

"Solo, look!" Fiolla pointed to an open hatch, this one set into the liner's outer hull. He ran to it and found that it gave access to a gun turret. The hatch had obviously opened at the first alarm. The twin-barreled blaster cannon was unattended; either its assigned crew hadn't made it to their station or the captain had recalled them.

Hiking himself through the hatch, Han settled into the gunner's saddle as Fiolla lowered herself into the gunner's mate's place. Through the blister of transparisteel enclosing the turret they could see the pirate craft, a slender predator painted in light-absorbing black, warping in adroitly on the passenger liner. The pirate was apparently going to match up against an airlock in the *Lady*'s midsection somewhat forward of the gun turret.

The emplacement was fully charged. Setting his shoulders against the rests, Han leaned against the padded hood of the targeting scope, closing his hands on the firing grips.

"What've you got in mind, Solo?" Fiolla queried sharply.

"If we start maneuvering the turret, they'll pick the movement up," he explained. "But if we wait, they will drift right across our sights. We can get off one volley, maybe even disable them."

"Maybe even get ourselves killed," she suggested tartly. "And everybody else into the bargain. Solo, you can't!"

"Wrong; it's the one thing I *can* do. Do you think they'll keep their word about not hurting anyone? I don't. We can't escape, but we sure can take a swipe at them."

Ignoring her protests, he put his shoulders to the rests and sighted through the targeting scope again. The pirate's menacing shape came into the edge of his field of fire. He held his breath, waiting for a shot at the raider's vitals, knowing he would get off only one salvo.

The control section didn't quite come into his line of fire and he let the crew quarters pass; they were probably empty, with most of the crew mustered at the airlock for boarding. The pirate wouldn't even have to put out her boats, thanks to the liner captain's meek surrender.

Han peered through the scope at the next length of enemy hull, then pushed himself away from the twin cannon and began drawing himself headfirst out of the gunner's saddle. "Let's go," he prompted Fiolla.

"What's this, the sudden onset of senile sanity?"

"Inspiration's my specialty," he replied lightly. "I just hope I remember the layout of this old M-class right. It's a long time since I shipped in one."

She trailed him forward again as he studied engineer's markings on the liner's frames, talking to himself under his breath. There quickly followed the hollow, heavy concussion of the pirate making fast to the liner's hull. Han skidded to a stop and drew Fiolla back into the temporary safety of a side passageway.

Not too far ahead a covey of passengers had foolishly gathered near a main airlock in defiance of the captain's instructions. Among them Fiolla recognized the priest of Ninn in his green vestments, an Authority assistant supervisor of plant inoculation from an agroworld, and a dozen others she had come to know. All of them shrank back from the pneumatic sounds of the airlock's cycling.

Then the passengers rushed away like game-avians flushed from cover as the airlock's inner hatch swung open and armed boarders poured into the passageway. The boarders, wearing armored spacesuits, brandished blasters, force-pikes, rocket launchers, and vibro-axes. They had the look of faceless, invulnerable executioners.

There were orders from helmet speaker grilles and cries from the passengers. The latter were ignored amid a great deal of rough handling. A takeover team dashed toward the *Lady*'s bridge with shock grenades, fusion-cutters, plasma torches, and sapper charges, in case the captain changed his mind about surrendering. A few of the boarders began herding feebly objecting passengers toward the lounge while the rest split up into teams and began a rapid search outward in all directions from the airlock.

Han led Fiolla to an inboard passageway and struck out aft again, still reading frame markings, until they came to a utility locker. Inside the locker was a hatch giving access to a service core that ran the length of the ship. Normally the hatch would have been secured shut, but it could, for safety's sake, be opened manually when the ship was on emergency status. Han undogged it and entered the service core, squatting among power conduits and thick cables. Ventilation was never good in these cores, and layers of dust had settled everywhere, deposited by the liner's wheezy circulators.

Fiolla made a face. "What good's hiding? We're liable to wind up adrift in a derelict, Solo."

"We've got a reservation for two on the next boat out of here. Now get in; you're letting in a draft."

She entered awkwardly, trailing skirt gathered in one hand, and climbed under him so that he could dog the hatch, then clumsily shifted position to let him lead the way. He noticed, in the process, that Fiolla had two very nice legs.

The trip soon had both of them dirty, hot, and irritable as they hauled themselves over, under, and between obstacles. "Why is life so complicated around you?" she panted. "The pirates would take my money and leave me in peace, but not Han Solo, oh no!"

He sniggered nastily as he loosened the clips on a grating and wrenched it out of his way. "Has it occurred to you yet that this isn't a pirate attack?"

"I wouldn't know; I get invited to so few of them."

"Trust me; it's not. And they sure could've found fatter, safer targets out in the fringe areas. They're taking an awful risk hitting this close to Espo patrols. And then there's all this nonsense about not launching the boats. They're after someone in particular, and I think it's us."

He was leading her in a strained, squatting progress over ducts and power routing, bumping heads on the occasional low-hanging conduit. There were only intermittent emergency lights, nodes that only slightly relieved the darkness. After what seemed like an eternity he found the hatch he had been searching for, just aft of a major reinforced frame.

"Where are we?" Fiolla asked.

"Just under and aft of the portside airlock," he said, jerking his thumb toward the deck overhead. "The *Lady*'s probably swarming with boarders by now."

"Then what're we doing here? Has anyone ever criticized your leadership, Solo?"

"Never ever." He ascended a short ladder and she followed dubiously. But when he tried the hatch at the top he found its valve frozen in place. Setting his shoulder to its wheel and nearly losing his footing did no more good.

"Here," Fiolla said, handing up a short length of metal. He saw that she had pulled loose one of the ladder rungs from beneath her.

"You're wasting your time doing honest work," he told her frankly, and set the rung through the wheel's spokes. The second try elicited a creaking of metal and the wheel turned, then spun. He cracked the hatch a fraction to have a look around and saw, as he'd hoped he would, the interior of the utility locker just off the airlock's inner hatch. In it hung the maintenance ready-crew's spacesuits and tool harnesses, waiting to be donned on a moment's notice.

Drawing Fiolla up after him, he swung the core hatch shut as silently as he could. "There shouldn't be more than a guard or two out there at the airlock," he explained. "I doubt that they're worried about counterattack very much; there won't be more than two or three firearms onboard the *Lady* all told."

"Then what're we doing here?" She imitated his unconscious whisper.

"We can't hide for very long. If they have to, they'll sweep the whole ship with sensors, and I doubt that there are any shielded areas. There's only one place where we'll get an escape boat now."

She caught her breath as she realized what he meant and opened her mouth to object. But he put a finger across her lips. "They're slavers, not pirates, and they're not going through all this trouble just to let us live. They want to find out how much we know, then wipe our tapes for good. I'm not sure how this will work out, but if you get to the *Falcon* without me you can have Zlarb's data plaque. Tell Chewie it's in the breast pocket of my thermosuit and he'll know it's all right."

She started to say something, but he put her off. "Fight *and* run, remember? Here's what you do."

The guard watching the main airlock had been following the boarding via helmet comlink. The ship was fairly well secured and search parties were going through their assigned areas.

A noise from the utility locker attracted his attention. Though difficult to identify through the sound-dampening helmet, it sounded like metal striking metal.

Holding his launcher ready, the guard hit the hatch release. It swung the hatch out of the way and he entered the utility locker. At first he thought the room was empty; it had been searched earlier. But then he noticed the figure crouching in a futile attempt to hide behind one of the ready-crew's suits. It was a terrified young woman wearing a torn evening gown.

The guard swung his weapon up at once and checked out the rest of the locker, but it contained only tools and hanging spacesuits. He stepped into the locker, motioning with the launcher, switching to external address mode. "Come out of there right now and I won't hurt you."

That turned out to be true in a way the guard hadn't foreseen. A weighty power prybar caught him across the helmet and shoulder, driving him to his knees. Despite his armor the guard was stunned for a moment and his shoulder and arm went numb. He fumbled for his comlink controls, but the blow had smashed the transceiver on the side of his helmet.

The woman dashed up to try to wrench the launcher away from him, but the guard fought to retain it. A scrabbling sound from behind him and another clout made the guard forget all about his weapon. Much of the impact was absorbed by armor and helmet padding, but the blow had been so severe that even the amount that penetrated knocked him out flat on his face, dazed, with a huge dent in his helmet.

Han Solo, still in the spacesuit by which he'd dangled from a hook in ambush, threw himself on the raider and quickly slipped a tool harness around him, drawing it tight to pin his arms. With another he bound the man's legs. Fiolla watched the entire process nervously, gazing at the shoulder-fired rocket launcher she held as if it had materialized out of thin air.

Han rose and gently took the weapon from her. He found it to be loaded with anti-personnel rounds, flechette canisters. Those wouldn't hurt a boarder inside his armored spacesuit, but they'd be graphically effective against unprotected passengers and crew members. Han would have preferred a blaster, but the old-fashioned launcher would suffice for now.

His voice was muted by the helmet he wore. "We don't know whether he's supposed to check in or what. All we can do is go. Ready?"

She tried to smile and he encouraged her with a grin. He closed the utility locker hatch behind him and in a moment they had crossed through the boarding tube and entered the raider craft.

The passageway there was empty. *They must have the whole panting pack out looking for us*, he thought.

Picturing the raider's hull as he had seen it when she'd warped in at the *Lady*, he started aft, heading for the boat bay that had made him stay his hand in the gun turret. He pushed Fiolla along in front of him and held the launcher at high port as if she were his prisoner. The spacesuit might keep him from being recognized as an outsider in the disorder of the boarding. It was, at least, worth a try.

He saw the caution lights and marker panels of a ship's boat bay ahead.

"You there! Halt!" he heard a voice behind him shout. He pretended not to hear, and gave Fiolla a shove on her way. But the voice repeated the command. "Halt!"

He spun on his cleated heel, brought the launcher up and

found himself staring at a face he recognized. It was the black-haired man who had appeared in the message tape, the one who was to have met Zlarb. He and another man in armored spacesuits, helmets thrown back, were digging at their sidearms.

But the pistols were held in military-style holsters, built for durability rather than speed. *Might just as well have those guns home in a drawer*, Han reflected dispassionately as he aimed. Fiolla was screaming something he couldn't take time to listen to.

Both men realized at the last instant that they couldn't outshoot him and hurled themselves back, arms covering their faces, just as he fired.

The antipersonnel round was set for close work; the canister went off almost as soon as it left the launcher, boosting the flechettes and filling the passageway with a deafening concussion. The slavers didn't seem to be hurt, but remained on the deck where they had fallen. Han fired another AP round at them for good luck and, grabbing Fiolla's elbow, ran for the boat bay. She seemed to be in shock but didn't fight him. He opened the lock hatch and propelled her through.

"Find a place and grab on!" He found time to bite out a malediction that he had come upon a lifeboat rather than a pinnace or boarding craft.

A blaster beam mewed past him and burned out an illumination strip further down the passageway. Han knelt in the shelter of the lock and cut loose with four more rounds, emptying the launcher at the figures pounding down on him. They all dove for cover but he didn't think he had gotten any of them.

Closing both hatches, he threw himself into the boat's pilot's seat and detonated its separator charges. Unlike the liner's boats, the raider ship's were still functioning. With a stupendous jolt the boat was blown from its lock. At the same moment he cut in full thrust and the lifeboat leaped as if it had been kicked.

Han swung hard, relying on steering thrusters alone here where there was no atmosphere to affect the tumbling boat's control surfaces. He piloted grimly to miss the liner's hull and looped up to put the bulk of the *Lady of Mindor* between himself and the slavers' vessel. Opening the boat's engine all the way, he vectored on until he was out of cannon range, then plunged toward the surface of Ammund.

He freed one hand from his struggle long enough to fling back his helmet.

"Can we outrun them?" Fiolla asked from the acceleration chair behind him.

"There's more to it than that," he said without taking his eyes from the controls. "They can't come after us until they sound recall and get all their men back from the *Lady*. And if they want to send boats after us, they'd better have some awfully hot pilots."

He heard a lurching and, despite the pull of the boat's dive, Fiolla drew herself up to the copilot's chair. "Sit down and stay put," he told her heatedly, if a bit late. "If I'd had to maneuver or decelerate just then, you'd be scraping yourself off the bulkhead!"

She ignored that. He saw something else had so shocked her that she was still feeling the effect of it. Knowing how resilient she was ordinarily, he divided his attention for a moment.

"What's wrong? Besides the fact that we might be vaporized at any second, I mean."

"The man you shot at . . ."

"The black-haired one? He's the one who left the message I told you about; he was Zlarb's connection." He turned to her sharply. "Why?"

"It was Magg," Fiolla said, the blood drained from her face. "It was my hand-picked personal assistant, Magg."

IX

IT was early in the morning of Ammuud's short day when spaceport employees and automata alike stopped work as sirens announced a defense alert. Reinforced domes folded back to reveal emplacements around the port and in the snowy mountains above. For a quiet little spaceport, Ammuud had an impressive array of weaponry.

A boat came out of the sky, catching the light. Its pilot hit the braking thruster, and the ear-splitting sound of its passage caught up with it. Turbolasers, missile tubes, and multibarreled cannons traced its descent, eager to fire should the boat show the slightest sign of hostile action. The defense command was already aware that a brief ship-to-ship action had been fought above Ammuud, and they were inclined to take no chances. Interceptors were kept clear, since it was a lone craft, and the entire sky was a potential free-fire area.

But the boat set down obediently and precisely at one side of the field by port control, at a spot designated. Ground vehicles mounted with portable artillery closed in around the little vessel while the larger emplacements went back to standby. The spaceport automata, cargo-handlers, automovers, and the like, their simple circuitry satisfied that there was no reason to discontinue work, returned to their tasks, with one exception. No one even noticed the labor 'droid who, still carrying a shipping crate, started off across the field.

As he cracked the boat's hatch, Han turned to check on

his companion. "Fiolla, you've got great judgment in hired help, that's all I can say."

"Solo, he passed an in-depth security investigation," she insisted, rather more loudly. "What was I supposed to do, have him brain-probed?"

Han stopped as he was about to swing down to the landing field. "Not a bad idea. Anyway, this tells us a lot. When you gained access to the slavers' computer pocket on Bonadan, it wasn't just because of miskeying. Magg's terminal probably had some sort of special-access equipment built into it; looks like he's the slavers' roving accountant, too, and maybe their security man as well.

"He sent you out on that scooter so you could be quietly taken out of the way. I'll bet he gimmicked up that fancy scanner-proof gun of yours, too."

Fiolla was fast on the recovery, he had to give her that. She had already accepted what she had seen and revised her ideas accordingly. "That doesn't make any of this my fault," she pointed out logically.

Han didn't answer, being busy staring into the barrels and emission apertures of a variety of lethal weapons, doing his best to look friendly and unthreatening. He showed empty hands.

A man in unmatched tunic and trousers stepped up, disruptor in hand. His uniform wasn't regulation but he wore a starburst insignia on an armband. Han already knew from inquiries that Ammuud was run by a loose and often competitive coalition of seven major clans under Authority subcontract. From the disparity of uniforms and attire it appeared that all seven clans supplied men to the port security force.

"What's the meaning of this?" the leader snapped. "Who are you? What happened up there?" On that last he gestured toward the sky over Ammuud with his pistol barrel.

Han dropped down from the open hatch and casually but conspicuously raised his hands while donning his sunniest smile. "We were passengers on the liner *Lady of Mindor*.

She was attacked and boarded by pirates; we two escaped, but I don't know what happened after we left."

"According to screens, the pirate has cut loose from that liner and run; we haven't got a paint on it anymore. Let me see your identification, please." The man hadn't lowered his sidearm.

"We didn't have time to pack our bags," Han told him. "We jumped the first lifeboat we came to and got clear."

"And just in time," added Fiolla, poised at the hatch. "Please help me down, darling?"

Several of the port police automatically closed in to assist. Fiolla looked very good, even with her gown ripped and dust from the utility core on her. She also added a convincing note to Han's story. He interceded before anyone else could help and, hands at her waist, lowered her to the field.

The officer in charge began rubbing his forehead. "It looks as if I'll have to take you to the Reesbon stronghold for further questioning."

But one of his men objected. "Why to the Reesbon's? Why not to our clan stronghold, the Glayyd's? There are more of us here than you."

Han recalled that Reesbon and Glayyd were two of the six controlling clans here on Ammuud. And the Mor Glayyd, patriarch of his clan, was the man Han and Fiolla were here to see. A quick look around indicated to him that the *Falcon* didn't seem to be on the field. Han resisted the impulse to inquire about his ship, not wanting to implicate Chewbacca in what was going on if he could avoid it.

But the problem of the moment involved being carted off to some clan stronghold. He wasn't sure yet what he would say to the Glayyd leader, but he knew he had no desire to be sequestered in the family home of the Reesbons.

"Actually, I'm here because I have business to conduct with the Mor Glayyd," he commented. That drew a scowl from the officer but, to Han's surprise, also evoked a suspicious look from the Glayyd men and women.

The first Glayyd clansman spoke again. "There, you see?

Do you deny that this is something that can be investigated by the Mor Glayyd just as honestly as by the Mor Reesbon?''

The officer and his kinsmen were in the great minority; he saw he could win neither by rank nor force. Han had the impression the port police forces were shot through with dissension. The officer's lips compressed as he conceded the point stiffly. ''I will summon a ground car; we'll have to keep all the weapons vehicles here at the port.''

Just then a slow metallic voice behind Han drawled, ''Sir, hadn't I best come with you? Or would you rather I remained here with the boat?''

Han did his best to keep his jaw from dropping. Bollux stood in the lifeboat's hatch, to all intents awaiting orders after an eventful descent and landing.

''I thought you two were alone?'' said one of the port police with a hint of accusation.

Fiolla was faster on the uptake than Han. ''There's just us and our personal 'droid,'' she explained. ''Do the Ammuud clans count machinery among the clan populace?''

Han was still staring at Bollux; he couldn't have been more surprised if the 'droid had danced his way out of a party-pastry. Then he got his brain into gear. ''No, you might as well come with us,'' he told the 'droid.

Bollux obediently lowered himself from the hatch. The officer was back, having spoken over the comlink in one of the weapons carriers. ''A car has been dispatched from the central pool and will be here very shortly,'' he told them. Turning to the Glayyd man who had given him the argument, he smiled bleakly. ''I trust the Mor Glayyd will report on this matter to the other clans quickly. After all, he has other . . . pressing matters that may call him away soon.''

The Glayyd people shifted and glowered, fingering their weapons as if the Reesbon officer had made an extreme provocation. The officer returned to his vehicle and, with the rest of the Reesbon people, departed.

The Glayyd man wanted to know more about Han's business with his clan leader. ''No, he's not expecting me,'' Han answered honestly. ''But it's a matter of extreme urgency, as important to him as to me.''

To forestall more inquiries Fiolla leaned heavily on Han's arm, eyelids fluttering. Putting a hand to her brow, she did such a convincing imitation of being close to collapse that further questions went unasked.

''She's been through a lot,'' Han explained. ''Maybe we could sit down while we're waiting for the car.''

''Forgive me,'' muttered the Glayyd man. ''Please make yourselves comfortable in the troop compartment of that carrier. I shall inform the Mor Glayyd of your arrival.''

''Uh, tell him I'm sorry if we're taking him from something.'' Han was thinking of what the Reesbon officer had said. ''What have we interrupted?''

The Glayyd man's eyes flicked over Han again. ''The Mor Glayyd is to fight a death-duel,'' he said, and departed to send his message.

Seated with Bollux in the troop compartment, Fiolla and Han pressed the 'droid for information. He gave them a brief summary of events following their parting on Bonadan.

''What'd you do when the escape pod grounded?'' Han wanted to know.

''I'm afraid Spray's timing wasn't all that good, sir,'' Bollux answered. ''I landed some distance from the city, but at least that kept me from being painted by their sensor screens or destroyed on the way down; defenses are very good here. I walked the rest of the way to the spaceport and simply made myself inconspicuous, awaiting your appearance. I must admit I'd been concentrating on incoming ships at their small passenger terminal; I hadn't expected you to arrive in this fashion. Also, I've managed to learn a good deal about the current situation here.''

''Wait; jet back,'' instructed Han. ''What'd you mean, made yourself inconspicuous? Where've you been?''

''Why, doing what 'droids are supposed to do, Captain Solo,'' Bollux answered both of Han's questions at once. ''I simply entered the port through the labor-automata checkpoint and began doing whatever work there was to be done. Everyone always presumes that a 'droid is owner-imprinted and task-programmed. After all, why else would a 'droid be working? No one ever questioned me, even the labor-gang bosses. And since I wasn't really assigned to anyone, no one ever noticed when I drifted from one job to another. Being a labor 'droid is very good protective coloration, Captain."

Fiolla was interested. "But that involved deceiving humans. Didn't it go against your fundamental programming?"

Han could have sworn Bollux sounded modest. "My actions involved a very high order of probability of contributing to your and the captain's well-being or even, if I may say so, of preventing your coming to harm. That, it goes without saying, overcame any counterprogramming forbidding deception of a human. And so, when I saw your boat land, I simply carried a shipping crate across the field until I was behind your craft and then entered it through the rear hatch. As I said—"

"Nobody noticed a 'droid," Han anticipated him. "When we're out of here I'll take care of that, if you like; we'll repaint you in flashy colors, how's that? Now what about this duel?"

"From what I've been able to learn listening to humans and talking to the few *intelligent* automata at the port, sir, there's an extremely rigid code of honor in force among the clans. The Mor Glayyd, leader of the most powerful clan, has been mortally insulted by an outsider, an extremely proficient gunman. The other clans won't intervene because they'd be happy to see the Mor Glayyd die. And, according to the code, no Glayyd family member is permitted to intervene either. If the Mor Glayyd fails to fight or his challenger is killed or injured before the contest, he'll lose all face and much of his popular support, and violate his oath as clan protector."

"We've got to get to him before this stupid duel," Fiolla exclaimed to Han. "We can't afford to have him killed!"

"I'm sure he feels the same way," Han assured her dryly.

Just then a car slid up, a wide, soft-tired ground vehicle gleaming a hard, enamel black.

"I've changed my mind," Han told the Glayyd clansman. "My 'droid here will stay with the lifeboat. After all, it's not my property and I guess I'll be responsible for its safe return."

There was no objection. Bollux reentered the boat and Han and Fiolla made themselves comfortable in the car's deeply upholstered interior. Glayyd clanspeople caught handholds and mounted the car's running boards.

The car was warm and comfortable, with enough room for a dozen passengers. A driver, backed by a guidance computer, sat on the other side of a thick transparisteel partition. The ride took them through the main part of the city. It was a rather ramshackle affair, its buildings being more often of wood or stone than of fusion-formed material or shaped formex. Street drainage was provided by open gutters that were frequently choked with refuse and pools of crimson-scummed water.

The people they passed showed a wide range of activity. There were trappers, starshipwrights, forestry service police, maintenance trouble-shooters, freight haulers, and street vendors. Among them jostled the young men of the clans and their carefully chaperoned kinswomen.

For all its faults and imperfections, Han preferred an open, brawling, and vital place like Ammuud to the depressing functionality of a Bonadan or the groomed sterility of one of the Authority's capitol worlds. This place might never be awash in profit or influential in galactic affairs, but it looked like an interesting place to live.

Fiolla frowned as they rolled past a row of slums. "It's an insult to have one of those eyesores in the Corporate Sector Authority."

"There're a lot worse things in the Authority," Han replied.

"Keep your lectures about what's wrong with the Authority," she shot back. "I'm better informed about that than you are. The difference between us is that I'm going to do something about it. And my first move is to get on the Board of Directors."

Han made a silencing motion, indicating the driver and the riders who clung to the car. Fiolla made a *hmmph!* at him, crossed her arms and stared angrily out her window.

The Glayyd stronghold looked like just that, a pile of huge blocks of fusion-formed material boasting detectors and weapons emplacements galore. The stronghold was set up against the rearing mountains at the edge of the city, and Han presumed that the peaks hid deep, all but impregnable shelters.

The car slid through an open gate at the foot of the stronghold and came to a stop in a cavernous garage guarded by young men, the Glayyd clan's footsoldiers. They didn't seem particularly wary and Han took it for granted that the car had been thoroughly checked out prior to admittance.

One of the clan guards escorted them to a small lift chute and stood aside as they entered, setting their destination for them. They rose quickly, and because the chute wasn't equipped with autocompensation gear, Han's ears popped.

When the doors swished open they found themselves looking out into a room far airier and more open than expected. Apparently some of those heavy blocks and slabs could be moved aside.

The room was furnished sparely but well. Robo-vassals and fine, if dated, conform-lounge furniture showed that the occupants enjoyed their luxuries. Waiting for the two was a woman some years younger than Fiolla.

She was dressed in a thickly embroidered gown trimmed in silvery thread and wore a shawl made of some wispy blue material. Her red-brown hair was held back by a single blue ribbon. She bore on her left cheek the discoloration of a recent injury; Han thought it the mark of a slap. She had a look of hope, and of misgiving.

"Won't you come in, please, and sit down? I'm afraid they neglected to forward your names to me."

They introduced themselves and found places in the comfortable furniture. Han wanted very much to hear her ask if he wanted something to drink, but she was so distracted that she ignored the subject altogether.

"I am Ido, sister to the Mor Glayyd," she said quickly. "Our patrolman didn't specify your business but I decided to see you, hoping it concerned this . . . current distress."

"Meaning the death duel?" Fiolla asked straightforwardly.

The young woman nodded. "Not us," Han said quickly, to keep the matter clear. Fiolla gave him a caustic look.

"Then I don't think my brother will have time to speak to you," Ido went on. "The duel has been twice postponed, though we hadn't expected that, but no further delay will be allowed."

Han was about to argue but Fiolla, more the diplomat than he, changed the course of conversation for the moment, asking what had prompted the challenge. Ido's fingertips went to the mark on her face.

"This is the cause," she said. "I fear this little mark is my brother's death sentence. An offworlder appeared here several days ago and contrived to be introduced to me at a reception. We took a turn through the roof garden at his invitation. He became enraged at something I said, or so it seemed. He struck me. My brother had no choice but to make challenge. Since then we've learned that this fellow is a famous gunman who has killed many opponents. The whole thing seems a plot to kill my brother, but it's too late to avoid the duel."

"What's his name, the offworlder?" Han asked, interested now.

"Gallandro, he is called," she replied. Han didn't recognize the name but, oddly enough, he saw from Fiolla's face that she had. *She keeps track of some strange information,* he thought.

"I'd hoped you might have come to prevent the duel or intervene," Ido said. "None of the other clans will, since they envy us and would like to see us in misfortune. And by the Code, no one else in our clan or its service can take my brother's part. But another outsider may, for the sake of either our interests or his own. That is to say, if it's a matter that directly concerns him."

Han was thinking that if he were the Mor Glayyd he'd be shopping around for a fast starship with the family jewelry in his pocket. His musings were interrupted by Fiolla's voice. "Ido, please let us talk to your brother; there may be something we can do."

After Ido, overjoyed, had rushed away, Han, ignoring the possibility of listening devices, exploded. "What's wrong with you? What can *you* do to help him?"

She stared back blithely. "I? Why, nothing. But you can take his place and save him."

"Me?" he howled, coming to his feet so quickly that he nearly bowled over a robo-vassal. The mechanical skittered back with an electronic screech.

"I don't even know what the fight's about," Han continued at high volume. "I'm here looking for someone who owes me ten thousand. I never heard of either of these people. Which reminds me, it looked like you knew about the gunfighter, what's his name—"

"Gallandro, a name I've heard before. If it's the same man, he's the territorial manager's most trusted operative; I've only heard his name once before. Odumin, the territorial manager, must be involved in all this; these must be the 'measures' Magg informed Zlarb about. If Gallandro kills the Mor Glayyd, it'll end your tracing of Zlarb's bosses and your chance to collect. But if you intercede for the Mor Glayyd, we might still get what we want."

"What about minor details," Han asked sarcastically, "such as if Gallandro kills me, for example?"

"I thought you were the Han Solo who said he could get more in this life with a blaster than with an open expense account. So this is your department. Besides, Gallandro will almost certainly withdraw when he finds out he'll have no chance of killing the Mor Glayyd anyway. And who'd dare face the great Han Solo?''

''Nobody wants to and nobody's going to!''

''Solo, Solo; you've eliminated Zlarb, seen Magg with the slavers, and heard what I've learned. Do you think they'll ever stop coming after you? Your one chance is to save the Mor Glayyd and get that information from him so that I can prosecute everyone connected with the slavery ring. And let's not forget the ten thousand they owe you.''

''Let's not ever. What about it?''

''If you can't get it out of them, maybe I can get you some sort of compensation. Reward to a citizen for a job well done, commendation from the Board of Directors, that sort of thing.''

''I want ten thousand, not a credit less,'' Han stipulated. Fiolla was right about one thing: unchecked, the slavers would undoubtedly keep coming after him. ''And no ceremonial dinners. I'll leave through the back door, thanks.''

''Whatever. But none of that's likely if you let Gallandro kill the Mor Glayyd.''

At that moment the door swished open, and Ido returned, her hand through her brother's elbow. Han was surprised to see how young the Mor Glayyd was; he'd assumed that Ido was a kid sister. But the Mor Glayyd was even younger. He wore a fine outfit stiff with braid and decorations of one kind and another, and a gunbelt that somehow didn't look right on him. He was slightly shorter than his sister, slim and rather pale. His hair, the same color as hers, was caught behind him in a tail.

Ido made introductions, but while she referred to her brother by his title, she called him by a more familiar name.

''Ewwen, Captain Solo wishes to intervene for you. Oh, please, please agree!''

The Mor Glayyd was unsure. ''For what reason?''

Han massaged the bridge of his nose with thumb and forefinger. Fiolla offered no hints, confident that he could come up with some plausible reply.

"I have, uh, business with you, a deal you might be interested in. It'll take some explaining—"

At that moment the comlink signaled for attention. The Mor Glayyd excused himself and crossed to the instrument. He must have activated a muting device as well; none of the others heard any part of the conversation. When he turned back, his face had become emotionless.

"It seems we lack time for your explanation, Captain Solo," he said. "The outworlder Gallandro and his second have appeared at the gate and will await me in the armory."

Steeling himself with *Think of cash!*, Han said, "Why don't I meet him for you?" When he saw he was going to get an argument out of this proud boy, he rushed on. "Remember your sister and your duty to your clan. Forget the point of honor; this is real life."

"Ewwen, please do," Ido implored her brother. "I beg it as a boonfavor to me."

The Mor Glayyd looked from one to another, almost spoke, held himself. "I couldn't yield this obligation to any member of my clan," he finally said to Han. "But my death would leave my sister and my kinsmen at the mercy of the other clans. Very well, I shall put myself in your debt. Let us repair to the armory."

The private lift chute carried them down quickly. The armory was a series of cold, echoing, vaulted rooms crammed with racks of energy guns, projectile firearms, and muscle-powered weapons along with work benches and tools with which to service them. Their footsteps resounded on stone as they made their way to a shooting range.

At the far end of the range and along the walls holotargets hung in the air, waiting to unfreeze into attack-evasion sequences. But it wasn't holotargets that were scheduled to be shot. At the nearer end of the range waited five people.

Han was fairly sure he could identify them—worlds with such an archaic and formal dueling code demanded about the same roster. The woman with the weary look on her face and the professional medipack slung from one shoulder would be the surgeon. In a gunfight at close quarters, Han doubted that her duties would extend beyond pronouncing the loser dead.

The older man in Glayyd household livery would be the Mor Glayyd's second; he had a lean, scarred face and was probably an instructor in arms or some such to his clan leader. Another man, in what Han had come to recognize as Reesbon colors, would be the other second. There was a white-haired elderly man standing aside and trying to conceal his nervousness; he could only be the match's judge.

The last member of the group was easiest of all to identify. Though Han had never seen him before, the sight of him set off internal alarms. He was slightly taller than Han but seemed smaller and more compact. Holding himself easily and gracefully, he wore a somber outfit of gray trousers and high-collared tunic with a short gray jacket over it. A trailing, supple white scarf, knotted at his throat, fell in graceful tails at his shoulder and back.

The man's graying hair had been cropped quite short, but he had long mustachios hanging at the corners of his mouth, their ends gathered and weighted by tiny golden beads. He was just in the process of removing his jacket. An intricately tooled black gunbelt encircled his waist, holding a blaster high up on his right hip. He didn't observe the common practice of studding his belt with a marker to indicate each opponent he'd beaten; he didn't look as if he needed to.

But it was the man's eyes that had set off most of Han's alarms, making him absolutely certain of the man's profession. The eyes were a deep, clear blue, unblinking, unwavering. They examined all the newcomers, remained for a moment on the Mor Glayyd and came to rest on Han, making a chilly estimate of him in a moment. The look the two exchanged left little to be said.

"As challenged party," the Mor Glayyd's second was saying, "Gallandro has chosen a face-off draw rather than the measured paceway. Your favorite weapons have been prepared, Mor Glayyd. All weapons have been examined by both seconds."

Still meeting Gallandro's eyes, Han took the final step. "I have a call on the Mor Glayyd's time. It's my right to intervene for him, I hear."

There was a murmur among the seconds and judge. The surgeon merely shook her head tiredly. Han went to where the mentioned weapons had been set out and began checking them over. He had passed on a variety of fancy shoulder and forearm rigs and was debating between two gunbelts that resembled his own when he realized Gallandro was standing next to him.

"Why?" asked the gunfighter with a clinical curiosity.

"He doesn't have to explain," objected Ido, who was ignored.

"My dispute's with the Mor Glayyd; I don't even know you," said Gallandro.

"But you know I'm faster than the kid," Han said pleasantly, holding up a short-barreled needlebeamer for examination. Then he met Gallandro's gaze, which was as placid as a pool's surface at dawn. All the important information was exchanged then, though neither man's expression altered and nothing more was said. Han had no doubt the duel would proceed.

Instead, Gallandro turned and intoned: "Mor Glayyd, I find myself compelled to apologize, and tender you my earnest plea for your forgiveness and that of your sister." He stated his case indifferently, disposing of an unpleasant duty, and made little pretext of sincerity. "I trust that you'll pardon me and that this entire unfortunate incident will be forgotten."

For a second it looked as if the Mor Glayyd would refuse the apology; having escaped a sure death, the boy wouldn't mind seeing Gallandro shot. Han was about to accept for him, not much inclined now toward a fast-draw contest, since it could be avoided.

But Ido spoke first. "We both accept your apology with

the proviso that you leave our home and our homeworld as soon as possible."

Gallandro looked from her to Han, who still held the needlebeamer. Gathering his jacket, the gunman inclined his head to Ido and prepared to go. But he paused to trade one last hard look with Han.

"Another time, perhaps," Gallandro offered with a brittle smile.

"Whenever you can work yourself up to it."

Gallandro nearly laughed. Suddenly, he had spun, dropped into a half-crouch, drawn his blaster, and put four bolts dead-center into each of four holotargets along the wall. He had straightened, his sidearm spinning twice around his finger and ending up in his holster, before most of the people in the room had grasped what he'd done.

"Another time, perhaps," Gallandro repeated quietly. He sketched a shallow bow to the women, the surgeon included, gathered the Reesbon second in by eye, and strode away, his steps carrying back to them loudly.

"It worked," sighed Fiolla. "But you shouldn't have traded digs with him, Solo. He seemed sort of—dangerous."

Han gazed at the four holotargets registering perfect hits, then back at the departing Gallandro. He ignored Fiolla's vast understatement. Gallandro was far and away the most dangerous gunman Han had ever seen; faster, he was nearly certain, than Han himself.

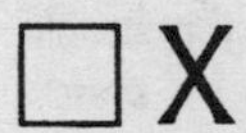

THE *Millennium Falcon* had found sanctuary by a small lake in a shallow valley high in the mountains beyond Ammuud's spaceport. Coming down the ramp, Spray was pleased to discover the previous night's windstorm had deposited no snow.

He found Chewbacca assembling an interesting collection of tools and equipment, including a metal tripod with telescoping legs, spools of light cable, supports, clamps, ground spikes, and a small sky-scan sensor unit. The skip-tracer inquired about the purpose of it all. With a few gestures, and growling in his own tongue by force of habit, Chewbacca made clear to Spray what he was about to do. In order to give them added protection, the Wookiee was going to mount the sky-scan sensor on the ridge line above them, where it would give a much wider area of surveillance than the *Falcon*'s equipment, surrounded by this little valley, could.

"B-but when will you be back?" Spray asked apprehensively. The *Falcon*'s first mate stopped himself from snorting derisively; the Tynnan had borne up well since the emergency landing and pulled his own weight, assisting in repairs and preparing meals. It wasn't Spray's fault if he wasn't used to survival living and wilderness situations.

Chewbacca made a quick motion with the tripod, as if spreading it and digging it in, and slapped its mounting plate, as if setting the sensor unit in place. The meaning was obvious; he wouldn't be gone long at all.

"But what about them?" Spray wanted to know, meaning

the herd of grazers moving up the slopes from a lower valley into theirs. The shambling beasts went at their usual slow, imperturbable pace, feeding on scrub, rock lichen, and such spring grasses as were exposed, their antlered heads rising and dipping as they carried on their endless ruminations.

Several herds had passed through the area, neither showing any interest in the *Millennium Falcon* nor any hostility toward Spray or Chewbacca. The Wookiee spread his hands to show that the grazers presented no problem. Some of his equipment he tucked into the floppy carryall held against his right hip by his ammo bandolier; the rest he tucked into the loops of a tool roll, slipping it over his shoulder by its pack-straps, then took up his bowcaster. Checking his weapon's action and magazine, he set off.

"And watch out for those things," Spray called through cupped hands, pointing aloft. The Wookiee looked up. As often happened, there were some of the pterosaurs of Ammuud, huge, long-beaked reptilian soarers, circling in search of prey. But, though they were usually to be seen singly or in pairs, perhaps a dozen of them were now quartering the sky.

The Wookiee looked askance at the skip-tracer and shook his bowcaster, snarling significantly; it was the soarers who would be well advised to take care. He set out again, his big, shaggy feet carrying him over the rocky ground and occasional patches of snow. His burden bothered him not at all.

He made good time and was soon leaning into the ascent to a high point on the ridge line. Atop it was a wide, level area and beyond the ridge was another, broader valley ending in a narrow pass. When he topped the ridge, Chewbacca spread out his tools and sat himself on a flat rock to begin assembling the sensor unit's tripod.

Once the mounting plate was locked into place on the tripod, he looked down to check on the starship. He couldn't see Spray, but that was no surprise; the skip-tracer was on the opposite side of the ship from the main ramp. What made his features cloud was the closeness of the herd of grazers;

their main flow plodded within twenty meters of the freighter, though they showed no inclination to investigate or molest her. Too, this herd seemed far larger than any of the others; its leaders were well on their way to the pass, yet its end wasn't in sight. More and more grazers were making their way up from the lower slopes. But the calves were staying well to the center of the herd's mainstream, with the bigger bulls tromping along in the lead and on the flanks, and the whole group appeared orderly and moving leisurely. Satisfied for the moment, Chewbacca returned to his work, running a check to ensure the unit was charged and functioning.

When a distant thunder reached his sharp ears, his head snapped up at once. The grazers, so quiescent and unthreatening a moment before, were now in stampede. So far, they were sweeping wide of the *Falcon*, but the herd began ranging out, the front of the stampede widening as Chewbacca watched, becoming a sea of shaggy backs and a forest of antlers. The soarers were making sweeping dives in along the leading edge of the stampede, emitting eerie wailing sounds.

The Wookiee wasted no time speculating on whether the flying things had started the stampede with air attacks to cut out weaker or slower grazers. Snatching up his equipment, he took in the surrounding terrain, searching for some shelter. More grazers were galloping up from the lower slopes and the stampede gained momentum every second. The animals were no longer lumbering, clumsy shufflers; in flight, they were six-legged powerhouses, the smallest adult among them weighing four times what the Wookiee did, traveling at high speed with the formidable impetus of fright.

But the narrow pass was already choked with struggling grazers, and as Chewbacca watched, the excess began to mill in a tossing of antlers and fill the lower valley. He put down his equipment and prepared to run, only to discover that he was already cut off. The grazers were flowing around the high point he had selected, avoiding its steep incline on their way to the lower valley.

A quick glance told him that the beasts were still avoiding the unfamiliar bulk of the *Millennium Falcon*, but if the backup from the pass reached that far, their reticence could change. The Wookiee hoped that Spray would have the sense to use the disabled starship's weaponry to keep the animals from damaging her further. By that time, of course, the grazers would be all over the ridge; they would start forging up the steeper slopes as soon as the pressure of the bottled herd grew great enough.

He held his bowcaster and took stock of his situation as objectively as he could, observing the animals below and the terrain around him. At length he decided that to try to work his way through the herd or even run with them would be suicide; they were aroused and in panic now and would be quick to attack any outsider among them. On the other hand—

He broke off in midthought as a shadow passed over him and a wailing cry warned him. He hit the ground rolling, clutching his weapon to him. Broad wings hissed through the air over him and sharp claws closed on nothing. The soarer swept onward, leaving a carrion reek in the air, screaming its frustration. A second, behind it, tried a swoop of its own.

The Wookiee came up onto one knee and threw his bowcaster up to his shoulder, lacking time to focus through the weapon's scope. There was the high twang of the bow, a simultaneous detonation as the explosive quarrel crumpled the soarer's wingtip. The flier veered, crippled.

Chewbacca fell backward, jacking the foregrip of his bowcaster to recock it and strip another round off its magazine. He got two more shots into the predatory flier as it half-fell, half-flew past him, putting yawning wounds in its rib cage.

The creature tumbled, dead on the wing. It came down among the stampeding grazers and in a moment was gone from view, trampled into a shapeless mass by hundreds of hooves. Another soarer had glided in, sheered off when it heard the explosive quarrels and come around for another pass.

Chewbacca realized now why the soarers had come together in such numbers for the migration of grazers. The stampede through the wild mountain country would inevitably produce casualties, leave behind the weak or injured and, too, strand refugees like himself, ripe pickings for the airborne pack. The soarers' primitive brains had recognized the chance for a feast.

The Wookiee brought up his bowcaster again and carefully sighted on the oncoming soarer. It stooped for him, claws open, long, narrow beak wide with its cry. He centered it precisely in his scope and fired directly into the gaping maw. The top of its boney skull disappeared and it nosed down at once, plowing into the ground. He had to jump back out of the way as the soarer's corpse, seeming to collapse in on itself, slid to a stop where he had stood.

With two of their number down, the soarers were more cautious about approaching the ridge. They tilted membranous wings and put distance between themselves and whatever mysterious thing had killed their companions, searching all the while for more approachable prey. Chewbacca stole a look back down at the valley.

The press of grazers at the pass was backing up toward him quickly. Even now a few of the beasts were pausing to mill around the lower part of the ridge. The Wookiee fired several rounds into the ground there, blowing showers of soil and rock into the air and sending off the terrified, bellowing grazers. But the swirl of the backlogged stampede moved more animals in toward the ridge again; they were too scared and too stupid to notice the cause of the explosions of a moment before. He would never hold them back, even if he had unlimited ammunition.

A tremendous racket, rising over the cannonading hooves, came from the *Millennium Falcon*. It was the ship's distress signals—hooters and klaxons combined with flashing lights, designed to attract the attention of searchers in case of crash or emergency landing. Apparently the grazers had begun to get too close to the ship, and Spray had resorted to this to save her. It was good thinking on the skip-tracer's part, but

Chewbacca knew he could look for little else in the way of help. He doubted if even the starship's guns could clear a secure path through the massed herd.

A soarer's cry sounded and he spied the creature rising from the cliff across the valley, bearing what looked like a stunned or injured grazer calf. The Wookiee growled an imprecation at the flier and wished for a second that he, too, had wings. Then he shook his fist in the air and bellowed wildly, for a mad inspiration worthy of Han Solo had just struck him.

As he worked out details, he slung his bowcaster and began rummaging through the equipment he had brought. First, the tripod. He clamped all three legs under his arm and got a firm grip on its mounting plate. Cords of muscle swelled in his arms and paws, and he gritted his fierce teeth in exertion. Slowly, he put the needed crease into the tough metal of the plate.

When he was satisfied, he put down the tripod and began to work furiously, casting occasional glances down to the growing turmoil in the valley as it surged toward his high ground. He had, he believed, the tools and materials he required; time was another question entirely.

He threw the downed soarer's carcass over onto its back without trouble; its bones were hollow and it had, for all its size, evolved for minimum weight. He jammed the bent mounting plate up under its chin, ignoring the ruin of its gaping skull, and fixed it there with a retainer from his tool roll, turning its screw down as tightly as he could without crushing the bone.

He spread two of the tripod's legs, extending them to maximum length, and lay them out along each wing. He curled the leading edge of the wings over the tripod legs and wrapped them two full turns at the tips, exerting his strength against the resistance of the wing cartilage. There was barely any fold at all near the wing joints, but it would have to serve. He had only eight clamps in his carryall pouch; four for each wing had better be enough. He tightened them down quickly to hold the tripod legs in place within the folds of the wing edges.

Stopping to check, he saw that the grazers were already thronging on the lower slopes of his high ground, packed tightly together, antlers swaying and flashing. He applied himself to his task with redoubled energy.

He drew the central tripod leg out along the soarer's body as a longitudinal axis. The creature was an efficient glider, but its breast lacked the prominent keel to which flight muscles are attached in birds, and that made fastening a problem. He settled, after no more than a few seconds' thought, on a row of ring-fasteners punched through the skin and passed around the creature's slender sternum. Fortunately, it had no more than a vestigial tail. He swallowed and tried to ignore its nauseating odor as he worked.

Then came his worst problem, a kingpost. Taking one of the bracing members he had brought, he thrust it up directly through the soarer's body next to the sternum, to stand a meter and a half out its back, and made it fast to the longitudinal axis. Then he fit the longest brace he had across the juncture, securing it to the other two tripod legs as a lateral axis. He didn't fret over the various vile substances now leaking out of the soarer; that decreased the weight, which could only help.

He spent a frantic several minutes cutting and fitting cable, with no time to measure or experiment, connecting wingtips, tail, and beak to the tip of the kingpost.

He had to pause when a group of grazers breasted the ridge, wild-eyed and quick to swing their antlers in his direction. He jammed a new magazine into his bowcaster and emptied it into the ground, filling the air with explosions that could be heard over the countless hoof-falls in the valley, driving the animals back down for the time being. But the valley was now filled and there would be no room for them below, he knew; it was only a matter of moments before a major part of the stampede covered the high ground and engulfed the Wookiee.

The soarer's grasping legs probably hadn't given it very good locomotion, but they made a plausible control bar once Chewbacca had stiffened them with supports, wired the claws together, and braced the shoulders with ground spikes. Then they, too, were cabled to wingtips, nose, and vestigial tail. The Wookiee dashed around the soarer's body, tightening down turnbuckles with no more than a hasty guess at the tension needed.

He heaved, thews bulging under his pelt, and lifted the animal framework, gazing down and hoping the stampede had receded and that he would be spared the necessity of testing his handiwork.

It hadn't; grazers were literally being borne up toward him by the pressure of those below. Another barrage from the bowcaster only made them fall back for a moment; the tightly packed bodies came at him again.

Chewbacca took his ammo bandolier, twisted it several times to tighten it, then slipped both arms through it as a harness and fastened it together at the front with a length of cable, hooking himself up to the framework where kingpost met longitudinal axis. He shouldered the weight of the soarer and slung his bowcaster around his neck. The body slumped but the extremely light, superstrong support materials kept it in deployment.

A grazer bull with antlers like a hedge of bayonets cut in toward him. The Wookiee skipped out of the way and almost collided with another knot of the animals. The ridge was being overrun. With nothing to lose, Chewbacca churned toward a dropoff, holding the soarer's reinforced carcass at what he hoped was the correct angle of attack, and launched himself.

He wouldn't have been surprised if the wings had luffed and, with no lift at all, he had gone tumbling into the stamping, snorting mass of grazers. But a caprice of the strong air currents along the ridge flared the flier's wings, bearing him along on an updraft.

He began to yaw, the soarer's beak moving to the right,

and pushed hard on the creature's braced claws to bring its nose around into the wind once more. Even so, his makeshift glider's sink rate was appalling. He raised his legs behind him and tried to distribute his weight for better control. He nosed up in an instinctive effort to get more lift, caring little about speed. He had flown powered craft of a design based on these same principles, but this was an entirely new experience. He nearly stalled and only barely got moving again.

Then a strong updraft off the ridge caught the soarer's wings, and a moment later he was truly flying. And for all the terror of unpowered flight, deadly panic of the milling grazers below, reek of ichor dripping down cables and supports from the soarer's corpse, the Wookiee found himself roaring and howling in elation. He started to dip the soarer's nose, but the experiment with pitch nearly sent him into a neutral angle of attack—and an abrupt descent. He instantly foreswore the exploration of new aeronautical principles.

Body centered, he made minor corrections and did his best to recall the devotional chants of his distant youth. Below him grazers thrashed and pushed, strident and frenzied, but the Wookiee now had the sound of the wind in his ears. The other soarers steered well clear of this new and bizarre rival. It was large and strange and therefore not to be trusted.

Chewbacca estimated that he was making better than thirty kilometers an hour and suddenly realized he had but one problem—getting down alive. He had angled toward the *Falcon*. The last of the herd had passed it now, and the freighter seemed to be intact. But his makeshift glider wasn't so inclined, and he found that any decrease in speed threatened to rob him of the lift that kept him aloft. Gradually, though, he cut back on both, bringing the soarer's nose back toward a neutral attitude, and brayed happily as he spied a good landing spot. The little mountain lake grew before him. He thought for a moment that he was about to overshoot it and began to experiment with a turn, hunching forward and pulling the soarer's bound claws back toward himself.

He didn't quite have time to conclude what went wrong;

the next moment, Chewbacca and a splayed carcass were gyrating toward the lake's surface. He caught a split-second flash of his own reflection before it parted for him with all the soft receptiveness of a fusion-formed landing strip.

The curt slap of the water galvanized him, though, helping him overcome the numbing cold. He fought to untwist himself, only to find that the soarer didn't float well; its wings settled around him and the weight of the metal framework bore him down. Reaching and wriggling, he still couldn't release himself from the improvised harness that held him to it. The bowcaster around his neck only complicated things.

He became snarled in slack cable and his giant strength meant nothing against the cushiony persistence of the lake-water. His breath, too much to retain, began to escape his lips in silvery bubbles as the Wookiee fought to free himself from the sinking glider. It became hard to see, and he found himself thinking about his family and his green, lush home-world.

Then he realized a dark shape was circling him, making quick motions and weaving in and out among the tangled rigging with a sure ease and suppleness. A moment later the *Falcon*'s first mate was being tugged toward the surface of the lake, which came at him like an unending, flawed mirror.

Chewbacca broke into the air and drew a breath with such enthusiasm that he found himself choking on it, splitting and coughing and mouthing salty Wookiee expressions. Spray got around behind to support him, swimming with deftness and agility despite the pair of heavy cutters he held in one hand.

"That was fantastic!" gushed the skip-tracer. "I've never seen anything like that in my life! I came after you when I realized you'd overshoot and land in the lake, but I never thought I'd reach you in time. The land just isn't my element." He pulled at the Wookie's shoulder to get him started.

Stroking for the nearby shore, Chewbacca decided he felt exactly the same way about the sky.

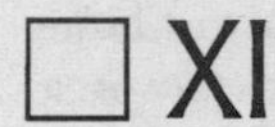

XI

"HIS name was Zlarb," Han said to the Mor Glayyd in that fortunate young man's study. "He tried to cheat me *and* kill me. He had a list of ships that were cleared through your clan's agency, but I haven't got the plaque with me right now. But if you could find his name in your records—"

"That isn't necessary. I know his name well," interrupted the Mor Glayyd, exchanging looks of extreme gravity with his sister.

"His bosses owe me ten thousand," said Han with something akin to fervor, "and I want it."

The Mor Glayyd leaned back, his conform lounger molding to him, and folded his hands. He no longer seemed quite so young; he was playing a role for which he'd been well groomed. Han wished he had hung on to one of those guns in the armory.

"What do you know of the clans of Ammuud and their Code, Captain Solo?"

"That the Code almost plotted your terminal orbit for you today," Han answered.

The youthful Mor Glayyd conceded, "A possibility. The Code is what holds the clans together yet keeps us from one another's throats. Without it, we'd revert to the backward, warring savages we were a hundred years ago. But betraying a trust or breaking an oath is also covered by the Code, and makes the violator a nonentity, an outcast, whatever his previous status. And not even a clan Mor is above the Code."

Oh, let me guess where this *is going*, Han simmered, but he said nothing.

"Those dealings my clan had with Zlarb's people fall into that category. We asked no questions; we accepted our commission for delivery and pickup of the ships without concerning ourselves with their use. Zlarb and his associates knew our practice; that's why they were willing to pay us so well."

"Meaning you're not going to tell me what I want to know," Han predicted.

"Meaning that I cannot. You're free to summon Gallandro back if you wish," returned the Mor Glayyd stiffly. His sister looked apprehensive.

Fiolla broke in: "Forget that; it's over with. But Zlarb's people broke faith with Han. Doesn't that mean anything to your Code? Do you shield traitors?"

The Mor Glayyd shook his head. "You don't see. No one broke faith with me or mine; that's the province of the Code."

"We're wasting our time," Han rasped to Fiolla. He was thinking of Chewbacca and the *Falcon*. He was willing to put aside his quest for the ten thousand for the time being; it didn't matter as much right now as the fact that Chewbacca was still somewhere out in the Ammuud mountains.

But as a parting shot he waved out at the city, at the departed Gallandro. "You saw what sort of people they are; you're throwing in with slavers and double-crossers and poisoners! They—"

The Mor Glayyd and his sister came out of their loungers so suddenly that the furniture slid on the slick floor. "How's that you say," the girl whispered, "*poisoners?*"

He'd said it thinking of the kit he had found on Zlarb and wondered now what nerve he had hit. "Zlarb was a Malkite poisoner."

"The late Mor Glayyd, our father, was killed with poison only a half-month ago," Ido said. "Had you not heard of his death?"

When Han shook his head, the Mor Glayyd went on.

''Only the most trusted of my clan circle know he was poisoned. It's unprecedented; the clans almost never use poisons, but we take precautions against them. And none of our food tasters showed any ill effects.''

''They wouldn't, from Malkite stuff,'' Han told him. ''Even some food-scanning equipment and air samplers miss it. And all a Malkite poisoner does to get around tasters is dose them with an antidote beforehand. The tasters never notice, and only the victim dies. Run tests on your tasters, and I bet you'll find antidote traces in their systems.''

He looked to Fiolla. ''The poisoning must be the suggestion Magg spoke about in the tape I found on Zlarb; I don't know how the duel bears on it.''

The Mor Glayyd had been rocked by what he'd heard. ''Then, then—''

His sister finished for him. ''We, too, have been betrayed, Ewwen.''

Han Solo checked his pocket to make sure the plaque given him by the Mor Glayyd was secure and tugged at the too-tight collar of the suit he had borrowed. Bollux was just finishing loading the lifeboat with guidance components—shielded circuitry rather than those damned fluidics!—provided from his own repair shops by the Mor Glayyd.

The boat had been moved here to the Glayyd yards so that its departure would be less conspicuous. The Mor Glayyd had shown a grim openhandedness when quick tests had borne out Han's suspicion that the food tasters' bodies contained traces of a Malkite antidote.

''You're certain you don't want us to accompany you?'' the boy was saying for the fourth time.

Han declined. ''That would draw too much attention if the slavers or the other clans are watching. I just hope the port defenses don't burn us out of the sky.''

''Many of my people are on watch today,'' the Mor Glayyd answered, ''and you're listed as a regular patrol flight over hereditary Glayyd lands. You'll go unchallenged. We'll be listening; if you need us, we'll come as quickly as we can. I'm sorry that your *Millennium Falcon* dropped beneath the detection ceiling when she bypassed the spaceport."

"No stress; I'll find her. But they should be getting the *Lady of Mindor* repaired any time now. Right after that, this place'll be alive with Espos. Do you think you can stall them?"

The Mor Glayyd was mildly amused. "Captain Solo, I thought you understood; my people are *very* good at not answering questions. None will violate the Silence, especially to Security Police."

Fiolla joined them. Like Han, she wore a borrowed Glayyd flier's snugsuit of gleaming blue and high spacer's boots. She'd been both awed and angered when she'd seen the names of Authority higher-ups who were implicated in the slaving ring by the Glayyd records, though the evidence was a bit tenuous, mostly official permits for ship charters and certifications for operation within the Authority.

"Please remember, Fiolla, we expect to hear from you when you've rooted out our enemies," the Mor Glayyd said. "If we can't work our own vengeance we will at least witness yours."

She promised soberly, "You will—and I know what a vow means to the Mor Glayyd. When I've gotten all this before an Authority Court I think I'll be able to keep you from prosecution. But I'd advise you to scrutinize future clients more closely."

The Mor Glayyd raised his hand in farewell. "We will not be used again, you may be confident." Ido kissed both Han and Fiolla on the cheek. Then brother and sister stepped back, as did their kinsmen and kinswomen. Within seconds the lifeboat lifted from its resting place, drifted into a departure lane, and sped up toward the mountains above the spaceport, hurtling between them and rising for the higher peaks beyond.

"How are you going to find them, anyway?" Fiolla, again in the copilot's seat, asked. "The sensors and detectors in this kettle aren't made for a tight search, are they?'' She moved aside a disruptor rifle given them by the Mor Glayyd, to give herself more room.

Han laughed, happy to be off the ground again. ''This wreck? You'd be lucky to find your own back pocket with the gear she carries. Even if she had a whole scoutship package, there'd be all these peaks and valleys and the ground clutter. But we've got this,'' he put a forefinger to his temple dramatically.

''If we haven't got something a little more high-powered than *that*,'' she said, mimicking his gesture perfectly, ''I hope there are some drop-harnesses aboard, because I want out!''

Han brought the little craft over onto a prechosen course, satisfied that he'd dipped low enough behind the peaks to be off the spaceport's detectors. ''We know the course Chewie was on when he passed over the port and *I* know how he thinks, how he pilots. I am now Chewie, with a damaged *Falcon* under me, one I've got to keep above three thousand meters, with limited guidance response. I know his style well enough to duplicate it. For instance, he'd never bank right off those three high peaks up there. You can't see enough of what's beyond to be sure of finding a high enough landing place to set down without blowing the rest of the fluidics.

''The *Falcon* would have enough emergency thrust to take the other cliff, and the terrain layout says there'll be more open space over there; you can see more of what you'd be getting into. That's the way my cautious old Wookiee pal likes things. He'll be looking for an out-of-the-way spot where he can set down, keep out of sight, try to do some repairs himself, and wait for me. I'll find him, don't worry.''

''You call this a plan?'' she scoffed. ''Why don't we just buzz along yelling his name out the hatch?''

His tone sharpened. ''I said *I'd find him*!''

Then Fiolla understood what desperate fears for Chewbacca's safety Han had been suppressing. ''I know you will, Han,'' she added quietly.

* * *

Spray, the skip-tracer, wound his sinuous body through the chilly water, fully at home, indulging in aquabatics and playful zigzags for the sheer joy of it, his tapered tail and webbed paws driving and guiding him with grace and power, his nostrils clenched shut tightly. The clear water in this small mountaintop lake, fed by underground springs and runoff, was cold even by Spray's standards, but his pelt kept him comfortable enough for short swims. As a youth, he had swum in much colder water, but he hadn't had the leisure for much swimming in a long time.

At last the Tynnan saw what he was looking for, one of the multilegged crustaceans that made its home in the lake's bottom. Spray was a bit short on air, having been frolicking when he should have been searching, he realized a little guiltily. He put on a burst of speed, hoping to catch the creature without a prolonged chase.

The crustacean didn't sense Spray's shadow or the pressure-wave he threw out before him until it was too late. It had barely begun to pick up speed when Spray seized it from behind—carefully, to avoid the pincers and walking legs. The velocity of his dive carried him down nearer the lake's bottom where, to his great surprise, his shadow scared up a second crustacean.

With a happy burble at the thought of the good lunch he would provide, Spray struck and doubled his catch for the day. When his air supply approached its limit, Spray headed for the lake's surface. He broke through with a happy squeal, spitting a jet of water high into the air and filling his lungs again.

He held his catch over his head, treading water and waving the crustaceans at Chewbacca, who stood on the shore. The Wookiee woofed happily and hungrily and waved back. By the time Spray was wading ashore, the *Falcon*'s first mate was already knee-deep in the cold water, holding an empty toolbag wide open. Spray dropped his prizes into the bag gingerly, and Chewbacca shut it at once; he ruffled the skip-tracer's furry head in approval. "You came along at just the right moment," said the Tynnan.

The freighter's rations had been all but depleted when Chewbacca had set her down, and no grazers had come near since the stampede. But Spray's skill had kept them fed, and they had split their tasks—Chewbacca staying busy with repairs and Spray taking on the job of meal procurement. Now they turned back for the half-kilometer trudge to the grounded starship. Water was already bubbling in an old inducer cowling that Spray had set over a thermal coil at the ramp's foot.

Their contemplation of a tasty meal was broken when Spray's head perked up, his ears swinging this way and that. Chewbacca craned at the sky and pointed, woofing an exclamation. A small boat or large gravsled had just crested the ridge and was now dropping in directly toward them.

The Wookiee pressed the toolbag into Spray's hands, leaving his own free to unsling his bowcaster. Not that the weapons would be much good against an aircraft, he reminded himself, as there was no cover near them. Luckily, Spray had the sense to imitate Chewbacca in remaining perfectly still. He realized that movement, more than anything else, would attract the attention of the airborne observer.

The boat passed over them, but even as it did, Chewbacca could hear the strain of its steering thrusters as its pilot came about for another pass. He pivoted, watching, then barked and roared with pleasure. On its second pass the boat waggled and went into a barrel roll. It could only be Han Solo.

Chewbacca plunged through the snow toward the freighter, yowling at the top of his lungs, making the shallow valley echo. Spray, clutching the writhing toolbag to his chest, followed in the Wookiee's wake as best he could.

When the lifeboat had settled next to the *Falcon*, its lock opened and Han jumped out. Chewbacca raced to him, kicking up an aftermath of churned snow, and began pounding his friend on the back and howling his delight across the valley from time to time. When the first wave of joy had passed, the Wookiee noticed Fiolla at the boat's hatch. He plucked her down and whirled her around in a carefully restrained hug, then set her on her feet.

Last to descend was Bollux. To him Chewbacca extended a friendly growl but withheld a helping paw, not wanting to imply that the 'droid needed assistance. A rumble of inquiry from the Wookiee and a thumb indicating Bollux's chest panels brought assurances that Blue Max, too, was present.

"We almost passed you by," Han said. "You're a little too good at camouflage." He meant the *Millennium Falcon*, which Chewbacca had permitted to settle until her landing gear was nearly retracted. The Wookiee and Spray had piled snow around the starship and spread clumps of scrub and more snow across her upper hull.

"But we noticed all those animal tracks detouring around to either side of her," Han added, "so I took a closer look." Spray and Chewbacca were tugging at the arrivals, urging them to come aboard. Han delayed just long enough to drag forth some of the new circuitry; he thought for a moment his copilot was going to weep at the sight of it.

Lunch was forgotten as they brought one another up on what had happened. Spray turned sheepish when his jettisoning of Bollux was mentioned. "To tell the truth, Captain," he said, "as I explained to Chewbacca here, I got the idea all at once and knew I'd have to act instantly." To the 'droid he said, "I truly apologize, but it seemed like the only thing to do, and I sometimes have trouble making snap decisions. I just plunged ahead with it before I could stop and dither. Perhaps the general impulsiveness was contagious."

"I fully understand, sir," Bollux answered graciously. "And as it worked out, it was quite fortunate for all of us that you thought and acted so quickly. Blue Max agrees with me, too."

They all thought it best to ignore the high-pitched hollow sounding *"Hah!"* that came from Bollux's closed chest panels.

Soon they were all at work. Bollux, Spray, and Fiolla began clearing away what they could of the piled snow, concentrating on exposing the cockpit, bow, and main thrusters. Han and Chewbacca strained at repairs with Blue Max, out of Bollux's chest emplacement and connected to the forward tech station to check for accuracy as each individual hookup was made.

As the fluidic components were removed one by one from the starship, Chewbacca took great pleasure in heaving them as far as he could; some of his throws were so impressive that Han regretted that it wasn't a formal athletic event. He pardoned his friend these excesses; the fluidics had been as much a curse as a blessing since they were installed.

As the replacements were made, the pile of discarded adaptors and jury-rigged gear grew. Because they knew intimately every cubic centimeter of their ship, they worked rapidly; they had originally installed the fluidics in such fashion that removal would be simple.

Activating another component, Han asked Max over the comlink how things looked from the tech station. "Checks out perfectly, Captain," came the computer's childish voice.

Pleased with the speed with which their labors were going, Han said, "We should take time to retune the engine power-curves for peak efficiency, but I'd rather get off Ammuud first. The biggest job's the only one left—the hyperspace control units. Shouldn't take more than—"

"Captain Solo!" Max's vocoder communicated urgency. "Trouble! Long-range sensors paint three blips!"

Chewbacca yipped a question at Han, who snapped a sharp response. "What's it matter who they are? They're not coming for a gala sendoff, that's for sure. No time for the hyperdrive. Seal up the hull." He called to Fiolla and the others "Get aboard; we're raising ship right now!"

Han sprinted up the ramp, leaving his first mate to close up the exposed systems. In the cockpit his hands flew back and forth across both his own and Chewbacca's sides of the console. Among other things, he flicked on the ship's commo board and monitoring outfit, though he doubted he'd pick up much in the way of transmissions from the bogies.

But a moment later, in the midst of charging the ship's weaponry, he noticed a blinking telltale on the broad-band monitor. He read the instruments; there was a steady signal coming from somewhere very close by. A fast scan by the direction finder told him its origin.

He recalled that he had left the disruptor rifle in the lifeboat. But Chewbacca had placed his gunbelt in the navigator's chair. Good boy! Fastening the belt around his hips and tying down the holster, he rushed back for the ramp.

Chewbacca noticed the blaster at once. "We've been popped," Han explained. "Somebody keyed the boat transceiver; we've been sending all along. It probably took them this long to pick us up among all the dips and crags." He was glaring meaningfully at Fiolla.

"After all this time," she said with amazement, "you still don't trust me."

"Name another nominee? Spray hasn't been near the boat and I sure don't remember doing it." He beckoned his partner. "We've got work to do, pal. Spray, you too. Bollux, go with our other guest to the forward compartment and watch her. And brace your chassis for some rough weather." He started back for the cockpit, and Fiolla headed for the forward compartment without another word.

Han ushered Spray into the navigator's chair, directly behind his own, and all three buckled themselves in. He thought about sending out a distress signal to the Mor Glayyd, but a glance at the commo board ended that; one or more of the oncoming craft was jamming, and he had no time to try to circumvent the interference.

Bringing thrusters up to a hover, he retracted the ship's three-point landing gear the rest of the way. Over the low tumult of the engines he asked the Wookiee, "How good a pilot is he?" He jerked a thumb at Spray. The first mate made a so-so motion of his hairy paw but nodded, which meant that while the skip-tracer might never make the Kessel Run, he would be adequate in a jam—which this was. "Splendid," Han said unenthusiastically, and cut in main thrusters. Kicking up fountains of steam and mud and clumps of scrub growth, the *Millennium Falcon* blasted free of the remaining snow and shot off into the sky.

Han let his copilot take the controls and left his seat to bend over Spray. "Here it is: we haven't got hyperdrive because we didn't have time to reconnect it. That means we can't duck out of this one. Sensors say those are small, fast jobs coming for us, maybe interceptors, and sooner or later they'll overhaul us. We can't outrun them but we can outfight them *if* Chewie and I can man the turrets. That means somebody's got to pilot, so unless you feel like manning a quad-mount—"

"Captain," gasped Spray, "I've never fired a weapon in my life!"

"Sort of what I figured," sighed Han. "Take a seat here." Scratching his hand nervously, Spray sat unwillingly in the pilot's seat while Han adjusted it and pushed it closer to the console. Spray poked his buck-toothed snout up to various indicators, scopes, and gauges; with his inferior eyesight he was, of course, primarily an instrument pilot. But he obviously knew what he was doing.

"Just keep shields up and try to angle with their attack runs," Han instructed, "and try to preserve her resale value, if that inspires you. Otherwise, nothing fancy. Just leave the rest to us."

He and his partner made their way to the central ladderwell that led to the top and belly turrets. "I wish there was another way to do this," Han confessed.

"Dowwpp," the Wookiee responded.

Han climbed toward the top turret and felt the vibrations along the ladder that told him his copilot was descending. He hauled himself into the turret, seating himself before the quad-guns and donning his headset.

Ship's gravity was altered here, permitting him to sit with his back perpendicular to the ladderwell without feeling a downward drag. In the same way, Chewbacca would be sitting in the belly turret facing directly "downward" without being pulled against his seat's belt.

Glancing over his shoulder, Han could look directly down the ladderwell at his friend's back. Chewbacca flipped him a quick wave, and each of them ran his battery through a few test-traverses, making sure the servos responded to control grips and tracked accurately.

"The usual stakes," Han called down, "and double for kills in the Money Lane." Chewbacca woofed consent.

Spray's voice, shaking with tension, came up. "I have three confirmed blips on approach. They should be on your screens by—*they're on us!*"

JUST as Spray apprised the two partners of the oncoming craft, the newcomers announced their own arrival unmistakably. The *Millennium Falcon* quaked, her shields claiming huge amounts of power as cannon fire incandesced against her.

"They're breaking!" Spray yelled, but both Han and Chewbacca could already see that from their targeting monitors. Clutching the handgrips of his gunmount, Han traversed the quad-barrels astern to address his natural target, the uppermost of the vessels overtaking his ship. He knew the Wookiee would be on the one falling deepest into his own field of fire. They'd been through this sort of thing before; each knew the area of his responsibility and how the other worked.

The targeting computer drew up intersecting lines in two parallel grids and showed Han an arrowhead of light representing the bandit. From a lifetime's habit, Han divided his time and attention between computer modeling on the tiny screen and visual ranging. He never entirely trusted computers or any other machine; he liked to see what he was shooting at.

The target swept in, even faster than he had expected. It was, as he had thought it would be, a pinnace, a ship's fighting boat. *So, our friends the slavers are still with us.*

At the same time he was squeezing off quick bursts, trying to bracket the pinnace. The quad-guns slammed away in alternating pairs, but the pinnace had picked up too much speed; it was into his gunsights and out again before Han had a chance to come close.

The starship shook like a child's toy as her defensive mantle struggled to deal with the blasts of the pinnace's cannon. Han registered, distantly, the sound of the belly guns and Chewbacca's frustrated howl as the Wookiee, too, missed on the first pass.

Then, instead of one triangle of light on his targeting monitor screen, Han saw two. He brought the quad-mount around hastily, its servos protesting, throwing him deeper against the padding of the gunner's seat.

A pinnace had come in from directly astern, its blaster fire bisecting the *Falcon*'s upper hull precisely. There were deep vibrations as the starship shuddered from the fire. Han couldn't stop himself, when he saw the volley walking along the hull at him, from throwing an arm up to protect himself. But deflectors held, and in a split second the pinnace had swept by with its two companions to come to bear for another run.

The pinnaces were perhaps twice the size of the lifeboat Han and Fiolla had stolen. They were fast, heavily armed, and nearly as maneuverable as fighters. Lacking hyperdrive, there was no question of outrunning them; the *Falcon* could only make a fight of it.

The freighter tilted and sideslipped as Spray attempted an evasive tactic. Han, his aim spoiled, yelled into his headset mike. "Nothing fancy, Spray. Just go with their strafing runs and cut into their speed advantage; no aerobatics!"

Spray trimmed the freighter. The pinnaces had broken right and left with the third ship going into a steep, rolling climb for an overhead attack. Han held fire, knowing they were out of range, and bided his time. Spray headed the freighter deeper into the high mountains.

The pinnace that had broken left now dove abruptly and came in under the *Falcon*'s belly. Han could hear the reports of Chewbacca's guns as he brought his own weapon around, its four barrels pivoting and elevating on their pintles in response to the commands of the targeting grips.

He tried for the diving pinnace. Outside the ball-turret the quad-guns responded minutely to the least adjustment of his controls. The computer limned aiming grids, plotted the pinnace's estimated course and speed, and predicted where it would be. Han slewed his seat around, hands clenching the grips, and four cannon barrels swung to follow suit. He opened fire and the quad-guns pounded red destruction at the bandit. He scored a partial hit, but the pinnace's shields held and it managed to evade his fire almost instantly.

"Swindler!" he howled, tracking the pinnace in a hopeless effort to connect again. There was the sound of a distant explosion and a triumphant roar echoed up the ladderwell. Chewbacca had drawn first blood.

The third pinnace swept past, taking a course almost at right angles to the one Han was still tracking. The newcomer got off a sustained burst that splashed harmlessly off shields, but there was a surge from the *Millennium Falcon*'s engines. The ship's defensive mantle was in danger of failing, having taken extreme punishment from the sustained, well-directed fire of the attackers.

Realizing he couldn't catch up with the one he had just missed and ignoring his comlink, Han yelled down the ladderwell, "Chewie! One in the Money Lane!"

Because of the *Falcon*'s design, a flattened sphere, and the position of her main batteries at the precise top and bottom of the ship, her turrets' fields of fire overlapped in a wedge expanding from the freighter's waist all the way around. This overlap was what Han and his first mate called the Money Lane; kills scored there counted extra, since it was a shared responsibility; their standing wager on who was better with a quad-mount carried a double payoff for hits in the Money Lane.

But right now Han didn't care if he ended up owing the Wookiee his shirt. Chewbacca brought his weapon around and just barely failed to get a bead on the pinnace out in the

Money Lane, chopping the air behind it with crimson cannonfire.

"Spray, keep your eye on the long-range sensors," Han called into his mike. "If their parent ship sneaks up on us, Interstellar Collections will have nothing to auction off but a gas cloud!"

The ship missed by Chewbacca came up into Han's field of fire. He led it, reaching out for it with red cannon blasts, but the pinnace's pilot was quick and threw his ship out of the line of fire before his shields gave. The enemy scored on the *Millennium Falcon*'s upper hull, and the freighter bucked. Han caught the smell of smouldering circuitry.

"Captain Solo, there's a large vessel moving up rapidly from magnetic southwest. At current courses it'll close with us in another ninety seconds!"

Han was too busy to answer the skip-tracer. Hearing his first mate's frustrated growl at a near miss, reverberating in the ladderwell, he saw the ship the Wookiee had just lost. It arced out beyond the bow mandibles, its pilot going into a fast bank as he realized he'd flown into another line of fire.

Han didn't bother with the targeting computer but tracked by eye, catching the pinnace at the slow point in its turn with a sustained burst. A moment later the pinnace disappeared in a fireball, shreds of it hurled outward.

The third pinnace, coming about for another run, swerved to avoid the explosion of its companion, rolled, and was again in the Money Lane. Han's and Chewbacca's fire probed at it simultaneously. It, too, became an eruption of enormous violence.

Han was instantly at the ladderwell, not bothering to climb down but sliding with toes clamped to its side-pieces, braking himself with his hands, worrying about the oncoming mother ship.

As he reached main deck level, he found Chewbacca swarming up the rungs beneath him. The Wookiee crowed happily and Han found time to sneer "What d'you mean, *pay up*? *I* made the kill in the Money Lane; you never even touched him!''

Chewbacca snarled as they dashed together toward the cockpit, but the issue of who owed whom had to be dropped. Once Chewbacca was in place, Spray squirmed out of the pilot's seat, breathing with relief as Han dropped into it.

''That ship's coming at vector one-two-five-slash-one-six-zero,'' Spray said, but Han had already read that information off the console. Bringing the starship's helm over and accelerating, he angled all deflectors aft with one hand, belting himself in with the other.

Spray had taken on more altitude than Han would have liked. With the hyperdrive still inoperable, things boiled down to a simple race. His best chance to deny the enemy a clear shot at him was to put the planet between them.

He was still increasing speed, the engines' rumble growing louder and louder, when the *Falcon* was jolted by a teeth-rattling explosion. Checking combat information feeds, Han found that the approaching mother ship was firing from extreme range even though its shots had little chance of penetrating the freighter's shields at this distance.

Their pursuer was indeed the slaver, the would-be ''pirate'' that had stopped and grappled the *Lady of Mindor*. That left him nonplused about Fiolla's part in matters and why the lifeboat transceiver had been left keyed open. Surely the slavers were out to get Fiolla, too?

Then he had no more time for imponderables; the slaver ship was closing the gap between them and nothing he did seemed to make any difference. She was an extremely well-armed vessel, easily three times the *Millennium Falcon*'s size, and fast in the bargain.

If we had had time to retune the engines, Han carped at himself, *we'd be highstepping away from them right now.*

A voice crackled over the open commo board. ''Heave to, *Millennium Falcon*, or we fire for effect!'' Han recognized the voice.

He switched his headset to transmit mode. "No free meals today, Magg!"

Fiolla's onetime assistant said nothing more. The pursuer's shots came closer; the shields' drain on the *Falcon*'s power grew acute. Han trained batteries aft by servo-remote. The slaver with her heavier guns was still out of range. Though Han flew a twisting, evasive course, parting the cold air of Ammuud with a high whistle of speed, he knew the slaver would soon close. All he could hope for was that inspired piloting, more than a little luck, and a well-placed salvo to damage the slaver would get him clear.

He brought his ship out of a quick bank with a flourish, sideslipping as thick streams of turbolaser fire belched past to starboard, just missing the *Falcon*. He thought, *we could still make it, unless—*

Fulfilling his silent fear, the freighter wobbled and shook herself as if in the throes of a fit. Instruments confirmed that a brute tractor beam had fastened onto the *Falcon*. Her maximum effort failed to free her.

With the freighter held fast, the slaver closed rapidly. In another moment, Han knew, their pursuer would be on top of them. He tried not to be distracted by regrets; his hands flew across the console and he lacked even the time to tell his copilot what he was about to do.

Han brought the *Falcon* about at full power, just barely overcoming the drag of the tractor, redeploying defensive shields to maximum over the upper half of his ship's hull. Before the startled pilot of the slaver vessel knew what was happening, the *Millennium Falcon* had come about, reversing field in the tractor beam, and dived under his bow. Evading the tractor projector set in the bottom of the slaver's hull took an extra twist and full power from the freighter's already overworked engines, using both the tractor's draw and the *Falcon*'s thrust to snap-roll free of the beam.

Dumbfounded fire-control officers began redirecting their gun crews' aim, but the suddenness of the freighter's evasion had won Han the advantage of surprise.

Streaking under the length of the slaver, Han fired salvos from his top turret and waited with some dread for the moment his shields failed. But they didn't, and Han's wild aerobatics eluded all fire coming from the surprised slaver.

Nearly. There was a monumental jarring. Such of the *Falcon*'s alarms and warning lights as were not already alive came on. Chewbacca, taking damage readings, hooted worriedly as Han accelerated again, leaving the slaver to match him if she could.

He turned to Spray. "Some of that new stuff we put in today must've been hit; I don't get any readouts from it. Try the forward tech station and see if you can find out anything."

The skip-tracer staggered off, lurching this way and that as the ship swayed around him. Reaching the forward compartment, he found Fiolla and Bollux still seated in the acceleration couch. From the tech station's chair Spray began examining readouts and squinting into scanners and scopes, twisting in the chair and scratching at his hand nervously.

"Does your hand still hurt, Spray?" asked Fiolla.

"No, it's much—" he started to say, then stopped and swung his chair around to face her with a shocked look. "I meant—that is—"

"Somatigenerative treatments always leave the skin itchy, don't they?" Fiolla went on, ignoring his protests. "You've been scratching since we got here. Solo told me he bit the hand of whoever jumped him in the hangar at the Bonadan spaceport. It *was* you, wasn't it?" There was little of inquiry in her tone, more of statement.

Spray was very calm. "I forgot how bright you are, Fiolla. Well, yes, as a matter of fact—" The *Falcon* quaked again; the slaver was gaining on her once more.

"And you left the lifeboat transceiver keyed open, too, didn't you?" she snapped. "But how? Han was right; you *weren't* anywhere near that boat."

"I did not," Spray declared soberly. "That, you may believe. I hadn't expected things to go quite this far, either; I abhor all this useless violence. This will end soon; your ambitious former assistant is close."

Still not sure she credited any of what he had said, she told him, "You know I'm going to tell Han, don't you?"

Bollux turned red photoreceptors from one to the other, wondering if he dared leave them alone long enough to inform Han of what he'd heard.

Then the *Falcon* jolted again in response to a barrage. "I doubt if that would make any difference now," Spray stated calmly. "And it's in your own best interests, Fiolla, to cooperate with me; your life has reached a critical juncture."

Han and Chewbacca had run out of options. The slaver had fastened her tractor on them again. This time there would be no survival value in a sudden reversal; the next volley would almost certainly penetrate shields and convert the *Millennium Falcon* into an explosive nimbus.

Han was busily training batteries for a last futile salvo in an attempt to avert death. But the volley didn't come. Chewbacca began pointing at the sensors and hooted excitedly. Han gaped, wanting to rub his eyes, at the size of the ship moving up hard astern the slaver.

She was an Espo destroyer of the old Victory class, close to a kilometer long, an armored space-going fortress. Where she'd come from wasn't as important to Han as what she would do.

The tractor beam pulling at the *Falcon* dissipated; the slaver had seen the destroyer, too, and wanted no part of her. But the Security Police battlewagon had tractors of her own, mightier than the slaver's. Suddenly the *Millennium Falcon* and her pursuer were both held in an inflexible, invisible grip.

Somebody aboard the slaver had the bad judgment to try a volley at the destroyer. Cannonade splashed harmlessly off the Espo's immense shields and a turbolaser turret in the warship's side answered, opening a huge hole in the slaver's hull and evaporating most of her power plant.

The slaver offered no further resistance. She was drawn up, uncontesting, into the gaping boarding lock in the destroyer's underbelly. The *Falcon*'s commo board sounded with a general override broadcast: "All personnel in both captive ships remain where you are. Follow all instructions and offer no opposition." There was something familiar about the voice. "Shut down your engines and lock all systems except commo."

Since the slaver was already occupying the destroyer's boarding lock, the *Falcon* was eased down toward the ground, the vast bulk of the battlewagon settling in over her, blocking out the sky. Relaxing to the inevitable, Han extended his ship's landing gear; the *Falcon* could never break from this tractor beam, and he had just seen the stupidity of trying to slug it out. He shut off his engines and cut power to weapons, shields, tractors, sensor suite.

He nudged his partner. "Keep your bowcaster ready; maybe we can make a break for it when we're outside." If they could get away, perhaps the Mor Glayyd could use a couple of good pilots. If not, there was nothing to worry about anyway, except which periodicals to subscribe to while in prison. But Han was determined to go out kicking.

The Espo craft descended until it was no more than fifty meters above the grounded *Falcon*. By leaning forward in the cockpit, Han could see the captive slaver ship. A boarding tube, no doubt packed with combat-armored Espo assault troops, was extending itself and fastening to the slaver's main lock.

Now, Magg, see how you like it, thought Han. It was only a knot of satisfaction in his long string of bad luck, but it was something. He savored it while he could.

From another lock in the destroyer a safety cage appeared, lowered by a utility tractor beam, coming down slowly and silently. The safety cage was a circular, basketlike affair with high guardrails and an overhead sling for hoist work. Within the cage, where Han would have expected a flock of trigger-happy Espos, there was only the man who had given the instructions over the commo a few moments before.

It was Gallandro, the gunman.

GALLANDRO approached the *Falcon* at a sedate pace. When he stopped, looking up at the cockpit, his hand moved to his belt and brought something up. A moment later the gunman's voice came over the commo board, obviously channeled through the Espo warship.

"Solo, can you hear me?" Rather than answer, Han flashed the ship's running lights once. "Oh, come now, Solo! How can you be surly to the man who saved your skin?"

Easily, Han reflected, *when he's so slick and so fast with a blaster.* But he opened his headset mike. "It's your play, Gallandro."

There was satisfaction in the other's tone. "That's better; isn't cordiality more pleasant? I'm sure that even you can grasp the realities here, Solo. If nothing else, you're a pragmatist. Kindly open your main hatch and come down, if you'd be so good, and we'll sort out this entire affair."

Han considered suggesting that Gallandro go sit in a converter, but one glance up at the great underbelly of the destroyer changed his mind. Turbolaser emplacements, twin and quad batteries, missile tubes, and tractor beam projectors were all aimed at the freighter. *One wrong move and we'll all be random energy.* He sighed and unbuckled his seat belt. Perhaps something outside would change the situation, but he knew nothing he could do there in the cockpit would help.

He turned to find that Spray had been standing at the rear of the cockpit, watching him. A moment later Fiolla appeared next to the Tynnan. It occurred to him that she might have some use as a hostage, but in view of the number of times her life had been in real danger already, he doubted that threatening her would deter Gallandro; the man seemed to know what real ruthlessness was. Besides, Han wasn't sure Gallandro would believe Han could kill her in cold blood, even now.

"Your friends have shown up," Han told her bitterly. "The Authority has things well in hand. There ought to be that big promo in this one, Fiolla."

She moved away toward the main hatch. Spray gave Han an odd look, then followed after. Encountering Bollux in the passageway, Han nodded at him. "Step into the cockpit and keep a photoreceptor on things, old-timer. If we don't come back the ship is yours, unless Interstellar Collections grabs it. Good luck; business has been lousy lately."

When Han got the hatch open he found Gallandro waiting at the ramp's foot. The gunman met his stare with a polite inclination of the head. "I mentioned earlier today, Captain, that there would perhaps be another occasion."

The invitation was obvious. Han thought about hooking for his blaster but, recalling Gallandro's incredible speed, set it aside as an option he could take later. Han was prepared to believe that the man confronting him was his equal or better with a sidearm.

Gallandro saw that in his expression and evinced a certain disappointment. "Very well then, Solo. You may keep your blaster for now, in case you change your mind. I don't suppose I need to tell you how many weapons are trained on you right now; please don't do anything abrupt without letting me clear it beforehand."

Han and Chewbacca stepped off to opposite sides of the ramp's foot, but Gallandro stayed far enough back to keep them both in view. The Wookiee, as aware of the situation as Han, kept his bowcaster slung at his shoulder.

Han was expecting to see a profuse greeting or at least a

cordial welcome for Fiolla. But Gallandro accorded her only a suave smile and sketchy bow, and waited expectantly.

Spray was last down, coming at his slightly uneven dry-land gait, the tip of his tail brushing the ramp, some moisture from his recent swim still gleaming in his pelt. Gallandro bowed to him deferentially, although the gunman never lost sight of Han.

"Odumin," Gallandro said, "welcome, sir. You've brought yet another project to a successful conclusion. You haven't lost your touch for field work, I see."

Spray made a depreciating gesture, squinting up at the tall, aristocratic gunfighter. "I was fortunate, old friend. I must confess, I find I much prefer administration."

Han, who'd been gaping from one to the other while Chewbacca made little strangling sounds, finally got out "*Odumin*? You're the territorial manager? Why you treacherous, mutinous worm, I ought to—" Words failed him for a fate sufficiently horrible.

"That's hardly called for, Captain," Spray chided, sounding wounded. "I *did* start out as a skip-tracer, you see. But as I advanced myself in the structure of the Corporate Sector Authority, I found it expedient, as a nonhuman, to use others as go-betweens and remain an anonymous figure. In this slavery business, which extends to my own deputies and officials of the Security Police, I found myself obliged to do my own investigating with the help of a few trusted aides like Gallandro here."

He laced his webbed fingers together and assumed the introspective air of a teacher. Han found himself listening despite his fury.

"It was a very convoluted problem," Spray/Odumin began. "First, there was the evidence that you had taken off of Zlarb, which, you see, led you to Bonadan and convinced me that you were the slaver. At the spaceport, when you headed for the hangar, I concluded that you were about to depart the planet. There were materials at hand, a pair of work gloves and an industrial solvent that could double as an anesthetic; that prompted an overly hasty decision on my part to attempt to take from you whatever information you possessed in such a manner as to make you suspicious of your, um, confederates. But you turned out to be a resourceful man, Captain."

Han snorted. "I still can't believe you worked up the guts to jump me, even with the lights out."

Spray drew himself up to his full height. "Don't make the mistake so many others have; I'm more capable than I appear. With your superior eyesight neutralized, you would almost certainly have grown dizzy from the fumes before I; I can, after all, hold my breath for protracted periods. But immediately after our struggle, Gallandro here, who'd been running a check on you, informed me of your true identity. I decided I'd found my solution."

Han's brows knit. "Solution?"

Spray turned to Chewbacca. "Remember our board game, and the Eight Ilthmar Gambit, a lone combatant sent in to draw out an opponent? Captain Solo, you were that playing piece, my solution. The slavers knew you were no security operative and that you couldn't appeal to the legal authorities. You compelled them to acts that made them vulnerable, as you can see, to me."

That made Han remember something else. He looked to Fiolla. "What about you?"

Spray answered for her. "Oh, she's precisely what she said she is: an ambitious, aggressive, loyal employee. The housecleaning required by this whole business will leave some prime job slots in my organization; I plan to see Fiolla amply rewarded. My deputy territorial manager's position will be vacant quite soon, I should think."

"A plush job with the Authority," Han spat, "worst gang of plunderers who ever infested space."

"Not everyone can outfly them or rob them blind, Han," Fiolla said. "But somebody inside might bring change, as Spray's been trying to do. If someone had the right position, she might do a great deal of good."

"You see?" Spray's question was filled with approval. "Our attitudes are complementary. For all your daring and ability, Captain, you'll never do appreciable damage to an organization of the Authority's size and wealth. I submit to you that beings like Fiolla and myself, working within it, may accomplish what blasters cannot. How can you fault her for that?"

To avoid answering, Han looked to Gallandro. "What was the challenge all about?"

The gunman's hand moved in an airy dismissal. "The Glayyd clan constituted a particular problem; their records are connected to a destruct switch manned by loyal clan members. We couldn't risk going in and taking the evidence only to have it destroyed in the process.

"The elder Mor Glayyd mistrusted the slavers and they suspected him of planning to extort more money from them. They aren't the type for faith in human nature, you see. The slavers made secret overtures to the Reesbon clan and when the elder Mor Glayyd learned of it, he began making roundabout contact with Spray, fearing his clan was going to be betrayed. He was poisoned very soon thereafter, of course, partly at Zlarb's suggestion, as it seems.

"I preceded you all here; after the *Falcon* made her emergency landing, Odumin—sorry, sir, *Spray*—managed to contact me. I saw an opportunity to use the peculiar structure of their Code to put the Glayyds in your debt, Solo. It wasn't very difficult to make myself available to the Reesbons, and as far as they're concerned, they're the ones who originated the idea of having me challenge the new Mor Glayyd to a duel."

"A marvelous inspiration," applauded Spray. "And it was also at your suggestion that the Reesbons contrived to key open the lifeboat transceiver?"

Gallandro shrugged modestly, twisting his mustache. Han wanted to kick himself. And everyone else present. "Wait a minute, Spray," he objected. "How'd you contact him? You were stuck out in the mountains."

Spray was suddenly chagrined. "Er, yes. There were commo techs standing by for my signal, but I had to have uninterrupted use of the *Falcon*'s facilities in case Gallandro wasn't immediately available."

He turned to the Wookiee. "And that involves an apology I owe you. To keep you away from the ship for the requisite time I frightened those grazers into stampeding with a flare gun, meaning only to isolate you on the ridge for a time. I had no idea there'd be so many of them, or that you'd be endangered. I'm truly sorry."

Chewbacca pretended not to hear him, and Spray didn't press the issue.

"So you're just another hired gun," Han said to Gallandro. "Is that right? An errand boy on the Authority's chain?"

The gunman was amused. "You've got a lot of time to put in before you're ready to pass judgment on me, Solo, whereas I've been in your place already. I've done it all, but I got tired of waiting to die in some senseless manner. So I've given up sleeping with one eye open, and in return I've got a future. Don't be surprised if you feel this way yourself, somewhere down the line."

Never, Han thought, but he found Gallandro to be more of a puzzle than ever.

"With Magg and the others in the slaver ship, and the evidence that's come to light, I should think our case will be incontestable," Spray said with satisfaction.

"Then you won't be needing us?" Han said hopefully.

"Not quite true," the territorial manager admitted. "I'm afraid I can't simply let you go, though I'll do what I can to elicit leniency for you."

Han made a skeptical face. "From an Authority Court?"

Spray looked pained, squinting at Han, then away. Seeing the empty safety cage, he said, "Gallandro, did you bring no men? Who's going to fly the *Millennium Falcon* back to port?"

"They will," Gallandro announced, indicating Han and Chewbacca. "I'll go with them, to make sure they behave."

Spray was shaking his head vigorously. "This is sheer recklessness. Needless risk-taking! I know you didn't enjoy reneging on your challenge, but that was in line with your employment. There's no need to be provocative!"

"I will bring them," Gallandro repeated coolly. "Don't forget that I work for you under certain agreed-upon conditions."

"Yes," Spray lisped softly to himself, stroking his whiskers. He turned to Han. "This is Gallandro's affair; I cannot interfere. I advise you most emphatically against any rash acts, Captain Solo." He extended his paw, offering a friendship-grip. "Good luck to you."

Han ignored the extended hand, staring directly at Fiolla, who wouldn't meet his gaze. Spray looked to Chewbacca, but the Wookiee conspicuously clamped both hands on the sling of his bowcaster and gazed off into empty air.

The territorial manager sadly withdrew his hand. "Should you both succeed in avoiding imprisonment, I would advise you to leave the Authority as quickly as you can and never, never return. Fiolla, we'd better be going. Oh, and Gallandro, please make sure you obtain Zlarb's data plaque from Captain Solo."

He started off at a slow amble, tail dragging the rocky ground. Fiolla fell in at his side without a backward glance. Gallandro extended his hand to Chewbacca. "I'm afraid I can't have both of you armed, my tall friend. I'll take the bowcaster."

Chewbacca growled, showing long fangs, and might have tried for a shootout right then and there. But there was no doubt that the gunman could kill the Wookiee where he stood and maybe get Han as well. At least, Gallandro seemed confident he could.

"Pass it to him, Chewie," Han ordered. The Wookiee looked at him, snarled again at Gallandro, and reluctantly handed his weapon over stock-first. Gallandro was careful to stay out of reach of those shaggy arms. With a gesture to the ramp, he invited them aboard.

"It's nearly that time, Captain Solo," said the gunman.

Just about, Han agreed to himself, and preceded Gallandro up the ramp.

"Now," said Gallandro contentedly when they were aboard, "if your copilot will be good enough to prepare the ship, you and I will get that data plaque." He caught Chewbacca's eye. "Warm up your engines only, and don't do anything rash, my friend; your partner's life hinges on it."

The Wookiee turned to go and Han led the way toward his quarters. The cramped cubicle was in the same disarray as when he had last seen it, with clothes and equipment strewn on the sleeping pallet and the tiny desk and chair. The pallet's free-fall netting had somehow come unstrapped from its retainers and hung from the bulkhead. A used mealpack tray sat atop the desk reader.

Han ignored the clutter and stepped to his minuscule closet as Gallandro put the bowcaster aside. With the gunman watching him carefully, Han reached his right hand into the inner pocket of his thermosuit, feeling for Zlarb's security case. But as he groped for it he found that the case's clip was engaged, hooked through the top edge of the pocket.

That Wookiee's a big, ugly genius! Han thought, instantly covering the disarm button with his forefinger and drawing the case out, separating it from its clip. He offered it to the gunman.

Gallandro put out his own right hand willingly. It had occurred to him that Han might take advantage of the brief distraction and go for his blaster while Gallandro's right hand was on the case. He was more than happy to let Han try it if he wanted to. But while both men's right hands were still on the security case, Han simply moved his finger off the safety.

The two cried out as a surge of neuro-paralysis washed up their arms like an absolute-zero lightning bolt. The security case clattered to the deck as they both clutched numb, useless arms to their sides.

Gallandro gritted his teeth and glared at Han, who slowly and cautiously flicked open the tie-down of his holster. Gallandro's own left hand started for his holstered weapon but he realized what an awkward move it was and that Han hadn't gone for his blaster yet.

Han tugged at his gunbelt until his blaster sat, butt-forward, on his left hip. Gallandro, smile gone, did the same with his own tooled holster. Their hands were close to their weapons now.

"Had to change the odds a bit," Han grinned amiably. "Hope you don't mind. Whenever you're ready, Gallandro. The stage is yours."

The gunfighter's upper lip now held beads of sweat among the strands of his mustache. His hand began to tense, fingers preparing for the unfamiliar task. Han almost went for his gun then, but curbed himself sharply. Gallandro would have to be the one to decide.

The gunman's left hand drooped loosely, as he abandoned the effort. Chewbacca, unable to ignore the outcries he'd heard, appeared at the hatch. Han snatched the blaster from Gallandro's tooled holster and pressed it into his first mate's midsection as he dodged past him. "Hold onto him! I'm getting us out of here if I can!"

He was reading instrumentation from the moment he entered the cockpit at a full run. He stopped himself with the heel of his left hand against the console and vaulted into his seat. The engines were hot but, as per Gallandro's orders, guns, shields, and everything else but commo were cold.

The neuro-charge hadn't been crippling; the feeling in his right arm was already coming back. *For all the good it'll do me*, he frowned to himself. He was shocked at how little time had passed since he'd entered the ship; Spray and Fiolla had only now finished the long walk back to the cage.

He smashed his fist against the console. "Look at this! If I had firepower I'd have two perfect hostages under the guns. Or if I had tractors, I could haul 'em back here."

"There're other ways to handle cargo besides tractors," said a high-pitched vocoder. "Isn't that right, Bollux?"

"Blue Max is quite correct, sir," drawled the labor 'droid

from the navigator's seat, from which he'd been keeping a photoreceptor on things, his plastron open. "As a general labor 'droid, I might point out—"

Han cut him off with a bloodcurdling war whoop and screamed back over his shoulder, hoping his copilot would hear, "Chewie! Hold onto your pelt; we're taking the long shot!"

He brought up full engine power. Giving the *Millennium Falcon* entirely too much acceleration, he tore off from a dead standstill to scream along under the belly of the destroyer, retracting landing gear as he went. Even with full braking thrusters he barely made a tight bank, throwing himself against the console as Bollux floundered for a handhold. Lining up his shot, he applied more power.

The safety cage, suspended halfway up to the access lock on its utility tractor, was before him with unbelievable speed. With more instinct than skill, Han made microscopic, split-second corrections in his course and hit braking thrusters again. The starboard bow mandible slipped through the cage's sling-arm.

Han accelerated again, carefully but extremely quickly, tearing the cage out of the utility tractor's grasp. "Go ahead, go ahead," he taunted the mountainous destroyer, whose weapons still tracked him. "Shoot me; you'll blow your territorial manager to *particles*!"

But no fire came. The *Falcon* shrieked out from under the Espo warship's belly; everything had happened with such suddenness that Han had snagged the cage before fire-control officers could decide what to do. Now they were powerless to intervene without endangering their superior. But the destroyer rose majestically and fell in behind the freighter in close pursuit.

Han was beside himself, laughing, howling, stomping his boots on the deck, but still piloting with utmost care; if anything happened to Spray and Fiolla now, the warship would surely eradicate the *Falcon*. He was relieved to find that the cage's sling-arm appeared to be firmly seated across the bow mandible.

Chewbacca appeared, pushing a ruffled Gallandro along before him. The Wookiee thrust the gunman into the commo officer's seat, then took his own. Gallandro was smoothing his mustache and straightening his clothes. "Solo, was it necessary to have this behemoth body-press me to the safety cushioning?" Then he noticed what had happened. Grudging admiration crept into his voice. "You seem to have gained the advantage, Solo. Congratulations, but please control yourself; the territorial manager is an extremely reasonable fellow and I'm sure he'll agree to any sane terms. I don't suppose that your unconditional release would be too much to ask. Oh, and perhaps afterward we can try that draw, for curiosity's sake. You may drain my pistol's charge first if you like; I'd just like to know what would've happened."

Han spared him a quick, disdainful look from the touchy business of guiding the *Falcon* smoothly and levelly through the hard, rocky peaks of Ammuud. "You *pay* to see the cards Gallandro; you folded."

The gunfighter nodded politely. "Of course; what could I have been thinking of? There will be other occasions, Captain. These circumstances were unique."

They both knew that was true; Han swallowed his next taunt. "If your arm's coming around, you can warm up the commo board and contact the commander of that gunboat back there. Tell him I want time and room to finish repairs on the *Falcon* and a little more on the side for a head start. No stunts now, or they'll be picking Spray up with blotters."

"Arrangements will be satisfactory," Gallandro assured him calmly, "with adequate safeguards for both sides." He set to work at the commo board.

Han cut his speed back, satisfied that there would be no fire from the Espos. He knuckled his copilot's arm. "That was a cute move. What made you rig up the security case's clip?"

The Wookiee answered with a string of the honks and

grunts of his own language. Han turned his face back front, so his expression wouldn't show. It was highly unlikely that Gallandro understood any Wookiee, and he wouldn't know, unless he saw the pilot's face, how Chewbacca's reply had bewildered him.

Because Chewbacca hadn't connected the security case's clip. And that left only one other person who had known where the case was. Han half-stood, half-leaned forward to look down through the canopy at the gently swaying safety cage. Spray was huddled miserably in the lowest corner of the dangling cage, webbed fingers clutched at the guardrail and its meshwork. He was making a courageous effort, it seemed, not to become airsick as he pondered the sudden reversals of fate. Han figured that even with this turnabout, it had been a good day for the territorial manager; he resolved to trade grips with Spray before they again parted company.

Fiolla, unlike her superior, was braced more or less upright, clinging to the sling-arm and staring up at the cockpit. When she saw Han gazing down, a slow and secret smile crossed her face.

Knowing how well she could read the slightest kinetic movement, he mouthed. *You are one very, very sharp future Senior Board Member.* He saw a laugh escape her then and she made a small, mocking bow of the head.

He pulled back down into his seat. Gallandro had raised the destroyer and was remonstrating with her skipper.

"I might just have to hang onto one of my hostages a little longer," Han interrupted. "To make sure you keep your end of the deal." Gallandro swiveled his chair around in surprise. "And don't get yourself in a lather, Gallandro; you'll get her back if your word's good." He went back to flying, checking sensors for a suitable landing spot. One more thought occurred to him.

"By the way, Gallandro, find out how much cash the purser has in his vault." He snickered at Chewbacca's questioning bark. "What d'you mean, 'what for?' *Somebody* owes you and me ten thousand for services rendered. Or did you forget?''

Gallandro, teeth clenched, went back to his argument with the Espo captain. Chewbacca's happy guffaws rang as the Wookiee pounded his armrest, the vibrations traveling through the deck. Han leaned forward again and blew Fiolla a heartfelt kiss.

HAN SOLO AND THE LOST LEGACY

A book for Linda Kuehl
and, with particular gratitude,
for John A. Kearney

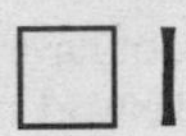

HAN Solo nearly had the control-stem leads hooked up, a sweaty job that had him stuck under the low-slung airspeeder for almost an hour, when there was a kick at his foot. ''What's holding things up?''

The leads, now gathered together in precise order, sprang free of his fingers, going every which way. With a scalding Corellian malediction, Han shoved against the machine's undercarriage, and his repulsor-lift mechanic's creeper slid out from under the airspeeder.

Han leaped up instantly to confront Grigmin, his temporary employer, the color on his face changing from the red of frustration to a darker and more dangerous hue. Han was lean, of medium height, and appeared younger than his actual age. His eyes were guarded, intense.

Grigmin, tall, broad shouldered, handsomely blond, and some years younger than Han, either didn't notice his pit-crewman's anger or chose not to acknowledge it. ''Well? What about it? That airspeeder's an important part of my show.''

Han attempted not to lose his scant temper. Working as pit-crewman to Grigmin's one-man airshow on a circuit of fifth-rate worlds had been the only job he and his partner, Chewbacca, had been able to get when they found they needed work, but Grigmin's unrelenting arrogance made the task of keeping his outmoded aircraft running nearly unbearable.

''Grigmin,'' Han said, ''I've warned you before. You put

too much strain on your hardware. You could stay well within performance tolerances and still complete every maneuver in your routines. But instead you showboat, with junk heaps that were obsolete when the Clone Wars were news."

Grigmin's grin grew even wider. "Save the excuses, Solo. Will my airspeeder be ready for my afternoon show, or have you and your Wookiee sidekick decided you don't like working for me?"

Masterpiece of understatement! Han thought to himself, but mumbled, "She'll be in the air again if Fadoop gets here with the replacement parts."

Now Grigmin frowned. "You should have gone for them yourself. I never trust these useless locals; it's a rule I have."

"If you want me to use a starship for a crummy surface-to-surface skip, you'll have to pay the expenses—up front." Han would sooner trust a local like the amiable, gregarious Fadoop than a shifty deadbeat like Grigmin.

Grigmin ignored the invitation to part with some cash. "I want my airspeeder ready," he concluded and left to prepare for the next part of his performance, an exhibition of maneuvers with a one-man jetpack. *Maneuvers any academy greenie could do*, Han thought. *These backwater worlds are the only place anyone would pay to see a feeble act like Grigmin's.*

Still, if it hadn't been for Grigmin's needing a pitcrew, Han Solo and the Wookiee, Chewbacca, freelance smugglers, would have been on the Hurt Vector. He adjusted his sweatband, toed the mechanic's creeper over to him, settled onto it, and pulled himself back under the airspeeder.

Groping half-heartedly for the control leads, Han wondered just what it was that made his luck so erratic. He had had strokes of good fortune that rivaled anything he had ever heard of, but at other times. . . .

He barked his knuckles, swore a mighty oath, and mulled over the fact that only a short time ago he and his Wookiee partner had held the galaxy by the tail. They had defied a slavery ring in the Corporate Sector, held the Authority's dreaded Security Police at bay with a Territorial Manager as hostage, and come out of the deal ten thousand credits richer.

But since then there had been needed repairs for their starship, the *Millennium Falcon*, and monumental celebrations on a dozen worlds as they put the Corporate Sector behind them. Then there had been ill-fated smuggling ventures: a ruinous try at clotheslegging in the Cron Drift; a failed Military Script-exchange plot in the Lesser Plooriod Cluster; and more, each adventure bringing a little closer that day when they would find themselves among the needy.

So they had ended up here in the Tion Hegemony, so far out among the lesser star systems of the vast Empire that the Imperials didn't even bother to exert direct control over it. In the Tion tended to congregate the petty grifters, unsuccessful con-artists, and unprosperous crooks of the galaxy. They ran *Chak*-root, picked up R'alla mineral water for the smuggling run to Rampa, swiped, ambushed, connived, and attempted in a thousand ways to fuel careers temporarily at a standstill.

Han considered all this as he carefully gathered the leads, once again separating them delicately. At least with Grigmin, Han and Chewbacca were paid, once in a while.

But that didn't make it any easier to take Grigmin's high-handedness. What particularly irritated Han was that Grigmin considered himself the hottest stunt pilot in space. Han had entertained the idea of taking a swing at the younger man, but Grigmin was a former heavyweight unarmed combat champion. . . .

His musings were interrupted by another kick that jolted his boot. The control leads sprang from his hands again. Furious, he pushed off against the airspeeder's undercarriage, jumped off the mechanic's creeper, and, combat champion or no, launched himself at his tormentor . . .

. . . and was caught up instantly against a wide shaggy chest in a frightfully strong but restrained hug and held a half-meter or so off the ground.

"Chewie! Let go, you big . . . all right; I'm sorry."

Thick arms muscled like loops of steel released him. The Wookiee Chewbacca glared down from his towering height, growling a denunciation of Han's manners, his reddish-brown brows lowered, his fangs showing. He shook a long, hairy finger at his partner for emphasis and tried straightening the Authority Security Police admiral's hat perched rakishly on his head, his lush mane escaping from beneath it.

The admiral's hat was just about the only thing the two still had from their adventures in the Corporate Sector. Chewbacca had taken a fancy to its bright braid, snowy-white material, glossy black brim, and ornate insignia during an exchange of hostages just before their hasty departure from that region of space. In his people's tradition of counting coup on their enemies, the Wookiee had demanded the hat as part of the ransom. Han, pressed by events, had indulged him.

Now the pilot threw up his hands. "Enough! I *said* I was sorry. I thought you were that vapor-brain Grigmin again. Now what?"

Han's giant copilot informed him that Fadoop had arrived. Fadoop stood nearby on her feet and knuckles, an unusually fat and outgoing native of the planet Saheelindeel. A short, bandy-legged, and densely green-furred primate, she was a local wheeler-dealer who flew an aircraft of sorts, an informal assemblage of parts and components from various scrapped fliers, a craft which she called *Skybarge*.

Pulling off his sweatband, Han walked toward Fadoop. "You scrounged the parts? Good gal!"

Fadoop, scratching behind one ear with a big toe, removed a malodorous black cigar from her mouth and blew a smoke ring. "Anything for Solo-my-friend. Are we not soulsealed buddies, you, me, and the Big One here, this Wookiee? But, ahh, there is a matter—"

Fadoop looked away somewhat embarrassed. Working the quid of *Chak*-root that swelled her cheek, she spat a stream of red liquid into the dust. "I trust Solo-my-friend, but not Grigmin-the-blowhard. I hate to bring up money."

"No apologies; you earned it." Han dug into a coverall pocket for the cash he had gotten in advance for the airspeeder parts. Fadoop tucked the money away swiftly into her belly pouch, then brightened; a twinkle sparkled in her close-set, golden eyes.

"And there's a surprise, Solo-my-friend. At the spaceport, when I picked up the parts, two new arrivals were looking for you and the Big One. I had room in my ship, and so brought them with me. They wait."

Han reached back under the airspeeder and drew out his coiled gunbelt, which he always kept at arm's length. "Who are they? Imperials? Did they look like skip-tracers or Guild muscle?" He buckled the custom-model blaster around his hips, fastening the tiedown at his right thigh, and snapped open his holster's retaining strap.

Fadoop objected. "Negatron! Nice, peaceful fellows, a little nervous." She scratched her verdant, bulging midsection, making a sandpaper sound. "They want to hire you. No weapons on them, at least."

That sounded reassuring. "What do you think?" Han asked Chewbacca.

The Wookiee resettled his admiral's hat, pulling the gleaming brim down low over his eyes, and stared across the airfield. After a few seconds, he barked a syllable of affirmation, and the three started off for Fadoop's ship.

It was high festival on Saheelindeel, formerly a time of tribal reunions and hunting rituals, then of fertility and harvest ceremonies. Now it incorporated elements of an airshow and industrial fair. Saheelindeel, like so many other planets in the Tion Hegemony, was struggling to thrust itself into an age of modern technology and prosperity in emulation of the galaxy at large. Farming machinery was on display as well as factory robotry. Vehicles new to the wide-eyed Saheelindeeli but obsolete on more advanced worlds were in evidence, along with communications and holo apparatuses that delighted the touring crowd. In an exhibition game of shock-ball, the charged orb sizzled between players wearing insulated mitts; the winning team was using a zoned offense.

Off in the distance, Grigmin was looping and diving in jetpack harness. Just seeing him again put Han in a more receptive frame of mind to meet Fadoop's passengers. Passing by the reviewing stand, he saw the Saheelindeeli's grizzled matriarch holding the elaborate trophy she was to present that afternoon for the best thematic float or exhibit. The fair's theme was *Fertility of the Soil, Challenge of the Sky*. Favored heavily to win was the opulent float entered by the Regional Fork-Pitchers' Local.

At last Han and his companions arrived at Fadoop's slapdash cargo ship. Despite her reassurances, Han was relieved to see the new arrivals were not Imperial stormtroopers—"snowmen" or "white-hats," as they were called in slangtalk—but an unassuming pair, human and humanoid.

The humanoid—a tall, reedy, purple-skinned type whose eyes, protruding from an elongated skull, held tiny red pinpoints of pupil—nodded at Han. "Ah, Captain Solo? A pleasure to meet you, sir!" He stuck out a thin arm. Han clasped the long, slender hand, trying to ignore its greasy skin secretions.

"Yes, I'm Solo. What can I do for you?"

The human, an emaciated albino wearing a sunproof robe, explained. "We represent the Committee for Interinstitutional Assistance of the University of Rudrig. You've heard of our school?"

"I think so." He vaguely remembered that it was the only decent advanced school in the Tion Hegemony.

"The university has concluded an Agreement of Aid for a fledgling college on Brigia," the albino continued.

The humanoid took up the conversation. "I am Hissal, and Brigia is my homeworld. The university has promised us guidance, materials, and teaching aids."

"So you should be contacting Tion Starfreight or Interstellar Shipping," Han noted. "But you came looking for us. Why?"

"The shipment is completely legal," the gaunt Hissal hastened to add, "but there is opposition from my planetary government. Though they can't contravene Imperial trade agreements, of course, we still fear there might be trouble in making delivery and—"

"—you want someone who can look out for your stuff."

"Your name *had* come to us as a capable fellow's," Hissal admitted.

"Chewie and I try to avoid trouble—"

"The job pays rather well," interposed the albino. "One thousand credits."

"—unless there's some profit in it. Two thousand," Han finished, doubling the price automatically even though the offer had been more than fair. There ensued a few moments of haggling. But when Han pressed the university representatives too sharply and their enthusiasm began to waver, Chewbacca issued a howl that made them all jump. He didn't much like crewing for Grigmin either.

"Uh, my copilot's an idealist," Han improvised, scowling up at the Wookiee. "Luckily for you. Fifteen hundred." The albino and the Brigian agreed, adding that half would be paid on consignment, half on delivery. Chewbacca pushed his gaudy admiral's hat back on his head and beamed at his partner, overjoyed to be lifting off again.

"So," said Fadoop, slapping her belly merrily with both hands and one foot, "that only leaves telling that fool Grigmin good riddance."

"It does, doesn't it?" Han agreed. "He'll be doing his big stunt display any time now." He rubbed his jaw and studied the ungainly, stubby-winged vessel that stood nearby. "Fadoop, can I borrow old *Skybarge* for a few minutes?"

"No questions asked. But she's got cargo onboard, several cubic meters of enriched fertilizer for the agricultural pavilion." Fadoop relit her cigar.

"No problem," Han told her. "Warm up your ship. I'll be right back."

* * *

Having already amazed the unsophisticated Saheelindeeli with his hover-sled, jetpack, and repulsorlift swoops, Grigmin began his grand finale, an exhibition of stunt flying with an obsolete X-222 high-altitude fighter. The triple-deuce looped, climbed, dove, and banked through textbook maneuvers, releasing clouds of colorful aerosols at certain points to the delight of the crowd.

Grigmin came into his final approach, putting the limber and lean ship through a fancy aerobatic display before coming in toward a precise landing. He didn't realize, however, that a second ship had come in after him on the same approach his fighter had taken. It was Fadoop's cumbersome *Skybarge* with Han Solo at the controls. To show what he thought of Grigmin's flying ability, Han took the tubby ship through the same display the exhibition flier was just completing. But, coming into his first loop, Han feathered his portside engine.

The green-furred Saheelindeeli gasped collectively and pointed the second ship out to one another with a great commotion, forgetting to watch Grigmin's landing entirely. They expected to see *Skybarge* plummet from the air. But Han completed the roll, deftly working with the nearly empty craft's stubby wings, control surfaces, and chugging engine. On the second roll, he feathered the starboard engine, too, and went into a third with zero thrust.

Shrieks of fright from the crowd and their tentative race for cover abated as they saw that the unwieldy aircraft was still under control. Jumping up and down, pointing with fingers and toes, they sent up a ragged cheer for the mad pilot, then a more forceful one, reflecting the Saheelindeeli affection for grand gestures, even insane ones.

Grigmin, who had exited from his ship virtually unnoticed, threw down his flight helmet and watched *Skybarge* in mounting fury. Han coaxed the third roll out of his homely vessel and waggled her down toward the strip.

But only one landing wheel emerged from its bay. Grigmin grinned at the prospect of a crash; but unexpectedly the ship bounced off the single wheel, trimmed handily, and settled a second time as another landing wheel lowered. She bore on the reviewing stand with surprising grace and rebounded from two wheels.

As *Skybarge* neared the reviewing stand, the crowd parted before her, clapping their hands and feet in high approbation. The ship waggled her tail in midair, extended her third and last landing wheel, and rolled cleanly for the reviewing stand. By that time Grigmin was so distracted that he didn't notice the cargo ship heading directly for his precious triple-deuce fighter.

Too late! Slam! He could only dodge out of the way as *Skybarge* rolled by. Han threw a wicked grin at him from the cockpit.

Skybarge's high, heavy-duty landing gear permitted her to pass directly over the low, sleek fighter. With consummate skill, Han flipped open her cargo-bay doors and suddenly an avalanche of enriched fertilizer dumped directly into the fighter through the open cockpit canopy.

The Saheelindeeli began applauding madly. *Skybarge*'s overhead cockpit hatch popped open, and Han's happy face appeared. He inclined his head graciously to acknowledge the ovation as Grigmin was being elbowed farther and farther away by the press of the crowd.

From the reviewing stand the matriarch's voice wheezed through the crackling public address system. ''First prize! Trophy to *Skybarge* for best exhibit, *Fertility of the Soil, Challenge of the Sky.*'' She waved the tall loving cup as her advisers whistled and stomped their feet in glee.

THE *Millennium Falcon* rested on Brigia's single spaceport landing field. She looked very much like the battered, much-repaired, and worn-out stock freighter she was, but there were incongruities. The irregular docking tackle, oversized thruster ports, heavy-weapons turrets, and late-model sensor-suite dish betrayed something about her real line of work.

"That's the last of the tapes," Han announced. He checked the offloading on his hand-held readout screen as Bollux, the labor 'droid, stumped past, guiding a repulsorlift hand truck. The automaton's green finish looked eerie in the glow of the irradiators with which the ship was now rigged. Brigia was flagged in all the standard directories, thus requiring phase-one decontam procedures. The ship's environmental systems circulated broad-spectrum anticontamination aerosols along with air. Han's and Chewbacca's immunization treatments would protect them against local maladies, but they were nonetheless eager to be away.

Han watched Bollux head for the steam-powered freight truck parked near the ship. The glare of the landing field's illumigrids showed him the Brigian workers, all volunteers from the budding college, arranging crates, packing canisters and carry-cases that the *Falcon* had delivered. They conversed animatedly among themselves, thrilled with the new broadcasting equipment and especially with the library of tapes.

Han turned to Hissal, who had accompanied him on the

flight and who was to be the college's first president. "The only thing left to get outboard is your duplicator."

"Ah, yes, the duplicator, our most-awaited item," commented Hissal, "and the most expensive. It will print and collate material at speeds our own presses cannot match and synthesize any paper or other material from the raw constituents it contains. This, from a device that fits into a few crates. Amazing!"

Han made a noncommittal sound. Bollux was returning, and Han called down the curve of the passageway, "Chewie! Secure the main hold and crack open the number two; I want to get that duplicator off and raise ship." From aft echoed the Wookiee's answering growl.

"Captain, there's one more thing," Hissal went on, drawing a pouch from beneath his lateral folds. Han's right hand dropped immediately to his blaster. Hissal, sensing his breach of decorum, held up a thin hand in denial.

"Be of tranquil mind. I know that among your kind it is customary to offer a gratuity for a task well done." Hissal plucked a curl of bills out of his pouch and extended it to the pilot.

Han examined the bills. They had a strange texture, more like textile than like paper. "What *is* this stuff?"

"A new innovation," admitted Hissal. "Several Progressions ago the New Regime replaced bartering and local coinages with a planet-wide monetary system."

Han slapped the sheaf of minutely inscribed bills against the palm of his flying glove. "Which gives them a hammerlock on trade, of course. Well, thanks anyway, but this stuff isn't worth much off-planet."

Hissal's elongated face grew even longer. "Unfortunately, only the New Regime may hold off-world currency; thus, all equipment and materials for our school had to come by donation. The first thing the New Regime did when it accumulated enough credits was bring in a developmental consulting firm. Aside from the currency system, the firm's main accomplishment was to profit from a major purchase of military equipment, which included that warship you saw.''

Han *had* noticed the ship, a pocket-cruiser of the outmoded Marauder class surrounded by worklights and armed guards.

''Her main control stacks blew on her shakedown cruise,'' Hissal explained. ''Naturally, there are no Brigian techs capable of repairing her, and so she remains inert until the Regime can muster enough credits to import techs and parts. That money could have brought us commercial technology, or medical advancements.''

Han nodded. ''First thing most of these boondock worlds do—no offense, Hissal—is pick up some toys to build their image. Then their neighbors run out and do the same.''

''We are a poor planet,'' the Brigian told him solemnly, ''and have more important priorities.''

Han declined further comment on that subject. Bollux had returned and was waiting for Han's next order, when suddenly there was a distant screeching of steam sirens.

Han walked down to the ramp's hinged foot. Closing in from all sides were rows of lumbering metal power wagons, petro-engines chugging, sirens ripping the night, high wheels making the landing field tremble. Arc-spotlights swung to converge on the *Millennium Falcon* and the freight truck.

Han shouldered past Hissal and dashed to the ramp head. ''Chewie! We've got problems; get into the cockpit and charge up the main guns!'' He rejoined Hissal halfway down the ramp.

The college volunteers stood surprised and unmoving on the bed of their truck, unsure of what to do. In moments the cordon of power wagons had been drawn tightly. Doors flew open and squads of figures came leaping from the vehicles. They were obviously government troops, carrying old-fashioned solid-projectile firearms. But something about their uniforms seemed odd. The troops wore human-style military regalia ill-suited to the gawkish Brigian anatomy. Han surmised that remnants and leftovers had been foisted off on the unsuspecting New Regime as part of their overall military purchase.

The soldiers marched in badly fitting battle harness, far-too-loose helmets perched precariously on their heads, filigreed epaulets sagging forlornly from their narrow shoulders, embroidered dispatch cases flopping against their skinny posteriors. Their legs and feet were too narrow for combat boots, so the warriors of Brigia wore natty pink spats with glittering buttons over bare feet. Among what Han assumed to be their officer corps were an abundance of medals and citations, one or two ceremonial swords, and several drooping cummerbunds. A number of troopers with no detectable talent were blowing bugles.

In moments, the soldiers had taken the shocked college volunteers captive at bayonet point. Other units advanced on the starship.

Han had already grasped Hissal's thin arm and was dragging him up the ramp. "But, this is an atrocity! We have done nothing wrong!"

Han released him and plunged through the main hatch. "You want to debate that with a bullet? Make up your mind; I'm sealing up."

Hissal hurried up the ramp. The main hatch rolled down just as the troops reached the ramp's foot; Han heard a salvo of bullets ricocheting off it.

In the cockpit, Chewbacca had already activated defensive shields and had begun warming up the engines. Hissal, trailing Han, was still protesting. Han couldn't take the time to reply; he was completely absorbed in readying the ship for takeoff.

The volunteers were being dragged, pushed, and thrown into confinement in the waiting wagons. The few who protested were summarily struck down and towed off by their slender, strangely boned ankles. Han noticed that the Brigians' war-bannered personnel carriers were, in fact, garbage trucks of an outdated model.

Chewbacca made a grating sound through clenched teeth.

"I'm mad about our money, too," Han replied. "How do we get the other half if we can't get a delivery receipt?"

The troops were taking up firing positions in ranks around the starship. "They couldn't have waited another ten minutes?" Han muttered. A Brigian stepped out in front of the firing lines. Because of the glare of the spotlights, Han had to shield his eyes with his hand to see that the Brigian held a loudhailer in one hand and an official-looking scroll in the other.

Han donned his headset and flipped on an external audio pickup in time to hear "—no harm will come to you, good friends from space! The peace-loving New Regime requires only that you surrender the fugitive now onboard your vessel. The Brigian government will trouble you no further."

Han keyed his headset mike over to external-speaker mode. "What about our pay?" He avoided looking at Hissal, but kept one hand close to his side arm.

"Agreements can be reached, honored offworlder," the Brigian below answered. "Allow me to come onboard and parley."

Han keyed his mike again. "Pull the soldiers back and turn those spotlights off. Meet me at the ramp, no weapons, no stunts!"

The Brigian passed his loudhailer to a subordinate and motioned with the scroll. The ranks fell back and the spotlights flickered out; the martial garbage trucks withdrew. "Keep an eye on things," Han instructed his first mate. "If anyone moves wrong, let me know."

Hissal was outraged. "Is it your plan to treat with these hoodlums? Legally speaking, they haven't got a receptacle to *skloob* in, I assure you. The courts—"

"—don't concern us now," Han interrupted, motioning him aside. "Go find a seat in the forward compartment and don't worry; we won't hand you over to them."

With great dignity Hissal corrected him. "My concern is for my friends."

Bollux, the labor 'droid, was waiting in the passageway,

the crated duplicator components loaded on his handtruck. In his measured drawl the automaton asked, "What are your instructions, Captain?"

Han sighed. "I don't know. Why is it I never get the easy jobs? Go up forward, Bollux. If I need you, I'll holler." The machine's heavy feet clattered on the deckplates. Chewbacca yeowled that the area was clear.

Han pulled his blaster. The main hatch rolled up, and at the ramp's foot waited the Brigian. He was taller than Hissal, broadly built for his species, his color a little darker than average. He wore a chrome-studded battle harness, rhinestone shoulderboards with dangling brushes at the ends, several colorful aiguillettes, a salad of decorations, and impressive, red-sequined spats. A plume bobbed from his tilting helmet.

Han beckoned warily. The creature marched up the ramp, the scroll tucked under one arm. Han stopped him at the head of the ramp. "Shuck the harness and the tin lid and toss them back down."

The creature complied. "Welcome to our fair planet, fellow biped," he said with an effort at heartiness. "I am Inspector Keek, Chief of the Internal Security Police of the very progress-minded New Regime of Brigia." He cast his harness and helmet away with a racket of clanking metal.

"I figured you weren't the Boosters' Club," Han said wryly, making the inspector raise long, skinny arms high. He cautiously poked at the security chief's lateral folds to make sure he had no hidden weapons there. Keek wriggled. This close, Han could read Keek's medals. Either these, too, had been obtained secondhand, he thought, or the inspector was also spelling champ of the planet Oor VII.

"All right, into the forward compartment there. Best behavior now; I've had all the games I'm going to play today."

Entering the forward compartment, Keek gazed without comment at Hissal, who was seated in an acceleration chair near the holo-gameboard. The inspector found his own seat by the tech station. Bollux had seated himself on the curved acceleration couch behind the gameboard.

Han rested one hip on the gleaming gameboard. "Now, what's the hitch? I've got my clearances. The Imperials aren't going to be too happy about you local enforcers trying to hijack an authorized shipment."

Keek spoke with forced jocularity, "Ah, you scaredy-*norg* human. Nothing's wrong! The benevolent Inner Council held an emergency session when word of this transaction reached them and placed all teaching materials and off-world literature on the restricted list." He waved the beribboned scroll. "I have here the Edict, which I am to present to you."

"And just who's the flaming Inner Council? Listen, slim, no little slowpoke world alters Imperial trade agreements." That he himself had often broken Imperial laws—shattered them to fragments would be more accurate—was something he chose not to mention.

"We are merely here, my troops and I," Keek replied evenly, "to take temporary custody of the cargo in question, until a Tion representative and an Imperial adjudicator can be summoned. The arrests were strictly an internal matter."

And the Tion representative and the Imperial adjudicator would undoubtedly come with price tags attached, Han reflected. "So who pays me?"

Keek attempted to smile; he looked preposterous. "Our supply of Imperial currency is depleted just now, due to repairs to our spacefleet. But our Treasury's note, or our planetary currency—"

"No play money!" Han exploded. "I want my cargo back. And besides, one run-down gunboat is no *spacefleet*."

"Impossible. The cargo is evidence for the trial of certain seditionists, one of whom you've been deceived into sheltering. Come, Captain; cooperate, and you'll be well received here." Keek winked, with effort. "Come! We'll pass intoxicating liquids through our bodies and boast of our sporting abilities! Let us be jolly and clumsy, as humans love to be!"

Han, who hated being played for a sucker worse than anything, gritted his teeth. "I told you already, I don't want any of your homemade cash—"

A sudden thought struck him, and he jumped up. "You want part of my cargo? Keep it! But I'm going to come across to Hissal with what's left."

The security chief seemed amused. "You seek to extort me with educational materials? Come, Captain; we're both worldly chaps."

Han ignored Keek's attempt at flattery. Carrying a power prybar, he began breaking packing straps from a crate on the hand truck. "This is a duplicator, just the thing to set up a college press with. But it's a top-of-the-line model, and it's versatile. Hissal, I'll take that tip after all."

Confused, Hissal handed over the Brigian currency. Han showed them one of the duplicator's components.

"This is the prototyper; you can program it for what you want or feed it as a sample. Like this." He inserted a Brigian bill and punched several buttons. The prototyper whirred, lights blinked, and the original bill reappeared together with an identical copy. Han held it up to the light, eyeing the duplicate critically. Keek made choking sounds, comprehending now that the pilot was holding his planet's entire monetary system hostage.

"*Hmm.* Not perfect," Han noted, "but if you supplied the machine with local materials, it would work. And for different serial numbers on each bill you just program that into the machine. That consulting firm must've been a cut-rate operation; they didn't even bother to set up a secure currency." The New Regime had obviously been the victim of aggressive salesmanship. "Well, Keek, what do you—"

Keek had snapped the end off his scroll's wooden core and pointed it directly at Han, who didn't doubt for a second that he was looking down the barrel of a gun.

"Lay your pistol on that table, alien primate," hissed Keek. "You will now have your automaton take the hand truck and he, you, and the traitor Hissal will precede me down the ramp."

Han gave Bollux the order as he carefully put his blaster on the gameboard, knowing Keek would shoot him if he tried to warn Chewbacca. But as Keek reached to take possession of the blaster, Han inconspicuously touched the gameboard's master control.

Miniature holo-monsters leaped into existence, weird creatures of a dozen worlds, spitting and striking, roaring and hopping. Keek jumped back in surprise, firing his scroll-weapon by reflex. A beam of orange energy crashed into the board, and the monsters evaporated into nothingness.

At the same instant Han, with a star-pilot's reflexes, threw himself onto the security chief, catching hold of the hand holding the scroll-gun. He groped for his blaster with his free hand, but Keek's shot had knocked it from the gameboard.

The security chief possessed incredible strength. Not stopped by the pilot's desperate punches, Keek hurled him halfway across the compartment and brought his weapon around. Just then Hissal landed on his shoulders, making Keek stagger against the edge of the acceleration couch. The two Brigians struggled, their arms and legs intertwining like a confusion of snakes.

But Keek was stronger than the smaller Hissal. Bit by bit he brought his weapon around for a shot. Han got back into the fight with a side-on kick that knocked the scroll aside so that the charge meant for Hissal burned a deep hole in one of the safety cushions.

The scroll-gun was apparently spent, and Keek began to club Hissal with it. Han tried to clock him, but Keek knocked the pilot to the deck with stunning force, then turned to grapple with the other Brigian, their feet shuffling and kicking around the downed human. Unable to get around them and recover his blaster, Han tripped Keek. The inspector sank, taking Hissal with him.

Suddenly the scroll, which Keek had dropped, rolled into Han's palm. As Keek was kneeling over the fallen Hissal, Han swung the scroll, connecting solidly with the security chief's skull. Keek's lank body shook with spasms and stiffened. Hissal merely pushed him, and the security chief toppled to the deck.

A roar came from behind them. Chewbacca, seeing his partner unharmed, was visibly relieved. ''Where were *you*?'' Han cried. ''He just about put out my running lights!'' Rubbing the bruises he had received, Han recovered his pistol.

Hissal, collapsed in an acceleration chair, tried to catch his breath. ''This isn't my usual line of endeavor, Captain. Thank you.''

''We're sort of even,'' Han replied with a laugh. Keek began to stir, and Chewbacca the Wookiee snatched him to his feet with one hand. Keek, strong as he was, had better sense than to resist an enraged Wookiee.

Han covered Keek's small bud of a nose with the muzzle of his blaster. The security chief's bulging eyes crossed, watching the weapon. ''That little trick of yours wasn't nice, Keek; I hate sneaks even more than hijackers. I want Hissal's people and my cargo back onboard this ship in five minutes or else you're going to have the wind whistling through your ears.''

When Hissal's freed colleagues and the controversial cargo were back onboard, Han brought Keek to the ramp's head. ''The Empire will hear of this,'' the Brigian vowed. ''It's the death sentence for you.''

''I'll try not to lose sleep over it,'' Han replied dryly. With the ship's forged papers he had used this trip, he doubted any law agency would be able to trace him. Moreover this would be, by the preoccupied Empire's lights, a very minor incident. ''And do yourself a favor: don't try anything funny when you get clear. There's nothing on this planet with enough fire power to take this ship, but you might make me mad.''

Keek looked at the other Brigians. ''What of them?''

Han sounded casual. ''Oh, I'll drop them off somewhere away from the noise and the crowds. It's legal; a spacer can contract for a surface-to-surface hop if he wants. We're going to take a long orbit, so Hissal can try out his broadcasting rig, hook it into ship's power systems.''

Keek was no fool. ''With that much altitude and power, he'll be reaching every receiver on the planet!''

''And what do you think he'll say?'' Han asked innocently. ''Something about what the New Regime's pulling? It's nothing to me, of course, but I told you pulling a gun on me would be a mistake. I'd be thinking about early retirement if I were you.''

Chewbacca gave the security chief a shove to start him on his way. Han closed the hatch. ''By the way,'' he called over to Bollux, ''thanks for handing me that scroll during the fight.''

The 'droid replied with characteristic modesty. ''After all, sir, the inspector had said it was for you. I can only hope there'll be no repercussions, Captain.''

''What for?''

''For destabilizing a planetary government to get even for having your ship shot up, sir.''

''Serves them right for cheating!'' Han Solo declared.

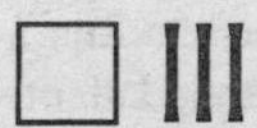

HAN stepped into the sunlight of Rudrig's brief afternoon with the balance of his pay safe in his pocket. Around him the spires, domes, towers, and other buildings that housed this part of the university stood in harmony with the lacy flowers, thick-boled trees, and purple lawns.

The university made use, in one fashion or another, of the entire planet. Its vast campuses and housing, recreation, and field training sectors were scattered over the globe. Students from all over the Tion Hegemony were compelled to come here or else leave the Tion entirely if they wanted advanced education of top quality. Centralization wasn't the best method of offering schooling, Han supposed, but was symptomatic of the languid, inept Hegemony.

He idly studied passers-by for a moment, noting many species flocking between classes, holding conversations, or playing assorted sports and various instruments. Stepping gingerly across a broad boulevard between rolling service automata, quiet mass-transit vehicles, and small ground-effect cargo transporters, he ascended a low access platform and boarded a local passenger beltway. It zipped him along between huge lecture halls and auditoriums, theaters, administrative buildings, a clinic, and a variety of classroom configurations.

Reading the glowing route markers and recalling the coordinates he had memorized from a holo-map, he stepped off the beltway again at that sector's spa, an annex of its sprawling recreation center. He had just started for the spa when he heard a voice. "Hey there, Slick!"

Han hadn't gone by that nickname in many years. Still, as he turned he kept his right hand high and near his left lapel. Though the carrying of weapons was prohibited on this quiet world, having one, Han's pragmatic philosophy ran, was a risk he was willing to take. His blaster was suspended slantwise, grip lowermost, under his left armpit and was concealed by his vest.

"Badure!" His right hand moved away from his blaster and closed in a grip on that of the old man who had called him. He used Badure's own nickname, "Trooper! What are you doing here?"

The other was a big man with a full head of hair going white, a sly squint, and a belly that had come to overlap his belt in recent years. He stood half a head taller than Han, and his grip made the younger man wince.

"Looking for you, son," Badure responded in the gravelly voice Han recalled so well. "You're showing up good, Han, real good. It must be a Wookiee's age since I've seen you. Which reminds me, how is Chewie? I was trying to find you two, and they said at the spaceport that the Wook rented a groundcoach and left word for it to be dropped off here."

Badure—Trooper—was a friend of long standing, and he seemed to have come on hard times. Han tried not to take notice of his faded, patched laborer's tunic and trousers or the scuffed and torn work boots. Still, Badure had held on to his old flight jacket, covered with its unit insignia and theater patches, and his jaunty, sweat-stained beret with its fighter-wing flash. "But how'd you know we were here?"

Badure laughed, his belly rolling. "I keep track of landings and departures, Slick. But in this case I knew you were coming."

Much as he liked this old man, Han was suspicious. "Maybe you'd better tell me more, Badure."

He looked pleased with himself. "How do you think those university types got your name, son? Not that it doesn't get around as is; I heard about that stunt at the Saheelindeeli airshow—and some rumors from out in the Corporate Sector, and something about water smuggled down the Rampa Rapids. I was here tracking down a few things on my own and heard someone was asking about capable skippers and fast ships. I passed your name along. But before we go into that, shouldn't you be saying hello to my business partner here?''

Han had been so preoccupied that he had ignored the person standing beside Badure. Chiding himself silently for this unusual lapse in caution, he looked her over.

The girl was short and slender, not long into womanhood, with a pale face and disorderly red hair that hung limply. Her brows and lashes were so light that they scarcely showed. She wore a drab, baggy brown outfit of pullover and pants, and her shoes appeared to be a size too large. Her hands had seen hard work. Han had met many men and women just like her, each bearing the stamp of the factory drone or mining-camp worker, lowest-echelon tech or other toiler.

She in turn studied him with no approval whatsoever. ''This is Hasti,'' Badure said. ''She already knows your name.'' Indicating the flow of beings moving around them to and from the busy spa, he gestured that they continue toward the entrance.

Han acceded, moving slowly, but a sideways slide of the older man's eyes confirmed something. ''What do I watch for?'' he inquired simply.

Badure laughed and said, more to himself than to Han or Hasti, ''Same old Han Solo, a one-man sensor suite.''

Han's thoughts were on Badure. The man had been his friend many years before and his partner on various enterprises a number of times since. Once, in an uncomfortable situation stemming from an abortive Kessel spice run, Badure had saved both Han's and Chewbacca's lives. That he should have sought them out here could mean only one thing.

''I won't waste your time, kid,'' Badure said. ''There are some that would like to see my hide hung out to dry. I need a ship with punch, and gait to spare, and a skipper I can trust."

Han realized that Badure wasn't going to be first to mention the life-debt the two partners owed him. "You want us to put our necks in the slot for you, is that it? Trooper, saving someone's life doesn't give you the right to risk it again. We're finally ahead of the game; do we owe it all out again this soon?"

Badure countered in neutral tones. "You're answering for the Wook, too, Han?"

"Chewie'll see it my way." *If I have to reason with him with a wrench!*

Hasti joined the conversation for the first time. "*Now* are you satisfied, Badure?" she asked bitterly.

The old man hushed her gently. To Han he went on, "I'm not asking you two to work for nothing. There'd be a cut—"

"The thing is, we're flush. Uh, in fact, we can cut some loose to see you through for a while."

He felt he had gone too far and thought for a moment that Badure was going to swing at him. The old man had made and spent a number of fortunes and had always been openhanded to his friends; but the offer of charity to himself had the ring of an insult. Favoring Han with a venomous look, Hasti put a hand on Badure's arm. "We're wasting time; our luggage is still at the district hostelry."

"Clear skies, Han," Badure said in a quiet voice, "and to the Wook as well."

Han gazed after the two long after they had disappeared on a passenger beltway.

Determined to put the incident out of his mind, he entered the spa. It offered specific creature comforts to a huge variety of human, humanoid, and nonhumanoid species. There were zero-gee massagers, ozone chambers, effluvial rinses, and many other options for humans; mud tanks for visiting Draflago; dermal autostrippers to service a Lisst'n or Pui-Ui; gill-flushes for any of a number of piscine or amphibian life forms; and as many other ablutive and restorative amenities as could be packed into the huge complex.

Inquiring at the central information area, Han discovered that Chewbacca was still enjoying the pleasures of a full-service grooming. Han himself had meant to take a leisurely cycle of soaking, sauna, massage, and pore cleansing, followed by a visit to the tonsorial center. But his encounter with Badure and Hasti left him feeling in need of a more active and distracting program.

He undressed in a private booth, storing gun and other valuables in a lockbox and feeding his pleated dress shirt, clothes, and boots to an autovalet. Then he dropped several coins into the slot of an omniron and stepped inside, keying it for maximum treatment.

In fifteen-second cycles icy water sprayed at him, sonics vibrated his skin and flesh, waves of heat lashed and nearly seared him, needle-streams of biodetergents lathered him, walls of swirling foam broke and surged through the cubicle, air nozzles hosed their blasts, and emollients were rubbed on him by vigorous autoapplicators.

He withstood the brunt of these processes and took on more cycles, finding he couldn't shake the image of Badure. Telling himself he had done the shrewd thing did no more to improve his state of mind than did the elaborate bubble bath he was taking, he concluded. So he terminated the omniron's program short of its allotted time, recovered his cleaned clothing and shined boots from the autovalet, donned his blaster, and resettled his vest. Then he set off to find his partner.

Chewbacca was in the portion of the spa reserved for its more hirsute clientele. Following the light-strip directory system helpfully placed along the floors, Han found his friend's treatment room. Checking the room's monitoring screen, he saw the Wookiee floating in a zero-gee field, arms and legs splayed. He was near the end of his session; every individual hair had been given a light mutual-repulsion charge to separate it while dirt, particulate matter, and old oils were removed. Now new oils and conditioners were being gently applied. Chewbacca wore a toothy grin, luxuriating in the treatment as he floated like a tremendous stuffed toy, his billowing pelt making him seem twice his normal girth.

Turning from the screen, Han noticed two very appealing young human females who were also waiting. One, a tall blond in an expensive jumpsuit, spoke into the ear of her companion, a shorter girl with ringlets of brown hair. The second girl wore a sportier outfit of shorts and singlet; she eyed Han speculatively. "Are you here to meet Captain Chewbacca, sir?"

Mystified, Han repeated, *"Captain . . ."*

"Chewbacca. We saw him walking across campus and we had to stop him and talk. We're both taking courses in nonhuman ethnology, and we couldn't pass up the chance. We've studied the Wookiee language tapes a little, so we understood a bit. Captain Chewbacca told us his copilot would be coming by to meet him. He invited us to go with you on a groundcoach ride."

Han smiled in spite of himself. "Fine with me. I'm Captain Chewbacca's first mate, Han Solo."

He had just established that the brunette's name was Viurre and her blond girlfriend's Kiili when Chewbacca emerged from the treatment room. The Wookiee, settling his admiral's hat on his head at a rakish angle, wore a beatific grin; his shaggy coat, now glistening and lustrous, floated lightly on stray air currents.

Han sketched a sarcastic salute. "*Captain* Chewbacca, sir, I've got the whole crew standing by for orders."

The Wookiee *wuffed* in confusion, then, remembering his assumed role, rumbled a vague reply that none of them understood. The girls promptly forgot Han and closed in on the Wookiee, complimenting him on his appearance. "I believe you ordered a groundcoach, *Skipper*?" hinted Han.

His partner *awoo*ed confirmation, and they all set off. "What have you found to be the essential differences in the life-experience on Wookiee worlds?'' Viurre asked Han earnestly.

''The tables are higher off the floor,'' the pilot replied without expression.

When they arrived at the carport, Han goggled and shouted, ''Tell me this is the wrong slip!'' Kiili and Viurre ''oohed'' in delight, while Chewbacca beamed fondly at the vehicle he had selected.

It was over eight meters long, wide and low to the ground. The groundcoach's sides, rear deck, and hood were paneled in dazzling scarlet *greel* wood that had been lacquered and polished and lacquered over and over until its metallic gleam seemed to go on forever through the fine grain. The coach's trim, bumpers, door hinges, latches, and handles were of silver alloy. It boasted an outlandish crystal hood ornament—frolicking nymphs in a swirl of gauzy, windblown veil-dresses.

The driver's seat was open to the weather, but just behind it and a luggage well was an enclosed passenger cab, also paneled in *greel* wood, complete with elaborate, hanging road lamps, tasseled bunting, and running boards and handrails on either side for footmen. Astern the cab was another luggage well between a pair of ludicrous meter-high tail fins bejeweled with all manner of signaling and warning lights. From the coach's primary and secondary antenna whips fluttered two pennants, several streamers, and the furry tail of some small, luckless animal.

''Too austere,'' Han muttered sarcastically, but he couldn't resist popping the coach's hood. A massive, fiendishly complicated engine squatted there. But Chewbacca quickly silenced Han's denunciations and amazed the two girls by throwing open the cover of the midship luggage well. It contained, due to his thoughtful arrangement, a heroic picnic lunch.

Kiili and Viurre had piled into the driver's compartment, investigating controls, dials, the sound system, and stowage drawers. Chewbacca was running an adoring palm over a quarter-panel when Han blurted out, "I bumped into Badure today, just as I was coming into the spa."

Forgetting everything else, Chewbacca barked a question. Han glanced away. "He wanted to hire us, but I told him we didn't need the work." Then he felt compelled to add, "Well, we don't, do we?"

Chewbacca howled furiously. The two girls studiously ignored the argument. "*What* do we owe Badure?" Han hollered back. "He made a business offer, Chewie." But he knew better. *Wookiees will honor a Life-Debt over anything else; he'll never walk away from it,* Han thought. Chewbacca growled another angry comment.

"What if I don't want to? Are you going to go after him without me?" Han asked, knowing what the answer would be.

The Wookiee regarded him for a long moment, then uttered a deep *Uurrr?*

Han opened his mouth, closed it, then finally answered. "No, you won't have to. Get in the bus."

Chewbacca yipped, knuckled Han's shoulder, ambled off around the coach's stern, and climbed in. Han slid into the driver's seat and swung his door shut.

"*Captain* Chewbacca and I have to go track down a pal," he told Kiili and Viurre brusquely. Then to himself he added, *I knew this would happen; I never should have told Chewie. So why did I?*

Kiili, twirling blond hair around one finger, smiled. "First Mate Solo, what should we talk to the captain about?"

"Anything. He just likes to listen to people talk." Han gunned the engine and expertly pulled the powerful coach out of its parking slip. "Tell him how he's ruining a great afternoon," Han encouraged her, then smiled. "Or sing some off-color ditties, if you know any."

Kiili eyed the contented Wookiee uncertainly. "*He* likes *those*?"

Han smiled engagingly. "No. I do."

IV

REMEMBERING that Hasti, the young woman with Badure, had mentioned the district hostelry, Han zoomed off in that direction. The scarlet monstrosity of a coach, riding its low ground-effect cushion, handled smoothly and responded well for its size.

One long arm along the back of the driver's seat, Chewbacca tilted his admiral's cap down and listened while Kiili and Viurre described the life of an undergraduate student of nonhuman ethnography.

They didn't have to enter the hostelry. Badure and Hasti were waiting at an intercampus shuttleskimmer stop near the building. Han pulled over to the curb with a belch of braking thrust, and he and Chewbacca jumped out, followed by the two girls. The Wookiee hugged the old man, giving out joyous sounds. Hasti regarded Han coolly. "Attack of conscience?"

Han angled a thumb at the Wookiee. "My partner's a sentimental fellow. Do you feel like telling us what we're getting into?"

Indicating Viurre and Kiili with a slight nod, Badure cleared his throat meaningfully. Viurre took the hint and, dragging the tall blond with her, was suddenly inspired to inspect some nearby foliage. In confidential tones Badure asked Han, "You must've heard of the ship called the *Queen of Ranroon*?"

Chewbacca quivered his nose in surprise, and Han's eyebrows shot up. "The treasure ship? The story they use to put kids to bed?"

"Not story," Badure corrected, "*history*. The *Queen of Ranroon* was crammed full with spoils from whole solar systems, tribute to Xim the Despot."

"Listen, Badure, crazies have been hunting that ship for centuries. If she ever existed, she was either destroyed or someone plundered her long ago. You've been watching too many holo-thrillers."

"When did I ever go chasing vacuum?" the old man countered.

A good point. "You know where the *Queen* is? You've got proof?"

"I know where her log-recorder is," Badure announced so confidently that Han found himself believing it. The vision of a treasure arose, a treasure so stupendous that it had become a synonym for phenomenal wealth, more than a man might squander in many lifetimes. . . .

"Let's get going," Han proposed. "We're not getting any younger." Hasti's derisive look didn't faze him. Then he noticed that Badure's face was drawn with tension.

Following his gaze, Han turned to see a black groundlimo slowly cruising toward them. Han drew Badure over to the coach, encouraging Hasti to move as well with an inclination of the head. Chewbacca, who had already thrown Badure's and Hasti's light baggage into the passenger cab, was also on the alert.

Someone in the limo had noticed their reaction. The black groundcar accelerated sharply and veered straight at them.

"Everybody into the coach," Han yelled as the limo jumped the curb and screeched to a stop, blocking the coach's front cowling. Badure began pushing Hasti into the coach's front seat as Chewbacca, unable to carry his bowcaster on this peaceful world, glanced around for a makeshift weapon.

Figures tumbled from the limo as Han drew his blaster. The blue concentric rings of a stun charge reached out and caught Badure, who had just propelled Hasti out of the way.

She fell backward across the seat; Badure staggered. She managed to grab him and pull him onto the driver's seat just as Han fired an answering shot.

By then a half-dozen beings had emerged from the limo with weapons of one kind or another. Han's hasty return shot caught the stun-gunner, a red-beaked humanoid, in its long, feathered arm. Two male humans armed with needlebeamers ducked as Han's shots shattered two of the limo's windows. The assailants, seeing that they had a fight on their hands, made a general migration toward the ground.

Chewbacca was clambering over the midship luggage well to help Hasti when she, hanging on to Badure with one hand, kicked the engine over and threw the scarlet coach into reverse. Two of the attackers who had been closing in found themselves pouncing on empty air. With a tremendous bump, the coach climbed the curb in reverse. Chewbacca had to cling to a decorative lantern to save himself, and Han jumped aside to keep from being run down, as Hasti hit braking thrusters, kicking up clots of purplish turf and exposing the rich gray soil of Rudrig.

"Well, pile on, Solo," she shouted at Han. He barely got to a running board, seizing a footman's handrail, before the coach surged forward.

Hasti didn't quite clear the end of the obstructing limo. The coach bashed it aside, half-rotating the black vehicle and crunching in its own nose cowling with a shower of *greel* wood fragments. Chewbacca cried out at the damage. As they lurched past, Han directed a suppressive barrage at the limo and its passengers, more intent on clinging to his life than on accuracy.

Hasti swerved to avoid a robo-delivery truck, thereby slamming Han up against the cab and nearly wrenching Chewbacca from the lamp, flipping him over with a snap that twisted his neck and sent his prized admiral's hat flying in the breeze. The Wookiee keened, grief-stricken for the lost headgear.

Over the howl of the coach's engine and the blast of its slipstream, Han yelled, "They're coming after us!"

The black limo was already slewing around to give chase. Han brought his blaster up. At that moment Hasti, ignoring a traffic-robo, tore into an intersection directly toward a slow-moving maintenance hauler that was towing a disabled freight 'droid. The girl set all her weight against the steering-grip yoke and hit the coach's warning horn. The first two bars of the Rudrig University Anthem sounded majestically from the coach's fractured hood. The maintenance hauler dodged with a bleep of distress and barely missed taking the driver's side off the coach.

The coach streaked straight down the thoroughfare now. Holding his abused neck stiffly, Chewbacca began inching forward again in order to take over the driving duties. A double column of students and visitors on an orientation tour chose that moment to enter a crosswalk, and Hasti hit braking thrusters.

Chewbacca flew head-first into the driver's compartment and hit the floor, his feet sticking up into the air. But even under those conditions, he had the presence of mind to notice that Badure wasn't completely aboard, and he clutched the stunned man's clothing to tug him into the coach. Hasti noticed her companion's dilemma and gave the coach a snappy cut so that the passenger door swung shut. Though hampered by wires of pain lancing through his neck, the Wookiee began extricating himself.

Just astern, Han had managed to pull himself inside the passenger cab and saw that the limo was closing in rapidly. He smashed the cab's crystalline rear window with a hard blow from his blaster. It cracked in webs, split, and fell away. Clearing away the shards, Han leaned his forearms across the empty sill. The coach's bouncing made the macro-sights useless, so he waited for a clear shot.

Chewbacca had hauled himself up and was yelping loudly at Hasti and gesturing madly. She somehow understood his meaning and hit the couch adjustment controls, which started up the servo-motors. Hasti held tightly to the control stem as the couch moved from under her, leaving her in a tense stoop. The Wookiee slid in behind her, whisked her out of the way, then took over the controls. Hasti turned at once and saw to her relief that Badure was unhurt. He was already stirring, throwing off the stun charge's effects.

The Wookiee proceeded directly through an intersection without benefit of right of way, aware that the limo, still chasing the coach, was zooming along between towering buildings.

Taking a fast curve, Chewbacca came abruptly up to a road-repair site. Far back in the mirror's reflection he could see the limo closing in. He gunned the engine, bursting through illumi-panel markers, smashing warning light-banks aside, and hurling two robo-flagwavers, still diligently waving their flags, several meters into the air. But his hopes for a safe route through the site were dashed when he rounded the turn; the roadbed had been excavated completely, side to side, the shoulders torn up right up to the building faces.

Chewbacca slowed, calmly considered his options, and decided he would have to offer his pursuers a head-on challenge. He hit the accelerator and swung the steering grips over for a smuggler's turn. The long coach leaped forward into a precise end-for-end spin, destroying several more danger indicators, its lift cushion kicking up dirt and debris. Then it sped off in the direction from which it had come.

Han leaned out a side window. As the limo bore down on them he propped his forearm through a handrail and opened fire, scoring hits on the limo's hood and one in the center of its windshield. Prepared for a terrible impact, Chewbacca uttered a piercing cry and Hasti began hugging Badure. Han could make out terrified expressions among the limo's occupants.

At thc last moment the limo driver wavered, declining the imminent head-on, and the black vehicle swung aside. Ripping through a dense Mullanite lattice-sculpture of thick creepers, slewing across a stretch of purple lawn, and—after bowling aside several long planters and snapping support columns—the limo ended up on a portico outside the local Curriculum Committee headquarters.

Chewbacca brayed his delight, but Han called a warning as the limo started up again. Chewbacca, glancing at the several rearview mirrors and single aft viewscreen, made a hard right turn to high speed by dint of sheer strength applied to unwilling controls.

The coach's left side rose, and the Wookiee took advantage of his momentum to snag another quick right into a side avenue, hoping to break off the chase. Unfortunately, he had swung the long coach onto the up-ramp of a major ground-transport artery. But he had the presence of mind to apply a Han Solo adage: when it won't help to slow down, pour it on! So he slapped toggle switches for full boost and auxiliary guidance thrust.

The immediate problem was a refuse-collection robo-dumpster making its way up the ramp. Its cyberpilot system was in a quandary over this unusual obstruction. Chewbacca, still exploiting centrifugal force, hit his offside thrusters and took the groundcoach full tilt against the ramp's safety fence.

The fence, part of a traffic-control design scheme based on very forgiving systems, gave and bent outward as the Wookiee barreled along with half the coach on the ground, half up on the wilting fence. Han, dragging himself up off the cab floorboards, took one look ahead and hit the deck again. The robo-dumpster edged toward the opposite side of the upramp and the two weighty vehicles passed each other.

The coach had lost its outermost rearview mirror post and part of the picnic lunch, and debris from the jostled dumpster was splattered across its meter-high red tail fins. Chewbacca was baying in utter exhilaration, an ages-old Wookiee war cry.

Hasti had just finished fastening a seatbelt across herself and Badure when the coach roared onto the main artery. Seeing that he was heading the wrong way on a high-speed road, the Wookiee hugged the outside wall while he assessed his situation. He kept one finger on the horn button, sounding the first two bars of the anthem over and over. All factors considered, Chewbacca felt, things were going fairly well.

Han, back in the passenger cab, held a somewhat different opinion. The black limo had taken advantage of Chewbacca's descent and was still on their tail. The intercom wasn't working, so Han pushed up the cab's forward window and shouted, "They're still on us!"

The Wookiee growled an irritated reply, then spotted his opening. He turned the steering grips with such emphasis that the yoke groaned on its stem, threatening to snap. But the coach managed to fishtail across three lanes of oncoming traffic, and Chewbacca hung in the center lane while awaiting shifts in the configuration of the traffic.

Automatic safety systems had taken notice of the potential massacre, and suddenly sequential warning lights began to flash, cautioning other drivers where the danger lay. Overhead illumi-markers and danger panels began flashing along the way, and those vehicles operating under autocontrol were brought to a halt at the shoulder by Traffic Central Override.

Meanwhile, Han, clinging to the rear window frame, saw the limo coming on. Its driver was having an easier time, following the trail the Wookiee had blazed. Han braced his right shoulder against one side of the frame and his left hand against the other to draw a steady aim. Just as he fired, Chewbacca, having lined up another gap in the oncoming traffic, hauled at the steering grips and cut hard for the center divider. Han's shot went wild, blowing a small hole in the tough fusionformed road.

Chewbacca came at the divider as directly as he could, aware that it was built to resist collision. He hit it with the coach's accelerator open, keeping his enormous foot down hard on emergency-boost auxiliaries. The engine wailed. Hasti clung to Badure.

The coach burst through a double retaining rail, taking two lengths of railing with it. Chewbacca then swooped up the sloped center abutment; two lanterns fell from the coach, and its curb feelers, he noticed, had been sheared off. Han tangled both fists into embroidered safety belting and set his feet against the cab's front wall.

The coach shot through the fence at the top of the abutment, the durable links stretching, then bursting with a titanic jolt that sent the remainder of the picnic lunch arcing into the air. Crashing down the abutment and through a second section of railing, they bounced into the traffic lanes now headed in the appropriate direction, if at illegal velocity.

Maneuvering smartly, the Wookiee avoided any other collisions. The coach sped along, intermittently shedding trim and pieces of smashed *greel* wood. Glancing out a side window, Han found himself the object of the surprised scrutiny of a gowned senior professor, a stalk-eyed creature in a robohack. Chewbacca accelerated and left the hack behind.

Less than a minute later, the black limo appeared at the crest of the abutment and descended through the swath of destruction left by Chewbacca. It, too, slid into the traffic lanes. A man, holding a long needlebeam rifle in his hands, stood up and poked his head and arms through the sunroof.

Han left the cab, swung from the handrail with one foot on the running board, and dove into the driver's compartment. "We've gone and made them mad," he hollered. "Escape and evade, old buddy!"

But even as Han exhorted his partner, Chewbacca was throwing the coach through zigs and zags, ignoring lane divider illumi-strips, applying full power though a disconcerting black smoke had begun to roil from the vehicle's engine. At last, the rifleman, his eye at his weapon's scope, fired.

A needlebeam sizzled at one of the scarlet tail fins, setting the lacquered wood afire and shearing off its tip as taillight circuitry blew. Han stood up, one hand firmly on the windshield and blaster gripped in the other. He replied with a hurried shot of his own; the bolt splashed harmlessly onto the pavement.

A second rifle beam hissed through the cab. "Get us out

of here before they cut us in half!'' Han yelled to his first mate.

Smoke from the hood now roiled more thickly. The Wookiee spun the steering-grip yoke, veering and putting an enormous robo-freighthauler between the coach and the limo. Another needlebeam, missing them, burned across the freighthauler's rear end. The last view Han had of the limo was of its driver trying to maneuver for another clear shot. He shouted to Chewbacca, ''Pump your braking thrusters!'' The Wookiee did so without question, accustomed to his friend's mad inspirations. When the freighthauler outstripped the coach, they found themselves even with the limo.

The surprised rifleman started to bring his weapon up, but Han fired first. The marksman, clutching his smoldering forearm, dropped back through the sunroof. Han's second shot blew out a piece of the limo's door. Two or three beings were trying to elbow their way up through the sunroof to set up a rocket launcher. If they couldn't stop the coach, they'd settle for blowing it all over the landscape.

Han felt the coach surge and looked around. Directly in front of them was the freighthauler, its long rear gate bouncing on the road. Its bed was half empty, a pile of construction rubble heaped against the front wall. An overpass loomed in the distance; Han quickly grasped his first mate's plan, holstered his weapon, and clung to Badure and Hasti for his life.

The coach jumped up the hanging rear gate, engine pouring black smoke, auxiliary thrusters overloading. Chewbacca pumped braking thrusters once to time his maneuver, then hit full power and the front-lift thrusters designed to help the coach negotiate low obstacles. The coach shot up the pile of rubble at the front of the cargo bed and soared into the air, the Wookiee plying his controls frantically.

Then the overpass was beneath them, and through some miracle it was unoccupied just then. The coach hit with an impact that collapsed its shock-absorption system, burned out its power routing, broke all the remaining lanterns, and shattered the cab windows. It slid, then ground to a halt against the overpass sidewall, crumpling its hood and popping its doors.

Coughing, Han and his first mate pulled Hasti and Badure from the wreckage. The black limo was already far down the road, forced along by the flow of traffic. Chewbacca, surveying the demolished groundcoach sorrowfully, sniffled and moaned to himself.

Wiping her eyes and choking, Hasti wanted to know: "Who ever told you two morons you could drive?" Then, noticing Chewbacca's gloomy look, asked, "What's wrong with him?"

"He figures he'll have a hard time getting his deposit back," Han explained.

Police groundcruisers and aircraft, converging under Traffic Control's direction, were already beginning to gather farther down the highway. Since Chewbacca had elected to leave the road in a unique manner, it would probably take the local authorities some time to piece together what had happened.

"QUIET down and sit still." Han took a firmer grip on his first mate's head.

The Wookiee, seated in a rump-sprung, sweat-stained acceleration chair in the *Millennium Falcon*'s forward compartment, stopped squirming but couldn't stifle his whimpers. He knew his neck injury had to be tended right away. Han, standing behind him, shuffling for a better stance, held his friend's chin clamped in one elbow. He pushed the palm of his hand against the Wookiee's skull.

"How many times have I done this now? Stop complaining!" Han began to apply pressure again, twisting Chewbacca's head up and to the left. The Wookiee dutifully fought the urge to rise, crimping his long fingers on the arms of the acceleration chair.

Meeting resistance, Han drew a deep breath and, without warning, yanked the thick-maned skull with all his might. There was a cracking and popping; Chewbacca yipped and snuffled pitifully. But when Han ruffled his friend's fur compassionately and stepped back, the Wookiee rubbed his neck and moved his head without pain. He immediately went off to prepare the starship for liftoff.

"If you're through ministering to the afflicted, Doctor," Hasti said from her seat by the gameboard, "it's time we got a few things settled."

Leaning against the tech station, Han agreed. "Let's put them on the table and see what we've got."

Badure, fully recovered from the stun charge, was sitting

next to Hasti. To avoid conflict, he took over. "I met Hasti and her sister, Lanni, at a mining camp on a planet named Dellalt, here in the Tion Hegemony. It was a small plunder operation; I was contract labor there."

He ignored Han's surprise. *Things have been worse than I thought for him*, the pilot realized.

"And things weren't too much better for them," Badure went on. "You know how those camps can be, and this one was about the worst I've seen. We three sort of watched out for one another.

"Lanni had a Pilot's Guild book and flew a lot of work runs, surface-to-surface stuff. Somewhere she had picked up a log-recorder, one of the ancient disk types. No ship has used one in centuries. She couldn't read the characters, of course, but there was a figure most beings in this part of space know, the *Queen of Ranroon*."

"How'd a log-recorder get to Dellalt?"

"That's where the vaults are," Badure said, and that brought some history back to Han. Xim the Despot had left behind legends of whole planets despoiled, of mass spacings of prisoners and other atrocities. And Xim the Despot had ordered that stupendous treasure vaults be built for the tribute to be sent him by his conquering armies. The treasure never arrived, and the vacant vaults, all that remained from Xim's reign, were a minor curiosity generally ignored by the big, busy galaxy.

"Are you telling me the *Queen* made it to Dellalt after all?"

Badure shook his head. "But somebody made it there with the log-recorder disk."

"The disk is in a lockbox in the public storage facility that set up operations in the old vaults," Hasti told him. "My sister was afraid it would be taken from her, for the mining company runs surprise inspections, barracks searches, and sensor frisks. So she diverted course on a freight run and made the deposit."

"How'd she get it in the first place? And where is she

now?'' Han saw the sobering answer on both their faces and wasn't surprised. The opposition, he had already learned, was in deadly earnest. He abandoned the subject.

''So, off to Dellalt before that rental agent comes looking for his groundcoach.''

But Badure, slapping his ample belly, announced, ''We have one more crewman coming. He's on his way now. I canceled our public-carrier reservations so the line will refer him directly here.''

''Who? What do we need him for?'' Han was reluctant to involve too many in this treasure hunt.

''His name is Skynx; he's a ranking expert on pre-Republic times in this part of space. And he reads ancient languages; he's already deciphered some characters Lanni had copied from the log-recorder disk. Good enough for you?''

Conditionally. Somebody, Han saw, would have to decipher the disk to find out what had happened to the *Queen*. Removing his vest, Han began disencumbering himself of the shoulder holster. ''Next question: who's the opposition?''

''The mine operators. You know how the Tion works. Somebody pays someone in the Ministry of Industry and gets a permit. The mining outfit carves up the terrain any which way, grabs what it can, and gets out long before any inspectors or legal paperwork catch up with them. They usually get their financing from some crime boss.

''This outfit's run by twins. The woman's name is J'uoch and her brother's R'all. They have a partner, Egome Fass, their enforcer. He's a big, mean humanoid, a *Houk*, even taller than Chewie there. All three came up the hard way, and that's how they play.''

Han had buckled on his gunbelt and holster and transferred his blaster. ''So I saw. And all you want is for us to get you to Dellalt and get you off?''

Just then the intercom carried the Wookiee's news that someone was signaling for permission to board. ''That'll be

Skynx," Badure told him. Han passed word to admit the academician.

"If you'll get us to the vaults and off Dellalt again," Badure resumed, "I'll pay you twice your usual first-asking price, out of the treasure. But if you throw in with us, you and the Wook can split a full share of the take."

Hasti cried, "Half-share!" just as Han protested, "Full share each!" They glared at each other. "Wound up a little too tight are we, sweetheart?" Han asked. "How're you going to get there without us, flap your arms?" He heard Chewbacca's footsteps moving toward the main hatch.

Hasti's temper flared. "For one hop, you and that furball want a full cut?"

Badure held up his hands and bellowed, *"Enough!"* They quieted. "That's nicer, kiddies. We are discussing major cash here, plenty for everybody. The breakdown's this way: a full share for me because I got Hasti off Dellalt alive and Lanni passed what she knew along to both of us, equally. Two shares for Hasti, her own and poor Lanni's. And for you, Skynx, and the Wook, half-shares each at this point. Depending on who has to do what in the course of finding that treasure, we renegotiate. Agreed?"

Han studied Badure and the seething red-haired girl. "How much are we talking about?" he wanted to know.

The old man inclined his head. "Why not ask him?"

Badure indicated the individual who had come onboard and was following Chewbacca into the forward compartment. *Now why did I assume he'd be human?* Han wondered.

Skynx was a Ruurian, of average size—a little over a meter long—low to the ground, his natural coat a thick, woolly amber with bands of brown and red. He moved on eight pairs of short limbs with a graceful, rippling motion. Feathery, bobbing antennae curled back from his head. Skynx had big, multifaceted red eyes, a tiny mouth, and small nostrils. Behind him rolled a baggage-robo with several crates and boxes on its flatbed.

Skynx paused and reared up on his last four pairs of extremities. The digits on his limbs, four apiece, were mutually opposable, deft, and very versatile. He waved to the humans. "Ah, Badure," he called in a rapid, high-pitched voice, "and the lovely Hasti; how are you, young lady? This fine Wookiee I've already met. So you would be our captain, sir?"

"Would be? I *am*. Han Solo."

"Delighted! I am Skynx of Ruuria, Human History subdepartment, pre-Republic subdivision, whose chair I currently hold."

"What do you use it for?" Han asked, eying Skynx's strange anatomy. Seeing no reason to delay where cash was concerned, he inquired, "How much money are we after?"

Skynx poised his head in thought. "There's so much conflicting information about the *Queen of Ranroon*, it's best to say this: Xim the Despot's treasure vessel was the largest ship ever built in her day. Your guess, sir, is no less plausible than my own."

Han leaned back and thought about pleasure palaces, gambling planets, star yachts, and all the women of the galaxy who hadn't been fortunate enough to make his acquaintance. Yet. Chewbacca snorted and returned to the cockpit.

"Count us in," Han announced. "Tell the baggage clunker to leave your stuff right there, Skynx. Badure, Hasti, make yourselves at home."

Hasti and Skynx both wanted to watch the liftoff from the cockpit. When they were alone, Badure spoke more confidentially. "There's one thing I didn't want the others to hear, Han. I had my ear to the ground, heard about some of the crazy jobs you've pulled. Word's out that somebody's looking for you. Money's being spread around, but I haven't heard any names. Any idea who it might be?"

"Half the galaxy, it feels like sometimes." There had been many runs, many deals, jobs, and foul-ups. "How should *I* know?" But his expression hardened, and Badure thought Han had a very good idea who might be seeking him.

* * *

Han stood in the middle of the forward compartment, listening. The tech station and most of the other equipment in the compartment had been shut down to lower the noise level. He could feel the vibrations of the *Millennium Falcon*'s engines. He heard a quiet sound behind him.

Han spun, crouching, in execution of the speedraw, firing from the hip. The target-remote, a small globe that moved on squirts of repulsor power and puffs of forced air, didn't quite dodge his beam. Its counterfire passed over him. Deactivated by his harmless tracer beam, the orb hung immobile, awaiting another practice sequence.

Han looked over to where Bollux, the labor 'droid, sat; his chest panels were open. Blue Max, the computer module installed in the 'droid's chest cavity, had been controlling the remote. "I told you I wanted a tougher workout than that thing's idiot circuitry could give me," Han reprimanded Blue Max.

Bollux, a gleaming green, barrel-chested automaton, had arms long enough to suggest a simian. The computer, an outrageously expensive package built for maximum capacity, was painted a deep blue, whence came his name. Part of Han's post–Corporate Sector splurge had included the modification the two mechanicals had requested, because without them he and the Wookiee might never have survived. Bollux now contained a newer and more powerful receiver, and Max had been provided with a compact holo-projector.

"That *was*," the little module objected. "Can I help it if you're so flaming fast? I could cut response time to nil, if you want."

Han sighed. "No. And watch your language, Max; just because I talk like that doesn't mean you can." He took the combat charge his weapon usually carried from its case at his belt.

Badure was reclining in one of the acceleration chairs. "You've been practicing all through this run. You're beating the ballie every time. Who's got you worried?"

Han shrugged, then added as if by afterthought, "Did you ever hear of a gunman called Gallandro?"

Both of Badure's thick eyebrows rose. ''*The* Gallandro? You don't bother yourself with small-timers, do you, Slick? So that's it.''

Han looked around. Hasti, at her own and Badure's insistence, had commandeered Han's personal quarters—a cramped cubicle—for some secret purpose. Chewbacca was at the controls, but Skynx was present. Han decided it didn't matter if the Ruurian heard.

''I backed Gallandro down a while back, didn't even realize who he was. See, he had to let me do it at the time because it was part of a bigger deal he was working. Later on, though, he wanted to settle up.''

Sweat gathered on his forehead with the memory. ''He really *moves*; I couldn't even follow his practice draw. Anyway, I pulled a stunt on him and got out of the mess. I guess I made him look pretty bad, but I never thought he'd go to all this trouble.''

''Gallandro? Slick, you're talking about the guy who single-handedly hijacked the *Quamar Messenger* on her maiden run and took over that pirate's nest, Geedon V, all by himself. And he went to the gun against the Malorm family, drawing head bounty on all five of them. And no one has ever beaten the score he rolled up when he was flying a fighter with Marso's Demons. Besides which, he's the only man who ever forced the Assassins' Guild to default on a contract; he personally canceled half of their Elite Circle—one at a time—plus assorted journeymen and apprentices.''

''I know, I know,'' Han said wearily, sitting down, ''*now*. If I'd known who he was then, I'd have put a few parsecs between us, at least. But what does a character like that want with me?''

Badure spoke as to a slow-witted child. ''Han, don't make someone like Gallandro back down, then walk away making a fool of him. His kind live on their reputations. You know that as well as I do. They accept no insult and never, never back down. He'll make you his career until he settles with you.''

Han sighed. "It's a big galaxy; he can't spend the rest of his life looking for me." He wished he could believe that.

There was a sound behind him, and he threw himself sideways out of his chair, firing in midair, rolling to avoid the remote's sting-shot. His tracer beam hit the dodging globe dead center. "Good try, Max," he commented.

"You strike me as being very adept, Captain," Skynx said from the padded nook over the acceleration couch.

Han climbed to his feet. "You know all about master blastermen, don't you?" He appraised the academician. "Why'd you come on this run anyway? We could've brought the disk to you."

The little Ruurian seemed embarrassed. "Er, that is, as you probably know, my species' life cycle is—"

"Never saw a Ruurian until I met you," Han interjected. "Skynx, there're more life forms in this galaxy than anyone's bothered to count, you know that. Just listing the sentient ones is a life's work."

"Of course. To explain: we Ruurians go through three separate forms after leaving the egg. There is the larva, that which you see before you; the cycle of the chrysalis, in which we undergo changes while in pupa form; and the endlife stage, in which we become chroma-wing fliers and ensure the survival of our species. The pupae are rather helpless, you'll understand, and the chroma-wings are, um, preoccupied, caring only for flight, mating, and egg-laying."

"There better be no cocoons or eggs on this ship," Han warned darkly.

"He promises," Badure said impatiently. "Now will you listen?"

Skynx resumed. "All that leaves for us larval-stage Ruurians is to protect the pupae and ensure that the simple-minded chroma-wings don't get into trouble—and to run our planet. We are very busy, right from birth."

"What's that got to do with a nice larva like you raising ship for lost treasure?" Han asked.

"I studied the histories of your own scattered species, and

I came to be fascinated with this concept, *adventure*,'' Skynx confessed as if unburdening himself of some dark perversity. ''Of all the races who gamble their well-being on uncertain returns—and there aren't that many, statistically—the trait's most noticeable in humans, one of the most successful life forms.''

Skynx tried to frame his next words carefully. ''The stories, the legends, the songs, and holo-thrillers held such appeal. Once, before I spin my chrysalis, to sleep deeply and emerge a chroma-wing who will no longer be Skynx, I wish to cast aside good sense and try a human-style adventure.'' Saying the last, he sounded happy.

There was a silence. ''Play him the song you played for me, Skynx,'' Badure finally invited. In the upholstered nook he had occupied for most of the trip, Skynx had set up his species' version of a storage apparatus, a treelike framework used in lieu of boxes or bags. From its various branches hung Skynx's personal possessions and items he wished to have close to him. Each artifact was an enigma, but among them was apparently at least one musical instrument.

Han had heard enough nonhuman music to want to forgo listening. Though he might be passing up decent entertainment, he might also be avoiding sounds resembling somebody's unoiled groundcoach. He changed the subject hurriedly.

''Why don't you show us what's in the crates instead?'' Han looked around. ''Where's Hasti? She should be in on this.''

''We'll be making planetfall soon, and she has preparations to make,'' Badure said. ''Skynx, show him those remains; they should interest him.''

Skynx rose, shook out his amber coat to fluff it, and flowed smoothly out of his nook. Hoping that ''remains'' didn't refer to the sort of unappetizing objects he had seen in museums, Han stepped up to the crates with a power prybar. At Skynx's direction, he opened a container and whistled softly in astonishment. ''Badure, give me a hand getting this thing out of the crate, will you?'' Between them they strained and lifted out the object, setting it on the gameboard.

It was an automaton's head. More correctly, it was the cranial turret of some robot out of ancient history. Its optical lenses were darkened by long radiation exposure. It was armored like a dreadnought with a coarse, heavy gray alloy Han didn't recognize. The assorted insignia and tech markings engraved into its surface were still visible and readable. Han expected the speaker grille to spew a challenge.

''It's a war-robot. Xim the Despot built a brigade of them to serve as his absolutely faithful royal guard,'' Skynx explained. ''They were, at that time, the most formidable human-form fighting machines in the galaxy. This one's remains were recovered from the floating ruins of Xim's orbital fortress, possibly the only one that wasn't vaporized in the Third Battle of Vontor, Xim's final defeat. There are more pieces in those other crates. There were at least a thousand just like this one traveling onboard the *Queen of Ranroon* and guarding Xim's treasure when the ship vanished.''

Han opened another crate. It contained a huge chestplate; Han knew he would never be able to uncrate the thing without Chewbacca's help. In the plate's center was Xim's insignia, a death's head with sunbursts in the eye sockets.

Bollux entered, chest panels open wide to let Blue Max perceive things as well. These two machines had been combined by a group of outlaw techs and had been instrumental in Han's survival at an Authority prison called Stars' End several adventures ago. Bollux and Max had elected to join Han and Chewbacca, exchanging labor for passage, in order to see the galaxy.

''Captain, First Mate Chewbacca says we'll be reverting to normal space shortly,'' the 'droid announced. Then his red photoreceptors fell on the cranial turret, and Han could have sworn they abruptly became brighter. In a voice more hurried than his usual drawl, Bollux queried, ''Sir, what *is* that?'' He went over to examine the thing more closely. Max studied the relic as well.

"So very old," mused the 'droid. "What machine is this?"

"War-robot," Han told him, sifting through the other crates. "Great-grandpa Bollux, maybe." He didn't notice the 'droid's metallic fingers quizzically feeling the shape of the massive head.

Han was mumbling to himself. "Reinforced stress points; heavy-gauge armor, all points. Look how thick it is! You could run a machine shop off those power-delivery systems. Hmm, and built-in weapons, chemical and energy both."

He stopped rummaging and looked at Skynx. "These things must've been unstoppable. Even with a blaster, I wouldn't want to mix with one." He slid the lid back on the crate. "Find yourselves a place and get comfortable, everybody. We'll revert from hyperspace as soon as I get to the cockpit. Where's Hasti? I can't hold up the whole—"

His jaw dropped. Hasti—it had to be her—had just swept into the forward compartment. But the factory-world, mining-camp girl was gone. The red hair now fell in soft, fine waves. She wore a costume of rich iridescent fabrics in black and crimson; the hem of her ruffled, wrapfront gown brushed the deckplates, and over it she wore a long quilted coat with voluminous sleeves, its formal cowl flung back and its gilt waist sash left open. Her steps revealed supple, ornamentally stitched buskins.

She had applied makeup, too, but with such restraint that Han couldn't tell what or how. She was cooler, more poised, and seemed older than Han recalled. Her expression dared him to make a crack. One side of him was trying to tally how long it had been since he had seen anyone this attractive.

"Girl," breathed Badure, "for a second there I thought you were a ghost. It might've been Lanni, standing there."

An hour ago I'd have said she couldn't find romance in a prison camp with a jetpack on! I'm slipping, Han thought. Then he found his voice. "But why?"

While Hasti inspected Han distantly, Badure explained. "When Lanni diverted course on a freight run to store the log-recorder disk at the vaults, she changed into this local outfit Hasti's wearing so word wouldn't leak that a woman from the mining camp had been there. Fortunately she gave us the rental code and retrieval combination before she was killed by J'uoch's people. Hasti must look as much like poor Lanni as possible, in case any of the vault personnel happen to remember her sister."

Hasti motioned back toward Han's quarters. "Nice wallow you have there; it looks like the end of a six-day sweepstakes party."

His reply was cut short by an angry caterwauling from the cockpit. It was Chewbacca insisting that Han come up for the reversion to normal space. "I wonder if I wouldn't be asking too much to view the procedure from the cockpit?" Skynx said to Han.

"Sure; we'll find some place for you." Han met Hasti's aloof gaze. "How about you? Care to watch?"

She pursed her mouth indifferently. Skynx left off observing what was, as far as he could conclude, a variation of human preening/courting rituals and excitedly hurried toward the cockpit, followed by Badure. Han, weighing Hasti's expression, decided neither to offer his arm nor to touch her in any ushering-along gesture.

None of them noticed Bollux, who remained behind, contemplating the war-robot's head, his cold fingers resting on the imposing armored brow.

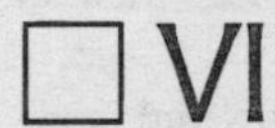

DELLALT had, in its heyday, been a prominent member of a strategic cluster during the pre-Republic phase known locally as the Expansionist Period. That importance had run its course. Altering trade routes, increased ships' cruising ranges, intense commercial competition, social dislocation, and the realigning power centers of the emergent Republic—all had long since converted the planet to a seldom taken side trip, isolated even from the rest of the Tion Hegemony.

Dellalt's surface boasted far more water than soil. The treasure vaults of Xim were located near a lake on the southernmost of the planet's three continents, a hook-shaped piece of land that crossed Dellalt's equator and extended almost to its southern pole. Around the vaults stood Dellalt's single large population concentration, a small city built by Xim's engineers. The travelers studied it during their approach.

Heavy weapons emplacements and defensive structures around the city were now gutted ruins filled with crumbling machinery. Broken monorail pylons and once grand buildings, falling back to dusk, were overgrown with thick dendroid vines. Recent construction was sparse, poorly planned, and done with crude materials. There was the wreckage of a sewage- and water-treatment plant, indicating just how far back Dellalt had slipped. Badure mentioned that the planet harbored a race of sauropteroids, large aquatic reptiles that lived in a rigidly codified truce with the human inhabitants.

Port officialdom was nonexistent; a bureaucracy would have been an unprofitable expense, something the Tion Hegemony avoided. Han and Badure, intending to attract attention, made a show of stretching and pacing as they came down the ramp to a landing area that was no more than a flat hilltop showing the scorches of former landings and liftoffs. Their breath crystallized in the cold air. Han had donned his own flight jacket. Glossy, cracked, and worn with age, it showed darker, unweathered spots where patches and insignia had been removed. He pulled his collar up against the wind.

Below them the decaying city spread out along slopes leading down to the long, narrow lake, part of Dellalt's intricate aquatic system. Han estimated from the condition of the landing area that it saw no more than three or four landings per Dellaltian year—probably just Tion patrol ships and the occasional marginal tramp trader. The planet's year was half again as long as a Standard one, with a shorter-than-Standard mean day. Gravity was slightly more than Standard, but since Han had adjusted the *Millennium Falcon*'s gravity during the flight, they scarcely noticed it now.

People came running up from the little city, laughing and making sounds of greeting. The women's attire was like Hasti's, with variations of color, layering, and cut. Male dress tended toward loose pantaloons, padded jackets, all manner of hats and turbans, and pleated, flowing cloaks and robes. Children copied their parents' appearance in miniature. All around these humans were packs of yipping, loping domestic animals, grainy-skinned quadrupeds with needle-like teeth and prehensile tails.

Han asked who owned the single building on the field, a decaying edifice of lockslab that might be used as warehouse or docking hangar. The owner appeared quickly, making his way through the mob with curses and insults that no one seemed to take personally. He was small but heavily built, and his scraggly whiskers failed to hide pockmarked cheeks and throat that had been ravaged by some local disease. His teeth were yellow-brown stumps. Crude or nonexistent medical care was too common on fringe worlds for Han to feel disgust anymore.

He inquired about the building. The language of Dellalt was Standard, distorted with a thick accent. The man insisted that rental terms were so minor a problem that there was no reason to waste Han's time, that the outloading of cargo could begin at once. The pilot knew that to be a lie, but confrontation was a part of Badure's plan.

Bollux appeared and began making trips between the starship and the building. At first the perplexed droid found himself surrounded by screaming, laughing children and snarling, snapping domestic quadrupeds. But the cousins of the building's landlord threatened, cursed, and slapped them away, then formed an escort to see to it that the labor 'droid could work in relative peace. Still, many eyes followed the gleaming Bollux; such automata were unknown here. The landlord's cousins opened one of the building's doors just wide enough for the 'droid to enter and leave. He began stacking crates, canisters, pressure kegs, and boxes inside.

The crowd milled around and under the *Millennium Falcon,* timidly touching her landing gear and gawking up at her in amazement, yammering among themselves. Then someone noticed the Wookiee, who sat looking down from the cockpit. Shouts and shrieks went up; hands were thrust at the Wookiee in gestures meant to repel evil. Chewbacca gazed down on all the activity impassively, and Han wondered if it had occurred to any in the crowd that his first mate was manning the freighter's weaponry.

A considerable pile of cargo containers had already accumulated in the building when, with his cousins stationed around its main doors, the landlord abandoned his effusive welcomes and named an enormous rental fee. Badure shook his scarred first under the landlord's nose, and Han shouted a threat. The landlord threw up his hands and besought his ancestors for justice, then insulted the offworlders' appearance and the circumstances of their birth. His cousins let the 'droid continue stacking cargo in his building, though.

* * *

Each time Bollux left the outbuilding, one of the cousins swung the door shut with a creak of primitive hinges. Waiting until she had heard that sound for the third time to be certain of the routine—and having timed the 'droid's purposely slow trips—Hasti pushed the lid off her shipping canister and stepped out, lifting her hem carefully and rubbing her cramped neck.

Anyone seen leaving the starship would have been trailed all over town by the crowds. That in turn would have made recovery of the log-recorder impossible. Badure's plan had circumvented all that.

The building had a small rear door. Everything was as Badure had predicted—on a backward world like Dellalt, the landlord could ill afford expensive locking systems on each door. Therefore, this rear door and the larger hanging door were secured from the inside, with only a smaller door set in the larger one equipped with a lockplate. Not that that mattered. Han Solo had given Hasti a vibrocutter in case she had needed to force her way out. But she needed merely to move the bolt and then emerged into the light behind the building, shouldering the door closed again.

Peering around the corner, she could isolate at least three different centers of furor. In one, Han Solo and Badure were squared off with the landlord, insulting one another's antecedents and personal hygiene in best Dellaltian haggling style; in another, people were pointing at and debating hotly over Chewbacca's origin; and finally, the landlord's cousins were battling the crowd so Bollux could keep filling the building with the containers they would later confiscate if the offworlders didn't meet the exorbitant rental fee. All the Dellaltians seemed quite happy with their unscheduled holiday.

At that juncture another distraction, also planned by Badure, occurred. Skynx ambled down the ramp, ostensibly to confer with Han and the old man. An astonished shout went up from the crowd, and most of the people tagging along after Bollux went at a run to see this new wonder.

Making sure her compact pistol was safe in an inner pocket, Hasti set off, keeping the building between herself and the field. She had draped the cowl over her head and went unnoticed. She had been in the city before, sent from the mining camp with Lanni to make minor purchases. Recalling the layout of the place, she set out for Xim's treasure vaults.

Pavement laid when the vaults were new had been chewed and disintegrated by use and time. The streets were rutted and hard-packed in the middle and muddy along the sides where slops had been dumped from overhanging windows. Hasti prudently kept along the middle way. Around her people ran, limped, or were carried toward the landing area. Two cadaverous oldsters, members of the local aristocracy, were carried past in an opulent sedan chair borne by six stooped bearers. A buckboard drawn by two skeletal, eight-legged dray beasts followed.

Three drunks lurched out of a drinking stall, arms around one another; they were waving ceramic tippling bowls in the air, sloshing liquor. They regarded her for a moment, then elbowed one another. Under the native code of ethics a woman was fairly safe, at least in town, but Hasti kept her eyes to the ground and her hand near her pistol. But the celebrants decided that the starship merited their attention first, or they would be excluded from an event the rest of the city would talk about all year.

Picking her way through a city that seemed to be falling apart before her eyes, Hasti as last came to the vaults of Xim the Despot. The vaults were contained within a sprawling, cameral complex of interlocking structures, immensely thick-walled and, in its day, impervious to forced entry. Still, thieves had gotten in over the years and, finding only empty vaults, yawning treasure chambers, and waiting bins and unoccupied shelves, had soon departed. Only the occasional wanderer or scholar of the obscure came here to tour Xim's barren edifice now. The galaxy was rich in sights and marvels worth the seeing and easier to reach; there was little of allure in the haunted emptiness here.

In the vaults' worn and pitted façade were engraved Xim's insignia of the starburst-eyed death's head and characters from an ancient language: IN ETERNAL HOMAGE TO XIM, WHOSE FIST SHALL ENCLOSE THE STARS AND WHOSE NAME SHALL OUTLIVE TIME.

Hasti paused for a glimpse of herself in the gleaming stump of a fallen column, hoping she resembled her sister sufficiently. She fumed at the memory of Han Solo's sudden change of attitude toward her—first fussing over the buckling of her seatbelt and then his reckless—but expert—planetfall, done to impress her. Either the oaf couldn't see how much she disliked him or, more likely, refused to accept it.

At the top of the steps she crossed the wide, roofless portico and passed through the vaults' single, gigantic entranceway. The interior was cool and dark. There was a vast circular chamber under a dome half a kilometer in diameter, a mere vestibule to the huge vault complex.

But this outermost chamber was the only part of the vaults in use anymore. Hasti's eyes adjusted to the light of weak glow-rods and tallow lanterns guttering smoke into the cavernous room designed to be lit by monumental illumi-panels. Farther in toward the center of the place was a small cluster of work tables, partitions, and cabinets—the administrative annex for the minor activity the vaults still housed.

A few Dellaltians, carrying data plaques, old-fashioned memo-wire spools, and even a few sheafs of paper computer-printout, passed by her. Hasti shook her head at the primitive operation. But, she remembered, the vaults had very few tenants. The Dellaltian Bank and Currency Exchange, a minor concern, was one, while the Landmark Preservation Office, charged with looking after the abandoned labyrinth with almost no resources, was that grouping of desks and partitions.

A man approached her from the semigloom—tall, broad-shouldered, his hair as white as his forked beard. He moved briskly; at his heels was an assistant, a smaller, grimmer man whose long black hair was parted down the middle and showed a white blaze.

The tall man's voice was hearty and charming. "I am steward of the vaults. How may I help you?"

Holding her chin high, Hasti answered in her best approximation of a local accent. "The lockboxes. I wish to recover my property."

The steward's hands circled one another, fingers gathered, in the Dellaltian sign of courtesy and invitation. "Of course; I shall assist you personally." He spoke to the other man, who departed.

Remembering to walk on his right, as a Dellaltian woman would, Hasti followed the steward. The vaults' corridors, musty with age, displayed mosaics of colored crystal so complicated that Hasti couldn't interpret them. Many of the pieces were cracked, and whole stretches were missing; they arched high overhead into shadow. Here, their footsteps resounded hollowly.

At last they came to a wall, not the end of the corridor but a partition of crudely cut stone that had plainly been mortared into place after the original construction. Set in the wall was a door that looked as if it had been scavenged from some later, less substantial building. Next to it was an audio pickup. The steward pointed to it.

"If the lady will speak into the voice-coder, we can proceed to the lockbox repository."

When Hasti's sister had told her and Badure about depositing the log-recorder disk she had told them the box-rental code and retrieval combination, but had mentioned no voice-coder. Hasti felt the pulse in her forehead and the thumping in her rib cage quicken.

The steward was waiting. Leaning to the audio pickup she said, as if in mystic invocation, "Lanni Troujow."

* * *

"My last offer," Badure threatened for the fourth time, resorting to hyperbole common on Dellalt, "is ten credits a day, guaranteed three-day minimum."

The landlord shrieked and tore hairs out of his beard, beat his chest with his free hand, and vowed to his ancestors that he would join them before letting plundering offworlders steal the food from his children's mouths. Skynx took it all in, amazed by the carefully measured affrontery of the hagglers.

Han listened with one ear, worried that Hasti might not have been able to get away from the landing area undetected. There was a tug at his shoulder; it was Bollux. "I noticed this altercation, sir. Shall I continue to outload our cargo?"

That meant Hasti was away. Badure heard and understood. "Get everything back onboard until this son of contaminated genes, this landlord, bargains reasonably."

"Unthinkable!" screamed the landlord. "You have already made use of my precious building and diverted me from my other pursuits. A settlement must be made; I hereby hold your cargo against the arrival of the Fact-Finders." He and Badure swapped deadly oaths.

The landlord called the old man a horrible name. Skynx, quivering in excitement, immersed himself in the spirit of the thing, antennae trembling. "Devourer of eggs!"

Everyone stopped, glancing at the diminutive Ruurian, who swallowed, appalled at his rash outburst. The landlord departed, along with much of the crowd, hurling back epithets and leaving his cousins to guard the outbuilding. From somewhere, the cousins had produced bolt-operated slug rifles with hexagonal barrels and long, lens-type scopes.

Back onboard the *Falcon*, Badure threw himself into a chair. "That landlord! What a freighter bum he'd have made!"

Han grabbed Bollux. "What happened?"

"The men guarding the building entrance kept looking through the door after me as I deposited the cargo. It was some time before they became bored and gave all their attention over to Badure's performance and Skynx's appearance. Hasti was no longer in her crate, and the inner door was unbarred. At Blue Max's suggestion I resecured the door."

"Tell Maxie he's a good boy," Badure said. "I like you two; you've got a touch of larceny in you."

Bollux's chest plastron swung open, the halves coming apart like cabinet doors. Blue Max's photoreceptor lit up. "Thanks, Badure," he said, sounding smug. Han told himself. *I should keep an eye on that computer or he'll end up wearing juvie-gang colors and packing a vibro-shiv.*

Just at that moment, Skynx appeared with Chewbacca, who had just left the cockpit. The Wookiee was holding the metallic flask of vacuum-distilled jet juice the partners kept under the control console for special occasions. "Skynx," Badure said, "I think it's time to strike up the band."

Skynx flowed to the acceleration couch and on up into his nook. He began taking objects from his treelike storage rack. "If you have no further tasks for us, sir," Bollux told Han, "Max and I would like to continue our study of Skynx's tapes."

"Whatever you want, old-timer."

Bollux crossed to the tech station, where he and the computer resumed their perusal of the ancient records Skynx had brought along. The labor 'droid, who had worked his way across the galaxy and had already outlived one body, possessed an almost sentient streak of curiosity, and Blue Max was always ready to absorb new information. The two mechanicals were particularly interested in technical data and other references to the giant war-robots of long-dead Xim.

Skynx, sitting up on his rearmost two sets of limbs, took and held a miniature amplified hammer dulcimer in the next set and two hammers in each digital cluster of the next. He strapped a pair of tympanic pulsers around himself, tapping experimentally with the digits of his next-higher limbs. Above those he fastened a pair of small bellows to pump air to a horn held in his uppermost-but-one set of extremities. In the uppermost he took up a flute of sorts and tried a few runs. The sound was like the wind cones Han remembered from his own homeworld. He wondered what kind of brain could coordinate all that activity.

Skynx launched into a merry air, full of sudden runs, bright interplay and humorous progressions, and impudent catches made to sound as if the instruments or Skynx's limbs were getting out of hand and taking their own course. The Ruurian made a great pretense of distress and bewilderment and a desperate effort to bring his extremities under control again. The others laughed, particularly Chewbacca, whose Wookiee chortles made the bulkheads ring. Badure rapped time on the gameboard and even Han was tapping a toe or two. He opened the flask, took a swig, and passed it to the Wookiee. "Here, this'll put some curl in your pelt." Chewbacca drank, then sent the flask along. Even Skynx accepted a drink.

They demanded another number after that, and a third. Badure eventually jumped up, both hands over his head, to demonstrate the Bynarrian jig. He capered around the compartment as if he were twenty kilos lighter and as many years younger.

At the height of the Bynarrian jig the ship's hatch signaled. Badure and Chewbacca rushed off, eager to see what Hasti had brought back. Bollux and Blue Max looked up from the strobing rapid-readout screen, and Skynx began extricating himself from his instruments.

"Step one completed!" he said in his quick fashion. "Skynx, of the K'zagg Colony, off on a treasure hunt! If my clutch-siblings could see me now!"

But when the Wookiee reentered the compartment, he slumped dejectedly over to his partner and sank into the couch, head in hairy hands. *Bad as that?* thought Han. Badure followed, one arm clasped around a despairing Hasti. She took a sip from the flask, coughed, told her story quickly, then took another.

"Voice-coder?" Han exclaimed. "Nobody said anything about a voice-coder."

"Maybe Lanni never realized her voice was being printed," Badure replied.

"That steward," Hasti muttered. "I should've jabbed my gun into his bellybutton and offered to glaze his gallstones for him."

Han handed the half-empty flask to his copilot and rose. "Now we do it *my* way." He headed for the cockpit, pulling on his flying gloves. Chewbacca fell in behind. "Want to know how to make a withdrawal? Stick around."

Badure hurriedly interposed himself between the two partners and the main passageway. "Steady there, boys. Just what've you got in mind?"

Han grinned. "Swooping down on the vault, blowing the doors with the belly-turret guns, going in, and taking the disk. Don't bother getting up, folks; it'll all be over in a minute."

Badure shook his head. "What if a Tion patrol cruiser shows up? Or an Imperial ship? Would you care to have a hunter-killer team on your neck?"

Han made a move to step around him. "I'll chance it."

Hasti jumped up. "Well, I won't! Sit *down,* Solo! At least consider the options before you risk the death penalty for all of us."

Chewbacca awaited his friend's decision. Bollux watched impartially and Blue Max with a certain excitement.

"Some forethought might not be out of place here," Skynx contributed in a very subdued voice.

Han disliked complications and subterfuge, but his hasty action was stayed, for the moment, by the conviction that being dead was the least interesting thing in life. "All right, all right; who's hungry?" he asked. "I'm sick of ship's rations. Let's go see what kind of meal we can get in town. But if nobody thinks of a new one, my plan still goes." He clipped the flask to his gunbelt while Chewbacca gathered up his bowcaster and bandoleer of ammunition. Badure found the small purse of local currency he had brought, and Bollux shut his plastron halves on Blue Max.

Hasti saw Skynx shedding his instruments. "Hey, I never got to hear anything."

Badure looked around. "Bring them along," he bade Skynx. The Ruurian began tucking his instruments into carrying cinches he fastened around himself.

Pulling on his flight jacket, Han shut and sealed the hatch behind them. Storm clouds had moved in, and electrical discharges illuminated the clouds in strange flashes of red. Badure pointed out that the landlord's cousins had disappeared. "They probably figured out they were guarding empty boxes."

"More likely they didn't want to sit around in that leaky barn," Hasti reasoned. The rest of the onlookers who had been watching the starship from a distance, mostly children and the domestic yappers, were gone as well.

They set off downslope with Bollux bringing up the rear. Up this high, away from the docks, the streets were poorly maintained and lighting was unknown. They didn't get far.

Han was first to sense something wrong—everything was too quiet, too many ramshackle windows were shuttered. No lights were showing and no voices could be heard anywhere nearby. He grabbed Chewbacca's shoulder, and the bowcaster came up, the blaster appearing at the same time. By instinct, they stood back to back. Hasti had her mouth open to ask what was wrong when the spotlights hit them.

Han recognized them as hand-held spots and, figuring that a right-handed man would be holding the spot as far out with his left as he could, took an estimated aim.

"Don't!" a voice ordered. "We'll cut you all down if anyone fires a shot!"

They were surrounded. Han holstered his side arm, and the Wookiee lowered his bowcaster. Humans and various other beings appeared in the glare waving rifles, riot guns, slug-shooters, and other weapons. Han and his companions were easily disarmed and their equipment examined. Skynx chittered in terror while their captors pawed his delicate musical instruments, but he was allowed to retain them.

Three individuals strode forward to search the captives. The smaller two were mainbreed human—twins, a young man and woman who shared traits of thick, straight brown hair and widow's peaks, startling black-irised eyes, and thin, intense, pale faces. The third personage hung back, a looming hulk in the light backwash of the spots. Han remembered the name Badure had mentioned: Egome Fass, the enforcer.

The twins approached them, the female in the lead. "J'uoch," murmured Hasti, shivering.

The twins' faces held the same rigid, lethal composure. "That's it," J'uoch replied quickly. "Where's the disk, Hasti? We know you went to the vaults." She gave Han a chilly smile. Then the smile vanished and she turned again to Hasti. "Give it up, or we burn down your friends, starting with the pilot here."

Chewbacca's great arms tensed, fingers curling. He prepared to die as he would be expected to, head of a Wookiee Honor Family, his life so intimately intertwined with that of Han Solo that there existed no human word for the relationship.

Han, in turn, was choosing among several tactics, all of them suicidal, when Bollux spoke. "Captain Solo mustn't come to harm. I will open the *Millennium Falcon* for you."

The woman eyed him. It hadn't occurred to J'uoch that the 'droid would be cleared for ship access. "Very well. All we want is the log-recorder disk." Han, in the grip of adrenal overload, stared at Bollux and wondered what was going through the old labor 'droid's logic stacks. One fact did not escape him: he had heard high-pitched communication bursts exchanged between Bollux and Blue Max.

Their captors herded them back toward the *Falcon*. Too late, Han understood why the Dellaltians had scattered. He just hoped the two machines had a workable plan.

Bollux, climbing the ramp, was at the main hatch lock with several of J'uoch's people near. Strangely, just as the main hatch rolled up into its recess, the 'droid chose to swing his chest panels open. Then Han and the others heard Blue Max's high-speed burst signals.

An ear-splitting hiss of a hurtling object echoed through

the air. One of the men who was guarding Bollux was lifted off his feet by terrific impact, and in the next moment was stretched headlong on the ramp. Another captor, farther down the ramp, was slammed in the shoulder and knocked through the air.

''Run for it!'' Blue Max shrilled. As suddenly as that, chaos broke loose.

VII

THE two strongarm specimens still standing at the top of the ramp ducked instinctively. Something small and fast swooshed past Han, knocking the humanoid who had been guarding him off his feet. Bollux pivoted to follow the action.

From the now-exposed Blue Max more high-pitched beeps issued forth. Han realized with some amazement that the computer module had managed to summon the remote target-globe from the *Falcon*'s interior and was using it as a weapon.

Before J'uoch's people could react, Han yelled, *"Hit 'em!"* He grabbed the nearest opponent's weapon, a slug-shooter carbine with a drum magazine and, twisting his leg behind the other's, toppled him over.

Badure rammed his elbows back into the face of his guard and turned to grapple with him. Chewbacca was less fortunate. Preparing to enter the fray, he was unaware that the massive Egome Fass had stolen up behind him. The enforcer's hard fist crashed into the base of the Wookiee's skull.

Chewbacca staggered, nearly falling to his knees, but his tremendous strength bore him up again. He turned groggily to give battle, but Egome Fass's first blow had given the enforcer a formidable edge. He avoided Chewbacca's slowed counterpunch and landed another blow, bringing his fist down on the Wookiee's shoulder. And this time the *Falcon*'s first mate went down.

Badure was having a difficult time with his second guard, who was young and fast. They struggled, feet shuffling in the dry dust, but just as the older man was gaining the upper hand by dint of weight and reach, he was tackled low around the knees and went down.

The tackler was Hasti. She had seen that J'uoch's men on the ramp were about to open fire on Badure. Propelled by its repulsor power and forced air, the remote globe had taken two antagonists out of the fight. J'uoch was shooting at it with Hasti's confiscated pistol, missing, and screaming orders that her troops ignored.

Han had retrieved the carbine, knocking his opponent away with a stroke of the weapon's butt. He spotted his partner struggling to rise as Egome Fass hovered over him. The enforcer's hood was thrown back, and in the light spilling down through the hatch, Han saw the humanoid's huge, square jaw and tiny, gleaming eyes set far back under thick, bony ridges of brow.

Han clamped the carbine stock to his hips and squeezed off a burst. The weapon stuttered with a deafening staccato and reeked of burned propellant. A stream of slugs plucked at the enforcer's chest but only ripped away fragments of cloth. Egome Fass was wearing body armor under his outsized coveralls. Before Han could adjust for effect, the humanoid lunged for cover.

A wash of white fire flared on Han's right. Turning, he saw that it was a power-pistol shot aimed at Badure by a man on the ramp who missed because Hasti had just tackled the old man. But it hit the man with whom Badure had been struggling. He shrieked once and died as he fell.

Han grabbed Chewbacca's elbow as the Wookiee struggled to his feet, shaking his head to clear it. Retaking the *Falcon* was impossible; the two remaining guards at the ramp head were kneeling in the shelter of the hatchway and firing into the night. "Get back!" Han hollered to his companions. He moved back, firing in brief bursts, followed by Hasti and Badure with Skynx scuttling rapidly behind.

The spotty return fire, hasty and poorly aimed, never came close. But one guard, a leather-skinned creature with a horny carapace, blocked Bollux's retreat. Blue Max beeped, and immediately the remote flashed out of the darkness, striking the creature from behind and knocking it over. Since the remote couldn't operate at any great distance from the starship, Max gave the signal that sent it jetting back onboard.

The labor 'droid hurried after the others, bounding in long strides made possible by heavy-duty suspension. The group ran, bounded, and scuttled to the edge of the landing area. All the while Han raked the field behind them to keep J'uoch's people pinned down. Then the carbine went silent.

"Drum's empty," he said. Off in the night he could hear J'uoch railing at her followers and calling for a comlink.

"She's posting a guard on the ship and calling for reinforcements," Badure announced. "We'd best lose ourselves in town for a while."

The group descended through the city in an informal race, past shuttered shops and locked doors. No lights could be seen; the Dellaltians who had seemed so curious earlier wanted no part of this lethal dispute among offworlders. Leading the others, Han plunged into an alley, followed it to a market plaza, and hurried down a trellised side street that smelled of strange foods and fuels.

They came to a factory district. Pausing in the shadows, the humans and the Wookiee leaned against a wall and fought for breath while Bollux waited impassively and Skynx, with a superior respiratory system, checked his carrier cinches to make sure that none of his precious instruments had been damaged.

"You should've snagged a gun," Han puffed, "instead of worrying about that one-man band of yours."

"These have been making music in my family for a dozen generations," Skynx replied indignantly. "And I'm sure I don't know how I could've wrested a weapon away from some malodorous ruffian four times my size."

Han gave up the argument and checked the nearby rooftops. "Can anybody spot a ladder or staircase? We have to see if they're trailing us."

"Now I can be of help there, I believe," Skynx announced. A nearby pole supported fiber-optic cables for in-town communications; wrapping himself around it, Skynx spiraled up the pole, protecting his instruments carefully. Since all the buildings were one-story affairs, he had a good view of the surrounding area.

Having reconnoitered, Skynx corkscrewed his way down the pole again. "There are search parties working their way down through town," he told them. "They have hand-held spotlights; I assume them to be using comlinks." He tried to hide his fearful quaking.

"Did you see their ship?" Han asked eagerly. "It must be around here somewhere. Perhaps we could pick up some fire power there."

But Skynx hadn't spotted it. They decided to try to skirt the search parties' pattern and see if they couldn't get back to the *Millennium Falcon*. Skynx's feathery antennae wavered in the air, attentive to vibrations. "Captain, I hear something."

They all held their breath and listened. A rumbling swelled until it shook the ground. "Looks like J'uoch got through on the comlink," observed Badure over the tumult. An enormous vessel mounted with heavy guns was hovering above the landing area, its floodlights playing over the city. The fugitives pressed backs into the shadows.

The ponderous lighter couldn't hover and search for long; instead she descended. "There'll be more manpower onboard her," Badure warned. "Skynx, shinny up and take a look. Be careful."

The Ruurian went up a nearby line-pole and was down again almost at once. "The big ship must have dropped off parties down in the lakeside area," he told them urgently. "I saw them spreading out, coming up the hill. And there's a group of three coming down this way from above. One of them is carrying Chewbacca's bowcaster."

The Wookiee growled ominously. Han agreed, "Let's take care of them, but *good*." No one mentioned surrender; it was plain J'uoch would do anything to get what she wanted.

The search party flashed hand-held spots into alleys and doorways. Teams were being organized to scour the rooftops; virtually every trustworthy being who could be spared from the mining camp had been armed and brought to the scene.

The man leading this particular party, the man whose carbine Han had appropriated, carried Chewbacca's bowcaster and had tucked Han's blaster into his belt. He had seen a Wookiee bowcaster used in the holo-thrillers and was determined to get even with the two by downing them with their own weapons. He was delighted, therefore, to see a looming, shaggy shape step out of the darkness before him.

Blocking his companions in the process, the man with the bowcaster took a stance and fired. But Chewbacca ducked at the last instant, knowing that the man's unfamiliarity with the feel and aiming characteristics of the bowcaster would cause a first-round miss. In a flash the Wookiee hurled himself forward.

The man gave the bowcaster's foregrip a yank to recock it and strip another round off the magazine for a second shot. But he got nowhere; the weapon's mechanism was set for a Wookiee's brawn and length of arm. Before he could cast it aside and pull out Han's blaster, a mountain of angry brown fur descended upon him.

The other two searchers fanned out to either side. One was felled immediately as Han Solo stepped out of the shadows and knocked him out with a swipe of the carbine's butt. The other was stunned by masonry brickbats flung by Hasti and Badure.

Han adroitly snatched his victim's pistol and fired at the brickbat-stunned searcher. Yelling, the man clenched his calf and fell. Meanwhile Chewbacca had separated his man from the bowcaster and thrown him against a wall. The man crashed with an impressive thud and slid to the ground.

"You'll live," Han decided, toeing over the man he had shot and waving his recaptured blaster, "*if* you make some worthwhile conversation. How many guards on my ship?"

The man licked his fear-parched lips. "Ten, maybe twelve. A few actually onboard, the rest around her."

"What about the ship you came in?" Hasti asked their captive. "The first one, not that big lighter."

Han slightly depressed the blaster trigger.

The man gasped. "Backslope of town, below the landing area, in the rocks."

Badure came up, having collected the comlink dropped by the bowcaster thief. "Sonny boy, you just bought yourself a future." Then he told them that J'uoch's spaceboat was grounded on an expanse of flat stone, with only two men guarding her. "I've grown to dislike unnecessary killing," Badure explained, setting an appropriated stun-gun for maximum dispersal. He squeezed the trigger, and blue rings of energy leaped outward. Immediately the two guards collapsed. Badure and Hasti patted them down for whatever weapons or equipment they might have, then Han climbed into the boat and moved to the pilot's seat. "Fueled and ready!"

Chewbacca, examining the copilot's side of the board, *woofed* a question.

"No. We won't leave Dellalt without the *Falcon*; we couldn't get out of the system with this baby carriage anyway," Han replied. "We'll jump out of their search locus, then work out our next move." He began throwing switches and punching instructions into the flight computer.

A warning sounded and the board lit up. Chewbacca threw his head back and yeowled his frustration. From the console rang J'uoch's voice: "Attention, landing boat, attention! Why are you attempting to violate instrument lock? Guard detail, answer!"

"I need tools; they've got the board locked down," Han said urgently. Chewbacca dug long fingers around the edges of the utility locker's door and ripped it away. Han was busy unfastening the console's housing latches. The Wookiee grabbed some implements from the locker and handed them to Han, and soon the partners were attacking the lockdown mechanism, ignoring J'uoch's vehement transmissions that crackled in the background.

Chewbacca howled in triumph, neutralizing one security circuit. "Got the other," Han crowed. But their elation disappeared as they heard the thunder of mass-lift thrusters.

"She's coming after us in the lighter!" Hasti yelled from the hatchway. "How soon can we lift off?"

"She's too close with those heavy cannons," Han rasped. "But at least we'll have a diversion. Get clear!"

The others ran for it. There was a chart readout on the console; Han slipped it into his vest and, with one foot out the hatch, inserted a series of instructions into the console. Automatic sequence cycled the hatch shut, and the boat lifted off.

Han hurdled a rock and crouched in its shelter with the others, and they watched the spaceboat rise into the night sky. The lighter was already on a close interception course; it seemed to Han a good time to get as far as possible from the liftoff site. Having distracted those on the lighter, the fugitives moved off in a ragged line. Chewbacca kept rearguard and, wielding a clump of dry red shrubbery, eradicated the few prints they'd left on the rocky terrain.

The spaceboat picked up speed, following Han's programming. The lighter's heavy artillery spoke, and tremendous spears of green-white energy made a brief noon in the Dellaltian night. The first salvo missed but gave the gunners their registration. The second hit dead center, several beams converging on the small boat at once. It exploded in a fireball, leaving a few scraps of burning wreckage to flutter from the sky.

"Capturing us wasn't such a big priority after all," Badure observed.

They had barely reached the temporary shelter of a rocky outcropping and hidden themselves among the boulders when the lighter returned with a rumble of brute thrusters and settled in where the boat had lifted. In moments the area was swarming with armed searchers sweeping hand-held spots.

The stunned guards were quickly discovered, the ground examined.

"They're buying it!" Hasti whispered with muted elation. The searchers noted the prints left by Han and the others when they had approached the boat but missed any sign of departure, thanks to Chewbacca's painstaking work. The dozing guards were lugged aboard the lighter and the rest of J'uoch's employees embarked. Thrusters flared again.

Han's mind was racing. Now that they were armed and J'uoch apparently believed them dead, they had a chance of retaking the *Millennium Falcon*. Han expected to see the lighter land next to his own ship, to take away the guards onboard. Instead, the larger vessel hovered above the freighter. The *Falcon*'s ramp was up, her ramp-bay doors closed. Han suddenly understood what was happening.

He threw himself forward at a flat-out run, bellowing at the top of his lungs, with Chewbacca only a step behind. No one on either ship heard them, of course; the lighter, its hoisting gear making loud contact with the freighter's upper hull and achieving tractor-lock on the smaller ship, lowered her mechanical support booms. In the same manner as she transported mining equipment, the lighter lifted off with the *Millennium Falcon* tucked up tightly to her underside.

The lighter veered south, gathering speed and altitude as she went. Han slowed to a stop. In despair he and Chewbacca watched their ship being borne away across the lake and over the mountains beyond. The others caught up.

"They think the log-recorder disk is onboard, isn't that it, Captain?" Skynx asked, somewhat in shock. "They searched us and didn't find it and tried to kill us, so they must assume we left it onboard the *Falcon*."

"Where are they headed?" Han asked tonelessly.

"Straight for the mining camp," Badure answered. "They'll have all the time and privacy they need to tear—to search her thoroughly."

Han pivoted on his heel and walked off toward town. A drizzle was starting.

"Where are you going? Where are *we* going?" Skynx yelped as the others hurried after.

"I want my ship back," said Han simply.

☐ VIII

"IT'S a lamebrained scheme, even for you," Hasti was saying. Han peered into the grayness and wished Badure would return.

The drizzle had become a freezing-cold downpour during the night, then slackened to a drizzle again. Han and the others, awaiting the old man, had taken shelter under a tarp behind piles of cargo in a broad-eaved wooden warehouse by the docks. They were sipping sparingly from the flask, which had remained clipped to Han's gunbelt throughout the night's action.

They were damp, bedraggled, and miserable. Han's hair was plastered flat against his skull, as was Hasti's. Drops fell from Skynx's matted wool, and Chewbacca's pelt had started exuding the peculiar odor of a wet Wookiee. Han reached out and patted his friend's head in a gesture of consolation, wishing there were something he could do for Bollux and Max. The two automata, abiding patiently, were worried that their moisture-proofing would fail.

"You haven't got a prayer of pulling this off, Solo," the girl finished.

He swiped a damp strand of hair off his forehead. "Then don't come along. There'll be another ship through here any year now."

A man in a shabby cloak appeared, splashing through the puddles, bearing a bundle on his shoulder. Han, his blaster's scope set for night shooting, identified Badure. The old man crouched with them under the tarp. Having acquired a cloak from an alley-sleeper, he had contrived to buy four more. Han and Hasti found that two fit them passably well and even Bollux could don one stiffly, unaccustomed as he was to the extraordinary feel of clothing. But the biggest cloak Badure had brought could barely contain Chewbacca; though its hood managed to cover his face from casual observation, his shaggy arms and legs stuck out.

"Maybe we could wrap him in bunting, like mittens and leggings," Badure suggested, then turned to Skynx. "I didn't forget you, my dear Professor." With a flourish he produced a shoulder bag, which he held open invitingly.

Skynx shrank back, antennae wobbling in dismay. "Surely you can't mean. . . . This is unacceptable!"

"Just until we're out of town," Han coaxed.

"Um, about that, son," Badure said, "maybe we should lie low awhile instead."

"Do what you feel like; this could be a bad hike. But they're probably tearing the *Falcon* apart at that mining camp."

"Then what's the point in going?" Hasti remonstrated. "It's a couple of hundred kilometers. Your ship'll be in pieces."

"Then I'll put her back together again!" he near-hollered, then calmed. "Besides, how did J'uoch and company show up so fast, unless she's got contacts here? We'd be sitting targets, not even to mention the average citizen's dislike of offworlders. We could end up bunking in the local slams."

Badure looked resigned. "Then it's the Heel-and-Toe Express for us."

The rain was letting up, the sky lightening. Han studied the chart readout he had picked up. It turned out to contain a complete survey map of the planet, dated but in exacting detail. "At least we had the good luck to get this."

Hasti sniffed. "You spacers and mariners and aviators are all alike: no religion, but plenty of superstition. Always ready to invoke luck."

To forestall another verbal skirmish, Badure jumped in.

"The first thing is to get across the lake; there are no connections south on this side. No air service anywhere, but there's some ground transport over there somewhere. The only way across is a ferry service run by the natives, the Swimmers. They're jealous of their territory and they charge a fee."

Han wasn't sure he wanted to be transported by one of the sauropteroids, the Swimming People of Dellalt. "We could hike around the lake," he proposed.

"It would take us five or six extra days unless we could negotiate a vehicle or get our hands on some riding animals."

"Let's check the ferry. What about food and equipment?"

Badure looked askance. "What about lovely ladies and hot food? There'll be settlements along the way; we'll have to improvise." He blew his breath out, and it crystallized.

"Are you coming or staying?" Han asked Hasti.

She gave him a scalding glare. "Why bother asking? You'll lean on people until there's no choice left."

The moderately safe and comfortable adventure envisioned by Skynx had become a very real struggle for survival, but this Ruurian practicality made his decision simple. "I believe I'll remain with you, Captain," he said. Han almost laughed, but Skynx's simple tone of pragmatism and self-preservation lifted his opinion of the Ruurian a notch.

"Glad to have you. All right; down to the docks and across the lake."

Skynx crawled unwillingly into the bag, which Chewbacca then shouldered. They proceeded in a tight group, with Badure in the lead and Hasti and Han on the flanks. The Wookiee and Bollux kept to the middle of the group in hopes that in the poor light and rain they would be mistaken for humans, one extremely tall, the other barrel-chested.

Skynx poked his head out of the bag, feathery antennae thrashing. "Captain, it swells awful in here, and it's cramped." Han pushed him back down, then as an afterthought gave him the flask.

The docks and their moored embarkation floats were already busy. Leaving the others in the partial concealment of stacks of cargo, Han and Badure went to inquire about passage.

Though the docks had space for many of the tow-rafts used by Dellalt's native sauropteroids, only the middle area seemed busy. Then, scanning the scene, Han saw one lonely raft off to the right. Though Badure had briefly described the Swimmers, Han still found them a startling sight.

Men were loading cargo aboard the tow-rafts, which were tied at the embarkation floats. Tow-lines and harnesses bobbed as the rafts waited in the water. Beyond them lazed twenty or so sauropteroids, circling or treading water with flipper strokes of immense power. They ranged from ten to fifteen meters in length, their heads held high from the water on long muscular necks as they moved in the lake. Their hides varied from a light gray to a deep green-black; lacking nostrils, they had blowholes at the tops of their long skulls. They idled, waiting for the men ashore to complete the manual labor.

One of the men, a burly individual with a jeweled ring in one ear and bits of food and droplets of breakfast nectar in his beard, was checking cargo against a manifest. As Badure explained their needs, he listened, playing with his stylus.

"You will have to talk money with the Top Bull," he informed them with a smirk Han didn't like, then called out: "Ho, Kasarax! Two seeking passage here!" He returned to his work as if the two men no longer existed.

Han and Badure went to the dock's edge and stepped onto an embarkation float. A sauropteroid approached with a few beats of his flippers. Han surreptitiously moved his hand closer to his concealed blaster. He was ill at ease at seeing Kasarax's size and his hard, narrow head with its fangs longer than a man's forearm.

Kasarax trod water next to the float. When he spoke, the blast of sound and fishy breath made both men fall back a bit. His pronunciation was distorted but intelligible. "Passage is forty *driit*," the creature announced, a hefty sum in Dellaltian currency, "*each*. And don't bother haggling; we don't fancy that down here at the docks." Kasarax blew a spout of condensing moisture out the blowhole in his head to punctuate the statement.

"What about the others?" Han murmured to Badure, indicating the rest of the sauropteroid pack.

But Kasarax caught Han's query and hissed like a pressure valve. "They do as I say! And I say you cross for forty *driit*!" He feinted, as if he were going to strike, a snakish movement that rocked the float with turbulence. Han and Badure scrambled onto the dock as the men there guffawed.

The man with the manifest approached. "I'm chief of Kasarax's shore gang; you may pay me."

Han, red in the face, was growing more furious by the moment at this high-handed treatment. But Badure, glancing toward the lone raft they had noticed earlier, asked, "What about him?"

A lone Swimmer was down there, a big, battle-torn old bull, watching events silently. The shore-gang chief forgot his laughter. "If you enjoy living, ignore him. Only Kasarax's pack plies this part of the lake!"

Still fuming, Han strode down the dock. Badure followed after a moment's indecision. The shore-gang chief called, "I give you fair warning, strangers!"

The old bull reared up a bit as they approached. He was the size of Kasarax, his hide a near-black, net-worked with scars. His left eye was gone, lost in a long-ago battle, and his flippers were notched and bitten. But when he opened his mouth his tremendous fangs gleamed like honed weapons. "You're new faces to the docks," he said in a whistling voice.

"We want to get across the lake," Han began. "But we can't meet Kasarax's price."

"Once, human, I'd have towed you across as quickly as you please and carefully, too, for eight *driit* each." Han was about to accept when the creature cut him off. "But today I tow for free."

"Why?" Ham and Badure asked together.

The bull made a burbling sound that they took to be a laugh, and shot a blast from his blowhole. "I, Shazeen, have vowed to show Kasarax that any of the Swimming People are free to work this dock, like any other. But I need passengers, and Kasarax's shore gang keeps those away."

The shore gang was gathered in conference, grouped in a knot of perhaps twenty, and shooting murderous looks at Han, Badure, and Shazeen. "Can you meet us somewhere farther down the shore?" Han asked the native Dellaltian.

Shazeen reared, water streaming from his black back, looking like some primitive's war god. "Boarding here at the dock is the whole point! Do that and I will do the rest, nor will any of the Swimming People meddle with you; it's Shazeen they must deal with, that is our Law, which not even Kasarax dares ignore!"

Badure pulled thoughtfully at his lower lip. "We might go around the lake."

Han shook his head. "In how many days?" He turned to Shazeen. "There are a couple more passengers. We'll be right back."

"If they menace you on the docks, I cannot interfere," Shazeen warned. "That is the Law. But they won't dare use weapons unless you do for fear the other humans, the ones who've been driven from their jobs, will have cause to intercede."

Badure clapped Han's shoulder. "I could stand a little cruise right now, Slick." Han gave him a wicked grin; they started back.

The others were standing where they had been left. Hasti held a large cone of plasform that contained a mass of lumpy, pasty dough, which she and Chewbacca were eating with their fingers. She offered some to Badure and Han. "We were starving; I picked this up from a vendor. What's the plan?"

Badure explained as they shared the doughy stuff. It was thick and gluey but had a pleasing flavor, like nutmeat. "So," finished Han, "no shooting unless we have to. How's Skynx?"

The Wookiee chortled and held open the shoulder bag. The Ruurian lay in a near-circle, clutching the flask. When he saw Han, his faceted red eyes, which were somewhat glazed, grew wider. Skynx hiccupped, then chirped, "You old pirate! Where've you been?" He flicked an antenna across Han's nose, then collapsed in chittering laughter.

"Oh, great," said Han, "he's tight as a scalp tick." Han tried to recapture the flask, but Skynx curled into a ball and was gripping it with four limb-sets.

"He said he's never metabolized that much ethanol before," said Hasti, looking slightly amused. "That's exactly how he said it."

"Keep it then," Han told Skynx. "But stay down; we're going for a ride."

Skynx's muffled voice came from the shoulder bag, "Perfect idea!"

They made their way back to the dock. Men from Kasarax's shore gang blocked their way to the embarkation float. Others, not of the gang, had appeared and leaned against walls or stacked cargo, carrying spring-guns, firearms, and makeshift weapons. Han remembered what Shazeen had said: these people had been forced out of a living by Kasarax's racket. None had been willing to risk riding with Shazeen, but they would see to it no weapons were used to keep Han's party from doing so. The rest of the shore gang was scattered around the docks, holding weapons of their own. As Han understood it, any shooting would trigger a general bloodbath, but anything short of that was allowable.

When Han was within a few paces, the shore-gang chief addressed him. "That's close enough." Several of his men were whispering among themselves, seeing the size of the cloaked and hooded Chewbacca.

Han moved closer, giving out a string of bland cordialities.

He had the impression that the man was a good brawler and thought: Victory first; questions later! The chief reached to shove him back, with a warning. "I'm not telling you again, stranger!"

How right, agreed Han silently. He speeddrew, blindingly fast, and placed his gun against the chief's head. The man was shoving and warning one instant, falling the next, with a look of surprise on his face. Han had time to backhand another man and give the shore-gang chief a stiff shove, such was the surprise he had generated. Then he had to duck a truncheon, and the scene erupted.

One young shore-gang member swung an eager one-two combination at Bollux, a short set-up jab and a long uppercut that would have done considerable damage to a human. But the youth's fist gonged off the 'droid's hard midsection and rebounded from his reinforced faceplate. As the boy cried out in agony, Hasti stepped around Bollux and brought the barrel of her gun down on his head.

Another shore-gangster reached for Han, who was otherwise occupied. So Badure stopped him with a forearm block and lashed out with his foot, kicking high and hard. His antagonist dropped. They had done well enough for the moment, but now the rest of the shoregangsters pressed in vengefully.

Then Chewbacca joined the brawl.

The Wookiee had stepped back to shuck the shoulder bag and put Skynx out of danger and to lay down his bowcaster. His hood still pulled low, he selected two men, shook them hard, then hurled them up and back in either direction. A swing of one long arm brushed another man back off the dock; Chewbacca kicked out in the opposite direction, connecting with a man who had lunged at Hasti. The man flew sideways, tumbled twice, and stretched out full length on the dock.

Two men tackled the Wookiee from either side. He ignored them, his legs as sturdy as columns beneath him. He struck out all around him, felling opponents with each blow.

The fight raged around Chewbacca, a flock of flailing, desperate shore-gangsters swarming at him. Spoiling for a fight since he had been downed by Egome Fass's treacherous attack, the Wookiee obliged them. Bodies flew back, up, over. The *Millennium Falcon*'s first mate restrained himself to spare needless bloodshed. His companions found themselves left out of the riot with only occasional assistance to be rendered in the form of a tap on the head, a shove, or a shouted warning.

Chewbacca found time to give each of his legs a shake, and the men straining at them were flung loose. Those who remained standing made a concerted charge. The Wookiee spread his arms, scooped up all three of them, and dashed them against the dock. One of them, the gang chief, who had recovered from Han's blow and reentered the fight, pulled a punch-dagger from a forearm sheath.

Han angled for a clear shot then, whatever the consequences. But Chewbacca caught the chief's movement. The Wookiee's head snapped around, his hood falling back for the first time, and he unleashed a full-throated roar into the shore-gang chief's face, drawing his lips back off his jutting fangs. The chief turned absolutely white, eyes bulging, and managed to produce the smallest of squeaks. His punch-dagger fell from limp fingers. The snarling Wookiee, having attended to all the others, set the man down and put one forefinger against his chest. The chief fell backward to the deck, trying to draw breath.

Hasti grabbed Chewbacca's bowcaster and her dropped cone of dough; Badure held the sack containing Skynx, from which emerged chitters of hilarity. Han grabbed his partner's arm. "Gangplank's going up!"

They dashed for the embarkation float, hopping one by one to the tow-raft. Shazeen, who had watched the whole encounter, loosed a blast from his blowhole. Closing a nictitating membrane over his eye, he ducked beneath the water to reemerge with his head through the tow harness, commanding, "Cast off!" Badure, last in line, brought the raft's painter with him.

They had expected Shazeen to move off quickly, but the Swimmer warped the raft out slowly. When he had put a few dozen meters between the raft and the dock, he slipped the tow harness by submerging, then resurfaced to nudge it to a stop with his rocklike snout. "That was some fine thumping!" he hailed. Throwing his head back, he issued an oscillating call that rolled across the water. "Shazeen salutes you," he clarified.

"Uh, thanks," Han replied dubiously. "What's the holdup?"

"We wait for Kasarax," Shazeen answered serenely.

Han's outburst was forestalled when another sauropteroid surfaced next to Shazeen, whistling and hissing with mouth and blowhole. "Use their language, woman," Shazeen chided the newcomer, who was smaller and lighter of hide but nearly as battle-scarred as the big bull. "These are Shazeen's friends. That pipsqueak there with the hairy face can really *thump*, can't he?"

The female switched to Standard. "Will you really oppose Kasarax?"

"No one tells Shazeen where he may or may not swim," replied the other creature.

"Then the rest of us are behind you!" she answered. "We'll keep Kasarax's followers out of it." The lake water swirled as it closed over her head.

"Drop anchor!" shouted Han. "Cut the power! Cancel the reservations! You never said anything about a faceoff."

"A race, a mere formality," assured Shazeen. "Kasarax must pretend now that it's a right-of-way dispute, to conform with the Law."

"*If* he can get passengers," Hasti broke in. "Look!"

Kasarax was having trouble getting any of his shore gang aboard his tow-raft. The clash at the dock had put doubt in them; now they were having second thoughts about being dragged into the middle of a Swimmer dispute. Their chief, too, hesitated.

Kasarax lost his temper and thrashed himself up over his tow-raft, half onto the dock. Men drew back from the enormous bulk and the steaming, gaping mouth. Kasarax bent down at the chief.

"You'll do as I say! There's nowhere you can hide from me, even in that shelter you built under your house. If you make me, I'll dig you out like a stoneshell from the lake bottom. And the whole time, *you'll hear me coming*!"

The shore-gang chief's nerve broke. White-faced, he scurried aboard the tow-raft, pulling along several unwilling followers and browbeating several others to accompany him.

"Mighty persuasive lad, that nephew of mine," reflected Shazeen.

"Nephew?" Hasti burst out.

"That's right. For years and years I whipped every challenger who came along, but I finally got tired of being Top Bull. I drifted north, where it's warm and the fish are fat and tasty. Kasarax has been running wild too long; partly my fault. I think shore folks put this takeover nonsense into his head, though."

"Another victory for progress," Badure murmured. Kasarax was nudging his tow-raft up even with Shazeen's.

"Anyway, don't worry," Shazeen told them. "The Swimming People won't attack you, so don't use your weapons on them, or you'll turn it into a death-matter. That's the Law."

"What about the other humans?" Han called, but too late; Shazeen had gone to confront Kasarax. The shore-gang members had brought along their harpoon spring-guns and a variety of dockside cutlery.

The two bulls churned the water, trumpeting to one another. At length Shazeen switched to human speech. "Stay clear of my course!"

"And you from mine!" Kasarax retorted. They both plunged for their tow-rafts, flippers beating with full force, diving for their harnesses and creating rolling swells. They reemerged with heads through harnesses and snapped the towing hawsers taut. The hawsers creaked with the strain, wringing the water from them. Water gushed up from the rafts' blunt bows, breaking in spray and foam. Everyone on both rafts fell to the deck, snatching frantically for a handhold.

Kasarax and Shazeen breasted the water neck and neck, shrilling challenges to one another. Han began to wonder whether a hike around the lake wouldn't have been a better idea after all. *Why do I always think of these things too late?*

TOWING hawsers thrummed like bowstrings. The rafts moved forward with surges matching the Swimmers' rhythms.

Han clasped the low deck rail. The water teemed with sauropteroids, both Kasarax's cronies and Shazeen's supporters, who had been kept from work by Kasarax's alliance with the shore gang.

Long, scaled necks cut the water; rolling backs and broad flippers showed with each dive, and the spray of swimming and blasting blowholes made it seem the rain had resumed.

"Chewie!" shouted Hasti, who was hugging a rail stanchion, "the bag!"

The shoulder bag containing Skynx was sliding aft. Badure rolled from a stern-rail corner and caught it, wrapping his legs around a stanchion. Skynx popped out of the bag, his big red eyes more glazed now than before.

Taking in their situation unsteadily, the Ruurian scuttled up halfway onto Badure's head, his antennae bending in the breeze, clinging resolutely with every digit he could spare, and hurled the empty jet-juice flask into the air, cheering, "*Weee-ee heee-ee!* I bet five *driit* on us!" Spying Kasarax's raft, he added shrewdly, "And five more on them!" He sank back down into the bag, which Badure closed over him.

The rough ride didn't trouble Han nearly as much as the fact that this was no ordinary race. The two bulls were straining, neither able to gain headway against the other. Kasarax made a bid for the lead, then another, but Shazeen matched his spurts and held the pace. Han could hear their booming grunts of effort over the rush of the wind and the slapping of water against the rafts.

Kasarax changed tactics, slackening his line. Shazeen followed suit. The younger creature changed course in an instant, cutting across Shazeen's path just behind his elder. He ducked under Shazeen's towing hawsers and pulled hard. His tow-raft came slashing after, hawsers brushing at angles under Shazeen's.

Han saw the shore-gang chief hoist a broad-bladed axe; Kasarax's men obviously intended to sever Shazeen's hawsers when the hawsers came up against Kasarax's raft's bow rail. The pilot drew without thinking; a blaster bolt flickered red across the water, and the axehead jolted, sparks arcing from it, a black-edged hole burned through it. The shore-gang chief dropped it with a cry as his men ducked.

Someone else grabbed the axe and swung it as both rafts and the Swimmers towing them were dragged and slewed around by each other's momentum. Han's aim was spoiled and the axehead descended. Perhaps it was an off-world product with an enhanced edge; in any case the axe parted a hawser with one blow and bit into the bow rail. Shazeen's raft swung, coming nearly side-on, with the unbalanced pull of the remaining hawser.

The chief had the axe back, ready to chop the other hawser. Han was aiming carefully at the axe when Shazeen changed course in an effort to see what had happened. The remaining towing hawser dragged across Kasarax's raft's rail, catching the shore-gang chief and pulling him overboard. At the same moment Shazeen's maneuver bumped his own raft into a trough. Han lost his footing, slipped, and fell, whereupon the blaster flew from his hand.

The chief was still clinging to Shazeen's remaining tow-hawser, lower body in the water, sawing at it with a knife. Han couldn't spot his blaster, but was determined not to let that second line be severed. The gang chief was working at the hawser, Hasti was shouting something about not starting a firefight, and Badure and Chewbacca were yelling something he didn't want to take time to listen to, being in no mood for a debate. Losing patience, he threw off his flight jacket, stepped over the bow rail, sprang, and began drawing himself down the hawser, hand over hand, his legs wrapped around it, the higher swells wetting his back.

The shore-gang chief felt the vibrations in the hawser, saw Han, and sawed more furiously at the tough fiber. The chief took a moment to slash at the pilot. Han suddenly realized how impetuous he had been, as if another man entirely had occupied his body for a moment. He didn't quite avoid the stroke and the knifepoint cut across his chin. The water pulled at them both.

But Han avoided the back-slash with dexterity gained in zero-gee acrobatics drills. He lashed out flat-handed in a disarming blow, and the knife plunked into the water. As the knife fell, the shore-gang chief began to lose his grip on the hawser. He grabbed at Han, and both men plunged into the water. The lakewater was agonizingly cold and had a peculiar taste.

Han dove as deeply as he could, his clothes dragging at him. Underwater he heard the thud of the raft's bow striking the chief's head. Cheeks puffed, the pilot glanced up through the icy, dark water as the raft passed over him, and then surfaced just behind it. He grabbed for the stern rail, missed, and was himself grabbed.

Chewbacca pulled his partner over the stern rail in one motion just as the raft began drifting to a halt. Shaking wet hair out of his eyes, Han gave an involuntary cry of surprise, seeing why they had stopped. Kasarax's maneuver had been Shazeen's needed provocation for combat under Swimmer Law. Both the monstrous bulls had ducked out of their tow-harnesses; now they met in resolute battle.

They charged into collision, a butting of great heads whose report sounded like the crack of a tree trunk, and an impact of muscular necks and broad chests that sent waves racing outward. Neither seemed hurt as they circled for position, flippers whipping the water into foam. The shore-gang boss was paddling toward his raft, eager to be out of the behemoths' way.

Han felt Bollux's hard finger tap his shoulder. "You'll no doubt be wanting this, sir. I caught it before it could go overboard, but you didn't seem to hear me call you." He passed over Han's blaster.

Without taking his eyes from the battle, Han promised, "I'm doubling your salary," ignoring the fact that he had never paid the 'droid a thing.

Kasarax wailed; he had been too slow on the withdrawal after nipping Shazeen. The older bull hadn't gotten a full grip with his fangs, and Kasarax had gotten away, but now blood flowed down his neck scales. Kasarax, wild with rage, charged again.

Shazeen met him head-on, each of them trying to butt and bite, to press the other under the surface, shrieking and trumpeting. Shazeen failed to repel a determined assault by Kasarax and slid back as the younger creature surged up over him seeking a death grip on his uncle's throat. But he had been too eager. Shazeen had drawn him out and now the older bull dropped his pretext and dove, rolling. His blunt tail slammed Kasarax's skull, and the younger combatant fell back in pain. They resumed butting heads, biting, thrashing flippers, and colliding with one another.

"Hang on!" warned Hasti, the only one who had thought to watch for other danger. The raft shuddered and timbers splintered as the bow was tipped into the air.

It was one of Kasarax's followers, a very young bull from the looks of him. He had closed crushing jaws on the raft's stern, shaking it, spouting wrathful blasts from his blowhole. He tore a meter-wide bite out of the raft, spat the wood aside, then came at them again. Han set his blaster to maximum power.

"Don't kill him!" Hasti shouted. "You'll have them all down on us!"

As the sauropteroid butted the raft, nearly capsizing it,

Han bellowed. "What do you want me to do, sweetheart, bite him back?"

"Leave it to them," she answered, pointing. She meant the other Swimmers, who were closing in. Kasarax's over-eager follower had ignited a general fray. One—Han thought it was the female who had surfaced at the dock and offered support to Shazeen—kicked up an impressive bow-wave, making straight for the raft. But once again the creature closed jaws on the raft's stern.

The trick's to keep on breathing till help arrives, Han told himself. He spied the cone of gooey dough Hasti had brought, still more than half-full. He reached for it, calling, "Chewie! Lock hands!"

Han got to unsteady feet. The Wookiee reached out his long arm and caught Han's free hand, steadying him. The young bull had seen him coming and opened its maw, but when he pulled up short it closed its jaws with a crash and blew a geyser of spray through its blowhole.

When he saw the edges of the blowhole vibrate with the indrawing of breath, Han jammed the cone of dough down on it as hard as he could. It landed on the sucking blowhole with a peculiar *shloop*!

The Swimmer froze, its eyes bulging. Into what air passages and chambers the dough had been drawn, Han couldn't begin to guess. The creature shook, then exploded in a sneeze that convulsed him, kicking up a fountain of water and nearly blowing Han off the raft with the fish-scented gust.

At that moment Shazeen's friend arrived. She hit the younger creature and they battled furiously. All around, pairs of the creatures rolled, ducked, bit, and butted in pitched combat. Scaled hides took tremendous punishment and the sound threatened to deafen the humans; the turbulence promised to capsize the raft.

Han kept his attention riveted on Shazeen and Kasarax, thinking, *If that old bull loses, it'll be a wet stroll home. And the fish are biting today!*

Both bulls were torn and injured, chunks missing from

each one's hide and flippers. The older one moved slowly, worn down by his nephew's youthful endurance. They rammed together for another fierce exchange. Surprisingly, Kasarax went under.

Shazeen sought to follow up his advantage but failed to keep track of his antagonist and circled aimlessly. The air was so full of pealing battle cries that Shazeen took no notice of his passengers' warnings. Kasarax had slyly and quietly surfaced behind his uncle and to his left, in the blind spot resulting from his missing eye. The younger Swimmer lunged with jaws gaping for a lethal grip at the base of his uncle's skull.

But Shazeen moved with abrupt speed, coming around and bringing his head up sharply, tagging Kasarax's chin with the boniest part of his foreskull. The crack echoed from the opposite lakeshore. Dazed by the terrible blow, Kasarax barely had time to wobble before Shazeen had his throat tightly between black jaws.

"That old con artist!" Badure whooped. Chewbacca and Hasti hugged, and Han leaned on the rail, laughing. Shazeen was shaking his nephew's head, mercilessly, side to side and forward and back, but refraining from the death bite.

At last Kasarax, head bent back at a painful angle, no fight left in him, began a pitiful croaking. All around him, combat ceased at the sounds of ritualistic surrender. When all the others had separated, Kasarax was released and allowed to tread water meekly while his uncle stormed at him in the sibilant language of their kind.

With a final, piercing rebuke, Shazeen sent his nephew off with a hard butt of his head. Kasarax submitted, then stroked slowly away to haul his tow-raft back the way he had come. His followers trailed him in disarray, convoyed by Shazeen's victorious supporters.

Shazeen moved to his own raft, feeling the pain he hadn't allowed himself to show his enemies. Bleeding from fearsome wounds, his scarred, one-eyed head battered and torn, he asked, "Now then, where were we?"

"*I* was in the drink," Han reminded him. "*You* were hauling the raft around to take out the shore-gang boss. Got him right in the bulb, too. Thanks."

The old bull made a gurgling sound resembling a chuckle. "An accident, peewee; didn't I tell you it's un-Lawful to meddle in a human squabble?" He gurgled again, bringing his wide chest against the raft's stern and shoving toward the opposite shore.

"What about your nephew?" Hasti wanted to know.

"Oh, he's through trying to make the lake his own pond. Fool idea would have gotten him killed sooner or later anyway, and he's too valuable to waste. I'll need a deputy soon; haven't got many more scraps like that one left in me. These youngsters always think they're clever, going for my blind side."

"I still wouldn't trust him," Han warned.

"You don't trust *anybody*," Hasti chided.

"And you don't see me getting my flipper bit, do you?" he retorted smugly.

"Oh, Kasarax will be all right," Shazeen said. "He just thought he wanted us to fear him. He'll like it better once we respect him; all but the worst ones come around, given the chance."

The far shore had come up quickly. Shazeen propelled them toward it with a few more hard strokes, then flipped over and shoved them on with a sweep of his rear flippers. The raft nosed onto the strand, lifted on the crest. Han stepped onto the damp sand.

The others followed him. Badure had a rather sick Skynx slung over one shoulder. The female who had saved Shazeen's passengers surfaced next to him, obviously concerned.

But her eye fell on Hasti, whose cowl had fallen back to display her red hair. "You had a rougher ride this time, human," the Swimmer observed.

Hasti registered confusion. "Wasn't that you," the Swimmer female asked, "back before Kasarax took over? Sorry;

the hair and, what do you call them, the clothes, are just the same.''

Hasti whispered, ''Lanni! These are her clothes!''

Badure asked the female what this passenger had done.

''Just came across and asked people questions about those mountains there, waved a little machine in the air, then went back,'' she replied.

Han, pouring water from his boot, looked up at the mountains rearing to the south. ''What's up there?''

''Nothing,'' answered Shazeen. ''Humans don't usually go up there. Fewer come back. They say it's just desolation up there.'' He was studying Chewbacca, who had doffed the hated cloak, Bollux's gleaming form, and the now-reviving Skynx.

''I'd heard that,'' agreed Badure. ''The mining camp lies on the far side of the mountains, Han, but I'd reckoned we'd go around. Why should Lanni have been interested in them, I wonder?''

Han stood up. ''Let's find out.''

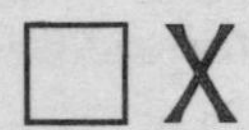

X

THE terrain lifted away from the lakeshore in a series of rolling hills carpeted with soft, blue moss that cushioned their steps. Han was gratified to see the moss spring back when they had passed, thereby obliterating the group's prints.

Supplies were no problem. The workers on this side of the lake, all members of Kasarax's shore gang, had departed in haste on seeing their leader defeated, fearing the blood-vengeance of the non-gang members. Calculating a ten- to twelve-day march through the mountains, the party had carefully picked through the abandoned storage buildings for provisions and equipment.

They had filled their packs with jars of lake crustaceans marinated in syrup, plastic cartons of the doughy stuff Hasti had first sampled, tubes of pickled vegetable slices, bags of meal, smoked fish, cured meat, and some hard purple sausages. Even though they carried capacious water bladders, they were relying on finding more water in the mountains. According to the survey map, there were abundant run-offs and fresh springwater throughout the area. Those who wore clothing had gathered cold weather gear. Han had pulled off his wet clothes, settling for a Dellaltian outfit until he could dry his own, and contrived a bandage for the knife cut. Practicality had made Hasti exchange her robes and gown for an outfit suitable for an adolescent boy. They had also found thick, insulated bedrolls.

There were no riding animals or power vehicles to be found. But Han didn't mind, trusting unfamiliar beasts no more than he did the aged and breakdown-prone Dellaltian machinery. Bollux, who could bear a heavy pack and yet consumed no water or food, found that his popularity had increased. They felt lucky to have him along, knowing none of the local domesticated animals or ground vehicles were suited to the mountain terrain and aircraft were few and far between on Dellalt. They had found some lengths of rope, but no other climbing gear. Neither had they found medicine or a medi-pack, additional weapons or charges, commo or navigational gear, heating unit, or macrobinoculars or tele-eye, though the scope on Han's blaster would be some compensation for the last. For shelter, they had brought along a wagoner's tent they found in one of the abandoned buildings.

And they were armed. In addition to Han's side arm and Chewbacca's bowcaster, they also had the weapons captured from J'uoch's forces. Badure carried the stun-gun he had already used and a brace of long-barreled power pistols. Hasti had a compact disrupter, a dart-shooter loaded with toxic missiles, and a blaster, but the latter was nearly exhausted because Han had used it to recharge his own. Skynx declined to bear arms, which his species never used, and Bollux's basic programming, the 'droid said, prohibited him from using them as well.

Ascending the foothills, they kept the ridge lines between themselves and the region behind, though Han doubted anyone was taking time to try to spot them. The collapse of Kasarax's racket was probably occupying everyone's attention. Gusting winds tore across the open hills, pressing at the resilient moss and stirring the travelers' hair, clothing, and fur. The country was stark and vacant. Lacking a second comlink, they decided not to put out a point-walker, but rather to rely on the wide field of surveillance they could maintain.

Chewbacca took the lead, treading the blue moss lightly for all his size, testing the air with black nostrils flaring. His blue eyes moved constantly, his hunter's senses keenly attuned. A dozen paces behind trudged Bollux. The labor 'droid had opened his chest plastron a crack at the computer's demand, and Max was taking in the view.

Next came Badure and Hasti side by side. Skynx followed after, carrying only his musical instruments because none of the packs fit him and he couldn't have borne much weight anyway. Undulating along, he kept pace without difficulty.

Han brought up the rear, frequently casting glances behind, making minute adjustments in the balance and shoulder-strap padding of the makeshift pack he had thrown together. He lined up prominent terrain features and did his best to keep track of their direction and course, since that was the only way they would have of orienting themselves to the surveying map. From time to time he thought about the treasure, but the open countryside and the brisk wind made him happier than he would have admitted. In a way, they reminded him of the freedom of space travel.

The group moved on throughout the morning with deliberate speed, Han stopping frequently to scan his blaster's scope for some sign of pursuit. But as Dellalt's blue-white primary climbed the sky and none appeared, they slowed a bit, saving strength for the long journey.

Skynx dropped back to talk to Han. The Ruurian had a rapid metabolism and so had recovered from his bout with the flask. Han, who had been walking backward for a few paces while he checked the rear, pivoted around in step. It occurred to him that Skynx must be thoroughly disillusioned with human-style adventuring.

"Hey, Skynx, break out that hip-pocket orchestra of yours. We're out in the open anyway, like a bug on a canopy. A little music won't make things any chancier."

The Ruurian complied eagerly. Using his lowermost four sets of limbs for locomotion without decreasing speed, he took up the tympanic pulsers, bellows-horn, and flute. He began a human-tempo marching tune, one for marching overland rather than for a parade.

The small pulsers held a catchy beat, the bellows-horn

tootled, and the flute skirled. Han resisted the quickened pace, but enjoyed the music.

Badure squared his shoulders and fell into energetic stride, sucking in his overhanging stomach and humming with the music. Hasti smiled at Skynx and strode along more quickly.

Chewbacca tried to stay in step, although Wookiees don't generally take to regimentation. The process was awkward for him. He achieved a kind of animated swagger, though not even remotely in time. Bollux, however, fell right into step, mechanical legs pumping precisely, arms swinging, chin held high.

They trod blue moss; cold wind made the landscape seem barren and free. In this manner they proceeded over the hill.

They were well up into the heights when the blue-white sun set. The few lights of the city came on, far below and behind them. Outcroppings of rock had begun to appear, rising from the blue moss. They camped at one of these ledges, under an overhang that would afford some protection from wind. There was no fuel for a fire.

As they settled in, Han established priorities. "I'm going to check the area with the scope. Chewie will take first watch, after he eats. Badure, you take second and I'll take third. Skynx can have the wake-up duty. Is that all right with everybody?"

Badure didn't mention Han's assumption of leadership, being content with the arrangement. "What about me?" Hasti asked evenly.

"You can have first watch tomorrow, so don't feel left out. Would it be straining our bonds of affection to ask to borrow your wrist chrono?"

Teeth clenched, she threw it at him, then he and Chewbacca set off. "You're welcome!" she called after him. "Who does he think he is, anyway?" she said to the others.

Badure answered mildly. "Slick? He's used to taking charge; he wasn't always a smuggler and a freighter bum. Didn't you notice the red piping on the seams of his shipboard trousers? They don't give away the Corellian Bloodstripe for perfect attendance."

She considered that for a moment. "Well, how did he get it? And why do you call him Slick?"

"You'll have to get that first part from him, but the nickname business goes back to the first time I met him, way back."

In spite of herself, she was curious. Skynx was also listening with interest, as were Bollux and Blue Max. The two automata decided to hear Badure out before shutting down for the night; their photoreceptors glowed in the dusk.

It was becoming colder fast, and the humans pulled their cloaks tighter, Badure closing his flight jacket. Skynx curled his woolly form to conserve body heat.

"I'd been a line officer, had a few decorations myself," Badure began, "but there was the matter of a floating Jubilee Wheel I was running onboard the flagship. Anyway, they reassigned me to the staff at an academy.

"The commandant was a desk pilot, off his gyros. His bright idea was to take a training ship, an old U-33 orbital loadlifter, and rig her so the flight instructor could cause malfunctions: *realistic stress situations*.

" 'Enough can go wrong without building more into a ship,' I said, but the commandant had pull. His program was approved. I was flight instructor, and the commandant came along on the first training mission. He gave the briefing himself, playing up the wise old veteran act.

"In the middle of it a cadet interrupted. 'Excuse me, sir, but the U-33's primary thrust sequence is four-stage, not three.' The kid was gangly, all elbows and ears, and had this big chow-eating grin.

"The commandant was cold as permafrost. 'Since Cadet Solo is such a slick student, he will be first in the hotseat.' We all boarded and took off. Han handled everything the C.O. threw at him, and that grin grew bigger and bigger. He really had put in a lot of time on that kind of ship.

"That crate had checked out one hundred percent, but

something went wrong and something blew; a second later we had all we could do to keep her in the air. I couldn't get the landing gear to extend, so I raised ground control and asked for emergency tractor retrieval.

"And the tractors failed, primaries and secondaries both, on the approach run. I just managed to get us up again. The commandant was white around the eyes by then; the crash wagons and firefighting machinery were deploying onto the field.

"Which was when Cadet Solo announced, 'The reservoir-locking valve on the landing gear's stuck shut, sir; these U-33's do it all the time.'

"And I said, 'Well, do you feel like crawling down into the gear bay and taking a wrench to it right this second?'

" 'No need,' the kid says, 'We can joggle it with a couple of maneuvers.'

"The commandant's teeth were rattling. 'You can't take a bulk vessel through aerobatics!' Then I said, 'You hope to sit in your mess kit. *I* can't, sir, because I don't know which maneuvers Slick over there is talking about. He'll have to do it.' While his mouth was hanging open, I reminded him he was ranking officer. 'Either you land this beast or let the kid try out his idea.'

"He shut up, but about that time there was a rumpus in the passenger compartment. The other cadets were becoming nervous. So Han opened the intercom. 'By order of the commandant, this is a full-dress emergency-landing *drill*. All procedures will be observed; you are being graded on your performance.'

"I told him he was playing fast and loose with what might be somebody's last moments, and he told me to go ahead and tell them the truth if I wanted a panic in the hold. I let it ride. Han took control back.

"The U-33 isn't designed for the things Han did to that bird. He took her through three inverted outside loops to free up the locking claws. Our vision began to go. How Han coaxed lift from those inverted wings, I'll never know: but he was smirking, hanging there from his harness.

"He went into barrel rolls to build centrifugal force in the reservoir. I thought he was going to rip the wings off and I almost took control back, but just then I got a board light. He had forced the valve open.

"But gravity could've swung it shut again, so he had to fly upside-down while the landing gear cranked out. The ship had begun losing altitude and the commandant was sort of frothing at the mouth, babbling for Han to pull out. Han refused. 'Wait for it, wait for it,' he said. Then we heard this long grinding sound as the landing gear seated, and a clang as it locked.

"Han snap-rolled, hit full reverse thrusters, and hung out all the hardware. We uprooted two stop-nets and only lived because we landed into the wind. Jouncer landing, I tell you.

"They had to help the commandant off the ship. Then they deactivated that ship for good. Han locked down his board, just like the rule book says. 'Slick enough for you?' he asked. I said 'Slick.' That's how the nickname started."

It was fully dark now. The stars were luminous overhead, and both of Dellalt's moons were in the sky. "Badure, if it happened today," Hasti asked quietly, "would you tell those cadets they might die?"

He sounded tired. "Yes. Even though they might've panicked. They had a right to know."

The logical next question, then, was, "Well, what're *our* chances, the truth? Can we get the *Falcon* back, or even survive an attempt?" Skynx, and the automata, too, hung on his reply.

Badure remained silent. Through his mind passed the options: lying, telling the truth, or simply rolling over and going to sleep. But when he opened his mouth to answer, he was interrupted.

"Depends on what we run up against," Han Solo said from the darkness, having returned so quietly that they hadn't heard him. "If camp security's loose, we could get away without losses. If it's tight, we have to tackle them somehow, maybe draw them out. Anyway, it means risk. We'd probably have casualties and some of us might not make it."

"*Some?* Admit it, Solo; you're so concerned with getting that ship of yours back that you're ignoring facts. J'uoch's got more hired killers than—"

"J'uoch's got portside brawlers and some small-time muscle," Han corrected Hasti. "If they were quality, they wouldn't be working for a two-credit outfit like hers. Handing some clod a gun doesn't make him a gunman."

He stepped closer and she could see his silhouette against the stars. "They have the numbers, but the only real gunman within light-years is standing right in front of you."

The craft was trim, sleek, luxuriously customized, a scoutship off the military inventory. Her approach and landing were exacting, and she set down precisely where the *Millennium Falcon* had landed several days earlier. Her lone occupant emerged.

The man was limber, graceful, though his movements were at times abrupt. Although he was tall and lean, his form seemed compact. His clothes were expensive and impeccable, of the finest materials, but somber—gray trousers and a high-collared white shirt with a short gray jacket over it. A long white scarf, knotted at his throat, fell in soft folds, and his black shoes shone. He wore his graying hair cropped short, but his mustachios were long, their ends gathered and weighted with two tiny golden beads, giving him a subtly roguish look.

Townspeople appeared and clustered around him, just as they had greeted the *Falcon*'s passengers. But something in this stranger's blue, unblinking eyes, something penetrating and without mercy, made them wary. He soon obtained from them the story of the *Falcon*'s arrival and removal by the mining-camp ship. They showed him the spot where the spaceboat had been destroyed by the lighter. Even scavengers had avoided the bits of wreckage, fearing radiation residues.

The stranger told the townspeople to disperse, and seeing the look in his eyes, they obeyed. He carefully removed his jacket and hung it inside his ship. Around his waist an intricately tooled black gunbelt held a blaster high on his right hip.

He brought certain sensitive instruments from his ship, some on a carrying harness, others attached to a long probe, and still others set in a very sophisticated remote-globe. Loosening his scarf, he made a patient examination of the area, working in a careful pattern.

An hour later he returned the equipment to his ship and rubbed the dust from his gleaming shoes with a rag. He was satisfied that no one had died when J'uoch's spaceboat had been destroyed. He reknotted his scarf while he considered the situation.

Eventually, Gallandro drew on his jacket and locked up his ship, then made his way into the city. He soon heard rumors of bizarre goings-on down at the lake and battles among the natives. He couldn't verify much about the outside humans involved, though; the only close-range witnesses, the shore gang of the sauropteroid Kasarax, had gone into hiding. Still, he was willing to credit the story. It was in keeping with Han Solo's wildly unpredictable luck.

No, Gallandro corrected himself. "Luck" was what Solo would have called it. He, Gallandro, had long ago rejected mysticism and superstition. It made it that much more frustrating to see how events seemed to conspire to impel Solo along.

Gallandro intended to prove that Solo was no more than he appeared to be, a small-time smuggler of no great consequence. That the gunman had doubtless given the matter far more thought than Solo himself was a source of ironic amusement to him. Using the vast resources of his employer, the Corporate Sector Authority, he had tracked Solo and the Wookiee this far and would, with only a little more patience, complete the hunt.

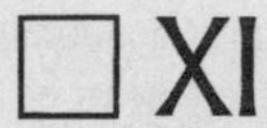

XI

"THERE'S something wrong," Han said, peering intently through his blaster's scope in the morning light. "I'm not sure, but— Here, you look, Badure."

"It just looks like a landing field to me," Hasti commented.

"Just because it's big and flat and has ships parked on it?" Han asked sarcastically. "Don't jump to any conclusions; after all, we may've stumbled onto the only used-aircraft lot in these mountains."

A stiff breeze at their backs blew down the narrow valley toward the field. It had been snowing heavily in the region; at the far edge of the flat area below, a snowfield sloped sharply downward toward the lowlands.

"It's not on any map I ever saw," declared Badure, squinting through the scope.

"Doesn't mean a thing," Han replied. "The Tion Hegemony's survey-updating program is running something like a hundred and eighty years behind schedule and getting worse. And these mountains are full of turbulence and storm activity. A survey-flyover ship could've missed that place altogether. Even an Alpha Team or a full Beta Mission might not have caught it."

Thinking it over, Han rubbed his jaw, feeling his growth of beard. He, like the others, was drawn and haggard from the march and had lost a good deal of weight. The knife cut across his chin was healing well enough in the absence of a medi-pack.

"Badure's right," Hasti said, holding the survey-map reader up close to her face. "There's nothing on her at all. And what's it doing out here anyway? Look, they had to have carved away half that cliff to build it."

Han was concentrating on the field with his remarkably acute vision. There, guidance lights and warning beacons were dark, understandable at a hidden base; but they seemed to be of a very outdated design. He could make out several craft that appeared to be about the size of spaceboats, and five larger ones. It was difficult to see any details because their tails and afterburners were pointed in his direction. Then he knew what was bothering him.

"Badure, they've got those ships parked and tied down with their rear ends into the wind." Since the craft on the field followed common aerodynamic design principles, the sensible way to position them would have been with their noses into the prevailing air currents.

Badure lowered the scope and handed back Han's blaster. "The wind's been steady, at least since last night. Either they don't care what kind of knocking-around their ships will take if a storm kicks up, or the place is deserted."

"We haven't seen a soul down there," Hasti said.

Han turned to Bollux. "Are you still getting those signals?"

"Yes, Captain. They originate from that antenna mast down there by the field, I would say. They're very weak. I only picked them up because the summit we climbed was close on a direct line of sight."

Han and Bollux had ascended that summit, a laborious session of trudging and scrambling and occasionally climbing, because of a suspicion of Han's. In the mining camp, Hasti and Badure had heard rumors that J'uoch and her partners were increasing camp security. Adding to that an apparent interest in the mountains on the part of Lanni, Hasti's late sister, Han thought it possible the mountains were seeded with antipersonnel sensors that were somehow tied in with the treasure. On the chance that, if there were sensors, they would be active rather than passive and therefore detectable, Han had taken the futilely protesting labor 'droid up to see if, now that they were approaching the lowlands, they could detect any signals. Using his built-in command-signal receiver, Bollux had tried all the standard calibrations and, when those yielded nothing, sampled others. Finally he had picked up a signal of a long-outmoded sort, and Han had taken a rough fix on it. The signal had led the group to this narrow valley, and the morning revealed what was apparently a landing field bracketed in stone.

They had been marching through the mountains for days; songs and high spirits had given way to sore feet, overworked servo-motors, aching muscles, and shoulders chafed by pack straps. The visit to the spa at the University of Rudrig seemed to Han like a dream of another life. According to the map, they were very nearly through the mountains.

That map had turned out to be their most important piece of equipment, allowing them to choose the easiest course. Nonetheless, they had hit a number of places where they had had to climb, where Skynx suddenly became a major asset. The Ruurian could scale or descend sheer rock faces, carrying one end of a climbing rope with him. Without Skynx, Han knew, they would still be somewhere far back in the mountains. As it was, their food was running low. Fortunately they had managed to find water on their route.

But even after they left the mountains they would still have to cross an expanse of open plains before reaching the mining site. A common thought was running through the group's respective biological and synthetic synapses: acquisition of a ship, even an atmospheric craft, would mark an end to their walking days. In addition, the field might offer supplies as well as transportation.

"Could this be what Lanni was curious about?" Badure wondered aloud.

"We'll see," Han decided. They had concealed themselves behind some rocks within a kilometer of the field. "Chewie and I'll go in first. If we give the all-clear sign, come on down." He demonstrated a broad waving motion, left to right. "But if we don't signal you within a half hour, or we give you *any* other kind of signal, get yourselves out of here. Write us off and try to reach the mining site, or double back to the city if that's what seems best."

Han and the Wookiee started shedding their extra gear. "I'm not so sure we shouldn't have stayed in the city," said Hasti.

Han tried to reassure her. "You would be if you'd ever done any time swabbing out the plumbing in some local lockup, doll. You ready, Chewie?"

He was. They moved out, taking turns advancing from cover to cover. Each awaited the other's hand motion before moving; they had done this sort of thing together before.

They observed no sentries, patrols, watchtowers, or surveillance equipment as they approached; but they felt no less uneasy. When at last they reached the edge of the field, they held a brief but heated debate conducted entirely in hand signals, over who would be first to step into the open. Each insisted that he should be the one. Han cut the dispute short, just before it devolved into an exchange of angry gestures, by rising and stepping out from the cover of the boulder.

Chewbacca, eyes roving the scene, bowcaster raised and ready, immediately shifted to a position from which he could give supporting fire. Han slowly moved across the open area, blaster out, nerves taut.

No shot or outcry came—and no alarm. The field was a simple expanse of flat ground—partly smoothed soil and partly rock that, from the looks of it, had been leveled a long time ago. Han wondered why somebody hadn't done a complete job and paved it over with formex or some other surfacing material.

He saw no buildings of any kind—only the primitive antenna mast, ground beacons, ground-control light clusters, and area illumination banks. He skirted the edge of the field, darting in among the rocks without warning to make sure no one was waiting in ambush.

He reemerged and continued working his way toward the parked ships. When he was satisfied that nobody had a gun turret or missile tube pointed at him from one of the craft, he approached them. And when he had come close enough to make out detail, he had difficulty speaking for a second.

What the flaming—"Hey, Chewie! Get over here!"

The Wookiee was out in the open instantly, racing toward him, bowcaster held high. His charge slowed to a distracted lope, then immobility as he saw what Han was talking about. He gave a bemused, lowing sound.

"That's right," Han agreed, slamming the side of one of the ships with his fist. It gave, leaving a deep indentation. "They're phonies."

Chewbacca came up slowly, shouldering his weapon, and took a firm grasp on the hatch of the next ship in line. He tore it off easily: it was merely a mockup constructed of treated extrusion sheeting and light structural alloys. He cast the hatch aside with a brayed Wookiee imprecation and leaned into the open hatchway. Light came through the clear pane used to simulate the cockpit windshield. The dummy ship, ribbed by support members, was gloomy, stale-smelling, and empty.

Han, examining the ships and the general layout of the field, was stumped. Nonetheless, he kept his pistol in his hand. The mockups were crude but had been made with obvious attention to details of landing gear, fuselage, propulsors, and control surfaces. They were copied—at least, he presumed them to have been copied—from models he didn't recognize and secured in place with lines of some artificial fiber.

His first thought was that this was a decoy base, part of some military campaign or defense system. But there had been no organized conflict on Dellalt or, for that matter, in this sector of space for years and years. Furthermore, this fake landing field must demand a certain amount of upkeep to be in the shape it was. A trick of J'uoch's? No logic sustained that.

Chewbacca was more instinctive. In his mind the place conjured images of some malign force using the field as a sort of trap, like those of the webweavers on the lower tree levels of his home planet. Nervously glancing around, eager to be away, he set one paw against Han's shoulder to get him moving.

The pilot shrugged off the paw. "Take it easy, will you? This place might still have some stuff we can use. Take a quick look around while I check out that antenna mast."

The Wookiee shambled off unenthusiastically. He made a rapid, thorough sweep of the area, discovering no watchers, no tracks, nor any fresh scents.

When Chewbacca returned, Han straightened from his examination of the instrument pods at the mast. "It runs off some kind of sealed power plant, a little one. It might have started broadcasting yesterday or been going for years and years. I gave the others the signal to come ahead."

Chewbacca whined unhappily, wanting only to depart from this place. Han was losing patience. "Chewie, I'm getting tired of this. There's receiver gear here that we can use to check for sensors and get a bearing on J'uoch's mining camp. This thing's been beaming for a whole day at least; if anybody in this miserable solar system were coming, they'd be here by now." That made the entire installation much more of a curiosity, he had to admit; but he didn't mention it, not wanting to make his towering sidekick any more nervous than he already was.

Badure, Hasti, Skynx, and Bollux soon appeared and, when they had looked over the bogus landing field, voiced surprise and mystification.

"This isn't any part of J'uoch's operation, I'm sure," Hasti said. Badure didn't add anything, but his expression conveyed discomfort. Skynx's antennae were waving a little erratically, but Han chalked that up to the Ruurian's timidity.

"All right," the pilot said briskly. "If we work fast, we'll be out of here inside of an hour. Bollux, I want to patch you and Max in on some of the equipment; one of Max's adaptor arms ought to fit. The rest of you fan out and keep your eyes open. Hey, Skynx, you feeling okay?''

The little Ruurian's antennae were waving even more pronouncedly now. His head wobbled for a moment, then he shook himself. ''Yes, I—felt strange for a second, Captain. Strain of the journey, I should imagine.''

''Well, hang in there, old fellow. You'll make it.'' Han started off with the labor 'droid while the others began spreading out.

Then he heard a panicked squeak and whirled to see Skynx collapse in a multilegged heap, antennae vibrating. ''Stay away from him!'' Han shouted.

Hasti fairly jumped back. ''What's happened to him?''

''I don't know, but it's not going to happen to us.'' They had too few facts to decide with any accuracy what was wrong with him; it could be a disease, or something natural to his peculiar physiology, perhaps even a part of the Ruurian life cycle. But Han wasn't going to risk having any other living members of the party contaminated. ''Bollux, pick him up; we're pulling out of here. Everybody else, cover.''

They formed a ring, weapons ready, as the labor 'droid hoisted the small, limp form and held it easily in his gleaming arms. Han barked out instructions. ''Chewie, take the lead.'' But as they moved out Han found his own vision becoming blurry.

He shook his head violently, which helped, but a surge of alarm made his breathing more rapid, and his heart began pumping furiously. They had only gone a few more paces when Badure, opening his flight jacket's collar, slurred: ''Whatever it is, I'm in it with Skynx.'' He collapsed to the ground without another word, but his eyes remained open, his breathing regular.

Hasti rushed to him, but she, too, was already unsteady on her feet. Chewbacca would have put out a paw to support her, but Han snagged a handful of his partner's pelt and pulled him back. ''No, Chewie. We've got to get clear before it happens to us.'' Han knew that they might be able to come back and help the others later, but if they succumbed now, no one was likely to survive.

Without warning, Han's legs gave way. The Wookiee, chugging like a steam engine, shifted his bowcaster to one hand and reached for his friend. His prodigious strength seemed to give him additional resistance to whatever was affecting the others. He considered running for it, for Han's statement that someone must get clear was correct. But the Wookiee code of ethics left no room for desertion. Tugging at his friend, he made a mournful sound.

Chewbacca wrestled his partner's slack body up onto his shoulder. Han, eyes still open, unable to speak, watched dully as the world spun by. Showing his fangs, the Wookiee put one broad foot in front of the other with determination. After a gallant struggle that brought him almost to the edge of the field, Chewbacca sank to his knees, nearly struggled up again, then pitched forward. Han regretted numbly that he couldn't tell his friend what a good try it had been.

Bollux now found himself in a crisis of decision—all actions and inactions pointed to members of the group coming to harm or dying. Resolving a course of action nearly burned out his basic logic stacks. Then the 'droid put Skynx down, and the Ruurian curled up into a ball by reflex. Bollux began the task of dragging Han Solo to safety. The pilot was, in the 'droid's evaluation, the one most likely to aid the others by virtue of his talents, turn of mind, and stubbornness.

As it happened, Chewbacca's fall had left Han in a position from which he could see Bollux approach. He wanted to tell the 'droid to take Chewbacca instead, but could form no words. Han's view of the 'droid was suddenly blocked by fantastic figures that leaped, capered, and circled around Bollux, gesturing and gibbering at him. They were dressed in bright costumes that were half-uniform, half-masquerade costume, and wore fantastic headgear, elaborate contrivances that suggested both helmet and mask. Even in his stupor Han registered the fact that they carried firearms of diverse types. Han thought them to be humans.

After a quick conference among themselves, the new arrivals began to push, pull, and shoo the distraught 'droid, forcing him out of Han's field of vision. The pilot was unable to move his head to follow the action.

A masked head thrust in close to him, examining him, but Han couldn't move back or even flinch. The globular mask bore a strong resemblance to a high-altitude or spacesuit helmet, but many of the details of instrumentation, pressure valves, hookups, and couplings were painted on. The air hoses and power-supply cords were useless tubes that dangled and swirled as the mask moved. Unintelligible words in a male human voice rang hollowly.

Han felt himself being lifted, but distantly, as if he had been packed in a crate of dunnage beads. Incidental views showed him that the same was happening to all the others except Bollux, who seemed to have disappeared altogether.

Then came a ride of uncertain duration. The lay of the land and the vagaries of the portage showed Han the rocky ground, Dellalt's blue-white sun, his companions being carried along by other captors, and then the ground again, with no predictability.

At last he saw a gaping hole in the terrain, an entrance to a subsurface area three times the size of the *Falcon*'s main hatch. The boulder that had hidden it was raised on six thick support jacks. Lowered, it would seal and camouflage the hole perfectly, Han knew, because he himself had prowled past it earlier in investigating the area.

Wide pleated hoses had been brought up from beneath the surface. Their pulsations indicated that a gas was being pumped through them, but Han could detect nothing by sight or smell. This was how they had been paralyzed, then; he concluded dizzily that the fantastic headgear he had seen contained breathing filters or respirators.

His bearers moved toward the opening. Suddenly darkness swirled all around him. Either he drifted into and out of consciousness or the lighting in the underground area was only intermittent; it was impossible to tell which. He knew that once or twice he caught sight of the sources of illumination: primitive glow-rods arcing over the tunnels, like tracer trails of rockets, in soft colors of blue and green and red.

Han was carried past many rooms that seemed to serve a wide variety of functions. Once he heard sounds of adults chanting, then of children doing the same. There were the rhythms of heavy machinery, whirring turbines and banging switching panels, racing gears and the spitting, crackling openings and closings of massive power bars. He smelled foods that were strange to him, and people, with all their various odors.

He tried to concentrate, either to find a way out of his predicament or to experience his last moments fully, but instead kept drifting into passivity.

His first indication that the paralysis was wearing off was when he was unceremoniously dumped onto a cold stone floor; he didn't quite let out a yelp but came close. He hurt where he had hit: his shoulder, back, and rump.

He heard someone—Badure, he thought—groan. Han tried to sit up. A bad mistake; a flare ignited in his forehead. He lay back down, knowing now what had elicited Badure's groan. He clasped his forehead, a major victory of movement, and ran his tongue over his teeth, checking to see if fungus were really growing there.

Suddenly an enormous shaggy face was hovering over him. Chewbacca hauled him up by great fistsful of his flight jacket and sat him up against a large stone. Han's faltering hand went automatically to his holster and found it vacant. That frightened him, but galvanized him as well.

He clamped both hands to his head, whispering so that it wouldn't come apart. "Best time to escape's the soonest," he told his first mate. "Kick the door over and let's leg it."

His friend *urrffed* with a disgusted gesture to the door. Han made a major effort and looked up, setting off little shooting stars on the periphery of his vision.

The door was barely discernible, an oblong of stone fitted

into the wall so tightly that barely a hairline crack showed. There was a glow-rod on either side of it, but the rest of the room was unlit. Han frisked himself—no tools, no weapons, not even a toothpick.

Badure and Hasti had been dumped together. Skynx was still rolled in a tight ball, but of Bollux there was no sign. The Wookiee plucked Han to his feet, and the pilot moved to one of the glow-rods and pulled it from its socket. The filament retained enough power to run independently for some time. Han moved farther into the chamber, waving the light as he explored; his partner trailed behind, huge fists ready.

''Check the size of this place!'' Han found the breath to whisper. The Wookiee grunted. The stone ceiling arced away into the gloom beyond the light. Han came upon row after long row of low stone monoliths, about the height of his sternum, twice as wide as they were high. He couldn't see an end to them.

A voice behind them made both partners jump. ''Where *are* we?'' It was Hasti, who had just recovered enough to rise and follow. ''And what are those things? Shelves? Work tables?''

''Runways?'' Han added, wincing at the throbbing in his head. ''Paperweights? Who knows? Let's look the rest of this granite gymnasium over.'' *At least*, he thought, *moving about would help counteract the paralysis. Best to let the others rest for now.*

But a search of the gargantuan room, which was about the size and shape of a medium spacecraft hangar, yielded no other doors, no other features at all, simply a vast space filled with the stone slabs.

''The whole mountain's probably hollow,'' Han conjectured, keeping his voice low. ''But I don't see how those hopping half-wits we saw could've done it.'' They started back toward the door.

Chewbacca uttered a low sound.

Han translated. ''He's saying how dry it is in here. You'd

expect it to be damp, from condensation if nothing else.'' Their footsteps clacked and echoed.

By that time Badure was sitting up and Skynx had uncurled. Interrupting one another with several simultaneous conversations and frequent crossovers, they established the bare facts of what had happened.

''What will they do with us?'' Skynx asked, not concealing his trembling.

''Who knows?'' Han responded. ''But they took Bollux and Max. I hope those two lads don't end up as drill bits and belt buckles.'' He regretted now his own and Chewbacca's abuse of the aircraft mockups on the landing field, and wondered if this was the standard treatment of vandals, recalling the Swimmer Shazeen's comment that few travelers made it through the mountains. ''Anyway, they haven't killed us out of hand; that's one thing in our favor, right?'' Skynx did not seem comforted.

''I'm thirsty,'' Hasti announced, ''and hungry as a Wookiee.''

''I'll summon room service,'' offered Han. ''Marinated range-squab for four, and a few magnums of chilled *T'iil-T'iil*? We'll get the place redecorated while we're at it.''

She snorted. ''You should get the auto-valet, Solo, and feed yourself into it; you look like a jet-juicer just off an eight-day twister.''

Amused, Han glanced at her, giving her a long-suffering smile. Then he sighed and sat down with his back against one of the stone slabs. Chewbacca lowered himself next to Han. ''Hey, partner; forward guard to your center's flanking slot, six win-lose units.''

Chewbacca fell into deep concentration, chin on fist, envisioning the gameboard match they would be playing on the *Falcon*. Without computer assistance, playing was much more difficult and involved, but it might help pass the time.

Hasti went to stand before the chamber's single door. Han looked up and saw that her shoulders were shaking, as was the glow-rod she held in her hand. He got up and went to comfort her, assuming she was weeping, but she pushed his hand away, and it dawned on him that she was trembling in anger.

Without warning, the girl flung herself at the door, swinging the glow-rod. It burst into splinters and a shower of sparks and blazing shards. She pounded the stone with the stump of the glow-rod, kicking it and beating it with her free hand, ranting maledictions she had learned in a life among the mining camps and factory worlds of the Tion Hegemony.

Han and Badure approached her when the worst of her rage seemed spent. ''Nobody's locking me under some old mountain to rot!'' she yelled. She swung randomly at the men with the battered stump of the glow-rod, and they found it more politic to duck than to grapple. ''Part of that treasure's mine, and nobody better try to cut me out of it!''

Puffing, drained, she shuffled over to where the Wookiee sat. Chewbacca had watched the proceedings curiously. Hasti dropped the glow-rod stump and sat down next to the *Millennium Falcon*'s first mate.

Han was about to say something, if only to comment on the intensity of her avarice, when a glissando from Skynx's flute sounded through the room.

The Ruurian still wore his instruments. They had been cradled to his middle, concealed by his woolly coat, when he had curled up. He was tuning them in an absorbed way, shutting out his current distress, having perched on the slab against which Chewbacca and Hasti sat.

Han went to listen while Badure stayed at the door to study it with the remaining glow-rod. In the halflight Skynx played a haunting tune full of longing and loneliness. Han dropped down next to Hasti and together they listened. The music made strange play with the acoustics of the vast space.

Skynx paused. ''This is a song of my home colony, you see. It's called 'By the Banks of the Warm, Pink Z'gag.' It's played at cocoon-weaving time, when the cycle's crop of larvae gather to go chrysalis. At the same time the previous cycle's cocoons open and the chroma-wings come forth to exude their pheromones, which draw them to one another. The air is sweet and light then; gaiety is there."

A large globule of emotion-secretion gathered at the corner of each faceted red eye. "This adventuring has been educational, but most of it is nothing more than danger and hardship a very long way from home. If I were ever to come to the banks of the Z'gag again, I would never leave!" He resumed playing the sad melody.

Hasti, gazing vacantly into the darkness, was disheveled, but looked attractive nonetheless, nearly as pretty as when she had been gowned and primped onboard the *Falcon*. Han slipped an arm around her and she leaned against him, scarcely noticing him.

"Don't fold until the hand's over," he encouraged her quietly.

She turned to him with a labored smile, brushing her dirty fingers against his stubble of beard, tracing the raw scar across his chin. "You know, this is an improvement, Solo. You're not Slick now, not so smooth and careless."

He leaned toward her and she didn't turn away. And then he kissed her. There was some question as to who was more surprised. Without parting, they settled into a more comfortable embrace, and gave the kiss serious attention. Skynx's music carried them along.

She shoved herself free at last. "Han, oh, I—stop it; please, stop!" He retreated, confused. "The last thing I need is to get involved with you."

Sounding wounded, he asked, "What's wrong with me?"

"You run all over people and you never take anything seriously, for starters. You joke through life with that silly smirk on your face, so sure of yourself I want to bounce a rock off your skull!"

She kept him at arm's length. "Solo, my sister Lanni inherited Dad's Guild book, so she had pilot's status here in the Tion. But I had to work any job I could get. Messhand, housegirl, sanit-crew, I've done them all in the camps, the mines, the factories. I've seen your type all my life. Everything's a big laugh, and you can charm the daylights out of people when you feel like it, but you're gone the next day and you never look back. Han, there are no *people* in your life!''

He protested, ''Chewie—''

''—is your friend,'' she cut him off, ''but he's a *Wookiee*. And you've got that pair of mechanical cohorts, Max and Bollux, and that hotshot starship of yours, but the rest of us are temporary cargo. Where are the people, Han?''

He started to defend himself, but she overrode him. Chewbacca, intrigued, forgot about his next gameboard move.

''I'm sure you drive the portside girls wild, Solo; you look like you just stepped out of a holo-thriller. But I'm not one of them; never was, never will be.''

She softened a bit. ''I'm no different from Skynx. On my birthworld there's a stretch of land my parents used to own. I'm going to get my cut of the treasure, I swear on my blisters, and buy it back if I have to purchase the whole planet. I'll build a home and take care of Badure, because he took care of Lanni and me. I'll have things of my own and a *life* of my own. I'll share it if I meet the right man, but I'll live without him if I don't. Solo, light housekeeping in a starship isn't my idea of a dream come true!'' She drew away from him and went to join Badure, pushing her fingers through the tangles of red hair.

Skynx finished his sad song, then lowered his flute. ''I wish I could see the home colony one more time, the air filled with the chroma-wings and their pheromones and the sounds of their wooing. What would you wish for, Captain Solo?''

Staring absently after Hasti, Han shrugged. ''Stronger pheromones.''

Skynx started. Then, sides rippling, began chortling in the Ruurian version of convulsive laughter, issuing chittering, high-pitched giggles. Chewbacca loosed a sustained howl of amusement, slapping his thigh with a huge paw, his mane shaking. That started Han chuckling ruefully. He reached up and gave Skynx a push; the Ruurian rolled over onto his back, tittering and kicking his short limbs in the air. A guffaw exploded from Badure and even Hasti, shaking her head in exasperation, shared the joke. Chewbacca, blue eyes tearing, slapped Han's shoulder, whereupon the pilot fell sideways, barely able to breathe for laughing.

In the midst of it all, the door swept open.

Bollux was ushered in and the door closed before any of them could do more than gape. In another moment they had congregated around the 'droid, elbowing one another, their demands for information and their questions interrupting one another's.

After a few seconds Badure shouted everyone down. They quieted, realizing he would ask the same questions as they anyway. "What's happened? Who are those people? What do they want from us?"

Bollux made the strangely human self-effacing sounds he employed in approaching a delicate subject. "There's rather a surprising story here. It's somewhat complicated. You see, long ago, there was—"

"Come on, Bollux!" Han shouted, cutting through the cybernetic rhetoric, "What are they going to *do* with us?"

The 'droid sounded dismayed. "I know it sounds absurd in this day and age, sir, but unless we can do something, you're all about to become, er, a human sacrifice."

XII

"BY which," Skynx said with a forlorn hope, "we may assume you mean *only* humans?"

"Not quite," Bollux admitted. "They're not really sure what you and First Mate Chewbacca are, but they've concluded they have nothing to lose by sacrificing you. They're discussing procedures now."

The Wookiee growled and Skynx's red eyes glazed.

"Bollux, who *are* these people?" Han demanded.

"They call themselves the Survivors, sir. The signal we picked up was a distress call. They're waiting to be picked up. When I asked them why they didn't simply go to the city, they became very vexed and excited; they harbor a great deal of hatred for the other Dellaltians. I gathered that that animosity is tied up with their religion somehow. They are extreme isolationists."

"How did you find all this out?" Badure wanted to know. "Do they speak any Standard?"

"No, sir," the 'droid replied. "They speak a dialect that was prevalent in this section of space prior to the rise of the Old Republic. It was recorded on a language tape in Skynx's material, and Blue Max had stored it along with other information. Of course, I didn't reveal that Max exists; he translated for me in burst-signals and I conducted the conversation."

"A culture of pre-Republic origins," pondered Skynx, forgetting to be scared.

"Will you forget the homework?" snapped Hasti, then

turned again to Bollux. "What's all this about sacrifices? Why us?"

"Because they're waiting to be picked up," said the 'droid. "They're convinced that life-form termination enhances the effect of their broadcast."

"So *we* stumbled in, a major power boost," mused Han, thinking of all those people who had disappeared in these mountains. "When's the big sendoff?"

"Late tonight, sir; it has something to do with the stars and is accompanied by considerable ritual."

We've got just one trump card left, Han thought, then said, "I think that'll work out just fine."

Their captors wasted no food or drink on them, which Han loudly proclaimed an indication that they had fallen into the hands of a low-class outfit. But they still had plenty of time to question Bollux.

The mountain warren was indeed a large complex, though it apparently housed what Bollux estimated to be no more than one hundred people living in a complicated family-clan group. Asked why he had been separated from them all, the 'droid could only say that the Survivors appeared to understand what automata were and held them in some awe. They had been adamant about the need to go forward with the sacrifice, but had bowed to his demands that he be permitted to see his companions.

On the details of the sacrifice Bollux was less clear. Ceremonial objects and equipment were being moved to the surface even as they spoke; the sacrifice was to take place on the mock-up landing field. Although the 'droid had been unable to locate the confiscated weapons, the captives decided that any attempt at escape would have a better chance of success if made on the surface. Han revealed his plan to the others, vague as it was.

"There are a lot of things that could go wrong," Hasti protested.

Han agreed. "The worst of which is getting sacrificed, which will happen anyway. How long until nightfall?"

She consulted her wrist chrono; there were many hours yet. They decided to rest. Chewbacca barked his gameboard move to Han, then settled down for a nap. Badure followed suit.

Han scowled at the Wookiee, whose gameboard move was extremely unconventional. "Just because we're going to be sacrificed, you're playing a reckless game now?" The Wookiee flashed his teeth in a self-satisfied grin.

Skynx appeared to be in deep conversation with Bollux, using the obscure dialect the Survivors spoke. Hasti had gone off to commune with her thoughts, and Han decided not to bother her. He wished urgently that the group could take some immediate course of action to dispel any brooding. None was available, so he settled into that—for him—most difficult of all tasks, waiting.

The opening of the door brought Han out of a troubled sleep filled with visions of strangers doing terrible things to the *Millennium Falcon*.

Then, abruptly, Survivors wearing their extravagant costumes dashed into the quiet chamber, carrying glow-rods and weapons, making resistance sheer folly. Their weapons were a fascinating assortment: ancient beam-tubes powered by heavy backpacks, antiquated solid-projectile firearms, and several spring-loaded harpoon guns of the sort the lake men used. Han's worse fear, that the Survivors would use their anaesthetic gas again and thus preclude any action on their captives' part, was unrealized. He found himself breathing easier for that; he had no intention of ending his life passively.

With shouted instructions and gesticulations the Survivors herded their captives out of the chamber. They formed a forward and rear guard, keeping their weapons trained watchfully so there would be no opportunity for mishap. Chewbacca rumbled angrily through it all and nearly turned on one Survivor, who had jabbed the Wookiee with a harpoon gun to hurry him along. Han restrained his friend; all the other Survivors were out of reach, and there was no place to hide in the stone corridors. They had no choice but to move as ordered.

This time Han got a clearer impression of the underground warren. The corridors, like the chamber in which they had been held, were carefully and precisely cut, arranged along an organized central plan, their walls, floors, and ceilings fused solid to serve as support. Thermal plates warmed them, but Han could see no dehumidifying equipment, though he was certain it must exist. Everything implied a technology in excess of what the Survivors seemed capable of fully utilizing. Han was willing to bet these capering primitives did simple maintenance by rote and that the knowledge of the original builders had been lost long ago.

He saw unhelmeted Survivors for the first time, mainbreed humans who, aside from an unusual number of congenital defects, were unremarkable. The prisoners passed heated, well-lit hydroponic layouts. The glow-rods and thermal plates in them made Han wonder about the power source; something suitably ancient, he presumed, perhaps even an atomic pile.

Badure's thoughts had been paralleling his own. "Regression," the old man said. "Maybe the base was built by stranded explorers, or early colonists?"

"That wouldn't explain their unreasoning shunning of the other Dellaltians," Skynx put in. "They must have taken elaborate precautions to avoid notice all this time, even in these desolate—"

He was silenced when a Survivor singled him out with the end of a beam-tube, gesturing with unmistakable fury. Conversation stopped. Han saw that Bollux had been right; the warren had clearly been built for many more people than now occupied it. In some stretches light and heat had been shut down to conserve power or had failed altogether.

They passed a room from which odd, rhythmic sounds issued. For just an instant when he drew even with the doorway, Han had a view of the interior.

Colored lights strobed in the darkness, flashing on the walls and ceiling in arresting swirls and patterns. Someone was chanting in the Survivors' tongue; underscoring the chant was the pulsing of a transonic synthesizer, as much felt as heard.

Han almost stopped short and had to step quickly to keep from being jabbed with a harpoon, thinking, *Hypno-imprinting! Crude version, but completely effective if you catch your subjects early enough. Poor kids.* It explained a lot.

Then they felt cold night air on their faces and their breath crystallized before them. They left the Survivors' warren by a different door than that by which they had entered.

The mockup landing field was a different sight in the night than it had been during the day; it was now a scene of barbaric ceremony. The stars and Dellalt's two moons brightened the sky; glow-rods and streaming torches lit the entire area, reflected by the sides of the dummy aircraft. At the edge of the ritual field, by the steep snowfield that sloped to the valley below, a large cage had been erected, a pyramid of bars, assembled piecemeal. Its door was a thick, solid plate, its lock in the center, inaccessible from within the cage.

Near the cage was a circle of gleaming metal, broader than Han was tall, suspended from a framework, suggesting an enormous gong. It was inscribed with lettering of an unfamiliar type, consisting of whorls and squares alternating with dots and ideographs.

Closer in, toward the center of the light, was a wide metal table, a medi-lab appurtenance of some kind. Near it were piled the prisoners' weapons and other equipment. The implication of the table hit them at once: a sacrificial altar.

Han was ready to make a break then and there; the pyramidal cage seemed firmly anchored to the rock, so sturdy that even Chewbacca's thews wouldn't prevail against it. But the Survivors had been through this procedure before. They were alert and careful, with weapons trained in clear lines of fire. Han noticed that the muzzles and harpoons were pointed toward the captives' legs. If the scheduled sacrificees made any wrong moves, the Survivors could shoot and still not be deprived of their ritual.

This decided the pilot against any immediate action. There was still a chance his plan would work, provided Bollux and Blue Max were flexible enough to adapt to circumstances as they arose. The 'droid was separated from the rest of them, complying with their captors as Han had instructed him.

The other captives were chivvied to the cage, ushered to the circular door plate that swung open on oiled hinges. It took every scrap of Han's resolve to enter the pyramid; once inside he stood there closely watching the Survivors' preparations.

The strange people were decked out in their finest garb. Now that he understood a little more about them, Han could interpret the Survivors' costume. A ground-crewman's blast-suit had become, over generations, an insect-eyed getup. Spacesuit speaker grilles had evolved into pointy-fanged mouths painted on imitation helmets; communication antennae and broadcast directors were represented by elaborate spikes and antlers of metal. Back tanks and suit packs were adorned with symbolic designs and mosaics, while tool belts were hung with fetishes, amulets, and charms of all kinds.

The Survivors whirled, leaped, and tootled their instruments, striking finger chimes and drums. Two of them beat the great wheel of metal with padded mallets, the gongings resounding back and forth across the valley.

With the prisoners' arrival, things began to build toward a climax. A man mounted a rostrum that had been set near the altar. A silence fell.

The man wore a uniform festooned with decorations and braid; his trousers were seamed with golden cloth. He wore a hat that was slightly small for him, its military brim glittering with giltwork, a broad, flashing medallion riding its high crown. Two aides set a small stand on the rostrum beside him. It held a thick circle of transparent material about the size of a mealplate.

"A log-recorder disk!" exclaimed Skynx. The others competed to ask him if he was sure. "Yes, yes; I've seen one or two, you know. But the *Queen of Ranroon*'s is back in the treasure vaults, is it not? What one is that, then?"

No one could answer. The man on the rostrum regaled the crowd, delivering loud phrases that they echoed back to him, applauding, whistling, and stomping their feet. Flickering torchlight made the scene seem even more primeval.

"He's saying they've been a good and faithful people, that the proof is there with him on the rostrum, and that the High Command won't forget them," Skynx translated.

Han was amazed. "You understand that garble?"

"I learned it as Bollux did, from the data tapes, a pre-Republic dialect. Can they have been here that long, Captain?"

"Ask the Chamber of Commerce. What's he saying now?"

"He said he's their Mission Commander. And something about mighty forces afoot; the rescue they've been promised will surely come soon. I—something about their generations of steadfastness, and deliverance by this High Command. The crowd keeps chanting 'Our signal will be received.' "

With a final tirade the Mission Commander gestured to the pyramidal cage. Until now Bollux had stood to one side of the proceedings, surrounded by gray-clad, masked Survivors who chanted and rattled prayer clackers at him, descendants of techs entrusted with maintenance of machinery.

But now the 'droid broke out of their ring, moving quickly to take advantage of the surprise he had caused. He crossed to stand with his back to the pyramid's door. The Survivors who had been about to fetch their first victim for the "transmission" wavered, still awed by the automaton. The 'droid hadn't been able to secure a weapon, a departure from Han's vague plan, but felt that he could wait no longer to make his move. Even in the rush of events Han wondered about the origin of the Survivors' reverence for mechanicals. Surely there had never been a 'droid or robot through these mountains before?

The Mission Commander was exhorting his followers. Bollux, his photoreceptors glowing red in the night, slowly opened the halves of his chest plastron. Blue Max, carefully coached by the labor 'droid, activated his own photoreceptor, playing it across the crowd. Han heard sounds of indrawn breath among the Survivors.

Max switched from optical scanning to holo-projection mode. A cone of light sprang from him; there hovered in the air an image he had recorded off Skynx's tapes, the symbol of Xim the Despot, the grinning death's head with the starburst in each black eye socket. From his vocoder came recorded tech readouts from the tapes in the language of the Survivors.

The crowd drew back, many of them thrusting their thumbs at Bollux to fend off evil. Max put forth more images he had taken from the information Skynx had compiled: an ancient fleet of space battlewagons in flight against the stars; the brilliance of a full-scale engagement with exploding missiles, flaring cannonfire, and probing lasers; battle standards passing in review, displaying unit colors that had been forgotten long ago. The entire time, the 'droid was surreptitiously edging to the pyramidal cage's door. While the crowd was riveted to Max's performance, Bollux manipulated the door's handle behind his back.

A yell went up from the assembled Survivors just as Bollux succeeded in throwing the bolt on the stubborn lock. Blue Max had projected a halo of the war-robot's cranial turret that Skynx had brought onboard the *Millennium Falcon*. Max held the image, capitalizing on their response, rotating it to show all sides. The Survivors jabbered animatedly among themselves, moving back from the frightening ghost-holo. Bollux stepped away from the cage door.

Max began running through all the other visual information he had stored about Xim's war-robots. Schematics, manual-extracts, records of the ponderous combat machines in motion, closeup details of construction, and full-length views. All the while, Bollux moved slowly forward. Step by step the crowd yielded ground, seemingly hypnotized by Max's projections. In the excitement and poor light nobody noticed that the cage door was now unlocked.

"He may not be able to hold them much longer," Han whispered. Bollux was now at the center of a near-circle of Survivors.

"Time to jump," Badure said.

Han agreed. "Make your way to the edge of the field. Nobody stops for anybody else, understood?"

Hasti, Badure, and even Skynx nodded. Unarmed, they could do little except run from the Survivors. Each individual would be responsible for his own life; stopping to give aid would be suicidal and expected of no one.

Han swung the door open slowly and stepped through. Shouting, gesticulating Survivors were still occupied with Bollux. The Mission Commander had left his rostrum to try to make his way through the crowd to Bollux, but was having trouble making headway through the press of his own people. Han waited while the others emerged.

Chewbacca slipped through the door and moved off like a shadow. Badure moved with less agility, then Hasti. Skynx exited and set off at once for the edge of the field. Low to the ground, he was nearly impossible to see. The Ruurian didn't pause or look back; he adhered to Han's directions completely, having acquired some of the necessary makeup of an adventurer. Han moved around the end of the cage to bring up the rear. He nearly backed into Hasti. "Where's Badure?" she mouthed silently.

They couldn't spot him at first, then made out the old man as he nonchalantly strolled around the edge of the crowd, heading for the abandoned altar where the weapons lay. No one paid him any heed; all of them were transfixed by Max's holos of a war-robot being put through its paces, firing weapons, and lumbering through basic infantry tactics.

''He's going for the guns,'' Han whispered. Chewbacca, who had also paused, stood with them, watching the old man's progress.

''We can't help him now; he either makes it or not. We'll wait at the edge of the field as long as we can.'' He didn't know if he was happy Badure was trying for their weapons, feeling naked and helpless without his blaster, or dismayed that the old man was risking his life.

Just then a Survivor sentry, coming in off his post, stepped out of the darkness and nearly stumbled over Skynx. The Ruurian chirped in fear and went into reverse. The guard's eyes bulged in amazement at the woolly, many-legged creature, then he fumbled for the flame-rifle at his shoulder, crying out an alarm.

A shaggy arm reached out and the weapon was snatched from his hands. Chewbacca's fist shot through the air and the guard was lifted, stretched out stiff as a post, to fall on the landing field, his left foot quivering.

People on the fringe of the crowd had heard the guard and repeated the alarm. Heads turned; in a moment the shout was taken up by many voices. Han ran, took the bell-mouthed flame-rifle, and slewed it in a wide, horizontal arc. A wash of orange fire streamed over the heads of the crowd. Survivors dropped to the ground, grabbing for their weapons and screaming conflicting orders at one another. Han could hear the shrieking Mission Commander trying futilely to bring order out of chaos.

Badure, having reached the altar, was out of the crowd's immediate line of sight. He shouldered Chewbacca's bowcaster and bandoleer of ammunition and began tucking weapons into his belt.

Shots were now being pegged across the field at them. ''Keep out of the way!'' hollered Han, elbowing Chewbacca behind him. He backed slowly, covering the withdrawal and creating a diversion for Badure. He directed his discharges into the ground between himself and the massed Survivors, making puddles of fire to spoil their aim and sending intermittent streamers of flame over them to force their heads down. A line of tracer bullets chewed up the field a meter or two to his right, and a pale particle beam barely missed his head.

The escapees needed cover badly, but their section of the field was open and offered none. Chewbacca, with sudden inspiration, ran for the gong and, back and arm muscles swelling with effort, lifted it from its support hooks, his widespread arms grabbing it by two carrying handles welded to its back.

The slugs, beams, and flames of the firefight dissected the air. The Survivors' shots were gaining in accuracy, though they weren't used to such a pitched battle. Badure, running in a low crouch to work his way back to his companions, was spotted by the crowd. Somebody let fly with an old rocket pistol, blowing up a clot of stone in his path. In a frantic effort to change course, Badure lost his balance, and Survivors' shots began to converge on him.

Chewbacca grounded the gong in front of Han as he and the others took shelter behind it. Projectile and energy weapons splashed and ricochetted from the shield; whatever the gong was made of, it was very durable material.

Han blazed away at the Survivors to keep them from pressing the attack against Badure. He had been spending the flame-rifle's ammo recklessly and knew he might soon find himself defenseless. Badure, struggling to rise, was having trouble. The Survivors' aim was zeroing in on him now, and he returned the fire as well as he could.

I warned him, thought Han. *Life-Debt or no, it's everyone for himself.* He had trouble selling the idea to himself, though.

Then the decision was taken from him. Issuing a deafening Wookiee battle cry, Chewbacca moved off, holding up the gong to protect himself. Han looked back and saw that Hasti and Skynx were watching him. The girl, he thought, would surely run to help Badure if he didn't.

"Don't just stand there," he snarled. "Get to cover!" He gave her a shove toward the edge of the field and dashed off the other way, laying down heavy fire as he sprinted, zig-zagging after the Wookiee.

"You crazy fur-face!" he roared at his first mate when he had caught up to him. "What're you doing, playing captain again?" Chewbacca took a moment from angling and maneuvering the gong for an irritated, explanatory growl.

"Life-Debt?" Han exploded, dodging around his friend into the open to snap off a pair of quick shots. "And who pays up if you lose us *ours*?"

But he maintained his fire, sideskipping along behind the straining, gong-toting Wookiee and bounding from cover to either side of him to get off a shot or two. Flames lit the scene, and the air was smoky and hot from the firefight. The flame-rifle's discharges were growing weaker, and its range was decreasing.

Skirting a section of field torn and ruptured by the battle, they finally reached Badure, who was pressed down flat on the ground, shooting with the pair of long-barreled power pistols. Chewbacca heaved the gong between the old man and the oncoming shots. Han coaxed a last feeble flicker from the flame-rifle, then threw it aside. Dropping to one knee, he helped Badure up. "Last bus is leaving now, Lieutenant-commander."

"I'll take a one-way on that," panted Badure, adding, "glad you could make it, boys."

Han snagged his own blaster from Badure's belt, and a sudden confidence steadied him. He stepped into the clear, crouched low, and let off a series of quick shots. Two Survivor marksmen who had been taking careful aim with heavy-particle beamers fell away in different directions, their wounds smoking.

Han ducked back, waited a beat, then stepped into the open again on the same side of the gong, eluding the aim of those who had been waiting to see him emerge on the opposite side. His bolts dropped two more enemies from the ragged firing line. But Survivor flankers could be seen in the wavering light, fanning out to either side in an effort to cut off retreat.

"Let's jump!" Han cried. Chewbacca began back-pedaling, still holding the gong, and headed for the field's edge as Badure and Han kept up the most intense fire they could, pinning down the Survivors facing them and impeding the flankers. Their energy weapons lit the night, answered by bullets, blaster bolts, needles, harpoons, particle beams, and gushes of flame. Han occasionally assisted the Wookiee's progress with a judicious shove.

Someone came toward them. Badure nearly burned the silhouetted form before Han batted the power pistol aside. "Bollux! Over here!"

The 'droid somehow made it to the gong's cover; they withdrew step by hotly contended step. A group of Survivor flankers was nearly in position to enfilade them, crouching by the antenna mast. Badure held both long-barreled weapons up side by side and fired at the flankers. Men fell and the instrument shorted out; the mast's power supply was drained in a swirl of energy, and the mast fell, wreathed in crackling discharges. It crashed into the rostrum and rostrum, frame, and log-recorder disk went up in flames.

Han heard his named called. Skynx and Hasti crouched at the edge of the field. Firing and scrambling, the others joined them.

"We can't retreat down that snowfield; it's too steep," Hasti declared, "and even Chewbacca couldn't carry that gong down. We'd make perfect targets out there."

Han dealt out a few more shots, pondering her reasoning and their lack of alternatives. Then Chewbacca, surveying the situation, barked a quick scheme to him.

"Partner, you *are* crazy," Han exclaimed, not without a certain respect. But he saw no nonfatal alternative. "What's keeping us?" He pulled the others closer and explained the plan. They readied themselves, having no time for fear or doubts.

Then Han yelled. "Chewie! Go!" The Wookiee backpedaled to the edge of the field, whirled, stooped, and laid the concave gong down, its curved surface indenting the hard, icy snowfield. Han fired furiously.

Badure dropped awkwardly onto the gong and grabbed a carrying handle. Bollux climbed onto the opposite side of the rim, locking servo-grips onto two more handles. Skynx swarmed aboard and clung tightly around the 'droid's neck, antennae flailing. Hasti braced herself next to Badure, and Chewbacca had to brace his broad feet in the snow at the tug of the gong's weight.

Han still stood, keeping up a heavy volume of fire. He shouted, "I'll pile on last!"

Chewbacca didn't take time to argue; he swept out one long arm, gathered his friend in like a child, and threw himself onto the gong. Shots from the Survivor flankers crisscrossed overhead. The Wookiee's impetus and weight gave them a quick start.

The gong gathered speed, spinning and sliding as it cut along the icy slope. Chewbacca lifted his head and uttered a foghorn-like hoot of elation, to which Skynx added a "*Weeee hee-ee!*"

The gong tilted and rotated to the left as it swished across the snow. Chewbacca threw his weight the other way; they bounced and slid on a fairly even keel for a few seconds, then hit a small rock outcropping in the snowfield.

They were airborne, all hands seeking a grip and flailing to stay aboard; to fall from the gong now and slide the rest of the way without protection would mean severe laceration by ice shards and shattered bones from the hardened patches and rocks.

They came down again with a breath-stealing jolt; everyone, miraculously, contrived to cling to the bucking, jarring gong. Han grabbed Hasti, who, in helping Badure, had nearly lost her own grip. The *Falcon*'s master encircled her waist with his free arm while she clenched a handful of Badure's flight jacket. Badure, in turn, had locked legs with Chewbacca, helping the Wookiee steer by leaning and tugging at the handles. Chewbacca, like the others, could barely see; their headlong speed through the icy air had stung everyone's eyes to tears and was numbing their exposed skin.

In leaning abruptly to the side, the Wookiee succeeded in guiding their mad descent around a prow of stone that would have smashed them all, but in the process he lost his balance. Bollux quickly shifted his central torsional member and secured his legs around the *Falcon*'s first officer's.

Badure held on to Chewbacca, too, reaching out with a free hand to help steady the Wookiee. But in doing so he saw he was about to lose Chewbacca's bowcaster and bandoleer. He cried out, his words stolen instantly by the wind, but Han was busy clinging to a handle and hanging onto Hasti and she to Badure, while Badure and Bollux were committed to keeping Chewbacca aboard. Meanwhile, the Wookiee devoted all his attention to what could only in the most ludicrous sense be termed "steering."

And so Skynx, facing the fact that only he was free to act, released his grip on the 'droid with all but his last set of limbs. He was dragged around at once, very nearly snapped like a whip, reaching with his free extremities. Just as Badure's scrabbling efforts to hang on to the bowcaster failed, Skynx got close enough to grasp the weapon and was abruptly thrown in the other direction as the gong changed course again.

The small Ruurian now clung to his only mainstay, Bollux, by the digits of his lowermost limbs, which clenched precariously on the 'droid's shoulder pauldron. But he determinedly hung on to the weapon and ammunition, knowing they might be needed badly and that there was no one to catch them if he failed. With each bump and rotation of the gong, Skynx felt his grip loosening, but he hugged his burden resolutely. One by one, he began to find purchase for his other limbs. Chewbacca felt him fumbling, shifted his leg as much as he was able, and Skynx managed to fasten two sets of limbs to the Wookiee's thick knee.

They were at the steepest part of the insane plunge, shearing through the snowfield, rocking in furrows, and smashing out of depressions in the surface. Several times Han saw energy beams of various hues register hits in the snow, but always far wide of their mark. *As targets go, we must be pretty fast and furious.*

He clung doggedly, fingers, ears, and face numbed by the cold, eyes streaming a constant flow of tears. "My fingers are slipping!" cried Hasti with unmasked fear. "I can't feel them."

Han knew with a sense of utter futility that he could do little to help her. He griped her as tightly as he could, hoping that his frozen fingers would hold.

Badure yelled, "We're slowing down!" Chewbacca bellowed pure joy. Hasti began to half-laugh, half-sob.

The gong had reached a gentler portion of the slope close to the foot of the snowfield and was losing speed moment by moment. The bumps and jolts became less dramatic, the spinning less pronounced. In seconds they were coasting.

"An excellent job, First Mate Chewbacca," Bollux was saying, when suddenly the gong's rim hit a slab of rock that lifted it into the air like a jump ramp. Frozen hands, servo-grips, Ruurian digits, and Wookiee toes, all lost their final struggle. The gong threw them free. Human bodies, the tubular Skynx, a yeowling Chewbacca, and gleaming Bollux sailed through the air on assorted trajectories, cartwheeling, tumbling, spinning—and falling.

XIII

HAN heard the whine of servo-motors over the moan of wind. From where he lay, mostly buried by the mound of snow he had scraped up on his landing approach, he could see Bollux draped belly-up over a low snowbank. The halves of the 'droid's chest plastron opened up and outward.

Blue Max's vocoder blustered. "Hey! Let's get moving; we're not out of it yet!"

A drift to Han's right sloughed and erupted. Chewbacca appeared, spitting out snow and rumbling an acid remark to the diminutive computer module.

"No, he's right," Han groaned to his partner. He raised himself on unsteady arms and gazed up the slope, foggily curious about whether his head was actually going to fall off or if it simply felt that way. A bobbing column of lights was wending its way down the snowfield from the Survivors' base. Their former captors were in hot pursuit.

"The short circuit's right on the money, folks; everybody up!" Han thrashed and floundered in the snow for a moment, then pulled himself to his feet and began beating his hands together to bring some sensation back.

Hasti was also struggling up. Han caught her hand and pulled her to her feet. She ran over to see to Badure. Chewbacca had just reclaimed his bowcaster and bandoleer from Skynx, whom he had dug free. The Wookiee growled his gratitude, patting and stroking the Ruurian's woolly back in a gruff gesture of thanks.

Hasti was chafing Badure's hand's and wrists, trying to get

him upright. Han moved to help and saw that the tip of the old man's nose and patches on his cheeks were whitened.

"He's getting frostbite. On deck, Trooper; time to depart the area." They pulled him up. Meanwhile, with Chewbacca's help, Bollux was once more upright.

Counting heads before striking off, Han spied Skynx bent over the gong, which had fallen face up, a flattened dome in the snow. The Ruurian was making minute examination of the whorls and patterns on the ancient metal, laboring to see in the light of moons and stars. When Han called him, the academician yelled back. "I think you'd better see this first, Captain."

They all gathered around him. His small digits traced the raised characters. "I thought I recognized these when I first saw this object, but I was too hurried to study them. All these," a splay of digits indicated groups of characters, "are technical notations and operating instructions. They have to do with pressure equalization and fastening procedures."

"Then it comes from a hatch," Badure concluded, his muffled voice coming through hands cupped to thaw out his cheeks and nose. "Some kind of decorative facing off an airlock hatch, a big one."

Skynx agreed. "A peculiar and rather ostentatious appointment, but that is the case. Those several larger characters there in the center give the vessel's name." He turned bulbous red eyes to them. "It's the *Queen of Ranroon*!"

In the middle of a tumult of voices—human, non-human, and electronic—Han stood imagining the treasure of entire worlds. Though cold, near exhaustion, pursued, and starved, he suddenly found himself charged with limitless energy and a dramatic determination to live and to claim the *Queen*'s wealth.

They were interrupted. Han's thoughts and the confused conversations springing from Skynx's revelation were cut short by a long note sounding in the night, a wail from a hunting horn or other signaling device.

That brought them all up short. The bobbing lights of the

pursuing Survivors' column were now well down the slope. Now and then one would drop from the line and disappear as its bearer lost footing on the treacherous snowfield and fell tumbling.

Led by Han, the escapees set out in a staggering string, helping one another as well as they could; fortunately, the snow wasn't very deep. They reached down to scoop up handfuls of the stuff to melt in their mouths, trying to relieve the dehydration of their captivity. Beating his gloved hands together, Han considered what the hatch cover might mean. Were the Survivors guarding Xim's treasure in their mountain warren? What had become of the *Queen of Ranroon*?

Hasti caught up to him in the struggling line of march. "Solo, I've been doing some thinking. The congregation back there isn't just tooting their horns to hear the echoes and let us know they're coming. I think they have patrols out and are calling the forces out on us."

He stopped, deriding himself for having been preoccupied with the treasure. Hasti repeated her reasoning to the others. "We're not too far from the snow line," Badure observed. "Perhaps that's the limit to their territory."

Han shook his head. "We messed up church for them and left quite a few of them in some pain. They're coming for blood and they won't stop just because the snow does. We'd better take up a better formation. Chewie, walk the point."

The Wookiee padded off quietly; cold and snow didn't bother him. Protected by his thick pelt, he slipped off, keeping to the cover of the increasingly frequent rocks and boulders. The others followed more slowly in his wake, slowed because they were bereft of his giant, supportive strength.

But within minutes the Wookiee was back to draw them down into the cover of a particularly large boulder and tell Han, in quick gutterals, what he had encountered.

"There're more of them, coming up this way," Han translated. "Chewie thinks we can hide here and wait them out. When they're past, we go on. Still and quiet, everybody."

They waited for oppressive minutes, straining to make no

noise, no shift of position or other movement that might betray them. Han slowly turned his head to check the progress of the Survivors from their base. The lights had made their way to the gentler part of the slope and fanned out for a ground search.

There was a slight sound, the smallest movement of rock and crunch of ice. Everyone tensed. A shape moved stealthily into view, keeping to available cover. The approaching Survivor was uncostumed but wore a hood and heavy clothing. The scout's head turned slowly, searching the area carefully as he went. Moments later another sentinel appeared, farther across the valley on a parallel course.

Han thought he understood. The valley widened abruptly from here, and a few sentries, farther along, might not be able to stop the escapees from getting past. The sentries kept moving warily. When they were well past the escapees' position, Han—using hand-touches to alert his companions and dictate the order of march—slipped out from behind the boulder. The servo-motors of Bollux's body were smooth and quiet, but sounded unbearably loud to Han. He could only hope the sound didn't carry over the wind and other noises in the night.

They had wound their way among the rocks for another half kilometer and gotten out of sight of the snowfield, and Han had just begun to let himself believe they were clear, when a yellow heatbeam flashed out of the night. It scored on a rock two meters to Bollux's right, throwing up sparks and globs of molten mineral.

Chill, shivers, frozen feet, and caution were forgotten. Everybody scattered for cover. Hasti brought her disrupter pistol up for a return shot but Han whispered, "Don't! He'll pick up your position from the flash. Anybody see where the shot came from?" Nobody had. "Then, sit still. When he fires again, we'll nail him. Aim for the point of origin."

"Solo, we haven't got time to sit here!" Hasti rasped fiercely.

"Then start tunneling," he suggested.

But instead she groped, found a stone that fit her palm, and heaved it. It clattered among the loose rocks. Another heatbeam flashed yellow from the shadows at the side of the valley.

Han fired instantly and kept on firing. The others, slower than he, joined a moment later with a torrent of blaster, power pistol, disruptor, and bowcaster shots.

"Hold it, hold it," Han ordered. "I think we got him."

"Do we move on?" asked Badure.

Han didn't think the light and reports of the shots would have been detectable back on the slopes. "Not yet. We have to be sure we won't get backshot. Besides, I saw a gleam of metal where the heatbeams came from. Maybe there's a vehicle there, or some supplies." He shivered from the mountain air. "Anything'd be a help."

"Then someone must investigate," Skynx declared and was away before anybody could stop him, flowing between the rocks with his antennae held low, nearly impossible to see. *I'll have to warn him about those heroics*, Han thought, *he's come a long way*. To break the tense silence, he whispered to Badure, "See what happens? First you go off medal-chasing to get our weapons back and now Skynx figures he's the valiant warrior."

The old man chuckled softly. "The guns came in handy, didn't they? Besides, it gave Chewbacca a chance to pay back his Life-Debt."

Han blinked. "That's right. Hey, what do you mean Chewbacca? We *both* came back for you!" Badure only laughed.

Just then Skynx called over excitedly, "Captain! Over here!" They went, slipping and stumbling with haste but still keeping low. They came to an overhang of rock, having to duck to pass under it. From the black regions within issued Skynx's voice. "I found a glow-rod, Captain Solo. I'll turn up the rheostat a bit." A faint glimmer showed them the Ruurian's face.

He had found a low, wide cave that reached in farther than

they could see. The body of the single sentry was sprawled in death, hit by several of their blasts. But what excited Skynx was what had been under guard there.

"Look, a cargo lifter!" Han took the glow-rod. "Hover-raft of some kind." He climbed into the open cockpit of the flatbed aircraft. "Looks like it was on down time; there're a lot of burned-out components on the floorboards, and the control-panel covers are still off."

He brightened the glow-rod. There were two more hover-rafts nearby, access panels open, gutted and cannibalized for the parts that had gone to repair the first. Han slid the notched hover bar down; the craft rose a bit.

He flicked controls; the board was clear. "Hop in; my meter's running."

They rushed to comply, ducking to keep from bumping heads on the cave ceiling. With one foot on a mounting step, Badure paused. "What was that?"

They all heard it—the sounds of running, voices, and the clatter of weapons. "Hot pursuit," answered Han. "No time to punch tickets, folks: stay gripped!"

He rammed up the impeller control, red-zoning the engine. The hover-raft shot out of the cave, nearly losing Bollux, who had been in the process of boarding. Badure and Chewbacca dragged him aboard.

The Survivors were closer than Han had thought; they had assumed positions around the cave and were closing in on it. The hover-raft zoomed from the cave near ground level, engines complaining. One or two Survivors had the presence of mind to shoot as the raft flashed by, but most either stood frozen or sought a lower elevation to keep from being run down. The few shots went wild, and Hasti put out a few rounds at random to keep the Survivors' heads down. The raft tore through a wide arc and headed down the valley.

"Where to, citizens?" Han grinned.

"Just turn on the heaters!" yelled Hasti.

The valley widened quickly, then gave way down to an open plain carpeted with bobbing, spindly amber grass. The hover-raft was equipped with rudimentary navigational gear. Han set a course for J'uoch's mining camp. Not wanting to use the raft's running lights, he cut his speed back and peered through the windshield, thankful it was a bright night.

The wind of their passage snatched the warmth out of the heater grids. Hasti discovered a folded tarp in one corner of the cargo bed and pulled at it, but stopped and called to the others. "Look at what they had onboard!"

Han couldn't turn from his steering, but Chewbacca, sitting next to him, pulled a handful of the tarp over the back of the driver's seat. Carefully fastened to the tarp were strands of plastic, meticulously fashioned to look like the amber grass of the plains. A camouflage cover.

"This crate comes equipped with an aerial-sensor, too," Han noted. "With a little warning and time to cover up, this thing would be just about impossible to spot without first-rate equipment." And the cave had been big enough to hold more rafts like this one. But that left the question of how a group of primitives like the Survivors, on a back-eddy planet like Dellalt, had set up an operation like this.

Han slowed just enough for Chewbacca to wrestle the collapsible canopy into place. They crowded onto the short couches of the cramped pilot-passenger compartment, lit by the glow of the dashboard instruments and Bollux's photoreceptors. Outside, the moons and stars lit a sea of waving grassland as it blurred under the raft's darkened bow. Eventually the heaters made some headway, and Han opened his flight jacket.

Badure sighed. "If that was the *Queen*'s log-recorder disk back there, we can write it off. The antenna mast destroyed it completely."

Han posed the question: "But how did the Survivors get it in the first place? I thought it was back in the vaults."

"They were talking like it's been theirs all along," Hasti put in, shifting in a futile attempt to find more room between Bollux and Badure in the back seat.

Skynx, in his best classroom voice, chimed in. "The facts,

as we know them, are as follows. Lanni somehow obtained the log-recorder disk and deposited it in a lockbox in the vaults. She evinced an interest in the mountains. J'uoch discovered her secret, or some part of it, and killed Lanni in trying to obtain the disk. And, here were the Survivors with either the same disk or one identical to it.

"Now, Lanni was a pilot, flying freight and operational missions, isn't that right? Suppose she happened to be airborne when the Survivors were holding one of their outdoor ceremonies, and either traced their signal or saw the light?"

Han nodded. "She could've landed somewhere, scouted, and bagged the log-recorder!" He trimmed the craft and corrected its course a bit.

Hasti agreed. "She could have. Dad taught her to fly, and a lot about wilderness survival and reconnaissance."

Badure picked up the thread. "So she put the disk in the lockbox and stopped off across the lake to see if she could detect a bounce or signal leakage or find out anything about the Survivors' base, or if she'd stirred them up. I bet the treasure's back there under the mountain."

They rode in silence for a time. Then Han spoke: "That would only leave two questions: how to get the *Falcon* back . . . and how to spend all that money."

Han's best efforts failed to nurse much speed from the antiquated raft. He kept the airwatch sensor on, depressed as low to the horizon astern as possible, but he detected no pursuit. He was still unsatisfied, having come up with no conclusions as to what the Survivors had been doing with those cargo craft, what the hatch face off the *Queen of Ranroon* actually meant, or how it was all connected with the treasure.

Dellalt's sun set off a purple dawn; grassland disappeared under the hover-raft's bow. They had nearly crossed the basin of grassland formed by a curve in the mountain range and were bearing toward the mining camp when Bollux leaned over the driver's seat and said, "Captain, I've been making communication monitoring sweeps as you ordered, listening for activity on the Survivors' frequency."

Han immediately became anxious. "Are they on the air?"

"No," answered the 'droid. "After all, their antenna mast was destroyed. But I also checked other frequencies mentioned in Skynx's tapes, and I've found something peculiar. There are transmissions on a very unusual setting coming from the direction of the campsite. They're odd because, although I can't pick them up clearly, they appear to be cyber-command signals."

Han's brow furrowed. Automata-command signals? "Mining equipment?" he asked the 'droid.

"No," answered Bollux. "These aren't the usual heavy-equipment patterns or industrial signals."

Badure turned the raft's commo rig to the setting Bollux had been monitoring but was unable to pick up anything clearly. Taking a bearing from the 'droid, Han changed course minutely and made a slow approach toward the mountains. Setting the airwatch sensor to full-scan, he readied Chewbacca and the others to pull the camouflage tarp over the raft at a moment's notice.

He came in slowly, taking his direction from the 'droid. They had already walked into one trap by investigating signals and, though it was important that they find out what these new ones meant, Han had no intention of being ambushed a second time. He lowered the raft's lift factor until it was bending the grass down, barely clearing the ground.

"Signals strengthening, Captain," advised Bollux.

They were approaching a rise in the plains, a ripple in the landscape preliminary to the sloping of the mountains. Han settled the hover-raft in behind the rise and got out of the craft. Parting the grass delicately, he and Chewbacca belly-crawled to the crest to have a look.

Less than a kilometer away the foothills began. Han squinted through his blaster's scope. "There's something down there, where that gully comes down to the plain."

The Wookiee agreed. They withdrew with care and told the others what they had seen. Sunrise was near.

"Skynx and Hasti, take lookout on the rise," Han directed. "Bollux and Badure, guard the raft. Chewie and I will move in; you all know the signal system. If you have to get out, at least you've got a boat now." None of them made any objections, though Hasti looked as if she wanted to.

The *Millennium Falcon*'s captain and first mate split off to the right and left of the rise, moving stealthily through the tall, amber grass, each of them keeping careful count in his mind. They had worked together so often that they automatically orchestrated their moves, without benefit of chrono or signal.

Han swept left, approaching the anomaly in the terrain that had attracted his attention. As he had thought, the lumps at the base of the foothills were a cluster of camouflage covers, a little too sudden and consolidated to be a part of the landscape. He saw no sentries or patrols, no surveillance of any kind, and so changed course to his right.

He heard something in the grass that might have been a small insect's buzz; the sound scarcely traveled a few meters. Han assumed his partner's signal had been sounding for a while.

He homed to it, parted a tuft of grass, and met his copilot with a grin. They talked in quick hand-motions; Chewbacca's recon had yielded the same results as Han's—with one addition; there was a guard, evidently a Survivor, walking a slow post. They made their plan and moved forward again. Han's first inclination was to use the stun-gun carried by Badure, but there was too much chance that someone would hear the discharge or see the blue light of the shot.

The sentry was dressed in common Dellaltian mode rather than in Survivor garb. He strolled along his circuit carelessly, armed with a Kell Mark II Heavy Assault Rifle. He carried the Kell at a sloppy shoulder arms. Like sentries in most of the places Han had ever seen, the man was convinced that nothing would happen and that he was walking guard for no good reason. He sauntered past, thinking thoughts of no great consequence—which was just as well. Those idle thoughts were dispelled a moment later when a hulking shape rose out of the grass behind him and expertly tapped him behind the ear with a bowcaster butt. The guard fell face-first into the grass.

Han retrieved the heavy-assault rifle, and the two partners made a hasty scout of the area. There were no more guards, but the thing that had attracted Han's attention through the blaster scope proved most interesting. All manner of ground-effect surface vehicles, all of them cargo models, were gathered there under camouflage covers, secured. A quick series of random checks revealed no cargo aboard any of them.

"What'd they need twenty flatbeds for?" Han wondered aloud as he waved his companions forward. "Plus two or three back at the mountain base?"

The others came up behind them. Badure explained that they had secured the stolen hover-raft with its own camouflage cover, behind the rise. They helped Han and Chewbacca in a precautionary smashing of the fleet's communication equipment. None of them could come up with a plausible reason for the strange gathering of craft either.

"There's a gully leading up into the foothills," Han said, jerking his thumb. "How far are we from J'uoch's mining camp?"

"Straight up that way," Hasti told him, indicating the gully. "We can work our way along a few ridge lines and we'll be there. Or, we could go along the valley floors and washes."

Han hefted the Kell rifle. "Let's move out now; we'll all go. I don't want to leave anybody behind in case we get a break and get the *Falcon* back; we can raise ship right away."

They started into the foothills, eyes darting nervously for any sign of ambush. Bollux, monitoring, picked up no evidence of sensors. The gully's floor had been sluiced by rains down to hard stone, scored and chewed as if heavy equipment had passed over it. They had seen no track or tread marks on the plain, but the resilient grass probably wouldn't have held them.

Bollux reported that the automata-command signals were much stronger now. "They're repetitive," the 'droid informed them, "as if someone is running the same test sequence over and over."

The gully cut through the first two ridges and gave out on the next, the highest they had reached. The ground here was all rock, still showing signs of the passage of what Han assumed to be machinery. That the Survivors had some special interest in J'uoch's camp was obvious; it remained to be seen if it had to do with the treasure. But uppermost in Han's mind was recovery of the *Millennium Falcon*.

They topped the ridge, advancing at a low crawl, to look down into the valley below. Hasti gasped, as did Skynx with a sound like a subdued hiccup. Bollux gazed without comment, less surprised than the others. Han's and Chewbacca's mouths hung open, and Badure whispered, "By the Maker!"

Now the fleet of cargo craft, the marks on the stone gully floor, the gist of the Survivors' ceremony—even the huge chamber in which they had been imprisoned—all made sense. Those monolithic stone slabs set deep in the mountain warren weren't tables, runways, or partitions.

They were benches.

And below were gathered the occupants that sat on those benches, at least a thousand of the bulky war-robots built at the command of Xim the Despot. They stood immobile, broad and impassive, mightily armored—man-shaped battle machines half again Han's height. They gleamed with a mirror-bright finish designed to reflect laser weaponry. Survivors moved among them with testing equipment, running the checks Bollux had detected.

"These are the ones!" Skynx whispered gleefully. "The thousand guardians Xim set onboard the *Queen of Ranroon* to look after his treasure. I wonder how many trips it took to ferry them all out here? And what are they here for?"

"The only possible reason's over there," replied Hasti, gesturing with her chin, raising up on her elbows. From their vantage point they could see J'uoch's mining camp, which straddled two sides of a great crevasse. The barracks, shops, and storage buildings were on one side, the kilometers-wide mining-operations site on the other, the two connected by a massive trestle bridge left from old Dellaltian mining efforts. The camp seemed to be operating as usual, its heavy equipment tearing away at the ground.

And on the side of the site, Han saw something that nearly made him whoop out loud. He pounded the Wookiee's shoulder, pointing. There, the *Millennium Falcon* sat on her triangle of landing gear. The starship seemed intact and operational.

But she won't be, Han caught himself up short, *if those groundpounders of Xim's get at her*.

At that moment there was a flurry of activity among the Survivors below. Their testing sequences were done. They scurried out from among the irregularly placed robots and gathered at a gleaming golden podium that had been set up on one side of the valley. A transmission horn projected from the podium, which was adorned with Xim's death's-head emblem. The Survivor on the podium touched a control.

Every war-robot on the valley floor straightened to alertness, squaring shoulders, coming to stiff, straddle-legged attention. Cranial turrets swung; optical pickups came to bear on the podium. The Survivor on the podium spoke.

"He's calling the Corps Commander forward," Skynx explained in a muted voice.

"I know that man on the podium," Hasti whispered slowly. Then more quickly, "I recognize the white blaze in his hair. He's the assistant to the steward of the treasure vaults!"

From the massed robots stepped their leader, identical to the others in his corps but for a golden insignia glittering on his breastplate. His rigid, weighty tread shook the ground, the epitome of military precision, his movements revealing immense power. He halted before the podium. From his aged vocoder came a deep, resonant question. Skynx translated in whispers.

"What do you require of the Guardian Corps?" the machine intoned.

"That with which you were entrusted is now in jeopardy," answered the Survivor on the podium, the steward's assistant.

"What do you require of the Guardian Corps?" repeated the robot, uninterested in details.

The Survivor pointed. "Follow the gully trail as we've marked it for you. It will bring you to your enemies. Destroy all that you find there. Kill everyone you encounter."

The armored head regarded him for a moment, as if in doubt, then replied: "You occupy the control platform; the Guardian Corps will obey. We will pass in review, as programmed, then go forth." The Corps Commander's cranial turrets rotated as he issued the squeals of his signalry.

The war-robots began moving, forming an irregular line, moving just as their commander had. Without cadence or formation, they grouped to one side of the podium. But as they passed it, the transmission horn's command circuitry automatically directed them to assume their review mode. From a massed group, they separated into ranks and files as they passed the podium, ten abreast, heavy feet rising and falling in step. With their Corps Commander at their head, the thousand war-robots marched, completing a circuit of the little valley.

Even the Survivors were hypnotized by it; the sight of their ancient charges walking again was nothing less than magical to them. Metal feet beat the canyon floor; arms as thick as a man's waist swung in unison. Han wondered if J'uoch's people wouldn't be able to hear their approach even over the sound of mining operations.

At some unseen signal from their Corps Commander, the robots stopped. The commander came around to face the podium with a rocking motion. From his vocoder boomed the words: "We are ready."

The Survivor on the podium instructed the robots to stand fast for a time. ''We go now to a vantage point, from which we will observe your attack. When we are in place you may proceed against the enemy.'' He and the other Survivors hurried off to watch the carnage. Presently the air was still, the war-robots waiting patiently, the only sound the distant buzz of the mining camp.

''We've got to get to the camp first,'' Han declared as they drew back from the ridge and got to their feet.

''Are you completely vacuum-happy?'' Hasti wanted to know. ''We'll get there just in time to go through the meat-grinder!''

''Not if we hurry. Those windup soldiers down there will have to go the long way around; we can run the ridge line if we're careful and get there first. The *Falcon*'s our only way off this mud-ball; if we can't get to her, we're going to have to tip J'uoch that the robots are on their way, or they'll rip my ship apart.''

He wished he could figure out why the Survivors were intent on destroying the mining camp and slaughtering its personnel. ''Everyone keep up. I'll go first, then Hasti, Skynx, Badure, Bollux, and Chewie on rearguard.''

Han put the heavy-assault rifle across his shoulders and set off, the others falling into their assigned places. But when Chewbacca beckoned Bollux, the labor 'droid hesitated. ''I'm afraid I'm not functioning up to specifications, First Mate Chewbacca. I'll have to come along as best I can.''

The Wookiee was torn by indecision for a moment, then trotted off after the rest, making it clear with hand motions and growls that Bollux was to come along as quickly as he could. The 'droid watched Chewbacca disappear from view, then opened his chest plastron so that he and Blue Max could speak in vocal-normal mode, as they preferred.

''Now, my friend,'' he drawled to the little computer module, ''perhaps you'll explain why you wanted us to stay behind. I practically had to lie to First Mate Chewbacca to do it; we may very well be left behind.''

Max, who had taken in the situation via direct linkage with Bollux, answered simply. "I know how to stop them. The war-robots, I mean; but we'd have to destroy them all to do it. We needed time to talk it over, Bollux."

And Blue Max related the plan he had conceived. The labor 'droid responded even more slowly than usual. "Why didn't you mention this before, when Captain Solo was here?"

"Because I didn't want him to decide! Those robots are doing what they were built to do, just like we are. Is that any reason to obliterate them? I wasn't even sure I should tell you; I didn't want you to blow your primary stacks in a decisional malfunction. Wait; what're you doing?"

The labor 'droid's chest plastron was swinging shut as he toed the edge of the ridge. "Seeking alternatives," he explained, stepping off.

Bollux slid and stumbled and plowed his way down the slope to the valley floor, working with heavy-duty suspension of arms and legs to keep from being damaged. At last he came to an awkward stop at the bottom amid a minor avalanche. Standing erect, he approached the war-robots, who waited in their gleaming, exact formation.

The Corps Commander's cranial turret rotated at Bollux's advance. A great arm swung up, weapons-apertures opening. "Halt. Identify or be destroyed."

Bollux replied with the recognition codes and authentication signals he had learned from Skynx's ancient tapes and technical records. The Corps Commander studied him for a moment, debating whether this strange machine ought to be obliterated, recognition codes or no. But the war-robots' deliberative circuitry was limited. The weapon-arm lowered again. "Accepted. State your purpose."

Bollux, with no formal diplomatic programming to draw upon and only his experience to guide him, began hesitantly. "You mustn't attack. You must disregard your orders; they were improperly given."

"They were issued through command signalry of the podium. We must accept. We are programmed; we respond.'' The cranial turret rotated to face front again, indicating that the subject bore no further discussion.

Bollux went on doggedly. ''Xim is dead! These orders of yours are wrong; they do not come from him; you cannot obey them!''

The turret swung to him again, the optical pickups betraying no emotion. ''Steel-brother, we are the war-robots of Xim. No alternative is thinkable.''

''Humans are not infallible. If you follow these orders, they'll lead to your destruction. Save yourselves!'' He could not admit that it would be by his own hand.

The vocoder boomed. ''Whether this is true or not, we carry out our orders. We are the war-robots of Xim.''

The Corps Commander faced front again. ''The waiting time has elapsed. Stand aside; no further delay will be tolerated.'' He emitted a squeal of signalry. The ranks of war-robots stepped off as one, arms swinging.

Bollux had to spring aside to keep from being trampled beneath them. His chest plastron swung open as he watched them go. ''What do we do now?'' Blue Max wanted to know. ''Captain Solo and the others will be down there, too.''

There was a quiver of sorrow in Bollux's voice modulation. ''The war-robots have their built-in programming. And we, my friend, have ours.''

THEY had worked their way to a ridge overlooking the outer perimeter of the mining camp before Han discovered Bollux wasn't with them. Han, incensed, slipped around a spire of rock for a look at the camp. ''I *told* that low-gear factory reject we needed him to monitor for sensors. Well, we're just going to have to be extra—''

Sirens began ululating through the camp. The travelers all hit the ground at once, but Han risked a peek around the spire. Now that they had been detected, information was more important than concealment.

The mining camp was swarming like an insect nest. Humans and other beings were running every which way to take up emergency stations. Those employees trusted by J'uoch were being issued arms and taking up defensive positions. Contact laborers were ordered by their overseers to retire across the bridge to the isolation and effective confinement of the plateau barracks area.

Han couldn't spot the sensor net he had tripped, but it was apparent that it had him pinpointed. Several reinforced fire teams were dashing to bunkers fronting Han's hiding place. Han saw that grounded near the *Millennium Falcon* and the gigantic mining lighter was another vessel, a small starship with the sleek lines of a scout.

Suddenly a response squad started up the hill to engage them, two human males with disruptor rifles, a horn-plated *W'iiri* scuttling on its six legs and bearing a grenade thrower, and an oily-skinned *Drall*, its red hide gleaming, lugging a gas projector.

Half-kneeling, half-crouching by the spire, Han dragged the old Kell Mark II around by its balance-point carrying handle. Knowing of the outdated weapon's powerful recoil, he braced himself before thumbing the firing stud. Blue energy sprang from the Kell's muzzle, tracing a broad line across the rock wall below. He was nearly knocked over backward by the Mark II's kick, but Chewbacca braced him. The rock sizzled, smoked, and shot sparks, then cracked, fragments and shards falling downslope. The response squad sought cover with gratifying freneticism.

"That should keep them off our necks until we can talk," Han judged. Cupping hand to mouth, he called out, "J'uoch! It's Solo! We have to talk, right away!"

The woman's voice, amplified by a loudhailer, rose from one of the bunkers. "Give me that log-recorder disk and throw down your guns, Solo; those are the only terms you'll get from me!"

"But she saw that we didn't have the disk," Badure muttered. "Didn't she guess that we couldn't get it from the lockbox?"

Han shouted down, "We've got no time to debate this, J'uoch; you and your whole camp are about to come under attack!" He pulled back suddenly as a barrage of small-arms fire opened up. Huddling back from it, the travelers clutched their heads in protection while energy- and projectile-searching fire probed the hillside. Rocks bubbled and exploded; shrapnel and splinters flew while explosive concussion battered their ears.

"I don't think she's going to be reasonable about this," predicted Badure.

"She's got to be," Han snapped, thinking of what would happen to his starship if the robots overran the camp.

The firing slowed for a moment, then, at some command they didn't hear, resumed even more heavily. "Face it, Solo," Hasti called to him over the din, "they want our hides and nothing less. The only way we'll get to the *Falcon* is if we can get to her while the robots are hitting the camp."

"When they're mixing it up with J'uoch's people? We wouldn't get two meters." At that moment the firing stopped again and a voice called his name from below.

Hasti was gazing at him alarmed. "Solo, what's wrong? You just went pale as perma-frost."

He paid her no attention but saw by Chewbacca's expression that the Wookiee, too, recognized the voice of Gallandro the gunman.

"Solo! Come down and negotiate like a reasonable fellow. We have a great deal to discuss, you and I." The voice was calm, amused.

Han realized that sweat was beginning to bead his brow despite the cold. A sudden suspicion hit him, and he threw himself up into the clear for an instant, just enough to ease the Mark II's barrel over the crest. The response squad was on the move and another was rushing to link up with it.

Han thumbed the trigger and hosed the barrel back and forth randomly. The heavy-assault rifle was a product of Dra III, made for the heavier, stronger inhabitants of that world, with its Standard-plus gravity. The Mark II's recoil forced him back a second time, but not before the play of its extremely powerful beam drove the advancing squads to cover once more.

"Spread out along the ridge or they'll outflank us!" Han ordered. His companions hurried to comply as Gallandro's voice came again.

"I knew you wouldn't have died in something as foolish as that uneven ship-to-ship action back at the city, Solo. And I knew the *Millennium Falcon* would draw you here in time, no matter what."

"You know just about everything, don't you?" Han riposted.

"Except where that log-recorder is. Come, Solo; I've struck a bargain with the delightful J'uoch here. Do the same, don't make things difficult. And don't make me come up there after you."

"C'mon, what's stopping you, Gallandro? There'll be nothing left of you but those little mustache beads!" Chewbacca and the others had taken up sniping at the response squads, pinning them down for now, but Han was worried about the armed aircraft in the mining camp.

The thought had no sooner formed than, scanning the sky, he saw a quick, dangerous shape swooping down at them. "Everybody down!"

The spaceboat, twin to the one that had been destroyed in the city by the lighter, made a quick preliminary pass at the ridge, its chin pods spitting. Anti-personnel rounds threw out clouds of flechettes; Han could feel the craft's afterblast as it darted by. He raised his head to see what damage it had done.

By some fortune the first pass, being hasty, had resulted in no one's being hit. But they were badly exposed there on the ridge; the next pass might well finish them all. Han pulled the heavy-assault rifle to him with a grunt of effort, pushed himself upright, and rushed out into the open on the back side of the ridge.

At the camp below, Gallandro conferred with J'uoch. "Madame, recall your boat; I'll trouble you to remember our deal." He spoke with a hint of impatience, as close to emotion as he ever let himself come. "Solo is mine, not to be killed by air attack."

Peering out of the bunker, she dismissed the objection with a wave of her hand. "What does it matter, as long as he's eliminated? My brother's using anti-personnel rounds; the log-recorder won't be damaged."

The gunman smiled, reserving his retaliation for a more convenient moment. He touched up his mustachios with a knuckle. "Solo is well armed, my dear J'uoch. You may be surprised at his resourcefulness, as may your brother."

Han raced over the open ground, keeping one eye out for available cover. Though hindered by the weight of the Mark

II, he adjusted it for maximum range and power level as he ran. He had thought about handing the weapon over to the Wookiee to let him shoot at the boat, but the *Falcon*'s first mate had little liking or affinity for energy weapons, preferring his bowcaster.

Han heard the boat begin its second pass. J'uoch's brother, R'all, dove at the exposed, fleeing man. Han threw himself into a troughlike depression in the rock, the Mark II clattering down next to him. The boat flashed past, so close that Han was in the dead area between the guns' fields of fire. Flechettes burst in long lines to either side of him. R'all flashed off, adjusting his weapons for a final pass.

Han got up, braced the Mark II's buttplate against the rock, and fired. Still the heavy-assault rifle's recoil made it jump and turn; the boat was out of range before he had come anywhere near it, and now was banking for a pass that was sure to find its target.

Han hitched himself around the stone trough and pulled the Mark II's bipod legs down. He had only one more trick left, and if that didn't work, he'd have no more worries about treasure, Gallandro, or the *Falcon*. Resettling so that his knees and the small of his back were higher than his shoulders, he wrestled the Mark II around and rested it on the incline of his legs. He set his feet against the bipod legs, holding the weapon tightly to steady it.

He squinted upward through the heavy-assault rifle's open sights. The boat came at him again. He bracketed it in the sights and waited until he heard the first concussion of R'all's fire.

Then he opened up, bracing the bucking Mark II with hands and feet, holding it fairly steady for the first time. The boat's pilot recognized his danger too late; an evasive maneuver failed and the heavy-assault rifle's full force caught the light boat, tearing a long gash in the fuselage. Control circuitry and power panels erupted and a gaping hole appeared in the cockpit canopy. The boat wallowed and shook, out of control, and disappeared in a steep dive, trailing smoke and flame. A moment later the ground shook with impact.

"R'all!" J'uoch screamed to her dead brother as she clawed her way out of the bunker. The boat had exploded on impact, scattering burning debris over a long, wide swath of ground.

Gallandro caught her arm. "R'all is gone," said the gunman with no particular sympathy. "Now, we will do this thing as we originally agreed. Your ground forces will encompass Solo's position, and we'll force him out into the open and capture him alive."

She wrenched her arm away, seething with rage. "He killed my brother! I'll get Solo if I have to blow these mountains apart!" She turned and called out to her enforcer, the hulking Egome Fass, who stolidly awaited orders. "Get the crew to the loadlifter and warm up main batteries." She was about to turn from him when an unfamiliar sound, rising over the fury of the boat's destruction, made her pause. "What's that?"

Gallandro heard it, too, as did Egome Fass and all the others in the camp. It was a steady beat, shaking the ground, the pounding of metal feet. The column of Xim's war-robots appeared at a spot farther along the mining camp's perimeter, having finished their roundabout march from their mustering place.

They came in glittering ranks, arms swinging, unstoppable. When their Corps Commander gave the signal that freed them from lockstep, they spread out across the site to begin their devastation. J'uoch stared in astonishment, not quite believing what she saw. Gallandro, fingering one of the gold beads that held his mustache, tried to remain calm. "So, Solo was telling the truth after all."

Up on the ridge, Chewbacca hooted to the exhausted Han, indicating the camp. Han wearily moved to the ridge and joined his companions in looking down on a scene of utter chaos. Their own presence had been forgotten by the response squads, fire teams, and other camp defenders.

The war-robots, faithful to their instructions, moved to obliterate everything in their path. First to feel the battle machines' power was a domed building that housed repair shops. Han saw a robot smash through the dome's personnel door while a half-dozen of his comrades set to work wrenching off the rolling doors. Pieces of lockslab gave way like soggy pulp, and a group of Xim's perfect guardians moved into the dome, demolishing work areas and heavy equipment, ripping down hoisting gear, and firing with the weapons built into their metal hands. Heatbeams and particle discharges flashed, throwing weird shadows within the dome. The building flared, pitted in a score of places. The robots' fire lanced the dome, probing the sky. More of them pressed in to tear apart everything they encountered.

It was the same elsewhere in the vast mining site. The war-robots, with their limited reasoning capacity, were taking their orders literally, devoting as much attention to devastating buildings and machinery as to attacking camp personnel. Whole companies of the war machines were moving among the abandoned mining autohoppers and landgougers, tow-motors and excavators.

The robots blasted and sprayed fire everywhere, making full use of their tremendous strength. One of them was sufficient to reduce a small vehicle to rubble in moments; for larger equipment, groups cooperated. Tracks were wrenched from crawlers, whole vehicles lifted off the ground, their axles snapped, wheels ripped off, cabs torn loose, and engines yanked out of their compartments like toys. A battalion moved toward a barge shell that contained the latest shipment of refined ore. The robots tore into it, swinging and firing, wrecking everything they encountered and hurling the pieces aside.

Meanwhile, others engaged the camp personnel in determined combat, turning the camp into a scene of unbelievable chaos. War-robots flooded through the operations site. "They're headed for the *Falcon*!" Han bellowed, then charged down the ridge. Badure's shouted warnings went unheeded. Chewbacca went racing after his partner; Badure took off, too, followed by Hasti.

Skynx was left alone, staring after them. Although going after his companions seemed a good way to ensure that he would never see the chrysalis stage, he realized that he had become a part of the oddly met group and felt acutely incomplete without them. Abandoning good Ruurian prudence, he flowed off after the others.

At the bottom of the slope, Han found his way blocked by one of the robots. It was just finishing demolishing one of the bunkers, kicking the fusion-formed walls to bits and hurling the larger chunks easily. The robot turned on him, its optical lenses extending a bit as their focal point adjusted. It lifted and aimed its weapon-hand.

Han quickly brought up the heavy-assault rifle and fired point-blank, knocked back several steps by the sustained recoil. His fire blazed blue against the mirror-bright chest. The machine itself was driven back a step with an electronic outburst and was ripped open. Han moved his aim up to the spot where the cranial turret was joined to the armored body.

The head came off, flying apart, smoke and flame gushing from the decapitated body. Han shot it again for good luck and the Mark II's beam came only faintly; the weapon was virtually exhausted. But it served to topple the robot, which landed with a resounding clatter.

More war-robots were reaching that part of the camp. Chewbacca descended to level ground, trailing dust and tumbling pebbles, just as another machine came at Han. The Wookiee threw his bowcaster to his shoulder and aimed. But his fire bounced off the robot's hard breastplate; he had forgotten his weapon was still loaded with regular rounds rather than with explosives.

Han threw aside the useless assault rifle and drew his blaster, setting it for maximum power. Chewbacca stepped back, removing the magazine from his weapon and taking one of the larger ones from his bandoleer. Han stepped in front to cover him in a stiff-armed firing stance. He squeezed off bolt after bolt, deliberately and with great concentration, into the approaching robot's cranial turret. Four blaster rounds stopped the machine just as it fired in response. Han ducked the heatbeam that split the air where he had stood. As the robot fell, the beam traced a quick arc upward.

Defenders that were sufficiently well armed were putting up stiff resistance with rocket launchers, grenade throwers, heavy weapons, and crew-served guns. Living beings and war machines were reeling back and forth in a storm of energy discharges, bullets, shells, and fire. Four robots lifted the reinforced roof off a boxlike hut as the men defending it fired frantically. Using a chattering quad-gun, the men's shots kicked up enormous clots of ground and blew away segments of the machines even as they attacked. More robots approached to join in; the crew, with barrels depressed, traversed their gun back and forth in a frenzy, taking a terrible toll. But even though several crew members used side arms in a desperate attempt to keep from being overrun, the roofless hut was gradually outflanked and disappeared behind a wall of gleaming enemies.

Not far away, a dozen of J'uoch's employees had formed a firing line in three ranks, concentrating on any robot that came near, and were thus far succeeding in preserving their lives. Elsewhere, isolated miners worked their way among the high rocks to exchange earnest fire with the machines, which couldn't negotiate the incline.

But many of the camp personnel were caught alone or unarmed, or were surrounded. The fighting was heaviest and fiercest there, the robots' implacability matched against the furious determination of the living beings. Humans, humanoids, and nonhumanoids dodged, evaded, ran, or fought as well as they could. War-robots simply advanced, overcoming obstacles or being destroyed, without any sense of self-preservation whatsoever.

Han saw a stocky Maltorran run up behind a robot with a heavy beamdrill cradled in its brachia and press it flush against the machine's back. The robot exploded, and the drill, exploding from the backwash, killed the Maltorran. Two mining techs, a pair of human females, had gotten to a landgouger and were making a resolute effort to break through the automaton lines, crushing many of them under the gouger's tremendous treads, maneuvering to avoid their weapons' aim. But soon the fire of many robots converged on them, finding the landgouger's engine. The gouger was blown apart with an ear-splitting explosion. Elsewhere, Han saw a robot grappling with three *W'iiri* who had swarmed onto it, tearing at it with their pincers. The machine plucked them off one by one, smashing them and tossing them aside, broken and dying; but in the next moment, the robot itself toppled over, disabled by the damage they had done it.

"We'll never get through to the *Falcon*!" Badure yelled at Han. "Let's get out of here!" More robots were approaching, and to attempt a return up the steep ridge under fire would be out of the question. The old man proposed, "We can withdraw across the bridge and take shelter in the barracks area!"

Han glanced across the crevasse. "It's a dead end; there's no other way off that plateau." He considered blowing the bridge behind them, but that would take the *Millennium Falcon*'s guns, or those of the lighter.

The latter ship was herself under attack. A ring of dozens of war-robots had formed around her, furiously firing while the huge cargo ship's engines strained to lift her off, her main batteries answering the robots' fire. Many of the robots' weapons were silent, their power exhausted, but more of the machines were gathering around the lighter every moment. Though the vessel's salvos wiped out five and ten robots at a time, sending them flying in heaps of tangled, liquefied wreckage, Xim's machines kept clustering to her, weapons-hands blazing, standing their ground. Soon hundreds were massed there.

Others turned their attention to Gallandro's scoutship, cutting swaths in her hull. The lighter rose unsteadily, her shields glowing from the concentrated fire, her heavy guns raking back and forth. Just at the moment it seemed she would reach safety, one of her aged defensive shields failed; after all, the lighter was an old industrial craft, not a combat vessel. The ship became a brilliant ball of incandescence, showering torn hull fragments and molten metal into the crevasse. The detonation knocked combatants, living and machine both, to the ground. Han was on his feet again in an instant, charging toward the *Falcon* with his blaster in his hand, determined that the same thing would not happen to his beloved ship.

So was someone else. Across the battlefield a ring of war-robots was closing in on the converted freighter, preparing to demolish her, their arms raised and weapon apertures open. Others were shoving the wreckage of Gallandro's scoutship toward the brink of the crevasse.

Another machine, far smaller than they, blocked the way to the *Millennium Falcon*, seeming fragile and vulnerable. Bollux's chest plastron was open, and Blue Max's photoreceptor gazed forth. From his vocoder tumbled the signals learned from tapes shown him by Skynx, amplified by the gear Bollux had cannibalized from the podium.

The advance stopped; the war-robots waited in confusion, unable to resolve the conflicting orders. The Corps Commander appeared, the death's-head insignia of Xim gleaming on his breastplate. He loomed over Bollux. "Stand aside; everything here is to be destroyed."

"Not this vessel," Max told him in the command signalry. "This one is to be spared."

The towering robot studied the two-in-one machines. "Those were not our orders."

Max's voice, directed through the podium's scavenged horn, was high. "Orders may be amended!"

The thick arm came up, and Bollux prepared for the end of his long existence. But instead a metal finger indicated the *Falcon*, and the command came: "Spare that vessel."

With signals of acknowledgment, the other war-robots moved on. The Corps Commander still regarded the labor 'droid and the computer module. "I am still not sure about you two, machines. What are you?"

"Talking doorstops, if you listen to our captain's opinion," offered Blue Max.

The Corps Commander stood stock-still in surprise. "Humor? Was that not humor? What have machines become? What kind of automata are you?"

"We are your steel-brothers," Bollux put in. The Corps Commander made no further comment, but continued on his way.

The waves of robots had thwarted Han's effort to reach his ship. One, stepping over the ruins of a crew-served gun and its slain crew, advanced toward the pilot. Han was looking elsewhere, helping Hasti fire blaster and disruptor shots at a machine approaching from the opposite direction. Han's shot scored the cranial turret; Hasti's, less practiced, sent its torso and limbs in a wild scatter. Badure was firing at still another, a long-barreled power pistol in each hand.

Chewbacca stepped into the path of the oncoming robot and triggered his bowcaster. Its staves straightened, and the explosive quarrel detonated against the robot's chest armor, holing it but not stopping it. The Wookiee held his ground, jacking the foregrip of his bowcaster and firing twice more, this time hitting the robot's head and midsection. The machine came on relentlessly. Its weapons-hands were raised, but their power had been drained in battle. Chewbacca backed a step and came up against Han, who was still firing the other way.

Then the robot toppled forward. Chewbacca, standing in its very shadow, would have leaped clear but realized that Han was unaware of his imminent danger. The Wookiee shoved the pilot aside with a sweep of his hairy arm but failed himself to avoid the tottering automaton. It struck him and pinned his right arm and leg to the ground. Skynx raced to him and began pulling ineffectually at the Wookiee.

Another robot chose that moment to step over the one Han and Hasti had just downed. Since Hasti's disruptor was drained, Han moved forward, then realized that his blaster's cautionary pulser was tingling his palm in silent warning that his weapon, too, was spent.

He whirled and called to his sidekick, then saw the Wookiee wriggling to extricate himself from under the fallen robot. Chewbacca paused long enough to loft his bowcaster into the air one-handed.

Han caught it, pivoted, dropped to one knee, and pressed the stock to his cheek. He squeezed, and the explosive blast blew up against the juncture of the approaching machine's shoulder and arm. The metal limb fell away, and the robot shuddered but kept coming.

Han tried to jack the bowcaster's foregrip and found, as had the man in the city, that his human strength was insufficient. He stopped himself from dodging out of the way; Chewbacca lay trapped, directly behind him. Badure, some distance away, couldn't hear Han's shouts for aid. Hasti fired at the machine with the only weapon she had left, the dart-shooter, but emptying the whole clip at it served no purpose.

Han avoided Chewbacca's efforts to swipe him out of the way and shifted his grip on the bowcaster, preparing for a last, hopeless defense.

THE war-robot seemed to block out the sky, a machine out of a nightmare. But abruptly its cranial turret flew apart in a blast of charred circuitry and ruptured power routing as a thread-thin, precisely aimed beam found its most vulnerable point. Han scarcely had the presence of mind to take a step back, nearly treading on Chewbacca, as the automaton crashed at his feet like an old tree.

He leaped up onto its back and scanned the battlefield. Far across it, a form in gray waved once.

"Gallandro!" The gunman gave him a bare, stark smile that held nothing Han could read. Han drew without thinking, then remembered his blaster was empty. Just then a robot appeared behind Gallandro, closing in on him, arms wide. Han never made a conscious decision, but pointed and shouted a warning.

The gunman was too far away to have heard, but he saw Han's expression and understood. He spun and ducked instinctively. The robot just missed with a blow of enormous power. With an incredible display of agility and reflexes, Gallandro seized the arm and rode the robot's recovery-backswing, at the same time putting two quick shots into its head. Letting go, he was flung clear to land lightly and put a last bolt into the robot as it fell.

Han watched the incident with awe. By far the most dangerous machine there was Gallandro. The gunman gave Han a sardonic bow and a mocking grin, then, like a ghost, was gone again in the swirl of battle.

The air was hot with the unleashed energies of the battle. With Skynx's and Badure's help, Chewbacca had squirmed free of the fallen robot, while Hasti stood nervous guard. Taking back his bowcaster, the Wookiee made a quick motion toward the robot that had so narrowly missed nailing Han and barked a question.

"It was *him*, Gallandro," Han told his partner. "A fifty-, maybe sixty-meter tight-beam shot." The Wookiee shook his head in bewilderment, mane flying.

There was nowhere to go except the camp living area, across the bridge. "Will you two stop chatting and get going?" Hasti called. "They'll have us surrounded if we don't hurry."

They started for the bridge at the best pace they could manage, a half-trot, each of them bearing a number of minor injuries and wounds. They moved in a defensive ring, Badure at the leading edge with his power pistols, Hasti to his right and Skynx to his left, with Chewbacca and Han bringing up the rear, back-pedaling and sideskipping. A metallic voice called Han's name.

Bollux somehow injected a note of immense relief into his vocoder drawl. "We're so glad you're all safe. The *Millennium Falcon*'s unharmed, at least for the time being, but I don't know how long that will last. Unfortunately, it's inaccessible just now."

Han wanted to know exactly what that meant, but Bollux interrupted. "No time for that now. I have the means to remedy our situation, sir," he told the pilot, resettling the signalry equipment he had taken from the robots' command podium. "But you'll have to get to the far side of the bridge before I can use it."

"You're on, Bollux! All right, everybody, scratch gravel!" They hastened away. The attack hadn't gotten as far as the bridge yet, but resistance was crumbling rapidly.

At the bridgehead Bollux paused. "I'll be staying here, sir. The rest of you must proceed across."

Han looked around. "What're you going to do, talk them

into suicide? You better stay with us; we'll take to the high ground on the plateau."

With a strange sincerity, the 'droid refused. "Thank you for your concern, sir; Max and I are flattered. But we have no intention of being destroyed, I assure you."

Han felt ridiculous for arguing with a 'droid, but insisted, "This is not the place to get noble, old-timer."

Seeing the war-robots converging on them, Bollux persevered. "I really must insist that you go, sir; our basic programming won't permit Max and me to see you come to harm here."

They departed unwillingly. Hasti walked with the tired Skynx beside her. Badure patted the 'droid's hard shoulder and trudged off, and Chewbacca waved a paw. "Look after Max," Han said, "and don't get yourself junked, old fellow."

Bollux watched them go, then searched among the rocks and boulders for a place of concealment at that end of the bridge.

Han and his companions slogged wearily across the bridge among others who had survived the robots' onslaught and were now falling back for a final stand. At the halfway point they came upon the body of a fallen mining tech who had died before she could complete the crossing, a *T'rinn* whose bright plumage was now charred and burned from combat. Han gently took a shoulder-fired rocket launcher from her lifeless claws, the weapon still containing a half-magazine of rockets. He was just standing up when a figure broke from the stream of retreating miners and attacked him, swinging an empty needlebeamer.

"Murderer!" J'uoch shrieked, her first blow grazing the pilot over the ear before he was aware of her onset. "You killed my brother! I'll kill you, you filthy animal!" Dazed, he pushed himself backward to avoid the blows she was raining on him, forearm up to protect himself.

Chewbacca would have torn the hysterical woman from his friend, but at the same moment he was struck from behind, a heavy blow from a thick forearm. The Wookiee fell to his knees, losing his bowcaster, as a huge weight fell upon him: Egome Fass, the enforcer. The two huge creatures rolled over and over, wrestling, tearing at one another. Retreating miners skirted the struggles, concerned only with staying alive.

Badure, weakened by the ordeal, waved an unsteady power pistol at J'uoch. But before he could fire, Hasti had thrown herself at the woman who had killed her sister Lanni. They whirled and fought, hacking and kicking at each other, finding reserves of strength in their mutual hatred.

Badure pulled Han up just as J'uoch got her forearm around Hasti's throat. But Hasti writhed free of the hold, dropped and turned, put her head and shoulder against the other's midsection and drove her back with feet churning and driving. J'uoch was shoved backward against the bridge's waist-high railing and toppled over it. She fell screaming, in a flurry of coveralls, reaching and thrashing. Hasti's momentum had carried her halfway over the rail, too.

Badure was there in time to pull her back from the rail, grabbing the material of her clothes. She sobbed for breath, her pulse pounding. Then it came to her that the roaring she heard wasn't in her ears, Chewbacca and Egome Fass had gone to war.

It had been the second time J'uoch's enforcer had struck the Wookiee from behind. What the *Falcon*'s first mate felt now could only pallidly be described as outrage. Han waved Badure off when the old man would have shot Egome Fass.

The two punched and grasped at one another while Han leaned against the rail to watch the honor match. "Aren't you going to help him?" Hasti puffed, her face showing the scratches and abrasions of her own match.

"Chewie wouldn't appreciate that," Han told her, keeping one eye on the rallying of robots at the end of the bridge. But he eased a pistol from Badure's belt in case the match didn't go as it should.

Egome Fass had gotten a choke-hold on Chewbacca. Rather than squirm out of it or apply an in-fighting trick, the

Wookiee chose to lock both hands on his opponent's arm and turn it into a contest of pure strength. Egome Fass was bulkier, Chewbacca more agile, but the question of brute force was still open. Their arms quivered and muscles jumped in the straining backs.

Bit by bit the arm was levered away from Chewbacca's throat. The Wookiee showed his fangs in savage triumph, and burst free of the hold. But Egome Fass wasn't done with tests of strength. He lunged at his antagonist for a deadly hug. Chewbacca accepted it.

They staggered back and forth, first the Wookiee's feet leaving the bridge, then the enforcer's. Both applied their full brawn in fearsome constriction. Egome Fass's feet were lifted clear of the bridge and stayed that way as the Wookiee held him aloft, muscles standing out like cables under Chewbacca's pelt. The enforcer's struggle became more frantic, less aggressive. Panic crept into his movements. Then there was a crack, and Egome Fass's body slumped. Chewbacca let go, and the enforcer slid limply to the bridge's surface. The Wookiee had to rest a paw on a support to steady himself.

Han teetered over with the rocket launcher over one shoulder. "You're getting decrepit; two tries to put away a bum like that!" He laughed and affectionately punched the Wookiee's shoulder.

"Enough, enough!" Skynx protested, tugging at Han's red-seamed trouser leg. "The robots are ready to attack; Bollux said we must be across the bridge."

Han didn't know how much chance the labor 'droid stood of stopping the steel horde, but he and the others obeyed Skynx's pleas. There was no one to stand with them at the end of the bridge. The miners who had reached it had gone either to put up barricades in the buildings or to find safe places among the rocks.

Han stopped as soon as his boots were off the bridge. He sat on the ground, looking back across the bridge. "We might as well face it here."

No one made any objection. Badure gave Hasti one of his pistols, while Chewbacca fitted a new magazine into his bowcaster. Hasti put one arm around Han's neck and kissed his cheek. "That's for a good try," she explained.

Bollux crouched in the jumble of boulders on the far side of the bridge. The mining-operations site was now completely razed. Machinery was burned and buildings were flattened, and no living thing could be seen.

The Corps Commander had mustered all his forces with high-pitched summonses. Other resistance had been crushed; all that remained was to annihilate the barracks area on the far side of the bridge, the successful completion of their first combat action in generations.

Bollux waited and didn't try to interfere. That would have been useless, he knew; they weren't so different from him. The machines gathered around their commander by the hundreds. The Corps Commander indicated the way with a long metal arm, gleaming like a statue of death in the blue-white light. He stumped toward the bridge, and his awesome troops crowded after him. And as the war-robots drew abreast of him, about to step onto the bridge, Bollux triggered the command signalry he had brought from the podium.

The Corps Commander fell into a marching step as the signals reached him. He didn't question them; the commands were automatic, military, geared to a segment of him that didn't doubt or ponder. Such was his construction.

Behind their commander the other war-robots responded to the signal as well, falling into ranks of ten, in step with their leader. Funneled onto the bridge, their ranks filled it from side to side. They stepped with meticulous precision. Metal feet tramped; arms swung in time.

"Will it work?" Bollux asked his friend.

Blue Max, tuned in with both their audio pickups, listened carefully, cautioning the 'droid not to bother him at this critical point. At Max's instruction, Bollux adjusted the marching tempo, matching the forced vibration of the robots' tread to the bridge's own natural frequency, creating a powerful resonance. The war-robots marched in to do battle for an overlord generations dead. The bridge began to quake, dust rising and forming a haze with the unified footfalls. Timbers reverberated, joints and stress members strained; the perfection of their marching made the robots a single, unimaginable power hammer. More of them poured onto the bridge and took up the step, adding to the concussions.

At last the bridge itself thrummed under them as Max found the perfect beat. All the robots were on the bridge, with no thought but to get to the other side and attack the enemy.

Han and the others rose, waiting. "I guess Bollux couldn't pull off his plan," Han said. The front rank, following their gleaming leader, had grown large. "We'll have to fall back."

"There's not much room for that," Hasti reminded him sadly. He had no answer.

Suddenly Skynx exclaimed, "Look!"

Han did, feeling a deep vibration through his boots. The bridge was shuddering in time with the robots' march, its timbers creaking and cracking with the punishment it couldn't absorb. Feet pounding, the robots marched on.

Then there was a rending snap; the vibration had found a member that couldn't support it. A timber bent and turned in its bed of press-poured material. The bed wouldn't accept the play and the timber twisted and split. All the supporting members at that side of the bridge gave way.

There were electronic bleats of distress from the war machines and the popping of aged rivets from the timber-joining plates. For a moment the whole doomed assemblage, robots and bridge, was suspended in space. Then all fell into the crevasse with a huge concussion, sending up clouds of rock dust and smoke and a wall of impact-noise that drove Han back from the crevasse's edge.

Wiping the dust from his eyes and spitting it out of his mouth, Han returned to the brink. Among the drifted dust and smoke he could see bridge timbers and the gleam of crumpled armor, the flare of circuit fires, overloaded power packs, broken leads, and shorted weapons. Suddenly Bollux appeared at the other side of the crevasse, waving stiffly, having divested himself of the scavenged equipment. Han returned the wave, laughing. *From now on those two are full crewmembers.*

A new sound made him look around in surprise and anger, mouthing a Corellian oath. The *Millennium Falcon* was lifting off. She rose on blaring thrusters, swinging out over the abyss. Han and Chewbacca watched in despair as they saw their ship whisked from under their noses despite all their efforts.

But the freighter settled gently on their side of the crevasse. They got to her just as her ramp-bay doors opened and the main ramp lowered, beneath and astern the cockpit. The main hatch rolled up, and there stood Gallandro. He welcomed them with a smile, his weapon conspicuously holstered. His fine clothing and beautiful scarf were soiled, but other than that, Han reflected, he looked none the worse for someone who had just waded through a horde of war-robots.

The gunman sketched a mocking bow. "I found myself obliged to play dead among the slain; I couldn't get to the ship until the robots had all left, or I'd have been of more assistance. Solo, those 'droids of yours are priceless!" His smile disappeared. "And so is Xim's treasure, eh? You're out for high stakes for a change; my compliments."

"You tracked me all the way from the Corporate Sector to tell me that?" Chewbacca had his bowcaster aimed at Gallandro, but Han knew that even that was no guarantee against the man's incredible speeddraw.

The gunman made a wry twist of his mouth. "Not originally. I was rather upset about our encounter there. But I'm a man of reason; I'm prepared to put that aside in view of the amount of money involved. Bring me in for a full cut and we forget the grudge. And you get your ship back; wouldn't that strike you as a fair arrangement?"

Han remained suspicious. "All of a sudden you're ready to kiss and make up?"

"The treasure, Solo, the treasure. The wealth of Xim would buy affection from anyone. All other considerations are secondary; surely that's in keeping with your own philosophy, isn't it?"

Han was confused. Hasti, who had come up behind him, said, "Don't trust him!"

Gallandro turned clear blue eyes on her. "Ah, the young lady! If he doesn't accept my offer, you'll be in a bad way as well, my dear; this vessel's weapons are functional." His voice went cold, the playacting evaporating. "Decide," he ordered Han crisply.

The defenders were beginning to emerge from the barracks, having seen the bridge collapse and the ship land. In another moment, escape might be much more complicated. Han reached out and pushed down Chewbacca's bowcaster. "Everybody onboard; we're back in business."

In moments they had lifted off with Han at the controls, uttering angry maledictions at the techs who had torn the starship apart in search of the log-recorder disk and reassembled her so inexpertly. "Why did J'uoch have the ship repaired, anyway?" Badure asked.

"She was either going to keep it for her own use or sell it," explained Gallandro. "She tried to sell me a lame story about her disagreements with you people, but considering the things I'd already discovered about your movements, the truth wasn't hard to guess."

Han brought the ship in to hover over the camp. "What about the other miners, the ones who lived?" Hasti asked.

"They've got food, weapons, supplies there," Badure said. "They can hold out until a ship shows up, or slog it over to the city."

Han was bringing the *Falcon* down again on the other side of the crevasse. A gleaming metal form waited there. Chewbacca went aft to let Bollux aboard.

"Like you said," Han found himself telling Gallandro defensively, "they're valuable 'droids."

"I said 'priceless,' " Gallandro corrected him. "Now that we're comrades, I'd never offend you by suggesting you've gone soft. May I inquire what our next move is?"

"Direct collection of intelligence data," Han declared, lifting off again. "Interrogation of indigenous personnel for tactical information. We're going to make a couple of locals sweat and find out what all this was about."

The Survivors who had activated the war-robots had decided to escape together in one large hover-raft rather than spread out across the plains in a fleet. A few passes and a barrage from the *Falcon*'s belly turret brought them to a halt. They threw down their arms and waited.

Han prudently left Chewbacca at the ship's controls. He and the others, weapons recharged, went to confront the Survivors. Hasti, first down the ramp, waved her gun at them, shouting, and fairly dragged one of them off the raft. Han and Badure had to pull her off the man, while Gallandro looked on in amusement and Skynx in confusion.

"It's him, I tell you," she yelled, straining to go after the frightened man again. "I recognize the white blaze in his hair. It's the vault steward's assistant."

"Well, clubbing him silly isn't going to help," Han pointed out as he turned to the man. "Better spill it, or I'll let her loose."

The assistant licked dry lips. "I can say nothing, I swear! We are conditioned in youth not to reveal the secrets of the Survivors."

"Old-fashioned hypno," Han dismissed it, "nothing you can't overcome if we scare you enough."

Gallandro stepped forward with a wintry smile, pulling his pistol in one fluid motion, adjusting it one-handed. A low-power, high-resolution beam sizzled into the ground at the captive's feet, blackening and curling the grass. The man paled.

Bollux had come up, his chest plastron open. "There's a better way," Blue Max advised. "Circumvent his conditioning, and we can find out anything we want. We can rig up a strobe and key it to the same light pattern the Survivors use."

Gallandro was dubious. "Query, computer: can you duplicate the Survivors' light pulses exactly?"

"Quit talking to me like I'm some kind of *appliance*!" snarled Max.

"Beg pardon," said Gallandro politely. "I keep forgetting. Shall we proceed?"

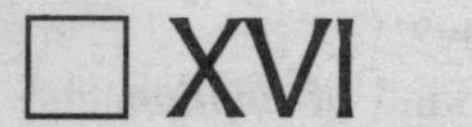

THE *Millennium Falcon* moved through the Dellaltian air at what was for her a conservative speed. Even so, Han was recovering the distance from the city in minutes.

Gallandro was off gathering equipment elsewhere in the ship, with Bollux's help. Hasti and Badure sat, respectively, in the navigator's and communication officer's high-backed chairs behind Han and Chewbacca. Skynx, his injuries dressed and treated, as theirs had been, was curled in Hasti's lap.

"It's hard to accept," Hasti was saying. "All these years. How could a secret be kept for generations?"

"Secrets have been kept for ages," Badure pointed out. "It was easy enough in this case; there're really two strata in the Survivors' organization. The dupes lived and died there in the mountains, maintaining the war-robots as a religious ritual, holding their ceremonies once in a while. Then there were the others, the ones who knew the secret of Xim's treasure and waited for the time they could use it."

"But they all got the conditioning as children, right?" Han asked.

"And when Lanni happened on the mountain base and got her hands on the log-recorder disk and put it in the lock-box at the vaults," Hasti murmured, her voice thick with sorrow, "she couldn't have known that the steward was part of the Survivors' apparatus."

Such had been the assistant's testimony once his conditioning had been overcome. The steward had sent the disk back to the Survivors' mountain warren as soon as it had come into his possession, of course. And he had contrived a nonexistent voice-coder to keep Lanni, Hasti, or anyone else from claiming it. He was aware that J'uoch had learned something about the disk from Lanni before killing her, and that the woman was actively seeking it. He had passed word to her through Survivor double agents that the *Millennium Falcon* had landed, knowing he couldn't cope with the starship if force were brought to bear on the vaults. He knew J'uoch could, and hoped that Hasti and the others and their ship would be destroyed in battle, and the matter closed.

But instead, J'uoch had mounted the ambush that had resulted in the capture of the *Falcon*. Not having found the disk onboard the starship, J'uoch had made pointed inquiries at the vaults. The steward had managed to put her off but, knowing it was only a matter of time until she used force to inspect the lockboxes herself and put him to a more harrowing interrogation, he ordered the long-dormant Guardian Corps sent out against the mining camp. The war-robots, maintained through generations for just such an emergency, had come close to accomplishing their purpose.

"So why are the Survivors still sitting on their money after all this time?" Han wondered.

"The Old Republic was stable and unbeatable," Badure answered. "They had no hope of moving against it, even with Xim's treasure backing them. It's only now, with the Empire having its troubles, that the Survivors smelled a setup they might be able to exploit, especially here in the Tion Hegemony. I bet small-timers everywhere are getting the same sort of idea."

"A new Xim, and a new despotism," Hasti mused. "How could they have believed it, even under conditioning?"

"They can believe one thing," Han said, watching the land roll by quickly beneath them. "The Survivors are about to suffer a capital loss."

"Shouldn't we have a bigger ship?" Hasti inquired.

Han shook his head. "First we make sure the treasure's

there, and put what we can in the *Falcon*. Then we unship a quad-battery and some defensive shielding generators. Gallandro and I will hold the fort while Chewie and the rest of you go find a bigger ship, about the size of J'uoch's lighter, say. It won't take too long."

"And what will you do with your share of the money?" Badure asked casually. He saw doubt and confusion cross the pilot's face.

"I'll worry about that when I've got a stack of credits so high I'll have to rent a warehouse," Han replied at last.

Gallandro, who had just entered the cockpit, carrying the equipment he had gathered, said, "Well put, Solo! Indelicate, but on target." He checked their progress. "We'll be there in a moment. I haven't ransacked a bank in a long time; there's a certain zest to it."

Han reserved his reply and put the starship into a steep dive. The *Falcon* dropped out of the sky ahead of her own sonic boom. Dellaltians near the vaults suddenly saw the vessel appear above them, its braking thrusters thundering, its landing gear extended like predatory claws. People scurried for shelter as the shock wave of the freighter's passage caught up with her, making the ground tremble and the buildings shake. She came to rest on the roofless portico outside the vaults' single door.

The *Falcon*'s external speakers whooped and wailed with emergency sirens and klaxons. Her visual warning systems and running lights were flashing at maximum luminescence. Bystanders would have difficulty seeing and hearing, much less interfering.

The ramp dropped and Han and Gallandro ran down, blasters ready, equipment and tools weighting them. Behind followed Badure, Hasti, and Skynx. The girl objected, "Are you sure there isn't some other way to do this?" Han had to read her lips, unable to hear her in the din.

He shook his head. Chewbacca had to stay at the controls, both because he knew the ship and because Han trusted only the Wookiee with care of the *Falcon*. Bollux stayed behind as well to keep a photoreceptor on instrumentation the first mate couldn't spare time to monitor. Han wanted at least two people to hold the main door, Hasti and Badure. He and Gallandro would do the searching, taking Skynx along to translate.

The area seemed fairly secure; the Dellaltians had no way to cope with an armed starship. Han waved to his partner in the cockpit, and though he couldn't be heard, added, "Fire, Chewie!"

From the *Falcon*'s top and belly turrets shot lines of red annihilation, playing on the closed door of the treasure vault. Smoke obscured the door in seconds as the quad-guns traced incandescent lines across it. Red cannonfire pitted and burned through material that had withstood generations of time and weathering, cutting glowing gashes in it. No weapon of its time could have penetrated it so easily, but in moments the door had been breached, pieces of it falling away. The reports of the gunfire added to the tremendous noise level.

Han signaled again and Chewbacca ceased fire. Smoke billowed away on the chill wind to reveal a yawning hole, its red-hot edges quickly cooling. "Armed robbery!" laughed Gallandro. "There's nothing like it!"

"Let's get inside," Han mouthed. They ran together and hurdled through the gaping door. Hasti and Badure followed a moment later. "Stay here and make sure you maintain com-link with Chewie," Han told them. Badure set Skynx down.

"Don't forget the defensive system!" Hasti called as Han, Gallandro, and Skynx raced off. Among the things their captives had revealed was the fact that the treasure vaults were equipped with defensive security devices; the presence of a firearm in any protected area would trigger automated weapons.

They went deeper into the gloom of the cavernous vestibule, abandoned by the Dellaltians, who had wisely sought other refuge. Han didn't see a man appear to one side, weapon raised, but Gallandro caught the movement, drew, and fired all in the same instant.

The steward cried aloud, clutching his middle, then collapsing to the pressure-pacted tile floor. The gunman kicked the steward's dropped disruptor away.

"You cannot, cannot," the white-bearded man moaned, half in delirium from his wound. "We have kept it, safe, unsullied since we were entrusted with it." His lids fluttered and lowered forever.

Gallandro laughed. "We'll make better use of it than you, old man. At least we'll get it into circulation, eh, Solo?"

Han, moving on, offered no answer. Gallandro came after, and Skynx rushed to catch up. They descended dusty ramps and broad staircases, the empty vaults all around them. At one point they lowered themselves by the cable of an ancient lift platform that no longer worked, complying precisely with the instructions extracted from the captive Survivors under hypno. Han marked their trail with a tint bulb. At the lowest level of the vault proper they came to a forking of the ways. Their information on the vault-complex layout went no further than this.

"It's off this corridor, one of the side tunnels," Han said. "Got your copy of the identi-marks? Good."

"The little fellow can stay with you, Solo," Gallandro replied, meaning Skynx. "I prefer to operate alone." He hitched up the straps holding his equipment and stalked away.

"Okay, stay sharp," Han told Skynx, and the search began. Soon they were absorbed in the intricate business of examining side corridors for the identi-marks described by their prisoners and copied by Skynx. These lowest levels of the vault proper were stale and seemed airless, layered with ankle-deep dust, and a gloom that resisted the beam of the hand-held spotlight. They passed room after room of empty bins and vacant shelves.

At last Skynx stopped. "Captain, this is it! These are the ones!" He was vibrating with excitement. To Han the side corridor looked no different from any other, ending as it did in a blank wall at the bottom of an obviously empty vault complex. But Skynx was right; the identi-marks matched. Han shucked his other gear and lifted a heavy-duty fusion cutter into place. Skynx, taking the com-link, tried to contact the others and inform them of the find, but could raise no response.

"The walls are probably too thick," Han suggested as he set to work. When it had been built, the wall would have withstood any assault that could have been made with portable equipment, but Han was beneficiary of a long technological gap. Chunks of the wall began to fall away. Beyond was the glow of a perpetual illumi-system.

Han set the fusion cutter aside hurriedly, anxious to see for himself. A treasure beyond spending! He could barely contain himself. He ducked and stepped through, followed by Skynx. The vault was dust-free, dry, and as quiet as when Xim's artisans had sealed it, moments before they were put to death, centuries ago.

His steps echoing in the stillness, Han smiled. "The *real* vaults; all the time they were right here!" Hunters had scoured this whole part of space for Xim's treasure because his vaults were empty and all the time there had been complete duplicates, right under the decoys. "Skynx, I'll buy you a planet to play with!"

The Ruurian made no answer, silenced by the weight of years hanging over the place. They followed the corridor through a few turns and came to a stretch where warning flashers blinked in their wall sockets, as they had been doing for centuries. This no-weapons zone was an antechamber to the true treasure vaults of Xim.

Han stopped, wishing neither to be burned by the defensive weapons nor to go on unarmed, aware he might face other dangers. He turned back with great reluctancc. At the fusion-cut opening, Gallandro waited.

Han paused and Skynx waited uncertainly. "We found it," the pilot told the gunman with a jerk of his thumb. "The real one. It's back there.'' He realized Gallandro had heard Skynx's transmissions after all.

Gallandro registered no elation, only amused acceptance. Han knew without being told that everything had changed. The gunman's abandoned equipment was stacked to one side, and he had doffed his short jacket, prelude to a gun duel. ''I said, the *treasure* is back there,'' Han repeated.

Gallandro smiled his frosty smile. ''This has nothing to do with money, Solo, although I postponed it until you and your group could help me find the vaults. I have my own plans for Xim's treasure.''

Han warily shrugged out of his jacket. ''Why?'' was all he asked, carefully unsnapping his holster's retaining strap and rotating it forward out of his way. His fingers stretched and worked, waiting.

''You require chastening, Solo. *Who do you think you are?* Truth to tell, you're nothing but a commonplace outlaw. Your luck has run out: now, call the play!''

Han nodded, knowing Gallandro would if he didn't. ''And this'll make you feel superior, right?'' His hand blurred for his blaster, the best single play of his life.

Their speeddraw mechanics were very different. Han's incorporated movements of shoulders and knees, a slight dipping, a partial twist. Gallandro's was ruthless economy, an explosion of every nerve and muscle that moved his right arm alone.

When the blaster bolt slammed into his shoulder, Han's overwhelming reaction was surprise; some part of him had believed in his luck to the end. His own draw half-completed, his shot went into the floor. He was spun half around, in shock, smelling the stench of his own charred flesh. The pain of the wound started an instant later. A second bolt from the cautious Gallandro struck his forearm and Han's blaster dropped.

Han sank to his knees, too startled to cry out. Skynx retreated with a terrified chitter. Swaying, clasping his wounded arm to him, Han heard Gallandro say, ''That was very good,

Solo; you came closer than anyone's come in a long time. But now I'll take you back to the Corporate Sector—not that I care about the Authority's justice, but there are those who have to be shown what it means to stand in my way."

Han gasped through locked teeth, "I'm not doing time in any Authority horror factory."

Gallandro ignored that. "Your friends are more expendable, however. If you'll pardon me, I'll have to see to your Ruurian comrade before he gets into any mischief."

He slapped a pair of binders he'd found onboard the *Falcon* around Han's ankles and ground the pilot's com-link under his heel. "You were never the amoralist you feigned to be, Solo, but I am. In a way, it's too bad we didn't meet later, when you were salted and wiser. You're pretty good in a fight; you might've made a useful lieutenant." He removed the charge from Han's blaster, tucked it into his belt, and sauntered off after Skynx, who, unable to get past the gunman, had fled back down the corridors toward the treasure vaults.

Gallandro moved cautiously, knowing the Ruurian was unarmed but counting no being harmless when it was fighting for its life. He rounded a corner to see Skynx cowering against the wall some distance along, gazing at him with huge, terrified eyes, paralyzed with fear. Around the far turn of the corridor he could see the reflected warning lights of a no-weapons zone.

Gripping his blaster, Gallandro smirked. "It's a pity, my little friend, but there's too much at stake here: Solo's the only one I can afford to take alive. I shall make this as easy as I can. Hold still."

Drawing a bead on Skynx's head, he stepped forward. Energy discharges flashed from hidden emplacements; even Gallandro's fabulous reflexes gave him no edge against the speed of light.

Caught in a flaring crossfire of defensive weapons, the gunman was hit by a dozen lethal blasts before he could so much as move. He was the center of an abrupt inferno, then his scorched remains fell to the corridor floor and the smell of incinerated flesh clogged the air.

Skynx uncoiled from his spot at the corridor wall bit by bit. He threw aside the warning flashers he had removed from their sockets along the corridor's wall. He gave silent thanks Gallandro hadn't noticed the empty sockets; a prudent Ruurian probably would have.

"Humans," remarked Skynx, then went off to rescue Han Solo.

"Not much left of him, is there?" Han asked rhetorically an hour later as he stood over Gallandro's blackened remains. Like the others, he had left his gun outside the no-weapons zone. Badure and Hasti had made temporary repairs to his shoulder and forearm with one of the ship's medi-packs. If Han received competent medical attention soon, there would be no lasting effect from Gallandro's blaster bolts.

Chewbacca was just finishing a careful examination of that corridor and the one beyond, running a thorough check along the walls to search out each weapons emplacement. He had opened each one with hand tools and deactivated it. Satisfied that there would be no danger in bringing power equipment and tools inside, the Wookiee barked to Han.

"Let's get busy; I don't like the idea of the *Falcon* being unmanned." When Skynx had returned with news of the gun duel, Chewbacca had moved the starship so that she blocked the main door, her ramp extended down through it. He had warped the ship's defensive mantle around and set her guns to fire automatically on sensor-lock should anyone come too close, one warning volley and then the real item. The Delaltians trapped inside on the starship's arrival had already surrendered and been permitted to leave; the *Falcon* would protect the treasure hunters for the time being, but Han didn't want to press his already overextended luck.

They gathered their gear and moved on. At the end of the next corridor was a metal wall bearing a Wookiee-high representation of Xim's death's-head symbol. Chewbacca lifted the fusion cutter to it and began slicing, splitting the insignia in two amid flying, flashing motes. Then he began carving in earnest. Heat washed back across him.

In short order there was a wide opening in the door. Beyond, bathed in the glow of illumi-panels that had been keeping the place bright for generations, was the glittering of gems, the gleam of metals, piles of strongboxes, and racks of storage cylinders in warehouse-sized shelf stacks that stretched from floor to high ceiling and away into the distance as far as they could see.

And this was only the first of the treasure rooms.

Skynx was quiet, almost reverent. He had made the find of a lifetime, a discovery out of daydreams. Badure and Hasti remained solemn, too, as they considered the size and wealth of the place, the impact it would have on their lives, and the memory of what they had gone through to stand here.

Not so Han and Chewbacca. The pilot jumped through the gap in the door, wounded arm held to him by a traction web. "We did it! We did it!" he shouted in glee. The Wookiee lurched after him, tossing his long-maned head back with an ecstatic *"Rooo-oo!"* They slapped each other, laughter echoing away into the piles of treasure. Chewbacca's huge feet slapped the floors in a thumping victory dance as Han laughed in joy.

Skynx and Badure had gone to open containers with Bollux's help, to examine Xim's spoils. Chewbacca offered to assist them. "Spread it out here!" Han enjoined him. "I want to roll around in it!"

He paused when he noticed Hasti nearby, eyeing him strangely. "I always wondered what you'd be like," she told him "when you found your big win, you and the Wook. What now?"

Han still rode the wave of elation. "*What now?* Why, we'll, we'll—" He stopped, giving the subject some serious thought for the first time. "We'll pay off our debts, get ourselves a first-class ship and crew, uh . . ."

Hasti nodded to herself. "And settle down, Han?" she

asked softly. "Buy a planet, or take over a few conglomerates and live the life of a good man of business?" She shook her head slowly. "Your problems are just beginning, rich man."

His joy was receding fast, replaced by a tangled knot of doubts, plans, the need for forethought and mature wisdom. But before he could berate Hasti for being a spoilsport, he heard Chewbacca's angry roar.

The Wookiee held a metallic ingot, frowning at it in disgust. He dumped a handful of them onto the floor in a chiming avalanche and gave the pile a kick that sent ingots skittering every which way. Han forgot Hasti and went to his friend. "What is it?"

Chewbacca explained with frustrated grunts and moans. Han picked up one of the ingots and saw that his copilot was right. "This stuff's *kiirium*! You can get it anywhere; Skynx, what's it doing in with the treasure?"

The small academician had located a vault-directory screen at the end of the nearest shelf stack, an old televiewer mounted on a low stand. He brought it to flickering life, and columns of ciphers and characters raced across the screen as Skynx answered distractedly.

"There would seem to be a great deal of it here, Captain. And a huge quantity of mytag crystalline vertices and mountains of enriched bordhell-type fuel slugs, among other things."

"Mytag crystals?" Han repeated in puzzlement. "They run those things off by the carload; what kind of treasure's this? Where's the *real* treasure?"

A belly laugh distracted him. Badure had found a canister of the mytag crystal and flung a double handful into the air. The crystals rained down around him, catching the light, as he convulsed in laughter. "This *is* it! Or was, an age ago. Don't you see, Slick? Kiirium is artificial shielding material, not very good by modern standards but a major breakthrough in its time, and tough to produce to boot. With quantities of kiirium to shield heavy guns and engines, Xim could field warcraft that were better armed and faster than anything else in space at the time.

"And mytag crystals were used in old subspace commo and detection gear; you needed lots and lots of them for any spacefleet or planetary defenses. And so forth; all this was critical war materiél. With the stuff in these vaults, Xim could have assembled a war machine that would have conquered this whole part of space. But he lost big at the Third Battle of Vontor, first."

"That's *it*?" Han bellowed. "We went through all this for a treasure that's *obsolete*?"

"Not quite," Skynx commented mildly, still bent over the screen. "One whole section is filled with information tapes, art works, and artifacts. There is a hundred times more information contained here than everything we know about the period altogether."

"I'll bet the Survivors have long since forgotten just what it was they were guarding," Hasti put in. "They believed the legends, just like everyone else. I wonder what did happen to the *Queen of Ranroon*?"

Badure shrugged. "Perhaps they plunged her into the system's primary after she offloaded the treasure, or sent her off with a skeleton crew to arrange misleading sightings of her and create a false trail. Who knows?"

Skynx had left the viewscreen and started a delirious dance, first on his hind limbs, then on the front ones, hopping and capering much as Han and Chewbacca had a moment before. "Marvelous! Miraculous! What a *find*! I'm sure to get my own chair funded—no, my own *department*!"

Han, leaning against a wall, slowly sank to a squatting position. "Artworks, hmm? Chewie and I can just stroll into the Imperial Museum with a bunch under our arms and start haggling, right?" He rested his forehead on his good arm. Chewbacca patted his shoulder solicitously, making mournful sounds.

Skynx gradually stopped cavorting, realizing what a disappointment all this was to the two. "There *are* some things of intrinsic value, Captain. If you choose carefully, you could fill your ship with items you could dispose of relatively simply. There would be some profit.'' He was fighting the urge to hoard the entire find, knowing that the *Millennium Falcon* could bear away no more than an insignificant part of it. ''Enough, I suppose, to get your ship repaired properly and have your wounds looked after in a first-class medicenter.''

''What about us?'' Hasti interposed. ''Badure and I haven't even got a starship.''

Skynx pondered for a moment, then brightened. ''I can write my own ticket with the university, an unlimited budget. How would you two like to work with me? Academic pursuits will be dull after this, I suppose, to a pair of humans. But there'd be generous pay and retirement benefits and quick promotions. We'll be years and years working on this find. I'll need someone to look after all the workers, scholars, and automata.'' Badure smiled and put an arm around Hasti's shoulders. She nodded.

That made Skynx think of something else. ''Bollux, would you and Blue Max care for positions? You'd be of great help, I'm sure. After all, you two are the only ones who interacted with the war-robots at any length. There's certain to be an effort to study their remains; we have a great deal yet to learn about their thought processes.''

Blue Max answered for them both. ''Skynx, we'd like that a lot.''

''*If* the locals don't march in here and take it all away from you,'' Han reminded them, as Chewbacca helped him to his feet. Seeing their concern, he added, ''I guess we'll leave you a portable defensive generator and some heavy weapons and supplies out of the *Falcon*. That'll give us more cargo space.''

Badure sounded uncharacteristically angry. ''Han, how gullible do you think the rest of the universe is? You always want to do the right things for the wrong reasons. Well, what will you do the day you run out of excuses, son?''

Han pretended not to hear. ''We'll punch through a distress call just before we make our jump out of this system. There'll be a Tion Hegemony gunboat here before you know it. Come on, Chewie; let's break out the handtruck and get the ship loaded before anything else happens."

"Captain," Skynx called. Han paused and looked back. "Here's a funny thing: I still think this adventuring was basically just danger and hardship a long way from home, but now that it's ended and we're parting company, I find myself saddened."

"Look us up for a refresher course, any time," offered Han.

Skynx shook his head. "I have much to do here; all too soon I'll be called away by my blood, when it's time to go chrysalis, then live a brief season as a chroma-wing. If you wish to see me then, Captain, come and look on Ruuria for the flyer whose wing markings are the same as my own banding. The chroma-wing won't recognize you, but perhaps some part of Skynx will."

Han nodded, finding no adequate way to say good-bye. Badure called, "Hey, Slick!" Han and his copilot looked to him and he laughed. "Thanks, boys."

"Forget it." Han dismissed the entire incident. He started off again with his sidekick, both of them moving with some pain due to their injuries. "After all, a Life-Debt's a Life-Debt, isn't it, *partner*?"

On this last note, he poked a knuckle into his copilot's ribs. Chewbacca swung angrily but not too quickly. Han ducked and the Wookiee backed off. "Look," Han said, "that's it for missions of mercy, all right? We're smugglers; that's what we know and that's what we're good at and that's what we're sticking to!"

The Wookiee growled concurrence. The others, surrounded by the endless shelf stacks of Xim's treasure, heard the discussion echo back from the corridor. Han broke into Chewbacca's rumblings with, "When the *Falcon*'s repaired and this wing of mine's fixed, we're going to try another Kessel spice run."

The Wookiee croaked an irritated objection. Han insisted. "It's fast money and we won't have to look at any dirt! We'll get Jabba the Hut or somebody to back us for a cut. Listen, I've got this plan . . ."

Just as they were moving out of earshot, Chewbacca's protests stopped. He and Han Solo shared some joke that made both laugh slyly. Then they returned to their schemes.

"There," Badure declared to Hasti, Skynx, Bollux, and Blue Max, "go the *real* Survivors."